THE LIGHT
OF OUR
YESTERDAYS

KEN HANSEN

ISBN 978-1-7328538-0-5 Paperback
ISBN 978-1-7328538-1-2 Hardcover

Cover and Book Design by Damonza
Maps by Christine Vande Voort

Published by Odium Odi Press, LLC

To Jenny, my own Sonatina,
who started me down this winding path
and held my hand all the way.

And to my mom,
who passed away within weeks of
the final editing of this novel.
She always gave me hope.

CONTENTS

GUIDES & MAPS

Guide to Characters by Group. vii

Maps Relating to the World in 1890 AH. x

PROLOGUES

Prologue, the First (Early 21ˢᵗ Century, AD) xiii

Incipit Prologus, Secundus (1890 AH). xv

PARTS OF THE STORY

First Part (*Prima Pars*)

First Part, the First: Confusion 1

Secunda Primae: Inspiratio *95*

Second Part (*Secunda Pars*)

Second Part, The First: Contemplation 167

Secunda Secundae: Quaesitum *281*

Third Part: Revelation (*Tertia Pars: Apocalypsis*) 403

APPENDICES

Appendix A—Detailed Excerpts from "Plinius's Condensed Study Guide for the Advanced Technologist Exam: History Since the Founding of the First Romanus Empire". 643

Appendix B—English-Language Contacts in Baqir Najwa's Cell Phone. 669

ACKNOWLEDGEMENTS 683

GUIDE TO CHARACTERS BY GROUP

Characters from Early Twenty-First Century AD:

Homeland Security and CIA Personnel:
Christian Huxley, Senior Terrorism Investigator, Department of
 Homeland Security
Kira Sampson (Huxley's assistant)
Deputy Undersecretary Blount (Huxley's boss)
Ken Mayer, Central Intelligence Agency

Huxley's Friends & Family:
Adona Huxley, Christian's mother
Hanna Elverman, Christian's one-time fiancé
Kadir al-Razin al-Asr, Christian's Harvard roommate

Israelis:
Captain Yadin, Aman Security Agency
Major Margolin, Aman Security Agency
Col. Brickner, Commander, Ramat David Airbase
Jacob Rosenthal, Israeli chemist
Rosenthal's two daughters
Mr. Riese, bodyguard to the Rosenthals

Afghans and U.S. Personnel Appearing in Afghanistan:
Abdul Saboor Anwari

Karim, Anwari's brother
Captain Granger, Captain, U.S. Army (friend of Anwari)
Half-Moon Mole (unnamed OGA or "Other Governmental Agency"
    employee)
Imam Rahini

Vatican Personnel:
Sonatina D'Amare, Deputy Director, Vatican Museums
Col. Zaugg, Commander of the Swiss Guard
Antony Cepini, Director of the Corp of Gendarmerie
Cardinal Armondo Fine, a former Catholic Cardinal

Members of Ungues Pardi:
Pardus, also known as the Ghost Leopard
Dracoratio, thought to be Pardus's lieutenant, possibly an alias of
    Esnanimen Kharun Udani, a former security agent with the United
    Arab Emirates
Baqir Najwa (possibly a member)

Others:
Jonathan Stirling, Professor of Archaeology and Acting Associate Director,
    Tel Megiddo Archaeological Excavation Site
Lieutenant Patismio, Chief Investigator, Italian Carabinieri
Dante Tocelli, Sapienza student and Tel Megiddo intern
Ahmed Jinnah, Analyst and Investigator, Pakistan Nuclear Security
    Agency (acquaintance of Huxley from Pakistani interrogation days)

Characters from 1890s AH:

Technologists of Roma:
Tomadus, prominent technologist and merchant
Stephanus, Tomadus's top assistant
Batu, Tomadus's friend and brain technologist
Ratan, psyche-technologist
Peregrine, former astro-technologist (later, a friend to Tomadus)

Officials of Roma, the Three Empires & their Permitted Religions:
First Consul Khansensius, leader of Romanus Protectorate

General Faisil, General in Sunni Muslim Empire
General Khameni, General in Shiite Muslim Empire
The Governor of the Palestinian Province
Abh Beyth Diyn of Jerusalem (Jewish leader)
Grand Imam of Palestinian Province (Islamic leader)

Demoseps in Tonquizalixco Tetepe:
Yohanan, one of the main leaders of the Demoseps (the "Boy on
    the Cover")
Decima, a Romanus supporting the Demoseps (Quintillus's daughter)
Raanan, principal Demosep leader
Achak, Demosep operative and good friend to Yohanan
Dekanawida, Demosep operative
Eliezer, Demosep operative

Romani in Tonquizalixco Tetepe:
Quintillus, prominent Romanus merchant living in New Åarhus, New
    Jutland (Decima's father)
Jochi, a Tetepian adopted by a Romanus family (Yohanan's sister)

Juteslams:
King Skjöldr
Vice Regent Hugleikr (right hand to the king)
Ædlehelten (young boy on train)

Members of the Way:
Isa, the man in the white robes, preacher and leader of the Way
Maryam, Isa's mother
Adin, one of the Ten (very large, simple man loyal to Isa)
Simeon, one of the Ten (Jewish)
Atuf, one of the Ten (Muslim)
Diego, one of the Ten (Jewish)
Anders, one of the Ten (Muslim)

Aztecs:
Emperor Acamapichtli X, Emperor of the Aztec Empire

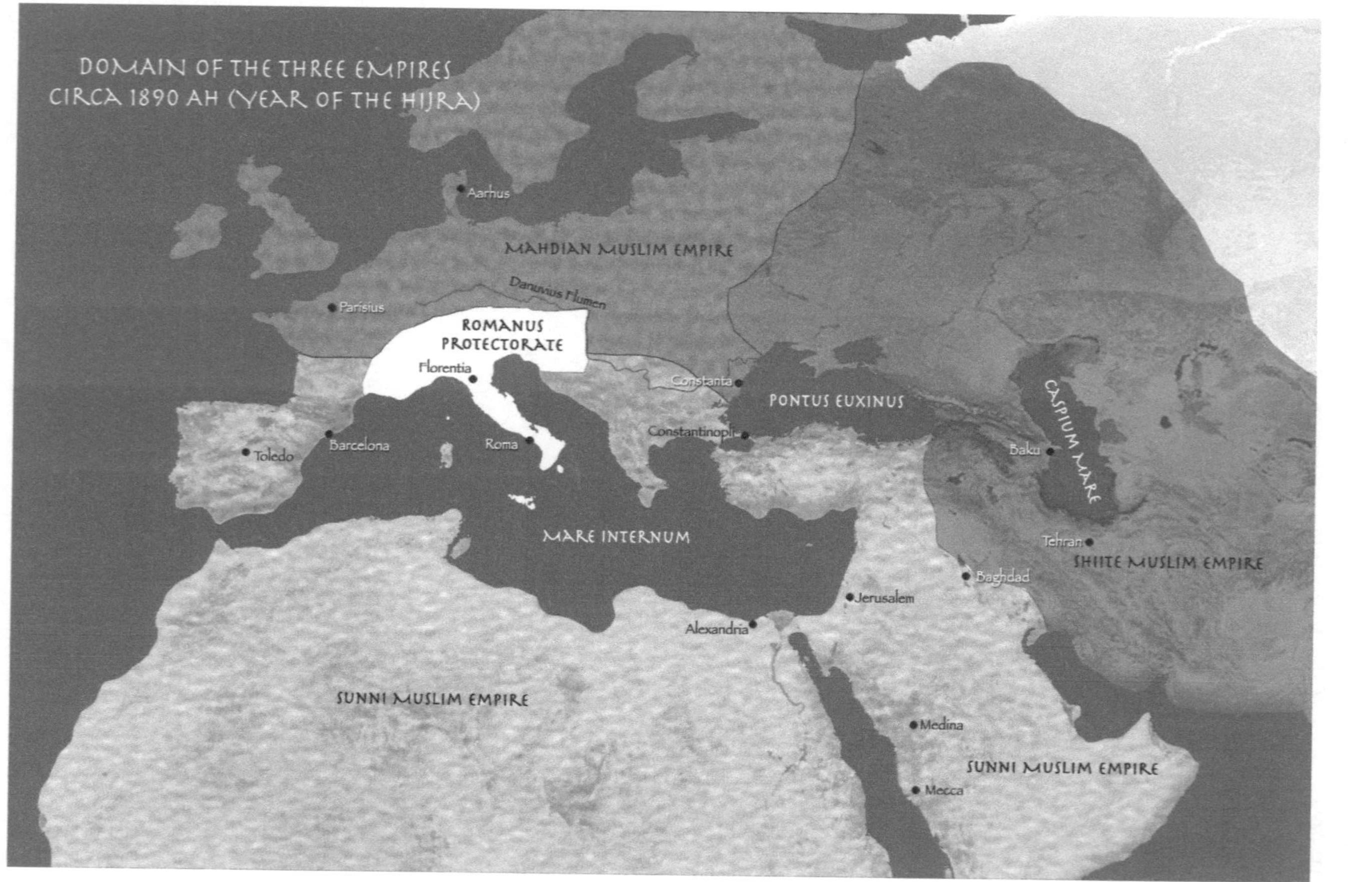

DOMAIN OF THE THREE EMPIRES
CIRCA 1890 AH (YEAR OF THE HIJRA)
MAHDIAN MUSLIM EMPIRE
SHIITE MUSLIM EMPIRE
SUNNI MUSLIM EMPIRE
SUNNI MUSLIM EMPIRE
ROMANUS PROTECTORATE
CASPIUM MARE
PONTUS EUXINUS
MARE INTERNUM
Danuvius Flumen
Aarhus
Parisius
Toledo
Barcelona
Roma
Florentia
Constanta
Constantinopli
Baku
Tehran
Baghdad
Jerusalem
Alexandria
Medina
Mecca

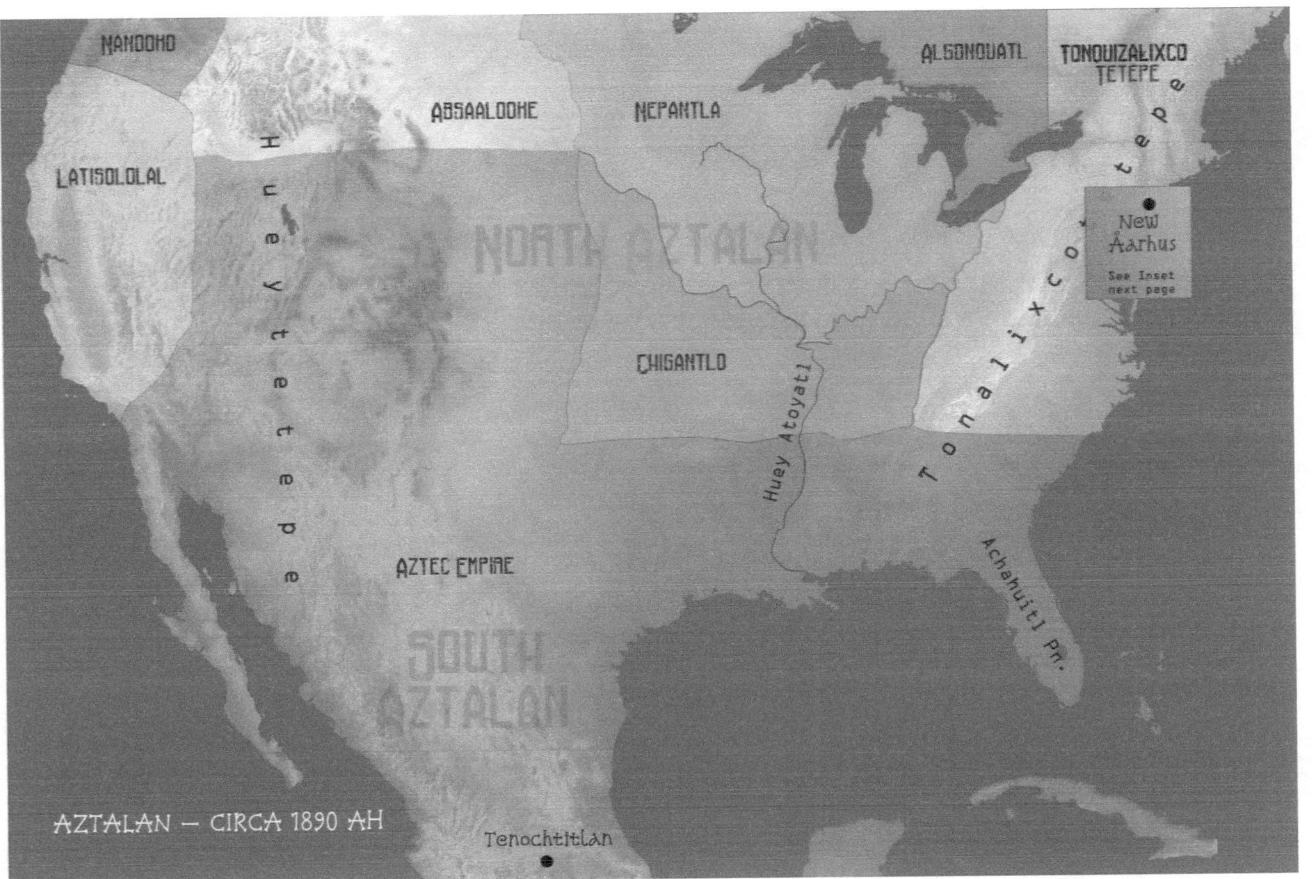

NAMOOHO
ABSAALOOKE
NEPANTLA
ALGONOUATL
TONQUIZALIXCO TETEPE
LATISOLOLAL
Hueytetepe
NORTH AZTALAN
New Åarhus
See Inset next page
CHIGANTLO
Huey Atoyatl
Tonalixcoxtetepe
AZTEC EMPIRE
SOUTH AZTALAN
Achahuitl Pn.
AZTALAN — CIRCA 1890 AH
Tenochtitlan

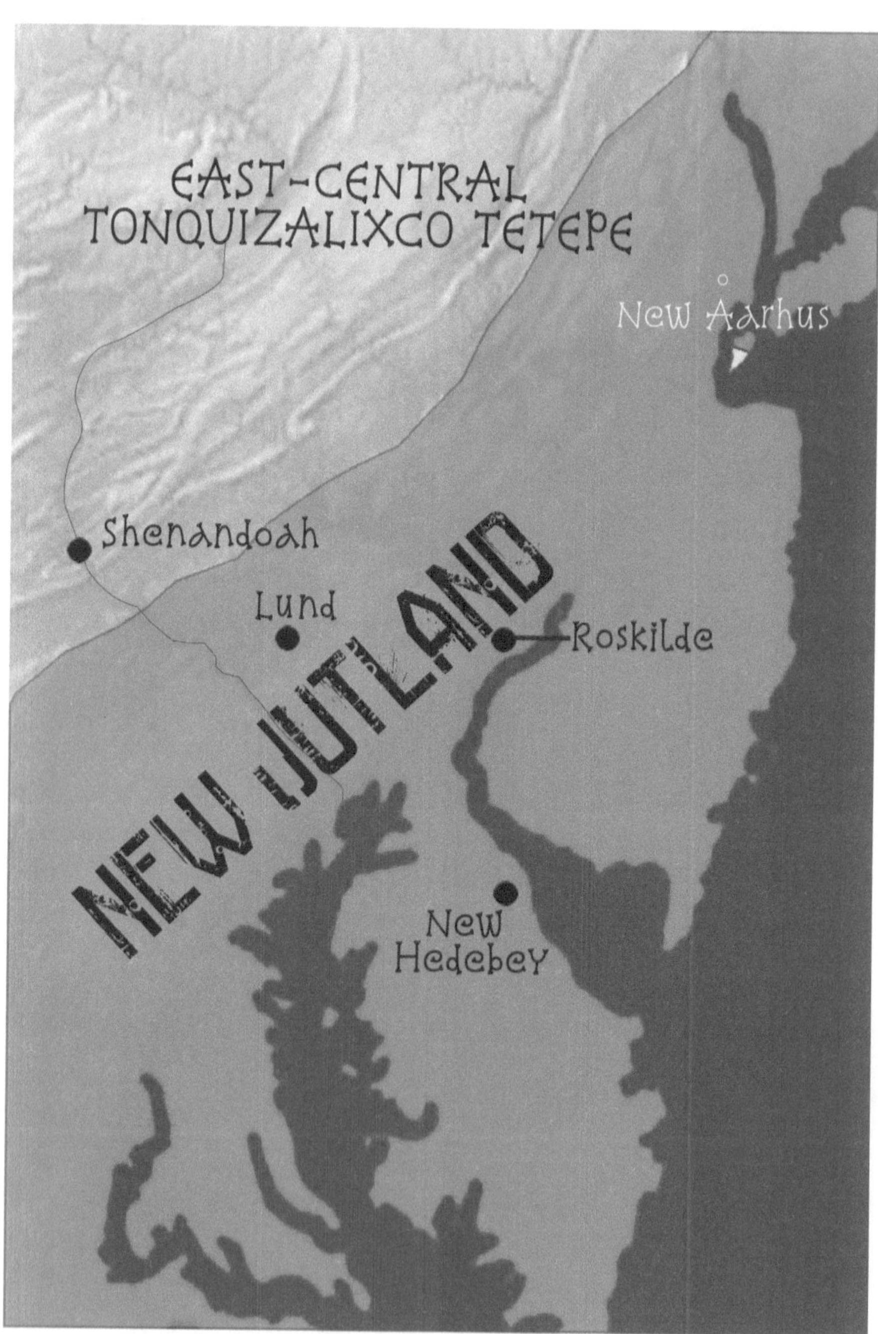

EAST-CENTRAL
TONQUIZALIXCO TETEPE
New Aarhus
Shenandoah
Lund
NEW JUTLAND
Roskilde
New
Hedeby

PROLOGUE, THE FIRST

(Early 21ˢᵗ Century AD)

H E CROUCHED UTTERLY still in the sweet blackness of the tunnel, a strange peace gripping him. The silence died prematurely when the other two began bolstering their courage with familiar chants that smothered his ears with tired clichés. "Quiet," he breathed. If he could see their eyes, they would be squinting suspiciously at his latest blasphemy. The men complied, nonetheless, and that was all that mattered. He needed to hear the sound of the engines. Timing. It meant success or failure, escape or capture, life or death.

A siren whirred to life a few hundred feet away. The fools must have finally noticed the incoming bombers on their radar. *Nearly time.* He felt the cold metal of the loaded weapon in his hands. *Old friend. Once again, give me truth, give me justice, give me life.*

Life? What life I have is forfeit. If captured, not even the Ghost Leopard could save him now. No, he would die fighting for this cause just as his father before him. The tunnel could provide a perfectly timed exit, but what was the chance the charges would seal off their retreat at just the right time? Everything seemed possible yet so improbable in this extravagant charade. No, this was little more than a disguised suicide mission. For what? His silent God? His dead father? His mysterious leader? And what had he done to earn this holy right, this sacred honor, this bloody curse? *The Ghost must have known. He always knew. Well, at least I have prepared.*

Father never had that chance. She will miss me, but yes, it is for her that I do this. Please forgive me for leaving you.

Jet turbines roared to life, momentarily tensing his every muscle. *Time.* He slid aside the pallet covering their tunnel. The three men climbed out behind the shed, remaining low in the early morning shadows nearly thirty feet apart. A hundred yards away, a fighter jet tested its engines. It awaited another jet being towed out of a nearby hangar. The two would take off together, scrambling as a second wave to meet a phantom enemy from the east.

The control tower stood several hundred yards away, just within range. He raised his arm and the other two each aimed their RPGs at the distant jets. A second after he flung his arm down, he heard the whoosh of the two rockets, their flaming tails trailing the explosives hurtling not ten feet above the ground. One rocket penetrated the shell of the first F-16, and the jet exploded. The other sped a foot above the fuselage of the other jet and crashed into the hangar. *A shame, but not mission critical.*

As he leveled his launcher toward the tower, he heard an explosion he hadn't expected. When it rumbled from below, the part of him that still longed to live pretended it was an earthquake or explosion deep in the bowels of the airbase. His brain knew better. The tunnel charges had triggered early, ending any hope for escape. *Why? Of course. Yet another clean ending for the Ghost Leopard.* Focusing on the tower, he pulled the trigger on his launcher, but he never saw the tower explode.

He never even saw the rocket leave the launcher. Instead, his eyes were blinded in a millisecond, though his brain never registered the appearance of the bright white light flashing from the weapon in front of his face. A rapture of bullets soon followed, but they simply compounded the corruption of his already dead flesh.

INCIPIT PROLOGUS, SECUNDUS

(1890 AH)

THE MAN IN the white robes stared at the images on the visi-scan, horrid images of the terror-stricken lands of Tetepe and New Jutland: first narrowly focusing on a mangled government building in the Juteslam capital; now pulling back to show dozens of bodies in the street, rescuers running between them as they desperately tried to assist survivors; now panning to the side to reveal the close-up of a blood-soaked woman being turned over by a rescuer, the woman's face nearly torn away, her arms still clinging to the few remaining fragments of her infant child; and finally cutting to a Tetepian village, thick black smoke rising slowly from the tangled remnants of the shelling, the whole scene evidencing the Juteslam's quick retribution for the shaitaanist Demosep bombing in the capital, with the camera now carefully avoiding the dead yet finding no living Tetepians either.

When the man in the white robes closed his eyes, a tear curled down his cheek. He kneeled on the ground and put his palms together. "Father, I shall follow your will in all things. Please, help me understand." After a few seconds, he sighed. "I can see that this man has suffered and now despairs. Though he has committed such terrible acts, good still dwells within him. I will guide him to the light, though I know he shall cry out before me."

A minute later, the man, still kneeling, swallowed hard. "Father, must we follow this perilous path? Will these other two human souls justify your trust by placing their faith in You? You must know they will suffer from Your great gifts rather than embracing them. Will they ever understand the truth? In any of our worlds? I could save them both. I could help them see… Yes, I know, they must choose for themselves… If You open their minds to the truth of their souls, will it be enough?" A few seconds later, the man nodded slowly, respectfully. "Of course, Your will as always."

FIRST PART, THE FIRST: CONFUSION

"Brief and troubled is our lifetime; there is no remedy for our dying, nor is anyone known to have come back from Hades. For by mere chance were we born, and hereafter we shall be as though we had not been; because the breath in our nostrils is smoke, and reason a spark from the beating of our hearts, and when this is quenched, our body will be ashes and our spirit will be poured abroad like empty air. Even our name will be forgotten in time, and no one will recall our deeds. So our life will pass away like the traces of a cloud, and will be dispersed like a mist pursued by the sun's rays and overpowered by its heat. For our lifetime is the passing of a shadow; and our dying cannot be deferred because it is fixed with a seal; and no one returns."

– The Old Testament—Wis 2:1-5

"The life of this world is like this: rain that We send down from the sky is absorbed by the plants of the earth, from which humans and animals eat. But when the earth has taken on its finest appearance, and adorns itself, and its people think they have power over it, then the fate We commanded comes to it, by night or by day, and We reduce it to stubble, as if it had not flourished just the day before."

– The Qur'an—Jonah 10:24

"Even now the ax lies at the root of the trees. Therefore every tree that does not produce good fruit will be cut down and thrown into the fire."

– The New Testament—Lk 3:9

CHAPTER 1

THE HOT, CRUSTY air barely slid through the window of the black Toyota Innova as they sat in traffic on Ha Teufa Blvd., just a few miles from Ben Gurion International Airport. "I apologize for the air conditioning, sir," said the Israeli lieutenant. "Thought we had it fixed."

Sitting in the back, Christian Huxley's belly gave him that little tug as his eyes narrowed. Add this last piece of garbage to the pile of crap he'd heard for the last day and a half. This whole charade stunk even more than that sweaty smell that emanated from the driver. Or was that his own stench from this heat? "How long to the base, Lieutenant?"

"An hour, perhaps a little more."

Huxley rested his chin on the crook of his left thumb and forefinger. The kid was not an Israeli, not really. Except in the sense that American Jews can quickly become Israeli citizens. He spoke perfect English with a recognizable accent. Probably refined at an Ivy League school or some liberal arts college in the East. Became an Israeli citizen and then began doing his part for the Jewish "homeland" for a few years before he would ultimately return to his cozy home in the States for a real job and life. Huxley grimaced. "Dumb Daring Dual." He could almost hear Hanna laughing as she joyfully invented another nickname for someone she refused to even try to understand.

But Huxley understood—he just felt sorry for the kid. By now that soldier must understand what he had gotten himself into over here: on constant watch for an enemy in and about his own land with guns and rockets and a deep hatred for his very fabric because why? Because even though the two Semitic groups prayed to arguably the same God, their competing articles of faith varied? Religion had that way of dividing people. But that certainly wasn't what this was really about anymore, was it? No, now it was all about hate.

"Lieutenant, how long you been here?"

"Here?"

"In Israel? You're from New York City, right?"

The lieutenant chuckled and looked back over his shoulder. "I guess not that long then."

"Ready to go home?"

"I don't know. Duty, you know?"

"Yeah." Duty. Huxley's own duty had taken him to many places where hatred had boiled over to war and terror and death. This place was no different. The Palestinians had nurtured a hatred forged in the fires of their reaction to the arrogance of a decaying colonialism then in its death throes. This sad, still paternalistic colonialism had clung so naively to the belief that it could solve one world problem without creating another, but it had once again failed.

Who could blame the Jews for wanting to establish their own state when they had been so mistreated and brutalized in Europe and Russia? And why would they want to go anywhere but return to their ancestral home? That was even before Hitler began systematically destroying the Jewish population in Europe.

Yet, who could blame the Arabs who occupied Palestine for wanting to control the destiny of the land they had lived in for so long? Powerless in the face of the British Empire and its American supporters after the Great War, they were forced to accept a growing stream of Jewish immigrants in their land. Following WWII, the Arabs could no longer view the immigration and parceling of their lands as anything more than an invasion sanctioned by world opinion. When they went to war—in their minds to defend their own homeland—the killing on both sides began in earnest and the hatred became their constant reality.

Huxley knew the Palestinians' hatred now ran broad and deep. It was the kind of hate people wallowed in after being beaten down again and again by someone they could only see as a foreign invader. It was the kind of hate that had seen fathers, brothers and sons suffer and die while rising up in a Quixotic effort to turn the clock back to a time over half a century past. It was the kind of hate that could never sink below a bubbling simmer and would too often boil over into new blood that fueled the eternal fire of their contempt.

Huxley despised the hatred of a whole people. Who could reasonably, impartially condone the hatred or violence on either side? Still, much of this story was an old one. He had heard this kind of lament and its many variants repeated in his interrogations across many troubled parts of the world, and the cause seemed always to be the same: ethnic groups historically wronged by each other but supported by powerful outside nations "protecting" their strategic geopolitical concerns, and neither side ever able to come to a lasting peace over their differences. You had to separate the politics and propaganda from reason and reality, but there was always some truth there—propaganda never grew so hot without at least a little truth to keep it burning. He understood the politics and power of hatred all too well, and he figured it likely was just this kind of hatred that had brought him to this land of milk and honey and on his way to the Ramat David Airbase.

Huxley peered out his window at the countryside. A long, flat plain planted with green and yellow crops lay to his right, interrupted only by a sudden sharp hill in the distance. Was that Megiddo towering over the famous plain of Armageddon?

He looked ahead at Ramat David. Terrorist activities against allies of the U.S. usually brought an investigator from D.C. or Langley. Still, why was he here? Though he had worked the more acute problems in Afghanistan, Pakistan, Iraq and Yemen and even a few in Sudan and Indonesia, he hadn't set foot in Israel in more than a decade. So why had the Israeli authorities insisted on him? Better yet, why had they even acknowledged any terrorist activity here? News of the attack had not hit the press. There was that report of a small electrical fire at the base, but that was probably a cover story from the Aman security agency. But then why ask for a particular American investigator? The Israelis never requested help unless they believed it to be politically expedient or critically necessary. Huxley couldn't see any political connection here. *So what do they need? And why do they need it from me?*

"What happened at Ramat David, Lieutenant?" Huxley asked, just for kicks.

"I don't think I could say, sir. You are scheduled to speak with Col. Brickner when we arrive in a few minutes. I'm sure he'll give you all of the answers you need."

What I need? More like what the colonel wants to leak. Yet, maybe the colonel would trickle out a few drops he could use.

❆ ❆ ❆

The slight folds of Abdul Saboor Anwari's eyelids nearly disappeared as he squinted through the glare of the mid-day sun blasting off of the Innova ahead. He smiled gently and scratched the dense stubble on his face as the target sped ahead on Highway 70. Anwari turned right onto Highway 66, southeast toward Megiddo. That was as close as he wanted to get to the Israeli air base. He looked back to the car disappearing down the highway to his left and said aloud, "If you are half as clever as he says, I will see you again soon, my friend." He picked up his cheap black flip phone and punched a few buttons. "He's almost to Ramat."

CHAPTER 2

A S THE TOYOTA pulled up to the security gate, Huxley pulled out his passport and Homeland Security ID. The lieutenant beat him to the punch. "Chris Huxley from U.S. Homeland Security, here on orders of Col. Brickner."

"Yes sir, I am aware of the orders. May I see your credentials, Mr. Huxley? Thank you, sir." A fifteen-foot-high concrete wall stood to the front, an electrified gate providing a silent barrier to the only entrance. After the corporal spoke a Hebrew sentence or two into his radio and punched in a few numbers on his computer screen, the gate slid open.

As they pulled forward, the gate closed behind them and they drove to the center of a concrete canyon about 15 feet deep and 40 feet in diameter. A single soldier wearing bomb-protection gear appeared with a German Shepherd. The soldier held an aluminum bar several feet longer than a broomstick with a handle on one end and a mirror and electronic detector on the other. After the lieutenant escorted Huxley away from the car with their hands on each of their heads, he and the dog searched the car, the dog sniffing around and through it, the soldier running the mirror and detector underneath it. When he finished, he patted down Huxley and the Lieutenant. After hand signals were given to guards on both sides of the enclosure, they reentered the Toyota, the second gate finally opened, and they proceeded into the military compound.

As the car weaved around the base, Huxley noticed a construction crew working to repair one of the aircraft hangers. Black carbon marks extended from the new wall in a burst pattern across a hundred feet of tarmac. Huxley smirked. Quite an "electrical fire." They hadn't had time to cover that part up yet.

Over forty minutes later, Col. Brickner finally strode out of his office. "I'm so sorry to make you wait, Mr. Huxley, but I've been detained."

Huxley rose and shook the colonel's hand. "That's fine, Col. Brickner. I'm ready to help. I'm looking forward to discussing the incident with you to see if there are any issues of concern."

"I'm afraid certain exigencies beyond my control have already intervened. I must leave for Tel Aviv immediately. Here, this is Major Margolin." Brickner motioned to an officer approaching from a secure doorway to the left. "He has been assigned to us from Aman. I'm sure you are familiar with our defense intelligence agency, which, of course, is investigating our little problem. The major is fully aware of all the facts concerning the incident and can speak with you at length."

"Okay, I think?" Huxley said tentatively.

The colonel looked down at Huxley's card, appearing to read from it. "Major, this is Christian Huxley, Senior Terrorism Investigator, Intelligence and Analysis Division, United States Department of Homeland Security."

"Nice to meet you, sir."

"Likewise, Major, but please, I would appreciate it if you would use Chris, not Christian. I believe that is what it says on the card, Colonel."

Col. Brickner looked at the card again and said, "So it does, so it does. But with that, I am afraid I will have to say goodbye, Chris Huxley." He nodded, turned quickly on his heel and began walking toward the door.

"But Colonel, I'd like to ask…"

The colonel disappeared out the door. The major stepped toward Huxley and directed him away from the door. "I'm sorry, Mr. Huxley, but the colonel is in a terrific hurry. Let's head to the briefing room where I have a team waiting to speak with you."

"A team?"

"Why yes, and they are very anxious to ask you some questions."

CHAPTER 3

THE BRIEFING ROOM could have been an interrogation center with a few extra props. In the center of the room, Huxley and the Aman team filled chairs around a plain metal table. The table was surrounded by bare white walls decorated only with a few patriotic portraits and area maps. A monitor protruded from the wall beyond the head of the table, and a whiteboard with dry erase ink stood in the corner. All of the briefing attendees were officers: two lieutenants, a captain and the major.

Huxley quickly eyed the Aman participants, searching for a weakness. It was quite a contingent for a simple debriefing. Maybe each officer had conducted a separate part of the investigation and thought it expedient to share his findings first hand with Huxley. *And maybe Jews will lie down with Muslims as their brothers next week.* The Israeli officers hadn't even introduced themselves.

Major Margolin cleared his throat. "Mr. Huxley, as you know, Ramat David suffered a terrorist incursion last week Thursday at approximately 0700 hours. Base forces repelled the invasion after several minutes. However, as you may have noticed on your drive in today, one hanger suffered significant damage, and one of our F-16s was totally destroyed and its pilot killed. While terrorist attempts here are not uncommon, such a loss of critical aircraft makes us take this investigation very seriously. Oh, I should mention that three terrorists were killed in the attempt."

"Do you have any background information on them or their associations with any terrorist groups, Major?"

"A little bit so far but not as much as we hope to discover."

"What little bit do you have?"

"All in good time, Mr. Huxley."

Huxley grimaced. What game were they playing? "Well then, what do you believe was their true target, Major?"

"Their mission was simple, and they succeeded to a small degree: destroy as many F-16s as possible. Each F-16 is worth more than $50 million to us."

"But you called this an 'incursion,' so it sounds as if they penetrated your security perimeter. Is that correct?"

Margolin's eyes widened slightly. "Indeed. Do you find that surprising?"

Huxley noted the careful tone of the major and the cold stare of the captain. "Yes, I do," he responded. "I saw your security on the way in, and I doubt it would be easy to breach. And the area outside the fence contains little or no cover for at least a mile, so it seems unlikely they could sneak up on the outside, cut the fence and move in without being detected by the security systems I saw on your perimeter. How could this happen?"

The major paused and glanced at the captain, a stout, powerfully built man in his late twenties. His thick, ruddy face dotted by several red bumps larger than pimples—more like carbuncles—generated a menacing look that had probably unnerved more than one of his detainees over the years. His black hair and the darker skin on his neck and hands revealed he was no transplant to this region but probably had suffered through some disfiguring accident or malady in earlier years. The captain waved his hands to an open posture. "These people are gophers, Mr. Huxley. They seem capable of tunneling miles by pure persistence. We found the head of such a tunnel hidden behind a grounds maintenance shed on the southwest side of this compound. Unfortunately, the remainder of the tunnel appears to have been destroyed, so we don't know yet where it originated. We've begun seismic testing to see if we can track it back to a local building and see if there are any other vermin trying to find their way in."

"I've heard of the tunnels coming from the Gaza Strip into southern Israel, but this far north?"

Major Margolin nodded. "We are only 7 miles from the north end of the West Bank. It was only a matter of time. There are quite a few industrial buildings within a couple of miles where they could have secretly removed the soil and the moved it out on trucks. We should have updated our underground sensors on the perimeter in the past year, but Col. Brickner, well…" He shook his head. "They showed up with RPGs just as we were scrambling F-16s to intercept a few ghosts."

"Ghosts?" asked Huxley.

"We scrambled after our radar showed four bombers approaching from the government-controlled sector of Syria. National radar later contested our radar data. It seems they appeared as ghosts only to Ramat David. We've checked the equipment since, but there's no malfunction."

"But that kind of planning and persistence would take years, and just to destroy an F-16 or two? Sure, F-16s are difficult to replace, but they are not the kind of propaganda pieces you would expect as the target of an obvious suicide mission. Has Hamas or anyone else claimed credit?"

"No. It is as if the terrorist groups do not even know. They often claim credit for any catastrophe—whether or not caused by them—but we have heard nothing. I think taking out a hundred million dollars of military hardware seems worth these gophers' efforts to me, but you may be right." Major Margolin looked down at his folded hands and then up again at Huxley. "So tell me, what do you think was their target?"

The major's tone seemed off and the captain's eyes never blinked. Huxley turned his head to each of the two men in order. "Quite difficult to say without knowing much more about Ramat David and what you might be keeping here other than fighter/bombers. Is there anything here that might seem a bit more, uh, interesting?"

Margolin stared into his eyes with a flat expression and said nothing for several seconds.

Huxley smiled back and elevated one eyebrow for effect. He had asked a forbidden question. *The major will never answer, but let's see if he wiggles a little.*

Margolin returned Huxley's smile. "The terrorists might have thought some other weapon system was located here, Mr. Huxley. You could always try proper channels, but it would be a waste of time."

The carefully chosen response said nothing and everything. They both knew Ramat David housed nuclear bombs available for deployment on its F-16s. Israel had undoubtedly developed a nuclear bomb similar to the B61 the U.S. had developed in the 1960s and previously had available for deployment on its F-16s. The tiny nation may even have created something akin to the more sophisticated B61-12 guided nuclear bomb that NATO had now developed. Although Israel had never officially admitted it possessed even a single nuclear weapon, everyone knew it did. Israel called this a policy of "nuclear ambiguity" and managed to never show up for the signing of any nuclear non-proliferation treaties. It was this solitary Jewish nation's ace in the hole, and everyone knew it.

The Israelis knew they had to protect those nukes with everything they had. The nuclear weapons at Ramat were stored deep in hardened vaults buried beneath the base and accessible only through complex security measures. It would take much more than a terrorist incursion to get at the devices. Huxley had checked with the CIA before his trip and knew the spy boys did not believe any nukes had been removed from Ramat David recently. Indeed, the movement of fissile material had not been detected by the sophisticated gamma ray and neutron detection satellites deployed by the U.S. around the globe.

"Sorry," Huxley said. "I'm sure you guys have it covered."

The major said, "I told you it's not possible. Besides, your country would know about any such event already, wouldn't it?" He smiled artificially. "In any case, such a matter would have deserved a slightly higher priority between our governments, don't you think?"

Huxley nodded gently. He was getting under the major's skin. He had better tread more carefully.

The major nodded back, but then leaned forward. "Now, let me ask you a couple of questions."

"Like what?"

"Well, one of the terrorists killed in the incident was named Baqir Najwa. Do you know him?"

Huxley's head jerked up slightly, and his nostrils flared a touch, but his face quickly returned to its normal countenance. *Keep that poker face, Hux.* He saw the captain studying him like an expert art connoisseur studies an abstract painting he's never seen before, trying to divine meaning from the lines of his face, the set of his chin, and the movement of his eyes. It was the same concentrated look Huxley often gave when he interrogated terrorists—when he wanted to see the truth oozing out of the detainee's expression. This was no briefing. It was an interrogation. *Be very careful, Hux. Figure out their angle and turn it on them. Get what you need and get out of here.*

"Yes, of course. If it is the same Baqir Najwa, I believe I may have met him a few years ago when he was at Guantanamo. He was released a few months later."

"What did you learn about him?"

Huxley smiled wryly. "Now I'm afraid that is something I would not be at liberty to tell you about, Major."

After Major Margolin looked at the captain across the table, the captain scratched his chin and said, "Look, we just want to understand this fellow. We don't need all of the specifics. Can you help us out?"

"I'm not sure that I can think of anything relevant to this incursion, Captain…"

"Yadin. Captain Yadin. Did Baqir Najwa know you well?"

"Know me? Not really, he was just a detainee there. I knew him, his background and that sort, but I would then, wouldn't I? Just like you probably know a bit about my background?"

Yadin glanced quickly at Margolin and back to Huxley. "Yes, but why would he know things about you?"

"Like what things, Captain?"

"Like about your mother?"

Huxley stiffened. *Keep it under control.* How did they know about that conversation? It hadn't been recorded. No, they had just researched his background and made a lucky guess. He leveled his voice and said, "I don't know what you mean."

Captain Yadin was about ready to launch into a diatribe about honesty and cooperation, the growing redness in his face giving it away, but Margolin cut him off, raising his hands and then pushing them palms down, slowly, gently toward the table. He turned toward Huxley and looked directly into his eyes. "Mr. Huxley, let us cut to the chase. Why would a former American CIA interrogator end up with his name and contact information in the iPhone of a dead terrorist who he had previously interrogated?"

Huxley raised his eyebrows, this time intentionally. "That would be very odd."

"Indeed, yet it is so. Can you explain?"

"I'm afraid you have me at a loss."

Major Margolin tapped the table a few times as he stared at Huxley. Then he tilted his head toward one of the lieutenants. "Show him the contacts entry."

The lieutenant stood up and moved over to an electronic panel near the monitor, which lit up and showed the entry in a standard iPhone contacts format:

Christian Huxley
CIA

work
703-486-0623

mobile
723-135-1171

other phone
413-333-4011

work address
Central Intelligence Agency
Washington, DC 20505

other address
2K927 Kings Ridge Dr.
Arden, DE 22329

Notes
A Th. Meet.
Mother: Maryam
Mobile-Other: Main

Huxley's face betrayed no emotions as he stared at the monitor. *They're looking for a response. Don't give them the satisfaction.* They probably figured that, in this room, in this context, with them breathing down his neck, he would leak out a little insight on his association with a dead terrorist. Instead, he smiled. "The guy may have my name all right, and the CIA's main number, but the rest is bogus. I've never even heard of the mobile or the other phone numbers or the other address. The notes are pure nonsense. My mother's name isn't even Maryam. And what is A Th. Meet? A Thursday meeting? I just came into the country today at your request. How could I possibly meet with him on a Thursday?"

Margolin replied flatly, "Of course, we checked on the information, and it does not correlate well to your known information, other than your former employment with the CIA. But there are always associates in these matters, are there not? And we did notice the zip code for your home address is very close to the zip codes in Alexandria, Virginia, where you currently reside. Do you think that is a coincidence?"

"Who knows? This is stupid. You have some metadata on the phone? Where has it been?"

Margolin smiled. "In and out of DC over the past month. Two weeks ago, he was in New York. Three weeks ago in Paris. A month ago in Boston."

That made Huxley more uncomfortable. With a terrorist question mark on his record, Najwa could only have traveled in the U.S. if he had snuck in. Worse yet, the dates and places seemed to match Huxley's own travel schedule over the past month. "You track down his calls and emails?"

"No emails either way. Strange thing is, he never received a call on the phone. He only made two—one to your home phone and one to your cell phone. What did he say to you?"

Huxley could feel the heat rising up the back of his neck. *Regain control. Time for a frontal assault.* He smirked and shook his head slowly. "Not a damn thing. I never knew he called. Look, I don't know what you are driving at, but it sure smells of a witch hunt. If you think this is evidence of some kind of secret association of this terrorist with me or the CIA, you are trying to find a pot of gold by farting at the end of a fading rainbow. It's nothing but a fairy tale."

"Fairy tale?" Margolin said.

"That's right." Huxley said. "Obviously, Najwa could have put this information in the phone for many reasons. He knew I had been in the CIA, so he puts in the CIA contact info. He does a few Internet searches and finds some other info, then he follows me around for a few weeks. Big deal."

"But why would he do that?"

Huxley laughed. "Are you kidding me? Maybe this guy wanted to target me in some way because he hated me so much. Or maybe something else is going on here. I don't know. But I can tell you this: I don't know this apparent terrorist outside of official channels, he is not a U.S. asset of any sort to my knowledge, and if he were, you know I couldn't tell you, and neither my government nor I have had anything to do with this 'incursion' into Ramat David. It's absurd. So let's knock off the crap and start working together to try to figure out what really happened here, and maybe, just maybe, we will both benefit."

Captain Yadin smiled broadly.

Huxley shifted in his chair. *This asshole thinks I protest too much.* Huxley lowered his tone, "So, Major, do you have anything else we can work with?"

Instead, the captain replied, "Why yes, we do, Mr. Huxley. You said your mother's name was misspelled, is that correct?"

"No, I said that is not my mother's first name at all."

"Interesting. Then why would he have included a contacts entry for your mother? Lieutenant."

The monitor screen switched to a new entry:

Maryam Huxley

home
993-485-0010

mobile
993-534-0120

home address
Apt. 3
3 Wiggin St.
Boston, MA 02113

Notes
—Forsaken & Deceased
—No? A dozen times at least.

Huxley scanned the entry. He threw his chest out and leaned in. Choosing the strongest tone he could muster, he said, "Well, this is just crap, crap and more crap." But when he saw "Forsaken & Deceased," his heart sank into his stomach. He unknowingly reached his left hand onto the top of the pants pocket and touched the outline of the object residing there. His thumb rubbed through the material of his pants over the bumpy center of the object along each of the four smooth, square, columnar surfaces projecting out from it. *Forsaken. She might have said that. Damn religion.*

Corpuscles bulging, Captain Yadin slammed his palm on the table. "Come on Huxley, are you telling me you don't recognize the home address?"

Huxley craned his head forward and focused on the address, continuing with his act. "Shit. Excuse me, Captain. Yeah, I think that might be my grandparents' old address."

"And your mother's when she was a child."

"I suppose."

"Still just a bunch of crap?" yelled Captain Yadin. The carbuncles on Captain Yadin's forehead were so red that they threatened to burst and shoot their venom into Huxley's face.

Huxley said, "It seems someone was trying to get my attention over here and they succeeded, because here I am."

"Precisely," Major Margolin interrupted the duel. He glanced quickly at Captain Yadin with a little squint.

Huxley held back a smile. A little truth had slithered out of the look on Margolin's face. He figured Yadin would not speak again.

Major Margolin's face relaxed and he looked back at Huxley. "Now, why is that, Mr. Huxley?"

Huxley grimaced, holding back a laugh at the major's ridiculous good cop ploy. "I have no idea though I plan to find out, and when I do, I may be able to share something with you."

"Thank you. We would appreciate that. But is there anything you can shed some light on right now?"

"I could only speculate."

"Please, Mr. Huxley. We've heard of your uncanny ability to ferret out terrorists' plans in their infancy. If you have any thoughts, any thoughts at all, they might help us understand this better and help both of our nations prevent a similar incident or perhaps something worse."

"Thank you, Major. I would say that Baqir Najwa must have conducted some research on me to find my grandparents' old address. They have been dead for many years. So why is the other information wrong? Moreover, he had my actual cell number if he called it as you have said, yet he included a fake number in the contacts entry. Was he confused? I doubt it. I suspect he was leaving a cryptic message for me."

"A message?"

"Yes. I don't know why, but it is the only theory that makes sense. I'll check these numbers and addresses and see if they lead to anything. I doubt they will, except as some kind of hidden code we must decipher."

"But if he wanted to send you a message, why wouldn't he just call you or send a message to the American Embassy or find some other typical way?"

Huxley leaned his chin on his thumb and forefinger. "A contingency plan. He only wanted the message out if he died."

"Why?" the major asked.

"Maybe he had been threatened by his fellow terrorists. Maybe they thought he had talked to me at Gitmo. Maybe he didn't like what they were doing. I don't know. Maybe he had some other reason for suspecting some-one else." *And maybe the message wasn't from Najwa at all.*

"OK, but why in the phone and why in a coded message?"

Huxley shrugged. "He may have thought others would see the phone before he died. Perhaps he thought there was a good chance his body would be found with the phone intact. It probably has nothing to do with this incident at Ramat David, but who knows until we figure it out? How did Najwa die in the incursion?"

"Misfired rocket," the captain said. "Exploded in his face. The phone was in a pack on his back and wasn't damaged."

"Is there anything more that you found on his body or on the iPhone that might give us more clues?"

The major responded, "Quite a few more contact entries, but nothing relating to you. Some are English. Most are Arabic. None seem real. Though we have had the same suspicions, we haven't been able to decipher any messages or codes."

"I'll get our guys working on it right away. Can I get a download of all of the entries?"

"Certainly, but do we have an understanding about sharing on this?"

Huxley nodded. "As long as it goes both ways."

"Of course."

"Is there anything else you have uncovered?"

"Nothing much. Najwa was found with this in his pack." The major gestured to the lieutenant, who produced a double-pointed metal pick with a six-inch wooden handle. A small jewel was centered over an engraved crown, itself centered between two letters in Old English script, "W" and "M". "Not sure how he was planning to use it, if at all, here. It may have been to dig the last few yards into the compound after the rest of the tunnel was destroyed."

Huxley snapped a picture of the tool. "Was anything else unusual happening on the base the day of the incursion?"

"Just typical ops."

"May I interview some base personnel."

"Certainly. The lieutenant will accompany you."

"Thank you, Major."

Two hours later a white cab picked Huxley up from the Ramat David Airbase and took him to a nearby hotel just outside of Mizra. While he was a bit disheveled and still a little emotionally shaken, he had weathered the storm. There was just too much garbage in those phone entries, and he was U.S. Homeland Security, after all. Huxley might help them, even if he had

had no part in this. If they didn't trust him, so what? *In this business, trust just gets you a knife in the back.*

They were letting this play out, following him to see if it led anywhere interesting. It was a method he had employed with a few of his own detainees. The detainee had to believe he was being released because of his "innocence." While Huxley could not be detained without all hell breaking loose, they had at least feigned some trust in him to find the answer.

Aman had also withheld something vital from him. Two corporals from a computer maintenance unit at Camp Rabin had visited Ramat early that morning. Huxley had uncovered this little gem after he excused himself to the restroom and slipped into the central waiting area for a few minutes. The friendly airman showed him the daily visitor logbook, laughed and told him, "When the air raid siren ended and we returned from the bunkers, those two geeks from Rabin were huddling in the corner under some tables with their hands over their ears. Lucky there wasn't any direct hit on the facility. Jerks said they had missed reviewing the air raid protocol for the base."

Huxley smiled. *I doubt that. I doubt that very much.*

CHAPTER 4

HUXLEY LEANED HIS head back and closed his eyes. The morning sun warmed his bare lower legs as they rested on the cast iron table he had dragged to the patio. The image stared at him from the darkness under his eyelids: meaningless phone numbers, his alleged address in a city he had never visited, and strange contact notes. He opened his eyes and glanced again at the Najwa contacts list downloaded to his iPhone, this time switching to the entry on Maryam Huxley.

He took a sip of coffee, Americano. It was like his early days as a code breaker at the CIA. He had always loved mathematics, logic and puzzles. It only made sense that they first recruited him out of Harvard as a code breaker, but he had found the work unsatisfying because he never had a chance to follow up on his discoveries. That was for the operators and investigators, which is why he eventually decided to join their particular fraternity.

Huxley stared at the entry. Baqir Najwa had gotten nearly every fact wrong except his grandparents' last address. Then there was the entry in the Notes section, which correctly identified his mother's emotional state before she had shriveled up. Who would know that? Najwa? Had Najwa somehow divined that from Huxley's response to Najwa's emotional plea?

"I have a wife. I have children," Najwa had said, his puffy face streaming with tears. "For Allah's sake, I have a mother just like you! What would your

mother say if she knew you tortured me because of my love of God? I am no guiltier than you. Why don't you go torture yourself?"

How could that terrorist have known the impact his plea would have on Huxley? How could he have known the emotional torture that was already tearing away at Huxley's world? It seemed far-fetched, yet the plea had remained, echoing into the prison corridors. It had stopped Najwa's pain and begun Huxley's anew. Huxley would never again interrogate detainees for the CIA. Still, how would Najwa have known that? And even if he had known, why would he have put it in a contacts listing?

Huxley sipped slow and deep from his coffee. Maybe "Forsaken" was just part of the message—not intended for him at all—just one of those unlucky happenstances.

He flipped between two address entries:

> 2K927 Kings Ridge Dr.
> Arden, DE 22329
>
> 3971 North St. Joan Way
> Kingston, Mass. 01723

The two shared one interesting five-letter combination: "kings" in "Kings Ridge Dr." and "Kingston." He had checked and found they were both partially real. There was a Kingsridge Rd.—close enough—in Arden, Delaware, as well as a Kingston, Massachusetts. Nevertheless, the addresses were phony.

The problem with the Kingsridge address required no digging. Some rural addresses in the U.S. used alphanumerics, but usually the letter was a cardinal point of the compass that came first to designate the general area of the route. Kingsridge Road was in the city of Arden, not in the countryside. Plus, the zip code was just wrong.

The Kingston address facially appeared more legitimate, but a simple search showed there was no St. Joan Way in Kingston. In fact, Kingston was originally part of Plymouth and settled by Protestant pilgrims in the 1620s. It would be rather strange and beyond ironic if one of its streets were named after a Roman Catholic saint who fought for the French Catholics against the English in the Hundred Years War and was eventually burned at the stake in pre-reformation England for her "heresy." It also seemed odd that the Commonwealth of Massachusetts in the entry was not abbreviated with "MA," the standard two-letter postal abbreviation in use for over sixty years; instead, the address used the old four-letter "Mass." abbreviation, even though "MA" appeared in the real address of his grandparents. Moreover, the zip code did not exist, though at least it was close to some other zip codes used in other parts of that state.

Huxley took another long sip and scratched the back of his head. *Two kings and some alpha-numerics that probably contain some kind of code. But what code?* There just didn't seem to be a starting point.

He thought about the many kings throughout history and mythology, but none of the numbers or other words seemed to work any magic with them. An Internet search showed that three kings were tied to St. Joan of Arc and her battles: Henry VI of England, Philip III of Burgundy, and Charles VII of France. Could something be involved with them? He couldn't see it. *I'm in Israel. What about its kings?*

Bruce Springsteen interrupted his examination, singing, "Meet me at Mary's place. We're gonna have a party!" The screen on his phone flashed "Kira Sampson, Homeland Security."

Huxley answered, "Hey Kira, whaddya got?"

A calm, youthful but confident feminine voice responded, "That depends, what do I get for staying this late to find the needles in your latest haystack?"

Huxley chuckled. "I'd rather you find a key than a needle. I never really learned to pick locks with long instruments."

"I thought you spy boys could break into Fort Knox with a hairpin."

"Yeah, well, I was never a lofty spy-type, so I guess they never taught me that particular skill. They just sat my butt down in a lonely prison with another lonely, desperate soul and waited to see which one started crying to be let out first."

"I can't see you ever crying, Mr. Huxley," Kira said.

"You've never seen me watch the end of Casablanca, have you?"

"No, sir. I didn't see you as the romantic hero type either."

"Now that's my problem," he answered with a sarcastic tone, "I'm so hopelessly romantic, I got no time to be a hero." They shared a laugh. "I tell you what," he continued. "If your little needle ends up getting me in the door on this investigation, I'll ask the muckety-mucks if they can give you another raise."

"You know they never give more than one raise a year. Department policy."

"Well, I didn't say you'd get one. I just said I'd ask."

Kira said, "Thanks a bunch, sir. I'll remember that the next time one of your favorite requests come in when I'm ready to punch out for the day. I'm not sure I deserve a raise for this one anyway. The terrorist's digging tool was an archaeologist's pick, just as you guessed. The crown suggests royalty, so you might think with the English script it originated in some place like England."

"Nah. I figured something more pretentious in the U.S. We love royal symbols even if we tend to despise monarchical rule. Probably some institution harkening back to colonial days."

"You got it. You sure you need my help?"

"Always."

"Well, the 'W' and 'M' in script are normally overlapped above the crown rather than separated on either side of it. You've heard of the College of William and Mary, haven't you?"

"Of course. It's one of the oldest well-bred academic institutions in the U.S. Not much of a football team, though."

"No, but they do have a rather prestigious archaeology department."

"Great. See if you can track that pick to someone in particular."

"Done. Professor Jonathan Stirling is on sabbatical in Israel. Apparently he has been digging for a year at Tel Megiddo."

"Interesting. Hold on." Huxley searched his iPhone map. "That's less than 10 miles from Ramat David. Is he still working there?"

"Sure is," Kira said. "Unless he is one of the dead terrorists."

"I doubt that. Hard for Aman to confuse an American professor for an Arab, unless—."

"No, I asked. He is as white bread as his name."

Huxley asked, "Of whom did you make these small requests in the middle of the night?"

"Well I managed to recall that little funding provision in the Patriot Act. Let's just say the dean of a college dependent on federal and state grants becomes very attentive when national security is at stake."

"I don't doubt it. But that means our professorial digger will have a jump start on a story when I speak with him. The dean probably called him and demanded an explanation right after you hung up."

"Sorry about that. You said you wanted this quickly."

"So I did," Huxley said. "Don't worry. I'm sure I will still find time to write that raise request. You get me a contact at Camp Rabin? I need to find out about those techie corporals."

Kira replied, "Still working on it. Got a call into DOD to see if we can find someone who can bypass official channels for you."

"Great. Call me as soon as you have it. And get some sleep."

CHAPTER 5

PROFESSOR JONATHAN STIRLING'S brow wrinkled just above his hand, which bisected his forehead to block the sun from his face. His eyes and nose crinkled beneath the hand, though his wire-rimmed glasses covered most of the crows' feet at the edge of his eyes. Beads of sweat already covered his sunbaked skin as he kneeled in a half-buried stairwell rising directly toward the east. With a small metallic tool in hand, Stirling was looking up the stairs at Huxley, who appeared like a two-dimensional shadow with the mid-morning sun at his back.

The professor remained still, staring at Huxley for a full five count. "What would an investigator from the U.S. Department of Homeland Security be doing on an old hilltop in Israel? I know you boys worry about evil terrorists from this part of the globe, but this is taking the Armageddon myth a bit far, don't you think?"

Huxley didn't skip a beat. "You never know if someone might take Revelation a bit too seriously, Professor. You guys don't have any weapons of world destruction buried under this hill, do you?"

The professor smiled. "You never know until you get to the bottom of things."

"My thoughts exactly."

The professor grinned and stood up, whisked past Huxley up the steps, grumbled something in Hebrew to an assistant, and then turned back to

Huxley. "Mr. Huxley, let's walk the site. I'll give you a little tour while we see if I can be of any assistance to you."

The two men began traversing the ancient city on a hill. To the uninitiated, it consisted merely of various piles of rocks, stairs, walls and platforms, all interspersed with a few palm trees; to an archaeologist, it was a vivid, historic painting. Stirling walked Huxley through two ancient stables that could hold nearly 500 horses in their hey day. The two inspected the hewn stone walls with basalt foundation standing at the foot of the wide Canaanite Gate, constructed to allow chariots into the city during the Bronze Age before the Jewish resettlement.

Nearing the end of the tour, Huxley said, "I'd like to show you a picture, if I could." Huxley pulled out his phone, tapped a couple of times and handed the phone to the professor. "Are you familiar with this instrument?"

"Ah, you found it. Seems like a long ways to travel to investigate the petty theft of a memento, though."

"A memento?"

"Yes. I was given this pick by my Department Chair on the occasion of my 25th year of service at the College."

"When did you last see it?" Huxley asked.

"A few weeks ago. I figured it had just gone missing in that wreck of a trailer I keep in the parking lot. But what does this have to do with Homeland Security?"

Huxley studied the professor's face as he answered, "This tool was found a week ago in the possession of a terrorist killed while trying to infiltrate an Israeli base."

The professor's eyes widened slightly beneath the rims. He took a deep breath, turned and coughed. "I'm sorry to hear that, Mr. Huxley. What was the terrorist's name?"

Huxley could see that the news had shaken the professor, even though he must have known Huxley was coming this morning. "I was hoping you might have some ideas on that."

"I see. Well, I don't see how I can help you. I don't know who took it. I wasn't even sure it was missing."

"So you did believe it was missing? Did you file a police report?"

"No, no. As I said, I did not know whether I had just misplaced it. In any case, I doubt that thing is worth much to anyone but me."

"It seems an odd thing to steal, don't you think?" Huxley asked.

"Precisely."

"Was anything else missing from your trailer?"

"Not that I have noticed. Have you peered within my trailer?"

A five-inch long black millipede crawled from underneath a rock by Huxley's foot, and Huxley's stomach turned a few notches as he drew his foot back. *Creepy-crawling things.* Still, they were far better than the rats crawling in the dark corners of an improvised detention cellar.

The professor took advantage of the pause in the questioning and returned to his narration. "This is one of the oldest areas of Megiddo that we have uncovered—about 6000 BCE, well before the end of the Stone Age. This site is incredibly resilient and kept being destroyed and rebuilt over thousands of years. We have found evidence of civilizations in different layers here from the Stone Age through the beginning of the Babylonian exile of Jews from this region. That would be around 587 BCE, when—"

The professor quickly pivoted and shouted in Hebrew to an assistant down the hill and began pointing toward a tour group that seemed to be getting a little too close to a rock wall on the Western end of the site. A little while later a tourist scampered out of the pit between Huxley and the tour group. "We have to live with these tourists trampling on our site, you know," said the professor. "The guides are supposed to keep them in line and off of our dig, but, as always, some guides are better than others. Unfortunately, it's how we get paid. Not much money in archaeology research these days. Government funds keep drying up. Now, where were we?"

"Who would have known that you had the memento?" Huxley asked.

"The memento. Yes, well, quite a few people, I suppose, since I occasionally employ it, or rather did employ it, on the site."

"You used a 25th anniversary memento in your everyday work?"

"No, not every day, mind you." The professor shrugged. "It is just one of those things I use to break up the tedium. While this job is unbelievably fascinating, just look around you, Mr. Huxley, you know that sometimes we can go for extended periods without any discoveries worth even a paltry cocktail party mention. I deploy the pick when I'm a bit in the dumps and need a reminder to stay the course. A new wonder often rewards the patient, Mr. Huxley."

"Have you had any members of your crew leave recently?"

"Oh, the workers come and go, particularly the locals. I wouldn't read much into that."

"Still, has anyone left recently?" Huxley asked.

"I would check with Professor Katzir. This is an operation of the Tel Aviv University, after all. I'm just here as a temporary associate director of this particular dig. Ask Katzir. I'd say we would have two or three local helpers who have left in the last month or so. This is a pretty good-sized dig."

"This tool, this memento, would it be useful for digging a tunnel?"

"Not much, I wouldn't think. No weight to it, is there? Delightful if you are finely picking away at debris surrounding delicate items—pottery and the like. But a tunnel? It would be a bit like a prisoner digging his way to freedom with a spoon. I suppose it could be done given a long enough time, but if he had a shovel and a heavy pick, it would be terribly more efficient."

The two were standing on the north end of the site. Huxley noticed a post with a vertical sign at the edge of the site, reading, "Let peace prevail" in both English and Hebrew. Huxley smiled at the irony: this was Armageddon. Huxley looked away from the dig and was struck by the gorgeous view. Tel Megiddo stood high above the wide plain to the north, the beautiful Jezreel Valley, formerly known as the "Plain of Megiddo" in Hebrew and the "Plain of Armageddon" in Greek. The sun gleamed off of enormous rectangular patches of yellow, brown and green fields interrupted here and there by small villages sporting squat houses on the vast plain. In the distance, the hills pushed upward, trying to reveal their magnificence through the haze of the day, while larger cities nestled comfortably at their feet. On a clear day, you could even see—

Huxley tilted his head slightly and then looked back at the professor. "Tell me, Professor, does anyone ever do any star gazing from here? It feels like a natural observatory."

"Oh yes. We had a big telescope out here a few months ago when Encke's Comet was shooting by. They had it set up just about here."

"Who brought the telescope out?"

"That would be Dante Tocelli. He was a bright one and seemed to have some kind of background in astronomy. Double major or something like that."

"Was a bright one?" Huxley asked.

The professor cocked his head and let out some air. "Well, I don't mean he's dead or anything. He returned to his university in Rome—Sapienza, I believe. He was just here on an internship."

"When did he leave?"

"About two weeks ago. But you need not worry yourself about him. He's a bright one. Not the type. I think he's a Catholic. I certainly don't think he's Arab. He has darker skin, but more of the northern Mediterranean type. And, of course, he possesses an Italian surname."

"You are probably right about that. Does the dig perform security background checks on interns?"

"Not that I'd know. You would have to consult with Katzir."

"Of course. Thanks for your help, Professor. I'll let you get back to your work."

"Certainly. And, uh, Mr. Huxley, since you have a picture of it, do you suppose you could manage to return that little memento to me?"

"I'll see what I can do."

Huxley turned back to the north and stared at the vast expanse of flat land lying to the north and east of Megiddo before Mount Caramel rising up some 8 miles away. About seven miles below, slightly to the east of north, the Ramat David Airbase seemed peacefully at rest.

The tour group clamored up the hill nearby. The tour guide droned on, "Before you lies the Jezreel Valley. It is peaceful now, but it has been the site of many important battles. Though this Tel was built over many thousands of years by many civilizations, one fact remained throughout—it was a critical juncture along a narrow pass and trade route connecting Egypt in the West with Assyria to the East. As such, the valley has seen great bloodshed. You may know it better as the 'Plain of Armageddon.' Napoleon once called it 'the most natural battleground of the whole Earth.'"

The tourist who had been chased out of the pit by the Professor spoke up, "I have heard there were many battles described in the Old Testament here. What are they and where can we find them?" With his sunglasses now propped on his head, the tourist was carrying a Bible and madly thumbing through it.

The tour leader smiled, enjoying the interaction of her group and the opportunity to demonstrate her preparation. "You are correct, sir. Deborah & Barak fought Sisera as recorded in Judges 5. Saul fought the Philistines here as stated in the first book of Samuel. Even the great Solomon battled an Egyptian Pharaoh here. Second Chronicles refers to that battle. And two of Judah's kings, Ahaziah and Josiah, died on this plain nearly two and a half centuries apart. Both can be found in 2 Kings."

Huxley's mouth opened slightly. He whispered to himself, "2 Kings. 2 Kings." He switched his iPhone to the downloaded terrorist's contacts list and stared at it. Something he hadn't noticed before. That note now made sense:

> 2K927 Kings Ridge Dr.
> Arden, DE 22329
>
>
> Notes
> A Th. Meet

Why Delaware? Why A Th. Meet? And why had he not seen this before? DE was not Delaware and there was no Thursday meeting. "2 Kings … DE A Th. Meet" was a message. 2 Kings meet death near this ridge. 2 Kings also referred to the book of the Old Testament that chronicled their deaths. The house number now made sense. He tapped Safari on his phone and fired up an Internet search. After a few moments, he found the passage right where he expected, at 2 Kings 9:27:

> Seeing what was happening, Ahaziah, king of Judah, fled toward Beth-haggan. Jehu pursued him, shouting, "Him too!" They struck him as he rode through the pass of Gur near Ibleam, but he continued his flight as far as Megiddo and died there.

Bingo. Megiddo is the answer. How about the zip code? He used it to punch in 2 Kings 23:29, confirming his suspicion:

> In his time Pharaoh Neco, king of Egypt, went up toward the Euphrates River against the king of Assyria. King Josiah set out to meet him, but was slain at Megiddo at the first encounter.

Huxley smiled broadly as that warm sensation returned to his gut at last. He felt eyes upon him and glanced up furtively. He saw the eyes of the wayward tourist with the Bible dart down and begin searching again through the Bible.

A little tail from my new friends at Aman? Undoubtedly, someone was here on their behalf, trailing and deciphering his moves, but this guy didn't look quite right. He certainly was not Jewish.

Huxley had seen the somewhat darker skin and slight fold of the eyelids before, in Afghanistan. One of the bigger tribes, the Hazara, shared some of their ancestors with Mongolians, such as Genghis Kahn. Something like one-third had the special star-cluster Y-chromosome marker tied to the great conqueror—probably the result of the exodus from Persia of Mongolian soldiers as their empire began to crumble behind them in the fourteenth century. Many of the Hazara obviously shared similar genes for eye shape as well. While most Hazara today were Twelver Shiites, a small minority were Sunnis.

Huxley wiped the sweat off his forehead. Hard to figure how Aman managed to turn an Afghan into their contractor, but they must have their ways. Huxley took a step toward the bible-carrying man. "Excuse me sir, but I found the references you were searching for in 2 Kings. They are 9:27 and 23:29. Great numbers, don't you think?"

The man gleamed back a smile. "Thank you sir. 2 Kings is a big book to search page by page."

Huxley returned the smile. That accent was Hazaran all right, but there was no fear in his eyes. Maybe he was not aware of the contacts entry. "You are welcome. Are you here on vacation?" Huxley asked, though he did not speak the words in English. He had used Dari Persian—probably the wrong dialect, but close enough.

The man's head jerked back, and for just an instant a micro-expression of fear appeared in the narrowing of his pupils and furrowing of his brow. Less than a second later, he smiled. In Dari Persian, he responded, "You speak my language. How delightful. Yes, I am here on vacation from my sad, war-torn nation."

"With a Christian Bible?"

"I cherish history, sir, and knew this was an area full of it, especially of the Old Testament sort. I must admit, though, I borrowed the book from that nice American lady in the group over there when I realized it would assist my understanding."

"You can read English?" Huxley asked. "How worldly of you."

"A symptom of learning to read orders from your military, I'm afraid." He switched back to English. "But I must go now sir. The group is leaving."

"Could I trouble you to take a picture of me in front of this valley? It is beautiful, and I loathe selfies so."

"Yes, of course."

Huxley pulled up his phone in front of his face, the main camera lens pointing toward the tourist, and touched a few buttons. "Let me see here, I have to get this camera off of selfie mode." He fumbled around for a few seconds. "There we go. Here now, just touch this button and I'll give you a big smile."

After the picture, they nodded to each other and parted. As the man hurried back to his tour group, Huxley switched his phone to view pictures and slid his own picture to the right. It was quickly replaced by a close-up headshot of the Afghan man with a pinched expression. *Rather clumsy of an operative to allow me to take his picture.* He sent off a message with the picture to Kira.

❈ ❈ ❈

Abdul Saboor Anwari sat in his rented white Volvo, which idled and poured AC onto his sweat-dripped face. Anwari stared ahead at nothing in particular, thinking. How would he explain his encounter with Christian Huxley to his controller? He was supposed to tail him, observe him, assist as necessary, and report back. There was nothing about contact, which meant, of course, contact was forbidden. But contact had been made. He had pushed a little too close, not realizing Huxley was so keenly observant. He had been warned about that, but the guy had been in a deep conversation with the professor. The professor had noticed him when he tried to get a little closer to hear their conversation, and that tipped Huxley's mind toward him. Now all might be lost. Huxley had made him, even speaking to him in his native language. *He looked at me like he knew me, like he trusted me, and I somehow almost felt like I could trust him. He is very good at this game.*

The flip phone's speaker started blaring a simple ring tone. He looked at the screen, but it could only be one person. He glanced at the side and ensured the encryption/decryption device was turned on. Although it didn't look like much, the chip stopped the NSA and other spy agencies from capturing key words in their massive supercomputers. Nevertheless, you couldn't be too careful. "Hello," he said in English, since Arabic would just attract more attention.

A deep, resonant voice spoke in English with an Arabic accent, "What is the status?"

"He gets Tel Megiddo."

"Good. Where is he now."

"He's at the site. He'll be leaving soon, I imagine." Anwari took a deep breath. "There is something else. He spoke to me in Persian."

"You made contact?"

"No, he did. He's pretty quick. I was just trying to be helpful."

"That wasn't the plan, was it? Contact is dangerous with him." The voice on the other end let out a deep sigh of disgust, followed by a short pause. "Did he ID you?"

"I don't think so," said Anwari, "but I was forced to admit to some of my background. I am a tourist. I think it will just stay there."

"Don't count on it."

Anwari closed his eyes, resting his forehead on his fingertips. *Am I in danger here?*

The voice continued, "Don't worry about it either. Remember, you are an Afghan hero. We may be able to use this. Keep your distance but track his movements. We don't want him seeing you show up nearby any time soon. He does not trust coincidence. I'll call tomorrow, same time."

Switching off the scrambler, Anwari pocketed the phone. Afghan hero? The Americans saw it that way. He couldn't tell if he was a hero or a traitor back then, so why should he believe it now? Images of that painful night smoldered in front of him. He closed his eyes and tightened his lips, holding the emotion in, recalling his pledge. *Inshallah.*

CHAPTER 6

"Another pint, Sir?" The barmaid at Sof Hfamim pub flashed her best tip-provoking smile at Huxley.

Huxley returned the smile. "Hmm, no, just water, please." He could use a good deal of logical insight, maybe colored by a little creativity. While another beer might pump up his creative powers a touch, it might undermine the clarity of his reason. He couldn't let the patterns escape him.

He had failed at Megiddo. Sure, he had found the initial clue in the contacts list and perhaps another strand to run down in Rome, but nothing came from his follow up with Prof. Katzir, the dig leader at Megiddo. He had a small lead, but something else kept gnawing at him: the apparent clues in the terrorist's contacts list. Why did the terrorist give him Tel Megiddo? There was something more here, and the two Huxley contacts in Najwa's phone held the key.

The "real" information in the contacts entries probably held no codes or clues, so what was left in the entry on Christian Huxley? He focused on the "Other" address:

2K927 Kings Ridge Dr.
Arden, DE 22329

Only the words "Ridge" and "Arden" had not been used by him to figure out Tel Megiddo. Ridge could refer to the hill or "Tel" of Megiddo at the archaeology site. Perhaps Ridge should be ignored, but did "Dr. Arden" refer to someone? He searched "Dr. Arden" on his computer and found references to a few random physicians and dentists, but nothing noteworthy. Probably just the props and costumes of the entry—pieces that helped disguise it as an apparently real address to the casual observer.

What about the note: "Mother: Maryam?" When he saw "Forsaken and Deceased" again, his stomach fell. He swallowed hard and returned his left hand back from the outside of his pants pocket, feeling the only tangible thing remaining from his mother. *No time to wallow in the depths of that despair.* Still, he couldn't help wading in for a few seconds.

His mother, Adona, had officially died over a year ago, but her mind had departed nearly a year before that. Would she have believed that her mythical soul sped away to Heaven as soon as her mind drifted away or that it would simply wait for the rest of her body to expire? No, she was a devout Roman Catholic, so her soul would sit and wait for her body to rot as long as her heart kept beating and her brain created a wavy EEG. To the church, it was like leaving a bad husband—death guarded the only exit door for souls and marriages (except for that little annulment technicality). Never mind that her personality had fled her, that she couldn't even remember him, let alone forgive him. He had to live with that tragedy as he cared for her that last year, all the while feeling the guilt enveloping him as the life oozed slowly out of her body. He had no time for this self-pity.

Huxley looked up and caught the waitress's eye and smiled. She returned the gesture, nodded and walked over to his table. "I've changed my mind. Get me a Guinness."

"Here's your water, sir. The Guinness will be here as soon as they finish slow pouring it. You know how that is."

"Aye, but 'tis part of its inherent beauty, me little lass."

She shook her head but smiled.

He returned to his own dialect and squinted slightly. "Seriously, I think I can make it that long."

"Thank you, sir."

He returned to the phone entry. Nearly every part of the Maryam entry must be decipherable. The grandparents' address fit his mother only as her childhood address, though his grandparents had lived there much longer. He had walked with his momma around the Italian neighborhood on Boston's North End when he was young. That was a few years before his father's "accident," when they were all visiting Nonna and Nonno. Even then it was one of the prettiest little neighborhoods in Boston. No grand old mansions towered over the neighborhood like in Beacon Hill, and no grand shops lured visitors like in the Back Bay; still, its little brick buildings felt quaint and ethnic, and at dinner time the scent of breads and sauces wafting out of the windows made the whole place smell like home.

He had walked with his mother by a beautiful church a few blocks away when his father went out to "mail a few letters." That was his father's little code for spending the afternoon at a local tavern in yet another feeble attempt to soak the ever-present depression out of his bones. On the other hand, maybe his father was finding other avenues for his afternoon entertainment even then—a form of escape that would not occur to Huxley until just before the "accident."

Although the church was pretty, he'd always been drawn more to its outdoor "Peace Garden." Filled with statues of various Catholic saints, the garden was an ideal spot for his mother to nurture him through his Catholic upbringing. She would point to each statue, quizzing him on the saints and their history. It gave him yet another chance to garner praise from his beloved mother. She was always so proud of him, and he loved to hear her tell him how clever he was. She often added, "Your brain is a gift from the Lord, my son. Use it for His good works. Every gift can be used for good or evil. You must trust your heart and fill it with God's love, and He will guide your way." Of course, if his father had been there, the rogue would have coughed up phlegm at Momma's pronouncement and then given Christian a knowing smirk behind her back.

Huxley's favorite piece in the garden was really a set of several statues. Mary, the mother of Jesus, stood in the center with her palms together, raised in prayer. In front of the Virgin knelt three unknown worshipers praying for the Holy Mother's intercession, while a sheep stood to the side. It was a lovely piece of art that told any thinking Christian that this was a Roman Catholic Church.

The fake name on the contacts' entry was Maryam Huxley. Was

Maryam a reference to his mother's devout beliefs? The earlier clue was a biblical reference, so perhaps this one continued the motif. When he searched "Maryam" on the Internet, two religious entries appeared. The first referred to a related form of the name, Mariam, the Hebrew name for the sister of Moses and Aaron. According to Exodus, she sang a victory song while gloating after Pharaoh and his army were drowned in the Red Sea:

> Sing to the LORD, for he is gloriously triumphant;
> Horse and chariot he has cast into the sea.

The second hit told him Maryam was the Aramaic and Arab equivalent to "Mary," the mother of Jesus Christ, who appears in both the Christian New Testament and the Islamic Qur'an. Since Mary and Jesus likely spoke often in Aramaic, it made sense that the entry in the contacts list would refer to her instead of Miriam from the Old Testament.

There were other fake parts of the contacts entry, such as the "other" address for Maryam:

3971 North St. Joan Way
Kingston, Mass. 01723

St. Joan Way was not a street in Kingston. Did this mean St. Joan showed the way north? How could Joan of Arc do that? Arc. Arc. That had another meaning. An arc in geometry is the segment of a circle. The degrees of an angle from the center to the endpoints of the arc on the circle are shorthand for the length of the arc. If you know the center and the starting direction, the degrees give you the new direction. Then all you need is the radius to get the next endpoint. This arc could show him the way. From where? Tel Megiddo.

He studied the address further. There were two sets of numbers—3971 and 01723—and a direction—north. He pulled up a map on Google Earth and made his origin the center of Tel Megiddo, since that was the starting point from the last clue. Degrees on a circle in math, or on a map or compass, always increased from 0 degrees at North to 360 degrees clockwise as you completed the circle. He used the first number as his degrees and used the army convention of two decimal places, making it 39.71 degrees.

He looked back at the address. Kilometers, or KM, was indicated by the capital K in Kingston and the capital M in "Mass." That explained the strange abbreviation of Massachusetts. MA would have created three capital letters, "KMA," which might have been too confusing. Using the same convention, he figured 17.23 KM, so he looked 17.23 KM from Tel Megiddo on an angle of 39.71 degrees and then zoomed in. He let out a little laugh. "I guess I should pat myself on the back—the Church of the Annunciation."

It all came together now: the angle and distance, Maryam, Mass, and the home address that represented the childhood home of Mary, not of Huxley's real mother. He looked it up on the Internet and confirmed his suspicions. The Church of the Annunciation was located in Nazareth, Israel. Catholics built the church over the reputed ruins of Mary's childhood home—the home she lived in before marrying Joseph and before bearing Jesus in her womb. It was known as the Church of the Annunciation because they believed Mary's childhood home was the site of the Annunciation—the moment when the angel Gabriel told Mary she would bear God's only begotten Son. The church would hold a Mass there at least every Sunday.

Bruce began singing about Mary's place on Huxley's cell. "Hello again, Kira. Good to hear from you during normal working hours."

"I don't know what 'normal working hours' are, but thanks. I got a contact for you at Rabin Army Base. Just sent it to your phone. We also have a hit on the picture you sent. He's Abdul Saboor Anwari, a former lomri baridman in the Afghan army who fought with us against the Taliban there. A lomri baridman is roughly equivalent to a first lieutenant."

"You know I was there, right?" Huxley said. "Anything special about his service?"

"The CIA has him down as a possible future operative. Well respected, speaks and reads fluent English, Dari Persian and Arabic. Got along well with his American counterparts. Oh, and he was a bit of a hero."

"What did he do?"

"First, he was great at sniffing out the Taliban in hostile areas. Seemed to have a sixth sense about it. He also saved a U.S. major's life once when his Black Hawk was hit by an RPG in Logar. Seems Anwari and his men fought off a Taliban contingent closing in on the survivors. Lost half his men and caught two bullets himself, but he kept them at bay until air support arrived."

Huxley rubbed his chin. "He still in the army?"

"Officially, yes," Kira replied, "but he's now unofficially inactive on a small salary. He led a few other missions as we were beginning to turn over the reigns to the Afghan army, but then he went on leave to help his brother, who was in Kabul mending from a Taliban attack in Jalalabad. Shortly after that, the Afghan army let him go inactive, apparently at his request. A bit odd, but they probably owed him after taking a couple bullets for his country. Not disabled, though. According to the CIA records, he maintains contacts with the army's intelligence agencies and occasionally provides some intel."

"Any suggestion he might be working for the Israelis?"

"CIA wasn't aware of any contracts, but Aman doesn't share those. Tough to tell."

"Could he really just be on a vacation in Israel?"

"Well," Kira said, "Israel approved his visa for that purpose a few weeks ago. There was some delay in the application, but it was granted after the Israeli state department did a background check with us on his military record. You would think Israel would expedite his papers if they used him as an operative, but the CIA tells me the visa thing might have been a ruse to keep us in the dark. Apparently they've done that before."

"Thanks. Anything else?"

"Just one thing," Kira said. "He seems to have traveled pretty extensively for a man with his limited income. Rome, Pakistan, Israel."

"You sure the CIA hasn't procured him as an operative?"

"I think they would tell me, wouldn't they?" she asked.

Huxley chortled with sarcasm. "You still believe in fairy tales, I see. No, Kira, not always. We Homeland folks look an awful lot like a troubling upstart cousin to the spy boys. They may invite us to their holiday dinners, but they aren't going to share much beyond that happy little meal. Any line on where Anwari is staying here?"

"He's at a hotel in Nazareth. I'll send you the info."

"Nazareth." Huxley nodded a few times. "All signs point north. Well, northeast anyway." This former Afghan lieutenant was looking more interesting by the moment. Maybe the lieutenant could use a new American friend. *Keep your friends close…*

CHAPTER 7

STANDING AT HIS bathroom sink, Anwari practiced the Wudu cleansing ritual perfectly, washing his hands three times, rinsing his mouth three times, and sniffing water into his nose—again three times. After completing these steps, he washed his face and arms three times and put his wet hands over his head and placed them around his neck and into his ears. Finally, he washed his feet—again three times. He always began with the right foot, just as he always cleansed his right arm and right hand before the counterparts on his left.

Anwari walked into the bedroom and faced south toward Mecca, raised both of his hands to his ears and said, "Allahu Akbar." He then began the opening prayer of the Salat in Arabic: "In the Name of Allah, the Most Gracious, the Most Merciful. All Praise is due to Allah alone…" He continued the Salat with prayers and bowing until he reached the Sujud. He prostrated himself on his knees, with his forehead and nose touching the stinking hotel carpet and said aloud three times in Arabic, "Glory to my Sustainer, the most High." He stopped with his nose still on the ground, sighed, and mentally rebuked himself for his lack of focus. The glory of Allah had been swept aside in his mind by an image of Christian Huxley.

Last night, he had watched Huxley emerge from the tavern near Tel Megiddo after sundown, pick up his luggage at his hotel near Mizra, and travel north to Nazareth—to the very hotel where Anwari was staying. It did not surprise Anwari that Huxley had traveled to Nazareth, but at this particular hotel on a night when he would have to pay for two hotel rooms 9 kilometers apart?

After finishing his prayers, Anwari stood up and glanced at his well-worn copy of the Qur'an on the desk. *Read it again. Find your way.* He spoke aloud: "Allah, be merciful for my transgressions. I seek to follow your words, but I am lost in their beauty. Help me find my retribution. No, not my retribution, but yours. Please help me see the right path. Let me be the instrument of your will and your vengeance, not of mine alone."

Anwari reached into his pocket and pulled out a faded and wrinkled picture of a man about his own age standing behind a much smaller woman with a red scarf around her head. She held her right arm around a young boy standing in front of her. In her left arm, she held a toddler still in diapers. They looked like they were all laughing at the camera.

"Karim, my brother," Anwari had said, "Try smiling a little. What's the matter, did little Samad drop a stink bomb in his diaper?" It had not been much, but the surprise had caused the needed effect—just the look he had wanted for a picture of his favorite family...

Anwari grimaced. Better days, despite the stinking Taliban. At least they had all been alive then, even though the Taliban had been so oppressive and cruel. He closed his eyes and looked up. "Help me find the path of righteousness, oh Lord, that you may forgive me and turn my evil deeds to good ones."

Anwari started a call on his flip phone.

"Hello," responded the familiar, deep, resonant voice.

"He has arrived here."

"In the city?"

"In the hotel," Anwari said. "A coincidence?"

"What do you think? There are probably 15 different hotels in that city, and many are American tourist quality. I think there is a very low probability of a coincidence."

"But he thought I was a tourist."

"He has identified you," said the deep voice. "It is of no matter. Let us use this to our advantage. He will seek you out today—let him. He cannot know your role in all of this. You must befriend him. Stick to your backstory. Americans are your friends. You are a tourist. Your friendship will give you the necessary cover to keep tabs on him."

Anwari stared out the window for a few seconds. "I fear he will see through me."

"You have been thoroughly trained by us, Abdul. Follow your training, act like yourself, but bury your emotions deep. Recall the good times in the Afghan army and let that replace your emotional state. He will not know what to think, and you can complete your mission successfully and gloriously. It is the will of Allah."

"I know I should hate him, yet I find myself liking him. What has he done personally to deserve your wrath?"

"Look," said the deep voice, "I know he can seem likable, but remember this: first and foremost, he is a tool of his government, just like Half-Moon Mole. As that tool, he has proven quite adept and plenty ruthless. He has persecuted your people in the depths of lonely prison cells where many still rot for no good reason. He ignores the consequences of his or his government's actions. You know all too well about those consequences. Do not forget that. Do not forget your past. Do not fall prey to his friendly banter, for it is nothing but a part he plays to his advantage. Play your own part, Abdul, but do not forget."

"Forget? How could I?" Anwari asked.

"Indeed."

After the phone disconnected, Anwari looked at the tattered picture of his brother and family again and picked up the Qur'an, turning to Sura 2, Ayat 190–95, for the hundredth time in the past week:

> Fight in Allah's cause against those who fight you, but do not overstep the limits. Allah does not love those who overstep the limits. Kill them wherever you encounter them, and drive them out from where they drove you out, for persecution is more serious than killing. Do not fight them at the Sacred Mosque unless they fight you there. If they do fight you, kill them—this is what such disbelievers deserve—but if they stop, then Allah is most forgiving and merciful. Fight them until there is no more persecution and worship is devoted to Allah.

If they cease hostilities, there can be no further hostility, except toward aggressors. A sacred month for a sacred month: violation of sanctity calls for fair retribution. So if anyone commits aggression against you, attack him as he attacked you, but be mindful of Allah, and know that He is with those who are mindful of Him. Spend in Allah's cause: do not contribute to your destruction with your own hands, but do good, for Allah loves those who do good.

Attack him as he attacked you. Yes. I am mindful of Allah. Am I not doing good? Do I overstep any limits? What are those limits? They let those who killed my brethren go on to kill other innocents. They remain disbelievers. They continue to persecute my people. What more do I need? These people are not innocents. He is not innocent. I am the tip of Allah's spear. And with my help, Pardus will change the world.

CHAPTER 8

HUXLEY PEERED OVER the top of his newspaper and saw Anwari strolling through the lobby's front door, his eyes darting around the room. Huxley slowly turned the page, deliberately lowering the paper to "accidentally" see Anwari full force. Tilting his head in apparent thought for a moment, Huxley smiled, stood and walked toward Anwari with his hand extended. "Excuse me sir. How nice to see you again. You remember me from Tel Megiddo yesterday, don't you."

Anwari extended his hand. "Of course. You are the man with the bible passages. I took your picture. I am sorry, but I do not recall your name."

"Huxley. Chris Huxley."

Anwari tilted his head slightly to one side and blinked.

Huxley saw Anwari's tell. *My first name surprised him.* "I believe I am now at a disadvantage, sir."

"Of course. My name is Anwari. Abdul Saboor Anwari. But what brings you to Nazareth?"

"Another stop on the tourist highway, I guess." Anwari gave him the same look. He had known who Huxley was, all right. The Israelis or whoever's responsible had apparently failed to train him on facial control.

Anwari replied, "Yes, likewise. If I see enough of these sites, eventually I may actually understand you Christians."

"Of course, though we Americans are not all Christians, I'm afraid."

"I'm sorry if I have offended you, sir," Anwari said quickly with genuine concern.

Huxley bowed his head slightly. "No offense taken. I am more interested in the historical aspects of these sites. I would like to see if I can figure out what they tell us about modern times." Anwari's face betrayed little to him, but the man's eyes had flicked just that little bit.

Anwari quickly responded, "I agree. Even those with no belief in God can see the tremendous historical value, I would think. I am alone, Mr. Huxley, and it appears you are as well. I think it is more enjoyable to visit sites with another history lover. Would you have any interest in accompanying me?"

"I would be delighted as long as we share a similar agenda. I'm off to breakfast and then to the Church of the Annunciation. Would you care to join me?" Huxley noted the slight smile that turned larger on Anwari's face.

"I am afraid I have already eaten this morning, but I would be happy to join you in the lobby, say in an hour?"

❆ ❆ ❆

Huxley's breakfast repast gave him time to reconsider the situation. He liked to do that in the morning before the day's agenda caught up with him. Sometimes he would run ideas by colleagues with a smattering of details; sometimes he would run hypotheticals by friends with so little detail that they had no idea what he was asking. His friends might not add much direct insight, but sometimes they would say something that inspired a new path for his thoughts. And sometimes his morning think tank worked pretty well even when he was alone in the tank.

So where was he, really? He needed to get to Rome and check out the archaeology student, Dante Tocelli, at Sapienza. Kira had dug up plenty already. The kid had apparently disappeared after his flight back to Rome, never reaching the university. Maybe he had just decided archaeology was no longer for him. Or maybe he was a closet terrorist.

Then there was the strange case of the missing soldiers. The two soldiers from Rabin Army Base had never returned after they had left for Ramat David early on the day of the incursion. In fact, his contact at Rabin had conceded unofficially that nobody had ordered them to Ramat David in the first place—computer maintenance was not due there for another two months. The Israeli army now feared both were kidnapped or dead. Aman surely knew this since they would have been involved in the investigation of the missing soldiers. Why had they not shared that with him? What do they fear?

Finally, the strange entries in the contacts listing seemed to keep churning out new clues. Kira had run down the phrase "No? A dozen times at least." It was a line from Shakespeare's *Measure for Measure*. Though he had taken a course on Shakespeare at Harvard, he could not quite recall the scene. She sent it to his cell, so he could study that more closely later, but it seemed unlikely the play would yield much.

The other English entries in the contacts might prove fertile ground. The owner of the phone spoke primarily Arabic, so why were some in English? Huxley understood English might seem necessary for Huxley to recognize the entries relating to him and his mother. Did the other English entries contain more clues? Those contacts just didn't seem real. Most of the contacts were supposedly located in the U.S., yet according to Homeland's records, Najwa had never traveled there. Still, he or somebody else must have followed Huxley or the cell would not have followed him around the East Coast. And so many of the entries employed improper capitalization. You might think Najwa was lazy, but the iPhone would automatically capitalize most of the words. So why had Najwa taken the time to un-capitalize words as he entered them? Also, there were just too many names, words and phrases that seemed unlikely or out of place. Perhaps the Church of the Annunciation would hold the answers.

The Boss started singing from his cell again. "Hello," answered Huxley.

"Mr. Huxley, this is Captain Yadin of Aman."

"Of course. Give me a minute." Huxley pointed to his phone and shrugged to the waiter and then headed outside away from curious ears. "What can I do for you?"

"You have not reported in. We have a sharing arrangement, and now I learn you have interrogated an Israeli Army officer without our presence or consent."

Huxley held back a laugh, imagining the red corpuscles bursting out of Yadin's forehead. "I'm sorry, but I was just beginning to consider some of the elements here, Captain. I was very surprised to discover that you had withheld information about two missing maintenance soldiers. Is there anything else you are hiding?"

"Well, I…I didn't see it as significant at the time, Mr. Huxley. We only just learned about it ourselves in the past few days. We still do not believe it is connected with the incursion at Ramat David. More likely the two were targeted on the road on the way back from Ramat."

"Seems like too much of a coincidence, don't you think? Have you checked your computers to see if anything was accessed by the maintenance workers that seemed unusual?"

Yadin cleared his throat. "Of course, but it was just a bunch of personnel records for those stationed at Ramat—sick days, vacation days and other low-level info for military and consulting personnel at Ramat. Anything important would have required high-level access accounts, even for the techies. I'm not sure why they accessed it, but I'm certain they had a reason. Might have had something to do with their maintenance duties, I suppose. Or maybe they wanted to check out where a buddy was going on vacation, but it seems unlikely that it could help any terrorists much."

"Have you alerted personnel about possible terrorist strikes during their vacations?"

"This is Israel. Every soldier knows he or she is always at risk anywhere he goes day or night, particularly when the soldier is not with his or her unit. And the Palestinians don't target consultants. Not enough of a media splash, as you would put it. But we have put out a high alert for all personnel, so do not worry."

"I'm afraid worry is my closest confidant," Huxley said. "Thank you for your time."

"You seem to be forgetting something."

"I'm sorry?"

"This is a reciprocal relationship," Yadin said flatly. "What have you found?"

"I thought you already knew. I seem to have a set of eyes on me."

"Not from us," Yadin said.

Huxley shook his head in disgust. *Yep, quite a reciprocal relationship.* "Okay. The clues in the contacts list seem to point to Nazareth. I'm checking that out further to see where it leads. The pick is owned by a professor from the College of William & Mary in Virginia. He is on sabbatical and doing work at Tel Megiddo. He said it was stolen."

"We figured that out ourselves, but the Professor didn't have much to add."

"Did you forget to mention that to me?" asked Huxley.

"We just tracked it down yesterday, so I am telling you today. But again, it led to nothing important."

Huxley grimaced. "Okay. I have a few other lines of inquiry that are rather vague at the moment, though nothing much real at this point."

"Well, let us know as soon as you do. What is going on in Nazareth?"

"I'm planning to visit the Church of the Annunciation."

"Whatever for?" asked Yadin.

"My mother recommended it."

CHAPTER 9

HUXLEY TOOK ADVANTAGE of the walk to the Church of the Annunciation to pepper Anwari with questions. Anwari always seemed to have a good answer but became quite vague when Huxley asked him how he afforded all of these trips on a soldier's meager wages.

"They call me a hero and so certain people with influence and cash seem to find ways to repay my service. I am fortunate, but I'm sure I will eventually become nothing to them and will need to make my own way."

When they reached the Church of the Annunciation, Huxley was struck by how the façade of this mid-twentieth century church managed to use white and tan stone to simultaneously create the feeling of a modern, yet ancient monument. A huge cupola stood high above the upper church used by Nazarene Catholics for their Sunday masses. The cupola was placed directly over the top of the cave thought by Catholics to be the place where Mary lived over 2000 years before. Above the cupola rested the "Light of the World," an enormous lantern representing Christ. Mosaics and paintings of Mary by artists from around the world adorned the upper hallways.

This version of the church had been completed in 1969—the fifth time a church had been built over the shrine of the Annunciation. It replaced a church constructed in 1730 and enlarged a century and a half later. The original shrine/church was built in the middle of the fourth century. It consisted only of a small altar within the cave thought to be the childhood home of Mary. The small shrine was rebuilt into a major church during the time of Constantine the Great, the Roman Emperor who nearly single-handedly changed the course of Christianity by throwing the weight of the Roman Empire behind the fledgling religion. He commissioned his mother, a devout Christian, to commemorate important events in Jesus's life with new churches. Israel still found itself with three of these well-known churches: the Church of the Nativity, the Church of the Holy Sepulchre and the Church of the Annunciation. The Church of the Annunciation was destroyed and rebuilt after various conquests by Muslims and crusaders. Franciscan monks were allowed by Saladin, a Muslim hero, to remain after he expelled crusaders in 1187, but their church was destroyed in the 13th century when Egyptian Baybers defeated the Seventh Crusaders. The Franciscans, never ones to give up easily, hung around as best they could until the ruling Muslims allowed them to rebuild the church in 1730.

When Huxley reached the large grotto beneath the main church, he knew the answer lay here somewhere. The interior of the grotto gave the entire space a surreal feeling, as if he had stepped into an enormous cave illuminated only with artificial light and smelling of moist, stale air with a hint of incense. This one hid a much smaller cave that was surrounded by various remnants of the ancient church buildings. His mother would have loved visiting this place. He felt like saying a Hail Mary just to complete this moment of reflection, but he could not bring himself to such a personal hypocrisy merely for nostalgia's sake. Though he had found nothing yet that suggested the terrorist Najwa had meant him to come here, the place certainly fit the religious motif Najwa had begun at Tel Megiddo; however, it had yielded no new insights.

He walked behind the main altar at the bottom of the steps to the center of the grotto and looked beyond the black iron gate protecting the old, freestanding stone foundation that surrounded a small archway. The archway seemed to link the site to the original cave where Mary might have lived. Just beyond stood another alter, this one smaller, covered with a white cloth with delicate lace patterns caressing four white candles and a bejeweled crucifix. The altar front was engraved with a decorative pattern and contained a quote following the sentiment of John's gospel, *"Verbum*

Caro Hic Factum Est"—Latin for "Here The Word Was Made Flesh." That was what the Annunciation meant to Christians, of course.

In Christian teaching, when Gabriel came down and told Mary she was with child, it was an acknowledgment that the Word, i.e., Christ, was coming from Heaven and being made into human flesh. Although Jesus was now becoming man, he had always been part of God. He did not start as a normal man and become something more through his acts on Earth. Some had read the synoptic gospels and Paul's letters that way, but the gospel writer referred to as "John" had clarified this view with the first chapter of his gospel account:

> In the beginning was the Word... And the Word became flesh and made his dwelling among us, and we saw his glory, the glory as of the Father's only Son, full of grace and truth.

It took several hundred years and the Council of Nicaea called by Constantine to get everyone on the same page. Well, maybe not everyone. There were a few remaining Arians after the council who still contended that the Son was not eternal and therefore the Word could not have existed from the beginning. They believed the Father came first and then the Son, for otherwise how could the Father truly have a Son? Arius and those of his followers who refused to accept the decisions of the Council of Nicaea were banished and became heretics. While the heresy remained in a weakened state and was even adopted by some of the barbarian tribes conquering Roman territory a century later, the universal church ultimately silenced their voice.

Was this Latin inscription the clue he sought? It seemed a bit too amorphous, ambiguous, antiquitous. *Wait, is "antiquitous" a word? No, it has a nice ring to it, but the right word is probably just good old "ancient."* Anyway, how could an engraving many centuries old be a clue to a 21st century terrorist plot? He kept searching.

Several bouquets of flowers had been set out just on the other side of the iron gate—offerings from the many visitors to the shrine. Some were fresh like they had arrived this morning; others were dried out and withering, soon to be disposed of by the grotto's Franciscan caretakers. The corner of a small white envelope with some handwritten English peered out from underneath one of the older bouquets. Huxley squatted down and reached through the grate, just able to reach the envelope. In artistic calligraphy, the cover read: *"My son, my son, why have you forsaken me?"*

Huxley's head jerked around. Anwari was still near the back of the grotto, examining other artwork hanging in the structure. Huxley pulled the envelope through the grate, walked away from the altar and sat down in one of the fifty or so chairs set up for Catholic Masses. The envelope must be the clue. Mary had never said Jesus had forsaken her, nor had he. It was Jesus who had said while hanging on the cross, "My God, My God, why have you forsaken me?" Many had thought he was lamenting his own suffering and wondering why God had not brought it quickly to an end. However, the words carried a much stronger meaning.

The words repeated the first line of what is now known as Psalm 22. At the time of Christ, the Psalms had not yet been organized by number. Instead, the common shorthand for referring to a particular Psalm was repeating its first line. According to Christians, although it was written over a millennium before Jesus's death, Jesus had referred to Psalm 22 while on the cross precisely because it had anticipated Jesus's end as well as its significance:

> My God, my God, why have you forsaken me?
> Why so far from my call for help,
> from my cries of anguish?
> …
> But I am a worm, not a man,
> scorned by men, despised by the people.
> All who see me mock me;
> they curl their lips and jeer;
> they shake their heads at me:
> "He relied on the LORD—let him deliver him;
> if he loves him, let him rescue him."
> For you drew me forth from the womb,
> made me safe at my mother's breasts.
> …
> Dogs surround me;

a pack of evildoers closes in on me.
They have pierced my hands and my feet
I can count all my bones.
They stare at me and gloat;
they divide my garments among them;
for my clothing they cast lots.
…
The poor will eat their fill;
those who seek the LORD will offer praise.
May your hearts enjoy life forever!"
…
The generation to come will be told of the Lord,
that they may proclaim to a people yet unborn
the deliverance you have brought.

No self respecting Christian would say Jesus abandoned his mother, so it must come as yet another scraping of Huxley's soul by the terrorist. Why?

Huxley stole a few furtive looks around the grotto and then opened the envelope and pulled out a white card with a gentle calligraphic design around its perimeter. The interior of the card contained more English in the same beautiful calligraphy as the cover:

I asked to speak with you, but you ignored me:
"'Who is my mother, who are my brothers?'
And stretching out his hand toward his disciples,
He said, 'Here are my mother and my brothers.
For whoever does the will of my Heavenly Father
is my brother, and sister, and mother.'"
So, my son, you may substitute my joy with God's will,
But do not find comfort among the harlots of Israel.

When Huxley reached the last line, he closed his eyes and sucked hard on his bottom lip. He began searching: not for yet another clue but his own personal redemption. The events of the past four years unraveled again in front of him. His whirlwind romance with Hanna Elverman had started all of this…

She had been beautiful, exotic and full of wit. He had thought that even when he had met her at Harvard, but then she was already in a serious relationship. They had become friends of a sort although he had always felt a certain shyness around her that he had not felt around other women. There had been her occasional coy smiles at him that suggested maybe she felt something too. But that was all.

He had not seen her in over fifteen years, and then there she was, lying at the poolside in this resort in the Maldives—laughing that familiar little cackle that could be amusing, charming and a bit grating all at once. He had often started chuckling himself without having heard anything funny but her laughter. When she laughed with you, it was highly infectious; when she laughed at you, it was highly noxious.

He was on leave for a week from his current CIA posting in Afghanistan. She was on leave semi-permanently from work in general and had been for many years. She had never married, yet never seemed to need work. Why bother when she could rely on a rich investment banking father, or a long-time Wall Street boyfriend, or some new, rich acquaintance hoping to set his boring life on fire. Huxley had little money, so he was a bit surprised when she seemed delighted to see him as he walked over to her from the poolside bar. The years had been good to her. At 37, she still sported the figure of an athlete, and any hint of wrinkles must have been carefully covered by expert makeup.

"A Crimson Cackler in paradise? Is that a new species?" he joked.

She turned away from her friend, paused while staring at him standing there in his swimsuit, and cackled again. "That's a pretty good nickname, Sko-B. You been thinking that one up these past 15 years?"

He smiled. Sko-B, short for Scholar Boy, the nickname his roommate had invented for him at Harvard when he discovered Huxley could afford to attend the college only on a full scholarship. "I never could keep up with you on nicknames. 'Sko-B.' That's an old favorite. But that'll be 'Scholar Boy' to you."

She returned the smile, more seductive this time. "Hey, the way you are looking right now, I'll call you whatever you want."

"I never knew you to be a flatterer."

"You never knew me when I could flatter you."

It ended up as his best vacation, ever. He remembered little of the native scenery or the local tourist jaunts, but he was pretty sure Hanna and he had seen some of them together at some point. All he could recall from that week was the glistening oil on her tanned skin, her goose bumps providing a perfect palette for his expert hands subtly stroking her back and shoulders; the intoxicating and intoxicated conversations leading to imaginary monarchies, where together they could correct all the world's ills; and the purifying moments of gentle bliss, their nearly naked bodies lying on a deserted beach while the waves roared their cacophonous approval.

From there it was only a matter of time before he proposed to her. But then came the heartache. No, she had not rejected him. She accepted with her normally flamboyant style. Employing her best coy, coquettish smile and feigning a pathetic southern accent, she replied, "Whatever shall I do with such a scandalous proposition as this? I do declare—a marriage between a Long Island Jewish Princess and Baltimore Catholic Altar Boy—how could that even be possible? Would not the stars realign and the earth shake to its very foundation?" She paused for effect, and added begrudgingly, "Ah, but I do love you, my little Scholar Boy, so perhaps we could, just this once, break with tradition and see if the world can survive it."

Unfortunately, her words proved less funny and more prophetic than he had believed. She insisted on a wedding before a judge, sans religion. She was of Jewish heritage, though non-practicing—no, non-believing. He had not attended Mass since his early college days, so it was no big deal, or at least he had tried to tell his mother that.

But his mother was crushed and would not relent. "If you marry outside of the church, son, how can I recognize you as man and wife? You will be living in sin. Is this what you want, Christian? Hanna really should convert, but that is her own choice. If she will not convert, can you at least marry her in front of a priest in a church? Please, do this for an old woman. I beg you."

Huxley could never refuse the rare plea from his mother. Unable to disappoint those sad yet loving eyes, he always obeyed. This time was no different. He now turned his pleas to Hanna. "Think about the bigger picture and try to put your own views aside. If you do not believe in God, then why should it matter if we appease my mother and get married in a Catholic Church?"

"What kind of hypocrite are you? You don't believe in God any more than I do. It sounds like a bad joke: 'So a Jewish atheist and a Catholic agnostic walk up to a priest and ask to be married...' It is absurd and a lie and I won't do it. And I won't subject my father, who does still believe in the God of his fathers, to watching his only daughter marry in a Catholic Church. Have you thought about that?"

"I love you, Hanna. But I also love my mother. She has been that little angel on my shoulder—my conscience—for my whole life. Don't do this. It will kill her. Your father accepted your atheistic views long ago. My mother still thinks she can save me. Please, reconsider. We can step out of the church as husband and wife and never look back. It is just a moment in time in your eyes but an eternity in hell fire for me in my mother's eyes. Can't you see that?"

Hanna screamed back at him, "A moment in time? That's what you think of me? A moment in time? At what moment in time will you grow up and break from your mother's skirt? Your angel. Your conscience. If she is the angel, am I the devil? Listen to yourself, will you?"

"I'm sorry. I didn't mean that. You're reading too much into my words. Please. I cannot do this to her."

Hanna shook her head and glared at Huxley. "But you can do this to me? I guess I don't know you after all. I thought you were strong, but you wilt at your mother's feet. You want a moment in time? Well remember this moment, Scholar Boy!" She ripped the engagement ring off her finger, slammed it down on the counter, and stormed out of their Georgetown apartment, never to return.

He spent weeks trying to clean up the mess to no avail. They still saw each other occasionally for a time, but something felt different. He even broke with his mother and told Hanna he would agree to a wedding in a synagogue if that would make her happy. But it was too late. It was as if, in those few moments, she had realized something about him that was irreconcilable with her very nature. His own interest in reconciling with her seemed to dwindle with the passing of time until the two just drifted apart. He had seen a side of her once again that he had almost forgotten—that blunt vindictiveness that scared the hell out of him. Nevertheless, he still longed for her. The longing led to pain, which led to anger. The anger would not let him forgive his mother for unraveling his happiness. His psyche needed someone to blame other than him-self, so he blamed his mother. He knew it was wrong, but he couldn't help it.

He never yelled at his mother, never wrote any screaming notes, and never left any nasty voice mails. He just stopped. He stopped driving to Baltimore. He stopped calling her. He stopped reading her letters. If she didn't exist, then neither could the pain. So for over a year, he pretended she didn't. And then she stopped calling, and she stopped writing, and he figured she had simply given up.

About a year and a half later, he learned of his mother's dementia. Her neigh-bor, a longtime friend, called him and begged him to return and visit her in the care center. Huxley had not even known she was ill…

Huxley was fondling the silver crucifix he had removed from his left pocket, running his thumb mechanically up and down the vertical post of the cross and over the tortured body of Jesus. It was the only thing his mother had left him when she had died a year later.

He had kept it, not for its religious significance, but just the opposite. He loved the crucifix because it reminded him of his mother and his love for her, which he demonstrated during that last year of her life, though by then she could not even recognize him. But he also hated the crucifix because it reminded him of the silly religious notions that had destroyed both his love for Hanna and his relationship with his mother. Religion seemed to find a way to divide people.

The crucifix meant more than that. It was a symbol that gave him clarity when others were lost in a sea of hate. He had encountered both many foreign terrorists and many "real Americans" who spewed hate in the name of their particular religion. But that often merely hid the true source of their hatred. No, religion was more often a means to an end, employed as a weapon by those with a lust for power or a compulsion for revenge who knew how to twist hatred out of love and squeeze chaos out of order.

It was no different between Hanna and him. She had not broken with him because of religion; she had run because of his unwillingness to bend to her will. After a year of sorrow, he saw that, in her selfishness, Hanna simply could not accept losing a battle for his emotions. The wedding skirmish had just uncovered a latent disease that would undoubtedly have brought their marriage to an early grave.

The premature death of their relationship didn't really matter to him any more. What mattered now was that he had lost himself in the emotional flood of the experience and abandoned, yes forsaken, his mother. The crucifix reminded him to lose the hate and lose the emotion. Yet he could not prevent emotions from flooding over him now as the white card in his lap kept shouting the old truth back to him and seemingly echoing it menacingly throughout the grotto.

Huxley looked up and saw Anwari standing over him.

"Are you all right, Christian?"

Huxley exhaled slowly and deeply, letting his cheeks and lips puff out.

"I thought you were a non-believer," Anwari said, "yet you hold a crucifix in your hand, and you look like this beautiful shrine has moved you nearly to tears. Is it more than merely historical to you? Has your soul been touched by this site?"

"Not exactly," Huxley said, his voice cracking slightly. "Just an old memory that haunts me from time to time." Huxley put the card back in the envelope and inserted it into his left jacket pocket. He looked once more at the crucifix and saw instead his mothers' withered face the day she died handing it to him in her defeated state. He fought back a tear and returned the silver object to his left pants pocket. "Have you found anything interesting, Abdul?"

"Oh, there were several beautiful mosaics of Maryam that caught my eye. They were quite beautiful."

"Maryam?" Huxley asked. "Oh yes, I forgot that the mother of Jesus has a place in your Qur'an. Have you studied art?"

"No, but I enjoy beautiful things. I noticed you were reading a small card. Did you find that here, or is that, too, a memento?"

"Perhaps both." Huxley stood up, still a little shaken. *But now I am more confused than ever.*

❆ ❆ ❆

Anwari looked around for any wayward ears, but the small park was still empty. "He was completely crushed by your little note. I thought he was going to cry like a baby, but he sucked it up when he saw me standing there. How did you know?"

The deep, resonant voice of Pardus said, "How could I not? Unfortunately for him, his life became an open book at the agency after he melted down with his mother's illness. He refused to take further interrogations. He seemed to have found a conscience. She had told him before that these tactics were the work of the devil and he was no better than the terrorists if he tortured them. That didn't seem to bother him until she fell ill. Her illness and his despair tore him apart. Officially, he was put on leave, but everyone knew his career was over. It was only when his former boss became the Deputy Under Secretary for Intelligence and Analysis at Homeland that he got the second chance he had hoped for."

"And how did you manage to get inside information from the CIA?"

Pardus paused for an uncomfortable period. "Let us say I have developed certain assets around the world. A few are highly placed; a few well placed. All are loyal. And if they were not, they could say little, because they know even less. It makes them less dangerous to me and to themselves. Unnecessary risks must sometimes be eliminated in the glorious fight for Allah. It is better to avoid becoming an unnecessary risk, do you not agree, Anwari?"

"Yes, sir. I understand you completely." Anwari closed his eyes. *Stop asking questions. Questions kill. Compartmentalize.* "By the way, I don't think Huxley has really figured out what this is all about."

"Do not underestimate him," Pardus said. "I suspect he will soon head to Rome. That is your next destination as well. We have need for some of your munitions expertise. With some luck, you will see Huxley there and be able to renew your growing friendship."

"Do you think it wise? What are the odds of another chance meeting?" Anwari asked.

"He already suspects you. Let him continue to do so, for he has nothing on you. And while he searches for answers and hopes to uncover your role, you can always help set him straight on his path. You must be subtle. Any direction he gains must not appear to come from you voluntarily. Let him draw it out of you so he believes he is using you to his benefit."

"I see," Anwari lied. How could he accomplish these subtle suggestions with someone as perceptive as Huxley? After a handful of conversations with the man, he had thought he had a bead on him, but now…had he fooled the investigator even a bit?

Pardus seemed to interpret his silence. "You are wondering if you have the skill to pull this off? Look, Anwari, nobody but you can do this. And remember: you do this for your brother—for all your brothers. You do this for Allah. You are his hands. You are his eyes. Let him be your heart. Together, we shall help Him remake the world."

CHAPTER 10

SEVERAL DAYS LATER, Anwari felt less like a terrorist and more like a true tourist as he sat beside the cooling waters of the sapphire swimming pool at the New Collossus Hotel in Rome. Pardus had told him to relax a couple days, meld into the tourist community, and maintain a casual watch for the target's patterns. It had proven easy duty, though he had kept struggling to turn his eyes away from the many young Western women in their tiny bathing suits. *Allah forgive me.* This time he had come to the pool area in the early morning, but the already steaming sun had brought others out to catch some of its rays before beginning their tourist jaunts through the historic city. He found some time to study the Great Book.

A shrill scream ten meters away jerked Anwari's eyes from his Qur'an, but it was merely one of the two girls—the ten-year-old—trying to regain her balance at the end of a diving board that seemed to jerk up and down with a mind of its own. Then he saw her older sister—the twelve-year-old—giggling as she jumped repeatedly on the board near its fulcrum. The younger girl finally lost her balance and fell, spiraling and flailing five feet into the pool. A few seconds later, she resurfaced, laughing. The older girl soon joined her in the pool, executing a nearly perfect airplane dive to the right, and they swam together toward the shallows.

Pretending to stretch and yawn, Anwari looked to his right, where he saw the huge man staring and smiling at the children. He was not their father. A black duffle bag sat beside his chair with the zipper open, a towel covering its deadly contents. The man began scanning down the poolside, pausing at the occupant of each lounge chair for a second. Anwari knew enough to return to reading his Qur'an.

"Mr. Riese, Mr. Riese!" called the older girl. "Would you throw us the ball?"

The large man by the duffle bag complied, batting the beach ball into the pool. The two girls bounced the ball to each other for a few minutes, but seemed to tire of the game. "Mr. Riese, Mr. Riese!" called the older girl. "Could you come play with us? You can be our net!"

Mr. Riese laughed. He grabbed his duffle bag and walked to the edge of the pool near the girls. "I tell you what," he said, "I'll sit hear at the edge and stick my leg up. You can hit it over the top."

The younger girl squealed with joy, but instead of hitting the ball over Mr. Riese's leg, she jumped up and hugged it with her two little arms, hanging a couple feet above the pool for a few seconds. Mr. Riese bellowed a low laugh and then kicked his leg up in the air, dunking it back down into the pool several times. Each time, the younger girl emerged with her head newly drenched, the joy escaping her body through raucous laughter. The older girl joined in on the other leg, and Mr. Riese began to scissor his legs to alternate the two girls up and down in the pool.

Anwari smiled, but carefully held back a laugh. He recalled his mission and frowned. He closed his eyes, breathed deeply and sighed. *Allah give me strength.* When his eyes opened, he saw Mr. Riese, still scissoring his legs, but staring at him. Anwari forced a smile and nodded slightly. Mr. Riese smiled back, and then continued another vigilant scan down the poolside. The sun had disappeared under some clouds and the first few drops fell to Anwari's bare legs. A good excuse for a casual exit.

❊ ❊ ❊

A couple kilometers away, Huxley sat near the large arch of the Osteria dell Commari, eating his "scrumble eggs" and bacon and sipping his caffè Americano. He liked to eat like the locals when he traveled, but toast, juice and a couple of sweet cakes just didn't suit him this morning. So he went for the tourist package and enjoyed a little taste of saturated fat and cholesterol while he awaited his morning meeting. He was staring out the front window of the restaurant near the Vatican, watching the rain come down in a steady stream while he rehashed the facts in his case.

Was Tocelli a lead or a dead end? Perhaps the kid just wanted to impress his bone-digging friends with his knowledge of astronomy. Maybe Tocelli had used his telescope simply to look at the comet rather than to spy on Ramat David; nevertheless, its placement on the site had been perfect. Tocelli's roommate had barely known his fellow Sapienza student and could not identify any of his friends. Huxley would have to track Tocelli's family and friends down in his native Florence. The roommate had given up one interesting fact—Tocelli seemed to have tried to hide some kind of employment with the Vatican. An electronic fob seemed to confirm that. It wasn't much, but what else did he have? Nothing, except the perplexing contacts list from Najwa.

The white card left at the grotto proved this case was personal. He had believed his name appearing in Najwa's contacts was just a little sign to draw him into the case, something Najwa had used to make a connection to an investigator who would find his killer. The Israeli Air Force had not killed Najwa, not really; his death had been preordained the moment he tunneled into the camp, and Najwa must have known it or he would not have brought his phone with him. But then why did he not just run away and contact the CIA or Homeland Security before the attack? The thing didn't quite make sense.

Then again, Najwa had always been an enigma. He had never actually been caught committing any terrorist activities. He was suspected only because of the activities of a few close associates, and he had always steadfastly maintained his innocence. The CIA released him, so they might have believed he was not involved. Or were they using him the same way the Israelis had tried to use Huxley? Was Najwa a little bunny released simply to lead them back to the rabbit hole?

What about the white card from St. Mary's grotto? It had hurled him back onto an emotional roller coaster Huxley thought he had managed to exit. The quoted material was right out of Matthew's gospel: "Who is my mother, who are my brothers... For whoever does the will of my Heavenly

Father is my brother, and sister, and mother." He had found that pretty easily with a Google search. It was apparently Jesus's way of telling his true followers that they were his family. The last two lines could be found nowhere in the bible or anywhere else, yet they were the lines that had ripped him apart. The mother told the son not to abandon her for Jewish harlots. The note might as well have mentioned Hanna by name. He knew the words were intended not only to intrigue but also to unnerve. And they had succeeded.

Though the calligraphic card had weakened him, it had also awakened him. Najwa could not have known enough about Huxley to write those words, so either Najwa had the help of someone in the CIA or Homeland Security or Najwa was himself a stooge. Who else with a stake in this would know about Huxley's mother? Only those who had seen Huxley fall at the CIA, but even that seemed far-fetched.

Though the card had set him off, it had provided no discernible pattern when matched with other entries in the contacts list. Could the next clue be hidden in something else at the Church of the Annunciation? His hand-written notes clarified nothing. Could the white card have been written by a different hand than the contacts list? Maybe someone else feared he would understand something at the church and knew how to distract him.

What about Aman? They might know much more about him than he had thought. They had their own contacts in the CIA and had good reason to ask about his mother, but then why the white card? Was Anwari their operative, just a harmless hero turned tourist, or does he play yet another role? Maybe Huxley had read too much into Anwari's expressions, yet Anwari had slipped and called Huxley "Christian" at the Church of the Annunciation. He might have guessed that was Huxley's given name, but why not Christopher? And why not just say "Chris?" No, Anwari must have had a dossier on Huxley before they even met. He was involved somehow.

Huxley opened the Najwa contacts list and looked at the remaining clues from the two Huxley entries. There was the quote from Shakespeare's *Measure for Measure:* "No? a dozen times at least." It had to be a clue, but to what? He really needed to re-read that play. He recalled from his class that some had argued the play was a religious allegory, but most experts thought of it simply as Shakespeare's criticism of hypocrites who judge others harshly in the name of God, patriotism or whatever else pumped up their fervor. Even the name of the play harkened back to the Sermon on the Mount in Matthew's gospel: "Stop judging, that you may not be judged. For as you judge, so will you be judged, and the measure with which you measure will be measured out to you." But how did the play fit into this terrorist plot? The path was far too murky.

"Mr. Huxley, so good to see you again." A woman stood next to his table with a soft, alluring smile. Her dark eyes and even darker hair complemented her slender nose and even slenderer body. She wore a designer suit with a skirt line just above her knees and held a black portfolio in her left hand.

Huxley stood up quickly and straightened his shirt. "Sonatina D'Amare, I did not think you would remember me. Thank you for coming." Huxley shook her hand and moved around the table to the opposite side, pulling the chair out for his guest.

"Of course, how would I forget the famous Savior of the Sistine Chapel?"

He blushed, bowed slightly, and returned to his chair, still smiling from the faint hint of a rose scent that had tantalized his nose from the back of her neck. He had certainly remembered her from that investigation many months ago, though he had only met her once. She had such a lovely way about her that the image had never quite evaporated from his mind. "Would you like some breakfast?"

"No. *Grazie.* Just a little *caffè.*" Huxley motioned to the waiter, and he brought her espresso.

"You make me feel like the piggish American that I am," Huxley said, motioning to the meager remains scattered on two of his plates.

She smiled. "Actually, I already ate a few bites at my flat this morning. You are hardly piggish, Mr. Huxley, except maybe for that little piece of egg on your lip."

Huxley snatched the napkin from his lap and wiped his mouth. He looked at the napkin, but it was clean.

She chuckled. "I'm sorry, I just couldn't resist. You are the *quintessenza* of manners, Mr. Huxley."

"Well, I always give it my best shot for such a..." *Don't push it, Hux. She might think you shallow.* "...for such an accomplished woman."

"*Grazie.* I hardly think the Deputy Director of an art museum should be so highly praised, but thank you, nonetheless."

Huxley beamed. "Come now, just an art museum? Next to the Louvre, the Vatican Museums can boast perhaps the greatest collection of art in the world."

She bowed her head a touch. "We do our part."

"You do, indeed. Now tell me, *Signora* D'Amare—"

"*Signorina.*" She tilted her head slightly and smiled softly.

"I see, *Signorina* D'Amare then, have you found anything on Dante Tocelli?"

"I am afraid not. We have no record of him in our employ, he is not among the interns we have used in the past year, and we do not have any record of any Dante Tocelli having been given any special research privileges in the past year. Is it possible your informant was mistaken?"

"Would you know if he were employed by another part of the Vatican? Perhaps the library or archives?"

"I have not checked, but I will see what I can do. Just how serious is this matter?"

Huxley sat back and rested his chin on his left finger and thumb. "I'm not sure, yet. Clearly some terrorists have died for some greater plan, but we do not yet know what that is. It could be minor, but I don't think so."

"Well, I am happy to help you if I can. The director of the Museums is still grateful to you for preventing those terrorists from destroying Michelangelo's masterpiece and has instructed me to provide you with any assistance that I can."

"And I thought it was just my charming personality."

"Well, that doesn't hurt matters any."

Huxley leaned over the table. "You might be able to help me out on something. Are you familiar with security devices in the Vatican?"

"Just those I have to pass every day."

"Do you need electronic security fobs to get through some doors?"

"Sure, a few of them. Why?"

"Can I see your fob?" he asked.

She handed it to him. It was attached to a lanyard along with her keys. No reference to the Vatican and no symbol appeared on it, just "Honeywell."

"Damn," Huxley said. "Oh, excuse my French. Dante Tocelli apparently had a fob with 'Vaticano' written on one side. The reverse depicted a symbol. It was described to me as a white cross inside of a square, with a circle in the middle and different coats of arms in two corners. The other corners had stripes in yellow and blue and possibly red. Does that ring a bell?"

Sonatina pulled out her cell phone and punched a few things into it. "Did it look like this?" She handed him the phone. The screen depicted a flag that matched the description. The title at the bottom read "Banner of the Pontifical Swiss Guard."

"The Swiss Guard?" he asked.

"Yes. It must be a security pass issued to Swiss Guard members or perhaps to some place restricted to the Swiss Guard."

"But he is Italian. They don't let Italians into the pope's personal Swiss protectorate these days, do they?"

"Not that I have heard," she said. "Maybe he was their guest or was helping them out with something."

"You think you could get me in to see the director of the guards?"

She laughed. "He is not a director. He is a colonel. The Swiss Guard is an army of sorts, you know."

Huxley sat back in his chair. "Ah, yes, I forgot about this last vestige of an imperial past. I guess I could use an education on everything Vatican."

"Is that how you see us, Mr. Huxley, as vestiges of the past? Do you think the pope is no longer relevant despite over a billion Catholics around the globe?"

"Sorry, I meant no disrespect. I was referring to the army and territory being left over from the vast Papal States back when popes served as pseudo emperors, not just religious leaders. I come from a Catholic upbringing, so I certainly appreciate the relevance of the pope."

"Come from? Are you non-practicing? Not even a holiday worshiper?"

"Let's just say a little too much holy water has flowed under my personal bridge over the years and kind of undermined the structure. But let's not discuss me. You seem to be a very intelligent woman. You didn't become the Deputy Director of the Vatican Museums without a fair amount of education. Do you have an art degree?”

“*Sì*. From *Accademia di Bella Arti* in Florence. But then I needed to actually earn a living, so I studied at *Sapienza* in marketing and administration. The combined degrees made me irresistible to art museums.”

“I can see that.” Huxley smiled, maybe a little too long. “You said you would help me any way you could, right?”

After Sonatina clasped her hands and tilted her head for a two count, she leaned forward and whispered, “Well, yes, within bounds of propriety, of course.”

Huxley grinned. It was a small risk, but he was stuck and needed a little push. He couldn’t see how they would matter to her, and if they did because of a Vatican connection to the plot, well, maybe this would jar a little truth out of her that he would otherwise never see. “Nothing strange, I assure you. Are you good at pattern recognition? I was just wondering if you would lend me your brain.”

“*Mi scusi?*”

Huxley tilted his phone toward her. “Here, take a look at these phone entries. They aren’t mine. They are some kind of clue, I think. Now, the parts that I have highlighted I have already used, so I think we can ignore those. But we have these numbers and these notes. Do you see the reference to ‘No? A dozen times at least?’ That is a reference to a Shakespearean play. Can you think of anything that can help connect the dots for me?”

Huxley watched Sonatina’s expression closely. She seemed neither surprised nor bothered by the entries.

She pointed at the phone display. “This is an entry for your *madre?*”

“No, that part is bogus. You ever try a scavenger hunt in college?” he asked.

“No, we studied art, not scavengers, though my professors often thought artists left tiny clues about palace intrigues in their works. The professors probably had too much time on their hands. You can see a pattern in almost anything if you look hard enough, no? Maybe that is what is happening here?”

“You might be right. Any ideas?”

"I see Arden," Sonatina said. "Is that not a forest in one of Shakespeare's plays?"

"Could be." Huxley did a quick search of "Arden Forest." It was the forest in "As You Like It." The more interesting find came from a side note: Shakespeare may have named the forest for his mother, whose maiden name was Arden. Once again it revolved around a mother. This started feeling right. Shakespeare somehow was a clue. He showed the result to Sonatina.

She shook her head and shrugged her shoulders.

Huxley replaced the phone in his pocket. "See, that was helpful. Maybe we should put you on this case. Anything more you can help me with?"

"I'll see what I can find out about Mr. Tocelli and the Swiss Guard and maybe get you an interview."

"Can we meet for a luncheon follow-up?" he said excitedly. "My treat and you name the place."

"That would be nice, but I am not free today."

"Tomorrow, then?"

"Certainly, if I have anything to add by then."

"You'll add plenty just by showing up, *Signorina* D'Amare. How about at noon? I'll stop by the Museum and we'll walk to your favorite spot."

"*Sì.* See you then." After she walked out of the restaurant, he noticed the rain had stopped and the sun now glistened off of her cheeks as she walked by the window. He smiled softly.

CHAPTER 11

DANTE TOCELLI CERTAINLY was a boring one. Other than his alleged contacts with the Vatican, Huxley could dig up nothing useful on the man. He'd been to Sapienza and discovered from a few professors that Tocelli was a good student who kept pretty much to himself. Nobody at Sapienza had seen him for over six months. The only interesting tidbit was that Tocelli had never majored or minored in astronomy. So why the telescope? He had to keep pressing.

After a wasted afternoon, Huxley found himself in St. Peter's Basilica in the Vatican. He wished he could explain why, but he always seemed drawn to this magnificent building when travelling to Rome. You could stand at the entrance and look down the enormous nave, its ornate columns and barreled ceiling leading the eye to the beautiful dome at the center of the transept and finally to the apse with the altar at the far end, yet somehow believe you were in a cathedral of more normal dimensions. Then your eyes would notice the movement of the little ants as they scurried through the transept and realize those were people and you were in an exceedingly large building—over two football fields long. It was not just the size that drew Huxley, though. Nor was it the basilica's sheer beauty and magnificence. There was something more, something deeper, but he couldn't place it.

As he filtered through the crowds, he came upon his favorite statue waiting behind bulletproof glass—the Pietà by Michelangelo. There Jesus's body lay in his mother Mary's lap, his face turned up. Mary cradled his head in her right arm and looked down at him with a surprising expression. It was somewhat sad, yes, but not overly sorrowful or tearful, not in agony over his death. It was more resigned, almost a look of expectation, of yearning to see him alive again. Michelangelo had chosen to depict Mary in her younger years, perhaps as she might have looked when Jesus was born, demonstrating the inner beauty she had always signified for the church. Unusual, too, were the relative dimensions of the two figures. Jesus's body seemed slight and undersized compared to the full breadth of Mary in her robes, reminding us of how she might have held him as a baby. Was it a deliberate allusion to Jesus's birth and death in a single statue?

Huxley could not help but think again about his own mother. She would have held him like that once. He could see her looking down at him with that same expression of expectation. But then he remembered holding her the same way, knowing she would soon die. It was too much, so he closed his eyes for a second, shook his head and turned around. There, through the thick crowds, he thought he saw his new friend. The man had quickly turned away and become lost in the crowd, but Huxley had recognized the slight folds in the eyes of his Afghan shadow. *So now he's in Rome.* Huxley smiled and walked toward the exit.

When Huxley's cell vibrated in his pocket, he walked out the basilica's doors and answered, "Hey, Kira, whaddya got?"

"That's it? Not even a stupid joke at my expense today?"

"Sorry, I've been a bit distracted."

"What, with that Vatican beauty, Ms. D'Amare?"

Huxley grimaced. *Am I that transparent?* "No. You get anything more on her?"

"Nothing worth reporting. Seems to be what she says. Hard to say about how deep her Vatican ties go, though. She's been there quite awhile now and keeps getting promoted."

"What are you suggesting?"

"Why not a thing. Listen, the boss needs to talk to you. Said I should transfer you. You need anything else?"

A few seconds later, Deputy Undersecretary Blount said, "Huxley, what are you up to?"

Huxley's eyes narrowed. "Uh, investigating the Ramat David incursion."

"Yeah, I know that. Why is Ken Mayer asking?"

Ken Mayer—the number one asshole from his CIA past. *Why, indeed?* "No idea. What did he say?"

"It's not what he said, but what he demanded. Wants the whole Ramat David file."

"You giving it to him?"

"What is there to give? Haven't had a report from you yet. You getting anywhere?"

"Hard to say."

"Yeah, well, if I hear it from the CIA first, you're going to have something hard in your backside. Care to share?"

"I would if I had something tangible. Just a bunch of false leads so far."

"You getting along with the Israelis?"

"Of course. They're my best friends."

"OK. Don't screw it up. If Mayer wants your ass, I can't cover for you. Too much baggage there."

CHAPTER 12

I N THE SMALL hours of the next morning, Anwari ran his thumb over the switch on the remote in his pocket, but left it in the off position. *No accidents. Timing is critical.* "We sure the vault area is still clear?"

Two Arab men dressed like Italian businessmen stood in the stairwell with him. One of them, Dracoratio, turned his head slowly toward Anwari. "Does it matter?"

"Of course. Allah does not want us to kill innocents."

"It will be clear. We distracted the night clerk for 15 minutes at least—you know that. You need to focus, Anwari. In one minute, this goes down. No hesitation. Is the bomb ready?"

Anwari pulled out the remote and flipped the switch. A red light appeared. He showed Dracoratio the light and nodded.

"Good." Dracoratio turned to the door and opened it a crack. "He's five doors down. We'll need to play this well. Anwari, stay here until we drag him back."

"You'll incapacitate him?" Anwari asked.

Dracoratio nodded and smiled. "Let's go." Dracoratio draped his arm over the other Arab's neck, and the two walked through the door. Anwari held it open a crack to watch. Dracoratio stumbled down the hotel hallway, the other Arab barely holding him up. He was singing badly in Italian. The huge man by the door stared at the two, his right hand reached behind his back and stayed there.

Now ten feet away and yelling "Ciao," Dracoratio opened his palms toward the man so he would see they carried no weapons. The other Arab's hands were also open. The huge man relaxed a bit. Dracoratio let go of the other Arab and stumbled into the wall and to the ground five feet from the huge man. The huge man did not move to help him. Dracoratio wavered on his hands and knees for a few seconds, giving the impression he just might vomit some of the liquor from his belly. "*Una sigaretta?*" he slurred, looking up at the huge man. The huge man said nothing, but shook his head.

"*Scusa, scusa,*" the other Arab said as he lifted Dracoratio up to his feet. Just as he reached his feet, Dracoratio stumbled again, this time right toward the huge man. As he moved toward him, Dracoratio lifted his left arm, hand open but back from the wrist. At the same time, his right arm dropped to his right pocket. Anwari heard a quick whooshing sound, almost like someone quickly exhaling hard out of a mouth not quite ready to whistle. The huge man began to fall, but Dracoratio and the other Arab caught him and dragged him back into the stairwell. Anwari saw the man's face up close and recognized Mr. Riese. He looked like he was sleeping, except he had a hole the size of a dime in his forehead, blood oozing out of it.

"You killed him," Anwari said.

Dracoratio smiled. "I told you we would incapacitate him." Dracoratio's expression turned serious. "Now, time for a little boom. I'll signal you."

All three men put on masks to fully cover their heads. Dracoratio and the other Arab headed back to the door, this time with AK-47s in their hands. When they reached the door, Dracoratio signaled and Anwari pressed the red button. They were nearly 80 yards away through 5 floors of concrete and steel and wood, yet Anwari heard the explosion and felt the building rattle. So did the occupants of the room. A middle-aged man opened the door, saying "Mr. Riese…" but he fell silent as the nozzle of the AK-47 touched his forehead. Anwari heard only the familiar shriek of a young girl as the door to the room closed behind the two intruders.

❁ ❁ ❁

Hours later, Dracoratio and the other Arab sat across the steel table from Anwari on steel chairs, the straps of their AK-47 rifles slung around the tops of the chairs next to them. Anwari's rifle rested on the table to his right. A clear plastic tube a little over a half-centimeter in diameter lay on the table, connected to a small metallic cylinder. They were in a cement-floored canyon, the walls of which were the many twenty-foot high steel shelves running in parallel rows nearly the 200-foot length of the room. Each shelf contained palettes loaded with boxes marked with Italian words, such as *ammoniaca, cloro candeggina,* and *acido sulfurico.* Overhead lights illuminated the little sitting area while the rest of the warehouse remained dark.

Anwari looked at the Arab leader opposite him. "Have you heard from Pardus yet?"

Dracoratio let out a breath that vibrated with a deep, tumultuous, vibrating tone, like the sound one might expect to hear from a dragon ready to breathe fire on its prey. "No," said Dracoratio in his gravelly, breathy voice. "Be patient. It is only 5 a.m. Let him sleep."

"How bad were the girls hurt? Do they need medical attention?"

"The 12-year-old tried to grab my mask and pull it off. She got what she deserved. She will survive. Might have broken her nose, but she was still breathing. The bleeding has stopped. The younger one came quietly after that."

"How about the wife?"

"She will awake soon enough."

Anwari nodded. "Is Rosenthal talking yet?"

"Have not tried. That is for Pardus. I think the chemist will respond to our leverage over his family."

"Won't Rosenthal assume you'll just kill them all afterwards anyway?"

Dracoratio grinned. "We wore masks. He shall believe we can let him go at any time. He just has to give us a little information and he and his loved ones are on their way home. He does not know where he is because he was blindfolded himself. We leave nothing to chance."

"I get that, but then why the explosive? I don't think you needed me on this. I just made a bunch of noise for nothing."

"Misdirection. Always get them looking for something else. You bomb the area of the hotel safe while we depart the hotel out the back door and nobody notices us. They figure the action is yet to come. We get here before they even know what they are looking at."

Anwari nodded. "Seemed to work."

"Yes, and it helps with the press, too. Pardus was explicit—he does not want this kidnapping hushed up by the government. Hard for them to do that when a bomb goes off. He said you would understand."

"I guess so," Anwari said. "You going to?"

"Going to what?"

"Let them go."

Dracoratio gave him a long, cold stare. "Not my call. Hold on." He pulled his phone out of his pocket. It was a flip phone just like the one Anwari had destroyed before he left Israel. "Yes, we have him. No problems. Safe made a noise and everybody ran toward it. Had to eliminate the BG—your new tube device worked to perfection. Anyway, we have them all and no glitches. What is next?" He listened for a few minutes. "Got it." He looked at Anwari and grinned. "Yes, he performed well. He will do. Certainly." Phone in hand, Dracoratio stretched out his arm toward Anwari. "He wants to talk to you."

Anwari snatched the phone. "Hello?"

"Excellent work, Abdul. You know what is next?"

"You want me to find Huxley?"

"Yes. Ensure he makes the connection. It is pivotal."

"What about the scientist and his family?"

"Dracoratio will take care of them. He can ship them out of the country and back to a safe facility. Then we can convince the Jew to cooperate."

"You going to torture them?" asked Anwari.

"No need. We will separate the family from him, and the good scientist will not know what to believe. We might have to hurt him a little just to make it real. But I do not think it will take too long—maybe a week."

"Then you'll release them?" Anwari asked.

"We shall have to see what is in the best interests of Allah, my friend. Nobody will get hurt unless they must for the cause."

CHAPTER 13

WHEN HUXLEY REACHED the entrance to the Vatican Museums, he saw the long line of tourists. He took out his cell and called Signorina Sonatina D'Amare. "I'm just outside. I think it may be easier for you to leave the building than for me to enter. Are you ready? Great, see you soon."

He looked up and saw Anwari, his *piccola coda*, listening to a tour guide, who held a red flag over her head. "That's right, sir, if you would like a tour, come with me and you can get right in. It is only twenty Euros more and you avoid the two-hour wait."

Anwari looked up at Huxley, feigning surprise. "Mr. Huxley? Mr. Chris Huxley? You too are visiting the Vatican art?"

"Yes, it is very unexpected, isn't it? What brings you to Rome, Abdul? You look a bit ragged, even for an old Afghan soldier."

"Well, I am a consummate tourist now, Chris, and this is one of the greatest places in Europe, don't you think? Anyway, I thought I was safer travelling as a tourist than fighting in the mountains of Afghanistan, but now I am beginning to wonder."

"What do you mean?" asked Huxley.

Anwari shook his head. "Terrible. Haven't you heard the news? A bomb went off at the New Colossus Hotel. I think I would rather be in a hazard zone where I can protect myself with my own weapon than in this city unarmed."

"Anybody hurt? What was the target?"

"TV said some Israeli chemist's bodyguard was killed. The chemist and family are missing."

"Any more details on the chemist?" Huxley asked. Anwari shrugged his shoulders.

Sonatina walked out of the museum entrance and began looking around. "Shit," Huxley mumbled. "Excuse me, Abdul, thanks for the info. Enjoy your tour."

Huxley walked quickly over to Sonatina. "*Buon pomeriggio, Signorina!* Thank you for coming." He placed his hand to his heart. "Unfortunately, I must now be the ugly American and apologize for standing you up. I just heard about an explosion at the New Colossus Hotel and I need to see if there is any connection. Please accept my apologies."

"But of course, Mr. Huxley. I understand completely." She paused for a second and then added with a smile, "You most certainly should get your ugly American body over there."

"Oh, I am crushed," Huxley said, feigning pain by placing both hands to his heart. "Could I make it up to you by amending the time of our date?"

"Our date?"

"Uh, our meeting, I mean. Could we meet for dinner tonight instead?"

"You must think I have no life."

Huxley bowed his head slowly. "Again, I apologize. I did not mean—"

"And you might be right. Could you pick me up here at seven?"

"Excellent." As she began to turn, Huxley added, "Oh, Signorina, do you have any information you would like to share with me now?"

"And miss an expensive dinner on an ugly American? *Non possibile!* See you tonight. *Ciao!*" She turned, flashed a smile and her pass at the guard, and reentered the museum doors.

Smiling as he shook his head once, Huxley watched her disappear through the doors, and then turned and pulled out his phone as he walked toward the cabstand on Viale Vaticano. A few moments later he was speaking with Captain Yadin of Aman. "Captain, I thought I would update you on my progress."

"Go ahead."

"I've got a dead end on the contacts list, unless you know where I can find the 17th Earl of Oxford."

"Oxford?" Yadin asked.

"Never mind. Bad joke, and it's rubbish anyway, as the English would say. I've been following a potential lead relating to an archaeology student without much luck so far. I'm in Rome."

"Rome?"

The excited tone in Yadin's voice told Huxley what he wanted. "Yes, and now I hear that an Israeli scientist and his family have been kidnapped from a hotel in Rome. You know anything about that?"

Yadin said, "So you are calling for information again instead of giving it out?"

"I just gave you what I know. What do you know?"

"We just heard ourselves. His name is Jacob Rosenthal."

"You seem to be a step slow," Huxley said. "Now you are going to tell me that he was working with the Israeli Air Force."

"How did you…?" Yadin asked. "Yes, he is employed by a local defense contractor. That is all I am at liberty to say."

"And he was working on a project at Ramat David?"

"I cannot say. What do you think?"

Huxley replied, "I would say he was the target of your little incursion there, wouldn't you?"

"Probably unrelated."

"You really believe that? Have you heard any demands from the terrorists yet?"

"No. We don't even know for certain that he was kidnapped. But we cannot find him, and he doesn't answer his phone."

Huxley looked around. Anwari had gone away. "OK, what was he working on at Ramat?"

"I already told you, I can't tell you where he works."

"So he was at Ramat."

"If he were there," Yadin said, "I would not be in a position to confirm that."

"And his vacation itinerary was on the list that was accessed?

"Yes."

Huxley grinned. *Interesting he would admit that.* "So why is this chemist so important?"

"I am not in a position to tell you that."

"Well, thanks for all of your wonderful insights on this, Captain."

"Huxley?"

"Yes?"

"This is even more important than either of us thought. We need to find this scientist soon. That is all I can say…here."

Tilting his head slightly, Huxley squinted into the distance. "Okay, I think I understand." *All he can say here? He looking for another way?* "Hold on a sec." Huxley quickly thumbed through the photo library on his cell. *Bingo.* "Captain, I seem to recall that you mentioned you have an interest in American cowboys. I just remembered that I have a few pictures that might interest you from my visit to the cowboy museum in Oklahoma. I know this is a personal matter, and, if your agency is like ours, you are not supposed to handle personal matters on your agency phone. Do you have another cell where I can text the pictures?"

Yadin did not hesitate. "Sure. I have your number. I'll send you a text and you can reply to it and send me the pictures."

"Sounds good. I will speak with you when I have more. Please remember to keep me informed as well."

Well, that was curious. Huxley had pegged Corpuscle Face as the hard-ass, play-it-by-the-book man. It now looked like Aman had him down as a more flexible resource. No doubt Aman wanted an off-the-grid channel of communication on this. No way Yadin would be flying solo here. It was a way the spy agencies sometimes operated so they could keep certain intel out of the official sharing arrangements to avoid disputes with their own fellow agencies—in this case probably the Israeli Air Force. He wanted to tell Huxley something that Aman thought could only be shared informally. He would have to wait for that text to know more.

Meanwhile, Huxley had other resources that could fill him in. He called for help from the home front. The phone rang six times before she answered. "Hey Kira, how are you doing this morning?"

She spoke slowly, "You do know that I actually need sleep to function, don't you?"

"Sure, but I'll bet it's a beautiful day in the District. Why not make it an early one and enjoy the sunrise?"

"I didn't get to bed but a few hours ago."

"What, up partying again?"

"Yeah, that's me, the party girl. Funny how my computer and I have such a blast together every night."

Better leave that comeback alone. "Okay, well, now that you are up at, hell it is already past six am there, can you track down some info on an Israeli scientist for me? Probably need to get to the Defense Intelligence Agency folks and try the CIA."

"I think I know the drill."

"Of course. There might be something in our own database, but I doubt it. The scientist's name is Jacob Rosenthal. He was just kidnapped in Rome along with his family. I think this is all connected with the incursion at Ramat David. I need the info yesterday or I wouldn't be calling you right now. Really. See what you can find."

Kira perked up. "Got it. Thanks for the new project. I was beginning to get bored."

"Glad to help. I also need you to get me hooked up with the ROS, the anti-terrorist unit of the Carabinieri in Rome. They'll be called in. I want to talk to the officers in charge of the hotel bombing/kidnapping. Call me soon."

Huxley hung up and noticed the text his phone had received while he was on the call. The short message read: "Here's the number. Have a meeting now. Send me the cowboy pictures and call me in a few hours so we can discuss them." Huxley texted the pictures and saved the number under "Captain Yadin, Home." He hoped he'd like the "home" version of Captain Yadin better than the "work" one.

⚜ ⚜ ⚜

Not an hour later, Huxley was in the thick of the kidnapping investigation at the New Collossus Hotel. "Nothing was taken from the bank vault?" Huxley asked, raising an eyebrow to Lieutenant Patismio.

Lieutenant Patismio's jet-black hair was slicked back underneath a black peaked military-style cap exhibiting the wavy silver emblem of the

Carabinieri. The red-bordered silver lapels of his black suit matched the red stripes on the sides of his pants and completed the uniform. His thick mustache remaining nearly still, Patismio said, "The explosion did not even open the vault. We think it was a pure diversion."

"For the kidnapping."

"Yes. When the bomb exploded, hotel security directed all of their resources to the safe—away from the kidnappers, apparently. They sent a signal to the Polizia station ten blocks away. The Polizia mobilized, quickly cordoned off an eight-block area and sent a team to the hotel. It was nearly a half hour later that we realized no robbery could have occurred."

"Did your men search all the vehicles coming through your cordon area?"

Patismio put his hands on his hips. "They are not my men. I am with the Carabinieri, not the Polizia. But yes, they searched every vehicle, questioned the drivers and detained anyone who was suspicious. But there was nothing. Certainly no kidnap victims. They would have seen them."

"But they were looking for bank robbers," Huxley said.

"It doesn't matter. In fact, that would have been even more suspicious. No, we have interviewed all of the Polizia officers and I don't believe that could have occurred. Besides, we think the kidnappers took the victims in the laundry van."

"The laundry van?" Huxley said.

"Surveillance cameras outside of the hotel showed a large black van with the logo of *Lenzuola Pulite,* a local laundry company. It left the rear of the hotel a minute after the explosion. We checked with the company and they had no trucks here this morning. It was a ruse."

"Any license plate or other info you can trace?" Huxley asked.

"No license plate was visible," Patismio replied. "We are looking at other video feeds in the city, but they are pretty sparse."

"When did you realize this was a kidnapping?"

"Our officers searched all the rooms, just in case the bombing perpetrators were holding out there. They found the bodyguard's corpse in the emergency exit stairwell near Rosenthal's room. He had an entrance wound in his forehead, and ceramic fragments were found in his brain. Looks like they used some kind of ceramic projectile. Not sure how they fired it. He'd been killed instantly and nobody in the hotel heard or saw anything."

Huxley looked at the wall for a few seconds. "Ceramic fragments and no sound. Did they find a tube or small compressed gas container nearby?"

"No. What you getting at?"

"Could be a purpose-built, compressed-gas weapon," Huxley said. "Best way to surprise a bodyguard if you have the resources to put one together. These guys are well-funded. Approach with a tube tied to the inside of the arm and swish—no loud bang to alert guests. Ceramic projectile tumbles around a few times after entering the guard's brain and breaks up. The big bodyguard falls without even knowing he's been hit. Then they snatch and grab the scientist and family."

"Could be. It looks like he was killed outside the door and dragged to the stairwell. Elevator was locked down when we arrived, so that would have reduced foot traffic."

"Makes sense. You have any other video from hotel security—maybe from yesterday and the night before?"

"We are going over that in detail now, but in the first run through nothing looked suspicious."

"Please send a digital copy to this Homeland Security server." Huxley wrote down the information on the back of his card. "Our facial recognition folks will see if one of the bad guys pops up. I'm sure you have Interpol working on that; still, we may have a larger database to search."

"Pictures from your drones over the battlefields?" Patismio asked.

"You never know. Can I see Rosenthal's room?"

"It's been gone over by our crime scene folks and sent off to RaCIS for analysis. They've photographed and inventoried everything already."

"You have their work on digital?"

"We have entered the 21st century here, Mr. Huxley."

Huxley nodded gently. "Sorry, plenty of places are behind the times, including in the States. Can I get a copy?"

"I have been instructed to cooperate in any way possible with you, so, yes, I'll have a copy sent to your server right away."

"*Grazie. Mi dispiace*, if I offended you, Lieutenant. You have been very professional and very helpful."

CHAPTER 14

"Is this dinner expensive enough for you to spill your guts to me?" Huxley asked in his best teasing voice.

"Just wait until I order the dessert," Sonatina responded. "If you agree to that, you can have whatever you want from me."

Huxley raised his eyebrows. "My mother used to say that great food brings out the best in people." He raised his glass of merlot and she followed with her pinot noir. "To a mutually beneficial relationship, then."

She frowned. "As long as your credit card doesn't bounce. I can't imagine they pay you government *ragazzi* enough for dinners like these."

"Hey, I get a $50 per diem from Homeland Security. That'll cover the salads and a quarter of your glass of wine."

She laughed. "I am not always this high maintenance, you know. Only when American agents want to squeeze top secret information out of me."

"It is my pleasure, but I'll try to avoid squeezing you too hard."

Sonatina smiled coyly. "That's your best move. I'm more of a peach than a grapefruit—squeeze me too hard, and I'll only bruise."

"Well, we wouldn't want that. I've always loved peach cobbler though."

"*Ahia*! Now you're slicing me up for your pie?"

"*Mi dispiace*, Signora D'Amare, I think I carried the metaphor a step too far."

"*Nessun problema.* I took no offense. Anyway, I think we have progressed to Sonatina, don't you think? May I call you Christian?"

"No, but you can call me Chris."

"That is what I remembered, but your assistant called you Christian when she set up our breakfast meeting."

"Sounds like her—she likes to mess with me. She probably heard your lovely voice and decided that would be great fun. I rarely use my full first name, not since my college days."

"Chris, then, though I think Christian suits you better."

He sighed. His damn name. If he had to explain it one more time... *No. Let it go.* He took in the ambiance of the restaurant. It was a place where Hanna would have fit right in: twenty-foot ceilings, ornate Italianate architecture with Romanesque columns, a dark wooden floor set off by the bright white of the linen tablecloths, and the thing Hanna would like most—waiters in black tuxedos. The woman sitting across from him now was very different than Hanna. Sure, she had that same playful manner, but she seemed to lack that dark little conceit that would hide in Hanna's shadows, emerging only when his guard had been lowered. At least he hadn't glimpsed a sign of that from Sonatina yet. *I hope I never will.*

Sonatina was beautiful but not bewitching like Hanna. Still, her generous smile and her dark yet glowing eyes radiated through him. It was charming the way she twirled the waves of her hair by her ear whenever she thought deeply. A tingle traveled down his spine. *Stop it. Lock it down, Hux. Play the game, get what you need, and get out before she breaks your heart.*

Sonatina broke the silence, "Where did you attend college, Chris?"

"Northeast U.S."

"Oh, whereabouts?"

"Boston area."

"Boston College?"

"Uh, close but not quite. Across the river." Huxley held up his hands. "Enough about me. You enjoy working at the Vatican?"

"*Si.* Mostly."

"Mostly?" Huxley raised his left eyebrow.

"Do not get me wrong, Chris, I love the museums, and most of the people are great."

"Most?"

Sonatina smiled but said nothing.

"Okay, I get it," Huxley said. "How did you end up there?"

"I had a few…opportunities…after school that I explored first, but I always wanted to come home."

"You left Italy?"

"*Si.* The Vatican does not hire many right out of school."

"No, of course not. Where did you go?"

"A few places. Singapore. Moscow. London."

"Moscow? You speak Russian?"

"Enough to get by. It wasn't the best place for me. At first, I thought Russia might enter an artistic renaissance of sorts, but with the organized crime and Putin bringing them back toward the cold war… I left as quickly as I could."

Huxley grinned. "I did not realize I was dining with such a world traveller. You almost put me to shame."

"I doubt that very much. What about you? Have you always been an ugly American spy?"

"Ugly yes, spy never." Huxley opened his palms to her. "I'm just a lowly investigator trying to find his way."

Sonatina rested her chin on her fist and gazed at him. "Yet you never seem lost."

Huxley chuckled. "If only perception were reality. Should we talk shop?"

"If you would like. Have you learned anything new about your case?"

"I was just going to ask you the same thing. The hotel kidnapping was no coincidence though I am afraid I cannot get into details." Details. He wished he had more of them. Damn Yadin had not answered when he called in the afternoon on his "home" cell. And Kira had called to tell him DOD and CIA were dragging their feet on his requests. Was Mayer holding this up? Maybe he would need to prod them himself. The only useful bit of information pointed back at the Vatican. He needed to keep playing his best hand here. "So what can you tell me about Mr. Tocelli and the Swiss Guard?"

"The fob you mentioned generally accesses most of the exterior doors of the Vatican and many of its interior doors."

"How do you know this?"

"It's not a state secret, and I do have an admirer or two among the Guard."

"How do they know?" Huxley asked.

"It is the card each Swiss Guard soldier is issued."

Huxley smiled. *Yep.* "Is Tocelli listed among the Guard? Is he listed anywhere?"

"No, I am afraid not. I can set up a meeting with Colonel Zaugg for you. Perhaps he will recognize the picture you showed me."

"Please do that. Did I show you this, yet?" He brought up a picture of one of the items found in the Israeli Chemist's room and handed it to her.

"A visitor's pass to the archives," Sonatina said.

"I thought so."

Sonatina sat up straight in her chair. "Tell me you are not one of those conspiratorial types who believe the archives contain a stack of secret Catholic documents that tell the real truth about Jesus and Mary Magdalene? The archives aren't really secret, you know."

"No?"

"No. The name of the place does not translate well into English, though they have used it since the Middle Ages. They really should be called not the 'Vatican Secret Archives' but the 'Private Papal Archives.' The pope opens them up to select researchers, but they aren't really owned by the Vatican itself. They are the property of the pope, and their ownership transfers directly to the next pope upon his election. Mostly personal papers and the like. Kind of like your presidential papers, but passed down from one pope to the next."

Huxley leaned forward. "Okay, I get it. Any thoughts, then, on why an Israeli chemist would want to see the pope's private papers, or why they would grant his request?"

"Who knows?" she asked.

He sat back in his chair. "You ready for that dessert? How about a chocolate espresso cheesecake?"

Sonatina smiled and licked her lips slowly. "I thought you would never ask."

Huxley's temperature began rising again, but then he felt a vibration in his pocket. "Excuse me, I am waiting on a few calls." Huxley motioned for the waiter. "Can you order for me?" He pressed his phone. "Hello, Kira, do you have something for me?"

"Hi Mr. Huxley, sorry to disturb your dinner with the *bellezza Italiana*, but Deputy Under Secretary Blount just called. He wants you on a plane heading back here tonight."

"I can't get a flight out tonight."

"Oh, yes you can. DOD has a flight coming back from Aviano Air Base in three hours. A Black Hawk will pick you up in one hour at the helipad coordinates I'm texting you."

Huxley frowned and shook his head. "They called a helicopter for me? What's up?"

"Looks like your inquiries created a little ruckus at CIA. They won't tell me, but something riled them up. Anyway, the boss wants a complete debrief on your mission tomorrow morning."

"Okay, hold on." Huxley stood up, motioned to Sonatina to eat dessert without him, and headed out of the restaurant. "What about the face recognition on the hotel tapes? You get any hits?"

"One big one," Kira said. "Esnanimen Kharun Udani was seen in the corridor of the hotel earlier in the day. Nobody even knew he was in Italy. You remember him, don't you?"

"We still haven't pinned any terrorist activity on him, have we? He keeps showing up around the time of some minor terrorist activities attributable to the group Ungues Pardi. But no direct link or cell phone activity or anything. He was in Guantanamo for a year and he didn't say a word. Some sheik from Dubai got him released. Said it must have been a mistake. Some huge coincidence. Udani was from the sheik's security staff and was just in the vicinity checking out dangerous places. Or some crap like that."

"You let him go?" Kira asked.

"Hey, it wasn't me," Huxley said. "He is our only link to Pardus. There has been suspicion that he may be Dracoratio, Pardus's reputed right hand man, but we have no confirmation that Udani even knows Pardus. Nevertheless, everyone else with a possible connection seems to have either ended up dead or ignorant about the boss. Pardus is a ghost—'the Ghost Leopard' we call him since Pardus is Latin for leopard. We don't even know who he is or what he looks like. Hell, we are not even sure of his ethnicity. For all we know, he and his group are just legends that get blamed or credited with a few attacks every year when the other terrorists don't want to take the blame."

Kira cleared her throat. "That's a bit more than I had on him. You on a personal quest or something?"

"Nope. But it's the guys you don't know who end up killing you, and we don't know Pardus. We got a location on Udani?"

"No sir. I'll let you know when we do. I do have one interesting bit of intel for you though."

"And that would be?" Huxley asked.

"The facial recognition software would not have even found him if it weren't for recent events—he wasn't even in the database. But I thought, just in case there is some connection, I'd run a special scan."

"Of whom?"

"Abdul Saboor Anwari."

Huxley leaned back and stared at the ceiling. "Shit, he was in the hotel?"

"He sure was. Now what was he doing there?"

"Maybe I've underestimated his role in all of this. Good work, again."

Sonatina was sitting and waiting for him at the table. A piece of chocolate espresso cheesecake stared her in the face while his tiramisu waited for him across the table. "*Mi dispiace,* Sonatina. It could not be helped, and now it looks like I will have to cut our evening short and catch a flight back to the States."

"Our evening? I thought this was just a dinner business meeting?" Sonatina smiled coyly.

Huxley tilted his head, smiling, and nodded a few times. "Of course. So back to business."

"Is there something else I can do for you?"

"Well, yes. I mean no. I doubt it." Should he trust her more? The Vatican could be involved somehow, so why not her? It was unlikely, but… Then again, if she were holding back, he might see that. He had mastered that investigative technique long ago—throw just enough out there so the person of interest thinks you trust them, then let their reactions and covers give them away.

"Have you decided, yet?" she asked.

"Decided?" He nodded softly. "I'm wondering if you've ever heard of Pardus?"

"The Leopard? You are speaking in Latin, now? I don't think so, unless he has changed his spots."

"He seems to change them continuously. Pardus may be the most elusive terrorist we have ever encountered. Some do not think he even exists."

"Then why is he important?"

Huxley smiled, slowly leaned forward and whispered, "He may be behind all of this."

Sonatina shook her head. "Really, when you get stuck, you turn to ghosts?"

He shrugged. "Anyway, I sure would like to figure out that contacts list."

"Don't your supercomputers at Homeland Security handle those patterns for you?"

"Perhaps." *They could try if I let them.* He had not reported the contacts list to Homeland. If his boss saw the personal connection, he would probably take Huxley off the case even though he was probably the only one who could figure out clues obviously intended for him.

Her eyes narrowed. "You haven't held that back from them, have you?"

He stared back at her. *She reads me well.* He gave her his best sly smile. "Who me? Why would I do such a thing? And what if I did?"

Sonatina looked down pensively for a few counts, then leaned forward, put her elbows on the table and rested her chin on her clasped hands above them. She spoke gently, "I think you are a clever man, Chris, but can you handle the emotional baggage?"

"Baggage?"

"Your mother has passed away, and the clues seem to involve her. 'Deceased and Forsaken?'"

Huxley winced. "That's not my mother. Her name wasn't Maryam."

"But your *madre*, she is dead."

"How did you know?"

"That is twice tonight you used the past tense with her, and each time there was a tone of sorrow in your voice."

Huxley's eyebrows rose.

"Did she die recently?" Sonatina asked.

"A year ago, but I don't want to talk about it."

Sonatina paused for a few seconds and then leaned forward. "That's fine, but you did ask me what I think. If you cannot even talk about your mother, will not your memories of her taint your consideration of the case? Someone obviously is messing with your head. Could it be this Pardus?"

Huxley stared at Sonatina a long time while she just smiled gently back at him. It was an image he would never forget and a statement that would continue to haunt him.

❁ ❁ ❁

An hour later, the image still followed Huxley as he awaited his lift to Aviano. Sonatina had read his past emotional state like she had known him well during that year of depression. But she had not. Was she just that perceptive from the few clues he had shared with her, or did she have some kind of inside information from someone else, someone who might have written the clues? She was wrong about one thing—he could handle the emotional baggage, couldn't he? His phone finally rescued him from his thoughts. The screen read *Captain Yadin, Home*. He answered it.

"Mr. Huxley?"

"Captain, I was beginning to worry about you."

"I am touched, Huxley. Look, this is off the books, you understand? You didn't get it from me or anyone else at Aman. You guys pieced it together for yourselves. We just talked about cowboys."

"Yes, I understand. What can you tell me?"

"Rosenthal—he is a chemist, but much more than that. He figured out how to block most of the gamma-ray and neutron signatures of fissile material—the special nuclear material in nuclear weapons. His method also blocks the radiograph imaging techniques employed by modern detectors. It has not yet been deployed by us, but we think it is possible that he could replicate his work in another sophisticated laboratory if he is given sufficient time."

"How much time?" Huxley asked.

"Unsure—a couple months, maybe. Could be less with proper motivation and resources. It depends on access to raw materials, the quality of assistants, the availability of lab equipment, and a variety of other factors."

"Are you familiar with our global capabilities?"

"Maybe."

"And?"

"We think it may block those detectors," Yadin said.

"You familiar with the Container Security Initiative, where we use detectors on container ships in foreign ports before they head to U.S. ports?"

"I am."

Huxley exhaled hard. "Well? Can it block those detectors?"

"I assure you that was not our goal, but it may be a corollary effect."

"Damn. So, according to your intel, if the bastard gets Rosenthal to cooperate and somehow gets hold of a warhead, it will be invisible."

"Pretty much."

"Then we are blind and the whole damn world may be at the whim of a nuclear terrorist?"

"That's why I'm alerting you. We must find him. But this did not come from Aman or anyone else in Israel. You'll have to follow up on the tech through other channels."

When he disconnected, the implications of Yadin's revelations hit him square. If the Ghost Leopard was seeking to develop the ability to hide a nuclear bomb from detection, then the terrorist must either have access to a nuke or believe he could soon secure one. When Huxley shuddered at the thought of a terrorist wielding that kind of power, he saw again the image of Sonatina smiling and challenging him. She had been innocent, compassionate even, yet her words burrowed deep into his core and managed to threaten him. *Emotional baggage. Someone was messing with him. Could it be Pardus?*

His mind was spinning nearly as fast as the helicopter blade approaching him from above. He must find the Leopard, but his only real clues were the puzzles he had begun to unravel. Yet if Pardus produced the puzzles, then would they not lead to a false end, or was something else going down? Huxley closed his eyes. He had to find the answers soon, or millions could perish at the hands of a ghost. Yes, he was chasing a ghost—a ghost of the apocalypse. Huxley laughed at the word and remembered the terrible images from Revelations that frightened him as a child. The images danced anew in his brain. There was the ghost rider on a red horse carrying a huge sword. When the horse reared, its hoofs nearly struck him in the head. Then the rider raised his hand toward Huxley, though the hand no longer held a sword but a nuclear missile. The rider laughed derisively in Huxley's face. Huxley opened his eyes and shook off the image while he approached the helicopter. *More religious baggage.* Just the kind the Ghost Leopard would use to confuse him. Yes, Huxley was chasing a ghost, but this one was not made of vapor and shadows. This one Huxley could catch and send straight to hell. If there were such a thing.

SECUNDA PRIMAE: INSPIRATIO

"Brief and troubled is our lifetime; there is no remedy for our dying, nor is anyone known to have come back from Hades. For by mere chance were we born, and hereafter we shall be as though we had not been; because the breath in our nostrils is smoke, and reason a spark from the beating of our hearts, and when this is quenched, our body will be ashes and our spirit will be poured abroad like empty air. Even our name will be forgotten in time, and no one will recall our deeds. So our life will pass away like the traces of a cloud, and will be dispersed like a mist pursued by the sun's rays and overpowered by its heat. For our lifetime is the passing of a shadow; and our dying cannot be deferred because it is fixed with a seal; and no one returns."

— Liber Prophetarum—W 2:1–5

"The life of this world is like this: rain that We send down from the sky is absorbed by the plants of the earth, from which humans and animals eat. But when the earth has taken on its finest appearance, and adorns itself, and its people think they have power over it, then the fate We commanded comes to it, by night or by day, and We reduce it to stubble, as if it had not flourished just the day before."

— Liber Prophetarum—M 10:24

"Even now the ax lies at the root of the trees. Therefore every tree that does not produce good fruit will be cut down and thrown into the fire."

— Liber Vitae—J 14:17

CHAPTER 15

TOMADUS OF ROMA first experienced the light just before unveiling his new invention at the Annual Lumenology Conference of 1890 (AH). He had chosen a stuffy title to fit the nature of the proceedings: "Computational Apparatus Employing Extreme Focusing and Amplification of Ultra-High-Frequency Photonic Logic Diodes." "Photon Computer" might sound more appealing to the masses, but the more technical name had served its purpose: over 200 of the most elite technologists from all over Roma had already registered.

He entered the huge exhibit hall and frowned. His lecture room awaited him on the other end of this mega-market maze, full of booths with robed men hawking various trinkets to the tech crowd. He set out across the floor, weaving and gently pushing his way between the masses.

A hawker from a nearby booth stepped in front of him. "My esteemed technologist, I can see you are in a rush. My new Tech-Sched will save you time."

"*No gratia.*" As he skirted by the man, Tomadus's crimson and white silk robe temporarily caught on the metallic edge of the booth. He could not rip it, not today. He slowed down and slid the robe off the corner.

Emerging from the throng, Tomadus saw the familiar face of a man in white robes among a group of men from the lower classes. Neither handsome nor ugly, it was a face he could never forget: long and gentle with thin lips, angular nose and high cheekbones, all framed by dark hair dangling down to his shoulders. He had seen him on the visi-scan news spouting something about saving the world—or at least saving everyone from themselves. So many pseudo prophets littered the landscape, but this one somehow seemed different.

As Tomadus stared, the man looked up and stared back for a few seconds. *His eyes*, Tomadus thought. *There is something haunting there.* Somehow, he felt like the man could see right through him. *No, that's not it. Not through me, into me.*

The man in the white robes smiled ever so softly, took a few steps toward Tomadus, and held out his hand. "Peace be with you, sir. My name is Isa."

Tomadus's eyes narrowed. *The guy doesn't bow but shakes hands like a Tetepian?* Yet some force drew Tomadus forward, pulling him closer, making him want to touch this man's hand. "And mine is—"

A hot-white light flashed across Tomadus's eyes and remained there for what seemed an eternity—glowing, piercing, searing a hole in his con-sciousness. An image burned in his mind, an image of a stranger dressed strangely, surrounded by others dressed even more oddly, with colored insignia on their chests and metallic symbols near their necks. But it was more than a mere image. He could feel the angst, the loneliness of this man, his thoughts repeating the word "forsaken."

The experience passed as quickly as it had begun. Confused, Tomadus ducked quickly and jerked his head around. Had his head been knocked silly by shrapnel? Had a Demosep shaitaanist slipped by security? No, he had heard no explosions, no screams, no body parts whooshing by. All seemed normal now.

Isa stood erect yet relaxed, his right hand moving to his heart and then slowly to his side, his face showing no apparent concern. His weightless eyes gently focused on Tomadus's own. "Peace, Tomadus," was all this man Isa said. Then he nodded slightly and turned slowly away.

Tomadus stood there blinking rapidly, trying to regain his bearings. *What the damnation was that?* Had he even told Isa his name? *Too much arak last night.* He craned his neck around from side to side, shook his head and strode toward the lecture hall. *Come on, refocus: photon logic, light amplification, spatial coherence…*

CHAPTER 16

TOMADUS'S EYES OPENED abruptly, fixing on the antique ceiling fan twirling gently above his room. The light from inside his dream seemed to cast a glimmer on his entire viewshed, washing over each blade of the fan with a yellow-white hue. He blinked a few times and realized he was shivering. The breeze from the fan quickly evaporated the sweat still dribbling down his naked body, chilling his skin. He could hear the thump of his heart, the great muscle contracting nearly every half-second.

It must have been a nightmare, but he couldn't remember a frame of it—except for the light. The same light that had flashed yesterday when he was with that preacher. There was something else. Shadows crept to the edge of his memory, just a tendril away, but they quickly slithered into the dark corners of his mind.

Yesterday he had achieved more than he had thought possible. An attentive crowd. An occasional, collective ooh or ah. A cheer when he finally unveiled the device. An exuberant standing ovation to conclude the demonstration. Never seen technologists do that before. And then that party that made him feel like one of the Three Emperors. He had bathed in the glorious steam of accolades for nearly a full day and fooled himself into feeling it would never end. But his old nemesis, that little creature in the depth of his gut, had snuck out during his slumber, opened up Tomadus's emotional valves, and roared in triumphant laughter, watching the gentle, uplifting steam seep out.

Tomadus sat up on the edge of the alabaster bed. The entire hotel room was adorned in white with the occasional interruption of an antique in dark mahogany, so obviously an attempt to capture the recent trend of modern Romanus nihilism mixed with a bit of the Mongolian Imperial touches from so many centuries ago. The two worked surprisingly well together and gave the entire room a feeling of great luxury. He smiled softly, feeling the warmth of success in his belly. *I deserve it, don't I?*

But then that little creature tugged from deep inside his belly and sent a tingle up his spine and down his arms. Not that pleasing little tingle that comes from an unexpected and joyous surprise. No, this was the sting of overwhelming dread, fear, and loneliness. He had struggled with the creature in his gut for so many years that he had almost forgotten the first time…

It was the year his beloved mother had died suddenly from the fever. His mother—hadn't he abandoned her? He shook his head. Strange—why had he just thought that? If anything, by succumbing to the fever, she had abandoned him to his great uncle. His great uncle was a hard man. That summer had been horrendous. Cast so quickly from the apex of adoration to the cesspool of contempt, Tomadus had turned to the streets to avoid lashings from the tongue and hands of a man who reminded him more of a slave master than a loving guardian. But the streets were unkind to him, and he had quickly found himself starving. Forgetting his mother's lessons, he had turned to petty theft.

It was only a loaf of bread and every bite had tasted like the greatest meal in his life. But then the creature stirred within him. At first, he thought he had eaten too much or the bread had been bad, but the feeling would not dissipate—not even when the baker ratted him out and he was taken to a delinquency ward in the Praesidium Sector. After his great uncle collected him, he nearly beat Tomadus to death, yet the creature continued to stir.

The creature finally quieted when the great uncle decided to rid himself of his new burden by dumping Tomadus at a work-for-scholarship boarding school on the north end. Tomadus never heard from his great uncle again. Quickly losing himself in work and study, Tomadus became the star of his class. Once again, he was the gentle prodigy his mother had cultivated and loved and adored before her death. The creature would not stir for several years, but it always returned—more as a warning than a curse—and eventually he learned to listen to it…

So the creature was chewing at his bowels to tell him something. But why now when all was going so well?

Despite a little abuse of *arak* and *vinum* last night, he remembered tidbits of the conversations at the party but nothing substantial. Everyone had been as drunk as he. Maybe it wasn't the creature at all. Maybe he was just reacting differently to the liquor this time. There was a perfectly good reason the empires banned alcohol outside of Roma, but he sure enjoyed partaking when he was home again. He rubbed his rough face with his palms a few times, shook his head, and stood up. "Go away, you beast!" This time the thing obeyed his command and crawled back into the deep recesses of his abdomen, falling asleep.

Tomadus began filling the tub and clicked on the visi-scan. Demosep shaitaanists targeting a governmental building in New Åarhus, trying to sow more terror in the minds of the Juteslam populace.

He smirked and shook his head. Couldn't they see that every bomb blast and every innocent maimed or killed just undermined what little support they had around the world? They showed courage, he would give them that, but they chose the wrong weapons. Why did they prefer bullets and bombs when wisdom and a little eloquence could seize the day? And now bullets and bombs seemed to be the only weapons they had left. Their irrepressible din had drowned out the soft voices of reason in the collective mind of world opinion.

That world opinion could no longer see Demoseps as the oppressed champions of an upstart political movement for democracy and self-determination in a little backward corner of the world. Now the world damned them as political extremists bent on killing innocent Muslims, well, Juteslams anyway, rather than accepting the Great World Peace of '39, who some in the Three Empires thought had been ordained and enshrined fifty years ago by Allah.

The visi-scan report went quiet and a little chime rang out three harmonious notes followed by a gentle male voice: "Sorry to disturb you, sir, but you have a call from the Romanus Imperium. Shall I put it through?" He reached down and turned off the bath. The voice repeated, "Sir?"

"Yes, please." The tri-tone chime repeated. "Hello, this is Tomadus of Roma. How can I help you?"

"Please hold for the First Consul." Tomadus's eyebrows rose and his mouth opened slightly. As he waited, he looked up at the visi-scan, which played without sound. Although the clips still covered devastation in the Tonquizalixco

Tetepe region, they had switched to a burning meetinghouse in a Demosep-controlled Tetepian village that had probably been shelled in reprisal by the New Jutland army.

Damn Juteslams, Tomadus thought. They were worse than the Demoseps. They enjoyed the military backing of the Three Empires, so they could afford to be magnanimous and search for a real, lasting peace. Instead, they used their military superiority to put their rather large boot on the Tetepians' necks every chance they got.

"*Civis* Tomadus, this is First Consul Khansensius. Let me congratulate you on your impressive presentation yesterday."

"*Gratias*, Your Eminence. I did not expect that level of interest from the Imperium."

"We believe that your invention has great potential in many applications. I would like to see you right away at my office in the Antiquus Sector. Could you be here in an hour? We may have a proposition for you. I will provide details at the meeting."

"Yes, Your Eminence, but—"

"Good. Can you bring the device with you?"

Tomadus looked down and scratched his head. "I, uh, I'm sorry, but it was shipped to my company's other office in Barcelona yesterday afternoon."

"Ah, that is a pity. Well, come here anyway. We have much to discuss."

"*Gratias*, Your Eminence. I will be there in an hour as you request."

Strange, thought Tomadus, *I don't remember representatives of the First Consul at the presentation.* He shrugged as he entered the bath. The visi-scan sound returned just as the screen switched to an image of the long conference hall from yesterday's Lumenology Conference. Showing uniformed security personnel leading a group of preachers out of the building, the visi-scan reported, "Members of the Way were escorted away from the conference to retain the strict sect neutrality demanded by the Florentia Protocol. The incident remained peaceful, but Way members were reminded dire consequences awaited anyone who proselytized their religious beliefs in the neutral Romanus Protectorate in violation of the protocol."

CHAPTER 17

"But, First Consul, computational applications will serve the greatest need." Tomadus pressed his chest further over the edge of the First Consul's antique walnut desk, its sides intricately carved with Mongolian warriors on horseback. "Look," he continued, "with extreme light focusing and amplification, I have made the dream of photon computers a reality. We could reach efficiencies that will allow light computing to revolutionize our world and economy. Don't you see it?"

First Consul Khansensius sat back in his leather chair, the ridge of his hooked nose clearly towering over the deep valleys of piercing brown eyes that now bore into Tomadus. The image might have caused Tomadus to bolt from his seat if not for the First Consul's gentle smile that somehow said everything would be all right. "Of course I do, *Civis* Tomadus. But that goal is one best left to you and your company. However, we are very impressed with the light amplification and focusing aspects of your invention."

"That drives the computational device, but they are merely tools. The photon computer is the thing."

"For you and your company Tomadus. We have other…uses in mind." The First Consul looked down and nonchalantly slit an envelope open with an ornate, three-jeweled letter opener.

Tomadus's stomach hardened. He closed his eyes for a moment and took a deep breath. *A diversion might help.* "That's a very handsome letter opener. Is it an heirloom?"

The First Consul beamed with pride and began telling him about how it was a gift from all three emperors and each jewel represented one of the Three Empires. Tomadus took the opportunity to survey his surroundings and consider his next tack.

No crowns or scepters adorned the room or the person of the First Consul; nonetheless, symbols of his power were palpable throughout. On the First Consul's desk stood two pictures, nearly identical. Each depicted one of the two principal Muslim emperors facing him as he bowed slightly in their direction with the grand Colosseum as a backdrop. A portrait on the wall behind his desk demonstrated his friendship with the third of the three emperors, Emperor Pepin XI. A map of Europe, northern Africa and eastern Asia on the far wall told the story of the Triumvirate partition of the Muslim world and the great influence of Roma and its First Consul in maintaining the peace among the empires. Of course, the golden gavel on his desk reminded visitors that it was he who led all meetings of the Triumvirate and mediated their disputes. The First Consul had no vote or right to make any decisions on their behalf, but his persuasiveness and consequent power were well known.

"Of course, it doesn't get much use—only for the correspondence I cannot trust to my staff—nevertheless, I travel with the opener because it subtly reminds others of my ties with the Three Emperors. Now, what do you plan for the invention?"

Tomadus snapped to attention with a smile and a nod. "I wish to market it throughout the world. It will take time, but it could benefit nearly every sector, from communications to manufacturing, from agriculture to technological research. Its bounds are endless. Can you see it? Its potential to facilitate networking is almost limitless.

"Networking? Of what? I have many networks now."

"Computing networks. The device should help us link them and thereby enhance our productivity."

"A laudable plan." He paused, again taking up the letter opener. "However, it will take a great deal of capital to accomplish it."

"Yes. My company could use some help. We are small and have few resources. With the assistance of your office and the Triumvirate, we could quickly expand around the globe and into every form of commerce, administration and entertainment."

"The globe?" The First Consul leaned in and lowered his voice. "Certainly you are not interested in helping the Triumvirate's enemies?"

"I...I...no, First Consul, I do not wish to help our enemies. But don't you think by enhancing the world's productivity, we will ultimately benefit the Three Empires?"

"Ah, but what if this falls into the wrong hands, Tomadus. Could it be weaponized?"

Tomadus sat back and sighed. "Weaponized?"

"Surely, you see the possibilities with your light focusing and amplification. We must protect it from...misuse."

"My staff will take measures to prevent that from happening. We are only at the prototype stage."

"That is good, Tomadus. However, the Three Empires would like to provide resources to both ensure those security measures are adequate and further develop your light amplification and focusing aspects—for purely governmental purposes."

"Are you planning to weaponize it? I am sorry, First Consul, but I do not wish to see my invention used for further bloodshed."

"No, no, I understand. We would not dream of such a thing. But we would like to explore its uses in defense of all the good the Triumvirate continues to bring to the world. You cannot be opposed to that, can you *Civis* Tomadus?"

Tomadus wriggled in his seat. *Careful. Read between the lines.* Any one of the Three Empires or the First Counsel could simply steal the device and dispose of him quietly. No, he knew he must feint working with them and find a way to turn this thing around. "No, First Consul, but the invention is quite complex. I imagine you would want my company's assistance in exploring these, uh, opportunities?"

"Of course. We will need your cooperation to help our people understand the device better. We will also provide you with some needed capital to address your own plans."

The creature began clawing at Tomadus's belly. He paused, breathing deeply to hold it down. "I suppose we can work something out. Here is my card, Your Eminence. Please have your assistant contact Stephanus at my office. He will arrange for some follow-up meetings with your technologists. Am I to assume that my company shall hold the rights to any inventions, subject to the government's customary unfettered rights of use?"

"Yes, yes, of course, as long as we can count on your cooperation."

"Then, I thank you for your proposal." Tomadus stood and bowed deeply to the First Consul. "May we each prosper through the great good we accomplish."

Tomadus exited the government building and glanced at the Colosseum that had been looming over the area for over 24 centuries—since over 500 years before the Hijra. He turned back toward the city center, walking briskly and searching for a communication pod. He reached one at the next corner near an auto news kiosk, slipped a coin in the slot of the pod, touched a few buttons and spoke into the fixed mouthpiece at the top of the pod. "Stephanus, this is Tomadus."

A younger man's voice trumpeted out of the top of the pod, "*Salve*, sir. I heard you pretty much lit up the Lumenology Conference yesterday. *Gratulor tibi!*"

"*Gratias.* It was nothing. The work was already done."

"You are getting attention beyond the tech crowd—even the visi-scan had a report."

"Maybe too much attention. Look, you are going to get a call from the Imperium's technologists. Be friendly, responsive, and sound very interested, but do not give them anything unless you have to. And do not give them any schematics or any confidential technical information under any circumstances without my consent. We need to slow play this thing for now. Got it?"

"Yes, sir. Are they going to help us with some of the development costs?

"I don't know about the costs yet. We'll have plenty of investors if we need them." Reaching his hand toward the pod disconnect button, he stopped and looked at the cover of *Tempus* Magazine in a nearby kiosk. "Hold on a second."

On one side of a split picture, the gritty and grimy face of a teenage boy stared up at him. The boy was handsome—his chiseled face simultaneously a picture of innocence and defiance. A lone tear ran down his right cheek. The boy had wrapped his arms around a young girl whose face was covered with intermingled blood, tears and grime. With her mouth open wide beneath horror-stricken eyes, Tomadus could almost hear her screams echoing out of the page. Behind her, in the background, stood a small, shelled-out house still smoldering. Near the house on the scorched lawn lay a silver, mangled Star of David. The second picture showed a synagogue burning, with old women dressed in black robes to the side crying and tearing their garments. Large block letters masked the top of both pictures, reading: "THE TEARS OF A HOPELESS REBELLION: THEN AND NOW."

The first picture had appeared over ten years ago when the Demoseps were making another appeal for help from the world. It had been banned in the Three Empires, yet managed to appear in the Romanus press for a brief few days, winning the Margaash Award for photojournalism. The censors had now allowed it to reappear, though perhaps the new spin made that possible.

Tomadus felt the creature prancing again. He rubbed the soft spot on his belly and grimaced. *That infernal thing again.* He had always felt sympathy for the innocents among the Tetepians, but now it seemed the creature was arguing that sympathy alone was useless. He knew that despair would attack him again if he tried to ignore the creature. He cocked his head and stopped massaging his belly as he looked back at the pod. Maybe he could help somehow. "How soon is my trip to North Aztalan?"

"Two weeks, sir."

"See if you can work in a side trip for a few days to Tetepe, particularly New Jutland.

"New Jutland, sir? Wouldn't that be a bit risky?"

"Perhaps. But maybe I'll find an ulcer remedy there." Tomadus clicked the button on the top of the pod and purchased a copy of the magazine. There, he already felt a little better. He folded the magazine under his arm and walked away.

CHAPTER 18

YOHANAN LAY IN the tall, moonlit grass on a hill beside the Susquehanna River. A pair of binoculars hung around his neck. Next to him lay a young woman wearing a tight black jumpsuit that revealed her athletic curves even in the darkness. A black stocking hat covered her blond hair. Both of them had darkened their faces and hands with charcoal. The two stared at the rail bridge below, listening intently for a distant rumble.

Yohanan turned his head toward the woman and smiled. Decima almost looked deadly in black although he wasn't sure if it was deadly to men in the carnal or carnivorous sense. Her blond hair, no matter how artificial in color, perfectly framed the work of art between her slender neck and long forehead. Her nose, tiny for a Romanus, complemented her slender lips. Her brown eyes contrasted with the blond hair, creating an exotic, alluring picture. He had known her for a long time, but more like a kid sister. Now that she had grown so beautiful, it was hard to hold back from less brotherly feelings.

She caught him staring at her. "What?" Decima asked.

"This is your first action, isn't it?" he asked.

"So?"

"You seem so serious, so deadly serious."

She turned her head slowly toward him. "You find something funny about a little death and destruction?"

"Look, I despise this more than any Demosep, but what is our choice? They don't discriminate between the innocent and the guilty. They show no mercy. If they don't give a damn, why should I?"

"Remember that little thing in your Torah called the Ten Commandments?" She raised her eyebrows. "I think one of them says killing is a bad thing."

"Yeah, I think I've heard of that, but we all know it refers to murder, not a justified battle against His enemies. I prefer to take my anthem from Jeremiah:

> Therefore the days are coming
> when I will sound the battle alarm
> against New Jutland of the Juteslams;
> It shall become a mound of ruins,
> and its villages destroyed by fire.
> Demoseps shall then inherit those who disinherited it.

"There seem to be a few modern references in there."

Yohanan looked back at the bridge and the mountains beyond. "Well, I find it a bit more satisfying to substitute the real combatants for the ones named in Jeremiah. I could just as easily keep the Amonites and Israel in the anthem. You know they're metaphors for our current battle."

"You call this action a battle?"

"Sure. They want to kill us. We kill them instead. What's it matter that they don't see it coming?"

"Aren't you concerned that innocent people will die down there?" she asked.

Yohanan snorted. "I doubt it. Many are soldiers of New Jutland. Anyway, they are all secondary to our main purpose here—to destroy the train and stop the shipment of weapons. We can't let the Juteslams think they can transport the instruments of our destruction through our lands without consequences."

"I agree. That's why I'm here. But I don't find it funny."

The stick in his gut poked him hard. "Nor do I, trust me. It makes me sick, actually." *No, too much. Can't seem weak.* He managed a sarcastic tone. "Hey, I'll probably even vomit a few times before I return home." *She'll never believe the truth of that.*

Decima shook her head and curled her lip, looking away.

He paused, turned his head toward her again and smiled wryly. "But I do find you funny."

"Why is that?"

"You're the daughter of Quintillus, a prominent Romanus merchant, beholden like other Romani to both the Three Empires and their local lackeys, the Juteslams. Absent clear and convincing evidence, the Jutes wouldn't dare touch you or your immense wealth, let alone oppress you as they have the Tetepians. Yet here you are, ready to destroy your empires' allies. Don't you find that funny?"

Decima turned her head slowly back toward the train tracks. "Romani are neutral. We are not one of the Three Empires."

"No, Roma is not neutral. It pimps for the Three Empires and their allies. Quintillus taught you that much. I know he understands that Roma is but a tool of the Three Empires, carefully crafted to keep the peaceful image of the empires free from our spilt blood."

"Keep my father out of this. You sound like one of those Anarchist nuts. If Quintillus heard you, he would give you a tongue lashing himself. Has he taught you nothing?"

Yohanan stiffened, his eyes narrowing.

She stared back at him. "Sorry. You've said you love him. How can you hate his country?"

Yohanan bit his lip hard. "I hate the Jutes. Roma and the Empires arm them. So how can I not hate Roma?"

Decima shook her head slowly. "You're wrong. Roma is just trying to keep the balance, what with the Aztecs and all, but the damn Juteslams want more. Roma may not be able to support you because of its position in the world, but plenty of us Romani still do."

Yohanan snorted. "And why do you fight?"

"I believe in the promise of democracy and the plight of the Tetepians."

"So do many who sit and watch from afar, as you could have. You could be in Roma right now toasting the First Consul's latest champion in the Colosseum. Instead, you live in squalor by the Susquehanna River. It's more personal for you, isn't it?"

"Let's just say Quintillus never wanted his only daughter destined to a lifetime of subservience to men. He raised me no differently than he would his only son, who you know he never had—except maybe for you."

Yohanan smiled softly. "Thanks."

"Yeah, well now that I am of age, I do not, like many Romanus women, long for the harem of a rich man in Roma or the Three Empires."

Yohanan shook his head with a smirk. "Can't see you doing that."

"No, fortunately my father did not seek such a match for me. You know he raised me to be independent, but where in the world could I truly do that except here? I want to be part of the answer, not getting fat and lazy in the inner courtyards of some old estate where Sharia law would protect—and restrain—me."

Yohanan laughed. "And so you kill to show the world it cannot restrain you?"

"I've never killed anyone."

"And yet, here you are." When Decima closed her eyes, he added, "At least I kill for the right reasons. The Juteslams deserve it."

Decima shook her head again. "You still act like the boy on the cover. You should grow up."

He grimaced. "We need to listen for the train." But he couldn't listen over the drumbeat of his own thoughts. *That damn cover.* He relived the old horror every time someone shoved it back into his face. His heart beat out of his chest and his body stiffened, the hatred looking for an outlet. They had found neither of his parents' corpses; instead, only a couple of limbs remained intermingled with the charcoaled debris. His night terrors were filled with the sound of the shell just before it hit, whistling through the space above their village. He had heard the siren and was running for the shelter with his sister Jochi in tow. When the blast knocked them over, he had rolled his sister under him to protect her from the burning debris raining down on his legs and arms.

What had his parents done to deserve the barrage? Nothing. Had they not avoided the Demosep shaitaanists and tried to live normal lives in Tetepe? But that was impossible in this constant war zone. People just died.

Senselessly, without reason. At the hands of your enemies, death reeked with the same odor of despair no matter why it came.

His mind kept racing. The Tetepian politicos had found him quickly and begun using his newly famous face to further their ends. He had become one of the voices of the movement before he had turned twenty. Eventually, his unwavering hatred had led him to volunteer with the militant arm of the Demoseps. A voice of the Tetepian people by day, he had become an instrument of Juteslam destruction by night, though the regret chewed slowly away at any sense of triumph. Before each operation, he flooded over these fits of regret by opening a well-worn valve to a cesspool of despair that ten years had not managed to drain from deep within his troubled soul. The ritual had always pushed him through, but afterwards he knew another piece of his humanity had ebbed back into the sludge. But what of her?

When a vibration from his chest stirred him, he grabbed the binoculars and stared down the tracks. "Are you ready?"

"I don't know. I...I don't think I can do it," she said. "You push it."

"No. It is your task. Now push it when I tell you."

Decima closed her eyes. The train began rumbling across the bridge. "Now."

She held her breath, closed the contact, and a small section of the bridge exploded, creating a ten-foot gap in the tracks—a gap through which the train quickly catapulted into the void below.

CHAPTER 19

TOMADUS STROLLED DOWN a winding street in central New Åarhus, the capital of New Jutland, with a tall, genteel man dressed in elaborate merchant's robes. The man's strong chin, square face and gentle eyes matched his smooth and graceful manner.

"So, are you interested?" Tomadus asked Quintillus.

"I am more than impressed with the demonstration of your device, *Civis* Tomadus. "It may bring many opportunities."

"So you see it, then?"

Quintillus nodded once. "But you must realize that it is of no use to us here in the hinterlands of Tetepe," Quintillus said. "Even in New Åarhus, most of my customers cannot afford anything but the most primitive technology. Visi-scan screens in the home are rare here. So I fear it will be many years before they can even dream of products employing your light computers. I am happy for the company of a fellow Romanus, but I am afraid you waste your breath. I wonder why you have even bothered to come this far."

Tomadus paused. If the purported reasons for his expedition to this backwater were that dubious to this transplanted Romanus merchant, would they be so to the authorities? He forced a smile back at Quintillus. "*Gratias, amicus meus.* But do not sell yourself or your market short. There are many businesses in New Jutland preparing to expand, to exploit this area's many resources. Think how they could grow with the use of some of my computational devices. We have only begun."

"Perhaps, but New Jutland is still surrounded by Tonquizalixco Tetepe. You must understand the situation. Who would risk a significant investment in technology here?"

"Let us not argue this point. I come here only to convince you to dream about the future. Dreams inspire our waking desires and those desires lead to big opportunities—for you and your customers. Sell these dreams to your customers, and, with a little help from my company, those opportunities could make you rich one day."

"I suppose it doesn't hurt to dream as long as I can keep one eye on my purse."

Tomadus laughed. "You can lock your purse and its contents away from me for now, *Civis* Quintillus. But you must dream."

"Dream?"

"Yes, and when you can see the future, be kind to yourself and contact my office. If we have not yet signed with an associate in this region, I am sure we could come to a satisfactory distribution arrangement with a Romanus merchant of your caliber. Until then, dream." Tomadus nodded with a slight bow and moved his right hand to his heart.

Quintillus repeated the gesture but then shuffled closer to Tomadus. "Tell me," Quintillus whispered, "Have others signed on?"

There was the opening. "Of course. My trip through this continent has succeeded. Our distribution network has already grown exponentially."

"Who shall I call if I am interested?" After receiving Tomadus's card, Quintillus nodded. "*Gratias.* Is there anything else I can do for you during your stay? Anything at all?"

Ah, the real opportunity he sought in this backwater wilderness. Sure Tetepe could eventually be a stable market, but returns would not pay his expenses here for many years. "Well, I understand you may have an *amicus* or two among the Demoseps?"

Civis Quintillus stopped walking and searched his fellow merchant's eyes. "Why would you think so?"

"You are rich and well-connected. I am building a network, and part of that network includes developing information that might be useful to me or to others. I am aware that you know many people throughout this area."

"I see. Why would you be interested in contacting them?"

Tomadus smiled. "You know the boy on the cover of *Tempus*? I heard you helped him years ago."

Quintillus's eyes narrowed. "What do you know about that?"

"He and his sister were orphaned. They needed help."

"It was a humanitarian gesture."

Tomadus smiled. "A beautiful thing. Maybe I can…continue your work. Can I meet him?"

Quintillus cocked his head for a minute. "I may have a contact or two I could reach with some trouble. Do you have a *stated* purpose for such a thing?"

Tomadus gave Quintillus an easy nod but held back the wink. "Purpose? Ah, yes, research, of course. I need to understand our markets better. Quite understandably, Tetepe seems to lack any real stability, particularly recently. I would like to see if I might better understand the course it will take in the coming years in light of—"

"The rebellion?"

"If that is your term."

Quintillus straightened. "It is the monarchy's."

"I am aware of that. That is the name we hear in Roma as well. What would you call it?"

Quintillus squinted into the sunlight at Tomadus. "I'm afraid I would have no other word at the moment."

"I see. You are rightly careful, *amicus meus*. What do the Demoseps call it?"

"Some call it a revolution, others a holy war. But most think it neither. They consider it nothing but a war to repel invaders, albeit from an invasion fifty years old. They are quite adamant that they have the right to defend themselves, even now, and by any means available."

"Do you agree?" Tomadus asked.

Quintillus grinned. "How could a Romanus merchant agree with shaitaanists who employ destruction and terror to secure their goals? And besides, they will soon vote on the peace accord. It may all be over soon."

Tomadus studied the merchant's eyes. Was that a little fear he detected or just concern? Should he read between the lines? "No matter. I simply wish to have some conversations for my own edification…and perhaps for some humanitarian purposes. Is that possible?"

"You would need to travel to Shenandoah by train. You will learn nothing from them other than their public rhetoric, which is never broadcast in New Jutland. But do not expect more on your own, they do not open up to strangers without a proper introduction."

"I could use a little assistance in that regard," Tomadus said.

"Perhaps I could find a suitable escort to facilitate the meeting."

Tomadus beamed back at Quintillus and nodded. "Excellent."

"It may take a few days. The escort I have in mind has not yet returned to the city. In the meantime, I insist that you stay with me. If we are to be partners in this…this venture, it is best we get to know one another better."

"Delightful. I think we shall be very good friends, indeed. *Gratias, amicus meus*."

CHAPTER 20

"You have all heard our kind emissary speak so eloquently of this wonderful proposal for peace. It is a peace, he says, offered generously by the mighty and benevolent King Skjöldr and brokered by the Romani, of course with the approval of the Three Empires. Our emissary is an honorable, elected representative of our district and a stately man of much eloquence, and I am sure we all thank him for his considered views."

A smattering of applause issued from the crowd of nearly a thousand in the Shenandoah town square. Tomadus noticed the grim faces of a few among the clapping throng, then returned his attention to the speaker at the center of the square, a handsome young man resembling the boy on the cover of Tempus; however, the years had matured his stature and washed away that lonely look of desperate longing from his eyes.

Tomadus looked to his right and saw his recent "escort," Decima, with her eyes focused on Yohanan. Her lovely name somehow befitted this daughter of Quintillus. Nobody would have guessed by a cursory look at her that she was a Romanus citizen. Her bright blond hair certainly lacked the traditional Romanus characteristics, but its dark roots and her dark eyes betrayed her heritage and told the astute observer she was simply employing the latest Romanus fashion.

"Our emissary confirms that this treaty will allow us all to live free and productive lives in our 'proper' environs," Yohanan continued. "Yes, the Sunnis, the Shiites and the Mahdians will return to the coastal cities, where they can live at peace with the Juteslams, provided, of course, that they restrict their worship only to their own homes and mosques. The Nahuatl must go southwest, to southern Tonquizalixco Tetepe, where they will receive economic assistance from the Aztec Empire, which has so graciously agreed to help in this matter. The Iroquois and Algonquin are to retreat to a part of their former lands in the northern Tetepe, but they will be provided assistance from the Juteslam Native Population Program. And the Jews, well, we are to be singled out and given this vast domain on the lee side of these mountains. It is such a rich land, full of pines and cliffs and little arable acreage, measuring less than one-tenth the size of the remaining New Jutland. I am sure we would have no problem flourishing here despite our population already doubling that of the Juteslams. The accord will permit us to pray as we wish and be left in peace. We are all so lucky to be granted our own little piece of Tetepian paradise." Yohanan's cynical tone caused a stir in the crowd.

Yohanan raised his hands and pushed gently out to the crowd and downward. The crowd fell silent. "I ask you this? Why? Why these divisions? Why would good King Skjöldr and his puppet masters want us to live apart now after nearly two hundred years of peaceful coexistence? Before the Jutes invaded this land, we were one people. For over two centuries we did not suffer the destructive wars of race and religion that befell our European overlords. Our peoples learned to accept their cultural differences and founded a new way grounded in cooperation, joint responsibility and the protection of all, including the weak. We call this democracy because we elect our own leaders, but we know it is much more than that. It is our right. It is our duty. It is our freedom."

The crowd began to cheer, but after a few seconds Yohanan raised his hands again to quiet them. "Now, Skjöldr and the Three Empires want to take this away from us. The emperors and their local lackeys all want the same thing. They want to divide us, to weaken us. But this is nothing new. They seek to move us toward waging war with our brothers instead of waging war with our overlords."

"Bastards!" a man in the crowd screamed. Another followed with, "Damn right!"

Yohanan raised the pitch of his voice, whipping up the crowd even more. "But why? Do they not seek peace? Do they not seek stability for Tetepe? Is that not what they have been preaching for fifty long years? Surely empires of such lasting power and tyrants borne of their dominion would not speak for one purpose and wish another?

"I do not need to tell you what they truly intend. We all know it deep in our hearts. We have suffered through their so-called good intentions for over fifty years. Many of our founding fathers came to this land centuries ago to flee the so-called benevolent intentions of their European and Asian masters. They want to bind us again to their lordship, steal our freedom, require us to submit to their imperial rule. Of course, they want all of this only for our own good, for our own protection.

"Well, again I ask you from whom are they protecting us? From the Aztec Empire? The Aztecs have long abandoned any attempts to influence Tetepe directly. From Nepantla or Chigantlo to our west? They are farmers, content to plow their fields, tend their crops and supply the world with food. Have you seen any indication that they wish to cross the Tonalixcotetepe? I have not. From whom do we need protection, then?

"Who then remains the real threat? The Juteslams, led by good King Skjöldr! For fifty years, the Juteslams have raided and destroyed our homes, driven us from our own cities, maimed and killed our brothers and sisters, our children and parents, our colleagues and friends. Now they offer peace? Protection? How can our enemies possibly become our protectors? I for one neither need nor want this kind of protection." Yohanan paused and held up his hands to the crowd and gestured all around. "Do you?"

"No," the crowd yelled together in harmony.

"This proposal is not about peace or protection but about slavery. It is a capitulation to that black-eyed demon Skjöldr and his imperial masters. It is no armistice; it is surrender to monarchy. If we are divided, we have already failed. Yet this peace accord promises little more than our division and leaves us to fight like dogs for the scraps left over from Skjöldr's table of plenty. Are you Skjöldr's dogs?"

"No!"

"Then let us not agree to submit our necks to his collars, to his leashes! I care not for a peace that puts us in chains at Skjöldr's feet. I care not for a piece of pitiful land that pits me against my brother for Skjöldr's entertainment. And I care not for a slice of life that requires me to prostrate myself before this pathetic despot and beg for his benevolence. Peace without freedom is slavery. And I for one refuse to give this despot my neck to be locked with his chains! And so for me, give me liberty or give me death!"

The crowd roared and began chanting repeatedly, "Liberty or death! Liberty or death! Liberty or death!"

Tomadus watched Yohanan step off the center stage of the square and shake hands among the crowd. When Tomadus met up with Decima, he said, "Quite a display."

"Yohanan has a way with the people."

"Can we meet him now?"

"Follow me."

They made their way through the crowd to a small tavern off the square, where Yohanan was surrounded by a small group just in front of the door.

Yohanan moved forward to meet them. "And here you are again, my little apprentice. Did you enjoy my little talk?"

"As always, Sir Agitator."

Yohanan glanced at Tomadus. "A new friend?"

"I'm sorry. This is a friend of my father's, Tomadus of Roma. He seems very fond of you and your movement. My father asked me to introduce you two. Tomadus, this is Yohanan, whom I fear we must now call First Citizen."

"First only to the gallows, I'm afraid. It is always nice to meet a friend of Quintillus. Welcome, Tomadus."

Rather then exchanging bows, the two shook hands, and Tomadus's world unraveled. The white light had seared through his brain again; however, this time the vision unwound with much more than a quick vignette. Another world swirled rapidly through his consciousness and threatened to split him in two. He could not breathe. He felt he was no longer in this space, this time, this reality. He nearly fainted but caught himself on his knee and released Yohanan's hand.

"Are you well, sir?" Yohanan asked. He shot a glance at Decima.

Ten or twenty seconds later, Tomadus reopened his eyes and stood up. His heart was trying to pound out a new opening in his chest. He tried to forget the memories and control the feelings of despair pulsing through him. He took a few deep breaths while the two ushered him into the tavern to a waiting wooden bench beside an open oak table. *Why do you torment me just as I am trying to do something good? Isn't this attempt the answer?* After a few more deep breaths, he was able to say, "I, I am sorry about this, my friends. I will be fine. Please, just give me a few more moments."

"What you need is a drink." Yohanan signaled a waiter and three glasses of beer arrived.

Tomadus took a long draught. Now smiling again, though a little glassy-eyed, he addressed them both: "Forgive my weakness. I must seek a physic-tech when I return to Roma."

"I'm sure it is nothing serious," Decima offered.

"You are probably right." He turned to Yohanan. "Sir, that was a magnificent and rousing speech. I have heard reports of your eloquence. Still, I had not imagined anything quite like that."

"I simply speak from the heart. The words just seem to come as I need them."

"Then you are truly gifted, for the First Consul's best speechwriters could not have equaled it."

"Well, I am sure they could, if they were allowed to convey the truth."

"That certainly may be the case on occasion, but it is a consequence of public administration, is it not?" said Tomadus. "I noticed you glossed over the civil war among your own peoples on this soil a few hundred years ago almost like it had not happened."

"Ancient history. The important point was that all of our cultures ultimately came together to form one democratic republic that has endured for two centuries and must continue despite the onslaught of the Juteslams and their foreign masters." Yohanan took a long draught from his beer and sighed. "Tell me, Tomadus, what brings a Romanus merchant to our little town in the wilderness?"

"Just this." Tomadus reached in his backpack and pulled out the *Tempus Magazine* he had recently purchased. "You recognize the picture, of course?"

"It is the picture that keeps me alive. Without this, Skjöldr would have put me to death years ago on suspicion of shaitaanism. But they have no proof, only a vague suspicion. And without proof, they cannot afford to make a new martyr of the famous son of a martyr. And so I can speak with impunity to my neighbors, but only where my voice cannot be heard by the outside world. They will not allow me that far."

"You are banned from the visi-scan?"

Yohanan frowned and nodded.

"Have you seen the article before?" Tomadus asked.

"No, only the first picture from ten years ago. The second is new, though unsurprising. The slant of the article…well, it was not what I would have hoped."

"Yes, the rest of the world began to back you after the massacre ten years ago. But that has changed. *Tempus* is just reflecting world opinion, which now views your cause as hopeless and your tactics as barbarian. Hence, your fight for freedom is now merely a barbaric rebellion gone bad."

Yohanan gritted his teeth. "You came thousands of *milia passuum* across the Atlantic to condemn me and my people?"

"No, my friend. I am sorry if I have offended you. I spoke only of world opinion, not my own. I do not wish to condemn you. I wish only to help you."

"Help? How? Do you have an army hiding in your robes?" Yohanan asked.

"Violence will never solve your problems."

Yohanan snorted. "What are you, a diplomat from the First Consul, lobbying for the peace accord? You do not feel our despair."

"I know despair plenty, though not your own. But that is of no matter. Please understand, I agree with much of your speech. The Tetepians should not sign the accord."

"Then we must wage war," said Yohanan.

Tomadus spread his hands, palms up. "What war? You speak of war, yet you have no armies. You are a pathetic little insurrection against the might of the Three Empires, who you correctly point out are behind Skjöldr. War means death, to you and to your ideals. You must not wage war. You must wage peace."

Yohanan stiffened. "You speak in circles. How can we wage peace but not sign the peace accord."

"Peace is a state of mind, not a piece of paper. Sign no accord, continue to live throughout as much of Tonquizalixco Tetepe as you would like. But live together. Continue your democracy together. And give the Jutes no justification for further destruction because of your Demosep shaitaanism. World opinion will turn back in your favor. With some luck, I may be able to help you get your message out and convince the world of the injustice being done here. Eventually, a real and lasting peace could be possible."

Yohanan looked at Decima and then stared hard into Tomadus's eyes. "You are a dreamer. We will be slaves. They banish us from the coasts to these hinterlands. They ignore our elected representatives. They respect nothing of our democracy. The peace of which you speak is not possible."

"Have not the Demoseps already been fighting the Juteslams for 50 years? What has it gained you except more death and despair?"

Yohanan looked down at his beer but said nothing.

"So why do you believe more of your desperate tactics will change the outcome? Can you not see that this constant militant insurgency failed years ago? Fight not with your bullets but with your words. Fight not with your bombs but with your hearts. With my help, the world will notice and come to your aid."

"What, lay down our weapons and open our throats to our enemies? Are you insane?"

"If they attack you, then defend yourselves. But stop terrorizing the Juteslam people. End your shaitaanist ways. You must accept reality for what it is. Despite your greatest hopes, the Juteslams will not simply dissolve into the ocean. They are here to stay. Accept that they are part of the answer, rather than simply your mortal enemy, and find a real and lasting solution."

"Peace with invaders?" Yohanan asked.

Tomadus raised his eyebrows. "I would hardly call them invaders. They came to Tetepe nearly seven centuries before your people came to this land."

"But they abandoned it for nearly three centuries before my people arrived. I don't think they really have any claim to this land other than nostalgia."

"Nostalgia? Do you think they all wanted to be forcibly marched west by the Aztec Empire? Do you think they look back with longing at their cities being utterly destroyed and their culture stripped bare?"

"They were nothing but raiders," Yohanan said, "Vikings with a little religion. They killed and maimed for glory, honor and loot and called it a Jihad. You cannot blame the Aztecs."

Tomadus leaned in. "Do not belittle this culture because it is not your own. They are a proud people with proud traditions. They took on an empire that was far stronger than they knew. They were too proud to quit. Their Nordic traditions viewed that as surrender. They refused to quit even when they were moved to a strange land and were subjected to second-class status over the centuries, treated almost as slaves by the Latisilolals."

"And now they treat us as slaves," Yohanan said acerbically.

"This is all in the past, and I do not wish to take their side here. I merely ask that you and your people try to see the world from their eyes. It can be enlightening."

"Their mortars light us up plenty. You can call them by another name if you wish, but we shall always know them as invaders."

Tomadus drew back. "For now, let us agree to disagree on this point, my friend. Regardless of whether they have any rights, they have certainly overstepped those bounds with the help of a few interested governments. Though I believe it can ultimately be set right, you must understand there is no solution where the Juteslams simply disappear, even at your able hands."

Yohanan smiled. "How about they move back west?"

"You know that will not happen. Move on. Keep your democracy. Defend yourselves, but do not attack the innocents. Eventually, the tide will turn."

Yohanan replied slowly, "We have fought them for fifty years."

Tomadus emphatically shook his head. "They have beaten you down for fifty years. There has been no real fight for forty-eight of those years. There must be another way. We must find that."

"Well, when you find the magic answer, I'll still be here, trying to survive with the rest of my people. If you can help, I welcome it, but I hope you do not expect us to obey you."

Tomadus grinned. "Obey? I had thought that word was not even in your lexicon. But I must rest now. Thank you for taking the time to speak with me. Let us continue this discussion another time. I hope you find a solution that brings a lasting peace." Tomadus stood up, bowed slightly and left the tavern.

∇   ∇   ∇

Yohanan thumbed his beer glass for a moment, then looked up and spoke softly to Decima, "What do you think of him?"

"Well, he is no spy," she said. "My father would know that. Quintillus told me he came to trust Tomadus after he spent a week at his home in New Åarhus."

"I trust your father's read. He is careful."

"Yes. Tomadus believes what he preaches, but the man has no experience here. He cannot truly understand our predicament. He thinks like many Romani. His simple solutions are cowardly and worthless to us. But according to my father, he already has money and some powerful ties to the Romanus government. He may prove useful to our cause at some point."

Yohanan looked up, rubbed his hands slowly over his face and sighed. "In the end, I wonder if he's right."

"About what?" Decima slammed her hand on the table. "Have you forgotten your own words from a few minutes ago?"

"My words are necessary for our people to remain strong, but I have always wondered if there is another way. I already have so much blood on my hands that they reek of death and decay. Can they ever be clean? Can we ever truly live again?"

"Only if we fight for what we believe in, Yohanan. Only then."

∇   ∇   ∇

Tomadus finished splashing water on his face as his searching eyes stared back at him from the mirror. *Who am I? Was Yohanan right? Am I insane? What is real and what is imaginary?*

Surely, he was a now-famous Romanus technologist and merchant who stood in front of a cracked sink in a bathroom in the Shenandoah Inn deep in the Tetepian backwater. *That is real, is it not?* Just as surely, for those few moments when the light had flashed, he was no technologist—he was not even a Romanus. He had found himself in a dream world where rows upon rows of buildings reached to the sky, towering over millions of people scurrying through and between them like rats in a giant maze. This image had dissolved and reformed into a white marble dome rising above a circle of Corinthian columns. The building was set on a hill above a grass plaza that extended for many *stadia*, guarded on either side by various official-looking buildings. Dwarfing even the Forum Romanum, the plaza seemed to reach toward an enormous stone phallic structure rising in the distance.

Again the image had dissolved, this time reforming into another reality, but a reality no longer vague and indistinct like a dream. He had been in an enormous basement or cave with an altar before him. He was searching for answers to perplexing words—words that he believed could help him uncover something evil. But the words had drenched him in black emotion and sent his mind scrambling through his past, through the heartache of love lost, through the superficial solace of blame, through the consequential abandonment and even greater heartache of another dear to him—his mother, lost. Not lost, forsaken. She was forsaken. Somehow Tomadus knew this as if he had been in the cave himself, as if the visions were part of his own past and the emotions still played upon his raw nerves. Somehow, he had become somebody else. He had lived, he had hoped, he had despaired—all in the mind of another man in another place, another world. But it wasn't another man. It was him. Yet it wasn't. *No, during those few moments, it was as real as the water dripping from this sink and the scratches disrupting the patterns of wood on this floor. So which is real and which is the dream?*

He knew he had to return to Roma to discover the cause of these strange visions that had nearly debilitated him. The vision had sprung on him just as he met Yohanan. Perhaps it was connected with the creature somehow. Though his North Aztalan business tour had found such great success, the creature continued to scrape away, reminding him of his one huge failure. Tomadus had been trying to find some way to assuage the creature and help the innocents here, but Yohanan would not, could not, listen to him. How could this embittered man, who had suffered so much, change his ways? It seemed impossible. Still, he respected the young man's passion for his people. He realized he must return again and find a way. The creature finally fell asleep.

CHAPTER 21

"Please do not laugh at me."

Tomadus's old friend Batu slapped him on the back. "I am not laughing at you, *amicus meus,* but at your rather absurd characterization of your dreams."

Tomadus had asked Batu to meet him at Angulus Taberna, their favorite hang out in Roma. "A few drinks—it's been awhile," Tomadus had said. He had failed to mention he would be seeking some insight from the brain technologist regarding his troubling visions. Now, he wondered if he had made a mistake.

"What is so absurd? You're a dream specialist. Do none of your many other patients dream of worlds they have never seen?"

Batu pulled the tobacco pipe out of his mouth and blew a perfect ring of smoke toward Tomadus. "It is exceedingly rare. Stories, yes. They are as fluid and subtle as the mind that dreams them. They consist of small slices of experience and images well known to us. Our minds, freed from the restrictions of conscious reason, reorganize those thoughts into semi-rational stories based on our hopes, our desires and our fears. But, at bottom, they are all based on our own experience. Our dreaming brains cannot truly create new faces, new places or new things. They are taken from our past. You must have seen thousands of images similar to these, and your mind has borrowed them to create a new world order for you. But you have seen nothing truly new. Yet you claim this world is completely foreign to you."

"The visions I see don't coincide with anything in my memory. Have you ever seen buildings so tall that we appear as but ants crawling in their shadows? And what do you make of the blinding light and the bizarre daydreams that seem to extend my night dreams?"

"The flashes of light concern me, but I suspect the dreams come because you have been overworking yourself," Batu said. "Do the flashes occur separately from the dreams?"

"No, they always come just before the vision begins—even when I am sleeping."

"I suspect they are part of the dreams themselves. We can hook you up to a monitor when you sleep just to be sure. Do not worry, Tomadus. It is not uncommon for those with physical and mental exhaustion to essentially fall asleep while apparently functioning. Their brains shut down for everything except movement. They become like sleep walkers and see in the daytime what they would dream during a normal sleep."

Tomadus set down his glass and sat back from the bar, shaking his head. "I have always worked long hours. And parts of these visions are not like dreams. They are real. Yes, they feel as if someone has implanted a visiscan monitor in my eyes and ears, so I can see nothing but these images and hear nothing but these sounds. Yet there is one important difference: I feel like I remember them as if they happened to me. In fact, I seem to instantly recall days at a time even though the light flashes for only a few seconds. Explain that, *amicus meus*."

"Sounds like a vivid hallucination. You haven't been smoking that peyote from Aztalan, have you? You know that is illegal here." Batu laughed, but Tomadus just stared back at him. "I tell you what, Tomadus, let me test you during one of your dreams. Although we cannot tell from our probes what you are dreaming, we can categorize them into several types of brain activity and thought. That will help us understand their nature better. Normally we do this solely for research, but in your case I think we can make an exception. I'll have to charge you a bit to cover costs. What do you say?"

"Is it dangerous?"

Batu shook his head. "The probes are just below the scalp. We don't drill into your skull or anything."

"When can we do it? Tonight?"

"Sometime when we haven't shared a bottle of *arak*. Perhaps tomorrow?"

"I dream the same even after I've had a few drinks," Tomadus said.

"*Amicus meus,* I need sleep and sobriety before digging into your brain. Tomorrow." With that, Batu stood up and walked out of Angulus Taberna in Roma.

Tomadus looked down at his shot glass. *Sleep? No, for then he would surely dream.* Those dreams scared him almost as much as the creature within unsettled him: though he knew both all too well now, he knew not why they came. And both filled him simultaneously with two nearly opposing emotions: curiosity and dread. He had thought the creature would take a vacation when he tried to help Yohanan and the Tetepians, for he had tried to accomplish what he thought was right and that had always seemed to help in the past. But the infernal thing and the constant dreams came back for more. Perhaps insanity was a good word for his condition. He ordered another shot of *arak*.

▽ ▽ ▽

"I guess we'll have to try again tomorrow." Batu, the brain technologist, stood over Tomadus, the lights in the room just flickering on while an assistant was removing the apparatus from his scalp.

"Why? Because you are glowing like the sun?"

"What? No. Wake up, Tomadus."

"I am awake, yet your aura remains." Tomadus sat up and reached toward Batu. "Are you an angel?"

"You are funny. You don't even believe in Allah and now you speak of angels? No, we will need to try tomorrow because your special dream did not come."

"But it did." Tomadus said.

"Not possible," replied Batu, shaking his head. He walked over to his desk and picked up his pipe. "You mind?" Not waiting for Tomadus's response, he struck a match and lit up. "Look, Tomadus, we have learned to distinguish between contemporary-reflective dreams and fantasy-projection dreams. The brain gives off very different signals for each."

"Contemporary-reflective dreams?"

"Yes, a dream where your mind reflects on events of the past few days, weeks or months and flashes through various critical images at hyperspeed. Our brains do that all of the time to select, refresh and reinforce key memories in our bio-chemical neuron structures. More than half of your dreams are like this. Oh, sometimes there are dreams of this sort that vary from your actual experience, but that is just the brain's way of suggesting subconsciously that you consider other alternatives in the future. Not the sort of new world order that you have described."

Tomadus frowned. "I tell you my memory of the dream is clear— and this world I see is not our own, not even close. I dreamed this man was in a huge basilica—like the *Basilica Maxentius*. But this was bigger, different, with a dome like the *Pantheon*, but just at its center. They called the building *Sancti Petri*, or something like that. Most of the men wore clothing that covered each leg separately and tunics that covered only their upper halves. I tell you it was no contemporary-reflective dream. This man—me I think—marveled at a beautiful marble statute of a woman dressed as if from our own world holding a half-clad man in her lap. The man appeared lifeless, yet he looked so familiar."

Batu took a deep pull from his pipe, leaned back and blew the smoke toward the ceiling. "Precisely. He looked familiar to you. You are just recombining different things you have seen recently in a slightly different way—the *Maxentius*, the *Pantheon*, the statue, perhaps of the Emperor's wife, and a man half clothed that you have seen before. It was no fantasy, no other world. No, I think you are just confused because of the procedure. Waking up in the middle of a dream can disorient you. You will be fine in a few minutes, but trust me, you could not have experienced an other-worldly dream. There are limits to our science, of course, but this is not one of them. The divide between these two main dream paradigms and the signals they provide have been established without exception for over a decade. Let us try again tomorrow."

"And what do your studies say about the flashes of light remaining even after I awake from a dream? Something else is happening here. And it is accelerating. If you were not my friend, I wouldn't tell you this, but I sometimes struggle to know what is real and what is fantasy."

Batu chortled. "As long as you can pay me from either world, please feel free to pick the one you like the best."

"And to think your mother said you had no sense of humor."

"Perhaps it would make sense for you to speak to my colleague, Ratan. He is a psyche-technologist who may be able to get to the bottom of this."

Tomadus grimaced but then nodded slowly. "At this point I'll try anything."

∇   ∇   ∇

A week later, Tomadus sat in a comfy chair feeling none too comfortable. He felt the dull pain coursing through every neuron of his brain, each cell trying to dispel the intense emotions of hope and despair filtering in from the other world. *Another day, another step into the quagmire of lunacy.*

Ratan, sporting a pointed head and beard, sat in the black leather chair, still staring at Tomadus. "So you have the same dreams while you are awake that you do while you sleep?"

"It's more complicated than that. The dreams are not identical, but they all depict the same world. Different stories, same general setting."

"But that is no different than anyone else, except for the day dreaming, of course. And that could be explained by exhaustion."

Tomadus exhaled deeply. "Do others dream of a world that is different than this one?

"I imagine we all wish for a better world from time to time, and that manifests itself in our dreams."

"Who said it was better? It is just different. In fact, I'm not sure—it might be worse. There is great hatred there."

"Whom do you hate?"

"Me? No. It is not me. I do not hate. At least, well, that's not what I was talking about. I am chasing hatred."

"Chasing hatred? Do you wish to hate?"

"No. No. I am chasing those who hate. I need to stop them before…"

"Before what?"

"I don't know. That part remains unclear."

"Perhaps the stress of your work bothers you. Tell me more about this feeling in your gut."

"I've had it since I was a child," Tomadus said. "It comes and goes. You probably would call it butterflies. However, this is much worse and feels like some creature is alive inside me. It usually occurs when I am most relaxed, not when I am nervous. It invades my thoughts, urges me to take actions against my interest."

"I see. And what do you think this, uh, 'creature,' looks like? Is he in your dreams? Is he the hatred you seek?"

"No. No. The two are separate…and yet…connected somehow. I can't explain it. I have no idea what the creature looks like. It is just a feeling deep inside."

"Have you been examined by a physic-tech?"

Tomadus sighed. "Yes. Just two weeks ago. He found nothing wrong physically. Look, it is more than a feeling and it is more than a dream, do you understand?"

"But you just said it was just a feeling and you described your night terrors as dreams."

"Yes, I know." Tomadus leaned forward and stroked his forehead. "They are feelings and dreams, but so much more. If I could describe them to you, I would. You called it a creature."

"No, you did," the psyche-tech said.

"Fine. Have you ever felt like something is inside of you, something that is part of you but you cannot figure out how to control it? Something that is watching and judging your every move?"

"You mean guilt," Ratan said.

"No. I know guilt. It's more than that. It is a yearning. Often a feeling of…dread, of hope that will somehow be lost if I don't listen, if I don't do what is right. And then when I do, he goes to sleep, and I feel the warmth of his body curling through my belly, rising through my chest and into my heart." Tomadus began to sweat. He looked down at his hands and then closed his eyes, sighed deeply and began again. "And the dreams—I can see them even as we sit here. I see them in my memory as if they were part of my own past. It's getting so that I'm finding it difficult to tell the difference between them and my real memories."

"Go on."

Tomadus continued, "And that was when the dreams came only

at night. Now, I sometimes just have new memories appear in my brain during the daytime at the oddest moments. The bright light always accompanies them. I don't know if I can bear it any longer."

Ratan began scribbling something on his pad. "Perhaps you need some rest and relaxation. A little separation from your daily troubles can help enormously. There is a quiet place here in Roma that I am considering for you. I will prescribe a medication that will help you sleep and even rest during the day."

"Sleep? Rest? I have no time. What else do they do? Will I be able to focus when I am awake?"

"Ah, you will feel a little duller than normal, but we can adjust the dosage if necessary. You will be fine."

"No. No drugs." Tomadus stood up. "I'm sorry, but I've wasted your time. I must go." Tomadus walked out of the room, out of the office building and onto Via Curiarum. If he'd said any more to the psyche-technologist, he might be committed to one of those derangement wards. He must find strength within himself, within his work.

He came to a communications pod already partially occupied by other *cives* who could easily overhear him if not engrossed in their own calls. That seemed to be the point of these pods—a deliberate theft of privacy. So be it. He placed a call to Stephanus. "Just checking on the network in North Aztalan. Have we received any more commitments?"

"You must have impressed them over there," Stephanus said. "We now have twenty-five merchants ready to sell the product when ready."

"Wonderful."

"There has even been some movement to the south: we've received written requests from several prominent merchants asking you to visit them in the Aztec Empire. Our organization in the Three Empires and Roma has been growing as well—no doubt due to advance sheets on the products and your speech at the conference. But, of course, we already had a substantial presence here, so the growth is a little slower. Nevertheless, it is already helping current sales of our other products. I think we will have a very good year, even if we miss the target for the new product launch later this year."

"Great news," Tomadus said. "Thanks for taking charge during these last few weeks. I have had a tough go of it. Still trying to get my head straight."

"No problem. You'll need to pull it together pretty soon, though."

Tomadus rested his forehead on his left palm. "Why? What's happening?"

"I can't hold off the First Consul's technologists anymore. They've threatened to shut us down if you don't turn over the plans or meet with them soon. I don't know when that would be, but it would be a disaster when we are trying to push this thing forward."

"You get anything more on their intentions?"

"Nope. They are more closed mouth than we are. Something about maintaining the stability of Roma and the Three Empires. Can't seem to get any more details out of them."

Tomadus frowned. "You see any alternatives?"

"None."

"Nor do I."

CHAPTER 22

"I am sorry, *Civis* Tomadus, but there was nothing I could do." First Consul Khansensius shook his head slowly. "I received first class requests from the offices of both emperors. If you had not decided to come to this meeting on your own, I'm afraid I would have had to send my agents to collect you. These generals wish to speak with you and convince you to cooperate. Despite my pleas—I have told them to give you a little time to assist us—they lack patience and press for results. I had no choice."

"This is Roma. Am I not a Romanus citizen? Have I no Romanus rights?"

"Of course, you have rights." The First Consul flashed his calming smile. "Still, you are wise enough to understand the difference between rights in theory and practice, no? Do not confuse the two, *amicus meus*, whether you speak of yourself or our country. We both see Roma as the magnificent independent nation it still is—the great grandchild of our ancient Romanus and Mongol forbearers who once nearly ruled the world, albeit almost a millennium apart. You can take pride in that, as do I. But under current conditions, we are both greater and lesser than that vision, are we not?"

Tomadus nodded.

First Consul Khansensius went on, "Roma is the arbiter of the world, or at least the Islamic empires. We maintain this through our neutrality. We have no religion, so we need not take sides in the great debates and conflicts between Sunnis, Shiites and Mahdians, or even the Juteslams, do we? We can even moderate problems involving the Jewish communities in Al-Andalus and Palestine, though we find that more difficult in Tetepe, of course. This arbiter status makes us a great nation and gives us considerable power. But it also imposes on us certain…realities."

"Realities?"

"We obviously cannot take sides, except at the request of our combined sponsors. Without a standing army, if we tried to separate ourselves from the Three Empires, we would be crushed. They permit us to serve as their arbiter because they need us to help them avoid the destructive wars and rebellions that plagued them for centuries. But make no mistake: we are neither their masters nor their equals, but their servants."

"Servants?" Tomadus said.

"Yes," said the First Consul. "Of course, we have the legal right to act independently, yet we always choose to exercise our independence by acting at their joint behest. The only time we truly act on our own is to resolve their disputes. And we do this diplomatically and without bias toward any empire. Any bias would condemn us all to an ignominious end. And so, *amicus meus*, when I get a call from an emperor or his staff, I listen. When I get a call from two emperors, I jump. When I get a call from all three, I prostrate myself before them and do as they please."

Tomadus closed his eyes and nodded slowly. His teachers had not quite taught him this, but he knew there was some truth to it.

The First Consul gently placed his hand on Tomadus's shoulder and spoke softly, "So have you the rights of a Romanus citizen? Of course. You have the right to market your invention under the Technologists Act of 1835. Even though the Romanus government will not stop you, will such laws protect you or your company against the might of the Three Empires? You know my hands are tied. I would personally love to help you all I can, but I am powerless."

Crossing his arms, Tomadus blinked a few times. What part of this impassioned speech was real and what part dispensed to advance the First Consul's political aims? He understood the reality better than the First Consul thought. Still, he was not so sure the First Consul was quite as powerless as he let on. The Three Empires relied on Roma not only as their arbiter in dispute among themselves but also as their proxy in conflicts around the globe. They would not cross the First Consul lightly. And Tomadus's invention should pose only a minor issue for them. Nevertheless, the First Consul impressed him with his candidness. Perhaps Tomadus needed to look at the situation and his relationship with the First Consul in a new light. "Your insights are helpful, First Consul. Tell me, before the generals arrive, what is your take on the situation in Tetepe?"

"Ah yes, I have heard that you visited there recently. Tell me what you think."

"How did you hear that?" Tomadus asked with a bit too much suspicion in his voice.

"We have paid attention to your movements, for your own protection, of course. A few inquiries with our friends there and we located you fairly quickly. What impressions did you draw?"

Tomadus drew his hands together, interlacing his fingers. *Be careful. Don't betray any sympathies. To him this must only be business.* "My impression, Your Eminence, was that it will be a very difficult place to market my products any time soon. I think the Demoseps will continue to fight for their freedom from the Juteslams for a very long time, and the Juteslams seem unlikely to relent."

"You see the Demoseps as freedom fighters, then, not as shaitaanists fighting a losing rebellion as they terrorize the good people of New Jutland?"

Tomadus stiffened as the hairs on the back of his neck pricked up. "They are what they are—I do not wish to label them. I tried to talk one of the Demoseps into ending any shaitaanist activity. I doubt I made much of a dent, though."

"I see," said the First Consul.

"Do you ever wonder if it will end? This bloodletting has gone on for fifty years now, with only intermittent stoppages as the sides take some time to lick their wounds. But the death and destruction always rears up again in waves. I thought since I was there I would see if I could do any good and improve business at the same time."

The First Consul looked right into Tomadus eyes. "The situation remains very…complicated, *Civis* Tomadus, very complicated, indeed. I have some sympathy for the Tetepian people myself. You may be aware that

I came from humble means and a war-torn area of Roma as a child. Like my relatives, most of these unfortunates are good people at the mercy of history. However, a small, violent group can ruin it for the rest. The only real stability is provided by the Juteslams, and, of course, we and the Three Empires would like the area to remain relatively stable."

"Do you think the last fifty years have been stable?"

"Relatively stable, Tomadus, relatively. A little instability helps us keep Tetepe from joining with the Aztecs and ultimately becoming a force against us. We do not want them to exploit their significant natural resources in ways that could harm Roma and the Three Empires, do we?"

"I see what you mean." *The strategic interests of the Three Empires trumps all.*

The First Consul continued, "And democracy, well, that is a dangerous and destabilizing path for any region, no? We must contain that ideology, if not destroy it altogether. Nevertheless, total instability in the region could impact larger global interests. Many powerful nations need access to those resources, you know. I do respect the Tetepians for their courage and stubborn refusal to accept the supremacy of others. But in the end, their efforts are doomed to failure."

"Do you think there is any chance we could bring peace to the region?" Tomadus asked.

"What do you mean, we? I understand the Tetepians rejected the peace accord Skjöldr offered. It was brokered by my administration. What hope is there for a lasting peace after that?"

Tomadus stared at the First Consul's eyes. *Do I leap? He seems to trust me, but he cannot openly agree. Still, he must see the truth.* "The Demoseps viewed that accord essentially as a proposal for their surrender—not as a peace among equals."

The First Consul put the tips of his fingers together and stared until Tomadus looked down and began fidgeting. "Perhaps," the First Consul said, "that may be the perception of the Demoseps. But perception is everything in politics, *amicus meus*. And the perception of the world today is that Skjöldr seeks an honorable peace while the irrational and violent Demoseps refuse it."

"What if…what if behind the scenes, Roma and the Three Empires pushed Skjöldr a bit to become a little more reasonable?"

"I'm afraid that is not possible under current circumstances. However, I see our generals have arrived." The First Consul rose as he nodded to the glass window of the meeting room door. "Let us see what they think is possible."

The First Consul's assistant was the first through the door. "First Consul Khansensius, *Civis* Tomadus, I present to you General Faisil of the Sunni Muslim Empire and General Khameni of the Shiite Muslim Empire." The two generals in dress uniforms placed their right hands on their chests and bowed slightly in the direction of the First Consul and Tomadus, who then returned the greeting.

"Welcome, sirs. It is an honor to meet with you here," the First Consul said, demonstrating a genuine tone of gratitude. "Please, have a seat at our table. Can I get you something to drink or eat after your long journeys?"

"No thank you," replied General Faisil. "We have little time. We would like to get straight down to this business."

"Of course, of course," said the First Consul. "I was just discussing the matter with *Civis* Tomadus, here. He has recently returned from North Aztalan on a business trip for his company. He is concerned about the unrest in Tetepe."

"I…I am merely interested in opening new markets there," Tomadus interjected. "Prospects are not good with this ongoing conflict. Now that the peace accord has been rejected, I fear there is little hope for a stable business environment there unless there is some way we could bring all parties back to the negotiating table. I would be willing to meet with Skjöldr personally to discuss it, if that could be arranged."

The two generals sat back. Faisil crossed his arms; Khameni put the palms of his hands together.

Tomadus studied the two men. Was that amusement in their eyes? *They're wondering what this tech-merchant thinks he is doing poking his head into diplomatic matters better left to generals, kings and emperors.*

General Faisal said, "Do not make the mistake many people do."

"What is that?"

"They assume the Three Empires support the Juteslams simply because they are Muslims. As you know, the Three Empires have their own religious differences and Roma has played an important role in helping us address those issues so we can remain united on other issues around the globe. But, doctrinally, we three empires are not far apart in our beliefs when compared with the Juteslams."

"You are all Muslims, no?" Tomadus asked.

"Yes, but because of their original isolation and Viking past, the Juteslams maintain a perverted view of Islam and the Qur'an. They drink alcohol and smoke tobacco like barbarians. They create craven images of the Prophet. They still worship their great ancestors, though they call it honoring their history. They are self-absorbed. Although they reflect many of the components of our religion and we respect that they found Allah in their isolation, they are no real kin to us. So do not assume that any support we may give them is because of their religion. That similarity may help soothe some of our citizens, but it gives others quite a little heartburn."

Tomadus nodded. "I see. Thank you for helping me understand that better, General."

"You are welcome. Now, please help us understand why there has been no progress on the transfer of your technology to Romanus government technologists. The First Consul had assured us of the transfer quite some time ago."

"I apologize," said Tomadus, "but I was in North Aztalan for some time and have had some medical difficulties since I have returned."

General Faisal leaned toward Tomadus, his broad shoulders seemingly blocking all of the natural light from Tomadus. "Well then, can we assume the schematics and detailed directions will be turned over to the Imperium's technologists this week?"

Tomadus wiggled in his chair, his chest clamping down on his beating heart. "General, I am curious about this. I had thought the Three Empires frowned upon us technologists since we are godless creatures. You surely cannot be interested in one of our inventions."

General Faisal frowned. "I am sure you understand that Roma helps us much in this regard. The Three Empires will not develop any technology, since we do not permit technologists to practice their crafts in our territories. But the Imperium in Roma can accomplish this on our behalf. We have no problem with our godless arbiter providing us with the tools we need. We simply choose not to engage in these lowly practices ourselves. So, again Tomadus, will you turn over the schematics and detailed directions to the Imperium's technologists immediately?"

Tomadus sat back. "I wish I could comply, but there are problems with the device. In good conscience, I cannot turn it over to you now. I do not wish to face any false claims penalties or imprisonment for improper practices. When we have the bugs worked out, we will contact your technologists."

General Khameni cleared his throat and put both hands on the table. "*Civis* Tomadus, you are too kind to so carefully consider the interests of our governments." He paused and smiled artificially. "However, I am afraid that you do not appreciate the nature of our interests. Time is of the essence. The Imperium's technologists are more than capable of working through any...problems."

"But General—"

"No buts. We want the imperial technologists to begin exploring the intense focusing and extreme amplification of light inherent in your design. You and your company will not be held responsible for any problems with the prototype. Those are to be expected."

"Thank you. However, once we discovered the problem, I'm afraid that we dismantled the device and began anew. I wish my team had not done that, but I was in North Aztalan and they thought it best. Anyway, it will be sometime before we can provide a fully-operational prototype."

General Khameni leaned forward and slammed the table with his fist. "Let me be blunt, Tomadus. You have plans, technical diagrams, research. Provide them to us today or we will shut your company down and search your offices ourselves. If we find the plans or prototype, your company will never be allowed to reopen. Am I clear?"

Tomadus looked back at the General, trying to hold back his fear, trying to overcome it. *They don't know I've hidden the plans and prototype away from my office the last few weeks.* "Crystal clear, but I am afraid I have nothing I can give you. Please feel free to search my office if you don't believe me."

General Faisal shot a glance at General Khameni and leaned forward.

"*Civis* Tomadus, sir, surely you see the benefits of cooperating with the Three Empires. First Consul Khansensius has assured us of your loyalty to the Triumvirate. If we can get this project going in the next two weeks, I am prepared to offer to pay you twenty-five million Romanus talents just for the designs. You can keep the rights to commercial applications. Our uses will be governmental only."

Tomadus breathed deeply. In one week he could make three times his company's earnings for all of the last five years. *I am stupid.* The creature stirred in his belly and that feeling of dread consumed him. He looked at the other three as he rubbed his abdomen and then opened his hands wide. "I don't know how to respond, General. That is quite a sizeable offer. But I doubt we can recover the information in that time period. What is the government's purpose, anyway?"

General Faisal said, "That is not something I can share with you, I am afraid. But I assure you it will be used solely to enhance the stability of Roma and the Three Empires. What if we could arrange a meeting between you and Skjöldr, with the express understanding that you were acting as a 'business diplomat' on behalf of Romanus technologists worldwide. Would that help you expedite matters?"

Tomadus felt the sinking feeling being replaced by a slight feeling of euphoria, the creature now withdrawing again after a small victory. Should not a clear good transcend the mere prospect of evil? Anyway, he couldn't keep them away forever. Eventually, they would find his prototype and his schematics and then he'd be sunk and they'd still get their way. Better to take their offer and swallow hard. And find other ways. "Two weeks, you say?"

"Two weeks."

Tomadus caught the First Consul nodding to him slightly. He had no real choice. "Okay. I have been troubled about Tetepe. Perhaps your solution will give me greater focus. General, I think I might be able to get you some schematics in two weeks. Will that do?"

"Marvelously."

The First Consul chimed in, "Excellent! Let us drink some tea to our good fortune." The First Consul's assistant brought a cup made of fine china before each of the four men and set a matching teapot in the center of the table. The First Consul himself poured all four cups of tea. He raised his cup, and the others followed. Then, with a slight nod, he said, "To our joint venture, then, may Tomadus's light amplification lead the way." They all repeated the phrase, smiled and clanked cups.

Once again, the bright white light burned through Tomadus's eyes and turned his mind upside down. His eyes widened and he began screaming wildly, uncontrollably, "They're all connected, you know—*Mater, Annuntiatio, Pardus, Armageddon*, Ramat David. They are all connected!" After a few seconds of this, he collapsed onto the table, spilling his tea on the two generals.

The First Consul was speaking when Tomadus awakened, though Tomadus's eyes were still shut. "My apologies, sirs. I do not understand what has come over him. I know he mentioned a recent medical malady. Perhaps this is a symptom of it."

General Faisal said, "What strange babbling: mother, announced, leopard and who knows what those other words were? Very odd."

General Khameni said, "We must obtain those plans before something worse happens to him. I fear he may be unstable."

"I am certain he will be fine," said the First Consul. "You will receive your plans."

Tomadus raised his head slowly. It felt like several construction workers had crawled into his ears and were trying to hammer their way out through his temples. When he moaned, the voices stopped. Gradually, he was able to lift his body off of the table and see the mess he had made. "I am sorry," he mumbled.

The First Consul touched his shoulder. "Tomadus, perhaps we should call an ambulance for you."

While Tomadus heard this, it made no sense to him. *An ambulance. To take me off to a derangement ward? No.* He couldn't afford that. Not now. "I'll be fine. Just need some rest."

CHAPTER 23

"I don't want to use Decima's father in this way," Yohanan said to the bearded man across the simple wooden table in an upper meeting room at the Shenandoah Inn.

Barely distinguishable from the pupils, the small, dark irises of Raanan's eyes now focused on Yohanan. "What's it to you? He is capable. He supports us. He is the only way in. What other choice do we have?"

Yohanan sighed. He never should have supported this egotist as the new Demosep leader last year. Yohanan looked around the table at the other Demoseps present. "Only the desperate narrow their alternatives to one miserable choice. We always have options. We could wait for another chance to kill Hugleikr. His life is not so critical to us. But Quintillus's life is. It is too risky."

Raanan shot back, "How do we know there will ever be another opportunity? Our spy networks are not so good that we can realistically hope for another chance any time soon. Quintillus can take care of himself. He is a master merchant and the Juteslams need him. If he is discovered, we can find a way to rescue him while he awaits trial before Skjöldr."

"Decima, what do you think?" Yohanan asked.

She looked at Yohanan with an air of disappointment, and then glanced around the table at the other members of the committee. "I agree with Raanan. We must kill Vice Regent Hugleikr. My father knows the risks. He has agreed to take them because our cause is just. He knows of Hugleikr's long reputation of hatred and cruelty. But even if they suspect my father, they would not dare trample upon his rights. Only Skjöldr could condemn him and only after a long trial. We could certainly find a way to remove him from that danger. But he will not be caught. This is a good plan. No, a great plan. And Hugleikr must die. We all agree to that."

Yohanan slowly rubbed his chin as he looked at Decima. She was too certain, too eager, too committed. She was just too damn new to the fight and had not yet tasted enough of its tragedy. *She could be reckless.* "A great plan?"

Achak, Yohanan's good friend and the Demoseps' best munitions expert, nodded and gave Yohanan that familiar wink of his. "Any day Hugleikr dies is a great day in my book."

Yohanan looked at his old friend and then at the rest of the faces waiting for him. Even Achak was telling him to go along. Of course, Yohanan agreed Vice Regent Hugleikr should die. As King Skjöldr's second in command, that vicious son of a bitch was the butcher responsible for the deaths of so many Demoseps and the shelling of so many more innocent Tetepians. If Hugleikr were out of the way, maybe the more moderate ministers in Skjöldr's council would gain greater sway. Maybe Skjöldr could break with the past. But risk Quintillus? That was like risking a second father's death.

"I agree with you, Achak," Yohanan said. "I quibble only with the plan. Yes, Quintillus is a respected merchant, but he is no warrior. Yes, he supports our cause, but he is no Demosep. He has never had to directly face the ugliness of this fight. It is wrong to bring him in so close now. Let us put our emotions aside. Forget that he is your father, Decima. For the moment, I will forget that he saved me from the streets after my parents perished. Let us forget what this man has already done for all of us. But let us remember what he still can do if we keep him safe. Without him and his contacts, where would we be? Where would we raise funds? Where would our spy network be? We need him in New Åarhus, and we need him there without any unnecessary suspicions from the Juteslams."

Decima responded even before Raanan could get in a word, "I agree, but this is a small task for him. It is not as if he is walking into the Great

Jutland Square with us. He will merely provide us with a little discreet access. Do you think I would want my father placed in danger?"

Yohanan sat back. Maybe she was right. The mission posed only a small threat to Quintillus, who was quite good at playing the part of a wily merchant caring little for politics except how it might affect his bottom line. Moreover, without Decima's support, Yohanan could never carry the day. "Obviously, I am in the minority here," Yohanan said begrudgingly. "I concede. Let's move on."

Raanan grinned and continued outlining the plan. "Okay. It looks like we are all agreed that the target and opportunity justify the risk. We can kill Hugleikr and make Skjöldr and his thugs look incompetent all at the same time. Quintillus holds the key…"

CHAPTER 24

THE DARKNESS SURRENDERED again to its own futility, no longer able to shroud her immense beauty. Yohanan was navigating his eyes over the figure of Decima, his only beacon the dim light of the moon shining through the porthole into the hold of the ship. Her own eyes were staring out of the porthole, searching for any lack of normalcy. Her expression was one of content, not worry.

"Always vigilant, I see," Yohanan said. "You have learned well. Thanks to your father, they know us only as a merchant ship, ready to unload in the Port of New Åarhus. He is a brave man, your father."

Decima turned away from the porthole for a moment. She smiled gently and looked down, away from Yohanan. "That he is. He believes in our cause but not our methods."

"I know. I'm surprised he agreed to help."

"He trusts me. And he knows the terror of Hugleikr all too well. Hugleikr has practiced his deadly craft in New Åarhus—even on Juteslams who are disloyal. We must kill him."

"Killing seems to suit you a bit more than when you blew up that train a few months ago."

"We all adapt," she said.

"Some better than others."

She smiled and Yohanan winced. "What do you think will happen to you when you are eventually caught?"

"I will never be caught. I am still the daughter of a prominent Romanus merchant. They know nothing other than my desire to help feed the poor of Shenandoah. If I am wrong, then I will fight to the death and take as many Juteslam scum with me as I can."

Slowly letting out a deep breath, Yohanan looked around the rest of the hold. Dekanawida and Achak sat on the other side, staring out their own portholes. It was a good thing his friend Achak had made it. That made up for Eliezer missing the rendezvous four hours earlier. That was unusual for his portly friend. A little obnoxious at times, Eliezer was not the favorite of many of the Demoseps, but he had always proven helpful to Yohanan in a pinch. But with Achak here, they had a sufficient crew to execute the plan.

When Achak caught Yohanan staring at him, he nodded back and winked.

Yohanan laughed and shook his head. His eyes focused again on Decima. "Don't you think the plan is a little too cute for our needs?"

"Raanan's plan is brilliant and elegant. This thing will unfold on visi-scan and will be replayed around the world. They will see what fools the Juteslams are. The Juteslams will realize they are vulnerable. And Hugleikr will die."

Yohanan sighed deeply and stared out the porthole.

A few minutes later, the horn sounded from the ship above, signaling their imminent arrival to the port authorities. The humming of the ship motors diminished until there was silence. He felt the sideways push of the tug as they listed momentarily to the side. His nostrils were filled with the heavy scent of sulfur from coal piled high on shore for export to the Three Empires. He heard the ropes being thrown overboard to the dock and the capstans twirling them taut.

As the gangplank was lowered, he listened carefully for the marching feet of a search crew. That was one of the big risks on this mission. The authorities could always insist on searching the ship right after it came to port, but it was rare, even in these troubled times. Typically, they would simply wait for the cargo to be unloaded and search the ship's crew as they left the docks. He heard only the sound of a single pair of feet crossing the gangplank.

A few minutes later he heard the coded knock on the door of their hold: three knocks, then two, then three. When Yohanan opened the door, Quintillus walked in. "Welcome to New Åarhus, Yohanan." Yohanan bowed to him respectfully, placing his hand to his heart. Quintillus repeated the gesture. Then they shook hands and embraced. A familiar, tingling warmth passed through Yohanan's arms.

Quintillus looked over at Decima and smiled. She ran to him and they hugged tightly. Quintillus did not seem to want to let go. His eyes were shut as he held her tightly to his chest for a good ten count. When he stepped back and looked at her, his glassy eyes betrayed his sentiment. "You have grown even more beautiful, my dear."

"Oh, Papa."

"Don't you think so, Yohanan?" Quintillus employed that wry smile he used whenever he deliberately embarrassed his daughter.

"Don't answer that, Yoh. He's just baiting you."

Yohanan responded anyway, "I have always found her as beautiful as you are kind, Quintillus. *Gratias.* Sorry to get you mixed up in this thing."

Quintillus pulled his lips in and nodded slowly, his head turning to make eye contact with the hold's occupants—each in order like an experienced orator. "You can all thank me by keeping to our agreed-upon parameters. Only Hugleikr dies. I know you Demoseps sometimes forget it, but these Juteslams are people too. Despite the propaganda, they don't all hate you. Many are innocents, and surely they do not deserve to die."

"The plan is perfect, Papa. The only other people at risk are Hugleikr's lieutenants, and they are nearly as guilty as he. The innocents, as you call them, will be far away behind the barriers. To address your concerns, we will install a fail safe just in case."

"I know, I know, my sweet daughter. But I have seen on the visi-scan far too many deaths of innocents from other schemes of your brotherhood. I know the Juteslams play up those tragedies, but they are tragedies, nonetheless. I want your word, all of you." He swept his hand around the hold, taking in the entire group. "Only Hugleikr, and maybe his lieutenants, will die."

All but Yohanan nodded their heads and made the promise. Quintillus looked at Yohanan, seeking some sign of his affirmation.

Yohanan returned only a gentle smile. "My friend, I promise you that I will do everything I can to prevent innocent deaths here. But I have seen far too much to promise you something I cannot completely control. Even if all goes well, I do not know what will happen in the aftermath. I do not know the reaction of the guards. There may be panic. It is always possible that innocents could die."

"Understood. Any panic by the Juteslams is the result of their own volition, and we know it is a tool for your escape. Now, I must get going. The guards are my friends and believe I needed to check my precious cargo, but they will begin to wonder if I stay too long. Good luck, my friends." Quintillus stopped, reached out to Decima, and, with his palms gently holding each of her cheeks, spoke softly, "Decima, you have always been twice my worth."

She laughed at his familiar little name pun.

"Stay safe," he added with a nod, and walked out of the cargo hold.

∇   ∇   ∇

Yohanan watched Quintillus nearly a hundred feet away as he passed the port guards and let out one of his quick and quaint little one-liners. The guards laughed and he turned back toward them for more conversation, this time offering each of them a cigarette. With that cue, the four Demoseps quickly crossed with their gear from Quintillus's ship down to the dock and up the gangplank of a much smaller vessel. This ship looked ancient, even in the moonlight. The long dragonhead and neck on the bow of the ship was intended to terrify anyone it approached near land or at sea.

The four in black ducked down on the deck and searched for the mini-hold trap door. Dekanawida found a brass ring embedded in the wood deck and signaled to Yohanan. Yohanan slid his index finger under the ring and pulled. The trap door rose up from the deck, revealing a space only a few feet deep running the length of the vessel, just deep enough for a little storage. Working together in silence, they managed to attach the explosive tubes to the inside of the hull and hide them with extra sailcloth they had brought for this purpose.

Yohanan examined the work and saw that the explosives were fully concealed. When ignited, they would blow a hole about five feet wide, destroying everything in its path. Based on past explosions, it should kill Hugleikr as far as twenty feet away. "Do you have the channel ready?"

"Almost done," Achak said. "I just need to install the barrier."

The Juteslams had fitted an oil channel into the Viking ship's rail twenty years earlier when Skjöldr began using the ancient Viking vessel as a symbol for the Konverteraften celebration. When poured with oil and lit by a torch on the side of the ship, the channel drew the flame up the rail and to the dragon figurehead on the bow. Skjöldr always had a sense of spectacle. This year, the spectacle would blow up in his vicious henchman's face. The Demoseps' newly installed channel cut underneath the built-in channel, allowing just enough of the oil to split off to a second path of flame, this one under the deck of the ship and down to the explosives.

"It's damn complicated," Yohanan whispered. "I would rather we just trigger the bomb directly."

"Come on," Decima replied, "you know it gives us deniability if the thing explodes en route. Plus, it is poetic justice that Hugleikr will light the bomb that kills him, don't you think? Imagine seeing that on the visi-scan! It will be glorious."

"If it works."

She exhaled hard and held up the tiny radio device. "Yoh, look, I promise I won't push the button until the devil is ready to light it. He'll get what he deserves. No one else will be hurt."

Yohanan nodded. She was right. The barrier Achak was installing was an adequate fail-safe. Until Decima triggered the barrier to move, it would block any of the flaming oil from reaching the explosives. But once the tiny barrier blew…

"OK, it's all in place." Achak said.

"The sun will rise in an hour and they will begin unloading Quintillus's ship," Yohanan said. "The guard changes in a few minutes and we'll have only a few seconds to cross the dock and get into the cargo containers with our Konverteraften costumes. Slip away from the cargo when you can and melt into the celebration in the city. We'll rendezvous tonight at seven, sharp. Let's go."

CHAPTER 25

YOHANAN STROKED THE beard he had grown for two weeks just for this occasion. It itched, but perfectly complemented the iron Viking helmet he wore. The helmet came complete with a set of riveted panels crossing at the crown. Together with the beard, the iron section hanging between his eyes and over his nose hid just enough of his face to keep others from recognizing him. The leather armor, sheathed sword and side dagger completed the picture of the ancient Viking warrior. Under normal circumstances, he would have stood out anywhere in New Jutland, but tonight he was among tens of thousands of "Vikings" who had converged on Great Jutland Square. The scene might have been the aftermath of some ancient battle, minus the blood and dead bodies. Instead of death, a slight hint of urine rose to his nostrils from the stone pavement. Undoubtedly, most of the warriors in the square had found covert ways to relieve themselves of the byproduct of intoxicants they had imbibed throughout the day—the last legal alcohol they would see for the full month of Konvertermaned.

Though Great Jutland Square rivaled some of the grand squares of Roma and the Three Empires in size, it lacked the majesty of their ancient structures and the wonder of their modern commercial towers. New Åarhus was still a fairly small city by world standards, but it was the capital of New Jutland, and Skjöldr had gradually made the square into his centerpiece for focusing the Juteslams on his hopes and dreams of inevitable grandeur. The square seemed to be watched over by two huge statues at opposite ends of the square: Helge the Great, the patriarch of the Juteslams, and Muhammad, the great Prophet of Islam. Any Muslim from the Three Empires would hide his eyes from the statue of Muhammad, fearing Allah's reprisals for what they would consider idol worship; however, to the Juteslam, the statue was but a natural extension of his respect for his nation's adopted religion.

A small canal nearly encircled the square, winding its way from the west harbor to the fore of Asgard Palace at the far north end of the square and back to the sea through the tidal East River. Around the canal, ornate pedestrian bridges appeared every one hundred yards or so, permitting access to the government buildings surrounding the palace.

The canal opened into a larger pond in front of the palace. The pond was decorated with tiered fountains dribbling water over and through statues of ancient Juteslam kings and heroes. Tonight part of the pond was blocked from the view of the square by a nearly five hundred square foot stage. The stage was protected from the crowd by a low fence line and police guards posted fifty feet to its front. The stage protected its occupants with a transparent, bulletproof acrylic shield. The stage also served as a makeshift dock for the old Viking ship floating in the pond, with its magnificent main sail still stowed in its yardarm and its oars pulled inboard stage side.

In this light, Yohanan could see the dragon's neck and head more clearly and understood how it brought its own form of terror to the people living near the coasts of this continent a millennium ago. The demonic head towered over the ship with mouth wide, ivory white fangs gleaming, nostrils flaring and eyes bulging.

When Yohanan was a boy and first saw this ceremony, the flame had shot up the rail of the boat and behind and into the dragon's long neck, eventually emerging as hellfire from the throat of the beast, spewing its fury a full five feet out of its open jaws. After a few seconds, the fire had burned itself out as its light was replaced by a lantern located at the top of the central mast, shining its beacon toward the front of the ship. At once the spectacle represented a tribute to Juteslams' ancient ways while still fitting their glorious story of conversion to Islam through the beacon of light.

The ship also served as a symbol of dominance over the remaining peoples of Tetepe. Tonight that symbol would breathe its flames out its side and devour the worst of the Juteslam leaders.

Searching the crowd nearby, Yohanan found Decima dressed as an ancient Viking shieldmaiden, complete with sheathed sword and wooden shield slung on her back, her dark leather armor clinging much too tightly to her breast. Yohanan smiled. *Damn, she always looks good in black.* He walked near her and nodded. "All set?"

"If you are. I heard from Raanan. We thought Eliezer was sick. Not so. Apparently he stayed home and then slipped away a few hours ago. Raanan's going looking for him."

"Not like him. You broke com silence during an operation?"

"He called Papa. Wanted to know if everything was on track."

Yohanan shook his head. "He knows better." He looked around a bit more and found Dekanawida and Achak. Their work was done. Hell, his work was done, if everything went as planned. They were all here to ensure a safe escape for the trigger, Decima. They just needed to stand around and act like stupid, drunk Vikings. That was pretty easy in this lit-up crowd.

The sound of grand marching music began to rise from Medina, the street running northwest from the square, with distant cheers becoming louder by the second. Several thousand Vikings turned nearly in unison, like an army on maneuvers, each soldier craning his or her head to see the oncoming parade cross the pedestrian bridge onto the square.

At the head of the parade, a marching band played ancient wooden flutes, pipes, animal horns and drums. Each band member wore a ceremonial helmet with protruding horns that no real Viking ever bore in actual combat. Behind them sat the night's special dignitary disguised as a mythical Viking king, with elaborate chain mail and battle-axe as props and an enormous helmet covering his huge head and face completely. He rode high up on a platform being dragged behind the band by four oxen. He sat on a throne covered in gold leaf calligraphy and surrounded with four dragon head posts burning torches. The platform depicted the seal of New Jutland and flew its flag. Walking beside the platform, ten soldiers held anachronistic rapid rifles at the ready.

The parade turned left and headed toward the stage. The band continued on, but the mobile platform came to a stop near the stage stairs. A security guard opened a door in the plastic-shield, allowing the mythical Viking king to leave the mobile platform and enter the stage. Several other men dressed in ornate Viking dress, undoubtedly Hugleikr's lieutenants, accompanied him onto the stage. They sat in ancient chairs with tall wooden backs intricately carved with various sea serpents.

The mythical Viking king walked to the podium and removed his helmet, revealing nearly orange hair. He raised his battle-axe to the crowd. A murmur, followed by a growing cheer, worked its way back through the huge square. A tall Viking next to Yohanan yelled as he looked through a set of binoculars, "It is Vice Regent Hugleikr!" Then the crowd around Yohanan began to applaud and cheer wildly.

Yohanan's lip curled as he exhaled forcefully through his nose. Did these men and women truly love this murdering madman? Or were they merely playing up their loyalty for the security cameras? Too often we blame leaders for their bloodlust, and rightly so, but do they not just embrace the wishes of the mob, who cry for blood when fear strikes them, whether justified or not?

After a few minutes, Hugleikr set down his battle-axe and motioned to the crowd to be quiet. The crowd refused to obey, which Hugleikr clearly enjoyed. Appearing to show some persistence, Hugleikr eventually managed to quiet the crowd. But he riled them up again with his first statement, "Welcome, Juteslams, to Konverteraften!"

After a few more calming gestures, he began his ceremonial speech, "My fellow Juteslams, we are here not only to celebrate our Nordic past but also to renew our welcome of Islam to our world."

"Allahu Akbar!" yelled several in the crowd.

"You and I are all dressed in ancient Viking garb to recall our people's great glory in coming to Tetepe over a thousand years ago. When our ancestors arrived in just a few ships from Jutland and found this wilderness, they encountered armed opposition from local warriors of the Algonquin and Iroquois tribes. Did they shrink from these barbarous attacks? No, and thank Allah, for our ancestors would have been swept into the sea and none of us would be alive today. Instead, though greatly outnumbered, they defended themselves against these savages and in only a little over a hundred years came to dominate the entire North Atlantic Coast of Tetepe. The ship you see behind me," announced Hugleikr, waving his arm outstretched toward the Viking ship, "this beautiful relic of our glorious past, was just one of many vessels that helped our brave warriors extend our domain on this continent." The crowd applauded.

Several Vikings had pressed between Decima and Yohanan. He took a step forward and saw her several feet to his right. He nodded slightly and she returned the gesture.

Hugleikr's arms drew apart as if trying to envelop the whole crowd. "Tonight, we celebrate this honored history. However, it shall always be only half of the story and half of the celebration. For without the second half we would have been lost, without our guide, without our master, without the great purpose that has kept us alive for these last nearly nine hundred years. Without Him, we would have shriveled up and disappeared when faced with the conquests of the Aztec Empire. We would have been assimilated into its culture like so many others before us. But we were strong. We were resolute. We did not waver. We may have come to this continent as a group of warriors who prayed to the false idols of Odin and Thor, but we became a true people when we turned our faith to the Most Gracious, the Most Merciful, the Most Just, Allah!"

Yohanan looked around at two guards making their way through the crowd with rap rifles at their side. One pointed at him, and he froze. Then the pointer laughed heartily to his buddy. Yohanan turned and saw behind him an enormous Odin weighing nearly 350 *librae*, patch over his eye, horns to the sky, spear in hand, swaying like a tree in the wind while a few smaller Viking friends struggled to keep him upright. When Yohanan turned back, the guards had already disappeared back into the crowd.

Hugleikr lowered his arms. "Tomorrow is the 878th anniversary of Helge the Great's conversion to Islam. And tomorrow we will begin our month of fasting and purification in honor of our Lord and the many great kings who have served him. But tonight, on the eve of this noble event, on this Konverteraften, we celebrate with joy the one true people who have been brought to the light of Allah on this continent, the Juteslams!" The crowd cheered loudly, and Decima, now a good five feet away, put her hands over her ears.

Yohanan jerked his head toward Decima. Had something dropped from her pocket? He shoved one Viking aside and stepped toward her and saw the crushed cup beneath her foot, a nearby Viking almost weeping at its spilt contents. Yohanan saw her return her hands to her pockets with no change to her expression. All was well. He looked back to the stage.

Hugleikr clapped for a few seconds, his thick orange locks and beard bouncing with each connection of his palms. "Yes, we celebrate you all. On behalf of our great King Skjöldr, I say, 'Thank you to each and every one of you.' For all of you Juteslams are honorable people dedicated to the will of Allah. But we all know that not everyone in Tetepe is so honorable or so dedicated. No, there are far too many evil ones in this land who choose darkness over light, destruction over peace, and certain death over life. They do this because they have never dedicated themselves to the grace of our Lord. They are unable to see the great generosity of Skjöldr, who in the service of Allah has offered them an olive branch of peace. Not just any peace. It is a peace that would embrace the holy among them whole-heartedly and bring them into our Juteslam fold. It is a peace that would mercifully allow the unholy savages to live separately with their own kind. It is a peace that would allow Juteslams to continue to protect themselves from the contamination of the filthy ways of the Demoseps."

Yohanan bit his lip hard and checked himself from shaking his head. He saw Decima with her head on a pivot, unable to restrain her reactions, even for the sake of the mission. Nobody seemed to notice.

Hugleikr's pitch only increased. "Yet this shaitaanist people, led by the Jews, reject our offer of peace. These shaitaanists think that by striking fear into our hearts, we will shrink from our beliefs and our duty to Allah. But they forget one important thing. They forget who we Juteslams are. They forget the blood that still burns in our veins. They forget that we are still Vikings." The crowed roared with approval.

"And like the Vikings who first came to these troubled shores a mil-lennium ago, we will not shrink from their barbarous attacks. We will not take one step back. We will, together, move forward. Now, please do not misunderstand me. I cannot promise you that more of our people will not succumb to heinous death at the hands of these killers. But I know, with your help, we can hunt down these barbarians, and soon, very soon, we will eliminate each and every one of these blights upon our peaceful society. To accomplish this, we must all be vigilant. We must all look around us for spies that undermine our society and serve the will of Shaitan, the devil. And we must all be resolute. Are you with us?"

The crowd roared back "Yes!"

Yohanan felt someone strike his left shoulder hard, the pain shooting down his arm. He whipped around, arms raised, ready to fight back. There lay Odin, out cold, his buddies trying to lift his drunken carcass off the pavement. Yohanan shook his head and moved to his right, looking back to the stage.

Hugleikr was gesturing with his fists in the air. "Then let us put these troubles aside for the moment and celebrate Helge the Great's noble conversion to our faith." He left the podium but took the microphone with him. He proceeded to near the front of the stage and lifted a large torch from its stand and began walking back toward the ship. "Our ancestors came to this world by the light of the stars and the glare of the dragons' eyes." He held the torch up high as he approached the ship. After a short pause, he added, "On this continent we found a new beacon for hope."

Another pause. Yohanan looked over at Decima and saw her glaring at the stage, her hand fumbling in her pocket. No doubt she was ready. *Not yet. Wait.*

Hugleikr continued, "And so, I light the dragon's breath on this ship as a symbol of the brave men and women who first came to this land seeking a new life and here found their great and powerful leader in Heaven." He began to lower the torch down to the ship's rail, but when it was less than a half foot from lighting the fire, he paused a moment, then raised the torch again. "But who am I to light this symbol of our greatness? I am a servant of you, the Juteslam people. Helge the Great was only one man converting to Islam; it took the people following his lead to make us a people of followers in the eyes of Allah. And so, I think it fitting that the people light the dragon's head tonight! Guards, open the doors and choose fifty good Viking volunteers." At that statement, the crowd surged toward the stage with thousands hoping to have the honor of lighting the dragon.

Yohanan turned in the direction of Decima, his mouth agape and chest thumping. At first, he could not find her. But then he saw her a good ten yards ahead of him, being shoved to the side by the surging crowd. He weaved his way as best he could through the throng, reaching her nearly a minute later. "Please tell me you have not tripped the barrier."

She looked at him with wild eyes. "I pushed the button when he lowered the torch. How could I know?"

"Can we defuse it?"

Decima shook her head.

Forty or fifty men, women and children were already on the stage. The guard closed the gate and held back the rest. Hugleikr ceremoniously handed the torch to the Juteslam closest to the old Viking ship. Yohanan noticed that Hugleikr walked to the other side of the stage, away from the ship and torchbearers, replacing the protective Viking helmet on his head.

"Dear God, he knows!" Yohanan said. "The bastard knows and he is going to let his people die!" Yohanan began fighting through the crowd toward the stage.

Hugleikr gestured and nodded toward the torchbearer and spoke into the microphone, "Light our history! Light our destiny!" He seemed to duck to the side of the podium.

When the crowed roared, no one could hear Yohanan screaming, "No!"

A moment before the torch's flame touched the rail, the oil's vapor caught fire and the flame began moving up the rail toward the dragon's neck. It disappeared into the back of the beast's scaly neck and moments later appeared as eyes of the monster glowing a bright red, followed an instant later by flames shooting out of the dragon's mouth.

A second later a fireball erupted at the side of the ship and instantly consumed the forty or fifty citizens of New Jutland. The horrible sound of the blast arrived a moment later, followed almost immediately by panic. Most of the crowd trampled over and through each other as they scrambled to escape the square, but a small group ran toward the front to help friends and family who lay dead or dying, smoldering on the burning stage.

Yohanan staggered back, his eyes staring at the mayhem that his hands had wrought, his heart consumed with guilt at the deaths of these innocent people.

Soon the speakers hanging to the left of the stage, for those on the right were ablaze, were filled with the now almost soothing voice of Hugleikr,

"Calm yourselves, Juteslams. Do not succumb to the terror of these monsters. Do not panic; you are in no further danger. Emergency fire and medical personnel have already arrived. We will give the victims of this outrage medical attention and save as many as we can. Do not approach the stage, for you will only cause more harm to your kin. The medical staff needs space. The firefighters need space. Our guards are surrounding the square. Be assured—we shall find those responsible." He continued in that voice for several minutes, and, gradually, the throngs began to obey.

Yohanan looked toward the stage. Twenty or so burly guards in full riot gear blocked the gate. In front of them stood the victims' loved ones, who just a few minutes earlier had been reveling in the great luck of their family and friends being given a once in a lifetime opportunity to light the dragon. Now they wailed and swore and begged the guards for access to their departed friends, parents and siblings. But the guards would not budge.

Within the chaos, Yohanan noticed a boy of about fifteen, his face blackened by the soot of the explosion, with tears streaming down his face. His arms comforted a young girl of about seven, her red hair covered with soot. She was screaming over and over again, "Mommy! Daddy!"

A shiver ran down Yohanan's spine. Frozen in place, he struggled to separate the pain of the present from the evils of the past. The two now merged in his mind.

A familiar hand caught him. A familiar voice shook him out of his stupor. "We need to get the hell out of here before the panic subsides," Decima said. "Come on Yohanan, snap out of it!"

The two began moving at a rapid walking pace toward Konge Street at the southwest corner of the square—the planned rendezvous point the team had set well before hell had unleashed its fury.

As Yohanan and Decima reached the corner a few minutes later, they saw their co-conspirators waiting for them. The guards were still trying to stem the flow of people from the square, but had not yet succeeded. Dekanawida and Achak were standing near the statue of Mohammed, a full forty feet from the closest officer. All four would be away from the scene and free to escape the square in less than a minute.

The entire time Hugleikr had been addressing the crowd with reassuring words through the microphone at the left of the stage. But now his voice rose to a feverish pitch. "As I promised, we have already discovered one of the perpetrators of this terror. Bring him to the stage!"

Yohanan looked at his group. No one was missing.

They all turned around to see four guards dragging a man up the stairs and over to Hugleikr, beating him with their batons every step of the way. The man crumpled down at the feet of Hugleikr. Yohanan could not see the man's face but could tell he was covered in his own blood and his hands were tied behind his back. The guards hoisted him up and faced him toward the crowd.

Though the stage was still too far away to see the details of the man's face, Yohanan's heart began to race. He reached into his costume and pulled out his binoculars and in one motion pulled off his helmet and put the binoculars to his eyes.

He saw the prisoner at first waver, but then, unable to stand, Quintillus fell to his knees on the stage.

"Who is it?" Decima barked, grabbing the binoculars from him and raising them to her eyes. "No!" she yelled. "No!"

Hugleikr stuck the microphone toward Quintillus's mouth and his words became audible to the crowd, "I am sorry. I am so very sorry." As tears streamed down Quintillus's face, he closed his eyes.

Hugleikr walked away from Quintillus. "You have heard him, good people of New Jutland. By his own words he has condemned himself. By the power vested in me as Vice Regent, I hereby declare this man, Quintillus of Roma, to be a shaitaanist, beyond the protection of the law and the court of Skjöldr. He will be executed on this stage right here and now." Hugleikr nodded to the guard, who then pointed his pistol at Quintillus's head.

Yohanan looked at Decima and the others, searching their eyes for what he should do.

Achak was the first to speak, "They won't shoot him now. They will torture him first to get our names. We are not safe here. We must go."

Decima whispered, "He won't do it. Even Hugleikr would not dare to execute Quintillus without a trial. He is protected by Roma. Hugleikr must be bluffing."

Yohanan stepped forward and looked them in the eye, each in turn.

"I'm sorry, but that is a risk I cannot take. Get out of here. Head back to Shenandoah without me. I owe this much to Quintillus."

Yohanan turned and began working through the crowd, yelling "Stop! I confess! I am responsible, not Quintillus! Don't kill him!" But the noise from the crowd drowned out his plea. Dekanawida grabbed Yohanan from behind.

Hugleikr, Vice Regent of the Kingdom of New Jutland, spoke once more, "You Demoseps have proven once again that you are nothing but murdering cowards! Well, here is what we do with murderers of women and children." He hesitated only a second, then yelled, "Fire!"

Yohanan screamed, "No!"

The guard pulled his trigger and Quintillus slumped to the stage, the blood pooling on the boards lying beneath his temple.

Decima screamed and Achak put his hand over her mouth and began dragging her back toward the statue.

Yohanan was staring at the stage, shaking his head, muttering, "I killed him. I killed them. I killed all of them. Dekanawida turned Yohanan around and escorted him out of the square.

CHAPTER 26

"Another double Gladiator, neat."

"Haven't you had enough?"

Not nearly enough, Tomadus thought, trying to stare back at the bartender while his head bobbed from alcohol and exhaustion. When the bartender walked away from his slumping body and served clientele on the other side of the bar, Tomadus yelled, "How you get a drink around here?"

Tomadus pulled himself up and looked up at the visi-scan above the bar. Predictably, the Imperium-censored news was replaying the horrid Konverteraften Massacre over and over, decrying the villainy of the Demoseps, but not bothering to mention that Hugleikr had executed a Romanus citizen live on the visi-scan. They showed only the conflagration and the soothing voice of Hugleikr. Then a voiceover reported that a Demosep spy responsible for the carnage had been killed when trying to escape. There was no mention of Quintillus's name at all. But Tomadus knew his new friend had died, because they showed Quintillus being dragged to the stage near the end of the report. He wondered if Yohanan and Decima were among those suspects rounded up by the Juteslams in the hours after the explosion.

Did it matter? He had failed. He had tried to silence the creature within through this meager effort at something good, but he had failed completely.

Shaitaanism continued and this visi-scan report would undermine any attempt at lasting peace. The carnage would go on, and the world would say, "See, I told you those people are barbarians. Democracy turns them into wild, violent dogs that cannot be trusted. They murder the innocent. They kill the children." And then they would put these horrible matters aside, away from their busy lives in Roma or the Aztec Empire, or the East Asian Empire, or the Three Empires, and they would act like it had never happened. It was just those crazies at the other end of the globe. Forget about it. Thank Allah for our own happiness. But they would remember—the next time somebody wanted to help the Tetepians or argued for democracy or tolerance for other religions or anything at all connected with any of the ideals of the Tetepians. No, they would say, they tried that in Tetepe and look what a disaster that was. Let them kill themselves. We'll all be better off. And it looked like maybe they were right. *Who the hell cares?*

The creature in Tomadus's gut began doing cartwheels on his stomach lining. *What the hell? I did what I could. What more can you ask? And now, look at me. I disgust myself.*

"Hey old buddy, how are your dreams?" It was Batu, pulling up a bar stool next to him. "Get me and my friend a couple more Gladiators."

The bartender shook his head. "I'll get one for you. He's had enough."

"Tomadus, you look terrible." Batu set his pipe on the bar and rested his hands on Tomadus's shoulders. "Dear Jupiter. How long has it been since you slept?"

Tomadus shrugged. "Days. The dreams. I can't sleep."

"Screw the dreams. You have to sleep, man. Come on, I'm taking you home."

"No!" Tomadus flung his elbow to shake his friend's hand from his arm.

"You are obviously upset. Is it that same dream?"

"No dream. Two worlds. I live in two worlds. You ever see St. Peters? Huh? Beautiful. Middle of Rome."

"What?"

"Course you haven't, because you're stuck in this world."

Batu shook his head. "You're rambling nonsense. Let me get you home and we can talk about it in the morning."

"No."

"Suit yourself, but I'm not leaving until you do."

Tomadus turned back toward the bar and fell off his stool, flat on the floor. Batu tried to help him to his feet, but he just stayed in a fetal position with his head between his hands, hoping it would all end.

The visi-scan reporter shifted to a different story: "Several members of the Way were arrested this morning in Neapolis for violating the Florentia Protocol. Released on bail this afternoon, the Way's leader, Isa, once again spoke for the group and ended with a plea."

Tomadus heard the voice of the gentle man in the white robes coming from the visi-scan above. "We have come as servants of *veritas*, but the Romanus hierarchy chose to arrest us for speaking the truth. What do they fear? We come from the Palestinian Province, and so have no earthly power, so what we say should mean nothing to them. And yet, our hands and ankles were bound. They tell us we must not speak of God to Romani in public. But how can we remain silent when so many souls cry out for help? The rocks themselves scream for justice, for love, for peace. I call to all of you who can see the light of our yesterdays and search for truth. Follow your yearning. Follow me, and I will lead you to paradise."

Tomadus's eyes opened abruptly. He sprung up like the *arak* had been washed from his bloodstream, staring at the visi-scan screen for a full five minutes, mouth agape. "The Light of our Yesterdays," he repeated. "Could it be that I am not alone?"

"What are you talking about?" Batu said. "He's just another cult crazy."

"Don't you get it? He sees what I see. He understands. The Light…the Light of our Yesterdays!"

"Tomadus, don't look for easy answers to your troubles in the incantations of soothsayers. It is pure coincidence."

"But he touched me when the light first started. He must be connected."

Batu shook his head.

"I'm telling you, he understands me. 'Search for the truth. Follow your yearning.' It is the creature."

"The creature?"

"You wouldn't understand."

"No, I wouldn't. Let's get you home."

Tomadus smiled and nodded. "I think I can finally sleep."

SECOND PART, THE FIRST: CONTEMPLATION

"We hear a cry of fear: terror, not peace."

– The Old Testament—Jer 30:5

"God does not change the condition of a people unless they change what is in themselves."

– The Qur'an—Thunder 13:11

"He will not speak on his own, but he will speak what he hears, and will declare to you the things that are coming."

– The New Testament—Jn 16:13

HUXLEY SAT WITH his hands holding his face, his elbows resting on his desk. He did not hear the knock on his door, but the warm feminine voice pulled him out of his wallowing brainstorm. "Mr. Huxley, sir, is there anything I can do?"

He sighed deeply and smiled, looking up toward the door. "How about have a seat and cheer me up?"

Kira Sampson, a godsend of an assistant in good times and bad, closed the door and sat in one of the chairs opposite his desk. She had that earnest look of the naïve college grad still trying to figure out why her bubble had just burst.

Huxley looked down at his desk. "I suppose the news is flying around the office already?"

"News? It was more like a weather report: 'Hurricane in the old man's office.' We couldn't help but hear a bit of it. Am I next?"

Huxley grimaced, shaking his head. "Blount won't hold it over you. I played the game a bit too close to the vest. 'Reckless,' he said. 'Almost criminal.' But you didn't know about the phone contacts. The funny thing is, I'm not sure how he found out. I was playing ball with my contacts at Aman, so the Israelis had no interest in blowing this back on me. Maybe they let it slip in official papers. Anyway, he and the spy boys are not too fond of having me lead an investigation that has become so personal.

Maybe if I'd told him earlier I could have convinced him, but now it's too late. At least he didn't take me off the thing completely."

She tilted her head a touch to the side. "How could he? You're the best investigator here, and everyone knows it."

"Thanks. I'm tainted on this one. 'Can't think straight. Too much family history.' So now I get to partner up with an old 'friend' from CIA, Ken Mayer. Unfortunately, he usually likes to bring a missile to a knife fight. He lacks subtlety and will try to go scorched earth and probably screw this thing up. At least he doesn't know…"

"Know what?" she asked.

Huxley looked her directly in the eye for a few seconds. He needed her in his confidence. "Have you mentioned anything about Anwari to anyone?"

She shook her head. "I ran those searches myself."

"Well, don't. It may be a key to solving this thing, and Mayer would just bring him in for a deep interrogation and blow the lead. I suppose they could backtrack your searches, but why would they? No, just keep it to yourself. If it blows back, just tell them I told you Anwari explained the coincidences to me and I told you to drop it. Got it?"

Kira nodded slowly, her lips just hedging up on the corners.

Huxley flashed a confident smile back. *She'll do just fine.* "Thanks. I probably should gather my thoughts. Run the contacts list I gave you through the pattern software and see if it comes up with anything. You can bet the spy boys are analyzing it already—had to download it to the boss this morning."

As she closed the door behind her, Huxley ran his hand through his hair. Where would this go? Mayer was a perfectly competent operator, at least when a light hand wasn't needed. But he didn't want Mayer up his ass again like at CIA. *You refuse to torture a guy and Mayer shines a spotlight on every little problem in your life and then declares you unstable. Asshole.* Mayer had been undercutting him ever since Huxley had called out his CYA bullshit at CIA. The guy always made sure he never took the blame for anything. His story may have matched the official record, but that official record always seemed to vary just enough to mask the real truth.

By now Mayer was poring through the report Huxley prepared in the transport last night. Mayer now knew the nuclear connection to the Israeli chemist but not the precise source. They would try to respect that. He knew about the Vatican connection, but was there really anything there? And he knew Dracoratio (or Udani) and Pardus were now the main suspects. Huxley would get a call this morning requesting a personal debriefing. And then Mayer would try to take over everything. Huxley couldn't let that happen, not when someone in the Agency had a big mouth—or worse.

❧ ❧ ❧

Biting his lip and rocking on his heels, Anwari let his eyes dart around the street. "Sorry, Imam, but he's gone. I saw him leave on a military helicopter last night. I have no idea where he is headed."

"No worries, Abdul. He is home safe in DC. You have done your job well."

Anwari tipped the bottom of the phone above his forehead and puffed the air out of his cheeks. Replacing the microphone by his mouth, he asked calmly, "Why? He isn't done here, is he?"

"The case finally caught up with him. Anyway, we are still on track."

"All right. I have nothing to do here. Can I help you with the chemist and his family?"

"No longer your concern," Pardus said.

"I could help on the interrogations."

"You would not want that, Abdul."

Anwari closed his eyes and breathed deeply. "There must be something—"

"Leave it be. I will take it from here. I have other plans for you. You might even get to take a tour of the Washington sights, but we shall see. Have you been questioned by the Carabinieri?"

"Why?" Anwari asked.

"You were at the hotel. They probably have some footage of you."

"I was a guest, remember? They would not have seen much of me. My face was covered during the op. No worries, as you say."

"All right. I shall be in touch. Until then, enjoy Italy. You are a tourist, remember?"

"Sure." Anwari closed the cheap flip phone. He had picked up the thing with pre-paid minutes and attached his scrambler chip from Pardus.

He was using a phone per week at this pace, but better safe than sorry. He walked back into the chemical warehouse and heard two of the guys cheering from the office. He walked into the office and saw the Al Jazeera network covering a bombing at a London train station: 25 people killed, including 10 women and 7 children. Funny how you always had to do the math to see how many adult men were killed. Another 45 had been injured.

The fat terrorist laughed. "When will the infidels learn? They will never hide from the hands of Allah. We are everywhere."

Anwari bristled. *Idiot. Christians are not even infidels. They are People of the Book.*

After a minute of watching the carnage on the television screen, Anwari walked out of the room and back outside to get some air. He pulled out the picture of his brother and the only family he could remember. He kept asking himself the questions that increasingly haunted his daily reflections. Is this life really for me? Is this even a life? Brother, is this what you really want from me? You asked for vengeance, but to kill innocents? Anwari recalled the scene of the two young daughters of the Israeli chemist being dragged away screaming, and his eyes became glassy as he fought back the tears.

He closed his eyes and the image of Karim reappeared for what seemed the millionth time:

His brother was lying in his hospital bed, his legs gone and his head wrapped with bandages, only one eye visible. The other eye had been left among the bloody pool of detached legs, arms and other body parts of his friends and family in the rubble of the house in Jalalabad. Karim was screaming at him in Persian, "You must avenge this, Abdul, or in the eyes of Allah, you are as guilty as those who maimed me and killed my wife and children!" Anwari had shuddered and thought, though he could never say it aloud, that he was already just as guilty, except for the spook and those bastards who protected him...

He had never managed to ask his brother to forgive him, but then his brother never really knew what he had done. Anwari looked up at the stars. *Allah, I beg of you, show me the way.*

CHAPTER 28

HUXLEY YAWNED AND grabbed his cup of coffee, but it was empty. *Shit.* After only an hour or two of shut-eye on the transport back from Rome last night, the sleep demons were beginning to haunt him. But he had to figure out the key to this damn contacts list. Something was trying to wriggle out of the mess, but nobody had figured it out yet—not even the CIA analysts.

As Huxley had expected, Ken Mayer had cornered him a few hours ago. Then Huxley's prediction had fallen apart. Mayer was letting him run with the case, or so he had said. CIA could not afford to blow the relationships Huxley had developed with D'Amare and Captain Yadin. They would work up an analysis, work on a few "extra" angles Mayer was not at liberty to disclose, and Mayer would run the show. Huxley would still be the front man on his part of the investigation.

It was better than Huxley had expected—too much better. Could Mayer be the mole? He had inexplicably given Huxley free reign. Maybe Mayer just viewed this as a dead-end case and wanted Huxley to be left alone as the eventual loser. The guy had never liked him, but that was taking professional dislike a bit too far. This thing involved nuclear weapons, and Mayer and his CIA chieftains knew it too, or they would not have called him back from Rome at a moment's notice. Nobody would use a case like this to get a little personal revenge, not even Ken Mayer. Had

Mayer suddenly become subtle? He'd just need to keep filing those partial "complete reports" with enough intel to keep Mayer off him long enough to solve this thing.

Solve this thing. Normally that seemed the inevitable conclusion to him, but so far the case had eluded him, at least today while his brain still muddled through its lack of sleep. The Shakespeare thing befuddled him. What kind of terrorist puts a Shakespearean quote into a clue? He stared at the printout he had made earlier today—the text from Act I, Scene II of *Measure for Measure*, with the quote from the contacts list underlined:

Lucio: If the Duke with the other dukes come not to com-position with the King of Hungary, why then all the dukes fall upon the King.

1. Gent.: Heaven grant us its peace, but not the King of Hungary's!

2. Gent.: Amen.

Lucio: Thou conclud'st like the sanctimonious pirate, that went to sea with the Ten Commandements, but scrap'd one out of the table.

2. Gent.: "Thou shalt not steal"?

Lucio: Ay, that he raz'd.

1 Gent.:   Why, 'twas a commandment to command the cap-tain and all the rest from their functions; they put forth to steal. There's not a soldier of us all, that in the thanksgiving before meat, do relish the petition well that prays for peace.

2 Gent.:   I never heard any soldier dislike it.

Lucio: I believe thee; for I think thou never wast where grace was said.

2 Gent.:   <u>No? a dozen times at least.</u>

1 Gent.:   What? in metre?

Lucio: In any proportion, or in any language.

1 Gent.:   I think, or in any religion.

Lucio: Ay, why not? Grace is grace, despite of all the controversy; as for example, thou thyself art a wicked villain, despite of all grace.

1 Gent.:   Well; there went but a pair of shears between us.

The passage seemed to be nothing more than a typical comic Shakespearean scene: a few scoundrel friends comparing the poverty of their virtue and wealth of their hypocrisy. They seemingly prayed for peace but not when it did not suit them—just as a pirate was willing to exclude that particular commandment from God that did not quite suit his trade. It was a nice introduction to this unusual Shakespearean comedy—the last the bard ever wrote. The point of the play seemed to be to question people who judged others but expected not to be judged themselves. But it was more than that.

Many thought the play had a problematic ending. In trying to remain true to the comedic form of the day, the play went for what has now become the usual happy Hollywood ending, but it seemed to fail miserably. Did the great Shakespeare fail? Perhaps; however, some experts saw his failure instead as a brilliant criticism of the classic comedic form. He had forced his main character, the Duke, to orchestrate events quite artificially to arrive at a conclusion that proved completely implausible and unsatisfying, yet still arguably "happy" by the standards of the day. By doing so, Shakespeare seemed to be saying, "See how stupid this is? I am moving on to something less hollow and more real." And so he did. He went on to write the greatest tragedies ever written, where everyone could die as they should, even if a bit too dramatically.

Huxley was dying himself here. Despite studying the whole play and this individual scene, no recognizable clue emerged. He tried putting words in the scene with words in the contacts list, but nothing worked. He looked at the characters names and tried to divine some relation to today's world, but nothing clicked. When he thought about the references to the Ten Commandments and the grace being said in "any religion," he figured he was getting somewhere, but nowhere arrived way too quickly. The other clues had all involved prominent religious places or events, so why not this one? And yes, this play touched on religion, but he could not grasp any answer that seemed to satisfy. Exhausted, he laid his head down on his desk for a moment. Maybe a ten-minute micro-nap would bring his senses back…

…He was dressed strangely, in multi-colored robes, as were all of those around him. They were in a huge conference hall filled with people hawking their wares as he tried to avoid them. Then he saw a man in white robes move toward him, introduce himself and shake his hand. When the man touched him, a blinding light filled his vision. For a brief moment, he had seen himself again in normal attire, back in Ramat David, thinking about his mother, his forsaken mother. Then the image disappeared and he saw the man in the white robes again, bowing toward him and smiling…

The phone rang Huxley awake. It was Ms. Blankenship, the receptionist. "Mr. Huxley, you received a call from the office of Ambassador Kadir al-Razin al-Asr. They said the ambassador had heard you were back in town and tomorrow morning would be an excellent time for the ambassador to, and I was asked to quote this directly, 'watch you flail harmlessly at squash balls.' Is this a joke, Mr. Huxley?"

He shook his head. It had been a month since they had played, a long time in the ongoing saga of Huxley getting schooled by the Kad-man in a sport Huxley didn't particularly enjoy. He had kept showing up anyway because it was the only chance he usually had to get breakfast with the busy diplomat who had once been his Harvard roommate. "Thanks. Can you call the embassy and let them know I'm up for another beating?"

A few minutes later, while he was still studying the passage from *Measure for Measure*, the phone rang again and he saw reception was on the line. "Yes, Ms. Blankenship, did that little bastard need to talk to me directly?"

"Uh, no, I don't think so, sir," she said. "Are you referring to the ambassador? His office said you two were 'on' at the usual time. But, no, you are quite popular today, Mr. Huxley. You have a call from yet another foreigner. Would you like to speak to a Sonatina D'Amare? She is calling from Italy and claims you know her, though I hardly understand how, given she sounds like a perfectly charming young lady."

Huxley improved his tone dramatically, "Sorry for my language, Ms. Blankenship. Sometimes I forget myself when it comes to my old friend, the ambassador. Yes, please, put her through." He waited for the click. "Hello, Ms. D'Amare, uh, I'm sorry, Sonatina, it is good to hear from you."

"Maybe you were right the first time, Mr. Huxley. Perhaps we should go back to our surnames after you left me so abruptly last evening?"

Huxley feigned a deep sigh. Thank goodness her tone had been light and playful. With a bit of melodrama, he said, "Sonatina, I apologize. I allowed events to overtake me, and, of course, your insights overwhelmed me."

"My insights? Into what?"

Huxley replied, "That's a state secret, I'm afraid. You'd have to torture it out of me."

"I'm certain I could find a better way," Sonatina said.

"Yeah, well, I guess when I'm in Rome again, I'll have to be careful. By the way, I'll be there next week. Can you set up a meeting with the Colonel of the Swiss Guard for me?"

"Of course. But your assistant could do that herself."

"Ah, but then I would not have a good reason to see you again, would I? You are my principal Vatican contact, so let's keep it that way. Maybe I can even scrape up a few coins for another dinner?"

"Are you trying to fatten me up for the kill?"

Huxley's brow furrowed as his eyes narrowed. *A strange double meaning?* "No, I...I just wanted to make up for my haste last evening. If at first you don't succeed..."

"Succeed at what?"

He stroked his chin. *Now I can't read her tone again.* "Well...I hope

I do not search for victory in the Pyrrhic sense." When she laughed, it gave him a chance to change the subject. "Seriously, given your tremendous insights thus far, might I impose upon your clever brain once again?"

"When you are so complimentary, how can I refuse?"

"*Grazie*. I assume you recall our little conversation about Shakespeare?"

"I do, but I do not recall helping you much," Sonatina said.

"Ah, but you have. I've been struggling with this thing most of the day without much luck. The play seems to fit, the reference to Shakespeare's mother seems to fit, but I need to find something more concrete."

"Well, I can hardly believe you'll find something concrete in a Shakespearean play."

"Why not?" Huxley asked.

"Well, it is not quite math, is it? It may consist of abstract concepts, but like any great art, the concepts are wrapped in multiple levels of meaning. And, of course, Shakespeare bound all of his meaning in poetry, which makes it much harder, even for those who speak English as their first language. Though I do believe he managed to demonstrate his mastery despite the constraints of his genre."

"Constraints? You mean the comedic form?"

"No, not the form of the play," she said, "the constraints on the language. So many English authors of the period wrote plays at that time in that silly iambic pentameter rhythm. The Lord knows it is a miracle anybody ever understands what the characters are saying."

That familiar tingle radiated down Huxley's spine and out his leg and arms. Somehow, he knew she had again shown him the way. Rhythm. What a dope he had been. Shakespeare was all about rhythm. He was a poet with very little rhyme, but a master of iambic pentameter. Only today's accomplished actors could pull off Shakespearean dialogue without the rhythm sounding artificial to a modern audience's ears. The great ones made the dialogue sing. He looked at the printout in confirmation:

"2 Gent.: No? a dozen times at least.
"1 Gent.: What? in metre?"

The clue wasn't about the nature of the play or the comedic form or even religion after all. It was the simplest of all codes in a child's codebook. One entry has the code, the next the translation. The words "in metre" provided the translation and the answer. By itself, "in metre" was useless. But he had an enormous set of meaningless English contacts from Najwa's phone to parse. The remainder of the contacts list must be coded in the same metre Shakespeare always used—iambic pentameter. That rhythmic system employed 10 syllables per line and placed a stress on every second syllable (iambic) for a total of five pairs of syllables (thus, pentameter).

Huxley was stirred from his deep thought by her melodic voice, "*Sei qui*, Christian?"

"Sonatina, *sei un genio*."

"I a genius? Again? What did I say this time?"

"It is uncanny, but you always seem to say exactly what I need to hear. Thank you again for your help. I have to go now. See you in a few days. *Ciao*." He hung up the phone, feeling renewed energy surging through his brain. He opened the contacts list and began scribbling out possibilities on a pad of paper. The effort would take him late into the night, but when he finally set down his pencil and smiled, he hoped it would not prove to be yet another Pyrrhic victory.

<h1 style="text-align:center">CHAPTER 29</h1>

"**S**ix-two," Huxley heard the Kad-man announce, and it registered somewhere in the back of his mind.

Since his muscle memory was well-developed, some part of his brain would tell his eyes to follow the ball travelling from Kadir's racquet to the front wall, this time arcing high off the wall toward the opposite back corner, and that memory would move his body roughly into a position for a chance at a shot, all without much interference from his cerebral cortex, which right now could not help but focus nearly all of its energies on the little enigma he had uncovered last evening.

From a seemingly meaningless set of English-language contacts in an Islamic terrorist's cell phone, using a code derived from a play by the greatest master of English drama, he had discovered a new poem.

"Seven-two," he heard Kad announce.

The poem was itself in iambic pentameter, which made the clue even more, well, poetic. Writing poetry was never his strength, but he knew when even the mere turn of a phrase in common prose felt poetic to him. This enigma was like that, but its greatest poetry derived not from the turn of a new phrase but from the turn of a new clue.

"Eight-two."

When Huxley had found the pattern leading to the poem, he had been pretty proud of himself. Iambic pentameter: the numbers two and five. It seemed like a simple algorithm. But he had to apply about fifty different permutations to the contacts list before settling on the right one. It wasn't just the pattern, it was the starting point and direction. Did it start at the beginning of the alphabet and work backward, or the opposite? Well, neither actually. Then he had tried thinking like a story and the puzzle had fallen into place. His entry and that of his pseudo mother, Maryam Huxley, had pretty much been used up. So he just continued with the "story" and moved to the next entry posted in English. When he had looked at the second "word" (he treated a number as a word) in the fifth fill-in space in that entry, the address for Donald Jacobs, it gave him the word "Just." He had continued "reading" by skipping to the fifth fill-in space after that (using English entries only). This one had been located in the "Company" section of the contact for "Chaiang Fenge Jiang." The company name was "Chaiang's take out." By choosing the second word, he had written "take." So now he had: "Just take." It had sounded promising. He had kept working at it and had to add his own punctuation occasionally, but the thing had begun to make sense.

"Nine-two," he thought he heard Kad bellow.

By the time he had finished decoding the contacts list last evening, he had written a nine-line poem in iambic pentameter, finishing with double couplets:

> Just take a look at her—do not believe
> The Word begot from altar writers past.
> We do believe, but just the simple Truth.
> We pray within The bawd, where only He
> Did soar so high above three centuries.
> Now cherish deep within our words of Lord
> The times her forlorn shrine has been restored:
> The main lies here all split apart in two,
> While source of thee doth hold a simpler view.

He had emerged from a long search in the cold darkness only to find himself surrounded by a dense fog.

"Son of a bitch!" Kadir screamed.

The stress in Kad's voice told some little part of Huxley's conscience mind that he had just won a point. He flashed a big smile.

Kadir shook his head. "I do not know why I bother serving so finely to you today, Hux. I hardly need it. Damned service fault just cost me a point."

Huxley shrugged at Kadir with a "Sorry you suck so bad" look, grabbed the little rubber ball, walked over to the service box and announced with pride, "Three-nine."

His smugness lasted only a few seconds more as Kadir quickly disposed of his serve with a perfect squeeze boast down the left wall. "Ten-three, game and match point," Kadir announced with quite appropriate in-your-face airs. The match ended in another five seconds with Kadir showing his big white teeth planted firmly inside a huge sarcastic smile. "Game and match for the Alumni Championship, my friend, unless you want to suffer through another one today? No? I did not think so. It was not exactly your best effort, was it? You getting out of shape or have you lost your edge?"

"Sorry." Huxley flashed his best deferential smile. "I know I didn't give you much of a game, master of the universe." He held his two arms straight in front of his body and bowed deeply toward Kadir.

Kadir laughed, grabbed Huxley around the shoulders and rubbed his head. "Now that is proper respect for one of your lowly station, Sko-B."

Huxley gave Kadir a quick pinch in the abdomen with his free arm, and the large man jumped and released him. "Sorry I allowed myself to be distracted by other thoughts during today's beating, master."

"Well, show some focus next time. You know it is hard to enjoy giving a good beating when your target fails to cringe from the pain."

"You always were a Kad, you son-of-a-bitch," Huxley responded.

They laughed and Huxley enjoyed the glow for a long time. That was why he played the man. The force of Kad's personality could make you feel like you really enjoyed the beating after all. A few days later, you were unsure why, but during those few moments with him everything felt a little lighter.

Thirty minutes later, the two men were seated in their favorite post-squash restaurant, eating American breakfasts, sipping coffee and comparing stories from the last month. "Have you seen Hanna lately?" Kadir asked.

Huxley winced. "You haven't mentioned her for years, so why now? You want to re-establish your Jewish relationships? I thought you forgot her ten minutes after you dumped her ass just before graduation."

"That is about right—the forgetting part, I mean. No big deal. I just thought I caught a glimpse of her a few weeks ago leaving a bar near the Capitol. I figured maybe she was in town to see you."

Huxley had a funny look on his face. "Not a chance. Haven't seen her since well before my mom died." He rubbed the back of his head.

Kadir drew back. "I am sorry I brought it up. How stupid of me. And just to set the record straight, I never dumped her, not exactly. I simply solved a little career problem with some adept diplomacy."

"Career problem?"

"Could you imagine how far I would have risen as an Arab diplomat with a Jewish wife? It doesn't matter that she is an atheist—where I come from she is still the enemy. So when the Harvard party was over I simply told her our backgrounds were incompatible with marriage, but we could still be 'close secret friends' if she liked. I knew she would fly away. I think she called me a 'Stinking Arab Pig' and stormed out. Not one of her more innovative nicknames, yes?"

Huxley laughed. "Sounds a bit too familiar. I wonder what she's up to these days?"

"You looking to renew your acquaintance?"

"Not a chance." Huxley tilted his head at Kadir. "You might as well know that I have a new target for my covertly-complicated, salaciously-sensitive, romantic affectations."

"Whoa. The Scholar Boy arises again. Where do you get that crap?"

"Women's magazines. You wouldn't believe the odd shit you can learn." They laughed.

"Who is this new mystery gal?" Kadir asked.

"An artsy Italian. You know you can't steal her because she is way too sophisticated for you." They laughed a bit harder.

"An Italian, you say? Then no doubt she would fall for my Arab-American accent and my amazing Arab visage. Most of the Mediterranean women do, you know."

Huxley choked and involuntarily spit his eggs out and onto his plate.

Then they both roared in laughter. After a few moments, Huxley regained his composure. "Why haven't you married? You too busy enjoying your playboy life? I imagine there are quite a few Arab women who could look beyond your putrid appearance and find some merit in your station in life?"

"Oh I have to fight them off, mostly because of my appearance, though. 'Putrid?' You have obviously been out of Harvard for too long, Sko-B. I am quite certain you must have meant 'heroic.'"

"OK, I admit a few woman might find you attractive, but then I suppose they would find out your nickname fits you, Kad-man."

Kadir grinned. "That is when I reel them in with the Ambassadorship and they discover I am actually a breath of fresh air. Every woman loves a man of peace."

"Is that your full title, Ambassador of Peace?"

"Close enough. Sure, my official title is still the United Arab Emirates' Ambassador to the United States, but do not forget I also helped found the Brotherhood of Arab Nations for Peace. All I have to do is combine the two and slur it a little and there is your magnanimous title."

Huxley shook his head. "You are a peace all right—a piece of work."

"Hey, you forgetting all the tips I have handed over to you Americans the last few years? You know I get crap from my own family for helping you so much. At least you could give me the title."

"Okay. Henceforth, I shall call thee, 'Ambassador of Peace.'" Huxley bowed deeply with great panache.

Kadir looked taken aback. "Like hell you will." They laughed again.

Huxley leaned forward and lowered his voice. "Speaking of terrorism, you haven't helped me out much lately. Care to give it a try? Maybe you'll free my mind for a better squash game next time."

Kadir's voice turned more serious. "Always glad to help, Hux. What have you got yourself into?"

"You remember when we used to participate in those elaborate scavenger hunt contests in Cambridge, the ones sponsored by Adams House?"

"Sure. Hey, we almost won our junior year until you decided you had to go study for a mid-term. The team fared none too well at that shit without you."

"It was plenty fun when it didn't matter, but now that it does matter, it kinda hurts."

Huxley told his buddy generally about the clues and where they had taken him. Since the investigation was still secret, he saved most of the details, but gave enough of the picture to get another perspective.

When Huxley finished, Kadir sat a long time with his palms together in front of his chest, his finger tips bouncing off of his closed lips, obviously lost in thought. After raising his head and eyes back to Huxley, he said, "I do not believe I can help you much. You seem to be making pretty good progress on your own. I will give it some thought and call you if something occurs to me. Right now, nothing. Sorry, Hux. I may be the Alumni Squash Champion, but it seems you remain the Alumni Scavenger Champ. Good luck."

CHAPTER 30

ONATINA'S HAND FELT soft and warm and supple. Huxley pulled it up to his lips and kissed it lightly, and then let their clasped hands drop between them. He saw her smile gently out of the corner of his eye, and he felt a touch flush.

After dinner, they had slowly strolled back toward the Vatican, finally crossing the Tiber at the *Ponte Umberto I*. The river gleamed both with white-yellow lights from the *Ponte Sant' Angelo* spanning the river ahead and with nearly a rainbow of reds, greens, blues and purples reflecting from the nighttime markets along the river's right edge. Above to the right in the foreground stood *Castel Sant' Angelo*, a nearly two thousand year old Roman mausoleum for Hadrian that had been converted over the years into a Roman Catholic fortress, prison and residence. Despite *Sant' Angelo's* massive size, it was still dominated by the majestic dome of St. Peter's Basilica ten blocks beyond, its cupola glowing in the night, infusing the atmosphere all around with self-assured awe.

Sonatina turned toward Huxley and grabbed his other hand. "Thank you again for dinner, Chris. And to think you did not even demand any secrets of me this time."

"Ah, but the night is young."

"That it is. What shall we do with the rest of it?" Sonatina smiled coyly, but as he leaned in toward her, she gracefully twirled and danced over the bridge, dragging him behind her with their still conjoined hands.

"Well, I suppose we could find a place to dance," he said.

She winked at him. "Let's just keep walking on such a beautiful night."

As they made their way through the open-air night market, Huxley released Sonatina's hand as he turned to pick up and examine a bauble offered by one of the rugged merchants. In the periphery to his left, a dark figure moved quickly about fifty yards away. He straightened up and tried to find the figure under the streetlights beside the river. Had the man, if it was a man, darted behind a tree or bush or sign? He waited about thirty seconds, but nothing moved.

When he turned back, he realized Sonatina had disappeared. When he scanned through the myriad of booths and lights dangling down, he saw her nowhere. He took a few hurried steps toward *Sant' Angelo*. Just when he began running, he saw her stand up from the other side of a kiosk not ten yards away. He slowed and walked around the kiosk, where he was surprised to see the face of a young boy grinning and gazing back up at her.

"*Prego, prego,*" Sonatina said to the child, gently patting him on the shoulder. She nodded to the elderly woman standing behind the kiosk before she saw Huxley approach. "Oh, there you are, Chris."

"I thought I'd lost you. Did you see the man behind us by the bridge?"

She shook her head. "Sorry."

"I should go check it out."

Huxley began turning back, but she grabbed his shoulder and turned him. "Not tonight," she whispered. "Can you give it a rest for one evening? The whole world is not out to get you, you know."

"Maybe." He looked at the little boy spooning something into his mouth. "What's with the kid?"

"He looked sad, so I bought him a little gelato. He looks much happier now, no?"

"You know him?"

"No. Why would you think that?"

Huxley smiled, the warmth flowing slowly through his body. Yes, he would give it a rest this evening. He had hoped to end the night quite differently, but something inside told him to slow down. *She's far too precious for that.* So his first real date with Sonatina ended at her doorstep, with a simple peck on her cheek. The warm smile she bestowed upon him in return told him he had made the right move.

❊ ❊ ❊

As the morning sun peeked over a nearby building, Anwari finished working the clay-like material carefully into the cable-connector box. The C4 felt natural in his hands. He had only produced a few actual bombs by himself, but he had defused many more during his days with the Afghan Army and the Americans. Once you removed the detonator, the shit was so stable you could light it up and heat your lunch with it and it still wouldn't explode—but you wouldn't want to stomp on it when it was lit. It needed both heat and enough pressure, but when they were both properly supplied by a detonator, all hell would break loose. So you could always be damn comfortable shaping the clay to fit your particular explosive needs—just keep the detonator away until you were finished. He had only learned how to do that after he had met Pardus and taken some specialized training, but already he had become a master "munitions expert" for the group.

Anwari closed the box and walked to the back of the van marked with the same logo as his overalls—the logo familiar to customers of a local cable TV provider. He pulled the electronics package out of the rear of the van and returned to the box. This was where he had to be careful. He mounted the controller on the inside cover of the box and then delicately inserted the detonators into the C4. He closed the box and looked around as naturally as he could. He had verified earlier that no cameras covered the narrow residential street. That was critical. Now he glanced around furtively and saw no one. Of course, someone could still be peering out a window, but with his cap, glasses and repairman uniform, he blended in perfectly, so any wandering eyes would not bother to look closely enough to identify him later.

❊ ❊ ❊

Huxley felt the vibration on his buttocks from the toilet seat as the Trenitalia train rumbled down the tracks toward that triumph of the

Italian Renaissance—Florence. Although it was somewhat unsettling going to the john on a moving platform, it gave him time for reflection. Florence boasted some of the greatest art the world had ever seen—from Michelangelo's *David* in the Academie d'Arte to da Vinci's *Annunciation* in the Uffizi, to Brunelleschi's red-brick masterpiece dome of *Il Duomo di Firenze*—but none of these were his destination. He was travelling to the home of Dante Tocelli to confirm what seemed to be yet another dead-end.

Huxley had obtained the address during his meeting with the Swiss Guard. At Sonatina's request, Colonel Zaugg had met with him yesterday and was joined by the Director of the Corps of Gendarmerie of Vatican City, Antony Cepini. The existence of this organization had surprised Huxley. In his naïveté, he had thought the Swiss Guard took care of all police matters within the Vatican. It turned out the Swiss Guard mostly protected the pope; conversely, while the Corps of Gendarmerie provided additional security for the pope (and had machine guns at its disposal), it mostly protected the Vatican City properties. Its officers were the uniformed police stationed in the city. But it turned out they were much more than that.

Director Cepini had admitted that Dante Tocelli had been employed by the Corps in a "special investigatory role" within the *Unità Antisabotaggio,* or Anti Sabotage Unit. The unit acted somewhat like the Vatican's own tiny Homeland Security branch. As an investigator with U.S. Homeland Security, Huxley figured he would have known about this little sister organization. Then again, he had not worked closely with the Vatican offices, even when he had foiled the attempt to blow up the Sistine Chapel.

After some poking and prodding by Huxley and a carefully placed reminder about the Sistine Chapel affair, Director Cepini had given him more details of Dante Tocelli's "special investigatory role." Tocelli had been recruited his first year as a Sapienza student. The Vatican had received some reports of radicals at the school planning demonstrations at the Vatican. Tocelli had been recommended by a trusted Vatican official, whose name Cepini and Zaugg refused to give. Tocelli managed to infiltrate the radical student group and discovered that the intel was overblown—a drunk student shooting off his mouth during a house party that happened to include various members of the group.

Now, a couple years later, Tocelli had been sent on a more danger-ous mission. The Vatican had received an anonymous tip about a terrorist attempt to blow up all of Vatican City. Though alleging a Muslim extremist plot, the tip explained more could be discovered at Tel Megiddo. Tocelli's archaeology background made him the perfect undercover investigator. When Huxley had pointed out that undercover investigators acting out-side of their own national boundaries are sometimes called spies, Director Cepini had scoffed: "He wasn't investigating another government or any-thing like that, for goodness sake."

Whether foreign spy or undercover investigator, Dante Tocelli had never relayed any terribly useful intelligence. Oh, he had reported a few times that there seemed to be something to the tip and that perhaps the Ramat David Airbase was somehow involved, but it was all vague and gen-eral. He needed more time to dig, and not just to uncover old staircases and stables. Then Director Cepini had received a coded message from him stating that a leopard may be involved. This had piqued Huxley's interest, and he had asked if Tocelli had used the name "Pardus." Yes, it is "leopard" in Latin, had come the reply. Tocelli had been expected to return soon and make a complete report. Unfortunately, they never received the final report nor heard from Tocelli again. According to the immigration officials, after Tocelli had re-entered Italy, he completely disappeared despite the Corps' extensive search for him. Yes, they had interviewed Tocelli's family in Florence, but the family had not seen him since he left for Israel. The Corps had never shared any of this information with U.S. Homeland Security because there did not seem to be any hard information to share. They had not wished to appear as fools, tilting at windmills.

The news disappointed Huxley. He had been looking for a terrorist but found just another terrorist hunter. At least it confirmed that Pardus had some involvement in the matter and that Tel Megiddo had served as some type of staging or planning post. Now, if he could discover what Dante Tocelli had planned to put in his report, he might have something tangible. It had made a trip to Florence worth the expense and time.

If this proved to be another dead end, he could track down Anwari and start pushing those buttons, but he seriously doubted that tactic would get him too far at this point. It might be easier to solve the poetic riddle he had discovered in the contacts list. The first two lines of the poem had been easy:

> Just take a look at her—do not believe
> The Word begot from altar writers past.

"Just take a look at her" was likely referring to Mary, who was depicted everywhere at the Church of the Annunciation. The rest of the two lines, "do not believe/The Word begot from altar writers past," seemed to be referring to the lines on the altar in the grotto of the Church of the Annunciation. He looked at his notes and saw the Latin reference to the opening of John's gospel and the Annunciation itself: "Here The Word Was Made Flesh." So the poem commanded him not to believe this.

The third line of the poem brought him to a full stop: "We do believe, but just the simple Truth." It seemed the "we" of the poem believed at least in Jesus, and so were Christians, but they contested the specific words of the altar because they believed in the "simple Truth." Did this mean they disputed the place of the Annunciation, the word "Here" on the altar, even though they believed in the Annunciation itself? So "The Word Was Made Flesh," but not "Here?" He had researched this possibility and found that just such a dispute had remained alive in Christianity. Catholics believed Mary had been visited by the Archangel Gabriel in her home, which was now the location of the Catholic Church of the Annunciation. The Orthodox Church believed the visit had occurred while she was drawing water from a well, and so their own Church of the Annunciation had been built there. But while that might be a truth, why was it a "simple Truth?" And how would the Orthodox Church, as stated in the fourth line, "pray within the Bawd?"

CHAPTER 31

ANWARI TOOK A seat in the café across from the station. From this spot he could watch the flurry of activity as trains arrived and departed and travelers scurried in and out of the main station entrance. He ran his thumb over the trigger on the remote control device in his pocket. The main switch was off, so there was little danger he would set off the explosive too early. He had to settle down and wait. But the waiting gave him time to think, which lately had troubled him.

Anwari had been surprised when Huxley discovered a connection to Dante Tocelli in Florence. Nevertheless, the man still did not get it. Though Huxley had proven to be quite clever, Pardus still kept outfoxing him. This latest touch would confuse matters plenty. And it would not be long before Pardus would help Anwari obtain a measure of revenge on the Americans. Revenge against Americans—a year ago, Anwari had never imagined he would feel that way...

He was angry and disillusioned from the disaster with his brother's family, but it had only made him want to quit the army, get away from the two-faced Americans, and go find a place to hide. Then Karim, staring at him with that one haunting eye, screamed the demand that still echoed in his brain. Anwari had paused and looked away in a moment of guilt but then tried to settle Karim down, whispering, "Be quiet, they will arrest you for such nonsense." And then Karim had become quiet, too quiet. But the peace had been achieved not through acceptance but defeat. The damaged artery in his brother's brain had burst and delivered him into Allah's arms at last...

❋ ❋ ❋

Returning to his seat, Huxley smiled at the two men still sitting in his booth. The older man, who looked old enough to be retired for quite a few years, smiled back through his short white beard and stood up, offering his forward-facing seat to Huxley to help with any nausea the rear-facing seat might have caused him. Huxley politely thanked the man, informed him he was not ill, and took his own seat. The man's travelling partner was twentyish—seemingly a bit too young to be the older man's son, though the two men seemed close, having employed both easy conversation and comfortable silences during the trip.

Huxley put his head against the window and thought he might drift off to sleep, but the conversation from the two men began to pique his interest. He listened with his eyes shut.

"I am so happy we were able to see the Vatican," declared the old man with a tone of true joy. "Could you believe the size of St. Peter's Basilica or the beauty of the Sistine Chapel? Where else could you find such magnificence?"

"Magnificence?" the boy said. "A magnificent waste of money that could have been used to help feed the poor. The Vatican is one of the last vestiges of a time when society threw away huge sums of money to prop up a myth that has long run its course."

The old man said nothing for a full twenty seconds. Huxley could hear him swallow hard before he spoke in a calm voice, "David, I cannot believe that is your true opinion. You are exploring your boundaries, are you not? A myth? Are you suggesting there is no God?"

The young man, David, cleared his throat but failed to loosen his larynx. "Yes. Look Father, I know I will never convince you, but do not expect me to believe. I have had years of biology and chemistry and physics at the university. I have studied the Big Bang and evolution and genetics. Man was not created in the Garden of Eden, the universe is not 7000 years old but over 13 billion years, and the Earth itself is over four billion years old. I just do not see how God enters into the picture. I am sorry."

Pretty smart kid, thought Huxley.

"These two are not mutually exclusive," the old man said.

"What do you mean?" asked David.

"Let us suppose there was a Big Bang and evolution as well. Do you think God might have had a hand in it?"

"I don't believe evolution requires intelligent design, Father."

Exactly, thought Huxley.

"Perhaps not, but let me ask you this: what came before the Big Bang?" the old man asked.

"It is impossible to know," David said, "but it may be the case that we have had many Big Bangs repeated over and over again as the universe expands and contracts over tens of billions of years."

The old man paused again, and then asked, "Okay, so let us take your supposition as fact for the moment. Still, what came before the first Big Bang?"

"Nothingness, I suppose," David said.

"Then what created the energy and matter from out of this nothingness?"

"I don't know. Nobody does. Maybe the energy and matter have always existed. Anyway, it doesn't matter, because it is clear there was no Eden, no Adam, and no Eve. The story is a myth. Science contradicts the teachings of the Church."

The old man sounded sad. "There you are wrong, David. The Roman Catholic Church learned its lesson about science long ago after suppressing Galileo and others and refusing to believe the Earth revolved around the sun instead of the other way around. We learned to focus on the spiritual and leave explanations of natural science to those who study it. The papacy has clearly stated that both the Big Bang and evolution are possible physical manifestations of God's creation. The Church takes no position on the scientific theories themselves."

"But they contradict Genesis!"

The old man said calmly, "Only if you read Genesis literally, but we do not. We see Genesis as a series of morality plays intended to teach humans about our inherent sin and how to distinguish right from wrong. Does it surprise you that God would do that? Does it surprise you that He would help us understand the struggle humans face as a species because we so often choose to separate ourselves from Him and His goodness? Does it surprise you that He would put a story of creation in the simplest terms that could possibly be understood by people of that time? No, David, read it for what it is: a reminder of how each of us as a human will always be imperfect and perhaps all too willing to allow evil into our lives when it suits our Earthly purposes. We follow Jesus and his teachings to overcome those failings of our species, but we can never be perfect. That is one of the great beauties of Jesus: he made it possible for our sins to be forgiven."

"It seems to me like you are rationalizing a clear conflict between the Old Testament and science through some smoke and mirrors by believing some biblical texts verbatim while ignoring others. Anyone can play those games. If there is a God, prove it to me."

Nice touch, Huxley thought.

The old man laughed. "You've got me there. Belief in God is a matter of faith. I cannot prove it conclusively to you with any fancy philosophical or scientific argument."

"Ha!" chortled the young man, David. "Then you must agree I am right."

"No, I simply ask you this in return: can you prove that God does not exist?"

David stared at his shoes. "Uh, I don't know."

"Well, let me cut to the chase for you. Nobody can conclusively prove whether God exists or not. It is a matter of faith. All the science in the world cannot prove this one way or another and I doubt it ever will. Oh, it can show some of our more primitive beliefs about God affecting the world around us are really the result of natural phenomenon and logical causes and effects, but this does not disprove the existence of God. Nor have the great philosophers offered any convincing proof. In fact, perhaps you have read works of the famous 18th century German philosopher, Immanuel Kant?"

David shook his head.

"My goodness," the old man continued, "Kant's writing still makes my head spin. He was quite critical of religion in many aspects and certainly was not a favorite of the Church, mind you, but he set out to prove or disprove the existence of God and ultimately concluded it was impossible to do either. He managed to effectively disprove many of the extant spurious proofs of God's existence that had been asserted before him, and that surprised a few religious folks back then, but it bothers few today. Proof is unnecessary. Belief in God is a matter of faith. And I fully agree it can neither be proven nor disproven."

"When a scientific theory cannot be proven or disproven, it is discarded. So why should I believe in God if nobody can prove He exists?"

"I challenge your assumption, David. The scientific method does not require a theory to be discarded if it has not been proven conclusively. If it fits the available facts, then it may continue until disproven. I ask you to give God the same respect."

This was too much for Huxley. He spoke as calmly as he could, although his insides were boiling, "I'm sorry, I couldn't help but overhear you. Could I bother you to butt into your conversation?"

"Please do," answered the old man.

"Is your God all-powerful?"

"I believe so."

"Does your God love all humans?" Huxley asked.

"Yes."

Huxley stared at the old man. "How can that be when He allows a beautiful human being to shrivel into an eggplant?"

"Excuse me?" the old man asked.

"Have you ever seen someone who suffers from the later stages of dementia? They waste away until they are virtually unrecognizable. Their personality changes. They become something else. They drool and snot runs out of their noses. They cannot control their bowels or bladders, and they don't even know it. They lose their human dignity. They suffer and those around them suffer. But worse yet, those who love them most cannot speak with them in any meaningful way. A son becomes a stranger to his own mother while watching her wither away to nothing. A stranger would never know they were once smart and proud and good. You tell me your God loves humans, but what kind of god could let that happen to a person he loved? I'm not saying your God caused it, but only that He must have let it happen if He exists. Why? Is He sadistic? Does He think we are worthless? Are we nothing more than rats in His grand experiment, kept fed when it suits Him and dying while He is busy working on some other plan on some other planet in this vast universe of trillions of stars? No, I don't believe a god who loves us would act in such a way. It is just one person's DNA suffering from a latent defect that finally manifested itself because of an environment corrupted by years of grief. There is no God, sir, and there is your proof."

David looked with terrified eyes at Huxley, but the old man leaned in toward Huxley and spoke softly, with eyes heavy and full of empathy. "I am so sorry for your loss, sir. I am sure it was quite difficult for you."

A strange warmth washed over Huxley's body and the tension seemed to flow out of his muscles. *Not the response I had anticipated.* This was an argument, not a wake, though the man's words were soothing somehow. This had become too personal. He'd forgotten his maxim of never arguing about religion or politics. He drew back. "Forgive me, I should not have inserted myself into your conversation. Please, accept my apologies."

The old man smiled. "No apology necessary. In fact, I prefer that you help us with this debate. Anything you might add could hit the ears of my nephew from another source when I am not present, and I would have no ability to respond. I would like him to hear both sides now."

Huxley nodded and leaned forward, somehow drawn to the old man. Then something the old man had said struck him as odd. "You said your nephew?"

The old man nodded.

"But he calls you father." Huxley said. "Unless…uh…are you a priest?"

"I am," the old man said as he nodded gently. "I have repeatedly asked David to call me 'Uncle,' but his mother, my sister, always emphasized my priestly title."

"Your sister? Is she travelling with you?"

David intervened, "She died earlier this year after a long battle with ALS. In the end, her body pretty much shriveled up, as you said, though her mind remained with her nearly to the end."

"I'm so sorry," Huxley said. "I meant no disrespect."

The old priest nodded. "Thank you. How could you know? David and I were quite close to her. Unfortunately, it seems we tend to see the ugliness of disease more closely in those whom we love the most. Now, if I could, I would like to address the point you made, if you are up to it."

"Please."

"Then I will answer your question with a question: how do you know God did not intervene in your case? I know it seemed miserable to you, but we are not competent to understand God's plans for us. He does not think as we humans do. I cannot tell you what might have happened here, but even with my human weakness I could construct a scenario where a kind and loving God might allow a loved one to live a while longer despite a debilitating illness. Were you able to spend time with her during this last stage?"

"Yes," Huxley said softly.

The old priest leaned forward and nearly whispered to Huxley, "Then perhaps God was helping you. Can you really know what your mother understood or thought when she was with you? I don't mean in the failing parts of her brain, though no doubt the chemistry was playing tricks on her, but in her heart, in her soul, if you will. You must have loved her very much, and I do not doubt she always loved you. And who knows if He intervened to call her to Heaven well before the disease would have run its natural course."

Huxley swallowed and looked at his lap and saw his left hand on his pocket. *Stop rubbing the damn thing!* His hand pulled away, but then his gut pinched again, so he put his hand back on top of the crucifix. "Thank you for that," he said to the priest weakly. After a few moments, strength returned to his voice. "I do not wish to argue with you, but I still cannot believe."

"Why is that?"

"Perhaps I, too, have been converted by science. I understand your response to the Big Bang and evolution. Still, it just doesn't ring true to my ears. I think man often accepts a mystical answer whenever science has not advanced far enough to give a complete explanation. But I believe at some point our greatest scientific minds will find the answer, a natural answer."

"I find that amusing. You challenge faith in God by giving your faith to future science?"

"I do. And though I realize it is not a perfect proof that God does not exist, all of the evidence keeps showing that the universe and life itself are explainable without any deities. How everything started may elude us, but perhaps we simply do not understand space-time well enough yet."

The old priest sat back in his chair. "You seem to see human knowledge as ultimately limitless."

"Sure. Why not?"

"Indeed. Do you have a dog?"

"No," Huxley said. "I had a little black and white one as a child. He was always begging food and licking my face. He was a joy. Why?"

"Did you teach the dog tricks—sitting, shaking his paw, rolling over, that sort of thing?"

"A few of them."

"And did the dog seem to figure out how to let you know when it needed to go outside to relieve itself?"

Huxley tilted his head and squinted. "Sure, he would stand at the door and bark."

"Did your dog ever read the New York Times?"

"What?"

"Do you know any dog that could do that?"

"Of course not," Huxley said.

"Do you think you could teach a dog to do that?"

"No, the structure of their brain is such that they cannot comprehend reading. That requires a level of complexity and abstraction that is not available to their brains."

The old priest smiled. "I see. Now, has any human ever really understood either the ultimate nature of God or the ultimate creation of the universe—not just the last Big Bang, mind you, but the actual creation?"

"Not really, but…"

"But what?"

"But that doesn't mean we couldn't," Huxley said.

"True, but like the dog, we don't know whether we ever will. We don't know whether our brains will ever have the ability to comprehend concepts that may be, as you put it, too abstract or too complex for our brain structures. Don't you think it is awfully arrogant of humans to believe they are so well evolved that they will figure everything out? By your own definition, we are animals like the dog, and the dog has limitations. Why do you believe humans have no such limitations? Could it not be that grasping the nature of God or the beginning of all things is simply beyond our ability to reason?"

Huxley shook his head. "Time has shown that we can figure out answers with the scientific method."

"Just as the dog has figured out how to ask you to let him out. I understand that this learning seems much simpler and remains of limited use because the dog cannot communicate its learning effectively to its offspring. Nevertheless, the dog has limitations and probably does not know it. Similarly, I believe humans have innate limitations, yet we are often too foolish or too stubborn to see them."

"Are you suggesting that we should stop trying? That we should assume that humankind has limits, so we should abandon further attempts to find the truth?"

"Heavens, no," said the old priest. "The value of the search alone is more than worth the effort. Humans must seek their answers—through science, philosophy and, yes, faith—but do not make the mistake of assuming that we always find that which we seek. Do not assume that the answer, if there is one, will be knowable by us."

"But these are very smart people, Father. I have to believe they will figure it out, even if not in my lifetime."

"So we are back to faith, then?" the priest asked.

"I suppose, in a way."

When Huxley's iPhone beeped, he excused the interruption and read the message from his friend Kadir:

> I considered your quandary some more and wanted to pass on a thought. The first clue used references out of the Old Testament, which is really just the Jewish bible, and the place was mentioned in that bible. The second clue used references from the New Testament, and the place is a Christian monument. Why wouldn't the third clue reference the third religion originating from Abraham—we Muslims and our bible, the Qur'an? Hope that helps. Best of luck!

"I'm sorry, Father," said Huxley, "I'll be back in a few minutes, though I'm not sure we have much more to discuss."

The priest filled his rosy cheeks, smiling and tilting his head. "Not a problem. But I think we have just begun."

❊   ❊   ❊

Anwari looked out the window of the little café to the Florence train station where he awaited Pardus's latest target. Pardus's plan would bring him still closer to avenging Karim and sticking it to those corrupt Americans who looked the other way over the death of so many Afghans. Too bad they backed up assholes like Half-Moon Mole instead of his buddy Captain Granger.

"SIGINT has confirmed the marketplace bombers hiding in this house in Jalalabad," Half-Moon Mole had said with his deep voice as he pointed at the map.

Anwari had called the spook Half-Moon Mole—not to his face but to Captain Granger—because the guy wouldn't give his own name, but you couldn't miss the large half-moon mole on his left cheek. The first time Anwari said that, Granger had laughed pretty hard but had warned Anwari to never, ever, say it to the man's face. "He's a prick, and he'll have a pound of your flesh for it," Granger had said.

Half-Moon Mole wasn't military, and when Anwari had asked, Granger just told him he was "OGA," Other Governmental Agency. That probably meant CIA. So, he was a self-important American intelligence ass who couldn't help pretending he was always in control. This OGA prick must have known Anwari had dug up the intel on the marketplace bombers himself. Anwari had always ensured his informers trusted that he would never disclose their names. And the extra money had made it easy for them to pass on a tip now and then. Of course, this bastard spook would want to take all the credit.

"We'll take a bird to within two klicks of the neighborhood at 2100 hours and work our way over from there," Granger said. "We don't want anyone running for it. We'll have one UAS up as our eyes in the sky and access to two fast movers loitering about ten klicks away. They'll carry JDAMs we can use in a pinch."

Anwari nodded. UAS was the military acronym for unmanned aerial system, what the rest of the world called a drone, and JDAM, or joint direct attack munition, was a guidance kit attached to a 500 to 2000 pound bomb that could be sent on its way from an F-16 or F-22 from miles up in the air (the fast movers loitering nearby). The thing could practically hit the little wart on your ass if you gave it the right GPS target. They were nice assets to have on a raid like this. "We got any jammers?" *Anwari asked.*

Granger smiled. "No, not for this. The force will consist of a small group so they don't see us coming. Intel has only 4 targets in the house. Might be a few armed friends with them. I got that right?" *He looked at Half-Moon Mole.*

Half-Moon Mole leaned both his huge hands on the table and stared at both of them. "Yeah, you got that right."

"Roger," *Anwari said.* "One thing, though. That area is residential. We sure it's cleared so we don't have any collateral damage?"

Half-Moon Mole sneered and narrowed his eyes at Anwari. "Yes, we are sure. Damn sure. That whole block was cleared out last week and all the residents are long gone and have not returned. These terrorists found it empty and began squatting this week."

"The whole block? So if we need the JDAM?" *Granger had asked.*

"Then use it. Look, we want you to grab these guys so we can get some further intel, but if you're in trouble, then use the JDAM. You're cleared hot," *Half-Moon Mole said.* "There's no one in that blast zone who's not the enemy. The target building is already designated as BG 1488."

Anwari said, "You sure people haven't—"

"Listen, Lieutenant," *Half-Moon Mole began, leaning forward on the table, bulging his triceps and narrowing his eyes at Anwari,* "I've seen your war record. Marvelous. You've uncovered a few bits of amateur intel along the way. Wonderful. But don't think you're the only source in town. Trust the professionals. If you can't do that, get out of the way."

Captain Granger moved between them. "Okay, we've got it. Anwari, you're in charge of the Afghan soldiers in the operation. I know you'll choose only your most trusted men. Need to ensure the mission isn't compromised, so keep OPSEC in mind."

"Got it." *Operational Security. No leaks to the enemy. Anwari smiled at Granger. The guy always had his back and usually let him learn from experience instead of just issuing condescending orders all the time. Oh, Granger would let Anwari know if he had screwed up, but just enough to drive the lesson home. And he knew he had screwed up plenty. But Granger and his guys knew how to fight like nobody else. And they were his brothers in arms, unlike that Half-Moon Mole prick, who could have been a poster boy for those Afghans who called Americans occupiers and infidels.*

This would be a small operation to ensure surprise, so he called on only ten men to complement the eight Americans. Officially, the Afghans were leading the operation as part of the turnover of forces, but everyone had known the American captain would be the one with links to the fast movers. Anwari and his men had learned a great deal about room and building clearing, but he knew it was still dangerous work—especially if the bad guys knew you were coming. He had needed men he trusted and could work well as a team, so he had handpicked soldiers he had known even before the latest war...

The waitress interrupted his concentration. "Would you like more *caffe, Signore?*"

"Sì," Anwari said. He shook his head. *How could I have been such a fool?*

❅ ❅ ❅

"Before you left," the old priest said, "you agreed that even with science you must ultimately return to faith to find the world's origins given what we know today. Is that right?"

Huxley settled back into his seat on the train. "I thought about that, and I don't quite agree. With science, I have seen evidence with my own eyes of what it can accomplish. So I don't have faith in science, I just trust it will ultimately succeed."

The old priest rubbed his beard. "I see. So you extrapolate from some evidence of the past to provide you with hope for an unknowable future?"

"I guess so. I understand it is a reach, but it is not as vacant as employing faith without any real evidence."

The old priest laughed. "I think I have given you the wrong impression. I said we cannot *prove* the existence of God. I never said there was no *evidence.*"

"What evidence?"

"Just look around you," said the old priest, gesturing toward the beauty outside of the train.

"But, Father—"

"No, stop. I know you'll just refer me to the theory of evolution." The old priest looked up and brought his palms together under his chin for a few seconds. "How about this? Consider the disciples of Jesus after his death. They put their faith in Jesus even though it meant death for all but one of them, and most were martyred in quite horrible ways. Do you think so many would allow themselves to be killed over such a long time for something they did not truly believe in? And were they not direct witnesses to what happened with Jesus? Is that not at least some of the 'past evidence' you seek?"

Huxley pulled his lips together and tilted his head back and forth. "I get it, Father, but how do we know what really happened back then?"

"You think they just made up all of the stories, even of their own martyrdom? Are you a conspiracy theorist or something? Can you imagine what it would take to make that up out of whole cloth and convert it into a religion when it was all against their own personal interests?"

"I don't know," Huxley said. "It all seems like fantasy to me. Maybe, if I had been there to see it, I could believe."

"So you are like Thomas, you must see it for yourself and put your fingers in Jesus's side to believe?" the old priest asked.

That tingle traveled down Huxley's spine again. He shook his head slowly, ran his fingers through his hair, and looked out the window.

The old priest leaned forward and touched his arm. "Look, I'm not asking you to believe here. But can you at least admit that even with science you ultimately must return to faith? It is just a different faith—a faith that all will eventually be knowable."

"I guess," Huxley replied.

"Then where should we put our faith? And must there be only one choice? I for one believe we humans have much to lose by losing faith in God."

"I have to disagree with you there, Father. Religion has often been a scourge on mankind. Look at what religious conflict causes today—Muslims kill Christians and Christians kill Muslims in droves in Africa. In the Middle East, Muslims try to kill the Jews as well as Muslims of different sects and all with the Christians caught in the cross fire, and the Jews respond by killing the Muslims as well. They have found no way to live with each other because of their religions. Even in the U.S., where religious differences have largely been tolerated, some Christian whack jobs have burned Qur'ans, killed doctors at abortion clinics and killed Sikh members at their mosque—the latter simply because they happened to wear turbans that made them look like Muslims."

The old priest listened with empathy and sadness drawn on his face and occasionally nodded.

Huxley continued, "And it is so easy to just blame so much of the world's conflict on Muslims, but consider the history of your own church, Father. It was a pope who called for the Crusades to kill Muslims and remove them from the Holy Land. Then, in the Fourth Crusade, the Crusaders stopped on their way at Constantinople, a Christian city that had broken with the Roman Catholics to become what we now call the Orthodox Church. Despite their religious similarities, the Crusaders decided it would be great fun sacking and pillaging the city. And in the years that followed the Reformation in Europe, some 8 million people died in the Thirty Years' War in the name of Catholicism and Protestantism. And that doesn't even touch on the people who were tortured or put to death by your religious leaders for heresy in the name of the Inquisition or the six million Jews who were killed in Nazi Germany merely because of their religion. History demonstrates that religion divides people and then kills them. No, I do not agree that humanity loses when it loses faith in God."

The old priest remained quiet for a few moments, clearly contemplating what Huxley had just said. "Unfortunately, I must admit that I could provide even more examples to support your thesis. No doubt we all have suffered through a shameful history. But does this shame arise because of God or because of man?"

"Well, since I dispute that there is a god, I can hardly say your God caused this mayhem," Huxley said. "Undoubtedly it was by men, yet in the name of the religions that worship Him."

"So it is not your argument that the belief in God itself has caused these events?"

"Without religion they would not have occurred," Huxley said.

"Do you really believe that?" the old priest asked. "You seem to be a very astute observer of human history, but now you want to argue that such evil arises only from religion? Do you really believe that or do you acknowledge that men will perform evil deeds even when religion is not at issue?"

"Of course. People rape, pillage and murder all in their own selfish interests all of the time. Evil is not limited to religion, but that does not mean that a considerable amount of the mass raping, pillaging and murdering in the world does not occur in the name of religion."

The old priest's brow furrowed. "That is twice you have said 'In the name of religion.' Why do you say that?"

"Because I rarely believe that the religious beliefs themselves actually support these heinous acts."

The old priest gently bounced his forefingers to his lips in deep thought for a few seconds. "I see. I would agree with you on that one. It would be unusual indeed that the core beliefs of any long-standing religion, including our own Christian faith, would command its followers to kill others, except perhaps in self defense. Some think the Muslim faith espouses the indiscriminate death of non-believers, but I do not myself agree with that assessment, do you?"

"No, I don't," said Huxley. "The extremists take a few words out of context and convert them to a mandate for terror. However, the Qur'an's core message and most Islamic teachers do not support that reading."

"Well then, do you think the words or actions of Jesus mandated that the leaders of the Church order the torturing and killing of heretics during the Inquisition?" the old priest asked.

"No."

"How about the battles during the Thirty Years' War between the Catholics and Protestants? Was war the solution taught to the leaders of these armies by Jesus?"

Huxley shook his head.

"And do you think that Jesus thought six million Jews should be killed to cleanse Europe for the Christians as Hitler seemed to believe?" the old priest asked.

"No."

"So then something else is going on here. What is it? In each of these

scenarios, what is the same with regard to the leaders of each of these historically evil actions?”

Smiling with his bottom lip protruding, Huxley nodded a few times.
“Men and women lusting for power, whether seeking to increase their
power or maintain it.”

“Precisely,” said the old priest. “God never told the leaders to commit
evil acts. Their core religious beliefs did not mandate their evil. Their evil
actions arose out of one thing—the desire to enhance or maintain power
by men and women for themselves or their institutions. Do you honestly
think the Thirty Years War was about religion? Or did German princes see
a way to break away from the bonds of the Holy Roman Empire that had
held them in check for so long?”

Huxley shrugged.

The old priest continued, “Undoubtedly, Hitler hated the Jews. But it
can hardly be said he was a religious fanatic. He seemed to see the Jews as
an ethnic impurity in his quest for Aryan greatness. This is obvious from
the fact that he made no distinction in his holocaust between practicing
and non-practicing Jews. The only criterion was ancestry. He was a fanatic
all right, but for himself and the fascist state he had created and the Aryan
race he dreamed would rule the world. The Jews served his propaganda
machine: they made a perfect scapegoat that could allow him to both steal
their property and force austerity on the German population while he built
his war machine.”

Huxley nodded slightly.

“Finally,” the old priest said, “do you think the Church really believed
that torturing heretics would save their souls as they professed at the time,
or do you think the misguided leaders of the Church feared that the here-
sies, if not stopped, would eventually undermine their power?”

Huxley rubbed his chin, eventually resting it on his interlaced fingers.
“I will concede your points, but they do not change the result. For while
leaders may seek evil ends for reasons that have nothing to do with their
core religious beliefs, they nevertheless use that religion to convince their
followers to support heinous acts as a matter of faith. The people would not
have agreed to these actions without the religion.”

The old priest closed his eyes for a few seconds. “I agree that the belief in God may be abused, and that, throughout history, it has been abused. But I do not agree that most of these heinous acts would not have occurred in the absence of religion. If you agree that men fought so-called religious wars for reasons other than religion, then why would you believe they would not have fought them in the absence of religion? Have not wars been fought without any references to religion at all? Were the most destructive wars in the history of man, WWI and WWII, fought because of religion? Or were they blatant exercises of power gone wrong? So if such destructive wars can be fought in the absence of religion, does it not follow that any war in the name of religion could also have been fought for some other causes? You mentioned Hitler, right?"

Huxley nodded.

"Then take the killing of the Jews by Hitler," the old priest said. "No doubt, the fact that these people were of a particular 'disfavored' religion allowed Hitler to make them something other than human in the eyes of his German people. But has not ethnic, class or other 'cleansing' of populations occurred even where the religious component was missing or not as predominant? How about the purges in the Soviet Union, the mass killings of Greeks, Armenians and Assyrians by the Ottoman Empire in World War I, the destruction of the urban class in Cambodia by the Khmer Rouge in the mid 1970s? These are but a few examples from the last century, but ancient history is filled with such destruction. No, I think if Hitler hadn't found the Jews as a scapegoat, he would have identified some other group and figured out how to manipulate his propaganda to support his agenda."

Huxley shot back, "But you cannot deny that differences in religion cause people to hate. It was hatred of the Jews among the German population that allowed Hitler to use them and then dispose of them like so much garbage."

"I do not disagree that people can abuse religion, even Catholicism, in that way. But it comes down to the fundamental law of hatred—it is all too easy for people to hate groups of people whom they see as 'others.' But that hatred of others is no special province of religion. People spew hatred for others for a variety of reasons, but at bottom it is because they are able to see that group as different from their own. All you have to do is listen to a right wing or left wing radio or television show and feel the hatred oozing from their mouths against those 'others' who think differently than them. Yet most of the world's religions teach love. Jesus taught us to love not just our friends but also our enemies. So how can this wonderful idea be twisted into hatred? Because the belief in God, like anything good, can be twisted and abused by those who choose to hate."

"What else has been so abused?" Huxley asked.

The old priest held out his hands. "Name something that is good and you can probably find a time or event where it was abused for evil purposes. Take fire. Without learning to control fire, where would humans be? Yet it is the harnessing of fire that has allowed us to create weapons that kill innocents, whether by exploding or shooting or creating a conflagration. Yet would you take away fire from humans as well? Or consider weapons themselves. Without them, how would civilized society defend itself from those marauders who would take away their freedoms? Yet put the same weapon in the hands of a murderer or someone we call a terrorist and how do we view the outcome? Do you agree that most things can be used for good or for ill?"

"Yes, I see your point," said Huxley.

"Then do not be surprised that the belief in God can be abused in this way, even if its very principles command against hatred. But neither should we allow some abuses to cause us to jettison our belief in God. As I said, we humans have much to lose by losing our faith in God."

"Okay," Huxley said, "we are back to where you started, so this time I'll bite—what do we have to lose?"

"The answers are infinite, but if I had to give you three, they would be Love, Hope and Contentment."

Huxley scoffed at this. "Really? I love, I hope, and I am content. You said hatred is not the special province of religion, but do you believe love, hope and contentment are?"

The old priest nodded. "Not in all of their aspects, but in their most important qualities."

"Like what?"

The old priest said, "Take Love. I have no doubt you love or have loved. You loved your mother. You have probably loved a woman. You may love one at this time. But do you love your enemies? Yet this is what Jesus teaches us. I admit it seems nearly impossible for humans to truly achieve in any universal way, yet there it is for us to remember. How much worse would the world be if we Christians did not remember this mandate from time to time?"

"But these words are purely aspirational," Huxley said.

The old priest grinned. "Ah, but this aspiration is the needle of God's compass for the world: without it we can accomplish little real good, for we will never know our proper heading; with it we may never reach the ultimate good, but we can come closer to God and do his work on Earth."

"I get this, but how many will ignore the needle regardless of their beliefs?"

"No doubt many will ignore this direction, and many of them will scoff at the few who do seek its guidance, just as many scoffed at Columbus when he set out for India. Of course, his goal turned out to be merely aspirational, yet he changed the world."

Huxley smiled and nodded a few times. "You have a way with analogies, Father."

"Thank you. You said that you hope. What is the nature of this hope?"

"I hope for many things." *Right now I hope to catch a terrorist.* "I have hope for mankind. I hope we will find a way to get along, to stop killing each other. And I hope we will reach the stars."

"These are beautiful things," replied the priest, "but do you believe in your heart they will happen?"

"I don't know."

The priest opened both of his arms toward Huxley. "How would you? And that makes all the difference. Will you live and will you die with the kind of hope that believes you will never truly die? Because of my faith in Christ, my hope is my belief: I believe that the world and my own soul will not end in death or nothingness. That is the strength of my faith. It gives me the confidence to know there is a God, a loving God, and in the end He will save us, not just collectively, but individually. God made us that promise when he sent us his only Son. Jesus will return to us. And along the way, we have to accept that God granted us free will for a reason. He would not lightly take that away from us. But I do believe that without God's guiding hand we may well have already destroyed this planet and ourselves a few times over. We speak of the evil deeds that people have unleashed on their fellow man, but how much worse it might have been without God and our belief in him to guide us through those terrible times."

Huxley flicked a nod to the side and stared out the window at the ground rolling by. He took a deep breath and looked back at the old priest. "I wish I could believe because death seems so much less frightening when it does not mean the end of all of us. I do not fear death for myself, but for humankind. I do not even know how to imagine that. You say God has saved us from this end. Well, what happens under your beliefs if God grows weary of our impertinence and gives up on us?"

The old priest looked at Huxley in total disbelief, "Then God help us all."

Huxley snorted at this intentional irony. "You also mentioned contentment, yet I am perfectly content."

"Are you? Could I ask you something personal?"

"Sure."

The old priest leaned forward and spoke softly, "Do you ever find yourself searching? I don't mean for anything tangible. No, I mean searching for meaning. Do you ever feel like something important to you is not quite there even though you cannot identify it? Perhaps you have felt like true happiness is just around the corner, just out of your grasp. You need only accomplish that one additional achievement that will bring you success, you need only acquire that one additional precious item that will make things complete, or you need only meet that one special lady who will bring you true love? It is a feeling that proves omnipresent yet elusive. You only realize it when you are alone or quiet and have too much time to think—too much time to feel. Normally, there is just a little emptiness in the pit of your stomach and you don't quite know why. Have you ever felt that way? I believe humans were meant to love God, and when we substitute for Him with other goals, we are never truly content."

Huxley stared at the old priest without saying anything for a long time. The man had been kind, thoughtful and considerate, yet somehow his words cut Huxley at his core. Huxley could not explain it, even to himself. He had to ask the question that was gnawing at him. "You admit you cannot prove the existence of God and it is a matter of faith. Okay, so what if you are wrong? Then you have wasted so much of your life and acted like a chump, haven't you?"

The old priest smiled softly. "I know you don't really believe that. Look, if I am wrong then I will still have followed the right path. Sure, we still make mistakes, and people still do bad things in the name of my religion. But I challenge you to look at the words and actions of Jesus and ask yourself if there is any moral path that could truly be more beneficial to mankind as a whole. If we all truly followed his guidance, we would be perfect. No matter how far short we may fall from time to time, I do not consider any such effort to be wasted, not by anyone." The old priest paused, staring deep into Huxley's eyes. "Have you ever asked yourself the reverse—what happens if you are wrong?"

Huxley looked down and said nothing. He pulled out his cell and looked again at his text from Kadir and smiled. Well that was his contentment for you. His friends always seemed to help him out at his lowest points—both in his life and in his career. He would look at the clues with Kadir's new angle in mind. The whistle blew as the train slowed and pulled into Stazione Santa Maria Novella near the historic district of Florence. Huxley returned his gaze to the old priest and his nephew. "Thank you for an engaging discussion, Father. I fear faith is far too personal to submit easily to debate even though the practice does help clear one's mind on occasion. I hope you two enjoy your visit to Florence. You will find it full of history and beauty."

Nodding gently, the old priest touched Huxley's shoulder. "I thank you, kindly, sir. I can tell you are a good and thoughtful man. While you may not wish it, I will pray your mind finds what you seek long before your soul discovers the truth."

CHAPTER 32

ANWARI LOOKED AROUND the empty café and said quietly, "Yes, Imam, everything is set. I await him now. I used a little less of the C4 than was recommended, but it should still work for our purposes. We don't want any collateral damage."

The deep, resonant voice of Pardus responded over Anwari's phone, "Very good, Abdul. You perform Allah's will. You concern yourself with unnecessary deaths even when you avenge an act of the Americans, who had no concern for the innocent lives of your brother and his family. But you understand, do you not, that such options will not always be available to you in the struggle against Allah's enemies?"

"Yes, Imam. I will follow your guidance as always, even to the point of my own death."

"There is no call for that as yet. But it is good to know if Allah calls, you will come."

"Thank you, Imam."

Anwari flipped his cell phone shut and stared at the table. Pardus wasn't an imam, not really, and Anwari knew that. But Pardus spoke with the authority of Allah's representative, and he certainly did his bidding against those opposed to Islam, so Anwari gave the man the respect he deserved. Pardus had never complained about it.

Anwari looked out the café window, where the sun had begun shining on the train station. No passengers yet though the train was due any minute now. Pardus was right, wasn't he? His brother's death must be avenged, and they would be careful not to kill any innocents. But Americans are not innocents—at least not their dirty agents.

No, the innocents were always the nameless individuals who suffered and died in obscurity whenever the plots of the powerful went awry. Sure, there would be apologies from American generals, but that didn't save them. No, to many arrogant Americans, these people were just statistics—a quantifiable number of men, women and children who unfortunately died in the latest attempt to kill the bad guys in Afghanistan, who they thought of as terrorists. But to many Afghans, the suffering and dead were those innocents who mattered most: their brothers and sisters, their mothers and fathers, their sons and daughters. And they suffered and died not because they were bad guys, but because they happened to be in the wrong place at the wrong time, like his brother Karim. Why had Karim chosen that night to take his family on a visit to see his injured friend?

Everything had gone as planned right up to the point the assault force was a couple hundred meters from the house. Then they had heard the report from the command post through their headsets, "UAS thermal camera has gone offline. Hold until we can recover." They had established a hasty defensive position, but someone might spot them and blow the mission. Then the news went from bad to worse. "All we have on UAS is visible light imagery. Can't see anything near the objective."

"Can you get a backup?" Granger asked.

"Not within the next 30 minutes. We've asked joint command ops to reallocate, but the nearest is assisting a TIC."

Anwari shook his head. They wouldn't move the UAS from troops in contact, not for this op. It looked like they might be blind.

The command post added, "Razor 6, without the UAS, will you abort?"

Razor 6, aka Captain Granger, looked at Anwari. "What do you think?"

"They could be gone by tomorrow, but without the UAS, we lose overhead observation on the objective. Could stumble into something or miss someone trying to envelop us."

"Agreed. So what do you do now?" asked Granger.

"Need to reassess the risk and our mission," Anwari said.

"That's right. What's your assessment?"

A new, deep voice came over the intercom, "Critical objective. We know about the recent bombing by these four, but it's probably just the tip of the iceberg. We don't want to lose the chance to bag these guys. No reports of mission compromise before the thermal went out."

Anwari gritted his teeth. Damn OGA bastard—just shut up Half-Moon Mole. Your ass isn't out here facing an armed enemy. He chose not to say those words and instead looked at Granger, who nodded back at him. Anwari asked, "Any other assets available to reestablish observation? 58 Delta? Apache? Any chance the thermal will come back up?"

"Apache could launch in ten minutes, but its another twenty minutes out," the command post reported. Last time we lost a thermal, it was down hard for a day. Unlikely the bird will come back up."

Anwari and Granger nodded at each other through the darkness, hearing only the intermittent barking of a few dogs in the distance. "Okay," Anwari said. "Should be only four of them. Worth the risk. Let's execute."

Anwari had established an inner cordon within 100 yards of the building. He looked through his night vision goggles, seeing three of the targets sitting in a few chairs on the lower level of the house. Anwari's men began moving quietly and quickly from covered position to covered position toward the target. A few seconds later, Anwari heard the slight explosion of a rocket propelled grenade launcher being fired. He turned instinctively and saw the bright trace of its path as the rocket motor ignited ten feet from the launcher. Shrapnel from a parked car ripped through two of his men. Then a hail of automatic gunfire rained down on his position from the roofs of several nearby houses. An ambush.

Captain Granger was issuing terse fire commands through his earpiece while all the soldiers sought cover, a few firing back trying to suppress the lead barrage. A few were caught in the open and tried to shield themselves in the small ditch across the street. Then a grenade launcher sounded off from behind them on the hill and rapid fire followed from the same direction. They were being engaged from two directions.

Granger asked, "Anwari, what is your plan?"

Anwari wondered why the captain had asked him for direction, but the answer came to him quickly: because Granger wanted Anwari to learn, even under fire. Anwari tried to mimic Granger's calm, assertive tone: "Let's try to outflank them. We'll concentrate on suppressing the automatic weapons to our front and move to a position that's covered from both sets of fire. Down this street to the east will work. We may be able to flank the position to our rear." He called for two of his old friends, Shafaq and Rahmati. "Focus all of your fire on the shooters on the roof at two o-clock. When you've suppressed them, we'll move up that street about two hundred meters. You withdraw when we reach the position. From there, we'll try to flank those guys on the hill to our six o'clock." Anwari turned to Granger. "Captain, can you guys lay down suppressing fire on the hill behind us? We'll take care of the rooftops ahead."

"OK, if that is your call, but don't forget about our other assets. Should we call the fast movers?"

Anwari regarded Granger. The captain had been disappointed he hadn't thought of the supporting assets, but there had been a slight note of pride in his voice, an acknowledgment his Afghan trainee was thinking his way through a tough situation tactically and without panic...

Anwari looked out the window at the station and then at his watch. *Focus on the task at hand, Abdul.* A few minutes later, he spied his target emerging from the train station.

❄ ❄ ❄

He had visited Florence before, but a couple of architectural masterpieces seemed to be calling him by name to Duomo Plaza, so Huxley walked a few blocks out of his way to once again see the beauty of the Duomo and the Baptistery that faced it. He marveled at the replicas of the set of bronze sculpted-relief doors by Ghiberti that were so stunning the great Michelangelo dubbed them the "Gates of Paradise." The replicas were placed on the East side of the Baptistery, where the originals (now in a Duomo museum) had stood for five centuries, guarding the octagonal building in which many of the Medicis and other famous Florentines, like Dante Alighieri, had been baptized. He turned to look again at the Duomo and thought for a second he might have glimpsed his old friend Anwari, but the man turned and disappeared into the crowd.

Huxley made his way south to the Arno River and over *Ponte Vecchio*, the old bridge filled with gold and jewelry shops that also held a private passageway built by Grand Duke Cosimo I de' Medici so he could walk secretly between his private residence and the government palace. Huxley wondered at the sheer arrogance of the Renaissance power broker, but then shook his head as he thought about similarities to the many wealthy elites who today wield power behind the scenes of American politics. Huxley stopped at the window of a gold shop in the middle of the bridge for a few seconds and casually looked behind him to see if Anwari might appear, but to no avail. Maybe the man he had glimpsed was just another tourist. Either way, when he returned to Rome he needed to track his Afghan friend down and begin squeezing out some information. For now he needed to focus on Dante Tocelli's family. He pulled out his iPhone to guide him the final steps through an old, charming neighborhood filled with narrow streets, three-story apartment buildings and bicycle racks. When the delicate mixture of fragrances wafted down from the flower boxes hanging from windows above, he smiled and raised his nose and arms to the sky, rejoicing. *Such a beautiful city!* And for those few moments, he forgot that the boundless distraction of beauty often conceals the subtlest of all treachery.

❁　❁　❁

Anwari took up his position on the park bench on the north side of the Arno. To any passersby, he was just another tourist soaking up views of the bridge over the river and snapping some pictures of the quaint surroundings with the large telephoto lens. That lens would allow him to see Huxley first knocking on the door and entering the flat and then his position in the home through the front window into the little dining room just a wall away from the cable box. He knew his timing would be critical. Timing always was, like that night in Jalalabad…

Shafaq and Rahmati had begun suppressing the machine guns. The enemy fire from the rooftops had almost ceased and Anwari was about to command the rest of his men to move when he heard another rocket fire. From the roof several meters away from the machine gun, an RPG headed straight for the truck Shafaq and Rahmati were using for cover. The truck seemed to splinter, sending shrapnel through their faces and chests. Anwari momentarily lost the demeanor of command, crying out, "No!"

He took a few deep breaths just as another hail of gunfire erupted nearby. Granger was yelling in his earpiece, "Anwari, you think its time to drop the

JDAMs?" The captain wanted Anwari to decide, but he was clearly making his own views known.

Anwari considered the situation. They were taking effective fire from two directions and already had four casualties. He had to think like an officer, protect his men. Half-Moon Mole had assured them that all civilians were out of the area. It was the right call. "OK, Captain, ask them to drop one 150 meters south of Bravo-Golf-one-four-eight-eight. You have a grid for the enemy at our six?"

Granger finalized the nine line requests for both targets while Anwari did what he could to suppress the machine guns to their front. A few minutes later, Granger said to the pilot, "Roger, Anchor, this is Razor 6. You are cleared and hot on both targets. My initials are Charlie Golf."

The pilot of the F-16 loitering over 20,000 feet up said, "Roger, Razor 6. You say I'm cleared hot into that neighborhood, right?"

"Roger, Anchor. I say again, you are clear and hot on both targets. Initials are Charlie Golf."

"Roger, Charlie Golf," replied the pilot. "Cleared hot on both targets. Tee Oh Tee in about 18 seconds…"

Anwari was brought back to the present by the image of Huxley appearing across the Arno through the long lens. He watched Huxley knock on the Tocelli's door and waited for a few minutes to be certain, all the while rubbing his thumb over the trigger switch on the remote in his pocket.

❁ ❁ ❁

Huxley sat in a chair with his back left to the front window. The Tocelli women sat on a couch to his right, a large crucifix hanging on the wall above them, guarding their souls from harm. "We have told everything we know to the Italian authorities, Mr. Huxley," said Tocelli's sister. "We have not seen Dante since he left for Israel. If there is anything we can do to help you find him…but nobody seems to know where he has gone."

She seemed honest enough. At least she showed none of the telltale signs of deception that typically covered the faces of those not well-practiced in deceit. Her middle-aged mother looked at him blankly, saying nothing. These two seemed to be suffering real distress. Huxley had hoped that maybe they were secretly protecting Dante Tocelli, but that hope had faded. He tried another tack. "*Grazie, Signorina* Tocelli. You said you do not know where he is, and I believe you, but it is critical we find him before it may be too late…for him. Did he say anything to you in his calls from Israel that might suggest in any way where he might have gone?"

"I don't believe so," she said. "What do you mean—'Too late for him?'"

"We believe he is in danger. Did he mention any place he might visit when he returned?"

She shook her head slowly.

"Did he mention a friend or a girl he might visit?"

She said, "He kept to himself and he never seemed to have many friends. I don't know of any girlfriend."

"When did you last speak with him on the phone?"

She looked up and then closed her eyes momentarily. "It was the night he told me he would be returning to Italy. We were overjoyed. But then he never came."

"Did he say anything on that call that might have seemed strange or out of place?" Huxley asked.

"Not that I can recall. He just talked about how great the site at Tel Megiddo had been and how he was excited to return to Sapienza. No, wait. He did say something strange about how small the world was after all. I asked him what he meant, and he laughed and said something strange like, 'Leopards may never change their spots, but a snake might when it molts.' I asked him if he had seen a snake while he was in Israel, and he said, 'An old snake from the old neighborhood,' but he wouldn't explain. Dante is that way, you know. He'll say clever things in some new way and then he'll laugh about it when nobody understands him. It didn't mean much to me, so I let it go."

"Interesting," said Huxley. "Did you mention this to the Polizia?"

"No. Why would I? I didn't think it mattered. Does it?"

"Possibly. Can you think of anyone from the neighborhood who he might think was a snake?"

"Goodness," she replied. "Who knows? He wasn't terribly fond of quite a few people, but he never really had any enemies that I can remember."

Huxley turned to Dante Tocelli's mother. "Are you aware of—"

He never finished the question. The pressure slammed into his head just as the sound overwhelmed his eardrums. He was thrown into the laps of the two women by the force of the blast as they were thrown to their sides. He could feel something dripping out of ears that now thundered their disapproval. A larger stream ran down the back of his neck. He looked up and saw the two women in fuzzy outlines moving at what seemed like a frame a second. With great pain and difficulty he turned his head back toward the cause of the trouble and saw a distorted image some thirty feet to his rear. It was a large hole to the outside where there ought to be a brick wall and windows. Long after this blur faded to darkness, a light flashed and a new scene seemed to appear, but then played repeatedly through his injured brain. He was staring helplessly at a television screen showing an explosion from a old ship and then bodies burning on a stage with chaos everywhere, except for a lone, soothing voice telling everyone to remain calm and another voice telling them the culprit had been caught and executed…

❦　❦　❦

Anwari stared vacantly out the window of the train back to Rome, trying to come to terms with the hollowness in his chest. Fleeing Florence under one of his alternate identities, he had walked over to the dining car when his stomach had gone AWOL on him. He could not find a way to eat before he pushed the button, and now he could not eat after. He ordered some *caffè* and a small *cantuccini* just to fit in. The ground rushing by just outside the train set him into an almost hypnotic trance. When he closed his eyes, all he could see was the explosion.

The fireball had nearly covered the side of the building. When it died down and the smoke lifted, he expected to see the hole in the Tocelli's wall. Instead, his mind replaced it with another image from his past…

A huge fireball had consumed several old buildings in Jalalabad and then continued to burn the remnants to the ground. All the automatic weapons from ahead and to their rear had gone silent.

The only sounds were of men screaming from beneath the burning wreckage. No, not just men. He heard women and children wailing and moaning and occasionally screaming in Pashtun and Dari. Anwari and the Americans cautiously moved forward seeking to care for as many as they could, but it was too late for most. Later it would be one of those unfortunate circumstances of war that would dominate the attention of Anwari's countrymen, but be largely ignored in America. He felt awful, but he had a job to do and kept doing it. Then he heard a voice he had heard so many times before. This time the voice was begging for help—not for himself but for his wife and sons. There lay his brother Karim, his legs now only bloody stumps and his head covered with blood, gesturing in the direction of a pool of blood and comingled body parts as he passed out from the pain.

Anwari had thought the explosion in Florence might cure him of this recurring image, but it had solved nothing. The pain remained, and his stomach told him a new pain had been added to the heap of his despair.

CHAPTER 33

WHEN HUXLEY OPENED his eyes, he was surprised he felt no pain. When he saw the clear tube running to his arm from the clear bag above, he closed his eyes again. More sleep would feel good. He drifted off into a dream. Once again, he was the man in the colored robes soaking his sorrows in that ancient tavern, but this time he heard that preacher in white robes calling him from the television, calling for all who searched for the truth to follow their yearning. The gentle smile of the preacher called him again from above the glowing white robes…

…Huxley's eyes opened briefly to a bright whiteness and glow. When he blinked and pulled back, he saw the white uniform of the nurse hovering over him and the bright hospital light shining down upon him. He closed his eyes again and fell asleep.

A few days later Huxley awoke again. This time his head was pounding, his ears rang with a high pitched distortion, but he fought through the urge to close his eyes, and sleep did not reclaim him. After a few minutes, he found the buttons to his bed and raised the back.

A nurse walked in smiling. "*Buon pomeriggio*, Mr. Huxley. *Bentornato ai vivi.* You know where you are?"

He shook his head.

"You are in Hospital Saint Maria Nuova in Florence. You know why you are here?"

Huxley mumbled in English, "An old friend wanted me to go out with a bang." He asked for some water.

Eventually, the physician came and examined him. He had suffered a fairly serious concussion and had been in and out of sleep and largely incoherent for four days. The lacerations on the back of his head might hurt, but they would heal just fine. He would need to stay for at least another week to recover and then should rest for another week or two before taking on any significant stress. Huxley asked about the two women in the apartment, and the physician said that they had fared much better than he since he had blocked much of the explosion from their path. They were treated for lacerations and released a few hours later.

Eventually, he managed enough strength to call Kira. "Had a bit of a setback."

"You call coming within a few yards of death a setback? Yes, we know all about it. The Carabinieri called the office. Then the thing hit the cable news stations: 'American investigator the target of terrorist bombing in Italy.' I'm surprised reporters are not at your bedside trying to get a sound bite from you. What the hell happened?"

"Not sure. Getting too close. Damn clue almost deciphered." Huxley closed his eyes. The pain this time pulled from between his temples and then reverberated to the back and down his spine. He grunted. "Got to… got to get back in the game before it's too late."

"You OK, Mr. Huxley?"

He was breathing hard. "Sure…just…just…you need anything else?"

"Well, you're supposed to call Ken Mayer at CIA as soon as you can speak. And the old man wants a full report as soon as you are able."

"Shit, don't need that. Thanks, I'll…uh…I'll try to handle it." Huxley grunted again as the pain returned from the rear of his head back toward his temples. "Tell them I was…I was a bit incoherent."

"Uh, the truth then?"

"What? Yeah. Can barely hold it together. I'll call them in a couple of days if I can."

"Don't bother. I'll give them a report and buy you a week or two. Just get better, OK?"

"Thanks. See if you can find that guy."

"Guy?"

"Yeah, uh…you know…the guy from the hotel."

"Udani—Dracoratio?"

"No, the other guy. The Afghan."

"Anwari."

"That's it. Find him, but keep it quiet."

"Boss, don't you need to start sharing a bit here?"

Huxley exhaled long and hard. "Can't let them screw this up." He may have forgotten Anwari's name for an instant, but he could not forget his place in his investigation. After he thought he had seen Anwari in Florence, he had nearly blown up. Anwari was his only live angle, and he wasn't giving the Afghan hero up to anybody else. Not just yet.

CHAPTER 34

TWO WEEKS LATER, Kira had not yet found Anwari. Not even suspecting such a search, Anwari waited with his crew without feeling the anxiety he had long expected for the upcoming operation. If the plan worked, no shots would be fired. The real job had been completed long ago through secret negotiations and timely payoffs. His crew was there as more of a transportation facilitator but stood by as well to ensure the mission's success. Anwari looked out at the scraggly plain before the distant mountains and almost felt at home, but not quite. Sure, he was used to wearing an army uniform, but the slight color and insignia variation made him feel like a soldier of fortune in a strange land. Still, the AK-47 in his hands felt like an old friend. The other five men in the truck were all professionals he could have mistaken for his old crew, but he could never hold them in such high regard.

Though this mission seemed minor, the ultimate consequences of its success weighed heavily on Anwari. Pardus had given him assurances that the infernal things would only be used as leverage to bring the Americans to their knees in negotiations. Nevertheless, he couldn't help running the key passages in the Qur'an about Qital over and over again in his mind:

Those who believe and do good deeds will be forgiven and have a generous reward, but those who strive to oppose Our messages and try in vain to defeat Us are destined for the Blaze.

Anwari nodded to himself. Yes, at worst we fulfill this message of the Qur'an, for these people certainly try in vain to defeat us.

> Those who have been attacked are permitted to take up arms because they have been wronged—Allah has the power to help them—those who have been driven unjustly from their homes only for saying, 'Our Lord is Allah.' If Allah did not repel some people by means of others, many monasteries, churches, synagogues, and mosques, where Allah's name is much invoked, would have been destroyed.

He crossed his arms and bit his cheeks. We have been driven from our houses. These people have continually found excuses to attack us everywhere we live. *We are justified in taking up arms.*

> [W]herever you encounter the idolaters, kill them, seize them, besiege them, wait for them at every lookout post…

> Kill them wherever you encounter them, and drive them out from where they drove you out, for persecution is more serious than killing.

Pardus had reminded him of these passages again and again as he recruited him to the cause. They were the guiding force of Qital, which many mistakenly called Jihad, though that was a much broader term referring simply to the struggle against evil for the sake of good. Qital meant precisely "armed struggle." He had read the passages over and over and memorized them.

The words near those passages gave him pause. Words like "do not overstep the limits: God does not love those who overstep limits." The context of these passages and had given him a different view before Pardus took him in. Pardus had explained his was the path of righteousness and revenge for the horrible deaths brought on his family by the onslaught of the Americans. This path would lead to Anwari's personal salvation. Had

Anwari merely closed his eyes to the Truth before Pardus, or was he closing his eyes now to justify his brother's demand still echoing down his spine?

The Americans had let him down. Not Captain Granger. He had been a good friend, a constant, his oak, but then the Americans cut the oak down. The inquiry had found him negligent.

Anwari had been disgusted when Granger had told him the news. "You mean to tell me Half-Moon Mole walks without any consequences?" Anwari asked.

Granger replied, "No, worse. They promoted him, at least that's what I heard through back channels."

"But the bastard deliberately lied to us! There was no sweep of the block the week before and I'll bet he knew that. He made that up just to get us to complete the mission. He wanted those terrorists bad, and he didn't care how he got them. I told the Colonel that. You told the Colonel that. Yet the asshole gets a promotion?"

"He's got more pull," Granger said. "You and I were the only ones in that briefing. He claimed some bullshit like he told us to watch out for the civilians instead of the other way around. It's a U.S. captain's and an Afghan lieutenant's word against a long-time spook."

Anwari shook his head, disgusted. "The OGA protects its own and they find us as scapegoats?"

"Not you, me," Granger said. "I called in the JDAMs. My initials were on the order. My order, my mess. No way getting around it. They see you as just backing me up 'cause we're friends. This won't hit your record. You blame them?"

"Damn right. You didn't kill my brother. Half-Moon Mole did. Are you telling me your country is so screwed up they refuse to see the truth? They want a murderer to go free? I want that bastard prosecuted."

"Won't happen, Abdul. Give it up. I'm sorry about your brother, really, it is a friggin' tragedy. But you know shit happens in war. Sometimes its easier for them to just chalk it up to that."

"Have you seen my brother? He's barely hanging on. Can you blame him that he wants revenge? Are you trying to make us all hate you?"

"Hey, come on," Granger said.

"Sorry. Sorry, I don't mean you. But you have to help me. We could go see the colonel together. Tomorrow, we could—"

❊ ❊ ❊

Huxley walked past the security gate at the Carabinieri's command center and looked for a cab. During the debrief with Patismio, he had struggled through the fuzzy corridors of his mind to give an adequate report without giving away Anwari. He wondered if Patismio had suspected something. Huxley knew he had better wait before tackling Mayer and Blount. In this state, they could squeeze his head until it popped off. He could not afford that, at least not with Mayer's motives remaining unclear. Even if Mayer were the mole, he still had to find the snake. He called Kira.

"Good to see you're still alive."

"Thanks. You OK?"

"Sure. Just keep dancing around Blount and Mayer. I think they are looking to shut down the music, though. You back in business yet?"

"The world is still such a dreamy place. Should I share a few with you?"

"God, no, I don't want any more of your baggage."

Huxley laughed. "You find our friend yet?"

"Nope. Italian Immigration confirmed he flew back to Kabul the day after the bombing in Florence. I got nothing else. Sorry."

"Keep looking. We have to find him."

"OK, can I—"

"No. No CIA. He's just a guy, remember."

"You don't make it easy."

"You want easy? I need you to get creative and see if you can come up with any possible leads on a snake from Florence?"

"A snake?" she asked.

"I know. This isn't easy or I wouldn't be asking you. Just see if you can find anybody who is originally from Tocelli's neighborhood and has some nasty personality defect. The term they used was "snake," so I'm looking for someone who was charged with fraud or corruption or something like that. This snake would have traveled to Israel around the time Tocelli was there. Check criminal and police records, newspaper and magazine articles, whatever. My guess is that the person was somewhat prominent at some point, if that helps. You got that?"

Silence.

"Kira, you still there?"

"Oh I'm here alright," she said. "I was just wondering if it would be better to feign a bad connection, but then you would just call me back with more impossible requests."

"Come on, you love a challenge," he said.

She sighed. "A challenge is climbing Mt. Everest. This is more akin to sprouting wings and flying to the peak."

"Better get growing those wings, then, so you can start flapping them madly at me. I have faith in you. You've worked miracles before. Can't I have another? I'll see what I can do to help you out on this one."

Huxley hung up and found one of his new friends in his contacts list. The man answered, "Mr. Huxley, good to finally hear from you. I was wondering when you would remember your Israeli colleagues. We had an understanding, right?"

The image of Yadin spitting into the microphone, red corpuscles bulging from his forehead, nearly made Huxley laugh, but he held it in.

Yadin shifted to a quiet, soothing tone. "Sorry to hear about the bombing. It was a relief to hear you had come out of it one piece. You gave us a bit of a scare."

"Aw, Captain, I didn't know you cared. You keep acting human and I may actually end up liking you."

"Well, we couldn't have that, could we?" Captain Yadin cleared his throat. "Anyway, what do you know?"

"Not as much as I would like. We still cannot find any real trace of Tocelli although I think I'm getting closer than someone would like. I did get one snippet of intel that I'm trying to track down, but it feels like a bit of a reach. Tocelli told his sister he had seen a snake from the old neighborhood while he was at Tel Megiddo. We are wondering if that might explain his disappearance."

"A snake?" Yadin asked.

"You got it. I know it's not much, but we'd like to cross reference some searches with your immigration database to see if we can find something. We are just looking for Italians in Israel during a three-week period. You game?"

"I think we could send you a partial database to use." Yadin sighed. "You will, as a good partner in this venture, tell us if you get any results?"

"Of course. Can we do this through normal channels so my assistant can get involved?"

"I don't see why not. Have her contact me."

Huxley scratched his head. "You have any more leads on the chemist or his family?"

"Nothing. No ransom notes, no contact. Looks like you may have been right. We need to find him yesterday, but we still have no real clues. Like a ghost nabbed them."

"That may be right. We think Pardus might be behind this, and he would have removed them from Italy as soon as possible. He may be back in your part of the world."

"Pardus?" Yadin asked. "You believe in the Ghost Leopard?"

"It's not a matter of faith, but our inability to find him does not mean he does not exist." *Crap, that sounded way too familiar.*

"Can we coordinate on this?" responded Yadin. "You get anything, let us know and we'll do the same."

"You got it. Let me ask you something, though. You going for a rescue if you find the chemist?"

"Sure, if we can pull it off quickly and with low risk. Between you and me, Jacob Rosenthal's brain remains the biggest single threat to the world while he remains alive. I doubt he will learn much from Pardus that would help us if he somehow survives. We would love to save him, but not at the cost of giving the Ghost Leopard more time to succeed."

"I take it you have what you need from Mr. Rosenthal already?"

Yadin laughed. "Nice try. I love you, but not that much. Anything else?"

"Just one thing since we are on such good terms now. You said a while back that you were not having me tailed. Now, I wouldn't blame you for not being straight with me given the situation, but it's critical that I know now whether my tail was sent by you."

"Of course you were tailed. You were a possible suspect at the time."

Huxley nodded. "Yeah, look, I don't need to know the tail's name, but could you tell me whether he had a black beard?"

"I doubt it."

"Why?" Huxley asked.

"Because I am not aware that she takes any testosterone."

CHAPTER 35

HUXLEY'S KNOCK ON Sonatina's door should have been accompanied by his intense excitement, but the bomb in Florence had changed all that. Now nearly three weeks later, his headache had dissipated, but a slight fog still obscured the lower corners of his mind. He should have waited until it cleared, but she might just raise his spirits when he needed it most. That hope suffered no disappointment when Sonatina opened the door to her apartment and flashed her most welcoming Mediterranean smile.

They ate a real Italian meal, not what you are served in a D.C. restaurant but the kind his mother used to make so many years ago. Risotto and meatballs with pomodoro fresco marinara. "Until tonight, I would not have believed that an artsy gal from *Firenze* could cook like this," he said.

"Florence is full of art, that is true, but have you ever eaten there? *Buon Appetito!*"

He smiled at her obvious pride in her hometown. "Where'd you grow up there?"

She looked down at her food. "Just southeast of *Ponte Vecchio.*"

After his head jerked up and his eyes widened, she quickly added, "I am sorry my old neighborhood was not so welcoming to you."

Huxley raised his voice, "You lived near the Tocellis? What the hell? Why didn't you tell me, Sonatina?"

"Tocelli is a common name in Italy. I never personally knew Dante or even that he lived in my neighborhood. *Mi dispiace.*"

Even when dessert arrived, Huxley kept fighting to remain engaged. His gut was sending out alarms, but he struggled to focus his troubled brain sufficiently to decode the feeling. After clearing the table, they moved to the divan and sipped some wine. Huxley could not quite bring his thoughts away from the Florentine coincidence. He remembered what Tocelli's sister had said and decided it was worth a shot. "Can you think of any snakes in your old neighborhood?"

"*Mi scusi?*"

"Snakes. I know it sounds odd, but apparently Dante Tocelli talked about an old snake from his old neighborhood making an appearance in Israel."

"I have no idea."

He watched her as she said this. Had she glanced up to her left even for an instant? Was she hiding something or was his paranoia running wild? "He said perhaps an old snake could change its spots when it molted even though a leopard could not." Again, he read her face as he said this, but it betrayed nothing.

"Leopard?" she asked. "Do you think that was a reference to Pardus?"

He smiled. "Good question. I'd love to know myself. If we can figure out the identity of the snake from the old neighborhood, then..."

She did not fill in his blank.

Sonatina took a few sips of her wine, sat back and crossed her legs. The hem of her dress inched up the shapely form of her thighs.

Huxley's eyes focused a little too sharply for a little too long. Was she trying to distract him?

She seemed to notice his glance and smiled gently back at him. "How is your decoding going? Have you figured that out yet?"

"Haven't had time to focus on it much since the explosion. Too many people to straighten out and too damn many reports to send—you'd think frickin' Mayer was trying to wear me down with administrative bullshit—and all with my head feeling like an overblown balloon."

"A balloon?"

"Yeah, since I haven't been thinking quite straight, I doubted I'd have much luck. A friend gave me an idea before the explosion."

"A friend? How well do you know him?"

"Very. He's my old roommate, but now he's an ambassador—the Ambassador of Peace."

"*Che cosa?*"

"Nothing—an inside joke. Kadir said I should think about Muslims and the Qur'an. He may be right, since the other clues involved Judaism and Christianity. It seems like a natural progression—just like history, in fact."

"Well, what is the problem, then? See what you can find in the Qur'an."

"It sounds easy, doesn't it? The Qur'an is a big book, though. You want to help? I doubt my faculties are up to it yet, but maybe you can make sense of it." He pulled out his phone and brought up the poem:

> Just take a look at her—do not believe
> The Word begot from altar writers past.
> We do believe, but just the simple Truth.
> We pray within The bawd, where only He
> Did soar so high above three centuries.
> Now cherish deep within our words of Lord
> The times her forlorn shrine has been restored:
> The main lies here all split apart in two,
> While source of thee doth hold a simpler view.

He looked at it and then at her, shaking his head. Her mere presence had already triggered new ideas in his brain. "Crap, I have been a confused fool. Look, the words on the altar at the Church of the Annunciation are translated from the Latin to: 'Here the Word was made flesh.' I thought it was simply that the Orthodox Church that did not believe the words on the altar, since they did not agree that the Annunciation happened at Mary's home. But it wasn't about the word "Here," it was about the entire statement on the altar. The Muslims believe Jesus was an important prophet, but not the Son of God. So they do not believe he is the 'Word.' And they praise Mary in the Arabic "Maryam" in the Qur'an itself. Do you have a laptop handy?"

"Si." She returned a few moments later from her bedroom with a MacBook Pro.

"Find an online copy of the Qur'an and then look up 'Mary' and 'Maryam.'"

Sonatina followed his directions and thirty seconds later the words flashed in English on the screen. "Look," she said, "there is a whole chapter on Mary—Chapter 19."

"It is called a 'Sura' by Muslims—Sura 19." They began reading the Sura quickly. It contained something familiar to them both—the story of God sending his angel to Mary with something akin to the Annunciation:

> [H]e said, 'I am but a Messenger from your Lord, come to announce to you the gift of a pure son.' She said, 'How can I have a son when no man has touched me? I have not been unchaste,' and he said, 'This is what your Lord said: "It is easy for Me—We shall make him a sign to all people, a blessing from Us."' And so it was ordained: she conceived him.

A few paragraphs later, they read about how others chastised Mary when she returned with a child. They declared her unchaste and were about to shun her. She pointed at the infant Jesus, suggesting the crowd speak with him. After the others asked how they could possibly converse with an infant, the infant himself began to speak, saying:

> I am a servant of God. He has granted me the Scripture; made me a prophet; made me blessed wherever I may be. He commanded me to pray, to give alms as long as I live, to cherish my mother. He did not make me domineering or graceless. Peace was on me the day I was born, and will be on me the day I die and the day I am raised to life again.

Other than giving the infant the power of speech and calling him a prophet, the reading could have been out of the New Testament, even to the point of discussing the day he would be "raised to life again." But then they read on and the distinction and language of the poem became clear:

> This is a statement of the Truth about which they are in doubt: it would not befit God to have a child. He is far above that: when He decrees something, He says only, "Be," and it

is. "God is my Lord and your Lord, so serve Him: that is a straight path."

Sonatina gasped. "Did you notice that Truth is capitalized in both the Qur'an and poem? This 'Truth' must be the 'simple Truth.' While they believe that God worked through Mary and Jesus, they do not believe he is the Son of God, so he could not have been the Word made into flesh as the altar writers had written. You have found your answer."

Huxley's smile quickly turned to a grimace. "Yes, my friend was right about the Qur'an, but what can I make of the rest of this poem. There is nothing in this Sura about "The bawd" or anything that "soars above for three centuries."

Sonatina's eyes widened and her smile beamed a ray of sunshine on him. "But you said yourself that it would have to be a place relating to Muslims. It says they, that is the Muslims, pray within the bawd, so it must be an Islamic mosque."

Huxley sat up straight, his grimace returning slowly to a grin. "Of course. Yes, you must be right. And maybe it was one of the tallest mosques for three centuries. But what is a bawd? And notice that "bawd" is preceded by an improperly capitalized 'The.' It must be a proper name that begins with some form of 'the.' Look up 'bawd' in the dictionary. I think I know the word if it is the root of 'bawdy,' but let's see." Seconds later, Huxley added, "Yep, it is a prostitute, a whore. But what can that possibly have to do with an Islamic mosque?"

"I don't know. Let's see," she said, "'The prostitute,' or 'The whore,' or maybe 'The madam.' You're right, none of them seems to make any sense. Could it be that we must translate it into another language? Arabic, maybe? Do you know any Arabic?"

Huxley nodded. It makes no sense there either." *Damn muddled brain.* He yearned for the old quick connections that now seemed to evade him.

Sonatina came up with another angle: "What if we search the Internet for key terms and see what we get. She began saying each search phrase aloud as she entered them: "'Let's try... 'Three centuries,' 'three hundred years,' 'Muslim mosque,' 'largest,' 'biggest,' 'tallest,' 'highest,'...there." She pushed enter. Several entries came up of Muslim mosques, including the largest mosque in the world, the Grand Mosque in Mecca, Saudi Arabia. They could find nothing that referred to three centuries or anything that could possibly relate to "The bawd."

Huxley sighed. "Well, it was a nice try, Sonatina. I think we'll have to sift through these to see if there is anything that could match. Wait, here is an entry on the 15 most fabulous Muslim mosques in the world. Let's start there." The article was nearly 10 webpages long, and he was impatient, so he began scanning the top of each mosque description until he came to the twelfth entry entitled: "Badshahi Mosque, or 'Royal Mosque,' in Lahore Pakistan." He looked at Sonatina, "Could it be that simple? 'La' is Spanish for 'The,' so 'The bawd,' or 'The whore' becomes 'Lahore?'"

They read on and found the answer a few sentences below:

> Able to hold 10,000 worshippers in the main prayer hall, with another 100,000 in the courtyard, the Badshahi Mosque was the largest mosque in the world from 1673 to 1986 (a period of 313 years).

Huxley looked at Sonatina with a ridiculous grin on his face. She returned the joy by flashing a soft, alluring smile. He could not resist. He grabbed her shoulders and pulled her to him, feeling her well-formed breasts against his chest. She squeezed back and it triggered something else in his body chemistry that he had missed for a long time. He rubbed her back and shoulders gently and whispered in her ear, "You are as much a genius as you are beautiful, Sonatina. *Grazie.*"

She returned the whisper, "Glad I could help, but it was all you, Chris, and you are pretty gentle on the eyes yourself."

He pulled back and kissed her on the lips, long yet softly. He had refused to trust himself to even this simple level of intimacy with a woman for several years. Since Hanna and her harangues. Since they had parted. Since he had abandoned his mother. *Damn, why do you think of such things at a moment like this?* He pulled back from Sonatina and forced a fake, weak smile.

"Are you alright?" she asked.

"Sure," he said, but he had lied to her, and she could tell. In that one precious, intimate moment, his mind had turned to his mother again, and all the troubles of the past returned. He cared for Sonatina, but he just couldn't focus on her any longer. *What did the priest say?* Perhaps God had kept his mother alive for him. For what? For his own personal purgatory on Earth? Yes, he had done everything he could for his mother that last year, but he could never forgive himself for abandoning her. So how could he possibly expect that she might have forgiven him, even if her brain had been able to form such a complex thought, or even if her heart or her soul could somehow overcome that weakness as the old priest had hinted.

"Chris, what are you thinking about?" Sonatina asked softly.

She was holding his hand, and he gripped hers tighter and smiled back. A tear was running down his face. "Have I ever told you about my mother?" *Why am I telling her this?* That feeling in his gut had become a torrent of liquid that wanted to flow out of his mouth, through the now open floodgates. She had become the only available basin for this unexpected outpouring.

"I know she passed away, and it has been too difficult for you to discuss."

"Maybe I should tell you why," he responded meekly. He spent the next hour trying to describe why the contacts list had spoken the truth when it proclaimed his mother had been forsaken. As he spoke, she held his hands, and the warmth of her touch washed over and through him. He had never been the touchy-feely type, yet somehow her tenderness in this moment gripped him deep within.

At the end of the long conversation, they sat, smiling softly at each other. He felt free, but exhausted and nearly limp. But there was something more. Could he confide even that with his newly found confessor? "This may seem strange," he said, "so please do not think of me as a nutjob, but have you ever felt a strange emptiness inside? No, not really emptiness—it is more like something or someone lurking in that deep hole in your gut, and it calls out to you. You don't know what it looks like, but it scares you, nonetheless. You try to pretend it doesn't exist. You feed it with your life's goals—your work and your relationships and your passions—and then, for a while, the thing disappears. But eventually the luster of those goals just dissolves into you like so much food and vanishes. Yet the hole remains, and when you have a quiet moment, the creature reappears, calling out to you, 'What do you seek and why?'"

She looked back at him lovingly but said nothing.

Huxley continued, "I don't know how to answer it. I keep thinking the answer will be there when I arrest another terrorist. But the thing never seems satisfied. The truth is, I don't know the answer to that question, and it haunts me."

Huxley wiped a tear from his eye. He had been babbling and had to stop. When he looked into Sonatina's eyes, he saw something he never quite understood. It was empathy, but it felt like something more.

She sat there looking at him for a few seconds and then looked down at his lap. She smiled and looked back into his eyes. "I think I understand. My advice to you is to trust your hands on this one. Maybe they understand the answer in your heart better than your brain may ever admit."

Huxley looked down at his lap and realized he had pulled out the crucifix and was rubbing it methodically with his left thumb. "Uh…no, no," he said, shaking his head. "That thing is there just to remind me of my mother. I don't even believe in God anymore," he said as he shrugged and returned the object to his pocket.

"Chris, perhaps you should reconsider. Think back to your youth. You may think you can destroy God in your heart, but that is impossible! He will be with you always."

"I don't know, maybe just in my dreams."

"Your dreams?"

"Yeah, I've been having weird dreams about the same people. But they are Arabs or something—at least they are dressed like them, with robes and the like. One is wearing fancy silk robes with various colors, but I don't really see his face—it is like I am him in the dream. In one dream, I think he saw me too. The other is always dressed in white robes. I could swear he looks like Jesus. When I was in the hospital, he seemed to be calling to me, asking me if I truly seek the truth."

Sonatina smiled broadly. "Perhaps that is God reaching out to you, telling you that you need him."

"Or maybe it was just a homely nurse telling me to come back to reality." He laughed awkwardly.

Sonatina stared back at him with a soft smile.

Huxley looked down at his hands again, at the crucifix. *God again?*

Why did they keep trying to pull him back there? His mother, the old priest—he laughed at what he had told the old priest. *It all seems like fantasy to me. Maybe, if I had been there to see it, I could believe.* Now the thing in his belly grabbed him, like it was dragging him closer to Sonatina, but then he sighed and pulled himself out of it. He looked back up at her slowly and said, "You don't happen to work for an old American priest, do you?"

"*Che cosa?*"

"Never mind."

"Chris, your answers lie here." She tapped him on the chest. "Trust them. Have a little faith and love will come back to you."

He smirked. "Then tell the thing in my gut to stop poking me there." He stood up. "Look, I'm sorry for being such a sap. I had a wonderful time. You are an inspiration. May I call you again?"

She smiled coyly and stood up with her wine glass in hand, raising it toward him. "To beautiful beginnings."

He left her apartment a few minutes later, his lips still smiling and his heart still singing. But then his mind turned again to the investigation, and his heart struck a discordant note. Sonatina always seemed to say exactly the words he needed to push his case forward, just as she had done tonight. *Just as Anwari had done before her.* Though he could see it coming from Anwari, he had to have his radar on high alert when he talked with Sonatina. The radar had been down tonight, but now the signals were beaming straight through.

What is really going on here? Is she mixed up in this strange terrorist plot? Is she tugging on my emotional strings to manipulate me? Is that why she is trying to drag me back to God? She had seemed so genuine: he had trusted her way beyond what his mind told him was safe. Yet he doubted he could ever truly read her, and that made him feel naked. Was she empathic or merely calculating? Was she loving or just deceiving? Was she a clever, beautiful muse or simply a brilliant, dangerous lover? And how could he ever know which?

CHAPTER 36

"The mission was a complete success, Imam," Anwari said into his latest cell phone. "The second package has now been attached to the special equipment and taken away by your agents. As far as we know, the authorities remain unaware that either package is missing."

"Excellent," Pardus replied. "You serve as Allah's right hand."

"Thank you, but I must tell you I still worry about this plan."

"Oh? Events seem to be moving ahead as I had hoped. Are you aware of something I should know?"

Anwari licked his lips, looked down and sighed. "I fear what might happen if the Americans do not react as you have anticipated. What if someone gets the wrong idea and goes through with this thing? I could not forgive myself, and, worse yet, I fear that Allah would never forgive me."

"Forgive you? Abdul, He will praise you and save a special place in Heaven for you. Remember, Allah has said, 'Fighting has been ordained for you, though it is hard. You may dislike something although it is good for you, or like something although it is bad for you: Allah knows and you do not.' This is difficult for you, Abdul, but it has been ordained for you because it is good. Do not forget you are on Allah's side."

"Yes, Imam, but did not Allah also say, 'Do not overstep the limits. Allah does not love those who overstep the limits.' And He told us, 'If they cease hostilities, there can be no further hostility, except toward aggressors.'

Is America really an aggressor? Al Qaeda's murder of Americans on 9/11 brought their wrath against those pigs who had been running my country. And, yes, the Americans have killed some innocents here, but I know they usually try to protect those who do not fight them. Does America, does the Vatican, really fit the enemy here? I am struggling to see it. Are we not overreaching the limits Allah has set for us? I only wish to do what is right."

"You wish to avenge your brother's death do you not?" asked Pardus.

"I killed him as much as they."

"Pfft. Abdul, you are confused," Pardus said. "You were co-opted by the Americans to help them in their wars against the Muslims and were an instrument of your brother's death only because you let yourself be swept into the infidels' control. You think their holy war against us started with Afghanistan? What about their attack on Iraq in 1990?"

"Iraq attacked Kuwait first. The Americans helped a Muslim brother against a Muslim conqueror."

"Huh? What propaganda is this? Is that what you think it was about? No, the Americans just wanted to secure the source of their ongoing addiction—oil from the Middle East. They chose to protect their main source—the Saudis—against the one emerging Arab oil power who refused to act at their behest. So they set Saddam up. Iraq attacked Kuwait after the American President had hinted his country would look the other way. And look what they have done to that part of the region ever since? It is a mess, with civil war in Syria and Iraq and those other idiots playing like they are a real army, though they are doomed to die in the desert. Do you think that is accidental?"

Anwari closed his eyes. "I don't know."

"No, it is not," instructed Pardus. "The U.S. benefits when Muslims fight each other. Everyone thinks the Americans want to stabilize the region. Bull. They and their oil buddies, the Saudis, want instability everywhere but where the oil pours out in the vastest quantities to the West—Saudi Arabia, Kuwait, and the UAE. As long as there is enough oil flowing, instability in Iraq and Syria serves their long-term interests. When the oil is threatened, the Americans come riding over the hill and kick some ass until they are satisfied the source of their addiction remains safe. But in the long term, no new opponent with any real power can arise. Hell, they would love to keep the Shiites in Iran down as well, but they have not yet figured out how to manage that. They staked Saddam as their horse for a time and then realized he might be more of a threat than Iran. So then they welcomed Iran into the fray in Iraq and Syria, hoping the thing ultimately would blow back in Iran's face and eventually destabilize it as well. And the Saudis smile right along with them."

Anwari bit his lip. He realized anything he said now would be dangerous.

Pardus continued his lecture, "The Americans need two stable nations in the region: Israel to keep the uppity Arabs at bay, and Saudi Arabia to keep the oil flowing and keep the calmer Arabs in line. And have you forgotten that the Americans have continually supplied military assistance to the biggest threat to Muslims in the world—Israel? Without the U.S., there is no Israel today. The Saudi's usually look the other way because business is just fine for them.

"I see," Anwari said softly.

"But forget all of this political underhandedness if it spins your head around or you want to look the other way and pretend everything is as America wants it to appear. You can forget it, but do not forget your brother, Karim. Have you forgotten his plea? Did he mean nothing to you?"

Anwari said, "No, I have not forgotten."

"Then you must also remember the screaming of women and children around him after the Americans attacked his friend's home? Do you remember him screaming for his wife and sons—your own nephews? They were like sons to you—that is what you told me. And then your American friends abandoned you and let his killer go free. When I first came to you, you were a broken down wreck. I showed you that the Qur'an provides the only true path, and it exhorts us to avenge those who try to kill Muslims. No, you must never forget: 'wherever you encounter the idolaters, kill them, seize them, besiege them, wait for them at every lookout post!' I know I will never forget these words of Allah. Have you?"

Anwari said dully, "No."

"I believe you," said Pardus. "Trust me. You are on the right path, my friend. Do not stray from that path or Allah may not be merciful. The Americans will accede to our demands and nobody will need to be hurt.

Even if something should go wrong with the plan, the result would end in glory and justice in the eyes of Allah. The disbelievers would feel the Blaze of Allah's eyes at the Day of Judgment."

Anwari said nothing.

After a couple seconds of silence, Pardus asked, "Are you still with me?"

Anwari's chest tightened. Honesty would end in death, so he responded with the conviction of a *wali*, "Of course, Imam. I am totally committed to you and Allah. I merely seek your wisdom to understand our purposes so that I may serve you and Him better. I only wish to do Allah's bidding."

"Of course, Abdul. I understand. I promise you we do this only for the glory of Allah to defeat His enemies."

CHAPTER 37

ANOTHER WEEK SEEMED to flitter by while Huxley fought to clear the decks with Mayer and Blount and even Patismio. Though he was anxious to resume the hunt at the Mosque in Lahore, Pakistan, Mayer had run him around in circles through his report until he finally seemed convinced that he knew everything. But Huxley had still managed to keep Anwari to himself. He shouldn't complain. At least the extra week finally cleaned out the remaining cobwebs in his head. As he drove to the airport, the international call finally connected. "Hey superstar, have you located Anwari yet?"

"Yes and no," Kira responded.

"Give me the 'yes' part."

"I know where he isn't—at his house in Kabul. I told you he flew back to Afghanistan the day after the bombing in Florence—that was nearly a month ago."

"Yeah, so he's not at home. Do you have an idea where he is?"

"No, and its not just me. I tried to locate him without help as you asked, but I finally had to reach out to our boys in Afghanistan."

"Son of a bitch. Sorry, excuse my French."

"That doesn't sound like any French I know."

"Sorry, I didn't mean anything. I told you we need to keep this out of certain channels."

"Don't worry. No CIA. Just a few trusted sources in the military that I know. No reports, just a friendly visit or two or three. Anyway, he seems to have gone underground. He landed in Kabul as expected, but from there, we don't know where he went. No report of him leaving the country, but no sightings in Kabul either. If he went home, it wasn't for long. I could find out more if you lifted the restrictions, but…"

"Thanks for reminding me of my little foibles."

"Little?"

"Okay, take it easy," Huxley said. "You are still my favorite assistant, right?"

"Yep, right up until they sack me for going along with your little act of deception."

"Deception? I just haven't gotten around to reporting this one little stray factoid yet. I really don't know anything for certain about Anwari."

"I'm sorry, I should have realized you would not want the facts to get in the way of a good story."

Huxley chuckled but then chose a more serious tone. "Hey, you still with me on this?"

"Sure, just yanking your chain."

CHAPTER 38

STANDING IN THE enormous *sahn*, or courtyard, Huxley understood why the Badshahi Mosque lasted three centuries as the largest mosque in the world. At 276,000 square feet, the courtyard could accommodate nearly five American football fields. The thing just swallowed you up and made you feel insignificant, which was probably its intent. And before him stood the beautiful red sandstone structure of the mosque itself in all its Mughal glory, with its 196-foot-high minarets, and three huge *qubbas*, or domes, each covered with a cone and topped with a tall spire reaching for the heavens.

Huxley walked toward the structure, searching for the next clue. He had not deciphered the last part of the poem yet, so he figured its lines might tell him more precisely where to look:

> Now cherish deep within our words of Lord
> The times her forlorn shrine has been restored:
> The main lies here all split apart in two,
> While source of thee doth hold a simpler view.

The line "The times her forlorn shrine has been restored" must have linked back to the Church of the Annunciation, since the feminine pronoun seemed unlikely to apply to this mosque. The shrine to Mary had been rebuilt five times, so the clue should be keyed with the number five. He saw some Arabic words on the entrance gate, but that inscription merely referred to the builder and its date, with no number five. No, the words he needed were "deep within" and must be "words of Lord."

He walked silently into the prayer chamber, or so they called it, though the word "chamber" seemed too inconsequential to describe the space. An arched niche stood in the center and was surrounded on its sides with five additional arches. Here the three Mughal-styled domes showed their interior magnificence. The entrance to the prayer chamber was paneled and enriched with marble inlay in lineal floral and geometrical patterns.

Huxley was admiring the beauty of the structure and almost had forgotten his purpose when he came upon some words in Arabic inscribed in the prayer chamber under the main high vault. They were the Kalimah: six general Islamic sayings memorized in Arabic by many Muslims in Pakistan and elsewhere. He smiled. Was this too easy? He looked at the fifth of the sayings, better known as the Kalimah Istighfar, or "The Word of Penitence." He pulled out his phone and searched for the most common English translation, the one the writer might have chosen:

> I seek forgiveness from Allah, my Lord, from every sin I committed knowingly or unknowingly, secretly or openly, and I turn towards Him from the sin that I know and from the sin that I do not know. Certainly You, You are the knower of the hidden things and the Concealer of the mistakes and the Forgiver of the sins. And there is no power and no strength except from Allah, the Most High, the Most Great.

Huxley laughed. "Well, there you go, Hux. That just about wraps it up for you. Time to head out and celebrate." He shook his head. *I still haven't got a clue, not really.* He scratched his ear and looked at his phone. He pulled up the last 4 lines of the poem again. The 5th Kalimah must be what the poem referred to as the "words of Lord." Hell, they even referred to the Lord. But what the heck was split in two? And what was the source? Maybe the docent could help.

As he turned to find a docent, he noticed a familiar figure quickly turn away from him and head across the hall. Anwari? He started walking slowly in that direction, and the man started walking more quickly away. Huxley picked up the pace, but then so did his target. He considered running, but he knew the guards might stop him and expel him for disrespecting this holy place.

The man stepped over a small red-roped barrier designed to keep tourists out of private areas. The security guard noticed and ran in front of Huxley, yelling in Arabic, "Sir, tourists are not allowed access to that part of the mosque."

Huxley stopped and watched as the man disappeared into the labyrinth of halls on the other side of the barrier, followed by the security guard. The guard returned a few minutes later, shaking his head and telling another guard through his shoulder radio that the man had fled the building out a side door.

Huxley returned to his quest and found a docent. "Excuse me, but could you help me with a question about the Kalimah over there?"

"Certainly, sir. How can I help you?"

"I am wondering where in the Qur'an I can find the words of the Kalimah Istighfar?"

"Nowhere directly, yet everywhere indirectly. The spirit, not the precise words, come from the Qur'an."

"Then where do they come from?"

"Where? Their source?"

"Source? Yes, exactly." Huxley smiled broadly. "What is the source of the Kalimah Istighfar?"

The docent rubbed his chin. "Well, it is somewhat disputed, but some believe it is derived from two Hadiths."

"Hadiths? Oh yes, those are official, non-Qur'anical collections of the words and deeds of Muhammad, right?"

"Correct. That is very good for an American who I must assume is not Islamic. Am I right? Have you nevertheless studied the Prophet?"

Huxley nodded. "Back in one comparative course in college. It has been a long time. Can you tell me which two Hadiths are the source of the Kalimah Istighfar?"

"Sahih Bukhari, Hadiths of Mohammed, Volume 9, Book 93. Oneness, Uniqueness of Allah, Hadiths numbered 485 and 534."

"Hold on, let me make a note of those." He pulled out his phone and began typing them into his notes. "So you said 9-93-485 and 9-93-534, right?" As he looked up and saw the docent nodding affirmatively, the numbers reached out from the page and slapped Huxley in the face. Rather than wincing in pain, he smiled. "Thank you, sir. You have been very helpful."

993485 and 993534: yes, he was sure of it. He brought up the Najwa contacts list and looked at the entry for Maryam Huxley, and there they were: "home: 993-485-0010; mobile: 993-534-0120." He had found the clue. Now he just needed to decipher it. He searched Google and came up with Sahih Bukhari, Volume 9, Book 93, Hadith 485:

> Abu Bakr As-Siddiq said to the Prophet "O Allah's Apostle! Teach me an invocation with which I may invoke Allah in my prayers." The Prophet said, "Say: O Allah! I have wronged my soul very much (oppressed myself), and none forgives the sins but You; so please bestow Your Forgiveness upon me. No doubt, You are the Oft-Forgiving, Most Merciful."

The clue seemed to be referring to the tenth word, which was "Apostle." Strange. Then he pulled up Hadith 534:

> Whenever the Prophet offered his Tahajjud prayer, he would say, "O Allah, our Lord! All the praises are for You; You are the Keeper (Establisher or the One Who looks after) of the Heavens and the Earth. All the Praises are for You; You are the Light of the Heavens and the Earth and whatever is therein. You are the Truth, and Your saying is the Truth, and Your promise is the Truth, and the meeting with You is the Truth, and Paradise is the Truth, and the Hell Fire is the Truth. O Allah! I surrender myself to You, and believe in You, and I put my trust in You (solely depend upon). And to You I complain of my opponents and with Your Evidence I argue. So please forgive the sins which I have done in the past or I will do in the future, and also those sins which I did in secret or in public, and that which You know better than I. None has the right to be worshipped but You.

Huxley counted the words to 120 and came up with "complain." "Apostle complain"—that just didn't seem right. He decided to count the two again and realized he must have counted a word twice on the way to 120. The clue was now "Apostle of." That made more sense, but Apostle of what?

He had used the "source," and that had held a simpler view. Obviously the remaining clue was more complicated. He spent a few minutes toying with a few ideas but just couldn't get what was meant by "The main lies here all split apart in two." He scanned the sources and the Kalimah for a word that matched, but the closest he got was "truth"—"Apostle of Truth." Maybe. But a Google search proved unsatisfactory.

Huxley walked out of the Badshahi Mosque and into the courtyard. He looked back at the structure one more time to imprint its beauty forever on his brain, but a few seconds later, the sound of his own name made Huxley's head jerk to his right. A moment later, his surprised look turned into a grin. "Ahmed Jinnah," he gushed, "How are you?"

A Pakistani man with a thin face and slight, pointy beard grinned back. "I am happy to see you here, Chris. What brings you to Pakistan?"

"Just a few loose ends."

"You still with the CIA? Still interrogating bad guys?"

"No, thank goodness. Homeland. You?"

"Yeah, I'm done with that myself. After you left, they pretty much shut us down anyway."

"I'm not surprised," said Huxley. "Hell, I was more surprised when they let us interrogate some of your own citizens. I figured when things turned a bit sour there, we wouldn't get much more cooperation."

"No comment, my friend. Hey." Jinnah leaned close into Huxley. "I'd like to speak with you privately for a bit. Can you meet me in Lahore?"

"What about?"

"Can't talk now. Tonight at 2100? You remember the Lahore Racing Club?

"Sure, we had a few laughs there."

"The Lahore Central Jail is just north of there. Across the street from it is a long warehouse. Go in the door on the left rear. No eyes on you."

"All right. That's a pretty remote area at night. You guys aren't into secretly nabbing any American Homeland Security investigators, are you?"

"Funny. See you then."

❃ ❃ ❃

"He seemed to pick it up," Anwari said into his cell. "I was quite far away. I think he might have seen me when he turned around. I couldn't let him find me there—too much of a coincidence. Anyway, I don't know if he has it figured out yet, but he has all the information he needs."

"Good. The plan continues to proceed, but you must ensure he solves the problem."

"How? I can't see him in Pakistan. Not now."

"You have a little time. Figure it out. He might be looking for you. Maybe you can make it easy for him if you return to Afghanistan and ensure the Americans know you are there. He will seek you out. You can be certain of it."

"It looks like a Pakistani friend sought him out at the mosque."

"Really? Who?"

"I took a picture. It's a bit grainy although you can still see the man pretty well. I'm texting it to you now."

A minute later, Pardus said, "Interesting. How long did they speak?"

"Just a minute or two. It looked like they had just lucked into each other, but what are the chances?"

"I agree. Keep an eye on Huxley for the moment. Let me know if they meet again. Let's see what he does in Pakistan. It may help us even more than I thought, but don't make contact yourself right now."

CHAPTER 39

THE STREET WAS dark as Huxley ducked into the service door of the warehouse. Nice place for a trap, but Jinnah had always been one of the good guys. When he saw Jinnah sitting back in his chair at a small table, he motioned to the single intense light hanging above. "You must miss the old days. You going to work me over, now?"

Jinnah shot back, "Only if you refuse to cooperate." The two laughed, and Huxley sat down.

"So what have you gotten yourself into that requires a secret rendezvous in such…austere surroundings?"

Jinnah's smile turned grim. "I'll need your word first, Hux."

"Word on what?"

"Make that a blood oath. You want to do the cutting, or shall I?"

"That serious, huh?"

Jinnah clasped his hands together and leaned forward. "So serious that if they trace this to me I know I will be executed, but not before they cut off both testicles and feed them to me as a parting snack. I need your word that you will bury my name so deep in the recesses of your consciousness that even I couldn't torture it out of you."

"I don't think you actually tortured anyone, if I recall correctly."

"Well, act as if I had then."

"You have my word. Now what's up?"

"In the last year, I moved into our independent nuclear security team. With all of your government's concerns about our ability to protect our assets, the government created an independent agency to keep an extra eye on them. I was transferred to the unit and became an analyst and investigator."

Huxley flashed a sly smile. "Spying on your own military. So how's that working out for you?"

"Pretty good until now. Just a few minor discrepancies now and then that I have corrected without much trouble. Despite what your press says, we really have a good crew ensuring the weapons do not fall into the wrong hands." Jinnah's brow wrinkled. "But now I have become worried."

"You have my attention."

"Are you familiar with how we safeguard our nuclear weapons from your government and the terrorists while ensuring nobody gets a quick trigger-finger on the inside?"

"Whoa, backup. You need to safeguard them from my government?"

Jinnah lowered his chin almost to his chest, giving Huxley an incredulous look. "Of course. A few years ago, your Secretary of State openly discussed that you had contingency plans for taking out our nuclear weapons if there was an emergency. Did you think we would just keep them all safe and sound where you could easily find them?"

"I got it."

"We also worry about the extremists in this country mounting a challenge for our weapons at one of our facilities. That is what most people fear. I tend to fear our own government a bit more. You know how power tends to shift around in this place."

"Sure."

"Fortunately, unlike your country, we have made it difficult for any one leader to have a bad day and decide to open Pandora's box. We don't mate our warheads to our missiles and have them ready to launch on a moment's notice as you Americans do. To do so here would be a bit too alluring to the terrorists and potentially a bit too tempting to whomever our current political leader is the next time India pisses him or her off."

Huxley nodded. "I have to tell you that we Americans appreciate your diligence."

"Thank you. But you Americans would also love to know where we have each weapon system kept, would you not?"

"Who me? I'm just a guy who is trying to stop a nuclear holocaust from happening, that's all. Nothing personal."

"No, but it does give my country a headache. If we cannot protect our nukes from you Americans, then you essentially own us. It would defeat the ace in the hole that has protected us from too much American intervention for the last thirty years. And we have no interest in turning that card into you."

"Okay, so what is your solution?"

"I like that. Humor me. Pretend you do not already know what I am telling you."

Huxley shrugged. *Jinnah probably didn't know our satellites tracked the nuclear signatures of every damn warhead they had, on the road or not.* "Look, Ahmed, I'm just a lowly investigator. They don't tell me everything about you guys, you know. But I might have heard Pakistan is putting warheads on trucks and driving them around the country. Hell, that's even been in the newspapers."

"Right. Well, we do not have other good solutions. Since the warheads are not mated with the missiles, we cannot deploy them quickly. But we do not wish to house them too close to the missiles or the very purpose of de-mating them will be lost. And if we keep them in a single location, your government will pretty quickly find them and then we become your neutered dog. So what is our choice?"

"You could at least run convoys of heavily armored vehicles ahead of the warheads for protection against theft by undesirables."

Jinnah shook his head. "I assume 'undesirables' excludes the CIA? Look, that too would defeat our purposes, since your satellites would pick those convoys up almost instantly. And a heavily armed group of terrorists might just be willing to pick a fight with one of those convoys after they determined the prize it contains. Instead, we have gone the stealth route. The trucks appear just like other commercial delivery trucks. They are filled with a sufficient number of soldiers and weapons to prevent any normal attack. And we have backups ready if something happens. But the real security lies in our stealth."

"OK, I have to admit this is nothing new, so I don't think the army should feed you your own stinking balls over this so-called intel."

"I am not finished. You are aware of recent tensions with India?"

"Of course. Why can't you two just get along?" Huxley grinned with his lips shut. "I'm kidding. I know the history of your wars with India and your own civil wars. To me it is just another story about another part of the world mucked up by British imperialism and the political morass created when much of its vast empire was dismantled after WWII. Now that India has elected a hawk to rattle its sabers about Kashmir again, your president chooses to rattle his saber back. But you both have nuclear weapons, so who are you kidding?"

"We have unmated nuclear weapons, remember? What happens if India shoots before we can respond?"

Huxley said, "But they follow the same protocols, don't they? So you should have plenty of time to mate up your weapons whenever they begin doing so."

"If we had perfect intelligence, which we don't."

"So what does this have to do with your security? Pakistan has not begun mating warheads with missiles, have they? That would be a problem."

"No," Jinnah replied, "but to deal with the current state of affairs, we have adjusted our routes and some are no longer exactly random. For example, you guys already know we have M-11 missiles housed in the Kirana Hills in the Sagodha Air Base, and we have some warheads that are housed in our nuclear production facility in Khushab Nuclear Complex." Jinnah gave Huxley a sarcastic look. "Right, you are looking at me like I'm giving you some big state secret. Nice acting job, my friend. But I know you know and I know you know I know, as they say. Anyway, even though the two facilities are only 30 miles apart by bird, they are over 70 miles apart by road due to the Jhelum River lying between them. If we were to continue running random routes out of Khushab, there would be quite a gap in time before we could mate the warheads with the missiles should an attack become imminent. Under our new procedures, we always want to keep a certain subset of warheads no more than ten minutes away from their missiles, so we need to keep a constant stream of trucks driving by the missile sites. It adds predictability, which I believe undermines the stealth of our mobile security program."

Huxley had to keep his poker face. He couldn't tell him that the CIA's satellites had already detected the route change. He managed his best concerned expression, wrinkling his forehead, narrowing his eyes and biting his bottom lip. "I see. This is serious. I'm not sure I can do much about it myself, though. It sounds like I need to run that up to the diplomatic boys and see if they can discuss it with your government."

"Don't bother. Look, that is only a small part of the problem. It gets worse—much worse."

Huxley sat up straight. "Go on."

"Well, about two weeks ago, after one of our warhead trucks passed by Kirana Hills and headed back on the southern route to Khushab, it made an unscheduled stop under a bridge. We know this because we always monitor the movement of the trucks through a coded GPS electronic signal sent out from an electronics package on the warhead casing. As soon as the signal disappeared under the bridge and failed to reappear, our normal protocol was triggered and we scrambled an additional security force and sent it to the area. At the same time, we contacted the captain leading the warhead team to assess the situation. He claimed there was no cause for concern, since the stoppage was due to a flat tire. Nevertheless, just in case of something nefarious, like an AK-47 pointed at his head, we sent several armored vehicles and several platoons of men to the site. By the time they arrived, the truck's front right wheel was off and being replaced by a spare without any apparent disturbance. The security team kept guard while the truck finished its repairs, and the truck and its troop returned to Khushab immediately thereafter. Upon arrival at Khushab, the warhead was returned to its high-security storage vault in the depths of the facility. So…no problem, right?"

"Sounds routine for you guys," Huxley replied.

"Sure, but then a few days ago, the same scenario occurred under another bridge. Again, the warhead was returned without any problems." Jinnah leaned forward, resting his elbow on the table and his chin on his fist. "But what are the chances of two flat tires on these two highly-maintained trucks in a few weeks? And there are only a few highway bridges in the whole region."

"Was it the same crew?"

"Good question," Jinnah said. "No, we rotate people among crews to prevent any possible conspiracies. The two crews were led by the same captain, however. We asked him about the coincidence, and he just replied, 'Can you believe my luck?' There was a minor investigation, but nothing came of it since the warheads were returned."

Huxley leaned back and gestured wide with his arms. "Why are you telling me this if the warheads were returned? Shouldn't you just take up additional security measures with your commanders?"

"Because I fear the warheads were not returned."

"What? Why? Don't they check the GPS, RFID and nuclear signatures when they return the devices to storage in Khushab?"

"Yes," Jinnah said, "but I wondered if those devices could be moved and the signatures faked. You do not need the nuclear codes to remove the GPS and RFID devices. The captain might have had access to those if he got close to his commanding officer. And any of the fissile material left behind would still create the gamma ray and neutron signatures when they were returned to the depot. I raised this possibility with my commanding officer and he told me he would he would look into it. Then I got stonewalled for a couple of days. When I finally reached him, he said he was told to stand down and that this was just a coincidence of two flat tires since all of the warheads were accounted for. He said any independent investigation would go nowhere."

"And so?"

"So now I worry there is some kind of cover-up."

"Ahmed, look, I trust your instincts, but in this case it feels like you are making something of nothing. Flats happen. Frankly, your roads suck. If they tell you the warheads were returned, why would you possibly think there was something else wrong here?"

"Well, I asked to interview the captain of the two crews again as part of a follow-up investigation. I am supposed to have access to all nuclear personnel. His commanding officer refused. He told me the captain had been reassigned to the north. I said I would travel there, and he said the captain was currently indisposed in a highly classified mission. Something didn't seem right, so I employed a little surreptitious security clearance I had obtained when helping my commanding officer with his computer a month ago."

"You hacked his password?"

"Hacking is such a harsh sounding word, my friend. I prefer to say that I managed to discover some internal intel that eventually proved useful."

Huxley winked. "Cute."

"Well, without it, I would not be meeting with you here. You see, with the password, I was able to access the classified personnel logs, and I discovered that all of the soldiers from both crews, including the elusive captain, had gone AWOL."

"Crap."

"That is what I did when I read it," Jinnah said, "right in my pants."

CHAPTER 40

LTHOUGH KEN MAYER had not sounded happy to be awakened in the wee hours of a Washington morning, he had perked right up when Huxley told him he was worried about some Pakistani nukes going AWOL. "How sure?" he had asked, his low voice reverberating through the phone with a hint of incredulity.

Huxley had revealed neither his source nor the details but had pointed to the Kirana Hills region with a few dates and asked Mayer to check it out. Now some eight hours later, bleary and red-eyed from chasing a sleep that his racing mind would not permit, Huxley sat slumping on the edge of the bed. He pulled out his phone and hit the button for Mayer.

"Huxley, I was just about to call you," said Mayer on the phone. "I think your intel is shaky at best. The satellite analysts have spent the day looking at data from that area and they swear no Pakistani warheads have gone anywhere we did not expect them to be."

"The satellites might not have picked it up," responded Huxley.

"Bullshit. They might lose a signature for a few seconds here and there, but they wouldn't just miss a warhead going astray for long."

"You are forgetting about the Israeli chemist kidnapping. The satellites might not be picking anything up because the terrorists are deploying his technology to cover their tracks."

"Shit. Wait a second, there is no way they could have duplicated that research already."

Huxley shook his head. "How do you know that? We don't even know the technology yet."

"Your Israeli contact told us any duplication would take a couple of months."

"It was his best guess. Now I'm guessing that the chemist might have been sufficiently motivated to rush it through. He wasn't creating this from whole cloth, you know. He just needed a lab to duplicate the process." There was nothing but silence on the other end. Huxley continued, "Look, Mayer, are you willing to take a risk on a nuclear terrorist based on a guesstimate from an Israeli captain? We need to do something and now. We need to get the Pakistanis to come clean on this."

Mayer said, "You haven't told me enough to escalate this to political. Who is your contact? I need to know if he is reliable."

"He is very reliable. I trust him. But I can't tell you his name. It would mean his certain death if it were inadvertently released."

"Look, you aren't a journalist protecting a source here. This is CIA. We are not going to let others know the names of our operatives."

Huxley bit his lip and closed his eyes. That may be true, but then again someone in CIA was working against him here. *It might even be Mayer.* "I understand, but I can't give it up. He has gone way out on a limb and I'm not going to put him in danger. Can you at least start making some inquiries through official or unofficial channels to see what you can find out from the Pakistanis?"

"I'll see what I can do, but I need more info from you." Huxley told him the story of the flat tires and Mayer was still unimpressed. Then he told him the soldiers had all gone AWOL. "Shit," said Mayer.

"I preferred 'crap,'" Huxley said.

"What took you to Pakistan in the first place?"

"Just checking out an old mosque for some inspiration."

"Oh, did you decide to visit it with a Pakistani friend?" Mayer asked.

Huxley's forehead furrowed. *What the hell is he getting at?* "No."

"Then why did you meet Ahmed Jinnah there?"

"You been following me?" Huxley asked.

"No, but we've had eyes on your friend, until recently."

"Until recently?" Huxley asked.

"Yeah, until he disappeared after your meeting last night. I suggest you sit tight until we can find out what's going on."

After the call, Huxley sat on his hotel bed a long time, staring at the wall. *What the hell happened to Jinnah? Are the Pakistanis watching him as well? Pardus? Jinnah was scared, but he hadn't seemed ready to run. What game is Mayer playing? He worried or trying to help? Forgot to tell Mayer about the next clue, though I still haven't deciphered it completely. Got to get to that. Maybe a wild goose chase…someone trying to distract me…but then why take me to Pakistan where the action has been? Mayer will drag his feet on this, but I can't just waltz into a Pakistani military facility asking questions. Maybe there's another way to force a play…*

❊ ❊ ❊

After a long shower, Huxley found himself having a light breakfast in a small café across from his hotel. His eyes were still droopy despite a third cup of coffee. He needed to get back to that infernal puzzle. *The main lies here all split apart in two.* The Kalimah Istighfar had come from two sources, but he had already used those.

He looked back at Narjwa's contacts entries. While the two phone entries in the Christian Huxley contact remained, nearly everything else had been used for a clue. The information in the Maryam Huxley contact seemed to have been exhausted. He had even used that strange "No, a dozen times at least" to figure out the poem. Wait. He turned back to the Christian Huxley contact. There at the bottom under notes was another strange entry: "Mobile-Other: Main." *Main. That must be it.* The main was split apart into the mobile and other telephone numbers. They had to be used together somehow. He pulled them up and started doodling with his translation of the Kalimah Istighfar, but nothing came out of it.

Huxley's phone began vibrating. It was Kira. "Hey kid, you got something good for me? I could use a pick-me-up."

"Always hoping to get you up, boss." She cleared her throat. "I mean I'd like to wake you up early just to compensate for all of the sleep you keep stealing from me."

"I'm sorry, but I seem to have lost my sympathy pail today. Haven't slept myself for more than a day."

"You that busy or should I be worried?"

"You'd be the first to know," Huxley replied. "What do you have?"

"We cross-referenced the names from Yadin with the names we were able to pull on Florence. Came up with a dozen people. I went through their backgrounds in Florence and a couple popped up with minor arrests. Nothing too significant."

"We don't know why Tocelli called the guy a snake, so let's check them both out."

"I did," she said. "One is already dead of a heart attack. I ran the other by Tocelli's sister. She didn't know him. Said she doubted her brother would have either, but she couldn't be sure. We are having him followed right now. He's here in the States. Seems to be on vacation in New York. Nothing suspicious so far."

"Good. Is that all?"

"Not exactly," she said.

"No?"

"No. I personally think that guy is just a guy."

"Why is that?" Huxley asked.

"Because with a little more digging I found something a bit more interesting."

"Please, entertain me. Maybe I'll even find a smile."

"Remember you thought there was a Vatican connection of some sort?"

Huxley rubbed his forehead. "Don't tell me the pope is from Florence."

"Funny," Kira said. "No, he's from the other hemisphere, remember?"

"Okay. So what is the connection?"

"Well it's not really a connection, more of a disconnection."

"Don't get cute. I'm too tired."

"All right. It seems there was a former cardinal visiting Israel during those three weeks—Armondo Fine. Although he wasn't originally from Florence, he did serve as a bishop there while Tocelli was growing up."

"Fine as in wine? That can't be right. How do you spell it?"

"F. I. N. E."

"That's pronounced 'Fine' in Italian. The 'i' is more like a long e and the e is not silent but soft. Anyway, you said former cardinal?"

"Sure did," she said. "The Vatican stripped him of his position and even his ordination as a priest a few years ago. 'Defrocked,' the press calls it, but its not like they ripped the clothes off him or anything. He had been working at the Vatican itself. Some thought the dismissal came because he was caught up in some of the pedophile scandals the Church was going through at the time, but the Vatican categorically denied it. They simply announced that his behavior was inimical to Church teachings and only the Church was harmed, so all information about the situation would remain within the Church. Since then, he has pretty much disappeared and been forgotten."

"Why do you think he's the one?"

"Tocelli's sister said Dante was an altar boy for the bishop in his early teenage years. Dante never liked the man."

Huxley grinned. "Sounds like a winner. Can we get some eyes on him?"

"Sure, if we could find him. He returned to Italy last week. Haven't located him yet."

"I'll see what I can do. Well done," said Huxley.

"Thanks, Boss. We make a good team, don't you think?"

"A good team?"

"Sure," Kira replied, "you solve the first piece, I solve the next. You solve another piece, and that helps me find another. Teamwork. And eventually the whole puzzle falls into place."

A strange, searching look came on Huxley's face. "Say that again." After she repeated the words, he said, "Team, hell, maybe you are the head coach and I am just a scrub. Thanks, Kira."

"Sure thing…I think…scrub."

He hung up the phone and looked back at his latest puzzle and started scribbling and talking to himself, "Take one and then another back and forth until the puzzle falls into place." There it was. The main clue had been split apart one by one into the "mobile" number, 723-135-1171, and the "other" number, 413-333-4011. He needed to re-mate the two in order, one by one, to make the main clue, which then would be 7-4; 2-1; 3-3; 1-3; 3-3; 5-3; 1-4; 1-0; 7-1; and 1-1. The first ordinal of each pair was probably the word, the second the letter. He applied that in order to the Kalimah Istighfar, starting with the seventh word and fourth letter and continuing from there, underlining each letter as he went:

> I seek forgiveness from Allah, my Lor<u>d</u>, from <u>e</u>very sin I com-mitted kn<u>o</u>wingly or unknowingly, se<u>c</u>retly or openly, and I tu<u>r</u>n tow<u>a</u>rds Him from the sin that I know and from the sin that I do not know. Certainly You, You are the knower of the hidden things and the Concealer of the mistakes and the Forgiver of the sins. And there is no power and no strength except from Allah, the Most High, the Most Great.

For a moment he was stuck. 1-0? How could there be a zero position letter in a word? He looked at what he had already. The code must include a two-digit word-letter combination: instead of 1-0 and 7-1, it was 17-01. That worked and gave him the full clue:

> I seek forgiveness from Allah, my Lor<u>d</u>, from <u>e</u>very sin I com-mitted kn<u>o</u>wingly or unknowingly, se<u>c</u>retly or openly, and I tu<u>r</u>n tow<u>a</u>rds Him from the sin that I know and from the sin that I do not know. <u>C</u>ertainly <u>Y</u>ou, You are the knower of the hidden things and the Concealer of the mistakes and the Forgiver of the sins. And there is no power and no strength except from Allah, the Most High, the Most Great.

"Democracy." The "Apostle of Democracy." That had to be right. He searched the Internet and found the names of several people in history with that nickname, including Francisco Madero and Lucy Maynard Salmon. Neither sounded right.

There was someone else, something from a childhood field trip. Then he saw it in the search: "Thomas Jefferson, the third president of the U.S., had many nicknames, among them 'Apostle of Democracy.'" So what now? Was he supposed to travel to Monticello again, to the Jefferson Memorial or to some other Jeffersonian site?

He searched Najwa's contacts list for "Jefferson." No results. He searched "Thomas" and it pulled up several entries with the first name

"Thomas." Eventually, he stopped at the one entry that listed "Thomas" as a last name: "Jeff Thomas, III." *Bam!* Sure enough, the address was in DC, near the tidal pool that reflected the Jefferson Memorial. *Looks like I need to go home.* Then he remembered why he hadn't slept all night. No way he could leave Pakistan just yet.

CHAPTER 41

ON HIS WAY to the Khushab Nuclear Complex, Huxley drove slowly north along the Sargodha-Faisalabad Road, looking a mile to the west through his powerful binoculars. He saw the roads of the restricted Sargodha Air Base leading around and under the strange rocky peaks of the Kirana Hills rising dramatically above the flat plain surrounding them. Though he had seen more on the CIA's satellite surveillance photographs, his direct presence at a site always seemed to lead him to a deeper understanding. Given the level of security around the base, Ahmed Jinnah and the CIA reports had been right: the hills acted as one of the main repositories of M-11 missiles. But the missiles didn't really matter now, since they seemed to have been ignored by the terrorists. Instead, the missiles merely explained the presence of warheads travelling around the roads nearby. Could he spot a warhead truck just by looking at it? Probably not.

Huxley found a little turnaround on the road and pulled over. He watched a few trucks go by for twenty minutes or so. They all looked like legitimate commercial vehicles, with no additional armor plating visible.

So Jinnah had disappeared. Maybe he'd been arrested by the Pakistan army. Or worse? With Jinnah gone and Mayer likely dragging his feet, he had to light a fire under Mayer's ass somehow. Then there was Cardinal Armondo Fine. Well, he's not a cardinal anymore. He needed to follow up on that. Hell, there's no time like the present. He could try his informal source first.

Sonatina answered on the second ring. "Chris? I was worried about you. Did you go to Pakistan? To the mosque?"

"I did, but I'm calling for something else." *Shit, wrong tone. I sound dismissive and I shouldn't be, at least not by her reckoning. Put your skepticism aside. She needs to feel the love.*

She had not. Sonatina responded quietly, "Is everything ok?"

"Sure, just having a tough day. How you been?" *There, much better.*

"Fine. Things are a little boring here since you left."

"What," he asked, "no bombs going off around the country? I seem to be attracting those lately." That had felt about right: a little dark humor disguised as light banter.

"You do seem to attract trouble. Maybe I should wear a flak jacket on our next date."

He laughed. "It might be awhile with this mess. I do need to ask you an important question, though."

"My," she kidded, "we've only had two real dates, Mr. Huxley. It's a little early to be popping important questions, don't you think?"

"Funny girl. Look, I know I've been a sap, but…" He shook his head. "Have you ever heard of Cardinal Armondo Fine?"

"*Alla faccia!* Is he the snake you were seeking? He was a Bishop in Florence and somehow slithered into the Vatican as a cardinal. Then they stripped him of everything. Yes. I think he fits the description. He has always been a viper."

Huxley winced. "You knew and you didn't tell me?" he asked.

Sonatina breathed out hard. "I would have told you if I had thought of it. Why else would you be asking about a former Florentine bishop?"

Her tone seemed a bit forced, or maybe a bit too practiced for what should be spontaneous righteous indignation. Huxley had to keep things calm. "Okay, I got it. Settle down. I'm sorry."

"It just seems like you don't completely trust me, Chris. I've done nothing but help you."

"I get it, Sonatina, and I agree, but you have to admit your clearance level is still kind of low, don't you think? You have to be a skeptical guy in this business, or you end up dead."

"I'm not the one trying to kill you. I'm on your side, remember?"

"Of course." Had his tone betrayed his thoughts? *Just move on.* "So, you know more about this cardinal?"

"Not really. Like I said, nobody from the old neighborhood loved him. I don't know why the Vatican promoted him, but then I don't know why they threw him out either. Most Florentines were quite happy to see him go. Not the kind of person you could ever trust, and trust is important, Christian, especially with me."

Huxley nibbled on his lip. Better to pretend he had not heard that verbal slap in the face. "You know where he is now?"

"No idea."

"All right, thanks again. And, hopefully, I can find a reason to come to Rome and see you again soon."

"Am I not reason enough?" Sonatina asked.

"Well, yeah, but trust me"—*shit, the wrong word*—"business calls and the customers are a little more than simply demanding right now."

"As long as you are saving the world, I suppose I can wait. *Ciao.*"

He hung up with a smile on his face, but it turned quickly to a frown. How would she have known what might be at stake?

An hour later, Huxley was driving south on the Jauharabad-Muzaffargarh Road, the Khushab Nuclear Complex to his right with the large cooling tower and its just-released column of smoke clearly visible. That was as close as he was going to get to this facility. He could have appeared at the security gate with his Homeland Security pass just for shits and giggles, but it would have gotten him nowhere. Even with some diplomatic assistance from the President, they would never allow a U.S. investigator on the property. But maybe, just maybe, he could guess at a truck carrying a warhead from the property and see how it worked in person. And maybe he would get a personal invitation from them to boot.

Just after reaching the southeast corner of the facility, he pulled into a roadside viewing area beside a bridge over Sher Garh Canal, which connects the Jhelum River just east of the complex with the Indus River to the west. If the satellite surveillance data was right, the target would appear out of the complex just north of the canal within an hour or two. He settled in, pulled out a camera with a nice-sized lens and seemed to snap a few photos of the complex across the canal, all the time acting as if he were taking pictures of the canal itself. They wouldn't know yet that he never actually pressed any buttons. Of course it was a crime in Pakistan to photograph a military installation. But this was just an energy facility, right? Nevertheless, he always made sure to have the canal carefully in the foreground.

Several trucks emerged from the security gate, but they all seemed legitimate, and they all headed south. He was beginning to wonder if he could spot a warhead truck when a large eighteen wheeler emerged from the security gate and headed north. While the truck looked perfectly normal through his camera lens, its engine sounded an octave lower and it accelerated very slowly, all as if the engine had been built for something very heavy. The warhead would not weigh too much, but maybe the significant shielding and armor on the truck did? Though the windows on the cab were slightly tinted, he could just see a driver…and a passenger riding shotgun. This one was worth a try.

How close could he follow without causing suspicion? No, how close could he follow and create some suspicion without putting himself in too much danger? He followed the truck for about thirty minutes on the Pakistani highways before it pulled off on a side road. He too pulled onto the single-lane road, and twenty seconds later the truck came to a complete stop, forcing him to do the same. Without warning, the rear doors were flung open, and out streamed a squad of Pakistani soldiers pointing AK-47s at his head. One soldier in the back aimed a missile launcher at the front of his vehicle—just in case he were stupid enough to make a run for it. Huxley appeared shocked and frazzled and held his hands high above the steering wheel, hoping that nobody was feeling particularly anxious to kill a nosy American today.

❁ ❁ ❁

The slight folds of Anwari's eyelids nearly disappeared as he squinted through the powerful binoculars at the glare of the mid-day sun blasting off the eighteen wheeler's metallic skin. The soldiers had surrounded the

American and Pakistani MPs were on the way. He made the call. "He's being hauled away by the Pakistani army."

"That wasn't the plan," bellowed Pardus on the other end. "How the hell did that happen?"

"Looks like he got a bit too anxious and decided to follow a loaded truck. They didn't appreciate it. I suspect he'll be taken to SAB."

"I need to get him out of there. There's nothing you can do about it. Go home. I'll let you know when I need you again. I'll take care of Huxley myself."

"But if he is in custody, then you don't need to worry about his investigation, so we can stop leaving bread crumbs to lead him astray."

Pardus grumbled back, "Not a chance. They will just assign someone else and I have way too much invested in leading him to the wrong hole to let these idiots keep him locked up. Remember, we need him to look to the District so he leaves the Apple alone."

Anwari's eyes narrowed. Apple. Pardus had never slipped before. Maybe he makes mistakes under pressure just like everyone else. "OK." He disconnected just as the Pakistani Army MPs flew by him on the highway heading toward Sargodha Air Base.

CHAPTER 42

ACCORDING TO AFGHAN immigration records, Anwari had never left the country. Hell, the authorities didn't have anything that proved he had even left his home in Kabul. With the good will of a few fellow terrorists with ties to Pardus, he was able to find his way through the mountains back to Afghanistan. Now at his apartment, Anwari thought he would catch up on some news and saw the CNN report from Israel.

Jacob Rosenthal, the kidnapped chemist, had been found earlier in the day near Tel Megiddo, barely alive, without much left of him. His tongue had been severed along with both of his hands. His eyes had been gouged out. An ambulance had rushed him to the emergency room of a hospital in Afula. A few minutes after he was admitted, he exploded, taking two doctors, three nurses and five other patients with him. Well, he didn't really do the taking himself, it was the bomb sewed into his stomach by Pardus's men that had managed all of the havoc.

Rosenthal's wife and two daughters were found dead later in the day in a concrete culvert nearby. The two girls were carrying typewritten notes that said only:

> And the earth shall be a waste
> because of its inhabitants,
> as a result of their deeds.

The news showed the smiling faces of the two girls from school pictures taken a few months earlier. Anwari turned off the television, fell back into his chair, and put his hands to his face. The images of the girls became confused as they warped into the scene of them playing in the swimming pool and then the image morphed again into his two smiling nephews. His head slipped lower in his hands, and his fingers covered his eyes. And Anwari wept.

❈ ❈ ❈

Huxley slowly rubbed the scabbed bump on the back of his head. He had taken quite a few hits to the belly, back and head during his short stay in the detention center at Sargodha Air Base. If Ahmed Jinnah had been handling the interrogation… But then his friend had disappeared, which is why he had to pull the damn stunt in the first place. If they wouldn't talk to him in his role as an investigator, maybe they might leak out a little intel to him if he were their interrogation subject. Unfortunately, he had discovered very little over the last day and a half. His interrogators either knew little or were trained well not to tip their hands. He had one more card to play, though it was risky to him and his friend. Their questions would be the same ones repeated over and over. He just needed to change one answer ever so slightly.

Huxley looked back up at his interrogator. "I'm sure you have verified by now that I am an investigator with Homeland Security. Don't you think it is about time you stop this nonsense and avoid a political situation between our nations?"

His tormentor said, "If you are who you say, then it will only go worse for you. You would be an American spy who deserves summary execution. And if you now lie, then you are merely an ordinary terrorist who can be assured of eventual execution. In either case, your only hope to survive with your body intact is if you tell us what you have done."

Huxley shook his head. *Too damn familiar.* "Look, we have been over this. You know I am not a terrorist because I work for the Americans against terrorism. And you know I am no spy either. For Christ sake, I work for Homeland Security, not the CIA. If you really think I am a spy, then what exactly did I spy on that nobody else in the country can see by simply driving on your roads on a daily basis?"

"You took pictures of the nuclear complex. We have video of you from our security cameras. That is a criminal offense punishable by five years imprisonment, even if you are not a spy. As a spy, it means death."

"Show me the pictures," replied Huxley. "I took pictures only of the canal and waterfalls at the bridge. And since you have not shown me those, I assume they were not even saved by the camera."

"You probably uploaded them to the CIA and then deleted them."

Huxley shook his head in disgust. "You know I could get a much clearer picture of your facility from our satellites than I ever could accomplish with a Nikon from the other side of the canal."

"Then why did you follow the truck?"

"I was lost. I was hoping it would take me to a city where I could get my bearings."

"When it turned off on a little side road?"

"Hey, half the roads here are dirt goat paths anyway. Why would I assume a paved road is too small to lead to a town?"

"What were you doing in Pakistan?"

Huxley felt the tingle on the back of his neck. *This is it.* "Look, I wanted to see the Badshahi Mosque, OK? I've told you that over and over." Now came the tricky part. He bit his lip and looked down, deliberately mumbling. "I would have been out of this God-forsaken country if I hadn't run into an old friend there."

The interrogator perked up, "What is this? An old friend?"

"It's nothing."

"Humor me."

"I shouldn't have mentioned it."

"Ah, but you did. Now tell me. Perhaps it could help you. You don't wish to die in this God-forsaken country, do you?"

Huxley looked up weakly, apparently giving up. "You know I used to interrogate terrorists, right? Hell, your government knows this because I did that right in this country in cooperation with them."

"And?"

"Well, I ran into a guy from your security group who used to help me with those sessions. Ahmed Jinnah. We were supposed to have breakfast the other day, but he never showed up. Do you know anything about that? He hasn't disappeared now, has he?"

The interrogator stared back at him, his face becoming more intense as the moments passed. "What do you know about that?" he shouted. So it was true, and they knew about it.

"Nothing. It's just that Jinnah never missed an appointment without calling. Not like him, you know. You have him in custody, too?"

"What? No. Why would we…?" the interrogator started.

Huxley held back a smile. So, somebody else had nabbed Jinnah, or he ran.

The interrogator stood up and walked around the room for a few seconds, then returned, leaning over Huxley and placing his hand on the table. "Do you have any knowledge of his whereabouts? Have the Americans kidnapped him?"

Huxley sat upright. *These guys are more lost than we are.* "Why would we do that? He is just my friend. What was he involved in? Does it have anything to do with that truck?"

"Answer my questions."

"I just did. Look, maybe I can help you if you tell me some more and let me contact Homeland. You guys wouldn't be missing anything else, would you?" Huxley eyed his interrogator. He never would have thought that a dark-skinned Pakistani could turn so many shades of red.

"What do you know?" screeched the interrogator.

Huxley smiled, despite himself. At least he withheld the chuckle. *Looks like I have all I need.* "Not a thing, just as I have been saying all along. I'm just guessing and trying to help you out. But you guys really seem on edge."

"Take him to his cell."

As Huxley entered his cell, he was given a nice little sleeping pill in the form of a rifle butt to the back of his head.

He awoke four hours later, still a bit groggy. A soldier was staring at him from above and holding a bucket. Huxley's face and shirt were soaking wet. "Really, you used a pail of water? Isn't that a bit cliché?"

"Let's go."

"Again? So soon?" he asked. "Come on, I don't have anything to add."

"No. Time to clean you up."

A half hour later Huxley was sitting in his street clothes in a cozy conference room, looking almost human. The door opened and a Pakistani colonel walked in with Ken Mayer trailing him. The colonel apologized to Huxley for the "terrible misunderstanding." Mayer said little, but nodded in his direction, so Huxley accepted the apology and replied that anyone could have made such a mistake under the circumstances.

It was not until they were on the highway to Lahore that Mayer said anything of importance. "When you went missing, I figured you had done something stupid. You can thank the diplomatic branch for convincing the Pakistanis to release you."

"Stupid? I was just gathering intel the only way I could while you sat on your hands in Langley."

Mayer shot back, "You lack patience, Huxley. It will kill you someday."

"And you lack insight, Mayer. It will get us all killed someday." Huxley saw Mayer grimace, the big half-circle mole on his cheek bulging out. No doubt someone was protecting Huxley at CIA. Otherwise, Mayer would have already pulled him off the case.

After ten seconds of silence, Mayer spoke again, "Well, it looks like patience has prevailed this time. The Pakistanis unofficially acknowledged that we just might want to be on the lookout for two warheads that apparently have gone missing."

"Probably because my urgency coaxed them into it."

"What do you mean?"

Huxley looked at Mayer with a wry smile. "I let on that we knew something was missing from their nuclear complex and so was Jinnah, who had called attention to it. The interrogator's babbling and facial expressions told me I was on the right path. They must have figured that if I knew about it, then the CIA knew too. They decided it was better for them to come clean and get help finding the infernal things."

Mayer shook his head. "I don't know about that, but I got a bit more information than just a facial expression to confirm it. Apparently, they thought the warheads were safely stored until they looked a little more closely and found two metallic shell replicas with a small amount of fissile material inside to give off a radiation signature. The RFID and GPS mechanisms had somehow been moved to the replica without setting off any alarms."

"Damn, sounds like what I told you three days ago. Any chance they are still in Pakistan, or is it too late now that we have waited?"

Mayer gritted his teeth. "They are doing everything they can to recover the devices and have now sought our assistance after obtaining appropriate assurances of secrecy to all of this. They have no idea, nor do we, whether the warheads are hidden in this country or have been shuttled out somehow. Our analysts are going over satellite data from the entire country for the past several weeks. Nothing so far. Oh, and I think you were right that the Israeli chemist completed his work for Pardus."

"How do you know that?" Huxley asked.

"Our satellites picked up no fissile material signatures from these incidents. What else could it be? Plus, the chemist exploded at an Israeli military hospital a day after you were captured by the Pakistanis. I can't imagine they need him anymore, can you?"

"Shit. Exploded?"

Mayer told Huxley about the incident.

Huxley shook his head and said, "What the hell are we doing to find these things?"

"What do you think? Everything possible. Every terrorism asset we have is on alert and searching. All possible resources are being diverted. And, of course, there's UNGARD."

Huxley gave Mayer an incredulous look and then looked away. Mayer should not have even said that name outside of the SCIF—a Sensitive Compartmented Information Facility—an area at DHS where they could talk about compartmented capabilities without any risk of electronic eavesdropping.

UNGARD, the nutty government acronym for Unified Neutrino and GammA Ray Detector, had just gone live in the last year. New integrated detection, background mitigation and signature correlation systems deployed on two Coast Guard vessels could allow detection of nukes passing between them on the high seas even if the ships were as much as twenty miles apart. As far as Huxley knew, it was still one of a kind and almost experimental. But he'd seen the data and the thing seemed to work even with heavily shielded nukes.

How could Huxley ask this without breaking protocol or flying back to DC? He looked back at Mayer. "You get more info from the Israelis to give us hope?"

Mayer looked his way. "The Israelis have suddenly become very cooperative, and we are now analyzing the device data they have provided. It's early but it's possible. There is strong concern about our other search detectors."

"Any expansion of the program I'm not aware of?'

"Nope." Mayer gave him a sour look. "Few months to a year. Pretty high tech shit."

Huxley shook his head. Damn, the one UNGARD was 15 miles away from the entrance to the Chesapeake Bay, protecting the approach to Washington and Norfolk. Without another… "So New York Harbor is exposed."

"Fricken naked, unless we can rely on the CSI detectors." Mayer said. "We have to find these nukes."

"Israelis told me CSI might not detect them."

"But they might?" Mayer asked.

"Not clear. Does it matter? These guys are obviously well funded. How much money would it take to get a CSI inspector to look another way in Shanghai? I don't care if they are Americans. A good enough story and enough money and someone will look away. Anyway, it doesn't take a container ship to carry a nuke, does it?"

"I suppose not."

"If we can find Jinnah," Huxley said, "maybe we find a trail to the warheads."

"Not likely."

"Why?"

Mayer looked at the road and then slowly turned his face toward Huxley. "Because two hours ago the Pakistanis found Jinnah near the Sulaiman Mountains along with all of the AWOL soldiers."

"Great. Let's talk to them."

"That might prove difficult since they just dug them up from a shallow common grave."

Huxley stared at the road ahead, holding back a tear. Jinnah dead. He had tried to act the hero, but…what a waste. No, not a waste. The Pakistani had died a hero, for without Jinnah how would they have discovered the missing warheads? The Ghost Leopard now had everything he needed to devastate two cities. Where would he stop? Hell on Earth? He looked up. He hoped Sonatina was right, for if there were such a thing as God, they just might need Him.

SECUNDA SECUNDAE: QUAESITUM

"We hear a cry of fear: terror, not peace."

– Liber Prophetarum—Jer 30:5

"God does not change the condition of a people unless they change what is in themselves."

– Liber Prophetarum—M 13:11

"He will not speak on his own, but he will speak what he hears, and will declare to you the things that are coming."

– Liber Vitae—D 16:13

H E HEARD HER pleas intermingled with the sound of rain splattering on the autumn leaves outside and smelled the subtle breath of slow decay that the drops now struggled so hard to wash away. But Yohanan could not help staring at the red fox's head on the opposite wall. The trophy was one of many that decorated the ramshackle, one-room hunting shack now serving as his residence. Was his visitor the fox or the deer? They were both beautiful animals, and her outward appearance might suggest she could be either. There the similarity ended. A doe moved through the forest in silence and with amazing grace. It ate only the vegetation and bounded away when an unknown sound unsettled its peace. Though it clearly was not the smartest animal in the forest, it knew well how to love and be loved. The doe befit her nearly a year ago, before he had introduced her to the Demoseps. On the other hand, the fox was cute and cuddly looking, but its pleasant outward appearance hid the sly deception that permitted it to steal past canine guards into the coop to kill the hens for its food. The red fox was a relentless, patient and intelligent predator who could leave but a few fluttered feathers as the only remains of its prey. *Yes, she has become the Fox and still cherishes the hunt.* He laughed aloud.

"Why are you laughing? Are you even listening to me? It's been months. Time for you to come back to the world, to the fight." Decima said.

"I'm sorry," Yohanan said, "I was distracted. Look, I hear you. I know you want me to return to Shenandoah and continue the Demoseps' fight. It's not possible for me anymore. I am so sorry for your father. Please forgive me. All I can do is stay here in his hunting shack and reminisce. He rescued me the last time, you know, when my own father died. How can I repay him now that I've killed him?"

"Damn it, for the hundredth time, you did not kill him. Hugleikr did. Or that traitor, Eliezer. Don't blame yourself. You could not have known. We tried to do something good—to rid the world of an evil man. We failed. There will be other opportunities."

Tomadus held out his hands to Decima and turned them around slowly so he and Decima could both see them clearly. "Can you not see the blood dripping from these fingers? I cannot go on."

"By Jupiter, Yohanan, stop it! You cannot take the blame for this. Those Juteslams died at Hugleikr's hands, not yours. Haven't you seen the visi-scan tape? He must have known about the plan—he knew that old Viking ship would explode. He moved away from the ship, put on his helmet and ducked just as the torch was brought to the rail. He knew!"

"Of course, he knew," Yohanan said flatly. "He always knows. He always wins. That changes nothing. Decima, when we set the explosives, we became responsible for everyone who died. Can you not see that? Did you not hear your father's own words just before they killed him? He was the least responsible, and yet he could not stop saying he was sorry. Does that mean nothing to you?"

"Yohanan, you are calling my father a murderer. You are calling me a murderer."

"No. You are not to blame. Your father was wholly innocent. It was my fault. I should have stopped it. I should have seen it coming."

"Stop this nonsense and return with me to Shenandoah," Decima pleaded. "There you can be with your friends and come back to yourself. We need you, Yohanan." She stroked his hair and cheek, and then said softly, "I need you, Yoh. Please."

He felt the string tighten inside his heart, the string she could always pull, but it would not matter today, for it pulled at nothing but a mass of misery. "Dec, I would return with you, for you, if I could, but I am paralyzed. I cannot leave this cabin. Not yet."

"When, then?" she asked quietly.

"When my eyes stop burning with those images. I hope that will be soon, but for now they consume me. Please, let me be. I will return when I am ready."

"All right. I'll leave. But do not despair, Yohanan. Stop blaming yourself. No one else does, especially me." They stood and embraced, and she walked out the door.

The next morning, another animal darkened his doorway. He grimaced and opened the screen door. "I didn't think I would see you here."

"Decima asked me to come," Raanan said. "I'm her last hope to rescue you from this emotional abyss."

Yohanan waved Raanan into the room and took a seat. He found his eyes focusing on the head of the bear on the far wall. Was that Raanan? No, black bears were actually pretty reasonable and gentle creatures given their size. Sure, you wouldn't want to be their prey, but they could easily kill humans if they so chose, and yet they would usually run away. Or maybe that was Raanan. He talked tough, but he never really personally entered the fray. No, Raanan was more like a boa constrictor, slithering along the ground and sneaking up on his food and striking at the last instant, allowing his unwitting prey just enough of the fading moments of life to recognize the beast strangling her. But no snakes decorated the cabin's wall. "What do you want?"

"I just want to help. Is this Quintillus's cabin? How did you avoid the seizure by the Juteslams of all of Quintillus's property?"

"This shack isn't in their records. He bought it ages ago but recorded it under another name—didn't want to be tied to the Demoseps. He came out here with me to avoid the crap the city dealt out. It was his refuge, but now it is mine."

"You do not need a refuge. You need to return to Shenandoah."

Yohanan glared back at Raanan. "I'd as soon return with you as I would sever my left testicle."

"Why are you so bitter with me? It was not my fault."

Yohanan shook his head repeatedly. "Not your fault. Not your fault. No, you are right. It was my fault for being so stupid to blindly follow the pathetic plan of a plain fool. You draw up your little plots and they sound so damn cute, but you seem to forget that innocent people die from your mistakes. I should have seen it coming. No, I did see it, and I let it go anyway. That was far worse. That was inexcusable."

The snake coiled back, hissing. "The pathetic plan of a plain fool? How was I to know that Eliezer was a traitor? How were you to know?"

"I keep hearing that Eliezer was a traitor, but I knew him well. How do we know he was a traitor?"

"You know he failed to show as planned," Raanan said. "Right after the disaster, I caught him trying to skip out of Shenandoah and head to New Jutland territory. He had a stash of cash he could not explain. The only explanation was a payoff."

Yohanan sat back, glaring at Raanan in disbelief. "Then bring him to me so I can question him."

"He's dead. I was overcome with rage and killed him on the spot for his treachery."

Yohanan shook his head. "He was a friend. He was devoted to democracy."

"No, he was a filthy traitor. A swift death was too good for him."

"So you became his executor with no judge and no trial. Not very democratic of you. Do you think you are Hugleikr?"

"Sometimes democracy gets in the way of what is right in the moment."

"And who are you to decide what is right? He's a convenient scapegoat for your failure. A dead stooge tells no tales. Did you take his blood money as well?"

Raanan clenched his fists. "Are you suggesting that I had something to do with the massacre?"

Yohanan's forehead creased and his eyes squinted slightly. "Not at all, but you are quite adept at shifting the blame for your failures. Maybe you want to kill me too."

Raanan stood. "I won't take this rubbish from you. You are a broken and beaten shadow of a man. No use to anyone, especially yourself."

"Get the hell out of my shack, boa."

Raanan squinted his eyes, shook his tilting head in obvious condescension, and walked out the door, slamming it hard.

CHAPTER 44

"I am looking for Isa, of that group, the Way. Do you know where he may be preaching?" Tomadus somewhat squeamishly asked the concierge of his hotel. At least he was in the Sunni Muslim Empire now, where looking for a man of God was not entirely out of place—if he had been of the correct religion. And in Toledo, in the middle of the Iberian Peninsula, even Jews were not entirely out of place.

The hotel concierge screwed his face up, looking at him like he could no longer trust his overnight guest. "You aren't one of those radicals hanging on his every word, are you? From the cut of your robes I can tell that you don't belong with that wretched throng that follows him everywhere. Look, this is a respectable hotel. We don't want any of that rabid element around here stirring up any trouble."

Tomadus smiled gently. Even in Toledo, where there was some modicum of tolerance for more than one religious view, there were many who hated anything that threatened their status quo. "No, sir, I could not be a follower of someone I have never even seen in person speak publicly. I am just curious and thought it would be a nice little diversion today."

"Well, that is understandable. Peculiar one, he is. I saw on his flyer that he is speaking at the south end of the old city, on the banks of the Tagus River. Not surprising that no mosque or synagogue will have him since his followers are all mixed up together. Imagine that!"

"South end?"

"Sure. About a twenty minute walk. Just go three blocks east and ten blocks south and you'll be pretty close. Easy walk down the hill but a tougher walk back."

"*Gratias*," Tomadus said. A walk would let him soak up the mid-morning sun and give him more time for reflection. After all, what was he really doing here in Toledo? Sure, he could afford a short respite from his work. Stephan could handle many of the day-to-day details now that he had put together a substantial international marketing and distribution network. Moreover, since he had delivered the schematics to the Imperium, the pressure should be off for now—unless their technologists figured out his crafty little modification. He and the First Consul had grown closer as a result, and the Imperium seemed willing to help him in his business. So now he had a little time to take a breath, but why not take his physic-tech's advice instead and travel to a fancy resort on the Mediterranean and relax? Because he knew he could not truly relax until he got to the bottom of these visions. From every angle that he had examined the problem, he kept seeing the man in the white robes.

Still, after Isa had uttered only a few strange words on the visi-scan to grab his attention, Tomadus had decided he should board an *aeronavis* and fly the 900 miles from Roma to see him speak in person? What could he hope to gain? Clarity? Sanity? The visions had begun when Isa had touched him. Then Isa had referred to the Light—the Light of Our Yesterdays. Isa had seemed to invite him personally to see him. Then over the last couple months the visions had grown clearer, more distinct. He could already recall so many things—so much intrigue, so much history, so much despair—from this other world and the strange investigator he seemed to be inhabiting. It was almost as if he had once lived there, sharing that man's memories, yet the visions kept coming with no clear purpose. But this preacher Isa was at the center of this. Yes, Isa must be the key to solving the puzzle.

At least Tomadus had not acted rashly. He had spent the past couple months and a considerable sum—one hundred thousand talents—trying to figure out if Isa was just another con man using a supreme deity to make some coin off those pathetic souls so desperate to hear answers to questions they did not even know how to ask. But his investigators had found nothing illicit and nothing that even smelled of greed by this preacher.

The Way had its wealthy benefactors who provided resources to the movement, but as far as his investigator could tell, the money never came back to Isa or his close followers for any kind of personal use or gain. They lived practically like hermits, sleeping in tents, occasionally staying in the homes of supporters for a meal and a shower, and moved about the world generally by foot, though they would occasionally take busses or trains or even ships. The Way seemed utterly bereft of corruption of any kind.

So if this Isa were like Tomadus, if he could actually remember a different world as if it were his own, then he must have some other angle on this preacher business. Why else would he seem to copy a religious icon from Tomadus's dream world? Isa's purpose did not seem to be profit, so maybe he wanted power. Or was it something else? Having exhausted his investigation from afar, Tomadus had decided to find out for himself. And perhaps he might discover something about the light and these visions and find some way to purge the constant scourge on his psyche.

Tomadus arrived at the southern hillside and looked down the steep banks to the River Tagus. A man was standing on a small raft moored at the edge of the river. It acted as a makeshift stage at the foot of a natural auditorium. As Tomadus worked his way down and through a large crowd, he could hear every word spoken by the gentle man in white robes.

"Do not think you are holy because you have come to hear me speak. You are all sinners. Who among you can truthfully claim to have followed God's will in all things? But do not despair. The greater the evil you have done, the greater the good you can do by returning to the Father. It has been said that those who take a life, which God has made sacred, who commit adultery, whoever does these things will face penalties, and their torment will be doubled on the Day of Resurrection, and they will remain in torment, disgraced. But it has also been said of these and other sinners, if they repent, if they believe and if they do good deeds, they will have their evil deeds changed by God into good ones, for our Father is most forgiving, most merciful. People who repent and do good deeds truly return to the loving hands of our Father."

As he heard this, Tomadus passed by a few men with turbans and robes speaking in Arabic. "He quotes almost directly from the Great Book, but calls Allah 'Father.' How strange."

His companion answered, "He is speaking of Allah figuratively. His message is love, and he wishes us to see God as our loving father. Beautiful."

As Tomadus made his way down the embankment, Isa continued to speak, his voice growing in volume and pitch. "Many who call themselves holy men or imams or rabbis have forgotten this: God forgives, for men are sheep and need a true shepherd to bring them back to their flock. How could your hapless shepherds forget what the Father proclaimed from above to his servant?

"Woe to the shepherds who have been pasturing themselves! Should not shepherds pasture the flock? You consumed milk, wore wool, and slaughtered fatlings, but the flock you did not pasture. You did not strengthen the weak nor heal the sick nor bind up the injured. You did not bring back the stray or seek the lost but ruled them harshly and brutally. So they were scattered for lack of a shepherd, and became food for all the wild beasts. They were scattered and wandered over all the mountains and high hills.

"I myself will search for my sheep and examine them. I will deliver them from every place where they were scattered on the day of dark clouds. I myself will pasture my sheep. I myself will give them rest. The lost I will search out, the strays I will bring back, the injured I will bind up, and the sick I will heal. Follow me and you will have rest. Repent, and our Father will be merciful."

A murmur arose from the crowd, particularly those with yarmulkes closer to Isa. Tomadus overheard one of them speaking with his friend, "What is this talk of sheep and shepherds? Is there any among us who is a shepherd or knows one? Have you ever even seen a sheep?"

The friend stroked his beard. "He quotes a great prophet from many millennia ago. Sheep and shepherds were everywhere then, so I have no problem with that part. But I think he claims to be the shepherd mentioned by Ezekiel, and we know the shepherd is God himself, so what can he be saying?"

Another in the group said, "He is speaking metaphorically. He is the new shepherd for the sheep, and he will help the Great Shepherd, God, gather his flock. He is chastising our religious leaders because they have failed us by merely condemning us without forgiveness and mercy. He understands we are all sinners and wants to help us return to the flock."

"Does he realize the danger of his words? He must know these words will eventually reach the Grand Imams and the Abh Beyth Diyn."

"I don't know. He doesn't seem to care."

Tomadus approached the river's edge, and Isa looked over to him and smiled. Tomadus nodded and returned the smile.

Isa looked back to the crowd. "There was a wealthy businessman in this area who had two sons, and the younger son said to his father, 'Father, give me the share of your business that should come to me upon your death.' So the father obtained an appraisal of his business and took out a loan from the bank for one-half its worth. This he gave it to the younger son in cash. Now the younger son immediately collected all his belongings and traveled to Roma, where he quickly squandered this inheritance through luxurious living, constantly visiting the many taberna, gambling establishments and brothels there. When he had freely spent everything, a recession hit the Romanus economy, and he found himself in dire need, but there was no work available in the local factories. Eventually, he found a local farmer who was willing to hire him to tend to his pigs, but paid him little. And he longed to eat his fill of the corn on which the swine fed, but nobody gave him any. Coming to his senses he thought, 'How many of my father's employees have more than enough food to eat, but here am I, dying from hunger.'

"So he got up and went back to his father. Upon seeing his son, his father was filled with compassion. He ran to his son, embraced him and kissed him. His son said to him, 'Father, I have sinned against Heaven and against you; I no longer deserve to be called your son; treat me as you would treat one of your employees.' But his father ordered his servants, 'Quickly, bring the finest robe and put it on him; put a ring on his finger and new sandals on his feet. Let us celebrate with a feast this very evening, because this son of mine was dead, and has come to life again; he was lost, and has been found.'

"Now the older son had been working late at his father's office, and, on his way back, as he neared the house, he heard the sound of music and revelry. He called one of the servants and asked what this might mean. The servant said to him, 'Your brother has returned and your father has hired the best caterer and invited all of his friends to celebrate.'

"The older son became angry, and when he refused to enter the house, his father came out and pleaded with him. He said to his father in reply, 'Look, all these years I served you and not once did I disobey your orders and I worked under you at your office, yet you never hosted even a small party for me and my friends. But when the son who swallowed up your property with prostitutes returns, you throw a lavish party with all of our friends.'

"The father replied, 'My son, you are here with me always; everything I have is yours. But now we must celebrate and rejoice, because your brother was dead and has come to life again; he was lost and has been found.'"

Isa looked around at the crowd for a few seconds and then added, "You must take these words and bind them to your own hearts."

When the crowd began to disperse up the hill and back into the city, Isa stepped off the raft and began walking down the shore, surrounded by his ten disciples. Tomadus stepped forward and one of the men confronted him. "What do you want with the Master? He needs his rest."

Isa turned and looked straight into Tomadus's eyes. "Tomadus, you have returned to me."

"You remember me?" Tomadus asked.

"Of course." Isa turned to the disciple. "It is all right, Simeon. Let him join us."

"*Gratias*. I never thought our paths would cross again."

"Yet here you are."

"I have come because you asked for me on the visi-scan."

Isa beamed. "I did?"

Tomadus nodded. "You said that all who can see the Light of Our Yesterdays and search for truth should follow you."

"So I did, Tomadus, for the people who walked in darkness have seen a great light. Upon those who lived in a land of gloom a light has shone. Do you search for the light of truth?"

"I search for understanding. If I comprehend you correctly, the Light of Our Yesterdays touches me often—far too often for my taste. Before I heard you on the visi-scan, I thought I was going insane. Have you too seen this other world?"

Isa looked around for a few seconds—first at the other followers and then at the sky above and the river to the south and the city to the north and finally back to Tomadus. "I see many things. To many, anything foreign becomes part of an unknown world from which they instinctively recoil. You must not be afraid, Tomadus, for you have been given a great gift. Your yearning aspires to greatness, my friend. Please, follow me."

"I'm afraid I don't quite fit into your little gang of preachers here." Tomadus waved his hand toward Isa's close followers. "I am a Romanus technologist and was raised from a child to believe in no god. I see you doing good things for people, and I respect you greatly for that. Nevertheless, your words that look to deities for answers are not written in my heart. I am sorry."

Isa smiled and clasped his hands together. "Did you listen to my sermon today?"

Tomadus nodded. "I noticed you drew from both Islamic and Jewish sources. I have not heard of the last story, though." *Well, not from this world, at least.* But the story had triggered a memory from deep within the other world, about a religion—Christianity—and a prophet—Jesus—both unknown to this world. Tomadus smiled. *Isa must have had similar visions and memories of that other world.* He looked back up at Isa. "In any case, it got me wondering, which are you, a Muslim or a Jew?"

"That story was for you," Isa said. "Hear these words. There were two men, one a Jewish rabbi and the other a Romanus citizen. Now, publicly, the Jewish rabbi was a model to members of his synagogue. He told them how to behave and how to eat, and how to praise God, and he was much admired by many of the people as a man of God. But behind closed doors, he led another life. He took money from his synagogue that was donated for the poor and used it for his own luxurious habits. He engaged in orgies with prostitutes that would make the Romanus emperors of old blush. And instead of seeking God's mercy and forgiveness for these transgressions, he told himself in secret not to worry about them, for if there were truly a God who could punish him, he would have been punished long ago.

"Now the Romanus citizen often said that he was no man of God, that he had never believed in such silly things. However, he always tried to help those who struggled with injustice. He gave shelter to the homeless and gave food to the hungry. He did not know why he did these things, which seemed clearly against his own economic interest, yet he knew they somehow helped him cope with that yearning, that feeling in his stomach that told him what was right. And he kept searching for an answer to that yearning."

Tomadus stared at Isa with his mouth agape. Had Isa had been talking about the creature within him? "Searching?"

"Yes, Tomadus. Now tell me, although one of these men is called a Jewish Rabbi and the other is called an Romanus atheist, who is closer to the Kingdom of Heaven?"

"I imagine the Romanus."

Isa said joyously, "Your imagination has always been on target, Tomadus. It is one of your greatest gifts."

Tomadus stroked his beard. "Okay, I get it, I think. What matters is what we truly believe and how we act on those beliefs. I cannot disagree with you. But what does this have to do with the Light of Our Yesterdays?"

Isa smiled. "Follow me, and you will find what you seek."

CHAPTER 45

THE TAGUS RIVER glimmered with the last few rays of a waning sun as Toledo rose above the far shore to the east. On the shore at the near edge of the river, mature maple trees intermingled among the twenty or so tents and nearly as many campfires, each crackling out its own garbled sermon as it warmed the congregation surrounding it. Beside one of the fires sat Diego, one of the group of Isa's closest disciples, better known as the Ten. Diego was playing an oud and singing softly. The smell of escudella made Tomadus's stomach growl. He smiled, nonetheless. He would soon satisfy that particular little animal with some good food; the other creature, the formerly insatiable one, had been lying silently in his gut throughout the day.

"What are you smiling about, Romanus? Thinking about one of your finer prostitutes in Roma?" asked Simeon. The speaker was tall and rotund, with a long, black, straggly beard. He reclined on his side by the fire on a blanket. But for the size of his belly, the man looked like one of the unfortunate homeless of Roma that Tomadus remembered all too well from his youth.

"No, Simeon, though if you long to meet one, perhaps I can set that up for you."

The others laughed. Simeon stared back. "Oh, I did not realize the atheist was also a pimp." More laughter.

Tomadus bit his lip for a second, then opened his mouth but stopped before his calculated wisecrack streamed out. Isa had said: *To many, anything foreign becomes an unknown world from which they instinctively recoil.* Yes, Tomadus was foreign to them and not just because he was from Roma. *Let it go.* "Simeon, I am sorry if I have somehow offended you with my presence. I am a Romanus, but fortunately I have not engaged in all of the known pastimes of my home. May I ask where you are from?"

Simeon looked back at him sideways and flashed a satisfied smile. "The Palestinian Province. Same as Isa. We go back over two years now."

"I see," said Tomadus. "You must be one of the early believers, very dedicated to the Way."

"Yes, I am dedicated to Isa."

"Then perhaps you should listen more carefully to his words." Tomadus got up and walked away from the fire and toward the women cooking the escuadella in a large pot over another fire not twenty feet away.

One of the older women walked toward him. "Do not let Simeon bother you. He is often gruff at first and forgets himself, but he is a good man. Give him time."

"Thank you for the advice. My name is Tomadus."

"Yes, I know. My name is Maryam. Isa is my son." She bowed slightly.

Tomadus returned the gesture with a deep bow. "Even your name."

"My name?" she said.

"Nothing, it is just a dream. And yet, even your name is the same."

"The same as what?" Maryam asked.

"The same as…never mind. It is but a dream. It is a pleasure to meet you. Your son has quite a following."

"It has grown so quickly. I never would have imagined so many people coming to hear him speak on a hillside in the Andalus Province. Then again, why should I be surprised?"

"Why, indeed?" Tomadus looked up at the stars and back to Maryam. "He seems to understand crowds. Has he always spoken in circles? I find it hard to get a straight answer from him, even in private."

"He gives your heart room to welcome the truth. Sometimes, your brain must find the answer on its own before it can comprehend what is before it."

Tomadus let out a little laugh, "I see the fig doesn't fall far from the tree."

As they talked, Tomadus noticed a very large man—probably as big as four and a half *cubitorum* tall and weighing 400 *librae*—slowly making his way over from the foliage near the camp. His enormous hands were cupped and joined together to form a large hollow ball. He seemed mesmerized by whatever was in his hands as he kept peeking inside the little space between his huge thumbs. He walked by the pots and pans stacked near one of the tents and tripped over several of them, creating an enormous ruckus. He looked down and shook his head with a frown for a second, but never lost the spherical coupling of his hands.

His giant grin quickly returned as he walked directly toward them. "Maryam, look what I found. It is a bug with a torch on its butt!" He opened the space between his hands slowly to let her see his captured treasure.

Maryam smiled gently at him and said, "Adin, that is a firefly. Isn't it beautiful?"

"Yes ma'am. It's very pretty."

"Can you give him his freedom now?"

Adin frowned a bit, looking first at his hands and then back at Maryam. "You mean let him go?"

Maryam smiled and nodded.

Adin tilted his head. "Then I won't have him anymore."

"Yes, Adin, but he will be free. Isn't that beautiful all by itself? And you can catch another tomorrow night and set him free as well, for surely where there is one firefly, there are hundreds more."

"Okay," Adin replied meekly. He bit the lower corner of his lip and exhaled hard, briefly closing his eyes tightly. With an exaggerated gesture, he looked up and opened his hands and arms quickly until they were stretched to the sky. The firefly flew away into the evening, twinkling as he moved away. Adin smiled and looked at Maryam, "He just said good-bye."

"Indeed, he did, Adin. Indeed, he did. Now, Adin, there is someone here I would like you to meet. His name is Tomadus, and he is from Roma."

"Hello, Tomadus from Roma. My name is Adin."

Tomadus let out a little laugh. "It is very nice to meet you."

"Adin, we are going to need more wood for cooking. Do you think you could go collect some?" Maryam said.

"Yes, ma'am."

The giant grabbed an axe and a lumber saw that looked like a little nail file in his hands and marched into the woods.

"Is he your son also?" Tomadus asked.

"Oh no. He joined us in the Grecian Province. He is one of the Ten."

Tomadus jerked up, his eyes squinting and mouth open a bit too wide.

"Do not be misled by his lack of guile," Maryam said. "Adin understands Isa more than most. The loving heart God gave him perfectly complements the wonder of his beautiful mind."

CHAPTER 46

THE LIGHT OF dawn was just peaking out to the east of the Tagus when the flap to Tomadus's tent pulled open, and a figure appeared. His body was surrounded by that familiar residual hue from Tomadus's dreams. Still dazed, Tomadus blinked a few times, and then rubbed his face and eyes. There stood Isa in the morning's glow.

"Tomadus, walk with me."

"As you wish."

They left the others sleeping in their tents, and in a few moments they were walking side-by-side, down a path by the river, the mid-autumn morning chill swirling wisps of fog over its surface. A hoopoe fluttered its wings as he swooped through and fed upon the swarming gnats above a few lily pads; several buntings sang their songs of joy from the treetops. The full-bodied fragrance of jasmine filled the air as the blooms clung to their last few weeks of life.

"Now that you have been with us for a couple of weeks," Isa began, "tell me your impressions of our little group."

"You want kindness or honesty?"

"Are you not capable of both?"

Tomadus took a deep breath. "Most of the Ten have welcomed me openly and they have made the time pass very quickly. A few others, particularly Simeon, seem to suspect me of some ill will toward you. I am not sure why. And, of course, your mother is pure joy."

Isa nodded. "I see you understand Maryam well. Simeon can be a bit of a bull, but he means well. He thinks he needs to protect me, and that causes him trouble occasionally. He believes you are a spy."

"A spy? For whom?"

Isa eyed Tomadus. "We are aware of your relationship with the First Consul and the Three Empires."

"That is a business arrangement. Nothing more. Do you think I am a spy?"

"Another label of no matter. I have nothing to hide. I speak in public, and if the First Consul wishes to hear my words, he can do so at any time. Simeon can tussle with trust at times. It will take him time to understand, but his faith is strong. Do you have faith, Tomadus?"

Tomadus looked up at Isa with a start, his eyes widening and his throat tightening. *Either I have faith or I am a spy? He must have an idea that I understand him.* "If you are asking whether, after these two weeks, I now believe in your God, the answer is still 'no.' But I do have faith in you, Isa. You have the ability to bring people together. You remind us all how to live moral and meaningful lives. I see the hope you engender in the eyes of the downtrodden. That itself seems a miracle in these times."

Isa nodded to him with a gentle smile. "Yet?"

"I am a man of science. I see the miracles proclaimed by your flock. You heal the sick and injured to degrees I've never encountered with Romanus physic-techs. But miracles? I have seen so many strange things in my mind's eye now that would undoubtedly seem to be miracles to any other Romanus technologist, yet I know they are real. So do I have faith? Yes, I have faith in you, Isa, to help those who need your help the most. And I know that if I were to believe in your God, I would certainly believe you served him well."

Isa stopped walking and turned toward Tomadus. "I see you answered honestly to your own mind, yet you found a way to be kind to me just the same. What of your search for truth?"

"I...I don't know. I had hoped to find others like me here, even yourself, but now I wonder."

"Others like you?"

"Yes. You proclaimed the Light of Our Yesterdays. A bright white light has flashed in my eyes while I have seen and heard and understood images from what I can only describe as another world. The first time it happened was when I met you in Roma at the conference. I thought that is what you meant." Tomadus stared down at his sandals. "Do you think I am insane?"

Isa began walking again. "What do you think this light is?"

"I do not know."

"Someday, you will."

Tomadus looked into Isa's eyes. "How do you know this?"

"The same way that I know you will eventually believe in me."

Pressing his lips together tightly, Tomadus blew his breath hard out his nose. "I do not wish to offend you, but may I be frank?"

"Of course."

"I haven't just seen images and heard things, I now have nearly complete memories of this other world, as if I lived there myself as another person in another time. I don't even know how they got there. I certainly do not recall specific visions of all of these memories, yet there they are, invading my thoughts. Still, you said 'yesterdays,' and I know it is not truly our own yesterdays, not as far as I can tell. The world is so different, but it is not the past. In some ways it is more advanced than our own world—medicine for instance—but in other ways… I wonder. At first, I thought I was going insane. Now I just want an explanation."

"How would this offend me?" Isa asked.

"Look, I remember that world almost as if I had lived there, including its history, its religions, its religious leaders. I remember much about Christianity, its history and its beliefs. Don't you understand?"

"And so?"

"And so, don't you remember it in just the same way?"

Isa stopped and turned toward him. "Why would you think so?"

"Isn't that where you got the idea for your mission, for the Way, for many of your speeches?"

"From this other world?"

"Yes," said Tomadus. "The connection is too strong to be denied. Look, what you are doing is wonderful. I have no intention of changing that. So what if it has been done before in this other world. I would never tell the others. Trust me. I just want to know I am not alone."

"You will never be alone if you follow me."

Tomadus frowned. *Can I say it directly without shouting, "FRAUD?"* This preacher did not deserve to be denounced. He was doing everything to help others, with nothing to help himself. So what if this gentle man had borrowed his life's work from this other world? He's using that knowledge for the good of mankind. *What can smoke this out without the taint of blame?* He smiled. "Are you not acting as Christ?"

Isa gently placed his hands on Tomadus's shoulders. "God is truly with you, no matter what you may believe, no matter what you may think you understand. But you must not yet share this understanding, even with the Ten."

Tomadus stared into Isa's eyes. *He can see into me, yet cannot understand my words. I don't believe in Christ. He must know that. I don't think I believed in Christ in the other world. Is it possible he really doesn't see that other world? No, he borrows from it, doesn't he? It cannot be coincidence, can it?* Tomadus put his hands on Isa's arms. "Please tell me directly so I may understand. What did you mean when you said 'the light of our yesterdays?'"

"You know the answer in your heart already. I am the Light—the Light of Our Todays, the Light of Our Tomorrows, the Light of Our Yesterdays. When you understand the Light, you will understand me. When you understand its source, you will understand yourself. Now, will you stay with me?"

Tomadus pulled back from Isa, never diverting his eyes from the preacher. "I'm sorry, but I must attend to my company for a few days. And I may be gone longer on a trip to the Aztec Empire. If successful, perhaps I'll be able to contribute a few talents to your cause."

"We must talk more in the future about your devotion to making money. But the Aztec Empire is our destination for the winter as well. Perhaps you would accompany me."

Tomadus cocked his head. "Perhaps. First, I need to stop in Tonquizalixco Tetepe to see a friend in need."

"A friend in need?"

"Yes, I had tried to reach him after all these months to no avail. I finally reached a mutual friend and discovered he could probably use a little of your medicine."

"My medicine?" Isa asked.

"Call it spiritual medicine. He has become despondent and disillusioned. You seem to have a way of rescuing the suffering from their mourning."

"What is his name?"

"Yohanan."

Isa smiled. "Of course, Yohanan. I will do what I can. We can meet the others in Tenochtitlan."

CHAPTER 47

H E WAS RUNNING toward Decima through a faceless, blurry crowd. He glanced ahead and saw Hugleikr up high, his huge head and orange hair bouncing to the cheers as he gestured to the multitude. Someone was climbing up the stairs. He desperately drove through the crowd, pushing the strangers aside. There, just a few yards away, he saw the device in her hands. "Stop!" he screamed. She smiled, ran and flipped the switch. Nothing happened. There was no sound but the repeated banging in his left ear.

Yohanan awoke with his clothes dripping in sweat. The red fox stared at him from the wall across the room. "Oh, hello, Decima," he said.

He realized the banging was coming from the door of the shack. The familiar female voice said, "Yohanan, I know you are in there. Let me in."

He wiped the cobwebs out of his eyes as he went to open the door. Decima stood there, beautiful as ever, but her beauty fell short of another standing beside her. The new woman smiled sweetly and lunged at him with arms open, "Yohanan!"

"Jochi!" He squeezed her tightly to him and did not let go. "I am so happy to see you, my dear sister." He pulled away. "You cannot remain here. Tetepe is too dangerous. You must return to Roma." He glared at Decima. "What have you done?"

"*Vah!* Don't blame her," said Jochi. "After all that's happened, I needed to see you. She simply showed me the way. Let us put aside these troubles and have a few laughs like the old times. It has been too long."

"I'm sorry, please come in."

"You two should spend some time together. I'll return tomorrow to see how things are going. I've brought some food," Decima said, handing him a satchel.

"Can I at least get you some tea?" Yohanan asked.

"No thanks. I'll see you tomorrow." Decima smiled and walked away into the forest.

"I'd love some tea. May I?" Jochi gestured to a chair by a table in the kitchen corner of the shack.

"Of course." He put on a pot of water and joined her at the table. "You have grown quite beautiful these past ten years."

She blushed. "The sun of Roma has been friendlier to my complexion than the shrapnel of Tetepe." When Yohanan grimaced, she said, "I am sorry, brother. I didn't mean—"

"No problem. You are right. This place is still a disaster. I'm so glad you were able to find a decent Romanus couple to take you away from it all."

"You know you found them for me. You sent me away. I was a little girl. At the time I felt abandoned. But I came to understand why you did it. I just wish you had come with me. I have missed you so."

"My place was here, amid the chaos. I still believe that, though I don't know how. What a wreck I've made of this world."

She gently grabbed his hands resting on the table. "It wasn't your fault. I heard about it from Decima. You must let it go."

As the pot began to whistle, he stood up to pour their cups. "I can't. The nightmare will be with me always, just like the rubble of our house. The wounds don't seem to heal." He put the teabag in the cup of water and handed it to her, and then sat down with his own. "The wounds will never heal. The best I can do is to find a clean bandage to staunch the bleeding. I'm searching for that now. The old bandage kept me alive, but I had to throw it away. It is dripping with blood—and not just my own. I need to find another way."

Leaning forward, Jochi said quietly, "I can be your bandage, Yoh. Come back with me. Get out of this hell. I'm sure I can talk my former guardians into helping support you until you get on your feet."

"The Romanus government will never let me live there. I would not wish to jeopardize your life there. It is dangerous enough for you to be here."

"You're exaggerating."

"It has gotten worse, especially since the…the disaster."

"I'm so sorry, Yoh." She grabbed his hands. "Let me help."

He smiled softly, nodded, then winked. "Well, you don't look much like a bandage, but you'll do as an antibiotic. You have already saved my life by coming." He glanced over at Quintillus's favorite shotgun hanging on the wall. "And since you are here, why don't we go hunting for some dinner like in the old days?"

Jochi looked squeamish. "Decima brought us dinner. I'm not sure I could…"

"It will keep. Let's go find a big pheasant like we did with Papa."

"Papa would never let me come, remember? I stayed home by the fire where it was warm."

"Well, then, you have something to learn."

CHAPTER 48

THE LAST SPRINKLES of sunlight were edging over the western Tetepian horizon when Yohanan came out of the woods holding Quintillus's favorite shotgun on his right shoulder. Jochi carried the fat pheasant he had shot.

"I'll start preparing the bird," she said. "You get some more wood for the fire."

As Yohanan gathered split logs from the stack behind the shack, he saw two familiar figures emerge from the forest. He quickly dropped the wood and took up the shotgun. As the men drew closer, he recognized Tomadus, his elaborately stenciled crimson robes betraying him as a Romanus technologist. The man next to him wore a simple white robe. Robes were not favored here; otherwise, that man would have fit right in as one of those desperately poor Jews of Tetepe.

"Tomadus, what are you doing here?" Yohanan asked.

"A fine way to welcome a friend."

"I am sorry. I don't get many visitors these days." The two shook hands. He looked at the man in the white robes. "And this is?"

"Isa, of the Palestinian Province. Isa, this is Yohanan, of the Tetepian hunting lodge, it seems."

Yohanan bowed his head for a moment and then reached his hand out to the stranger. "Welcome." Yohanan looked right at Isa's eyes. They were strangely gentle, comforting almost, but piercing, nonetheless. It was as if he were looking deep inside you, searching not for trouble, but for some pearl of goodness within that you did not even know existed. The eyes filled Yohanan with such warmth that he did not wish to look away.

"It is good to meet you, Yohanan. Tomadus has told me much about you."

"Please, come on in. You are both welcome for dinner."

They scrambled into the cabin, and there was Jochi tending to dinner preparations at the hearth. She turned and faced them, her cheerful smile doing its best to brighten up the dim interior of the shack.

Yohanan gestured toward the men. "This is Tomadus, a Romanus merchant and technologist, and Isa, who I am told comes from Palestine. Gentlemen, this is my sister, Jochi, who now hails from a prominent Romanus family herself."

"Stop it, Yoh." She laughed and then returned her gaze to the two men. "I am but a Tetepian in Romanus clothing, and not even that when I am here."

Yohanan had not seen that look on her before. Had Isa mesmerized her as much as him? Yohanan turned around and saw the same starlit gaze returned by Tomadus, which was peculiar on its own.

Tomadus stepped forward and bowed with his right hand to his chest. "I am delighted to meet you, madam, although the moment I saw you my heart began leaping as if I had seen you before." Isa repeated the gesture and Jochi nodded simply at both. Tomadus continued with a slightly pinched tone, "Yohanan, I was not aware your sister was living in Roma. I wish I had known." He turned back to Jochi. "I remember your picture, of course, although you were so much younger then."

The words had not been out of his mouth for more than an instant when Tomadus must have realized his mistake, for there could only be one picture. "Oh, I am so sorry, madam," he said with a slight nod. He turned to her brother and nodded, "Yohanan." He looked back at Jochi. "Jochi, I am a clumsy fool. Please forgive my carelessness."

"No need, sir," Jochi said. "Unfortunately, it is how people seem to know me." She was still staring, not at Tomadus, but at Isa.

Noticing this, Yohanan turned to Isa, took him by the elbow and began to escort him to the small sitting area on the other side of the room. "My sister has been living in Roma for nearly ten years now. Quintillus of Roma was kind enough to find her some guardians who took her away from this." He looked down. "He is no longer with us."

"Yes. My condolences."

"Thank you. Now, please, sit down. We don't have much here, but we will try to make it comfortable for dinner tonight. Tell me, Tomadus, why have you come to the backwoods of the hinterlands?"

"Let me be frank," Tomadus began. "I saw what happened to Decima's father on the visi-scan. I do not know the details, nor do I wish to. I tried to reach you, but could only reach her. She said you have withdrawn from your movement and fallen into some kind of depression. You remain in this remote cabin though the Juteslams do not pursue you. Decima seemed to be desperate to help you, so she asked if I could visit you. I brought a friend who I think can help."

Yohanan replied, "Sorry that you have come all of this way. Jochi is helping me. I will be fine."

"Then when will you return to Shenandoah?" Tomadus asked. "The people there need you."

"They do not," said Yohanan flatly. "I have failed as a leader. You were right, Tomadus, when we met a few months ago. The disaster confirmed it. Violence is not the answer. Yet I can find no good answers. I don't even know the questions anymore. I am powerless to fight the Juteslams even though they remain evil. They kill and they murder. When we retaliate, more innocents die. The blood has flowed so deep that I can no longer wade through it. And so, here I sit, powerless in my shack, killing only wild animals for sustenance. I'm sorry." He lowered his head and looked at the floor.

Isa said gently, "Do not be sorry for that, Yohanan, for you have come far. But you are still filled with much hatred for the Juteslams."

"Of course. They are beasts."

Isa leaned very close to Yohanan and said softly, "You must learn to love them."

Yohanan glared at the gentle man. "Are you crazy? They killed my parents. They killed Quintillus. They have killed so many of my friends that I have lost count. How can I ever love them?"

"You speak of Juteslams as if they are all one person," said Isa. "Did every Juteslam kill your parents? Did every Juteslam kill Quintillus or your friends? They have family and friends who have also died in this conflict. Until you love the Juteslams as people, you can never truly understand them. And until you understand them and they understand your people, you will always be at war, not just with them, but with yourself."

Yohanan shook his head, his lips tightly drawn. "Look, I know Hugleikr and Skjöldr are mostly responsible for this. I have already begged God to forgive me for the deaths of innocent Juteslams. But I will not weep at the death of Skjöldr or Hugleikr. They deserve to die."

"Can you condemn them to death by yourself?" Isa asked. "Are you the judge of their sins against God?"

"No, but I am the judge of their sins against my people."

"Do not seek to judge others, Yohanan, for he who judges must himself be judged. A man who cannot forgive cannot be forgiven."

Yohanan felt the heat of Isa's eyes penetrating his soul. *Yes, I'm sorry, but at least I killed with justice as my guide. How can you ask this of me?* He stared at the table legs and then closed his eyes. "I'm sorry, but I can never forgive them."

Isa grabbed Yohanan's hands gently. "Then you will always suffer. The pain you feel, that you have felt these many years, is masked by a glowing and growing hatred that blackens your soul. Lose the hatred, Yohanan, and reveal your own sorrow. Understand the sorrow, accept it, and convert it to love and forgiveness, not hatred and vengeance. It is only in this way that you can truly set your heart free."

"Yohanan," Tomadus said, "when we first met, you asked me to return when I found another way. Today you said you are searching for an answer and do not even know the questions. I brought Isa here because I think he could be the answer. He may be the other way you seek."

Isa continued to hold Yohanan's hands. Neither stirred, and the silence and connection between them seemed to unnerve Jochi. She walked over and began massaging her brother's shoulders. "It's easy for you two to say these things," she said sharply. "You haven't suffered the evil that my brother has endured throughout his lifetime. He saw his own parents…they…you wouldn't understand. He will never forsake them. He will never forsake his people."

Tomadus's eyes squinted as he tilted his head. "Forsake them?" he asked. He opened and closed his eyes quickly as if he were trying to recover from the brightness of the sun. "Why would he forsake them?"

"You ask him to find another way…to turn against his past."

"No," Yohanan said softly. He released Isa's right hand and reached up, gently grabbing her right hand in his and holding it to his cheek. A tear meandered from his opposite eye to his chin. "No, Jochi, Isa is right. The pain is so very deep, and I no longer know from where it comes. I fear my wounds bleed more than my own blood. Dear God what bandage could ever slow this intermingled liquid flowing out my veins? I am dead."

Isa said softly, "By saying so, you have saved your life. Follow me and those wounds will heal, even if you die."

The other three cocked their heads at Isa in confusion. Isa closed his eyes and whispered a prayer.

CHAPTER 49

"**Y**ohanan!" Decima shrieked from across Shenandoah Square. She ran up to Yohanan and jumped into his arms. He held her there for a few seconds in nearly the exact spot where he had delivered his anti-treaty speech just a few months before.

They separated, and she began speaking rapidly, "I'm so happy to see you here. I knew your sister and Tomadus would help free you from whatever had taken hold of you. We have made so many good plans in the past few weeks. I can't wait to share them with you. We just need to find someone who will…,well, let's save that for the meeting. I was just heading up there. Come with me."

"I'm happy to see you as well. But, please, wait a few moments. Here, have a seat on this bench. I want to tell you about my plans." The two sat down slowly, her narrowing eyes never leaving his. He looked down and noticed the ring on her finger. Its shining platinum was overshadowed by a triangle shaped by three gems: a ruby, a sapphire and a diamond. "Your father's ring."

"Yes. They let me have it. It's nearly all I have left of him."

"He will always be in our hearts. His love has given me the strength to seek another path."

"You've come up with a plan. Tell me about it at the meeting. Let's go. I'm sure everyone would want to hear your idea."

"I'm not talking about strategy, at least not what you are thinking."

"What then?"

Yohanan smiled. "I met an unusual man—Isa. He and Tomadus are heading to the Aztec Empire. I'm going with them."

"What? Why? Are they looking for military support? Can Tomadus pull it off?"

"No, Dec, just the opposite. They seek nothing but peace."

Decima's shoulders sagged and she frowned. "More of this peace crap from him. I hoped Tomadus would bring you out of your stupor, but I had no idea he would talk you into his own stupid ideas. We have a war to wage against these demons. Stay here and fight them with me."

Yohanan looked down. "I cannot fight. I cannot kill. Not anymore. The massacre took that out of me, and I don't believe more shaitaanism will save us any more than it has these past years." He looked into Decima's eyes. "We have to change the story. I have to change my story. I think this Isa may have some answers. He could help you, too. Come with me."

"Massacre? You sound like one of them. They killed their own people by luring them into harm's way. I would have thought the memory of my father would mean enough that you could never quit the fight. How could you do this to him?"

"Do you remember what your father said to us just before he left his ship at the dock that night? 'The Juteslams are people too. Despite the propaganda, they don't all hate you. They are innocents, and surely they do not deserve to die.' Do you remember that? Please do not condemn me with his memory. I am simply trying to honor his wishes."

She stared at him with eyes blazing and mouth agape. Her eyes quickly narrowed and became clouded with tears. She stood up, looked down at him, and poked her finger in his face. "Don't you dare condemn me with my own father's words. He was my father, not yours, no matter what you want to believe."

Yohanan felt that jab like a knife entering his heart.

She shoved the blade deeper. "My father understood the situation and gave his life for us, so we could continue the battle."

"No, Dec, he was truly sorry for what happened."

"He died for us, Yohanan, not for the Juteslams. Go wring your hands and join your cowardly friends. Leave the battlefield to those of us who are strong enough to deal with reality." She turned abruptly, strode briskly away and never looked back, disappearing into the crowd.

Yohanan frowned and shook his head. How can she not see that the Demoseps keep making the same mistakes over and over again? How can she not see that death begets death for us all?

CHAPTER 50

"**I** am in New Åarhus on business," Tomadus said into the pod. "I'm hoping to meet with King Skjöldr. Have your generals arranged that yet?"

The First Consul said, "You know they are not my generals, but in any case, it is too early for such a meeting."

"Have I not met my side of the bargain?"

"Yes, you have. I am told the technologists are making good progress with your schematics, though they seem to be struggling with the amplification module."

Tomadus scratched his beard. *Of course they are.* "Progress on what, exactly? You have left me in the dark."

"Patience, Tomadus. The empires impose limits on what can be shared. Remember, we are only trying to find a way to enhance our security."

Tomadus closed his eyes. *Advanced weapons can do much to enhance security.* "Why do you think it is too early to meet with Skjöldr?"

"Come, Tomadus, give it time. After the Konverteraften Massacre, nobody in New Jutland is in the mood to talk peace. We must be patient."

"Must we wait for more people to die?"

"We must wait until the time is ripe or you will be ineffectual. Now, you said you are there on business —is this Isa your new business partner?"

Tomadus paused. "Are you spying on me?"

"I receive daily reports on the movements of certain…individuals who our security forces believe require monitoring. Isa is one of those. Be careful who you choose as friends, Tomadus."

"He is a gentle man who simply helps others see how to seek God and live their lives morally," said Tomadus.

"Are you seeking God, now? It seems strange for a Romanus, especially a technologist."

"No, no, I am no convert, but he has a way with people that you cannot understand unless you meet him. He just helped my friend overcome deep despair. He can help others. I've seen it. I hope you get a chance to meet him before you form any opinion against him."

"I have no interest in forming any such judgment. I am simply passing on my concerns should others with far greater power than I choose to act. I trust you realize that if he crosses any of the Emperors, the tide may go out on him, and you may well be caught up in the undercurrent."

Tomadus looked around the room, searching for the right words. "Thanks for your advice. I appreciate you looking out for me, but I think you are too far removed to judge him. He is no subversive. He seeks only to guide men's souls toward good and seeks followers to help him."

"It is the search for an army of followers that concerns some people the most. You do know the tiniest mustard seed can grow into the largest plant?"

Tomadus sighed. "I understand. I am travelling to the Aztec Empire on business at the request of several prominent merchants there. He's travelling with me, so I will watch him and his group further. But I don't think you have any cause to worry here."

"The Aztec Empire? Do you feel safe travelling there?" asked the First Consul.

"Why shouldn't I?"

"Confidentially, the Aztec Empire has begun to move in a different direction from us. Their monarch is…unpredictable. The area is not entirely stable. We have provided travel warnings to Romani for some time for the area."

"If I paid attention to every travel alert from the Romanus government,

I would have no network in North Aztalan nor much of the rest of the world."

"Just be wary while you are there. Anything could happen, and our relationship with the Aztec Empire is not so strong that we could get you out in the event of some unfortunate…complication."

"Like what?" Tomadus asked.

"You never know with these things until they happen, *amicus meus.* What if this unstable government decided a Romanus merchant was a nice little bargaining chip for its current geopolitical aims?"

Tomadus said sarcastically, "Me, a bargaining chip? I doubt they have even heard of me down there. But I will try to be careful."

CHAPTER 51

VISIBOARD IN HAND, Tomadus walked quickly down the narrow streets of the central district of Tenochtitlan and thought about the past few weeks, trying to make sense of this trip to the Aztec Empire. It certainly had become a profitable venture for him. The four merchants he had met were among the elite of the Aztec Empire, members of the Emperors' court, and they had all signed on to sell his new products in different parts of the empire. Still, the veiled warnings kept coming.

Three of the four merchants had inquired about his association with this mysterious man named Isa and what he really wanted from the Aztec people by preaching to crowds in the city. "Doesn't he know we are neither Muslims nor Jews?" "Why is he pushing his god upon us?" "Does he know he will upset the Emperor?" "What do you think the Emperor may do?" They all advised him to end his association with Isa. When Tomadus had asked them for the reasons behind their warnings, each of them had gone mute.

Tomadus rounded the Confucian Temple and came into the northern section of Tlamatinime Ilhucaatl Plaza. The square was even larger than Great Jutland Square. It could fit probably five whole Colosseums without feeling too snug. Isa stood near a podium on a marble dais in the center of the square, speaking quietly with a small group standing around him. Isa's talk must have ended as most of the audience had begun to disperse;

however, a few mesmerized souls felt compelled to soak up a little more of the great man's aura. Tomadus could not see any of the Ten near Isa, but then noticed Simeon, Adin and a few others at the northeast corner of the square, resting on the grass near a pristine marble statue of Buddha. Yohanan was sizing up the statue, walking around and viewing it from every angle as Tomadus approached.

"I see our servant of the coin has arrived." Simeon guffawed. "How does your golden purse grow?"

"No quicker than your belly, my friend." They shared a hearty laugh.

"You missed the master's words to the Aztecs on their Tlamatinime Ilhucaatl Day," Simeon said. I cannot fathom why we waste our time here. We tell them about a God they do not know and do not love. Most of them are atheists or ancestor worshipers or lovers of the yin and yang. Worse yet, some praise this Buddha and look forward to returning from the dead as other creatures. What would you like to be: a goat, a cow or a pig? How about a snake? Would that fit you, Tomadus?"

A voice to Tomadus's left broke in, "Do not belittle other peoples' beliefs." It was Isa.

Atuf, one of the Muslim members of the Ten, spoke up, "But master, Simeon has a point. Why are we here? These locals are not People of the Book. They are infidels and cannot appreciate your words."

Isa sighed and sat down by them and most of the disciples followed his lead. Tomadus remained standing by the foot of the Buddha statute. "Let me tell you a story," Isa said. "A landowner went out at dawn to hire temporary laborers for his vineyard. After agreeing with them for the usual daily wage, he sent them into his vineyard. Going out about nine o'clock, he saw others standing idle in the marketplace, and he said to them, 'You too go into my vineyard, and I will give you what is just.' So they went off. He went out again around noon, and around three o'clock, and did likewise. Going out about five o'clock, he found others standing around, and said to them, 'Why do you stand here idle all day?' They answered, 'Because no one has hired us.' He said to them, 'You too go into my vine-yard.' When it was evening, the owner of the vineyard said to his foreman, 'Summon the laborers and give them their pay, beginning with the last and ending with the first.'

"When those who had started about five o'clock came, each received the usual daily wage. So when the first came, they thought that they would receive more, but each of them also got the usual wage. And on receiving it they grumbled against the landowner, saying, 'These last ones worked only one hour, and you have made them equal to us, who bore the day's burden and the heat.' He said to one of them in reply, 'My friend, I am not cheating you. Did you not agree with me for the usual daily wage? Take what is yours and go. What if I wish to give this last one the same as you? Am I not free to do as I wish with my own money? Are you envious because I am generous?'"

Isa looked in turn at each of the Ten, ending with a focus on Atuf and Simeon. "There are many rooms in my Father's mansion. Do not be jealous if he invites all whom he loves, no matter when or how. The Father has plenty mercy for us all."

Simeon and Atuf looked down at their sandals in silence.

Isa looked around at all of his disciples, "Do you believe you understand God in all his dimensions?"

"Dimensions? What do you mean?" responded Atuf.

"What do you think I mean?" said Isa.

"I do not know."

"Then how would you describe God?"

Atuf thought for a few seconds. "The Great Book says, 'He is One God: God the Eternal, the Uncaused Cause of all being...and there is nothing that could be compared to Him.'"

Simeon added, "Isaiah says, 'I am the LORD, there is no other, there is no God besides me. It is I who arm you, though you do not know me, so that all may know, from the rising of the sun to its setting, that there is none besides me. I am the LORD, there is no other.'"

Isa smiled at both of them. "Good. So it appears you both agree that there is one God, that there is no other and nothing can be compared to him."

"Yes!" the two answered together.

"But what if I told you that it is possible to have one God who appears to the world in different ways?"

"Impossible, for then there would be more than one God," replied Atuf.

"Not so." replied Isa. "Let us ask the technologist here. Tomadus, you are familiar with triangles, are you not?"

"Yes."

"Well, let us examine the triangle from geometry." Isa drew a small triangle in the dirt. "It is an abstract concept. You can define each angle of a triangle separately by describing its relative degrees and its orientation on a hypothetical grid. Would you say that these three angles can be viewed separately?"

"Sure," Tomadus said. "I can measure each angle without the others."

"And the measure of each angle could differ from the two others?" Isa asked.

"Yes, as long as they add up to 180 degrees, they can be any kind of positive measure and still make a triangle."

"So if you see one of those angles by itself, it might appear to be a different angle from the others?"

"Yes."

"And viewed separately, you might not even know each angle was part of a triangle?

"Yes."

"And so these are separate dimensions of the triangle, are they not?"

"Yes."

"What happens to the triangle if you take away one of its parts?" Isa rubbed out one of the legs of the triangle in the dirt.

Tomadus held out his hands and shook his head. "Well then, it is no longer a triangle."

"So the triangle needs each part to be a whole."

"Yes."

"Does this mean there is more than one triangle?" Isa asked.

"No, there is one triangle, but it consists of three different parts," Tomadus replied.

Isa smiled broadly and held out his arms wide. "Exactly. And so, I tell you, Atuf, and you, Simeon, you are wise when you say there is only one God. But do not assume he has but one dimension. Nothing requires Him to manifest himself to all of mankind in only one way. You and your people may see only one angle and believe that to be everything because that is what you have seen. But what if God has not shown you the whole triangle? And what if He has shown you the whole triangle, but your eyes have failed to see it?"

Simeon shook his head, mumbling, "It's all so confusing."

Isa nodded. "Do not worry, any of you. Let me ask all of you this: in the eyes of God, what is man's greatest purpose—to seek to understand the nature of God or the nature of man?"

Many of the Ten responded, only a few seconds apart: "The nature of God."

Tomadus paused and said alone, "What you say, Isa, about the nature of men."

Isa laughed. "And a child shall lead them. While most of you have your hearts in the right place, you stumble because you think about God with your human brains, limited as they are, and you forget your hearts. Let me ask you another question. Suppose you were a parent of a three-year-old child and you wanted to teach him something important. Would you explain to the child the intricacies of your own biological makeup, such as how cells work, how nerve cells interact with your brain, and how nerves signal your muscles to contract, knowing that this child could not possibly understand these things yet? Or would you instruct the child to never hit his baby sister because that was wrong, knowing that, with your perseverance, the child would eventually comply? Which would you do?"

Most of the Ten chimed in, "Teach the child never to hit."

"Of course," Isa said. "At that age, a child's brain cannot understand how a human body functions, but does it matter? The child need know nothing of the synapses firing in his parent's brain to understand the moral lesson. Now, human physiology may be utterly complex to the brain of a three-year-old, but it is infinitely more difficult for any human brain to understand the nature of God."

Simeon nodded.

Isa smiled gently. "So, then, why do you assume that God would try to teach you everything about his own nature rather than how you should act? And why does it surprise you that people understand the nature of God and the afterlife in different ways in different cultures? Do parents not respond to their children in different ways to explain the same thing depending upon their ability to understand at the time? Do not different cultures accept an understanding of truth based on their own experiences?"

Several heavily armed Aztec soldiers approached the group. Each held a rap rifle with a strap slung over his shoulder. Tomadus cleared his throat and nodded toward them. Isa turned around and stood up. The soldier with three stripes on his forehead moved ahead of the others. He was looking at the handbill for today's speech and scanning faces in the group. He held out the handbill toward Isa. "Are you the man who led this rally today, this Isa?

Isa responded, "Rally? I know of no rally. I was simply teaching them about truth."

The soldier replied, "Truth? Well, truth is pretty much what we choose to believe, isn't it? Truth. Look, speak straight with me, I am warning you. Are you the one who taught religion in the plaza today?"

"I am."

"Then you must come with us." The soldier nodded to the others with one stripe on their foreheads and they encircled Isa.

"Are you arresting him?" asked Simeon.

"Call it what you want. We are taking him to the Emperor." Then the soldier noticed Tomadus standing by the statue. "You there, are you the Romanus merchant?" He flipped over the handbill and referred to some handwritten notes on the back. "Tomadus of Roma?"

Yohanan stepped between them. "Why do you care? He is just a merchant."

"Did I ask you?" said the soldier. "Stay out of this or you'll be next."

Yohanan stood his ground. "You have no right to—"

"I have every right. Take him as well." Another soldier stood next to Yohanan with his rap rifle raised.

Tomadus stepped forward. "Leave him be. Yes, I am that merchant of Roma. Please, leave this man alone."

"You three have an audience with the Emperor. Anyone else interested in attending?" He paused and the others shrunk back. "No, I thought not. Now clear out."

Isa turned back to the group. "Be not afraid, my friends. We are in no danger, for it is not yet our time." He turned toward the first soldier. "Please, lead on."

Tomadus looked at Isa and shook his head. This Isa was such an eloquent and insightful student of the hearts of men, yet obviously so ignorant and naïve about the politics of his day.

CHAPTER 52

TOMADUS GRABBED HIS head as the pain seared through his brain. He fumbled for his neck and ears, but he felt no blood dripping down them. He had seen a wooden cross with a man, this Jesus that Isa now emulated, nailed to it. The cross hung behind two women seated near him—near this Huxley—in strange living quarters. The women had begun falling quickly to their sides as a hole appeared in a brick wall behind him and light seared through his eyes, into Huxley's brain and down his neck. The vision had faded to black until a new light exploded again. Then the visiscan screen appeared again with all of those bodies burning on the stage beside the Viking ship as Hugleikr kept calming the masses, and he had heard the voiceover inform all that the murderer Quintillus had been found and executed…

When the pain and the intensity of the glowing light receded a bit, Tomadus opened his eyes. There were no women or hole in the wall, no Viking ship, no dead bodies. Instead, he was sitting with Yohanan and Isa in a large, ornate room. He shuddered and breathed hard. *This man, this Huxley, can he see the horrors I have seen as well?*

"Well, at least it's not a dungeon," Yohanan joked. "I've seen a few jail cells in my time, and I can tell you they don't typically have forty-foot ceilings, marble columns, gold-leaf cornices and alabaster and jade sculptures."

Tomadus surveyed the huge hall and marveled at its ornamentation.

The marble dais in front of them held an empty marble throne inlaid with a tufted red velvet seat and back. The remainder of the dais was empty, except for a podium with a microphone far to its left. A small corridor trailed off the back of the dais and behind a wall of gold, silver and jade that reached the full thirty *cubitus* to the ceiling. Four of their former escorts were posted as guards at each of the four main ten-*cubitus* high double doors that opened into the hall. Isa sat quietly contemplating, perhaps praying, with his palms resting together in front of his lips and his eyes comfortably closed.

"We're in the Emperor's palace," said Tomadus. "He can pronounce us guilty of whatever crimes he chooses to invent. This is the Aztec Empire. He can do whatever he wishes."

From the rear corridor, a guard emerged wearing ceremonial colors of red, orange and green. He held not a modern rap rifle but an obsidian-tipped spear. He spoke loudly as if the enormous hall were filled with a large crowd, "All rise for His Majesty, the King of Kings, Emperor Acamapichtli X." One of the soldiers came over with his rap rifle raised, and the three prisoners stood in unison. A few moments later, a tall and powerful man appeared from the rear corridor to the dais. He wore an elaborate headdress made of gold and covered with jade, diamonds and other jewels. Pinned at his collar, his jade green robe hung to his calves; it wrapped around the sides of his ancient iron breastplate and short white skirt. Intricately designed red and orange cloths wrapped around his huge calves and accentuated his muscular upper legs. Ornately bejeweled sandals adorned his feet. In his hand, he held a spear similar to the ceremonial guard, but this one was tipped with a pointed diamond the size of two fingers. His thin mustache and thick beard seemed out of place in Tenochtitlan. He moved to the front of the dais and stared at the three men.

The ceremonial guard pronounced officially, "You shall approach His Majesty, the Emperor, on your knees." Tomadus dropped to his knees, followed by Yohanan. Isa remained standing, mute, staring directly at the Emperor.

One of the guards came forward and raised his rap rifle with two hands to butt Isa in the head from behind, but the Emperor intervened, "Stop! Do not strike him. You other two may stand as well. All three of you may approach on your feet. Indeed, we seek a private audience with these men. Guards, leave us. These men pose no danger."

The guard dressed in ceremonial garb said, "But your Highness, security concerns demand that I—"

"We will be the judges of our security needs. Leave us." Immediately, all of the guards disappeared out nearby doors.

The Emperor stepped down the dais and bowed slightly toward the men, his right hand raised to his heart in the manner of the traditional greeting in Roma and the Three Empires. "Peace be with you." The three responded with like gestures and words. The Emperor continued, "Isa of Palestine, welcome to my land. I have been following your progress abroad for several months now. I was delighted to see you come to Aztalan and our capital in Tenochtitlan. And now I am thrilled to finally meet you."

Isa nodded slightly. "Thank you, Emperor. You have taken your time in summoning us. We have been in your land teaching your people for weeks."

"Yes, I know. I am sorry my security personnel had to follow you, but it was necessary to ensure that I had made no mistake in my measure of you. Your display a few minutes ago told me that I had not."

"You were not offended by Isa's refusal to kneel?" Tomadus asked.

"A small test. I knew if Isa believed what he says, he would not kneel to me." The emperor motioned to the back of the dais. "Please let us continue this conversation in less formal quarters and with less formal attire. I came here straight from an appearance to celebrate Tlamatinime Ilhucaatl Day. I still wear the pomp of ceremony, and it itches so." He removed the headdress, pivoted and walked up the dais, motioning to the three to follow him down the rear corridor, which gave way to an anteroom, a marbled hallway, and finally a large sitting area overlooking the plaza below.

The Emperor turned toward them. "I apologize for the way my soldiers summoned you. That was a small part of my investigation. If you had resisted or tried to flee, we would not be having this conversation. But you acquitted yourselves as I expected, so here we are. Please, feel free to partake of the food and the fruit of the vine, for we have many good varieties here." He motioned to a table of plenty nearby. They partook with a glass each and claimed heavily cushioned seats in a circle.

"Why have you summoned us?" Tomadus asked.

The Emperor's left eyebrow rose. "Is that not obvious already to a famous technologist from Roma? I simply seek to speak with you, for not to discuss with a man worthy of conversation is to waste the man. To discuss with a man not worthy of conversation is to waste words. The wise waste neither men nor words. I have studied Isa from afar and know well that he is worthy of conversation. I have heard the same of you from merchant members of my court, Tomadus. This other man, Yohanan is it? Your reputation from Tetepe is well earned, is it not?"

"I have left my past transgressions behind. I am seeking a new path now."

"I see. Then I trust I will not waste my words on you, for a wise man who has faults does not fear to abandon them."

Tomadus tilted his head and narrowed his eyes. He was nearly certain he had heard similar aphorisms before, or at least bits of them, but it was so many years ago. Yet even the tone reminded him of his old teacher. "Your Highness, although you are an Aztec emperor, you appear well-trained in the words of the ancient Chinese master, Confucius. Were you educated in the East Asian Empire?"

"I see you remember your Romanus tutelage well," said the Emperor. "Sometimes I forget that your culture was infused with a little Asian flavoring when the Mongols occupied your Latin empire for so many centuries. No, Tomadus, I was educated here in Tenochtitlan. As I am sure you are aware, we too have enjoyed some of the benefits of Asian culture, for far longer than many foreigners realize. For example, today we are celebrating Tlamatinime Ilhucaatl Day, which translated means 'Feast of the Wise Men from the Sea.' You know of this?"

Tomadus shook his head. "Only vaguely, I'm afraid. There seems to be a bit of a reluctance on the part of Romanus state schools to teach much Aztec history."

"That does not surprise me. So allow me to enlighten you, my friends, for learning without thought is labor lost, but thought without learning is perilous. The event marked by this celebration occurred early in our empire, in 1034."

Tomadus asked, "1034? Is that AH—Year of the Hijra—or are you using an Aztecan calendar?"

"Yes, it is AH—the Year of the Hijra. I have used the year from your imperfect Muslim calendar because that is the best reference point for you, is it not? Or do you Romani now go by the year of the founding of Roma? I find it humorous that the precursor to your Roman Empire, Julius Caesar, promulgated a quite accurate annual calendar over 650 years before the Hijra of Muhammad from Mecca to Medina, yet your region of the world has chosen to adopt that flawed monthly Muslim calendar as if the world began on that date. But no matter, as long as we know we are referring to the same system."

"The date has great religious significance for the Muslims," Tomadus said. "We choose to follow their lead."

"Of course, as you do in a great many things," said the Emperor. "So the event occurred in 1034 AH, over three centuries after the founding of this great city. The empire was vast for that time, extending from the Sea to the Ocean and, in your lexicon, for over 250 *milia passuum* north and south of this city. Then it was but a loose conglomeration of tribute states, and any further expansion was limited by our meager means of transportation. Even if we could administer the outer regions, we had no advantage at arms other than our numbers to hold the outlying areas in check. The arrival of the wise men from the sea changed all of that—both for good and bad."

"Good and bad?" Tomadus asked.

"Yes. At first, many of my people thought these travelers were gods, for their technology and weaponry far exceeded our own. We understand now that they were troubled emigrants travelling from China, bound across the Western Ocean to the huge island-continent to the south. They had departed China just after economic stresses from the difficult Imjin War with the Nipponese had put them in opposition with the Wanli emperor near the end of the Ming Dynasty. They sailed in a ship a hundred times bigger than our own at the time. Their departure was, shall we say, promoted by the Chinese government, but these emigrants were told they could return only at the risk of death. It was lucky for us, for this motivated them to include among their cargo as much technology, agriculture and weaponry as could be useful in their new home. They also found it prudent to include among their number many skilled craftsmen."

"Why did they sail here?" asked Yohanan.

The Emperor replied, "Unfortunately for these wise men, they encountered the edge of a hurricane north of the equator that severely damaged their sailing ship. By the time they had repaired the ship, they had floated into the counter-current just five degrees north of the equator. And then the doldrums hit, with no wind for weeks. They could do nothing but float ever more eastward with the current until they were beyond any maps or charts known to them. As the current took them near the coast, it changed direction and carried them north to our shores. They landed nearly a hundred days later and a few weeks after they had expended most of their foodstuffs. The long voyage and their great hunger had weakened them, so they thought twice about seeking any conquest of our empire with their far superior weapons. There were only a hundred of them left, and eventually they knew they would have run out of ammunition. So wisdom prevailed and they sought refuge among the Aztecs. If we had been unfortunate enough to have a fool for an emperor, they would have been executed immediately as an outside threat. But Emperor Mochtezacatl demonstrated great vision and welcomed as opportunity what others saw only as peril. He accepted these travelers as counselors, technicians and teachers and slowly began to integrate their technology and agriculture into our own."

"It must have helped your economy," Tomadus said.

"To say the least," the Emperor said. "From them we learned many things we take for granted today—like the wheel. There had been little reason to invent that marvel in this land because there were no substantial beasts of burden to take advantage of it with wagons. But the wise men also brought horses and oxen and wheat. They taught us to make gunpowder, to smelt iron, and to build iron weapons, cannons and primitive guns. Within a few short years, they transformed us into a powerful empire. Emperor Mochtezacatl erected stelae as a tribute recounting their trip and innovations to our society."

"That all sounds pretty good. What happened?" asked Tomadus.

"Well, their arrival also devastated us. These Chinese travelers unwittingly brought to our continent new diseases. Measles, scarlet fever and small pox ravaged our population. It is believed that over a third of our people died from the new diseases alone in the ten years after the wise men arrived. Many of my people thought our gods were punishing us for taking

in these foreigners. Some of the people called for the foreigners to be sacrificed to the great god Huitzilopochtli at the Great Temple. But Emperor
Mochtezacatl placed all of the Chinese immigrants under his private protection. He proclaimed that their death at the hands of any Aztec citizen
would be equivalent to killing one of his royal family. This angered many of
the people, and several of the more independent kingdoms to the east soon
rebelled. Other kingdoms began to join them and eventually the people
of this city committed a great treason and rose up and killed Emperor
Mochtezacatl. The mob then rounded up all of the Chinese immigrants
and killed them. By then, some of the Chinese had married some of the
Aztecs and had produced young children. These mixed-race offspring were
temporarily spared by the mob, but only so they could be used as special
sacrifices to Huitzilopochtli."

Yohanan closed his eyes and hung his head, shaking it slowly from side
to side.

"Yes, Yohanan," the Emperor said, "I see you comprehend. These horrible murders cast a long shadow over our collective soul. Nevertheless, their
deaths came too late to undermine their technological contributions to our
Aztec Empire. They had brought us great weapons, so we killed them for
angering our gods, yet found no hypocrisy in using the new weapons to
greatly expand our borders. Expansion proved to be easy. The diseases that
had ravaged our population now ebbed in our empire just as they flowed
into other nations to the north and the south. As our new enemies fell, the
new emperor predictably claimed credit. The Chinese immigrants—these
wise men who made much of our great empire possible—were largely forgotten and their stelae removed."

"So why do you celebrate them today?" asked Yohanan.

The Emperor nodded. "Well that was nearly a millennium ago. It was
another 500 years before one of our early historians dug into the old legends, found the abandoned stelae and discovered the importance of these
visitors to our empire. With half a millennia of hindsight, we realized the
dreadful diseases from your continents would have come later anyway, with
the arrival in later centuries of the Vikings and other European peoples,
except our people would have been decimated at exactly the wrong time.
Instead, over time we had developed immunities and we had enhanced our

technology from the wise men from the sea. And through these advantages, we were able to eventually dominate the newcomers."

Yohanan nodded. "Hence the vast expanse of the Aztec Empire for centuries."

"Yes. It took 500 years, but this newly enlightened emperor finally acknowledged that our forbearers had mistreated these wise men from the sea. He pronounced a new celebration of Tlamatinime Ilhucaatl Day. Of course, his decision also might have been influenced by his efforts at the time to establish stronger relations with the East Asian Empire. The celebration has grown ever since. I personally have re-emphasized our connections with East Asia since I was handed the mantle of leadership fifteen years ago. Hence, you see a Buddha in the Tlamatinime Ilhucaatl Plaza and the many other symbols of Chinese culture interwoven with our traditional Aztec strength. Whether man or nation, each of us is strongest when he stands on both legs, don't you think?"

Not when the legs run in two different directions, Tomadus thought. While the conversation continued, Tomadus could hear little more. He began rubbing both temples with his fingertips, hoping to soothe the intense pain. The Emperor's history lesson had driven a wedge through his brain and into his soul. In his current reality, the story fit what he knew, though it added some interesting elements he had never considered. Wise men from the sea—no teacher had ever mentioned that in Roma. But his memories from the other world kept intruding as the Emperor spoke. The Aztec government and culture had been wiped out by the weapons and intrigues of the Conquistadors from Spain as well as by the blights of disease and religion that followed them. *No, that's not right. That is that other world.* There is no Spain, no France, no England and no Christianity. There never has been in this world. No, these bits of history existed only in his troubled mind, freshly warped by new visions of the Light.

So then he should not be surprised, even by this tale of wise men from the sea. But was this story another cause of the differences between these two worlds or just another effect of an earlier deviation? And, worse yet, he could not know which world was real and which was fantasy. The duality became incomprehensible and seemingly pinched every neuron in his brain. He had to find the answer before it split him in two. He had to find the right path or die trying. *Is Isa the answer?* With that thought, the pain vanished.

The Emperor was saying, "Very thoughtful, Isa. I see you appreciate that the wise men also serve as a metaphor for my efforts to shift the paradigm of this ancient world. Many do not understand that I seek to modernize us with an infusion of technology and understanding from abroad. They hold to their old ways. But this is a large empire with so many parts that have long been corrupt. Sometimes the people may be made to follow a path of action, but they may not be made to understand it."

Isa regarded the Emperor. "You seek to transform your country. I seek to transform your people's souls. I wish you well, but I see no place for us in this palace. I care not about any political influence, nor do I believe politics can truly promise man anything but sorrow. Change in society comes not from those who govern but from the hearts of the governed. Any other change will soon devour itself."

"You are wise to say this, Isa," replied the Emperor, "and I begin to wonder if you have studied Confucius as well. For the master once said, 'To put the world in order, we must first put the nation in order; to put the nation in order, we must first put the family in order; to put the family in order, we must first cultivate our personal life, we must first set our hearts right.'"

Isa smiled. "Well, he did have a way with words. Perhaps even he had a little guidance from above?" The two laughed. Isa looked at Tomadus. "Tomadus, you have been very quiet. I thought politics and technology would be of great interest to you."

"I am sorry," said Tomadus, "so they are. I have been distracted by the odd convergence of two worlds—but perhaps only in my own mind." He noticed the Emperor looked at him with a kind of wonder in his eyes. Tomadus thought about the Emperor's comment on the East Asian Empire and recalled the warning from the First Consul. "I do have a question for you, Your Highness, if I may?"

"Of course."

"You spoke of your renewal of Chinese culture and your renewal of ties with the East Asian Empire. Is that what concerns the Three Empires?"

"You know of this fear because of your friends in high places, no doubt.

Remember, Tomadus, a man's position need not reflect his inner qualities, and you should have no friends not equal to yourself. Nonetheless, let me answer your question. I suppose our ties to the East may concern them, but I think they may be more worried about our little cultural revolution here. Your friends in Roma and the Three Empires fear change more than anything. Their power is built on the vestiges of the past, and they fear that change will eventually topple them."

"How so?" asked Tomadus. "Forgive my forwardness, but as an Aztec emperor are you not also a symbol of stagnation after a millennium of imperial rule?"

"I can see how you might think so, but recall that I came to power by overthrowing a weak and corrupt man who was allowing our empire to shrivel up and die. Those who supported me then still understand the need to revitalize our world and look beyond the concept of empire."

Yohanan perked up and asked. "Beyond empire? Do you seek other ways of governance?"

"You do not believe I signed on for life, do you?" asked the Emperor.

"Is that not the way of emperors?" Yohanan asked carefully. "Most only leave power when they leave the Earth."

"That has been the paradigm, I'm afraid. I want to change that."

"Why?"

"Well, who will govern when I am gone?"

Yohanan replied, "Your oldest son—is that not the system employed by monarchies and many dictatorships?"

"No, I have no sons, nor am I capable of producing any offspring. And if I did, is it not possible they would not be up to the task?" He looked over at Tomadus. "Following the ancient tradition from Roma, I suppose I could adopt someone as my heir to the throne, but why? It is all the same. I cannot anticipate how my successor will rule once I am gone."

"Why? Can't you select someone you trust who will not change after your death?" Tomadus asked.

"One certainty is that people always change. They must, for the world changes around them, and should they foolishly choose not to change, they would change all the more."

"I don't understand," Yohanan said.

The Emperor sat back. "Let me see if I can make it plain. Such a person is like a stubborn, inexperienced sailor who must travel due east to reach a particular port. He sets out and finds himself lucky enough to have a perfect tail wind from the west for a full week. He makes such great progress that he begins to congratulate himself on his excellent handling of his sailboat. But then the wind shifts and blows directly from the east. Now, instead of adjusting his tiller to begin to tack his ship toward the east, this foolish and stubborn sailor says to himself, 'No, this method I have used in the past has worked well for me, so I will not change.' Eventually, despite the tiller, the wind and waves toss the bow of the boat around and he begins heading due west, back from whence he came. In his confusion and proud of his ways, the sailor smiles and says, 'See, I have not changed and I am sailing smoothly again. I was right; I know that if I keep my tiller straight I will always sail true. But I must say that I am very disappointed in the sun, which has succumbed to the vagaries of the world and now rises in the west and sets in the east.'"

The four men laughed heartily. Isa said, "Thank you for this fine, humorous tale. It makes your point so well." Isa turned toward Tomadus and Yohanan and spoke in a very serious tone, "The Emperor shows true insight, for this story reveals another meaning as well. I am the sun. You are the sailors. The winds are the many good, evil and unknown forces that affect this world. For each of you, the tiller is your own personal experience before we met. Now I say to you: follow not the way of the tiller, even if it has served you well, for your reliance upon it can make you a fool. No, use the tiller as it is intended—as a tool, but always find your way again by looking to see where the sun rises, for the sun will never lead you astray."

Tomadus stared at Isa and took a deep breath. *I want to believe him, but he demands something I cannot give: unconditional loyalty.* Were he and Yohanan to follow Isa even if their experience told them Isa was wrong, or worse, insane? It had been too much to ask. *I hope Isa will never lead us astray, but what if he does?*

The Emperor had remained silent and seemed to be contemplating Isa's proclamation. He opened his arms, palms toward the sky, and said, "Isa, you are indeed wise. Do you intend these words for me as well?"

Isa looked at the Emperor and smiled. "Though all men can be sailors, some have no present cause to sail eastward."

The Emperor laughed. "I'm afraid sailing is out of the question for me right now. But someday, who knows, a trip may be well earned or even necessary. For now, I seek a way to keep this empire from imploding when I sail away. As I said, Yohanan, everyone must change, so I choose not to put my assurances in the promises of any one individual. I must find another way."

Yohanan raised his eyebrows and leaned forward. "Have you considered democracy? It is the most resilient form of government over time, for it does not rely on any one man but on all the citizens."

"Well, I don't know if you mean a true democracy or a mere republic, but both have been tried and both were quite flawed and short-lived. Your precious democracy killed Socrates, did it not? And the Romanus Republic flourished for far fewer years than your subsequent Romanus Empire. Is that not true?"

Yohanan responded: "Our democracy has survived for nearly two centuries. We think we've solved the problem of the reckless majorities that killed Socrates by agreeing to minority rights and built-in checks and balances between parts of the government."

"And it has worked well within your own little province of Amer—, uh, Tetepe, my friend, but have you Tetepians flourished? No, you survive only because behind the scenes we have prevented the Juteslams from wiping you out. And if you were to grow and no longer have a common enemy as your focus, your little factions would soon grow apart. Whether you like it or not, the wealthy among you would eventually assume the mantle of power over those less fortunate, all in the respectable guise of representing the people."

Tomadus said, "I'm sorry to interrupt, Emperor, but did you say America?"

Looking a bit squeamish, the Emperor said, "No, I…I'm sorry, you must be mistaken. What is this thing you call America?"

"Perhaps I misheard. I am sorry." But he had heard it. The Emperor did not want to admit it. Tomadus could not push the Emperor now in front of the others, or the man might just lock the truth within for good. "Please, go on."

Yohanan took the cue, "Yes, Emperor, I am trying to understand you better. The people have the power to elect whomever they wish. Won't they elect those who meet their needs regardless of the size of the nation or where the wealth resides? If the wealthy govern best, then the people will vote for them, but if they do not, then the numbers will be against them and they shall fall."

"Hypothetically, I suppose you are right," the Emperor acknowledged. "Yes, the poor have real power, but in the end they do not, they cannot, exercise it. Your statement assumes that all voters will understand the situation well and act accordingly. But the wealthy tend to control the diffusion of information in large societies, and leaders who win elections tend to discover that they need the rich to win future elections. In the end, apathy arises among the poor because they feel none of those who seek office will truly help them anyway. So the wealthy will always dominate representative democracies in the long run."

Yohanan shook his head demonstrably.

"Oh, I understand," the Emperor said, "the rich may allow the middle class to appear to control things for a time, but when interests of the wealthy are truly threatened, they will assume power again, directly or indirectly. It is no different in empires, you know. I can only remain in power as long as enough of the elite with money and power believe it is in their best interests. Without them, my government will eventually topple. So in the end, what is really the difference between empire and democracy?"

"The difference is that democracy makes people free," Yohanan said. "If they make mistakes in selecting their rulers, it is a mistake of their own freedom. And if the wealthy have more power, they still choose, perhaps unwisely, to allow them to govern. But at least the people can feel they are free."

The Emperor stroked his beard for a few seconds. "I wonder, what is worse for a people— to be blindfolded and not see the cage that surrounds them or to have their eyes uncovered so they know the ugliness of their jailor? Look, I do not disagree that democracy has a certain allure, but do not believe it is a panacea. Despots rule in democracies the same as in kingdoms, and often from behind the scenes. Democracy may well be right for Tetepe or some other nation. It may even be right for the Aztecs at some point. We have not yet decided that. But do not fool yourself into believing in the perfection of any form of government. The superior man does not set his mind either for anything or against anything. What is right he will follow."

When Yohanan glared at the Emperor for a moment, Isa intervened, leaning over and grabbing Yohanan gently by the shoulders and saying in a low and slow voice, "Yohanan, your search is noble, but you search for answers to the wrong questions. Let government take care of itself, for governments are creations of men and will always remain the tools of their desires. Seek instead to change the hearts of men, and you will change the world." Yohanan looked with wonder at Isa, turned his head and then nodded slowly with his eyes shut.

Tomadus stared at the Emperor. "Your Highness, you seem to have thought so deeply about democracy that it almost seems as if you have studied examples of it personally. Since neither the Aztec Empire nor the East Asian Empire has ever seen it practiced, how have you come to this knowledge?"

The Emperor stared at Tomadus for a few seconds, apparently searching for something in his eyes. "It is true that there are not many examples to study. Perhaps I have formed an opinion too quickly without sufficient empirical evidence. I shall give that greater thought in the future. Thank you, Tomadus." The Emperor rose. "A fitting way to end this delightful and illuminating conversation, but now I must return to the drudgery of governance. Know that you are welcome to visit all of our empire, including our remaining territories to the north, whenever you see fit. I shall grant each of you a Letter of Transit that will allow you in any of our territories. Perhaps our paths will cross again someday, though I cannot sail east with you as yet."

The other men stood. "Before we part, please take heed, Isa of Palestine," the Emperor added. "In Roma and the Three Empires, danger may well await you and your followers. Most men of power do not tolerate novel ideas as well as I. They fear what they are unwilling to understand. If not removed, their fear saps their minds like an insidious poison. It renders them weak, consumes their thoughts, and blinds them to the consequences of their actions. They think only of how they must eliminate that fear at its source. If strong enough, a drowning man in the depths of fear will pull his potential savior under and kill them both, never realizing, if he had only conquered his fear, he might have been saved."

Isa nodded. "Thank you, Emperor. I am quite aware of this danger. Nevertheless, I must follow the will of my Father in Heaven."

"Then follow His will you must, but take care to watch out for enemies." The Emperor paused and looked directly at Tomadus, "Tomadus, protect him."

The Emperor clapped his hands and his guards reappeared. As Yohanan and Isa were led out, Tomadus hung back. "Your Highness. May I speak with you alone for a moment?"

"Of course."

"I need to ask you something," Tomadus said. "But I'm afraid you will think me mad."

"The man who asks may be a fool for the day, but the man who never asks will be a fool for life."

Tomadus looked up. *But will the fool for a day be put in a derangement ward in the Aztec Empire? No, he knows about the other world. Take the risk.* Slowly and calmly, he said, "America."

The Emperor sighed, "I believe we have had this conversation."

"Do you know of the Light? The Light of Our Yesterdays? Have you seen visions of the other world?"

The Emperor pinched his lips together for a few seconds, staring back. Then he spoke softly. "Tomadus, I can tell you are capable of seeing many things. That is wonderful. Everything has beauty but not everyone can see it. Perhaps you can see more beauty than others. I cannot answer your question, but allow me this warning: be careful, for what I said to Isa would apply doubly to you if you repeat whatever visions you may have had to the wrong people."

"You asked me to protect Isa. How am I to do that, and how do you really know he is in danger?"

The Emperor held up his hand. "Look, I have said what I have said. Remember, a man should study the past so he can define the future. And if a man were fortunate enough to study even more than the past, then what a future he could define! Farewell."

A guard ushered Emperor Acamapichtli X to a doorway that opened to another room and then closed behind him.

CHAPTER 53

THE REPETITIVE SWAY of the train car closed Yohanan's eyes and nearly delivered him into a well-deserved sleep. It had been difficult to contain his sadness when he had parted with Isa and Tomadus at the *aeroportus* in Tenochtitlan at the close of their winter together in the Aztec Empire. The sadness compounded with the growing weariness from walking so many miles every day, the southern Aztalan sun blazing down on his back, to bring Isa's message to so many who had never before even heard of the God of Abraham. Still, his spirits had soared during this goodbye when Isa had put his hands on Yohanan's shoulders and said, "You are in our Father's hands now, but I will be with you always. I know you shall walk a path of peace, for you will prepare my way."

Yohanan had asked, "And how shall I do this?"

Isa had answered, "When you follow the rising of the sun, Yohanan, you shall lead the rising of the sun, and you will find your way home."

Home—he had now almost reached Shenandoah. Shenandoah had no landing strips for *aeronaves* that had not been bombed out for years, so he had flown to New Hedeby and boarded this train that would take him through several Juteslam-controlled cities and ultimately to his home. As a Tetepian, he was required to sit near the front of the train, where the noise of the locomotives could be deafening. He might find a way to move toward the back after the last Juteslam stop in Lodbrok.

A door slammed, and a man said, "Tickets and papers please." Yohanan opened his eyes and handed over the documents to the conductor, who gave him a stern look, ripped the ticket and returned the passport marking Yohanan as a lowly Jewish Tetepian. Well, at least they still let him travel. He would change all of this. It may take years, but it would change. He would find a way.

Yohanan glanced out the window, barely able to keep his eyes open. The early March thaw had melted most of the snow, but the barren trees and the dormant grasses now cast a bleak brown hue over the landscape, desperately awaiting the renewal of spring. He slowly tilted his head toward the window, but before he could close his own eyes, he saw two little eyes staring at him from two seats to his front. When Yohanan smiled, the eyes quickly disappeared in front of the seat back, only to reappear a few seconds later, this time revealing beneath them a set of prominent freckles belonging to a very young boy. Yohanan quickly raised his eyebrows and opened his mouth wide, which again caused the head of the boy to duck for cover. He heard the ratcheting of mechanical gears, and a few seconds later, a small metallic toy appeared above the seat, caressed by tiny, awkward fingers. It depicted an ancient Viking and Aztec engaged in eternal combat, repeatedly clanging their swords against one another as the spiral spring within the clockwork mechanism unwound its worldly tension. When Yohanan let out a simulated shriek of fear, a giggling sound emanated from the forward seat, followed quickly by the appearance of the boy's now guarded face. Yohanan smiled gently and nodded to the boy. The boy grinned ear-to-ear and waved.

A woman sitting to the left of the boy looked back at Yohanan with a disapproving scowl while physically forcing the boy to sit and look forward. She tried to grab the toy out of the boy's hand, but he wrenched it away from her and held it tight to his chest. She leaned over the boy and whispered something in the ear of a man with three interlocking drinking horns tattooed on the back of his neck. The man turned slowly toward Yohanan and glared.

When the conductor reached the family, the man flicked his head toward Yohanan while looking at the conductor. "Are there still no seats available in the other cars so we can leave the filth in this car?"

"Yes sir. A few have opened up in the rear."

The man stood and corralled his son by his shirt collar, nearly dragging him toward the rear of the car, with the woman trailing a step behind, her eyes staring at Yohanan from above a handkerchief she held over her mouth and nose.

Yohanan felt the heat of anger rising within him, but he remembered Isa's words and suppressed it. He turned to watch them leave and was rewarded with a slow wave, twinkling eyes and a sly smile from the little boy as he opened his other hand to once again reveal the wind-up toy. Yohanan winked to the boy and nodded to himself as a different kind of warmth flowed through his chest. *Our future belongs to the children. We must stop schooling them in hatred. They are the foundation of a new beginning.*

Returning his head to the window, Yohanan nodded off to sleep. He was awakened by a bright flash that caught his eye from the ridge above the train. He stared intently and saw the movement of what appeared to be two prone bodies dressed in camouflage. One of the prone figures held binoculars, which reflected the late afternoon sun back toward the train. The other had what looked like a black box. Yohanan's fists clenched. *No!*

As he stood, an explosion rocked the train behind him, forcing it to an abrupt stop and catapulting him into the forward door. He might have passed out from his concussed brain, but the piercing sounds of huge chunks of metal squealing, crashing, and ripping apart would not let his body bring him relief. It sounded like a chain reaction of explosions competing with each other for his attention, eventually commingling in his ears as they grew louder and less distinct, and finally ending with a few intermittent bangs. Then silence for a few seconds as the all too familiar scents of smoke and burning flesh and blood began to fill his nostrils. A cacophony of screams and shrieks and squeals attacked his ears.

Yohanan managed to pull himself up. The train car was still upright, though it seemed askew on the track, with the trailing car at nearly a right angle to it. As he stood, the hammer in his head nearly pounded him back to the floor, but he caught himself on the door handle, slid it open, and stumbled out of the train. The locomotive to the front remained upright and on the rails. He turned and beheld the carnage to the rear. It looked as if God himself had picked up the cars in His Hands and dropped them in a refuse pile, their huge carcasses visibly expelling their last few breaths of heat into the cool March air. No, not God, not with this destruction.

He fought off the dizziness and nausea as the screams of women and children drew him ever closer toward the devastation. He looked up at the ridge, but the Demosep operatives, those agents of hate, had long disappeared into the wilderness. When he reached the first overturned car, he saw a young woman lying halfway out of one of the broken windows, blood covering her face. He shook his head slowly. When she coughed a fountain of blood, he knew she would be dead soon. He shivered. *What kind of future is ever possible when this is our present?*

He continued toward the back of the pile and found others who might be saved and tried to tend to their wounds just enough to leave them living and then move on to the ocean of humanity that lay further back within just moments of death.

In the fourth car back, Yohanan came upon the tattooed Juteslam man who had insulted him. The man lay impaled on a long piece of metal scrap peeled like a potato skin off the car in front. He heard a groan nearby and found the man's wife under another dead body, her arm twisted backward, broken. When he dug her out of the pile, her eyelids fluttered as she struggled to regain consciousness. As he laid her on the grass just outside the car, she opened her eyes fully, reaching both arms toward him. "No, Ædle! My little Ædlehelten!"

Yohanan felt the energy surge through him as he leapt back into the car's interior. He searched among the bloody piles of broken bodies, but the boy was not among them. Where could he have gone? He glanced outside to see if the boy had been thrown clear of the wreckage, but there was just too much rubble. He heard a tapping to the front of the car and noticed a door in the corner. *The toilet. The boy might have survived in that enclosed little space.* Yohanan raced forward, tripping madly over the piles of dead bodies and severed limbs. When he grabbed for the handle, it broke off in his hands. Another small tap sounded from within. Yohanan shouted, "Ædle, is that you?" No verbal reply came, but another tap followed.

His heartbeat racing, Yohanan scanned the car and found a splintered metal seat support that he poked between the door and its jamb. When he shoved this lever with all of his weight, he fell to the side while the door sprung open. Scrambling to his feet, he saw the boy's smiling reflection in the broken mirror on the wall. He moved closer and saw the boy's hand lying open, palm up. Resting on it, the metal toy fell silent as it tapped out the remaining energy from its last wind. But it did not matter, for the boy did not hear or see the warriors finish their battle. He could not. A triangle-shaped piece of the mirror had broken away from the wall and sliced several inches into his neck. Yohanan fell to his knees and wept.

CHAPTER 54

THE LATE WINTER sun had not yet settled below the mountaintops just west of Shenandoah when Yohanan took his familiar place on the platform in the center of the town square. The crowded square was already full of Tetepians anticipating another rousing speech from the man who had been the political mouthpiece of the Demosep movement for several years. He forced a smile and nodded at a few friends milling in the crowd. Everyone's anticipation might undermine their willingness to accept his new message—one he knew would differ so greatly from his past pronouncements. Maybe he could use that anticipation to his favor. He closed his eyes, and images of death, both old and new, still flashed through his brain. *I must make them understand.*

Yohanan took a deep breath and raised his arms to quiet the crowd. "My old friends, my brothers and sisters in arms, my fellow Tetepians, I come here today to speak to you of a Great Truth. It is a truth that has come to me slowly and only through much pain. It is a truth that many of you may not wish to hear. But it is a truth that resides in our very souls.

"Tonight, I do not speak of our suffering, for you already know the nature of this malady all too well. Yes, we have suffered here in the hinterlands of Tetepe for nearly fifty years, but that is a truth you need not hear me utter. You already know it in every ounce of your being.

"Nor do I speak of our democracy, for you already know of our great hope for the future of mankind. Yes, we have governed ourselves with justice and civility these past two centuries, but that is a truth not you, but the world, must hear. You already feel it deep in the recesses of your hearts.

"And I do not speak of our patriotism, for you already know we have all fought arm in arm for our country. Yes, we have tethered our lives and our fortunes to one another these past fifty years, but that is a truth that need not be mentioned. You already sense the warmth of its cloak every time we meet.

"No doubt, these beliefs remain as guideposts to each and every one of you. For we have all suffered, we have all chosen freedom, we have all acted as patriots. I will not ask you today to shrink even one *uncia* from any of these truths. You will need them not just tonight but tomorrow and every day that follows. You will need them to give you strength so that you may have the courage to accept the Great Truth that I reveal to you here today.

"I already hear some of you asking, 'What is this Great Truth?' I will come to that shortly. But first, please allow me to indulge in a little personal history. Most of you know much of my story. Who here remembers the day my parents were killed?"

A few in the crowd raised their hands and shook their heads.

Yohanan went on, "I recall the tragedy all too vividly: every day in my thoughts and every night in my dreams. Yes, I became famous around the world because of a picture of me and my wailing sister on the cover of *Tempus*. But while my own grief became a clarion call for our movement, we all know that you and I are really no different. For though no journalist was there to capture it, most of you have felt that horrid pain all the same."

Many in the crowd nodded their heads. A few of their faces were already full of tears.

"Now how did I respond to this agony? Probably the same as you: with deep, unabashed hatred, a hatred for the men who shelled my house, a hatred for Skjöldr and his lieutenants, and, yes, a hatred for all the Juteslam people. And all these years that hatred has been carried in my heart, in the depths of my soul."

Yohanan put his hands to his heart and looked at the crowd. He noticed an athletic, blond woman was slowly weaving her way toward the stage.

He held his hands out wide. "That hatred became the engine of nearly every significant action I have taken in the past ten years. It drove me to join hand in hand with the Demoseps in their battles against the Juteslams. This engine of hate heated my brain to its boiling point, so the focal point of my thoughts became revenge upon the Juteslams at nearly any cost. It fostered the growth of a cancer on my soul, so it could undo what conscience I had left and allow me to commit truly unspeakable acts. And it led me blindfolded to Great Jutland Square on a warm summer's eve, only to confront me with a horror revisited from ten years before of innocent blood spilled in front of children who screamed in agony and grief. But this time the blood was Juteslam blood, and this time the grief turned to thoughts of revenge against me and you and every single person standing here today. And that same glowing hatred forced me to witness my second father, the gentle Quintillus, publicly murdered. I have seen so many killed. By them, by us, by all who hate.

"So where has that hatred brought me? Where has it brought us? What good has this hatred done for us or for our people? I am not the first Tetepian to hate the Juteslams. This hatred began over fifty years ago. I have no doubt that this hatred fills most of your hearts today. So I ask you these simple questions, my fellow Tetepians: Has this hatred served us well? Has it returned us to our homes in the coastal cities? Has it improved our lives? Has it given us hope? Has it saved us from despair?"

Yohanan paused for effect. "NO! It has not and it never will. That is the Great Truth. My hatred—your hatred—has led us only to further death and misery."

Yohanan nodded sadly and surveyed the crowd. He saw the blond woman push her way past two burly supporters and disappear behind a stone column. He continued, "If this hatred has proven so self destructive, then why do we embrace it so? I will tell you why—because it is just too damn easy. When we are grief-stricken, our defenses lie open and the evil of hatred finds no door to bar its entry through the gate to our souls. There, while we are still weakened, it gains its foothold and begins to corrupt us from within. It acts like a virus in our brains that insidiously rescripts our thoughts so deeply that we cannot even tell a metamorphosis has occurred. And it is only with great courage, with great foresight, and with great wisdom that we can expunge this evil from our midst.

"And so I challenge each of you to see through the mist to the ugly snarl of this hatred that now chews at your soul. Seeing is only the first step, but a critical one, for until you can see this Great Truth, you will never be able to confront it. I warn you now that this step will not come easy. You must search the truth of your suffering, examine the goals of your democracy, and appreciate the pride of your patriotism. These truths do not conflict with the Great Truth. If you truly understand each of these truths, you will see that they do not support but oppose hatred. You, too, must oppose hatred and fight it with every fiber of your being. It took me ten long years to understand this Great Truth, but our Father in Heaven, our Lord and our God, has helped me to see it. With His guidance, you too will see it, and we together may rid ourselves of this evil and condemn it to its natural resting place in hell."

Several of the Demosep leaders shook their heads. Spittle was dribbling out of one leader's mouth and another's veins strained out his neck. Yohanan bit his lip hard. What would these men do when they were still so consumed by anger?

A woman Yohanan did not recognize walked forward and asked, "Do you agree that God teaches us to hate evil?"

"Yes, yes," Yohanan nodded, smiling as he stepped closer to the woman. "You should hate evil in all of its manifestations."

"But the Juteslams have murdered our friends and family without remorse. They are evil. And if they are evil, then by your own words, God demands that we hate them!" Some in the crowd cheered this proclamation.

Yohanan smiled gently and raised his arms to hush the crowd. "This logic of yours seems to ring true, but in the end it sounds a false note. Do not succumb to its phony charms! All of us can agree that some Juteslams committed evil deeds, but that does not condemn them all. No more than the evil deeds of some of us should condemn us all. Quintillus, himself once reminded me, 'Juteslams are people too. Despite the propaganda, they don't all hate you. They are innocents, and surely they do not deserve to die.' I heard him then, yet I did not feel the truth of his words. He was right, but none of us have listened. We, the Demoseps, have killed many innocent Juteslams ourselves over the years because of our glowing hatred. Who are we to kill innocents and then condemn others for doing the same?"

One of the Demosep leaders yelled, "An eye for an eye and a tooth for a tooth! These are commanded in our Torah. How can we be wrong to follow God's lead?"

Yohanan responded at once, "Whose eye and whose tooth? Do you think God tells you to take the eye of any innocent Juteslam because another Juteslam has taken your brother's eye? No. This statement from our Torah was never meant as a call for revenge. It was a limit upon the punishment of individual criminals so society would not unjustly take out its vengeance upon them. Who are we to condemn all of the Juteslams for the crimes of the few? The killing of innocents must stop!"

Raanan stepped forward and climbed the edge of the platform. "Enough of this traitorous talk. If we do not fight, the Juteslams shall either carry us away in chains or slaughter us like lambs. You said this yourself in this very spot, but now, in your weakness after Quintillus's death, you urge the opposite and condemn us for defending ourselves against these monsters." He waved his arms toward the crowd. "Do you wish to be in chains?"

The crowd erupted with cries of "We are not slaves! We are not lambs! Traitor!" Then a few others began yelling, "Quiet, let Yohanan speak!" and "Hear him out!" and "Shut up, it's Yohanan. You're a traitor for saying that!"

With the crowd throbbing behind him, Raanan glared at Yohanan, his fists clenched. "You little coward. You see what our people believe."

Yohanan wiped his forehead and gestured to the crowd. "I am no coward. I am no traitor, Raanan. You seem all too willing to claim treason when someone disagrees with you—or worse, to cover up your own failures. You raised the specter of treason against Eliezer to cover up your disastrous plan in New Jutland Square. When will you accept the blame for that instead of pointing the finger at a man we all know never once wavered in his sacrifice for our cause?"

"I could not have known of his treachery," Raanan yelled.

"His treachery," Yohanan continued. "The poor man could not defend himself against your charges because you chose to be his immediate executioner, without the benefit of a trial before his peers. If there were a treasonous act, that was it. It would be all too easy for me to ascribe your action to the blind hatred that I have denounced today. However, I fear your actions belie a motive even more sinister."

"You liar! You coward!" Raanan began lunging forward, his arms outstretched, but a few Yohanan supporters jumped between the two and pulled Raanan back into the crowd.

"No, Raanan, you speak of fighting again with the Juteslams, but where has it gotten us these last 50 years? It is insanity for we Tetepians to continue in the same old ways and believe the outcome will change." Yohanan waved his arms and looked around at the crowd. "Are any of you truly happy? Has this way—this path of destruction Raanan still advocates—has it led to anything other than misery?"

The crowd grew eerily silent.

Yohanan continued, "Raanan says you must continue this fight as you have or you will perish or be placed in chains. But this way of thinking will bring only more heartache and suffering. I am here to tell you there is another way. If the Juteslams try to invade our communities with their armies, then, yes, we must defend them. Warriors die in battle to protect their homes. But we must not kill the innocents. There has been no real war here for over forty years, yet people keep dying just the same. Some are fellow Tetepians. Some are Juteslams. Some are just little children." Yohanan swallowed hard and bit his lip, his eyes watering. "We kill each other and what does the world see? They see us as shaitaanists murdering innocent Juteslams and the Juteslams pounding us back with long-range shells in retribution. They see us only as the instigators, but they see the Juteslams as the defenders of their own land. Without the world on our side, we are doomed to failure. We must change that view. We must stop the killing!"

A woman from the crowd yelled out, "But Skjöldr withdrew the peace treaty after we rejected it. You stood here and told us to reject it. So how can we now do what you ask?"

"The peace treaty was deeply flawed. It would have divided us and deported us from our own land. No, another, honorable peace is possible, one in which we can live in peace where we wish within Tetepe. Our own hatred spurs the Juteslams actions. We must end the hatred on both sides.

We must accept that we will never remove the Juteslams from Tetepe. We must learn to live in this land with equality and justice for all, not just for Tetepians, but for each and every Juteslam. Yes, we fight when we need to defend ourselves, but we must learn to engage in peaceful protests and other civil actions against Juteslam injustices wherever they may exist."

"Peaceful protests?" Raanan laughed. "Are you crazy? They will just mow us down."

"The Juteslam leaders are not stupid. The world will sit in judgment, and they do not wish to be alone against the world. And it is to the world that we shall appeal. We have friends abroad. We can find others to aid in our cause. But we must lose the hate!"

Yohanan panned through the faces of the crowd. Though he was losing most of them, a few were still behind him. The most active Demoseps and a few of their leaders would side with Raanan, but even some of his old Demosep friends had nodded their heads when he had spoken.

The crowd parted as a beautiful blond woman made her way through it to the platform. It was Decima.

Yohanan grinned. Decima would come to his side and help him turn the crowd. He reached to help her up to the platform, but felt the slap of her hand on his forearm as she jumped up herself. When he looked in her eyes, her disgust punched him in the gut. *All is lost.*

She turned toward the crowd. "Most of you know me. I am Decima, daughter of Quintillus, the Romanus merchant who was murdered a few months ago for helping our cause. I saw him shot in the head as that filthy Hugleikr pronounced sentence on him without any trial or evidence. And I, for one, will never stop hating him and the Juteslams for it!"

Much of the crowd cheered.

"Yohanan speaks of peace, but he dishonors the loss of all our loved ones. We cannot rest until the Juteslams responsible for these atrocities suffer the same fate at our hands!" Another cheer.

"Yohanan would like you to believe the majority of Juteslams are innocents simply because they don't take up arms against us. He is wrong. By choosing to keep the demons Skjöldr and Hugleikr in power, they are just as responsible for the murders of Tetepians. That is right: the blood of your loved ones spilled on this very ground drips from all of their hands!

"So Yohanan can go perform his pathetic little peace protests and rot in jail if he wants. He would turn you into the same collared dogs of Skjöldr begging for scraps about which he complained two months ago when his head was still on straight. No, the Demoseps will not follow him, for he has lost his way. He has become a coward! We will carry on and fight against the hated Juteslams. Yes, I said, 'hated,' Yohanan. It is not a dirty word, for the Juteslams deserve our hate, and I for one will give it to them along with the bullets from my rap rifle! Let's go!"

The crowd cheered. Decima turned, waved the crowd to follow her, and then walked off the platform toward the edge of the marketplace followed by Raanan. Many fell behind them as they made their way to the tavern there. The rest of the crowd dispersed.

In the center of the square, still on the platform, Yohanan remained standing alone, looking down, devastated at the suddenness of his defeat and realizing the bleakness of his new reality: hatred always seemed to vanquish the truth, even the Great Truth. A few dozen stragglers walked up to him and thanked him for his encouraging words and deep courage. A few even offered to join him in his new struggle for peace. Achak strode slowly up to Yohanan with his head down. The two men embraced. When he pulled away, Achak nodded and winked.

Yohanan turned and looked at the small cadre of his fellow countrymen who accepted his message. It might not be enough, but it was a beginning. The images of death flashed again in his eyes and he closed them, and he saw Isa telling him he would prepare the way. He nodded his head. This was the way.

CHAPTER 55

THE FAMILIAR PATTERNS of Isa's address told Tomadus that he would soon arrive at that magical moment. After travelling with Isa and the Ten through the Mahdian Empire, Tomadus could now tune out the familiar stories while keeping a small part of his ear open for the shift, when some question from the crowd spurred yet another insight from Isa that Tomadus had never heard or considered.

Tomadus took these few minutes to take in the great beauty of the *Pontus Euxinus* as it slapped Tomis Beach with waves from the east. He enjoyed the warmth of the sun on his face for a few seconds until a gust from the early spring wind swept the warmth away. Isa was sitting on a raised platform on the beach, just a few steps from the sea, the sun high at his back in the late morning, its rays lighting up the faces of nearly a thousand curious locals standing below and in front of the ancient city of Constanta. He hoped they were not all local Constantans.

His squinted eyes scanned the faces for the powerful man with the oxymoron visage. Since they were less than a thousand *milia passuum* from the eastern edge of what was left of the Romanus Empire, Tomadus had asked the First Counsel to finally come see Isa for himself. He would not join the crowd but remain separate and protected. He looked above the seawall separating the beach from the city proper and saw the security detail first. He looked closer and saw the First Consul sitting on one of the few benches, alone except for the four guards standing around him and keeping the way in front of him clear. The First Counsel was looking at him. Tomadus nodded at the First Consul just as the question came.

A man wearing a salmon-colored cloth turban took a few steps forward from the crowd and asked, "Teacher, you have told us to be perfect, but we are only human. No matter how hard I try, I know I will still fall short of perfection. Must I truly attain perfection always to satisfy Allah and be welcomed into His kingdom in Heaven?"

Isa responded, "Follow me and you will find what you seek."

The man did not relent. "Yes, I know. But suppose I follow you and listen and try to do as you say but still falter? Am I damned for all time? Will Allah forgive me?"

Isa responded again, "You are a Mahdian, are you not?" The man nodded. "Then take some guidance from your Great Book, which tells you that Allah is most forgiving and merciful. To cleanse and purify, you should give alms to the poor, the needy, those who administer them, those whose hearts need winning over, to free the unjustly imprisoned and help those in debt, for God's cause, and for travelers in need. The Father is all hearing, all knowing. The Father Himself accepts repentance from His servants and receives what is given freely for His sake. Take action! Allah will see your actions, and then you will be returned to Him who knows what is seen and unseen."

Isa looked up from the man and stretched out his hands to the crowd. "All of you take heed. At the end of the age, the Son of Man will come and split the people into those on his right and left. To those on his right he will say, 'Come, you who are blessed by my Father. Inherit the kingdom prepared for you from the foundation of the world. For I was hungry and you gave me food, I was thirsty and you gave me drink, a stranger and you welcomed me, naked and you clothed me, ill and you cared for me, in prison and you visited me.' Then the righteous will answer him and say, 'Lord, when did we see you hungry and feed you, or thirsty and give you drink? When did we see you a stranger and welcome you, or naked and clothe you? When did we see you ill or in prison, and visit you?' And he will say to them in reply, 'Amen, I say to you, whatever you did for one of these least brothers of mine, you did for me.'

"Then he will say to those on his left, 'Depart from me, you accursed, into the eternal fire prepared for the devil and his angels. For I was hungry and you gave me no food, I was thirsty and you gave me no drink, a stranger and you gave me no welcome, naked and you gave me no clothing, ill and in prison, and you did not care for me.' Then they will answer and say, 'Lord, when did we see you hungry or thirsty or a stranger or naked or ill or in prison, and not minister to your needs?' He will answer them, 'Amen, I say to you, what you did not do for one of these least ones, you did not do for me.' And these will go off to eternal punishment, but the righteous to eternal life. Follow me and find the Way to salvation!" Isa walked off the platform.

The crowd murmured its approval. Some stayed, hoping for more words from Isa. A few dispersed. Tomadus nodded toward the First Consul and flashed a warm smile full of pride. The First Consul returned the gesture, and Tomadus breathed easier.

A group of young Mahdians walked up to Isa and began bowing to him and calling him the "Mahdi" and proclaiming that he would finally return peace and justice to the world. Isa smiled at this but neither acknowledged nor rejected their proclamation. When the men departed, Tomadus looked back at the First Consul only to see him shaking his head and frowning.

Several men carried a man whose limbs appeared shriveled and twisted up to Isa. One of the men begged Isa in Arabic to cure his brother. "I have heard the stories of your miracles. My brother has been crippled and in pain for these twenty years, yet I know that if you ask it of our Lord in Heaven, my brother will be cured. Please, I beg of you, help this poor man who has suffered so much." His brother looked up at Isa with a look of great longing.

Isa touched the crippled. "Your faith has healed him. Please, rise and walk and be in pain no more!" With this, the cripple stretched out, his arms and legs releasing from their corkscrew configuration, and he stood up and embraced Isa, tears pouring from his eyes.

Tomadus had seen Isa perform cures before, but nothing so significant or dramatic. Mouth open and eyes narrowed, he tilted his head and looked at the healed cripple and back again at Isa. He leaned over to Diego, one of the Ten, and asked, "How do we know this man who walked away?"

Diego chuckled and shook his head.

Tomadus said, "Then how did he do this?"

Diego looked toward the sky with his palms toward the heavens.

Tomadus looked at the cripple and tilted his head. *But there must be a scientific explanation.* Tomadus caught up with the former cripple as he walked slowly away with his brother. "May I see your arms and legs?" Tomadus asked. When the man showed his limbs, Tomadus saw strange light markings down them twisting along their axis. Were these part of Isa's cure? *No, they are merely differences in pigmentation.* The long twisted lines of skin had obviously been hidden from the beating sun for many years. He tried one more line of questioning, "What did the master do to cure you? Did he give you a drug? What did you feel?"

"He only touched me and my body tingled all over. I know not what he did, but I know Allah hears him."

Tomadus just nodded and walked back to the Ten and Isa, who was laying hands on several others with difficulties, and one by one they were apparently cured and began rejoicing and praising his name and that of God, sometimes using the name Allah and sometimes referring to him simply as Lord or Father. When the line of people seeking help ended, Isa and the Ten brought fruit and bread out of their backpacks, retreated to a quiet corner of the beach, said a prayer, and began to eat.

One of the local Jewish leaders approached the group and chastised them, saying, "Why do you and your followers break the tradition of the Elders? You eat without first washing your hands. Do you not understand that you are defiled?"

A local Mahdian elder nodded and added, "Yes, by the Hadith, the Messenger of Allah said, 'The blessings in the meal is by washing before and after it.' Yet you do not follow this tradition of our faith. What is wrong with you?"

Shaking his head, Isa set down his apple. "You hypocrites, you follow these human traditions instead of the commandments of God to secure your comfort and power." He looked at the Jewish leader and said, "How well you have set aside the commandment of God in order to uphold your tradition! For Moses said, 'Honor your father and your mother,' yet if a person says to father or mother, 'Any support you might have had from me is dedicated to God,' you allow him to do nothing more for his father or mother. You nullify the word of God in favor of human tradition."

Isa turned to the Mahdian. "Your Great Book says 'Let there be no compulsion in religion: Truth stands out clearly from falsehood,' yet your history is full of wars with your brothers brought to extend your sects to their people and leaders who force the conversion of infidels at the point of a sword."

Isa looked at the Jew and back at the Mahdian. "Isaiah spoke well about both of your peoples when he said, 'This people honors me with their lips, but their hearts are far from me; in vain do they worship me, teaching as doctrines human precepts.' Hear and understand. It is not what enters one's mouth that defiles that person. What comes out of the mouth is what defiles one."

The two religious leaders left without another word.

"But, Master, are they not right to criticize us for not following the law?" Simeon asked.

"Even you are still without understanding?" Isa asked. "Do you not realize that everything that enters the mouth passes into the stomach and is expelled into the latrine? But the things that come out of the mouth come from the heart, and they defile. For from the heart come evil thoughts, murder, adultery, unchastity, theft, false witness, blasphemy. These are what defile a person, not eating with unwashed hands."

Tomadus turned to see the First Consul begin walking away from the beach surrounded by several men of his security detail. Tomadus rushed up the stairs of the seawall and approached him. "First Consul, may I have a word with you?"

"Yes, ride with me." They both entered his official vehicle.

"Thank you for attending this gathering. What are your impressions of Isa?"

The First Consul paused for a few seconds, apparently in deep thought. Then he turned toward Tomadus with a funny smile on his face, not humorous, but strange, somewhat forced, with his lips too tightly drawn. "He does seem to want to help the poor. He is quite an orator and showman. I see why the throngs follow him. How do you suppose he pulled off that 'healing' of the cripple? It was quite impressive."

"Yes. I have no real explanation for it. I believe the man was actually a contorted cripple—did you see the paleness of the skin that had been hidden from the sun? But, what did you think of his message? His words span Jewish and Muslim traditions, but go beyond them both. They reach out to all—even to many Romani. He is a coalescing force."

"He speaks impressively, but is his message coalescing? I'm not sure. I am quite concerned that he did not correct the exuberant followers who called him the Mahdi."

"Does it not refer to a master in the Mahdian Empire?"

The First Counsel frowned and shook his head. "You do not yet comprehend the danger of these proclamations. The Mahdian Empire is separate from the Shi'ite Muslim Empire because the Mahdians believe that the Twelfth Imam, Muhammad al-Mahdi, disappeared in the third century AH and has remained in occultation, or spiritual hiding, ever since. According to their belief, he is an infallible descendant of Muhammad. He is similar to the messiah still anticipated by the Jews—except the Mahdians see the Mahdi as the Great Imam who will return peace and justice to Islam."

"What danger is there in that? Isa seeks peace for the entire world."

The First Consul sighed and frowned. "You are more sophisticated than that. If this Isa of yours gains enough followers who believe such things, what do you think the Three Emperors might do?"

"I don't know. He does not seek power. He did not call himself Mahdi."

"No, I doubt he even believes that, but our religious leaders may be troubled if they find him insincere. If he is a fraud, he will never bring the world together, but will drive it apart. The consequences could be ugly—for the world and for him."

Tomadus's heart almost stopped. "I have no doubt he is sincere in trying to bring the world together. Do not judge him by a few misguided followers. Do the religious leaders suspect his is a fraud or are you speculating?"

"I am only speculating as I look out for your interests, Tomadus. His sincerity is critical. If they do not believe him…"

"I understand. We must change their perspectives. I know he merely seeks to teach us to love one another. Could we convince these leaders of that?"

"Perhaps. We shall see. The time is not ripe. Please keep an eye on him and we will see when we can address it."

"I will do what I can." As soon as he had finished saying this, a twinge of guilt gripped Tomadus. Had he now become the spy that Isa predicted? *No. Never.*

First Consul Khansensius replied, "Good. Now I have some excellent news for you. I have secured a meeting for you with Skjöldr, though unfortunately you must travel to that wretched Tetepe."

Tomadus beamed. "*Gratias*, First Consul. I will travel there immediately."

"You are welcome, *amicus meus*. By the way, did I tell you about the progress our technologists have made on your invention?"

"No. Progress?" *Impossible. I left out a key part of the accelerator.*

"Yes. They seemed to struggle awhile and kept telling me something was missing from your diagrams and plans. I told them they must be mistaken, for I trust you so well. I told them we were trying to accomplish something that you had not attempted with your invention, so they just needed to work a little harder at it. Fortunately, with a few appropriate incentives and a few well-placed disincentives, they seemed to have discovered an ancillary method that solved the problem. *Gratias*, Tomadus, for your great service to Roma and the Three Empires. In due course, you will receive a more public honor, but be patient."

Tomadus paused in thought. He had not believed the Imperium's technologists could pull it off, but he had been a fool. The First Consul had just subtly informed him of his foolishness and then congratulated him on his service. *He knows of my deception, but I am still to be congratulated?* Tomadus saw the First Consul staring at him and awaiting an appropriate response. He forced a weak smile. "*Gratias.* You are most generous. I am happy I could help our protectorate."

"And you have, Tomadus, you have, believe me. I have appreciated your concerns in this matter, but we really never had much choice but to comply with the Emperors' generals, did we? But, perhaps, we might be a little more careful in the future."

Tomadus smiled. He could see the First Counsel sympathized with him and had probably taken extraordinary measures to protect him from the repercussions of his deception. "Of course, First Counsel, you are right," Tomadus said.

To this, the First Counsel merely nodded and smiled.

CHAPTER 56

TOMADUS BREATHED DEEPLY and followed his armed escorts through Skjöldr's Asgard Palace. It had been a whirlwind week: parting from Isa again, managing to find an *aeronaves* scheduled to hop across the seadromes to New Åarhus, and learning about Yohanan's fate as he waited for Skjöldr's assistants to finally schedule his promised audience with the king—a king who had undermined his initiatives even before he had arrived. And yet, he had pressed on. The creature within would not let him do otherwise.

As he walked toward Heorot Hall, Tomadus marveled at the opulence of the marbled corridors of Asgard Palace. Huge paintings of ancient Viking battles adorned both walls. The ornate walls led up some twenty feet to a barrel-vaulted ceiling inlaid with gold and decorated on each side with various images of Viking history. At the center of each segment of the barrel vault hung a picture of the Great Book open to the first page of a different Sura.

Tomadus knew little of these two traditions, but what he did know made the juxtaposition of Viking icons with the words of the Great Book seem nearly blasphemous. The Grand Imams in the Three Empires would have cringed at the association of the Great Book with the near idol worship of ancient Viking heroes. But this cultural merger would seem natural and appropriate to his palace host, who sat on his throne in the hall just beyond the huge wooden doors at the end of the corridor.

With a gentle push from his escorts, the doors swung open, revealing an enormous, lavish marble hall adorned with exquisite brass and wooden carvings of various shapes and sizes. Tomadus noticed that two types of carvings were repeated in several places in the room: three interlocking drinking horns and three interlocking triangles. The carvings repeated at odd intervals, though he thought he detected some kind of pattern to them, almost like a code.

Without warning, the familiar light flashed in his eyes and the other world opened up to him again. He saw an image of an enormous mosque in a strange land with Arabic writing on one of its walls. It referred to the Great Book. A shadow dashed past and his mind kept swirling as if the words meant something more than what they seemed. *Not now!* He shook his head and struggled to dispel the thoughts and feelings that had briefly overtaken him. Sweat dripped from his brow down his nose and to his lips. He dabbed his face with a section of cloth from his pocket.

The grand marshal announced, "Tomadus, a Merchant of Roma."

Tomadus looked forward and refocused his eyes on the plush scarlet carpet leading from the door to the back of the hall and a marble dais that rose nearly five feet above the floor. Tomadus composed himself and recognized the two men conversing quietly on the dais.

One man sat on the only piece of furniture on the stage—a massive, elaborately carved oak chair, which obviously served as a throne to this Viking clan. A large man, he wore a jeweled crown on his large head, while a plush violet cape covered his shoulders and upper arms. Beneath the cape he wore ancient Viking leather armor. The man's trimmed red beard revealed a strong jaw and high cheekbones set just below stone-cold, nearly black eyes.

Next to him stood a man with a huge head expanded by dark orange hair flowing out from his head, cheeks and neck. Tomadus could still see this demon on the visi-scan coldly calling out to the "cowards" of the Konverteraften Massacre after Tomadus's friend, Quintillus, had been dragged up to the New Åarhus stage before an immediate execution.

Hugleikr's angled visage rolled Tomadus's stomach and turned his hands to ice, and he fought an almost uncontrollable urge to either flee the palace or jump up and strangle the killer. *Control yourself.* Success meant burying his emotion deep. *Remember Isa's words. Love your enemies.* He took a deep breath, forced a smile and moved forward. When he approached the dais, he bowed deeply.

"Welcome, Tomadus of Roma," Skjöldr said. Hugleikr, still standing beside him, silently stared at Tomadus.

"I thank you, your Highness. You are most gracious to receive me. I bring greetings from Roma and the Three Empires. First Consul Khansensius sends his salutations, as do Generals Khameni and Faisal, at whose request I have made this journey."

"We are delighted to hear it. It has been a long time since we have shared a banquet with these men. Please, when you return, send my regards to them as well. We have been told you serve as an unofficial ambassador of Romanus merchants."

"I do, your Highness. As you know, I have made some efforts throughout North Aztalan to create markets for my photonic computer products. I believe New Jutland and all of Tetepe could benefit not only from my products but also from significantly enhanced trade with Roma and the Three Empires. I am here to explore that possibility."

Skjöldr glanced at Hugleikr and the second returned a tight-lipped smile. Skjöldr turned back to Tomadus and said, "We see. What is the nature of that exploration, for New Jutland has never restricted its trade with Roma or the Three Empires?"

"Ah, your Highness, I believe your confusion arises from the distinction between purely legal and otherwise practical restraints. I know we are free to trade by your law and our own, but most of my fellow merchants are quite reluctant to risk much capital in areas where the political situation is, shall I say, a bit unstable."

"Unstable?" roared Skjöldr, "We have been king for over 25 years. We hardly think New Jutland can be called 'unstable.'"

Tomadus forced a restrained smile. He had to be careful here or the meeting would end badly. He nodded gently. "Of course, since you have ruled longer than many monarchs of the world, the instability derives not from your rule but from the ongoing…situation…with the Demoseps and the Tetepians."

Skjöldr and Hugleikr exchanged a knowing glance again. "May I, your highness?" asked Hugleikr. Skjöldr nodded and Hugleikr looked directly at Tomadus. "Tomadus of Roma, we understand you visited Shenandoah yourself less than a year ago."

Tomadus's heart skipped a beat, but his outward composure remained intact. He smiled and nodded gently. "Yes, of course, Vice Regent, after the reports of my fellow merchants, I made the trip to assess the situation here. I am sorry to say that it brought me only greater worries for this region. For the sake of business, I am hoping, with the support of the First Consul, we might work together to find a way to bring the trouble you have faced for so long to a reasonable conclusion."

Skjöldr flashed a seemingly genuine smile. "We would welcome any assistance the First Consul could provide to help us deal with these troubles. We understand a certain alteration of your invention might at some point help us in that regard. We have done everything in our power to live in peace with these people, yet they seem to seek only murder and chaos. We propose rational peace terms, and they reject them out of hand and seek our deaths. We build up our cities, and they seek to tear them down. We go to Tetepe to help them maintain the peace and our soldiers are blown up on roadsides and railroads. These people are not rational. It seems their only goal is to exterminate us."

Tomadus had feared this view. "I understand your concerns, your Highness. Some of the Demoseps still struggle to see the situation through your eyes. However, with enlightened leadership, others may find a way to end the violence. The Tetepians, too, have suffered from this war and many demonize the Juteslams for it, just as you demonize them. But we have made some inroads with a few leaders who are capable of appreciating your point of view and understanding the need for peace. I hope that you will try to do the same."

Hugleikr laughed. "Do these so-called leaders include that rabble-rouser Yohanan and his paltry followers? Did you know that as we speak they are imprisoned for sedition and conspiracy to insurrection?"

"So I heard after I arrived in New Jutland. I have come to know Yohanan as a man of peace."

"Is that so?" said Hugleikr. "He was preaching his nonsense in Great Jutland Square and trying to rile up a crowd. They booed him and threw things at him, but he remained and caused a substantial disturbance. He and his group refused to disperse upon the demand of our security forces. They sat down in front of the palace and forced the security personnel to carry them to the prison below. The entire episode was clearly the start of a conspiracy to insurrection for which he and his cohorts will be tried and convicted."

"I see," said Tomadus. "Of course, there will be repercussions from the arrest."

"Repercussions?" Hugleikr asked.

"Yohanan was one of the few Tetepians who had begun to speak against violence. He had only a small following, but it was growing quickly. It is one thing to arrest shaitaanists, another to arrest peaceful demonstrators. It does not strengthen your position on the world stage."

Hugleikr lashed back, "Peaceful demonstrator? We have reason to believe he was behind the Konverteraften Massacre. Yohanan is no man of peace. We—"

Skjöldr put up his hand as to silence Hugleikr. "Speak no more of that terrible day. We wonder if you understand the situation completely."

"You may be right, your Highness." Tomadus bowed slightly. "I know only bits and pieces."

"You seem to see New Jutland and the rest of Tetepe only as it stands now," said Skjöldr. "But if you appreciated our history, you would appreciate the constant precariousness of our situation. The Juteslams are alone in our faith and it is only our enduring will to survive and our willingness to fight for our beliefs and culture that has prevented the extinction of our people. You must know that the Latisilolals—those fanatics from the west who started the last world war—nearly succeeded in destroying us forever as many of my people struggled to survive within their borders. They hated us more than the Aztecs before them and blamed us for all of their economic problems. We thank Allah that the Three Empires and the Aztecs joined together to defeat them and the North Asian Empire in the Great World War. Without His intervention, we may well have perished."

Tomadus nodded respectfully.

Skjöldr went on, "But He, with the assistance of the allied powers, helped us return to the land of our forefathers in New Jutland. The Tetepians had interloped on our land in our absence, but we still welcomed them as our brothers. What was the result? They tried to destroy us just as the Latisilolals had done. With Allah as our guide, we fought back and defeated this violent people. But now we remain surrounded by the red men who dominate this continent and the Jews who shout about the power of the people but wish only that we be swept into the sea. To you, we seem like a dominant power lording over the Tetepian people, but they are only a small part of the problem. To us, we are but a grain of sand on the beach of this vast continent, fighting the tide of intolerance for our beliefs and clinging with everything we have left to remain fast on the shore."

"So you see," said Skjöldr, "we must always remain vigilant. We cannot seem weak to anyone in this hemisphere—not even for a moment. If today we were to agree to unreasonable peace terms to end the violence of the Tetepians, tomorrow they or their brothers in arms around this continent would be imprisoning our leaders, burning our mosques, and raping our women. We cannot, we shall not, ever raise a white flag, even for a single battle, and even if that means we must fight them all to the last man. Such an ill-considered act would be the first step toward our own demise."

Tomadus nodded again, holding back his anger. He was not the first to hear this speech from Skjöldr, but it could not simply be propaganda. No, Skjöldr believed his own words almost as an article of his own faith. No doubt there was at its core some shining scepter of truth there, but it had long ago become encrusted with the residue of the corrosive power of hate. Only some unspeakable tragedy would ever reopen his eyes and his heart. No shaitaanist act by the Demoseps could ever accomplish that feat, for such attempts would serve only to further justify his ideology. For now, the best he could do was obtain Yohanan's release. "I understand, your Highness, but I wonder if you may have undermined your own goals by arresting Yohanan. I have heard he has argued that the Tetepians must relinquish any hope of driving the Juteslams away from Tetepe. He claims they must accept the Juteslams and seek an honorable peace. While he is in the minority, he has much sway, here…and abroad."

Hugleikr interrupted, "That makes him more dangerous, not less."

Skjöldr flashed a chastising look at Hugleikr and looked back at Tomadus. "You are wise, Tomadus. Perhaps there may be hope for Yohanan, yet. As long as he and his followers are willing to stay out of New Jutland itself, we think we shall pardon them and set them free. But if we ever discover anything about his involvement in the Konverteraften Massacre, we shall act without delay. I will have my guards bring Yohanan to you. Vice Regent Hugleikr is leaving on an important trip to Jerusalem and then Mecca for the Hajj. We have much to accomplish before he leaves. Please give my regards to the First Consul."

"Thank you, your Highness," Tomadus said with a bow. "With Yohanan's help, perhaps we can make progress on a true and lasting peace. May we meet again to continue our discussions?"

"Let us see where your efforts with Yohanan lead. And then we shall see."

CHAPTER 57

THE TWO MEN embraced at the top of the stairs before the Asgard Palace. Yohanan looked a bit disheveled. "I don't know what you did, but thank you for getting me released. Being thrown in prison for a good cause sounds better than it feels. I see most of my followers have already thanked you." He nodded toward the group awaiting them at the bottom of the staircase.

"My friend, I simply showed them the truth and the advantage of letting a man of peace go free. However, you and your followers are personally banished from New Jutland for the time being. They are happy to see you perform your rabble rousing for peace, but only among your own people."

"Well, I suppose I can always return to New Åarhus some other time with a camera crew ready to record my next arrest."

"Yes, but for now you will need to return to Shenandoah to convince Decima to join your cause. You need to build this movement."

"I understand, but the Fox is no longer in Shenandoah."

"The Fox?" Tomadus asked. "Is that some kind of code name?"

Yohanan shook his head. "Sorry, forgive my little quirks." Yohanan looked around for unwanted ears. He said in a low voice, "I heard Decima left the continent and has traveled to the Palestinian Province on Demosep business. Raanan is with her along with a handful of other Demoseps. It sounds like they may have plans for more disruption."

Tomadus closed his eyes a moment and exhaled hard. "You may be right. Hugleikr begins his travels to Jerusalem tomorrow."

"Damn. Then they are going to make another attempt at him. Fools! So be it. I will no longer have anything to do with them."

"No, you must. You are the only one who can talk Decima out of this nonsense. I've just opened up a dialogue with Skjöldr that could eventually lead somewhere, but if this happens, peace will be dead for years, and I fear for the destruction that will rain down on Tetepe for another generation."

"I agree, but what can I do? You did not see the look on her face when she denounced my Great Truth. She hates all Juteslams, but she especially hates Hugleikr. She wants her revenge. She will do anything to kill him."

Tomadus put his hands on Yohanan's shoulders. "You must try. What would Isa do? You must."

Yohanan looked down at the ground for a few moments, back at his small group of followers, and finally back to Tomadus. "I know you're right, but I doubt I can even get Letters of Transit into the Sunni Muslim Empire, let alone catch up with Decima and Raanan."

"The First Consul is the only one who can provide the Letter of Transit you need to get to Jerusalem. Without it, the Sunni Muslim Empire would never permit travel there by a rebel with known Demosep links. Let me make a few calls. Meanwhile, gather what you will need for the trip and join me at the *aeroportus* outside the city. We can board an *aeronavis* there and fly to Roma."

"Do you trust the First Consul?"

"I am beginning to. He arranged the audience with Skjöldr, and at least that led to your release. I think he trusts me. This will be a big test."

▽   ▽   ▽

The man with the black hair and beard bellowed out a laugh in Tomadus's face. Then he smiled and raised one eyebrow as he turned and showed the contents of his right hand—a scroll that unraveled to the floor. The scroll depicted many tiny identical black dots repeating in equidistant spaces in increasingly longer rows to form the shape of a perfect equilateral triangle. Below the triangle, "T_{36}" was written in the style of the math techs. It looked like each of the three perimeter "lines" of the triangle contained about 36 dots. The bearded man's eyes narrowed and he flung the parchment into the air, where flames immediately consumed it. The man roared again with laughter. Tomadus lunged and tried to grab him with both hands, but he simply disappeared, his laughter still echoing in Tomadus's ears.

When Tomadus's eyes opened, he quickly squinted them shut, opened them extra wide again, and then repeated the procedure several times until the afterglow of the dream faded, but he knew the strange vision would never completely dissipate from his memory. That man with the black beard, he was familiar. Huxley knew him, didn't he? Somehow, he looked different than in the other visions, like another he knew. *I must be obsessing about the First Consul. He too invades my thoughts.*

Leaning back in his chair on the *aeronavis*, he saw the vast blue ocean shimmering in the moonlight a few thousand feet below, its waves seemingly beckoning him home. He felt the *aeronavis* begin to descend again. When he looked ahead, he could just see another floating seadrome many *milia passuum* in the distance. This would be the third and last stop between the continents, where all fifteen passengers would disembark and eat a meal while the *aeronavis* refueled. The things took some getting used to with their landing decks some 70 *cubitus* above the water. Their huge columns looked like they must reach to the ocean floor, but that was impossible. Instead, they led to buoyancy chambers near the surface with huge ballast chambers far below to keep them stable. The whole unit was attached loosely to a floating buoy system that linked it to a massive concrete mushroom anchor submerged below with two long steel cables. The thing had its own power plant and could use propellers to maneuver slightly while anchored. It was the only way the *aeronavis* could fly over the Atlantic between the Three Empires and North Aztalan. Yet another example of the genius of the Romanus technologists.

Tomadus heard the deep breathing of Yohanan sleeping next to him, his head tipped back as far as the seat would allow. *Does this friend of mine hold the key? Together, maybe we can stop the dominoes of hatred before it damns Tetepe for another fifty years.* After he had thought this, the creature within again crawled out of the depths of his gut and began to howl. Tomadus shook his head. *Why now? I seek peace but find only despair. I am doing the best I can. What do you want of me?*

CHAPTER 58

YOHANAN SIGHED AND looked away, rubbing the back of his neck. Could he trust Tomadus's judgment here? He knew little about this First Consul, but Tomadus was right. Without his help, there was no way to get to Jerusalem, to Decima. And he must make the attempt.

If her plan failed on foreign soil, she would face disaster without any friends nearby to save her. Raanan's gang could not be resting their fate with Jerusalem's Jews, whose leaders had long been co-opted by the Sunni Muslim Empire in exchange for some modicum of freedom to practice their religion. Was something else going on here? And how did they even get into the country? They too were closely associated with the Demoseps. Even Decima's Romanus citizenship would not get her all the way to Jerusalem with the intel the empire undoubtedly possessed of her ties to the Demoseps.

"The First Consul will see you now," the assistant told them.

He saw Tomadus smiling with confidence. Yohanan followed him into the office of the First Consul. Clearly, Khansensius had more real power than Skjöldr, but the trappings of his office paled in comparison to Asgard Palace. The accouterments seemed to suggest he was just a simple background figure providing helpful services to the Three Emperors upon their summons. He played that role well. Yohanan saw Tomadus and the First

Consul exchange warm greetings, smiles all around, and he relaxed a few notches. *Tomadus must know what he is doing. I must trust him.*

Tomadus gestured toward Yohanan. "First Consul, this is my friend, an agent of peace, Yohanan, from Tetepe."

"I have heard much about you, sir. Welcome." The First Consul turned toward Yohanan with a slight bow, his right hand raised to his chest.

Yohanan returned the bow, but more deeply. "*Gratias*, your Excellency, and I have heard nothing but good about you from Tomadus."

The First Consul turned back to Tomadus. "Tomadus, I take it from your friend's presence here that your meeting with King Skjöldr went well."

"Not entirely. It was a start, but a small one. I fear something catastrophic must happen before Skjöldr sees any value in taking real steps toward reconciliation. But he did see the value of releasing Yohanan to allow him to preach peace to his people."

"I see," said the First Consul. "Yohanan, you seem to have found a Romanus merchant as your sponsor. I congratulate you."

Yohanan was about to reply, but Tomadus threw him a glance. "No, Your Excellency, I am not his sponsor, and he requires no such thing. I merely seek a peaceful end so we can make business inroads in Tetepe and perhaps stabilize a difficult part of the world in the process. Yohanan has had certain…experiences…that have given him the ability to appreciate the need for a peaceful resolution. In that regard, he may be critical to our success there."

"Our success?"

"Why yes, you do agree that peace in Tetepe would be to the advantage of Roma and the Three Empires, do you not?"

The First Consul stroked his chin. "Of course, on appropriate terms."

"Well, Yohanan and I are here today to ask for your help in achieving that goal."

"How could I do that?"

Tomadus said, "We require a Letter of Transit to permit Yohanan to travel to Jerusalem."

The First Consul stiffened and crossed his arms. "For what purpose?"

Yohanan watched Tomadus look at him and then back at the First

Consul. Would Tomadus break his word and tell the First Consul the whole story?

Tomadus spoke slowly, "I am sorry, but I believe it would be best if we do not go into details. Please, trust me that Yohanan is on a mission of peace."

The First Consul tightened his lips. "Tomadus, you and I have developed an excellent relationship, and I do trust your judgment in a great many things. However, you are asking me to give written orders that permit a man known to associate with shaitaanists to travel to one of the most holy cities of the Sunni Muslim Empire. Will you next ask me to allow him to travel to Mecca? No, I must know the reason."

Tomadus looked again at Yohanan, and Yohanan responded with a look of terror. Would Tomadus reveal Decima's involvement with the Demoseps? His friends would be arrested and executed in Jerusalem. Yohanan took the initiative, "I must visit a friend from Roma who is travelling there. It is critical that she return to Tetepe to help in my campaign. Without her, we will be lost."

"What is her name?"

"Decima, the daughter of Quintillus."

The First Consul raised his hand to his chin and stroked his beard a few times. "She too has associated with shaitaanists. This does not give me great comfort."

"I know I can convince her to join our peace movement. I just need to speak with her alone."

The First Consul raised his arms to his chest and placed his palms together with the tips of his fingers bouncing on his lips. When he spoke, he employed a greater tone of officialdom than he had previously revealed to Yohanan, "Tomadus, will you vouch for the importance of this mission?"

"Excellency, I can tell you that the success of his mission may be the only thing that will allow peace to return to Tetepe for many years."

"Then I will grant you the Letter of Transit, on one condition. I will contact authorities in Jerusalem and ask them to keep an eye on your activities there. They will report directly to me. I must protect myself from recrimination if your mission should fail."

"As you wish," Yohanan agreed. "I will do nothing to give you pause."

"See that you don't."

A few minutes later, Yohanan and Tomadus were walking in the shadow of the Colosseum back toward their hotel, the Letter of Transit in hand. "When will you leave?" asked Tomadus.

"The earliest *aeronavis* to Palestine is tomorrow afternoon," Yohanan said.

"Will you have dinner with me tonight before we part?"

"I'll have to pass. I'm visiting Jochi, my sister. You remember her from your visit to Tetepe?"

Tomadus grinned. "How could I forget? I felt as though I had already known her."

Yohanan looked hard at Tomadus. After an uncomfortable moment of silence, Yohanan said, "Anyway, why don't you travel with me to Jerusalem? You might help me find Decima."

Tomadus shook his head. "I would be of no help there, I am afraid. I will find Isa and seek his assistance."

"When you see Isa, tell him that I follow the rising of the sun, so I sail to Jerusalem."

CHAPTER 59

YOHANAN HAD GUESSED right. Ahead of him walked the Fox tugging at his heart with all her beauty and all her cunning. He had anticipated the Demoseps would spend a few days reconnoitering the site of Hugleikr's planned speech later that week. The visi-scan had invited those interested to assemble below the eastern stairs leading up to the Dome of the Rock. A few hundred feet to the left of the stairs, Yohanan had found a quiet corner behind some trees that still allowed him a decent vantage point. Sure enough, several hours later Decima and Raanan strolled not more than fifty feet from the base of the stairs.

The shrine had been built on the Temple Mount, where the first and second Jewish Temples had stood until destroyed by the Babylonians and the Romani. It was the site where many Muslims believed Muhammad had ascended into Heaven with the angel Gabriel to speak to God and receive instructions on the details of prayer. The stairs leading up to the shrine provided the perfect spot for Hugleikr to restate, for the entire world to see, the devotion of his people to Islam. It was a spot that the Demosep leader, Raanan, with his weakness for dramatic irony, would likely pick to end Hugleikr's life.

For over an hour, Yohanan followed Decima from a distance as she walked through Jerusalem. He wanted to speak with her alone, away from the influence of Raanan the Snake. After the two animals parted, the Fox entered a small café alone.

Her eyes bulged as he approached and took a seat at her table. "What are you doing here?" she said, her eyes glaring back at him.

"Rescuing the Fox from the Snake."

"What?"

"I know what you, Raanan and the others are up to here. If I have figured it out, don't you think the authorities have also?"

She looked around. "I don't know what you mean. I have always wanted to visit this holy city. Raanan and some other friends chose to join me." She looked straight into his eyes, yet if he had been ignorant of the truth, he could not have known she was lying, except for that one nervous tic: she was gently tapping Quintillus's master merchant's ring against her ceramic cup with her right hand. The triad of red, white and blue jewels glimmered with every bounce.

Yohanan broke the silence, "Do you think it may seem a bit too convenient that you are visiting Jerusalem at the same time that the Vice Regent of New Jutland is making a major speech at the Dome of the Rock?"

The Fox's face lost some of its color, but she said nothing.

Yohanan leaned his chest over the table. "Look, Decima, it's me. Stop the pretense. You have to know this is madness. It is just another one of Raanan's misguided schemes to show the world that the Demoseps can strike their enemies anywhere. It will end in disaster for you and for our people."

She sat back. "I am quite willing to die to avenge my father's death. Are you willing to die for your own beliefs, whatever they are?"

Yohanan looked down at his hands. "Why did you join the movement in the first place?"

"For the same reason you did, to end the domination of the Juteslams and preserve what little democracy remains in Tetepe. Democracy holds the best hope for women like me. The best hope for us all. It may be too late for me but not for those who follow."

"So why are you trying to destroy that democracy forever?"

She shook her head, leaned in, and whispered, "I plan to kill a tyrant who is an enemy of democracy."

"But don't you see the consequences of this plan? What good will it do even if you are successful? It will force Skjöldr to crack down on Tetepe even more. In the end, I fear our way of life, our democracy, will burn to ashes in the firestorm you ignite. Is that what you want?"

Decima sneered at him. "All people who have felt the sting of tyranny will applaud our actions. The world will have to face the depth of our convictions to gain freedom and preserve democracy. Anyway, he deserves to die at our hands."

"Can you condemn him to death by yourself? Are you the judge of his sins against God?"

"God?" she said sarcastically. "God no. I care not about the sins of this man against any mythical creature. But I am quite comfortable being the judge of his sins against mankind."

Yohanan grabbed her hands and said softly, "I once believed that myself, but I have found the answer lies in love, not hate."

Decima pulled her hands away from his. "More of your peace and love crap. I can't listen to that garbage, not now, not even from you."

"Then listen to this. Tomadus has begun a dialogue with Skjöldr to find an honorable peace. We think such a peace might be possible, though it could still take some time. But if you and Raanan carry out your intentions here, Hugleikr dies a martyr to his cause. A hero. Skjöldr will use his death to crush our democracy. You must stop this and allow us to do our work."

"I'm sorry, Yoh, but I will not suffer a fool's feckless folly. I once thought you brilliant and insightful. Skjöldr will never of his own initiative allow Tetepians to live in peace. We must force his hand. This is the only way."

Yohanan frowned and shook his head. "There are powers far greater than Skjöldr. Tomadus has the First Consul's backing. There is a real chance, but even that will fade if you do this. It is your way that condemns us to death."

"And your way condemns your people to chains and my father's name to oblivion. I will not rest until his killer dies a horrible death." She slammed down her cup, stood up and walked out of the café.

Yohanan sat in the café for another hour, seemingly alone, never noticing the man at the next table who had followed him into the cafe. He had loved her once. How much he could still love her if she could just overcome the hatred now consuming her. He kept shaking his head and resting his forehead on his fingertips, eyes closed. *There has to be some other way to stop the carnage and save her from herself, some way to abort the assassination.*

CHAPTER 60

THE SUN'S RAYS bounced harmlessly off the golden cupola of the Dome of the Rock as Yohanan cut through the crowd of several hundred who had decided to watch Hugleikr give his speech. The introduction by a local imam had already begun at the top of the stairs as Yohanan scanned the crowd for Decima and her Demosep cohorts. He found Dekanawida lurking near the back of the crowd, with a hood around his head and sunglasses hiding most of his face from security. Raanan the Snake was similarly dressed to avoid detection and was walking behind the crowd off of the Temple Mount, just far enough away to make a quick exit, just like a snake through a hole in the wall.

The crowd applauded the end of the introduction, and Hugleikr began his speech: "Thank you all for your kind reception before this great monument. This ancient city reminds me of the battles this great empire has had over the years to keep the holy land safe from those who would turn it to dust. You have all enjoyed safety and security for the past fifty years, but we, the Juteslams, continue to fight against the barbarians of Tetepe, who wish to undermine our Islamic way of life…"

Yohanan shook his head almost reflexively in disgust as he scanned the crowd. Nearly all were Arab men acknowledging Hugleikr's words. A few children sat on their fathers' shoulders. Guards patrolled through the crowd while two stood just in front of a three-cubit high temporary chain barrier securing the stairwell up to Hugleikr. An obviously pregnant Muslim woman, face hidden in a burka, hands in pockets, stood motionless behind the barrier. It seemed unlikely that a devout Muslim woman would be standing in this mixed crowd.

Yohanan began searching the natural stage at the top of the short stairs leading up from the pregnant woman. Hugleikr was employing his typically exaggerated gestures, just like he was in a much larger square in New Jutland. Yohanan searched for a likely bomb location. There was no temporary stage since they were just using the top of the short stairs for the speech. The microphone stand? It seemed too narrow to house a fatal bomb. How about one of the other dignitaries at the top of the stairs? All anti-Demosep types. Where else? Maybe they had planned some kind of rifle shot instead. He began scanning the trees to see if security had missed someone perched above.

He heard a gasp from the crowd and looked down toward the barrier, where the crowd had now parted slightly. Security personnel were making their way to the pregnant woman in the burka, who had apparently succumbed from the heat of the sun and was now lying on her side next to the barrier. Hugleikr paused his speech and asked security to bring the woman up the stairs, so she could rest in the shade near the inner wall.

With the assistance of the men in security uniforms, the woman stood up slowly and was beginning to be led around the barrier. As she passed the barrier, her right hand swung free, for the first time revealing the ring on her finger: large and platinum, with three stones in a red, white and blue triangle. Yohanan could feel the adrenaline rush through his body as his brain connected the picture.

He cut quickly through the crowd, pushing others aside as he made his way toward the base of the stairs. He watched the woman reach into the pocket of her robes and fumble with a small device with two wires leading toward the fetus within her body. Yohanan screamed, "Stop!" He knocked over two security men as he approached the barrier.

Decima now shook free of her surprised security helpers, ran up the stairs several steps, pulled off the burka and yelled, "Death to tyrants! Long live democracy!" She seemed to be pushing something on the device, but nothing happened. She stopped, jerking her head down looking at her right hand emerging from her pocket, her forehead furrowing, eyes narrowing and lips moving without a sound. Yohanan leapt over the barrier and bounded up the steps, yelling "Decima, don't! Stop!" The look on Decima's face changed to one of surprise as several bullets penetrated her chest. She fell backward down the stairs, the bomb and its wires at her midsection now visible to all. She rolled to Yohanan's feet. He lowered himself over her and tried to cover her from further harm. When he looked into her eyes, he saw a look of total disbelief. "I was so close. You were right," she gurgled. "Traitor!"

"Decima," he whispered, but her eyes had gone stone cold, her face frozen. Yohanan looked up at the security guards surrounding him just in time to see the blur of a rap rifle butt rapidly approaching his forehead. Everything went black.

TOMADUS FINALLY CAUGHT up with Isa in Corinth. Corinth was a city of ten thousand lying on the edge of the isthmus leading to the Peloponnesian Peninsula in the Grecian Province of the Sunni Muslim Empire. When Tomadus arrived, he discovered that most of the Ten had left at Isa's direction to spread his message to various parts of the Three Empires. Tomadus found only Adin and Maryam staying with Isa, all as guests of a long-time friend of the Way. Since the disciples had left, Isa had apparently spent most of his time meditating alone in the garden behind the home. Following Maryam's strict orders, Tomadus patiently waited several hours for Isa to emerge from his meditation. When Isa walked into the room, Tomadus jumped up and greeted him with a kiss on each cheek. Isa smiled and returned the gesture.

Tomadus said, "It is only when I am with you that I feel myself. I missed you these past couple of weeks."

"I always feel your absence," Isa replied. "Have you found your answers?"

"Not really, but I don't know. At least when I am with you I feel less terrified of my dreams."

"You refer to this other world you have mentioned?"

Tomadus nodded. "It can be terrifying to live in two worlds at once."

"Tomadus, be pleased you can see only two. Do you believe you have a soul?"

"A what?"

"A soul—the spiritual part of you that has the potential to transcend the limits of our corporal bodies."

Tomadus shook his head and smiled. "Where does this soul exist? I have never heard of a physic-tech who has found this organ in the body."

"Do not mock the things you do not understand. The soul is your spiritual essence. You cannot touch it or see it, and no surgeon can remove it."

"Then how do I know it exists?"

"Because it is God's greatest gift to you."

"That's a bit circular. Remember, I do not believe in a god. I don't even think my alter ego believed in a god in that other world."

Isa cocked his head. "Yet you believe in your visions, and you believe in this other world."

"But I see them with my own eyes."

"Yet nobody else can see them, so how can they possibly be real?"

"I just know they are."

Nodding, Isa flashed a warm smile. "Just as I know you have a soul."

Tomadus blushed. "What does this soul have to do with my dreams?"

"Everything."

"But how?"

"When you understand that," Isa said, "you will understand everything."

Tomadus sighed deeply. "If only I didn't feel so alone."

Isa said, "You are never alone, Tomadus, and you are not alone in this gift."

A spray of euphoria seemed to wash over Tomadus's body. "Where?" he asked quickly, "Where can I find another like me?"

Isa smiled. "You are unique, as are all of my Father's children, but if you need comfort, recall my words from that day on the edge of the *Pontus Euxinus*, at Constanta."

Tomadus searched his memory. That was the day the First Consul had first seen Isa speak. "Are you referring to your commandment to feed the hungry and visit the prisoners?"

"Do as my Father asks and you will have your solace."

Tomadus stared at Isa a long time, saying nothing. He would get no more on this subject from Isa today. Finally, he said, "I have news about Yohanan."

"How so?"

"He was imprisoned by the Juteslams for staging a peaceful protest in your name with some of his followers. I convinced King Skjöldr that it was wiser to release him and his followers as long as they left New Jutland."

"Yohanan has come a long way spiritually."

"He is on a mission of peace. He said to tell you that he follows the rising of the sun to Jerusalem."

Isa nodded gently. "Now there is a soul that has been touched. You could learn much from him."

"I let him know by podgram that we are here, in Corinth. He wonders if we could help him in Jerusalem. Shall we travel to Jerusalem and help prevent this terrible act? Surely you can do something. If you have a miracle left in you, it would truly be worthwhile there."

Isa shook his head slowly. "Their hearts are set, Tomadus. I am sorry, but I do not believe they can be turned through persuasion alone. Do not ask me to interfere with their free will to save your peace movement, which must stand or fall of its own accord. You still seek answers among the powers of the Earth. I seek only to save men's souls. Yohanan has understood this and now seeks the same. He must walk this path alone."

Tomadus grew hot, his face reddening. He gritted his teeth, closed his eyes for a moment and took a deep breath. "How," he began, "how can you turn away from our efforts against such injustice? You preach peace, and that is what we seek. It shall all blow away in an instant. How can you say you care about this world and then just ignore an evil you know you can prevent?"

Isa touched his shoulders. "Tomadus, you concern yourself with the problems of the day that lie at your feet, yet you cannot see through the mist of the coming storm. My Father in Heaven has a plan, and I must follow it. I am sorry, but sometimes the purposes of events are not readily perceptible to the human mind. You must trust that our Father loves us all as his children and desires only what is best for us."

Tomadus shrugged off Isa's hand. With his mouth open, he stared back at Isa, and then bit his lip. *I have misjudged him. He's all talk and no action.* His nostrils flared and his lips trembled, barely holding back the single word that kept trying to escape: HYPOCRITE. He noticed he was clenching and unclenching his hands and shaking his head. He could say nothing, so he turned on his heel and left the room.

Tomadus walked quickly through the living area into the corner bedroom and froze as he saw Adin kneeling by the bed with his back to him.

Adin was speaking aloud in his deep, yet almost childish voice, "Please don't let them fight, dear Lord. They need each other." Adin lowered his head into his hands and began to cry.

Tomadus stood silently at the entry. The simple truths this simple man could see when others might think his mind only weak. What would it be like to have such a simple and clear faith?

Adin looked up again toward the ceiling and continued, "I love them both, dear Lord. I know you do too. Please help Tomadus, dear God. He loves you even if he don't know it. Don't let him go away mad. Please, dear God, in Isa's name, I beg you. Amen."

Tomadus backed out of the room quietly and began walking back in. "Oh, there you are, Adin."

Adin flashed a big smile. "Hi, Tomadus! Are you OK?"

"I'm fine. Come, let us sit down and talk." The two took seats at the large oak desk near the window. "You have great faith in God, don't you Adin?"

"Faith?"

"Yes, you believe in God and love Him," Tomadus said.

"Of course. I love God with all of my heart. I love Isa with all my heart. So do you."

"How do you know that?"

"I can see it on your face. You love him and you believe in him. So I guess you have faith in him."

"I guess you are right, to a degree," Tomadus said. "I believe he loves those who need his love the most.

"Yes, that is why God helps those who can't help themselves."

"You mean the sick and crippled that Isa heals?"

"Tomadus, Isa doesn't do that."

"No?" Tomadus asked, eyebrows raised. *A revelation?*

"No. The Father heals them for him because he loves Isa and Isa asks him nicely for his help."

Tomadus's head went back and then nodded. "I wish I could believe that, but I cannot."

"Last week, Simeon and Anders were making fun of you because you don't believe in God. I told them to shut up. I said 'Look at how he believes in Isa. It is easy for you two to believe, because you have always believed in God, but Tomadus believes in Isa even though he cannot seem to find God.'"

The two men were startled by a male voice at the door. "The kingdom of God belongs to such as this. Tomadus, you should take notes and learn from this spiritual man, for whoever does not accept the kingdom of God like a child will not enter it."

Tomadus looked up and saw Isa standing by Maryam in the doorway, each smiling broadly.

"Adin," Isa went on, "I have a task for you. Can you come with me?" Adin nodded, and the two men walked out.

Maryam stayed and closed the door behind her. "I understand you have had a little spat with Isa, Tomadus."

"I don't know about that. I'd say I was disappointed he refused to help Yohanan in his quest for peace."

"You are a good friend to Yohanan, but you must remember that Yohanan is but one of the Father's instruments of peace and justice in this world. Yohanan does not always know the right way, as you have experienced. You seem to want to follow him, but your destiny lies with Isa, for he is the Light of the World."

"I'm sorry, but you sound like a very confident mother," said Tomadus, "or perhaps a very effective propagandist. The Light of the World?"

"Yes, an angel of the Lord told me this before he was born." She smiled gently. "Some of the Ten know of this. However, at Isa's request, we do not discuss it publicly. Isa wants the focus of his work to be on his words and actions today, not on the miracle of his birth, which he knows the skeptics would endlessly try to contest."

Tomadus leaned forward, his hands clasped. "Can you tell me about it?"

"Yes, I must." Maryam took the seat previously occupied by Adin and looked down at her hands, apparently gathering herself. After a few seconds, she looked back up at Tomadus. "I came from a very poor family and left to become a servant in the house of Yusef in Nazareth when I turned 14. Yusef was a very nice Muslim man with two Muslim wives. I worked hard for a couple of years to keep him and his wives and their sons and daughters happy. As a Jew, while in their household I had to be careful to ensure I did not violate any Muslim traditions or beliefs."

"Was that difficult?" Tomadus asked.

"Not really, but you might have thought so. While Yusef was always kind to me, his wives shared neither his views nor his manner. I have never known why, though I have a few guesses. I was told I was quite pretty then, so they may have worried about his intentions toward me. But he never once approached me with any improper words or actions. In a strange way, I think Yusef might have had a soft spot for me just because I was a Jew. His family had converted to Islam several generations before he had been born, and I think he still respected that ancient ancestry."

"Yusef's family was originally Jewish?"

Maryam nodded. "Now, despite some difficulties with his wives, I found I was generally well respected in the household, and I enjoyed my work there. I was able to send a few talents to my parents on occasion, and I was usually happy. Then a very surprising thing happened. I was asleep in my quarters and was awakened by the sounds of the gentle twinkling of tiny bells throughout my room. The room contained no such bells. The scent of subtle incense touched my nostrils. I had no burner in my room. Then an angel suddenly appeared out of nowhere."

Tomadus raised his eyebrows. "An angel?"

"Yes, an angel," she said. "He was there, yet not there. Do you know what I mean? I could have put my hand straight through his body, yet I could see him plainly, and he glowed with an aura I cannot describe. As I cowered beneath my sheets, he cried 'Do not be afraid, Maryam, for you have found favor with God,' so I came out of my cover and sat up on my bed. He said, 'Behold, you will conceive in your womb and bear a son, and you shall name him Isa. He is the Light of the World and will shine above forever.' Now, of course, I was astonished and I said, 'But how can this be, since I have had no relations with any man.' The angel said in reply, 'The Holy Spirit will come upon you, and the power of the Most High will overshadow you.'"

Tomadus shook his head. The story from the other world had become familiar to him. He knew Isa had found a way to copy Jesus for a very good purpose, but now Maryam was also in on it? It was too much.

Leaning her chin on her hands, Maryam sighed. "I thought I would be disgraced among my family and my household for carrying a child when I had not yet wed. Two days later, Yusef came to me and asked me if I was with child. I sheepishly told him the story I told you, worrying that I would be dismissed from his house at once. Instead, he broke down crying and told me that he too had been visited by an Angel of the Lord just the night before. The Angel had told him that he was a charitable man and must now show his duty to Allah by supporting this child of his servant, Maryam, who no man had touched. The Angel had told him that this child would be a great savior of the Jewish and Muslim people. Yusef then asked me to marry him and become his third wife to legitimize the child in the eyes of the people."

"Wait, Isa is not a Jew, but a Muslim?"

"In Judaism, a child is Jewish if the mother is Jewish. In Islam the reverse is true. So it depends on whom you ask. But does it matter? Yusef was a wonderful husband and father. He permitted me to teach Isa our Tanakh and Jewish traditions. Of course, he also taught him the Great Book and traditions of the Muslims. You once asked Isa whether he was a Jew or a Muslim and he did not answer your question directly."

"He rarely answers my questions directly," Tomadus chided.

"Well, in this case he would not answer your question because, in a sense, he is both and neither."

Tomadus squinted his eyes and scratched his beard. "So he was born in Nazareth?"

"No, in Bethlehem, but that is another whole story."

Tomadus smirked. *Of course it is.* It was incredible how much of the tale they had copied from the other world. *They must know of it.* Or was something else going on here. *What if they didn't know? What if this world was just a variation on the other world?* He looked up shaking his head at Maryam. When she squinted her eyes at him, he realized his body language and stopped. "Of course," he said, "because that is the city of David's birth."

Maryam smiled as she tilted her head. "I see you understand the significance. Now Isa grew to become a young and pious man, as Yusef and I knew he would. If it had not been for Yusef's other wives, life in those years would have been magnificent. But the two wives always resented me and never could quite treat me as an equal and certainly never treated Isa as an equal to their own sons. It did not matter to me because Yusef protected us from their intolerance and refused to allow them to use the sharp tongues they wished to lash at us. But then Yusef died suddenly at the age of 55. His eldest son, Jamal, from his first wife, inherited most of his estate. Dominated by a mother who hated us, Jamal ignored his duties under the Great Book and forced us to leave the property. We instantly became penniless and homeless.

"We returned to my birthplace in the Jewish sector of Nazareth, and Isa began to work at the carpentry trade to help us make ends meet. He began to attend synagogue and the people there were often amazed at his insights. But he also grew friendly with several local Muslims as well, and often discussed their beliefs with them, though he was shunned by some of the local imams. Then one day he was on the road to Capernaum to deliver some cabinets to a customer and saw a Muslim man lying naked and beaten on the side of the road. He, uh…,well, you have heard him tell the parable of the Jewish man who was robbed and beaten and left on the side of the road, have you not?"

"I think so," Tomadus replied.

"After several prominent Jews, including a rabbi, ignored the poor Jew, a Muslim came by and cared for him, taking him to a hospital and paying his bills. It was one of the stories Isa told about loving your neighbors and changing your perceptions so that 'neighbors' could include people more commonly treated as 'others.'

Tomadus nodded.

"Well," Maryam said, "he was like the Muslim man in the story, only in reverse, for he had previously been viewed by the Muslims as a Jew. The Muslim man who had been left on the side of the road never forgot Isa's act of kindness and mercy—nor did the man's family and friends. When Isa began his mission, this group soon began to follow him."

The door knocked and Maryam raised her voice, "Yes, come in please."

The host's servant came in with a piece of paper, and said, "I am very sorry to disturb you, but we have just received this podgram for Tomadus. It is from Jerusalem."

Tomadus thanked her and tore open the message. He stood and said quickly, "I must leave at once. Yohanan has asked me to collect his sister and bring her to Jerusalem as soon as possible. He does not explain why, but I fear the worst."

CHAPTER 62

YOHANAN SMILED BETWEEN the iron bars. "Thank you two for coming. Tomadus, you are not family. Why did they allow you in here?"

"I brought him with me as my public escort," Jochi said. "They did not turn him away."

Yohanan gripped the bars between them tightly. "Well, thank you, but please do not worry for me. I have accepted my fate."

"But, Yohanan, we can fight this," responded Tomadus. "You were trying to stop the assassination attempt. They must see that!"

"My friend, I am dead already. I was dead as soon as I set foot in Jerusalem."

"What do you mean? I'll hire the best *attornatus*. Isa will help us. And I can call the First Consul. You are in the right. You will be exonerated."

"There are no *attornati* in Sharia law, and the judge will not care about what Isa or the First Consul think. Besides, I am guilty."

"Stop saying that. You were trying to prevent the assassination."

"No, I am guilty. I killed Decima. I turned her into a killing machine, and then I let her go seek her vengeance. And by yelling to her, I alerted the guards at the very moment they were most trigger-happy. I should have found another way. I killed her just like I killed her father before her. I am responsible for the deaths of so many throughout my life that I can't even count them anymore. Don't you see, Tomadus, I deserve to be executed."

"Don't be stupid," said Tomadus. "You were in a war in Tetepe. You killed because you knew no other way to help your people survive."

Yohanan shook his head. "Is that what you told me that day in Tetepe when you wanted me to find another way? I think not, my friend."

"But you have found another way. Let's get you out of here now so you can continue that fight for peace. We need you, Yohanan, to help set Tetepe free."

Jochi had been staring at Yohanan and crying, obviously searching for something to say. She said softly, "Please do not give up. Fight this. Your friends need you. For God's sake, I need you."

Yohanan looked through the bars at Jochi for a long time with a sad look of deep sympathy on his face. He grabbed her hands in his and stroked her fingers slowly with his thumbs. "I am sorry, but I know it is my time. You'll be fine. Promise me that you will follow Isa and spread his message to Tetepe and the world. That is how you can best remember me."

Unable to speak, she nodded slowly, her eyes nearly shut, unable to hold back the tears.

Tomadus watched Jochi with a mixture of awe, sadness and déjà vu. The tears in her eyes darkly mirrored the cover of *Tempus*, but she was just a little girl then. There was something else in her manner, something deep in his corrupted memory. He strained for it, but it was still a tendril away. It languished beyond his grasp. He looked at Yohanan. "Do not abandon hope. I'll get you out of here. You're innocent. If anything, you are a hero."

"It does not matter," replied Yohanan.

"Why?"

"Because even if I am released, they will just find another time and place to put me to death. This is Hugleikr's doing. His men knew I was coming, and he outsmarted us once again."

"That's crazy."

Yohanan shook his head slowly. "Is it? Raanan and the others were in a cell next to me. Last night, I saw Raanan visited by a man I recognized as Hugleikr's security chief. Not an hour later, Raanan and the other Demoseps were released, smiling from ear to ear. I am now the only official scapegoat of this tragedy. Well, along with Decima, who was already sacrificed by that traitor."

"Raanan? A traitor?"

"Sure. Just before she died, Decima said, 'You were right. Traitor!' She looked into my eyes not with anger but with regret. When I saw Raanan released, it made me think again about what happened. I saw the look of shock and wonder on her face when the bomb on her belly failed to explode in Hugleikr's face. She had been so willing to sacrifice herself for the cause but suddenly realized Raanan had betrayed her. So she died knowing she had become Raanan's personal sacrifice to Hugleikr. Who knows what the Snake will get in return? No doubt Raanan had blamed poor Eliezer for his own treachery in the Konverteraften Massacre. She must have realized that the instant before she died. Hugleikr has won."

▽   ▽   ▽

Since there was no communication pod in the home of Isa's Corinthian benefactor, it had taken Tomadus nearly a day to contact Isa. After a few messages, they finally arranged for a call at a public pod in Corinth. Though he feared the authorities would be listening in, Tomadus saw no alternative to taking the call in his hotel room. And now he sounded anxious while Isa sounded far too distant.

"Isa, you must come. You know Yohanan—he is innocent—but he will be killed if we do not stop this charade. You have influence among some of the Muslims here. Please, I seek only justice and mercy for him."

"Tomadus, why do you seek for Yohanan on Earth that which my Father has already granted him in Heaven?"

Tomadus closed his eyes and breathed deeply. "He needs your help on Earth. I need your help. Please."

Isa spoke softly, his voice tighter than usual. "You know not what you ask. If you did, it would terrify you. It is not yet my time to travel the path Yohanan must now walk in Jerusalem. He must finish his part, for in his life and in his death, he is the voice in the wilderness."

Tomadus's muscles tensed and his cheeks flushed. *Again a man of words, not action, yet I keep following this hypocrite.* He took a deep breath and closed his eyes as they replayed the memory of Adin kneeling at his bed, praying for Isa and him. *Peace.* He said evenly, "Isa, I am very disappointed you feel this way. I am afraid I will have to resort to others for help."

"Do what you must, Tomadus, but be careful, for when you seek the aid of the wolf, you risk becoming his next meal."

Tomadus shook his head and hung up. *Wolf? The First Consul has done nothing but help me. I can only hope…* He placed a call to the First Consul, but was denied any access by his assistant.

After three more calls over the next several days, the First Consul finally answered. "Tomadus," he said, "you must have some big *coleonum* if you are calling me now. You promised Yohanan was on a mission of peace. They have demanded information on the Letter of Transit I issued. I have had to battle with the Governor there just to stop you from being arrested along with Yohanan."

"First Consul, thank you for keeping me out of this. For that I am grateful. I am very sorry for what has happened, but you must know that Yohanan is innocent!"

"I know nothing of the sort. The Jerusalem authorities have told me that he leapt the barrier at the critical moment. They know he was a Demosep. They think this whole peace thing was just a new cover for him."

"But he is an agent of peace. He was trying to stop the bomb, not set it off," Tomadus yelled.

The First Consul sighed. "Then why would he have met secretly with the shaitaanist in a café the day before the attempt? Yes, I told you both that I would have him followed. They heard the two talking for some time there—plotting, they say."

Tomadus shook his head. "He was trying to persuade her to drop the plan. It was only when he failed to convince her that he went to the site and tried to foil the attempt itself. Why else would he yell, 'Stop,' just before she rushed Hugleikr?"

"I have not heard anything about him yelling anything but encouragement. It sounded to me like he just attacked a couple security men. And when she died, he embraced her. How do you think that looks, Tomadus? He could have alerted the authorities."

Tomadus felt his muscles tighten as the blood rushed into them. "And be called a traitor by his own people and lose any chance of leading them back to peace? I vouched for the importance of his mission because he was the only one who could stop it and keep any chance for real peace in Tetepe. I tell you, on my honor, First Consul, I was aware of his plan to thwart the assassination attempt. He was no part of it! He and I had guessed they would make an attempt, but we had no proof. He thought he could stop it, but he was framed by the real culprits here—Hugleikr and Raanan."

The First Consul paused for a few seconds. "Raanan? The Demosep leader?"

"Yes," Tomadus said. He tried to catch his breath, slow his heartbeat. He leveled his voice, "Raanan was released after a visit from Hugleikr's chief of security. Raanan has been a traitor to the Demoseps all along and seems to be in league with Hugleikr."

The First Consul said nothing for quite awhile. "Those are strong accusations, Tomadus. You must be careful what you say. Let me consider your views further and see what I can do."

"That is all I can ask, First Consul. *Gratias*." When the pod disconnected, Tomadus thought long about his friendship with the First Consul. The man wielded so much power, yet he had tried to help Tomadus whenever he could. The First Consul had rarely promised much, but he had often delivered. *A true friend.* Perhaps that was also where his true faith should lie.

CHAPTER 63

TOMADUS FELT THE Jerusalem sun blasting down upon Muhammad Square. Sweat rolled down his brow as he closed his eyes and bit his upper lip. The top of the hour had passed without activity, but maybe this sentencing hearing was delayed for good reason. Perhaps the First Consul was still working his diplomatic magic. Although the Palestinian Provincial Governor's Minister of Justice had already declared Yohanan guilty in a closed-door "trial," there was always hope in the Sunni justice system right up until the very moment of sentencing by the Governor. Might the First Consul or one of his contacts in this empire be trying to convince the Governor to grant Yohanan leniency—or better yet, a pardon? At times like this, it helped to have friends in high places.

Tomadus opened his eyes and smiled at Jochi, hoping to exude the optimism that might help her cope with this proceeding. She looked up at him sadly, gazing gently into his eyes. But her eyes grew big and then she gasped at the dreadful clatter of the traditional procession entering the square on the right. Three ancient wagons rolled in on wooden wheels, each pulled by four magnificent draft horses. The first two wagons looked like ornate personal carriages that belonged to the royalty of a few centuries past. The last wagon appeared plain and stark, adorned above its platform only by rusted steel bars. Inside the mobile prison cell sat four men, each naked but for a single strip of clothing around their privates, metallic bracelets locked around their wrists and ankles, and metal collars locked around their necks. The prisoners seemed drugged or near exhaustion.

The first carriage arrived at the makeshift stage near the east end of the square. The door opened and a guard approached the door with an umbrella as a man dressed in a red robe with purple fringes emerged from the carriage. The Governor. Just as he reached the stage and came under the temporary canopy, the next carriage arrived and the same procedure was repeated, but this time with three guards and three dignitaries. The first dignitary wore a white robe and cap, his graying hair and beard trimmed neatly. The second dignitary wore a yarmulke above long, curly black hair that seemed to continue around to the hair hanging two feet below his chin. The last of the dignitaries was dressed in Romanus governmental robes. When the man glanced quickly back to the crowd, Tomadus swallowed hard. It was the First Consul.

Now several guards approached the third wagon, carrying spears instead of rap rifles. They unlocked the door and forced the prisoners to the front of the stage. The prisoners followed orders to turn and kneel facing the stage, away from the audience, their backs revealing blood oozing out of fresh whip marks, slowly staining the tops of their little white strips of loincloth.

The dignitaries displayed solemn expressions as they stood on a temporary stage, with the Dome of the Rock looming above and behind them. Tomadus now recognized the other two dignitaries as the Grand Imam and Abh Beyth Diyn of Jerusalem. The First Consul stood between them in a line just to the left and behind the Governor.

The Governor stepped to the microphone and spoke, "You four men have been convicted of capital crimes against Allah within the Sunni Muslim Empire and await sentencing. In the tradition of our glorious empire, I have the power to condemn you to death, commute your sentence, or grant you a pardon. However, execution awaits each of you unless the interests of justice and mercy demand otherwise. I shall hear each of your pleas, one at a time. Stand and approach the microphone when I state your name. Do you understand?"

The four men nodded their heads. The Governor announced the first name, "Rigoso of Andalus, you have been convicted of sodomy. What say you?" The prisoner on the far left stood up and approached the micro-phone, crying. "Please," he begged, "I have reformed. I will never commit this awful abomination again. I have a wife and two children who need me. If not for me, then please take pity on them and save me."

The Governor responded quickly, "Rigoso of Andalus, this is not your first conviction. We have granted you leniency in the past. I take pity on your wife and children. They have been shamed by your unnatural lust, and so you must die." When the prisoner fell to his knees and continued begging the Governor to change his mind, several guards came over and dragged him back to the holding area.

This process was followed for two additional prisoners, but with mixed results. The second prisoner was recalcitrant and argumentative, and the Governor immediately condemned him to death. The third prisoner admitted his guilt for stealing a loaf of bread from the Imperial market and begged forgiveness from Allah. He said that it was his first conviction, and he had stolen the bread only to feed his little brother, who was dying from malnutrition in the slums of Jerusalem. The Governor hesitated and asked, "Are you not a Jew? Then why do you beg for forgiveness from Allah?" The man told him he had converted to Islam and now saw the error of his former ways. The Governor seemed satisfied by this and commuted his sentence to five years hard labor and one severed hand at its expiration.

"Yohanan of Tetepe," said the Governor, "you have been convicted of attempted murder, mayhem and rebellion in connection with the thwarted assassination of our good friend, Vice Regent Hugleikr. What say you?"

As a bank of dark clouds covered the sun, Yohanan approached the microphone and looked up at the governor and then the other three men on the stage. His head remained turned toward the First Consul for a few seconds. Then he looked directly at the Governor. "Governor, I thank you for the opportunity to state my case before you and these people of Jerusalem. Others have begged for your forgiveness today, but I shall not do so, for I have done nothing in this empire that requires your forgiveness. I will ask for forgiveness, nonetheless, but not from you."

After a murmur rose from the crowd reacting to the prisoner's apparent insolence, the Governor raised his hand, and silence ensued. He seemed about ready to say something, but the First Consul stepped forward and whispered in his ear before returning to the other dignitaries. The Governor nodded. "Continue."

Yohanan looked at the crowd. "Many of you may recognize me from a famous photograph in *Tempus*, a photo taken moments after my innocent parents were splintered and burned and mutilated when one of the Juteslam shells ordered by Vice Regent Hugleikr struck their tiny home in Tetepe. My sister, Jochi, appeared in that photo too, crying helplessly at the sight of her parents' horrible death. She is here today as well, this time crying for fear of her brother's execution."

Tomadus looked down at Jochi and saw her shaking uncontrollably as the tears streamed down her face. She gasped for breath. He held her tighter to his chest under his arm.

Yohanan stared at the Governor. "That photo proved to be both a boon and a curse. For years it gave me instant credibility with the people of Tetepe. And no doubt I have survived the wrath of King Skjöldr and his Vice Regent for many a day simply because they thought it too imprudent to make a martyr of the 'Face of Tetepe.'

"But it also became a curse when I allowed it to define me. In truth, I became more than the Face of Tetepe. I became the face of anger and hatred against all Juteslams. Worse yet, in a misguided attempt to honor and avenge my parents' deaths, I chose to turn my life toward hatred and killing. Though some have called what I did shaitaanism, many Tetepians have called it heroic, and a few have even called it righteous. But I stand here today and call it by its proper name: murder. For just as surely as Hugleikr murdered my parents over ten years ago, I have murdered countless Juteslams since."

A collective gasp whooshed from the crowd. A few in the crowd yelled, "Murderer!" and "Execute him!"

His eyes steely, Yohanan looked at the crowd and back to the platform. "I am guilty of no murders or attempts or any other crimes within these borders. No, despite these ridiculous charges, which you, Governor, know to be untrue, I tell you now, as I go to my death, I did not try to assist in the assassination attempt on Hugleikr. No, Governor, I tried to prevent it. But that is of little import anymore. For I stand before my maker today and lay myself bare."

Yohanan looked up to the sky, arms outstretched to the heavens. Lightning smacked a thunderclap across the sky and into the square, where it reverberated a few seconds. A steady rain began falling, causing a few in the crowd to seek shelter among the awnings of nearby buildings. The prepared few pulled out umbrellas, and some of their friends sought refuge with them. Tomadus pulled up the hood of his robe and tried to shelter Jochi from the rain with his outer cloak. She curled her head under his arm and made no attempt to flee. No storm could move either of them away from this spot—not now.

After a few seconds, Yohanan bowed his head. "I would not be standing here if I had not met a most extraordinary man, Isa of Palestine. He saved me from myself. He helped me to see that my hatred led only to my self-destruction. He made me understand the beauty of love, peace, and forgiveness. I tell you, he is the one who was promised to us, the one who was promised to us all."

At this statement, the Jewish and Muslim religious leaders leaned in toward the First Consul and whispered something. The First Consul nodded, but remained quiet.

Yohanan continued, "Decima, whom you have already killed, would have said to me, 'See, you followed this man Isa foolishly, and it has killed us both.' But she would never have been further from the truth. For I know if I follow the rising of the sun, I will surely sail east and find my way to God.

"So I fought my rudder and came east to Palestine to prevent Decima from killing Hugleikr. You must admit, in that I succeeded, for is the beast not still alive? But I also succeeded in helping you kill the woman I loved. Although she carried great goodness in her heart, she could not overcome the darkness that had enveloped her soul when she saw her father murdered by Hugleikr before thousands in Great Jutland Square. I shall soon join her in a common grave on this Earth as our due punishment for our many offenses against God and man. I know Hugleikr will never suffer the same fate for even one of his many murders of my fellow Tetepians. I know when the powerful kill while praising justice, we men too often call their acts something else, something noble. It is a shame we often cannot see the truth of their barbarity through the bloody walls of our hatred. But it does not matter, for God will be the final judge, and though I die today, I go with faith that Hugleikr will truly die before me."

"Liar," someone yelled from the crowd and others repeated it. Then a few started chanting, "Execute him, execute him," but the Governor raised his hands above his head and the crowd went silent.

Yohanan said, "Despite this, I forgive him. I do. I forgive the Vice Regent of New Jutland. Not just him but his king as well and the troubled souls that follow them. I forgive them for their many despicable acts against me and my people. I forgive them all for their violent domination of the Tetepian people these last fifty years. And I forgive all of you here today, and, yes, even you, Governor, for your role in my death."

Tomadus looked down and shook his head. Yohanan was writing his own order of execution.

"I ask you all to repent for your sins, but first forgive others for theirs. The road to repentance travels through your own mercy and forgiveness. I do not seek your forgiveness, and I do not seek your mercy. But I do beg forgiveness from the only one who matters: my Lord and my God."

Yohanan dropped to his knees, his hands raised high together, his head back with eyes gazing to the sky. "In Isa's name, I beg you, dear God, to forgive me my sins as I forgive others their transgressions against me."

A few in the crowd, including Jochi, dropped to their own knees and prayed aloud for Yohanan. Another lightning bolt shuddered the square with the crash of its thunder. Tomadus could not pray; nevertheless, he lowered himself to his knees and held Jochi as she wailed in prayer.

The Governor paused a few moments, gathering his thoughts. The two religious leaders now circled the First Consul, whispering again, this time with their heads bobbing and jerking quickly as their faces reddened. When the entire entourage approached the Governor, he covered the microphone as they spoke. After they parted, Tomadus caught the eye of the First Consul, but he did not flash him the smile of Yohanan's deliverance. How could he after that speech? Instead, the First Consul looked right at Tomadus with a frown and shook his head slowly.

The Governor leaned into the microphone. "Yohanan, we have heard rumors of your eloquence, and now we see they do not exaggerate. But your persuasive power does not undo your crimes against Allah and the

State. You claim you tried to stop the assassination attempt, but you rushed the stage with Decima all the same and yelled, "Decima, don't stop!" just when she appeared to hesitate. And what many here have not heard is that we saw you meet with the assassin to plan the attempt the day before the good Vice Regent's speech. Yes, there are witnesses. And today you have given us clear motives for your crime.

"You slander the Vice Regent's good name and publicly call for his death. You profess a simple man from Galilee as your new prophet to hide your shame. Your words come from Shiataan, Tomadus, not from Allah, not from your God. You confess to the countless deaths of innocents. Therefore, in the name of Allah and the Sunni Muslim Empire, I hereby condemn you to death by *triangulum penetrans*."

Jochi screamed an elongated, "No!" Tomadus grabbed her in both arms and held her tightly.

The guards tied Yohanan and two others by the wrists behind the third wagon. The procession began moving out of Muhammad Square and heading up *Via Mortis*. The path led out of the old section of the city to an open area on a hill, where four giant triangular mechanisms awaited the prisoners. Tomadus and Jochi were able to work their way close to a gate at the edge of the old city. Jochi never stopped crying.

As Yohanan passed, he saw the two of them together and smiled. "Jochi," he said, "remember: follow Isa."

Jochi wailed uncontrollably.

As he was dragged ahead, Yohanan looked behind him. "Tomadus, remember to sail east. Protect him."

Tomadus cocked his head and nodded slowly as Yohanan was dragged away by the wagon heading up the hill.

The muddy road to the hill proved no obstacle to the guards as they led the procession up to the ancient place of execution. When the horses slipped, a guard merely whipped them, forcing them to pull the wagon harder up the hill, all the while yanking the prisoners behind and dragging them whenever they fell in the mud.

At the end of the procession, the three men were cut loose from their ropes and placed on three inverted triangular slabs. This took little time, since the contraptions simply applied electromagnetic force to the metal in the iron shackles around their necks, wrists and ankles. The triangular surfaces were made of the traditional painted wood, a design that might have dated back a millennium. But the updated design also sacrificed a little tradition for convenience: four well-placed magnets held each prisoner firmly in place, with feet at the bottom point of the triangle, hands at the side points of the triangle, and head to the top center. Each triangular slab was filled with hundreds of tiny holes spaced about an *uncia* apart and containing recessed metal cylinders about a quarter *uncia* in diameter. Tomadus had never witnessed execution by *triangulum penetrans,* but he had heard enough about its horrors to know the cylinders would soon fill with instruments of hell.

As the three condemned men hung on the inverted triangles for a few minutes, several impatient foreign observers in the crowd wondered if something had gone wrong. The men were just hanging there without any apparent pain. But then the holes on the triangles appeared to move and began to fill. Standing at a slight angle, Tomadus could see that small metal points were slowly emerging from the metal cylinders. It seemed almost imperceptible at first, except to the prisoners, who all began crying out in pain as thin needles punctured their skin. Blood began to trickle down the triangles from beneath their arms and legs.

This ugliness would have been over quickly if holes and needles had been located behind the prisoners' heads or heart, but that would have been far too merciful. Instead, the needles kept emerging slowly and steadily, progressing farther and farther into the prisoners' other body parts, including a few vital organs. The punctures failed to bring death swiftly. Each prisoner screamed out intermittently as the points breached a new organ. After awhile, the blood flowing down each triangle became intermingled with yellowish-brown fluids draining from various parts of the body.

Occasionally, a prisoner would pass out from the pain and a guard would check his pulse on a monitor connected to his wrist magnet. If the prisoner was not yet dead, a jet of water splashed from above into the prisoner's face, awakening him again to endure more pain.

After nearly thirty minutes of this utter agony, Yohanan opened his eyes, stared at the overcast sky with a look of amazement, and said, "There it is, the rising of the sun! I am your first sacrifice, but not your last, for

I have prepared Your way!" With that, Yohanan passed out again. This time, after the guard checked the monitor, no spray of water flowed into Yohanan's disfigured face. He was dead.

Jochi had buried her face in Tomadus's arms, so she did not see the end. Tomadus looked at her soft hair and back up to the *triangulum* and Yohanan's limp body. For the first time he could remember, Tomadus wept.

THIRD PART: REVELATION

(Tertia Pars: Apocalypsis)

"Thus I have searched among them for someone who would build a wall or stand in the breach before me to keep me from destroying the land; but I found no one."

– Liber Prophetarum—Ez 22:30

"By the fading day, man is in loss, except for those who believe, do good deeds, urge one another to the truth, and urge one another to steadfastness."

– Liber Prophetarum—M 103

"See that no one deceives you."

– Liber Vitae—At 24:4

"Isa replied, 'You know not what you ask. Can you drink the cup that I drink?'"

– Liber Vitae—An 10:38

CHAPTER 64

TOMADUS WAS BACK at his office in Roma but found it difficult to focus. It had been nearly a month since Yohanan's execution. He should have emerged from his deep mourning by now, but the heavy chains of lethargy kept dragging him down. Worse yet, the creature had returned in force, each day stomping around his gut like a tiger in a cage, restless and unsatisfied. But Stephanus's sheer exuberance had managed to pull Tomadus out of the haze as he updated him on the company's recent fortunes.

"Sir, you cannot believe the international reaction!" Stephanus said. "We have received orders from around the globe, even in the East Asian Empire. Our dealers in the Aztec Empire have been leading the way there and in their own empire. If only we could keep up with demand—we'll need to double or triple our manufacturing footprint and bring in more technologists as soon as we can hire them."

"Do we need more capital to fund that growth?" Tomadus asked.

"I think we'll be able to swing it with the profits being generated from the growth of our existing products. If not, we can always license others to manufacture."

"No, keep it in house—we'll be better off in the long run."

"You are probably right. I think we will all grow wealthy before long."

Tomadus snorted. "The eye of a needle."

"Whose eye?" Stephanus asked.

"Nothing. Just something he said to me."

"Who?"

Tomadus just shook his head. Three melodic notes rang through the conference room, and a gentle male voice said, "Sir, I am sorry about the interruption, but First Consul Khansensius would like to speak with you. Shall I put him through?"

"Of course," answered Tomadus into the device. "We'll continue the report later, Stephanus." Stephanus nodded and left the room.

"First Consul, so good to hear from you. To what do I owe this honor?"

"Greetings, Tomadus. Are you well?"

"I am improving. *Gratias*."

"Good. Good," said the First Consul. "Life must move on. We cannot always control events, Tomadus. The dead are already buried. Do not bury yourself in the past with them. There is so much to do."

"I suppose you're right."

"Now, you may remember that some time ago I promised you a medal for your great generosity in helping Roma and the Three Empires with your invention."

"I seem to recall I was not given much choice in that decision."

"Like it or not, you are a technologist hero, Tomadus. We would like to recognize you for your accomplishments. You will receive the Amicus Imperatorum Medal at a dinner to be held at the Pantheon next week. I am calling to ask you to attend."

Tomadus pulled in his bottom lip and sat back. Too much, too quickly. He had never really sought wealth and fame for their own sake, but now that they were on his doorstep, what would he do with them? The creature had clawed away at his gut and he knew the only answer that would quiet the thing, but he had refused him. Maybe it was time to listen again. Accepting the award might make him a hypocrite, but it could prove helpful in such a mission. And the First Consul had proven repeatedly that he was his friend.

"Tomadus, are you there? Can I count on you?" the First Consul asked.

"Of course, Your Excellency," replied Tomadus.

"Wonderful. Now, there is one other thing I wish to discuss with you."

Tomadus cocked his head. "Yes?"

"As you know, we have been closely following the activities of your friend Isa. We have great interest in him, particularly after Yohanan's speech."

"Are you now opposed to Isa?" Tomadus asked.

"No, no, of course not. That is the way of the Imperium. Tell me, are you aware of his current mission in Tetepe?"

Tomadus sighed. "I know he has been travelling there, but little more. I have been somewhat…preoccupied by my business of late, so I have not really kept up with his efforts."

"I see."

"Is there a concern?" Tomadus asked.

"Perhaps. Though his intentions may be good, there are a few who worry about the consequences of his movement in Tetepe and beyond."

"Consequences?"

"Yes," the First Consul said. "As you know, Tetepe presents a very delicate situation, not only to the region but also to Roma and the Three Empires. There is fear that Isa may tip this balance in a way that we cannot…control. The consequences could prove disastrous to Isa and his movement and to Tetepe in general."

"Isa is a man of peace. He has no political ambitions."

"Of course, but Isa has developed a large following among the non-Juteslam Tetepians. It seems most of Yohanan's former followers have joined his movement. Even a few of the Demosep leadership have lost their loyalty to Raanan and have instead found faith in Isa. And in the last week, a group of liberal Juteslams have invited him to speak in Great Jutland Square."

"A legitimate inroad to peace there?"

"If it were so simple. Remember that Skjöldr and Hugleikr still run New Jutland. They see his movement as a threat to their power and influence there and will use force, if necessary, to bring him down."

"Then we should intervene to protect him. I still think Isa is the best chance we have to bring peace to the region."

"Perhaps, but it is impossible in the current environment."

"Has New Jutland become too powerful?"

"Too powerful? No, but there are other considerations. Interventions have had a way of ending in major conflicts over the past half millennium.

Thank goodness Roma has calmed the discontent caused by constant meddling among the Three Empires. Nevertheless, we cannot always prevent interventions by the empires outside of our union—just as the last Great World War demonstrated. One small slip and the world could turn its restlessness again to war. We must be careful."

"That was so long ago," Tomadus said. "The world has been at peace for over fifty years now."

"You think so simply, like those at the end of the cold war."

"The what?" Tomadus blanched. Cold war? That term only had meaning in the other world. *Is it possible?* "I'm sorry, did you say 'cold war?'"

"Did I?" The First Consul cleared his throat. "Yes, well, I was simply referring to the ten years after the last Great World War when we came close to beginning another conflagration.

"I had never heard it called that."

"Well, perhaps I have coined a new phrase, then. Anyway, there are other, more specific concerns."

"Specific? You mean Isa?"

"Yes, I refer to Isa. You and I see him as a man of peace, of course. But this view is not shared by all within the Three Empires."

"The religious leaders?" Tomadus asked.

"They are skeptical of his purposes. One of them told me they do not even think he believes in God. They think he preaches merely to agitate the masses for some personal gain. The Grand Imams also have influence on the emperors. Until we can convince them of Isa's sincerity, I could never garner support for his movement in Tetepe—or anywhere else."

"He believes he performs God's will."

"You need not convince me, but we need a strategy to change the minds of the Grand Imams and even the Abh Beyth Diyn, who has significant influence in the Palestinian Province."

"I see. That reminds me, during the Governor's examination of Yohanan, I saw you whispering with the Grand Imam of Palestine and the Abh Beyth Diyn. What were they saying?"

The First Consul bristled. "That was a private conversation, Tomadus, so I am not at liberty to say. I will tell you this, though: Yohanan's speech was like a clarion call to these men. They had not quite appreciated Isa's significance before then."

"I was afraid of that."

"Yes, that troubles me as well. Tomadus, you have a personal bond with Isa. I thought you might help him understand the need to get these men on his side."

"I have not spoken with him for nearly a month. We are not as… close…as we once were."

"Perhaps it is time you rekindle your bonds. No offense, but Stephanus has proven quite adept at running your business in your absence. You could do more good with Isa."

"*Gratias*, First Consul. I will consider it."

"That is all I ask. I will see you at the ceremony. *Vale*, Tomadus."

The walls quickly closed in on Tomadus. He closed his eyes and still saw the image of Yohanan screaming on the *triangulum penetrans*. Isa might have prevented his death. He could have convinced Yohanan to keep going instead of sacrificing himself with that speech. Then the First Consul would have succeeded, but Isa had turned away. Could Tomadus now overcome his broken heart and listen to the creature?

Jochi had cried for so long under his arm. She had found the strength to pull herself together, yet she had not followed him back to Roma. Honoring her brother's last words, she had joined the Way and traveled with Isa to Tetepe. Isa had used Yohanan's death to spark the movement there. Tomadus had not been able to bring himself to follow, even though he longed to be near her, to be near him.

Tomadus knew he must return to both of them. While Isa could infuriate him, the man still remained the best hope for the world if Tomadus could just keep him from stumbling over the political cliff to his own destruction. Isa's movement remained too weak to fend off the likes of Skjöldr in the King's own domain. Without the help of the Three Empires, Isa would eventually be crushed and forgotten. The First Consul had hinted that help could come, but they had to convince the religious leaders of the depth of Isa's beliefs. Maybe they could address both in the same way. If he could broadcast Isa's words to the world, even the Juteslams would not dare take him into custody. And the religious leaders would see his true convictions. Tomadus felt the creature finally settle down. It could be the answer, and with his new wealth and reputation within Roma and the Empires, Tomadus might be able to engineer it. Now that would truly be glorious.

Or would it? People might think he believed in Isa's God, but that would be impossible. *Deities are for the weak. Faith is for the common man. I am a technologist. I live by logic and reason, by experimentation and data, by method and result. I have learned the laws of physics. The world is not determined by some perfect higher being but by the physical forces and reality of a world shaped by all too imperfect men. Yet what Isa says so often rings true to my ears. What is wrong with me? Have I gone soft? Do I really want to believe in Him? How can I? There is something that old priest said to me.*

Old priest? Damnation! Stop confusing your life with the man in the other world. Why does it invade my every thought? How am I connected with this Huxley? I could swear that I am he and he is I. I do not share his flesh, yet I sense his thoughts. I feel his angst. I know his pain.

Tomadus sensed the feeling washing over him. When the light flashed again and a new vision streamed quickly through his brain…

❄ ❄ ❄

…Huxley tried to sleep on the long jet ride home from Afghanistan, but too many inchoate thoughts kept swirling through his brain. The depth of his pain over the murder of Ahmed Jinnah surprised him. Sure, he had worked with the man for a few months in a few stressful situations in Pakistan, but that was five years ago, and they were never what you could call "close friends." Yet the feeling lingered.

Maybe it was because Jinnah seemed like his Pakistani alter ego: a pretty bright, dedicated guy who just wanted to stop the whole world from going to hell. No, not his alter ego—Jinnah was better than he. Jinnah had heroically overcome his own national patriotism and bias and risked everything: He had cared more about averting a terrorist tragedy than avoiding being forever marked as a traitor of his own country. Had Jinnah understood he was risking his own life and limb as well? *If I were put to the same test, would I choose the same way?*

That uncertainty sprinkled salt on an open wound festering within the strange guilt that kept clawing his troubled gut. Jinnah had died because of Huxley's mistake. Despite Huxley's caution, someone must have followed him to the meeting with Jinnah that night. Yet no matter how many times Huxley ran the scenarios over in his mind, he simply could not imagine doing anything differently. He had chosen neither the location nor the time of the rendezvous. Hell, he had not even contacted Jinnah in the first place. Nevertheless, the strange feeling remained.

Why was he always so damn morose about death? Was it just a selfish reflection of fear for his own inevitable end? No. He had faced death when he was with the CIA on several occasions—all without suffering from this macabre feeling of depression. Still, every death of friends and family had triggered his own despondency going way back to his youth. Geez, it probably went all the way back to the time of his father's "accident." Did he somehow blame himself for that one as well? *Shit, stop psychoanalyzing yourself, Hux.* He grabbed a pillow and put it between his head and the vibrating fuselage.

Sleep refused to come, and his caustic self-examination continued. Now his brain kept rambling through the kind of hypnotic questioning that often troubled him at night; however, it began expanding and terrorizing his conscience all the more.

Why do I care about another's death? Why should anybody? What are we but a blob of flesh, pre-programmed by a complex set of evolved biological codes and capable of converting energy to mass and back again? Why should one blob give a crap about another blob? Hell, why is there any morality at all?

Doesn't natural selection favor those who can pass more of their DNA onto the next generation? Who can do that best but the most powerful—those great men who, through conquest and power, can spread their chromosomes as wide as they wish? Does evolution, then, agree with Nietzsche that life is not a path to self-preservation but a will to power? Look at Genghis Kahn—he probably has more confirmed descendants than any person in history. Yet some powerful men, like Adolph Hitler and Julius Caesar, passed on none of their genetic material. No, evolution favors more than the individual.

DNA passes successfully to multiple generations only if the offspring continue to propagate the codes to future generations. A man could have a thousand grandchildren, but if they all die by killing each other, then the coding ends there. It must help if the offspring are able to work together and encourage the growth of the entire community. That requires some genetic predisposition for getting along with others and suspending the immediate needs of the individual. That in turn requires acceptance of rules of conduct. So when humans evolved to that level, our genetic code found a strategy that allowed it to dramatically accelerate its expansion. But hell, apes and monkeys live together in communities as well. So do many other species. So what separates our morality from theirs? Or are they the same thing?

Our morality. Is there a common morality shared among all humans? Not even close. What makes one set of rules good and another evil? For that matter, what makes one world perspective good and another bad? Do good and evil arise simply from our own subjective, socio-centric perspectives? Or is there something inherently right and wrong? But if evolution is the sole cause of human morality, then how can one society share mores that can be innately right while another society considers those mores innately wrong?

Do we judge these rules by which society is the most objectively successful in growing its population? Isn't that the ultimate arbiter of evolutionary strategies? Or do we judge them by which strategy we subjectively believe leads to the greatest growth for all? It seems stupid. Why is growth the determining factor at all? Earth already bulges at the seams from overpopulation. So have human societies outgrown natural evolutionary forces? But then what determines what is good and what is evil? Is it the nature of society? Is it my current society? And who in that society decides? And who decides if they decide correctly?

Is morality just about our agreement on a set of rules? Have we all entered into a social compact, as Hobbes and Locke would like us to believe? I get that for politics—we give up something (the right to do anything we want with whatever unpredictable consequences may occur) in exchange for the security, safety and relative predictability that comes from others agreeing to do the same so we can form a government.

But what does a social compact mean for individual morality? Why must I keep that social compact? Surely it is not because I must keep promises, for if there is no intrinsic morality, then keeping a promise itself has no intrinsic moral value. Then is it simply that I do not wish to be punished? But what if I know that I can commit murder without getting caught? Surely I understand that this behavior conflicts with the social compact, but so what? An unsolved murder results in no dire consequences to me. And without consequences, I cannot even say that I should refrain from the murder just to prevent others from committing murder. If I sufficiently cover up the crime itself, others wouldn't even know anyone killed the victim, so they have no reason to act differently themselves. And yet, even though all my self-interests seem to be aligned with committing murder in a particular circumstance, I can never imagine partaking in the activity. Why? What keeps me in line? Is it just the social programming I have received from societal propaganda since my birth? Perhaps that is the answer, but somehow it just doesn't feel right. There must be more.

Was the old priest right? Is there a value in believing in a God who prescribes right and wrong, so we don't have to? Why would we listen to Him when we don't have to listen to the very mores we have prescribed for ourselves? Maybe we realize, even subconsciously, that we can never completely hide our actions or even our intimate thoughts from an all-knowing deity. We will never be able to completely avoid punishment when God serves as the policeman, prosecutor and judge. Is this why we invent noble gods, to make us better able to live in societies? Or does this need merely confirm His existence? Is the old priest right regardless: Do we have much to lose by losing faith in God, whether or not He exists?

I once had faith, didn't I? Despite all of the sarcastic expressions of my old man, I still believed. On Sundays, I dutifully followed my saintly mother to Mass and served as an altar server. I never doubted there was a God. I doubted the words of my father quite often, but only my father on Earth. And when he died, my mother and I prayed to God to take my father's soul to Heaven, though I strongly doubted even then that He would seriously consider granting the request. Yet I never doubted then that He had the power to do so if He so chose, did I? Or was I just playing the role my mother had scripted for me as a child? I know I stopped going to church in college, but now it has been so long that I cannot recall whether I just lost interest or I actually made a decision to reject my faith. But I did decide at some point, didn't I? Now, although I desperately wish I could somehow believe in a god, my brain and my heart simply refuse. Why? What else is there to believe in?

How do others resolve their own doubts? Wait, what am I thinking? So many have no doubts. So many seem so absolutely certain that they know there either is or is not a god, and those who know there is a god seem to have no doubt their particular god is the only true one. But how do they come to that conclusion when there is no clear, demonstrable evidence to support their belief? The old priest was right—nobody has ever proven there is or is not a god, and likely nobody ever will. Then how can these people be so damn sure of themselves that they hate others for believing in a god, in another god, or in no god at all? Do they simply ignore reason when they argue so vehemently that they know a truth that is clearly unknowable? Or are they like the character in the Shakespearean play who "doth protest too much?" Yes, they are like the bully who uses his false bravado to conceal his true cowardice. Do they even truly believe what they say? I suppose that may be right for some, yet I have no doubt the old priest truly believed what he said: "It gives me the confidence to know there is a God, a loving God, and in the end He will save us." I saw it in the old man's eyes. He was not professing a mere hope—he knew. How does one attain a faith in the unknowable so strong that it truly becomes knowledge rather than mere desire? How could I ever know? How did he know? How did my mother know?

My mother, the little angel on my shoulder whom I abandoned. She had tortured me with constant recriminations about torturing the very prisoners that Jesus had told us to visit, to comfort. Prisoners? We were told they were only terrorists bent on our destruction. We had every right to use any means to prevent another disaster. But then Najwa's voice had reverberated from that prison cell, "What would your mother say if she knew you tortured me because of my love of God?" Huxley touched the bulging bruise on his own forehead, the mark of his own personal Afghan jailer, who seemed to have every right to use any means to prevent another disaster, or so that man had thought. *What would my mother have said to that if only she could have visited me…*

∇   ∇   ∇

…When the light subsided, Tomadus blinked a few times. By now, he had grown so accustomed to the invasions that he could often function while they flooded his brain. What might seem like a week of experiences might only take him out of this reality for a few seconds. This vision had passed in an instant. Nevertheless, Tomadus still suffered the emptiness, the sadness, the pain he shared with Huxley. He could see the shadows of the steel bars on the prisoner's face as the prisoner demanded Huxley's empathy, and the look of surprise when the demand was met.

Tomadus recalled Isa telling all his disciples to visit and comfort prisoners. It had seemed so strange at the time, but now he understood. Perhaps the message was for him. He had asked Isa if there were others who experienced the light like him, and Isa had responded, "Do as my father asks, and you shall have your solace." Solace…comfort…comfort the prisoners. Was it conceivable that was a hint? He could not possibly visit all of the prisoners in the Three Empires, even those in Roma alone. But was there another way?

Tomadus hit a button on the conference table and said, "Get me Servi Inquisitio." He need not be alone. With his resources, he could hire several dedicated investigators to work through the prisons for him and narrow it down to a few worth a visit. No, not just prisons. Better include the derangement wards.

CHAPTER 65

TOMADUS SIGHED AS he walked down the dank corridors of yet another dismal derangement ward. His investigators had identified ten of the unfortunate ones for his search. He had reviewed their backgrounds and begun his quest with the most promising candidates. That was six prisons and four derangement wards ago. So far he had merely discovered a few desperate souls whose damaged brains so longed for a different world they had convinced themselves that they now lived in them. Perhaps he suffered from the same illness, but at least he could see the difference between the two worlds. And none of the worlds envisioned by these helpless souls approached anything close to his other world. Would he ever find another like him? Had Isa merely confused him? *Am I simply insane?*

The psych-technologist led him to a painted concrete box of a meeting room containing only a small wooden table and two plain wooden chairs. In the corner stood a burly ward guard with an unkempt beard wearing a beige uniform. The psych technologist explained, "We cannot permit you to be alone with him, sir. He could be dangerous."

Tomadus sat at the table. "Has he ever shown any tendency to violence?"

"No, except to himself, but you never know with these cases. Blutus here is ready to provide protection for you if anything happens. I have other matters to attend to. Please excuse me." The technologist left the room. Blutus nodded to him and spat to his side, all the time keeping his well-sculpted arms folded on his enormous chest.

A few minutes later, the inmate Peregrine was brought into the room and took a seat at the table. He was tall and lanky, with a scruffy black beard, curly black hair and wild blue eyes that didn't fit his otherwise Romanus appearance. He smelled like he had not showered for a few months. "And who are you?" he asked.

"Tomadus of Roma. I would like to hear about your visions."

"Why? I'm no lab rat." He spat on the floor. "Leave me alone."

"I would be happy to do so, sir, if you could just enlighten me. If you are whom I seek, I might be able to help you."

"Help me? How?" the inmate said gruffly.

"I might be able to get you released from this place."

"Why would I want to leave such an elegant palace?"

Tomadus's lips curled tightly together. Crap, the guy was just another delusional inmate believing he lived like royalty. "You like it here?"

Peregrine looked up at him and with a big smile tinged with sarcasm. He said in a strange accent, "All things considered, I'd rather be in Philadelphia."

A tingle began in Tomadus's neck and spread down his back and through his legs. "Why would you want to be in the Sardis province of Anatolia?"

"You don't get it, but why would you? Just leave me alone," Peregrine said and then looked down in disgust.

Tomadus looked at Peregrine and felt the tingle continue down his arms. The creature within began pacing. Tomadus closed his eyes. There was some other Philadelphia—in the other world—yes. And that line by Peregrine was from an old movie. An old joke. He leaned forward and said, "You refer to another Philadelphia in another part of another world, don't you?"

Peregrine perked up quickly and nodded slowly as his eyes narrowed suspiciously.

Tomadus pursed his lips. He must give Peregrine hope but hold back the lifesaver until the man demonstrated Tomadus could be a rescue ship and not just another mirage on the horizon. "Tell me, sir, if we assume this

Philadelphia you mention was once in a place known as the United States of America, would you be able to tell me what state it was in?"

Peregrine's jaw fell. He stared at Tomadus a long time and a tear fell down his left cheek. "Pennsylvania. Dear God, how do you know about the United States?"

Now Tomadus fought off a tear. "Because I once knew someone who lived near Washington, D.C."

Peregrine began shaking and crying uncontrollably, his lips quivering. He grabbed Tomadus's wrists in his. The guard began walking toward the table, but Tomadus nodded that everything was fine. Peregrine whispered between sobs across the table, "I had begun to believe them—they said I was crazy—but the two of us could not have shared the same vision. I am sane! I am sane after all!"

The guard took a step forward and spat to his side, wiping his beard with his forearm. "Yes," Tomadus replied, "As sane as I. When did you have your first vision?"

"It was nearly three years ago now. I was an astro-technologist attending a conference in Genua, and I met a preacher in white robes."

"Isa?"

"Yes. How did you know?"

"Did he touch you?" Tomadus asked.

"He came over to me, and when he touched my shoulder, the light exploded in my mind. Ever since, I have been utterly confused and fearing these many visions."

"You and I should fear no longer, my friend. We are not alone. I will get you released to my custody, and we can visit Isa. As I have long suspected, he must be at the center of this. Together, perhaps we shall even discover the truth."

CHAPTER 66

"I seek a better understanding, Imam. I have studied these passages from the Qur'an that call for Qital. I have listened to many, including my mentor, who says they tell us to attack the Americans in any way we can. Yet I struggle to reconcile them with the feelings in my heart." Anwari was sitting in Imam Rahini's sparse quarters near his mosque in Kabul. This imam had argued for peace and tried to calm the incessant calls of a few other imams in remote parts of Afghanistan and Pakistan to attack the Americans everywhere. *I need to hear the other side.*

The imam stared back at him for a few moments and then smiled. "Abdul, you are not alone. These passages confuse so many, but why? If you read all of their words in their proper context, then their intent is clear. Yet those who wish to hate, those who wish to kill, those who wish to destroy, they convert a few of the words into their battle cry. However, do not be misled. These interpretations of our faith are not shared by most Muslims around the world."

Anwari nodded slowly.

Imam Rahini went on. "You must ask yourself, why? Why do they do this? I will tell you what I think. Not for the glory of Allah but their own. They use His words as weapons to move the disenchanted among us to undertake horrible deeds that no just man could ever fathom on his own, let alone consider righteous. You say your mentor has taught you these meanings, and I do not doubt it. But you must ask yourself, what does he truly seek—the will of Allah, or his own power or need for revenge?"

Anwari winced. "I do not know, for I do not truly know him. He says he serves Allah, but I have begun to wonder."

"It is good that you question his motives, for many who have gone before you have not. When you truly understand this mentor's real purposes, then you will know what course to take. You obviously have a goodly conscience, or you would not be asking me these questions, so let your conscience and Allah be your guide."

Anwari bowed slightly to the Imam. "Thank you, but can you tell me where my mentor is wrong? Take the passage from Ayah 2-191: 'Kill them wherever you encounter them, and drive them out from where they drove you out, for persecution is more serious than killing.' Does this not mean we should fight non-Muslims everywhere and kill them when we can?"

"Abdul, who in this passage is 'them?'"

"Some say it is all non-Muslims, but I do not believe it."

The imam nodded slowly. "Precisely. The terrorists love to pull this out and act as if 'them' refers to anyone who is not a Muslim, because they must therefore oppose Islam. But this passage comes immediately after the Qur'an says, 'Fight in Allah's cause against those who fight you...' Abdul, this passage contains nothing more than an appeal to Muslims for their own self-defense! How can you take this then to mean we should bomb innocents? Are those people fighting us?"

"Maybe not directly, but through their government. The American government fights us, and by their own principles, they are a government of their people, so the people are just as responsible."

"Do you really believe the Americans are fighting Muslims? Why would they do this when millions of Muslims live peacefully in the United States? Do you really believe they have a holy war against Muslims here in Afghanistan? You fought beside them, did you not? Were they trying to kill as many Muslims as they could?"

"No, of course not," said Anwari, "though many innocent Muslims have died."

"Yes, many have, for war kills many never intended as its targets. But answer this: how many innocent Muslims have been targeted at the hands of other Muslims, at the hands of the Taliban? Should there be a Jihad against the Taliban? And how about the civil wars that preceded the Taliban rule? Do you forget the horrors of those days as well?"

"No," said Anwari. *But at least my brother and family were still alive then.*

"Moreover, where does the Qur'an say we should target innocents because of their governments? That is quite a leap, don't you think? No, Abdul, this passage merely tells us it is not unholy to defend ourselves. But it is not an exhortation to murder. How can you read the entire Qur'an and believe such evil could be intended? And in the very provision you cite, what does it say so boldly, just to make it perfectly clear that we must always proceed cautiously when it comes to war? You know this. It says that even when we defend ourselves, we must not overstep the limits, because Allah does not love those who overstep the limits."

Anwari spread his hands wide, a look of bewilderment on his face. "But what are the limits?"

"The Qur'an itself says, 'If they cease hostilities, there can be no further hostility, except towards aggressors. A sacred month for a sacred month: violation of sanctity calls for fair retribution. So if anyone commits aggression against you, attack him as he attacked you, but be mindful of Allah, and know that He is with those who are mindful of Him.' Abdul, we must be mindful of Allah, and we attack only as we were attacked. So how can they really say this sanctions terrorism?"

"I see. What of Ayah 9:5, which tells us to kill the idolaters and seize them and wait for them at every lookout post?"

"Ah yes." The imam sat back, smiling. "This is a favorite among the extremists. But again, they take out of context that which is limited to a particular situation. They teach that the "idolaters" are anyone who is not a Muslim, and so it is fine to kill anyone who is not a Muslim. Do you think this could possibly be the intent of Allah? No, my friend, when the passage refers to idolaters, it specifically refers to the critical context that comes before it. We know this is true because it uses the article *ahdiya* in the sentence to refer to what has already been stated. What comes before it? Ayah 9:1 announces that Allah and Muhammad are annulling a specific treaty with the Pagans in Arabia. Ayah 9:2 and 9:3 give the Pagans a period of 4 months to travel to Mecca and repent. Ayah 9:4 further explains that this applies only to those Pagans who broke the treaty with Allah and Muhammad in the first place. As for the other Pagans who kept the treaty, "fulfill your agreement with them to the end of their term. Allah loves those who are mindful of Him."

Anwari nodded.

The imam continued, "So, Ayah 9:5 is merely telling Muslims that those who broke a specific treaty at that specific time should suffer the consequences. It is a call to war against a specific enemy at a specific time. Some Christians and Jews quote this as evidence that our religion seeks to destroy them, whether through terrorism or otherwise, but it is no more a sanction of terrorism against non-believers than the Hebrew bible's exhortation to Joshua to tear down the walls of Jericho is a sanction of war against all those who are not Jews."

Anwari asked, "If this is so clear, then why do the terrorists rely on it, and how do they get away with it?"

"Why, indeed, my friend? And now we have returned to my first question to you. Let me answer this question with another question: Do you believe that all who claim to act in Allah's name always do so?"

"Of course not. Many have their own interests in mind."

"Then why should it surprise you that these same people might abuse the words of the Qur'an to further their own interests? I am not saying they all disbelieve their distorted constructions. For many reasons, people of all ethnicities and creeds hold hate deep within their hearts for 'others' who they believe have wronged them, whether individually, a member of their families, or their ethnic groups or nations. As their hate grows like an insidious sickness, it devours the truth of their souls and the clarity of their minds. They convince themselves that others must die or be persecuted and, feeling the natural conflict within their hearts, they reach out to their moral creeds for justification and find that which they wish to discover and believe that which they wish to understand. We Muslims are not alone in this, for history and the world today is replete with examples from many religions and peoples."

"Yes, I agree." Anwari said.

"But history has rowed its heavy oars toward us now, Abdul, as so many

Muslims feel mistreated by those who rule this world and try to dominate us. This domination breeds hatred, and unspeakable acts follow. Now all the world begins to judge us not on the basis of our true faith, but on the evil works of those who distort our faith. Do not succumb to this path, Abdul, for you are too good a man. If your mentor believes in this distortion, leave him at once. And if you do not yet believe me, discover for yourself his true motives and act accordingly."

Anwari graciously thanked the imam for his insights and walked outside. This imam had confirmed his own feelings, but other militant imams had argued the opposite, had argued as Pardus had taught him. Whom should he believe? What was Allah's true will for him? "Allah, I beg of you, guide me on the straight path. Show me the way."

Anwari's cell phone rang—not the phone he used with Pardus but his everyday phone. He looked at the caller ID. Perhaps his short prayer had been answered.

"Abdul, it's Chris, Chris Huxley. It has been awhile."

"Yes it has. How are you?"

"I'm fine. Hey, I was thinking about you this morning."

Anwari tensed up. "You were?" he said slowly.

"Yes, I was showing a few visiting friends some sites here in Washington, and I thought it would be fun to give my new friend Abdul a guided tour. How about it? Are you still travelling around the world? Maybe you could come here?"

Anwari stiffened. *A trap? No, they could arrest me here and then I would have no rights, but in America...* "Perhaps. I would have to see if it would work for me."

"Great, why don't you check on it?" Huxley replied. "Sorry, but I cannot comp your travel here to the States. You'll have to get your sponsors to do that. I'm particularly looking forward to showing you the Jefferson Memorial. You haven't been there before, have you?"

Anwari nearly gasped, but held it in. The Jefferson Memorial was the last of Pardus's clues, but he had heard nothing concrete about it. Had Huxley now associated him more closely with the breadcrumbs? Anwari would need to speak with Pardus. Pardus. Was Anwari just falling in line with him again? Maybe this was the perfect time to make a break. *Is that Allah's will?*

"Anwari, are you there?" Huxley was sounding impatient.

"Yes, sorry. No, I have not been to that site. It sounds like a great idea."

"When can you get here?"

"Soon. I will let you know. Soon."

Anwari hung up the phone and then stared at it for over a minute, frozen with indecision. Either way, he had to call Pardus. He pulled out his secure phone and called.

"Yes?" said the deep voice on the other end.

"He just invited me for a little tour of his sites. He mentioned our friend, Tom, in particular."

"I see. He remains on track, but I wonder if he will ever understand. We might need to nudge him."

Anwari smiled. "Yes. I will go."

"No. Let me think about it. Timing will be critical."

"Yes, Imam." Anwari fingered his thumb and pinched his lips together. Should he tell him or would that condemn him to death? Pardus was probably having him followed anyway. It would be better for Anwari to confess himself. Maybe he could sort things out. "Imam?"

"Yes, Abdul."

"I met with Imam Rahini today."

"That filthy collaborator? What did he say?"

Anwari breathed deeply. "I just asked him about the provisions in the Qur'an we have been discussing, just to understand his perspective. As you might imagine, it differs from yours."

"Of course, since he has long been in the pay of the Americans."

"He claims his views are shared by most of the world's Muslims. He said Qital is essentially a doctrine of self-defense for Muslims, not a justification for terrorism. He argues that those who use the words of the Qur'an as such are fooling themselves to justify their evil actions."

"And what do you believe, Abdul?"

Anwari remained silent for longer than he wished. He would be writing his own death sentence, yet in many ways he was already dead. "I am sorry, Imam, but I find myself conflicted. I wish to serve Allah and satisfy my brother's call for revenge, but I do not wish to harm innocents. I cannot bring myself to believe that Allah would want it so."

"You speak of innocents. Who is innocent here, Abdul?"

"Most of the people in America and Italy who are at risk. If this goes badly, their blood will be on our hands."

"You call the Americans innocent, even when they elect the leaders who bomb our cities and bring armies to enforce their will upon us? Are they innocent when they watch on television and cheer their bombs lighting up our cities? Are they innocent when their taxes pay for weapons that destroy our villages, maim our children and murder our brothers? No, Abdul, they are no less guilty than their soldiers. These so-called innocents might as well have come here to kill us themselves."

Abdul looked down and closed his eyes.

Pardus went on, "And what of the Italians? In their midst, they preserve the relic of a misguided and blasphemous faith. What are the popes but guardians of a great myth of the divinity of a mere prophet? This ancient fairytale allowed a false apostle to expand a tiny Jewish sect by appealing to Pagan gentiles who were already accustomed to worshiping human gods. And this blasphemy survived these past two millennia in large part because of a long line of popes and their Vatican intelligentsia, who smothered dissent and declared themselves the sole oracle of their faith. I can think of nobody who more deserves to learn the hard lesson of Allah's true will. If the Italian people suffer as a side effect, so be it, for it is they who have chosen to sustain this bastion of sacrilege in their city."

"I understand, Imam," said Anwari slowly. *I've crossed the line. Just shut up, Abdul, and you might live.*

"Do you? Perhaps you do not appreciate the situation, my friend. Your useless desert imams can scream all they want, but they will not matter for long. I already have what I need to change the world. Change it will, and for the better."

Anwari bit his lip, but to his dismay it worked itself free. "How do you know it will be better?"

"Because I will reshape it in my own image."

Anwari's jaw dropped. *Holy hell, who does he think he is?*

Pardus continued, "Get on board, Abdul, or you risk being swept away by the next flood—though this one will flow with blood."

"Yes, of course, Imam," Anwari replied. Was his tone supportive enough? Did Pardus believe him? How could he when Anwari could not believe the man himself? Imam Rahini had proven prescient: when Anwari had tested his mentor's motives, the truth had quickly revealed itself. He had received his answer from Allah. "How about Washington? Shall I go?"

"No, stay there for now. I'll let you know when I decide."

"Thank you, Imam." Anwari hung up the cell phone and this time did not pause when he switched to his other cell to make a call. A few moments later he said, "I'd like a flight from Kabul to Washington, D.C., please—as soon as possible."

CHAPTER 67

Pre-occupied with thoughts of the next puzzle awaiting him, Christian Huxley left his car on Ohio Drive in East Potomac Park and walked along the Potomac toward the Jefferson Memorial without noticing his little tail. He had no reason to believe anyone would be following him in DC anyway, so he left caution aside and let his mind wander. He had hoped to view the Memorial with Anwari and see if the Afghan's eyes might lead him to his next step, but the man had never returned his follow-up calls. Huxley could wait no longer.

He had spent his waiting time studying the Jeff Thomas, III, entry. The clues, if any, were altogether too sparse. The entry read:

Jeff Thomas, III

home
202-693-4721

mobile
202-579-7979

work
202-987-1295

home address
Apartment three
1252 Maryland Avenue, S.W.
Washington, DC 20024

Notes
If I could play The Apostle, would I know
the truth?

Are the telephone numbers a deciphering key like the numbers in the Christian Huxley entry? At least that entry had specified the pattern when it referenced "Mobile-Other: Main." Here, the "Notes" section again held the only unusual clue: "If I could play the Apostle, would I know the truth?" If he was supposed to play Thomas Jefferson, the Apostle of Democracy, the Jefferson Memorial seemed to be as good a stage as any.

As he approached the memorial, he saw that its domed roof was supported by a large number of Doric columns. Could their number represent a clue? He counted them, counted the number holding up the front portico to the structure, and played a few mathematical games with the combinations and phone numbers in the telephone entry. No clarity emerged.

He approached the center of the structure and its giant statue of the Apostle of Democracy. If he assumed the statue's viewpoint, in a sense he would be "playing the Apostle." He stood at the base of the statue and followed Jefferson's eyes beyond the columns supporting the portico and beyond even the huge tidal pool that lay before it. His eyes finally focused on the historic building lying plainly visible just over a mile away: the White House. He could see no "truth" in merely pointing to the White House, unless that was the alleged target of the attack. He looked around some more and decided to take pictures of every viewpoint available to Jefferson's statue. The interior walls of the memorial were covered with four inscriptions containing excerpts from various Jeffersonian writings. The first was just behind the statue on his left and was pulled from the famous document Jefferson first drafted, the Declaration of Independence:

WE HOLD THESE TRUTHS TO BE SELF-
EVIDENT: THAT ALL MEN ARE CREATED
EQUAL, THAT THEY ARE ENDOWED BY THEIR
CREATOR WITH CERTAIN INALIENABLE
RIGHTS, AMONG THESE ARE LIFE, LIBERTY
AND THE PURSUIT OF HAPPINESS, THAT
TO SECURE THESE RIGHTS GOVERNMENTS
ARE INSTITUTED AMONG MEN. WE…
SOLEMNLY PUBLISH AND DECLARE, THAT
THESE COLONIES ARE AND OF RIGHT
OUGHT TO BE FREE AND INDEPENDENT
STATES…AND FOR THE SUPPORT OF THIS
DECLARATION, WITH A FIRM RELIANCE
ON THE PROTECTION OF DIVINE
PROVIDENCE, WE MUTUALLY PLEDGE
OUR LIVES, OUR FORTUNES AND OUR
SACRED HONOUR.

The second inscription to the statue's front left focused on certain Jeffersonian arguments about religious freedom:

ALMIGHTY GOD HATH CREATED THE
MIND FREE. ALL ATTEMPTS TO INFLUENCE
IT BY TEMPORAL PUNISHMENTS OR
BURTHENS…ARE A DEPARTURE FROM
THE PLAN OF THE HOLY AUTHOR OF
OUR RELIGION…NO MAN SHALL BE
COMPELLED TO FREQUENT OR SUPPORT
ANY RELIGIOUS WORSHIP OR MINISTRY
OR SHALL OTHERWISE SUFFER ON
ACCOUNT OF HIS RELIGIOUS OPINIONS
OR BELIEF, BUT ALL MEN SHALL BE
FREE TO PROFESS AND BY ARGUMENT
TO MAINTAIN, THEIR OPINIONS IN
MATTERS OF RELIGION. I KNOW

BUT ONE CODE OF MORALITY FOR
MEN WHETHER ACTING SINGLY OR
COLLECTIVELY.

The third inscription to the front right revealed various Jeffersonian views concerning liberty, education, and the evil of slavery (although he was himself a slave owner and probably fathered a child by a slave):

GOD WHO GAVE US LIFE GAVE US
LIBERTY. CAN THE LIBERTIES OF A
NATION BE SECURE WHEN WE HAVE
REMOVED A CONVICTION THAT THESE
LIBERTIES ARE THE GIFT OF GOD?
INDEED I TREMBLE FOR MY COUNTRY
WHEN I REFLECT THAT GOD IS JUST,
THAT HIS JUSTICE CANNOT SLEEP FOR-
EVER. COMMERCE BETWEEN MASTER
AND SLAVE IS DESPOTISM. NOTHING
IS MORE CERTAINLY WRITTEN IN THE
BOOK OF FATE THAN THAT THESE
PEOPLE ARE TO BE FREE. ESTABLISH
THE LAW FOR EDUCATING THE COMMON
PEOPLE. THIS IT IS THE BUSINESS
OF THE STATE TO EFFECT AND ON
A GENERAL PLAN.

Finally, behind him and to his right, the inscription reiterated Jefferson's famous penchant for keeping up with the times (indeed, he had once famously penned: "I hold it that a little rebellion now and then is a good thing, and as necessary in the political world as storms in the physical"):

I AM NOT AN ADVOCATE FOR FREQUENT
CHANGES IN LAWS AND CONSTITUTIONS.
BUT LAWS AND INSTITUTIONS MUST GO
HAND IN HAND WITH THE PROGRESS

OF THE HUMAN MIND. AS THAT BECOMES
MORE DEVELOPED, MORE ENLIGHTENED,
AS NEW DISCOVERIES ARE MADE, NEW
TRUTHS DISCOVERED AND MANNERS AND
OPINIONS CHANGE, WITH THE CHANGE
OF CIRCUMSTANCES, INSTITUTIONS
MUST ADVANCE ALSO TO KEEP PACE
WITH THE TIMES. WE MIGHT AS WELL
REQUIRE A MAN TO WEAR STILL THE
COAT WHICH FITTED HIM WHEN A BOY
AS CIVILIZED SOCIETY TO REMAIN
EVER UNDER THE REGIMEN OF THEIR
BARBAROUS ANCESTORS.

Huxley played with the inscriptions in his head, trying to find some recognizable pattern. He tried using the telephone numbers in the Jeff Thomas III entry to pull out letters or words from the inscriptions, but nothing came of it but gibberish. Perhaps he needed the NSA's decrypting computers, but some important piece seemed to be missing. Without more, the computers could prove useless.

Not divining any other codes, Huxley returned to East Potomac Park and glanced at the river. On the other side, a few large yachts were moving into their slips at Southwest Wharf. He shook his head and looked away, but his mind had already turned back to his father's death. *An accident. Bullshit.* He and his mother had pretended it was an accident when everyone must have known it was suicide. A man does not accidentally string himself up by the neck on cables hanging from the wharf's edge. No, that son of a bitch screwed an ambassador's wife and then couldn't face up to it when his nine-year-old son caught him in the act. *A gruesome way to kill yourself, though. To hell with that bastard.* Huxley swallowed and exhaled. *Focus on the investigation.* Slowly, the old, recurring, horrible images faded away.

Anwari must be the key here. The coincidences were just too great. The man was probably in the pay of Pardus and possibly his only link at finding the warheads. Huxley would need to get him here, but he had to play it right, or the Afghan hero would become just another corpse left mute in

Pardus's wake. Huxley pulled his phone out of his pocket, cruised his own contacts list, and punched "Abdul Saboor Anwari." Nobody answered. Had the hero disappeared again?

Crap, what else did he have—a bunch of words in old Jeffersonian writings and a spirited taunt about playing The Apostle? Playing. He looked at the Jeff Thomas entry again. The word "The" was capitalized before "Apostle"—why? If you wrote, "play the Apostle of Democracy," as in "play Thomas Jefferson," you wouldn't capitalize the article "the." Pardus had not been sloppy so far. Then maybe "The Apostle" is itself a title. When would you play something with a title of "The Apostle?" The clue was on a cell phone. Shit, that must be it: You play The Apostle not as an actor but as a gamer.

Huxley went back to his own contacts list and found the entry for his favorite Israeli captain and selected his "home" number.

"What do you have for me, Huxley?" answered Captain Yadin.

"Not much. But I have a hunch, and I'm wondering if you can help me with it."

"Didn't your mother teach you it was better to give than receive? You're always taking and never giving."

Huxley chuckled. "Sorry about that. I'm sharing what I can same as you. I'll tell you this—I had better figure out something soon or we may all be very unhappy."

"OK, you've got me spooked. Word is out you Americans are putting on a full court press, but we don't have the details. However, we are not feeling too great knowing Pardus no longer needs assistance from the one man who could help him hide nuclear warheads. That cannot be good. Is there something else you want to tell me about the location of another country's nukes?"

"You know I can't say anymore. I wish I could. Nevertheless, I desperately need your help."

"What do you need?" asked Captain Yadin.

"Najwa's phone. I downloaded the contacts list from it, but I'm wondering if there is something more on it."

"Sure, there are plenty of apps on it, including a few we've never seen before."

Huxley crossed his fingers. "You see a game called 'The Apostle?'"

"You noticed the Jeff Thomas entry."

"Yep. Is there a game?"

"A game?" Yadin said. "I don't know—we haven't been able to get anything from it. It just makes the screen go completely dark. There are no instructions, no graphics, no text at all. Just a blank, dark screen."

"You try to type in a password."

"Of course, but nothing's worked. Tried a bunch of things from the Jeff Thomas entry and then from other entries in the contact list. Nothing changed the screen. You have any ideas?"

Huxley sighed. "Not really, but this bastard knows me. Maybe I could tinker with it for a few days and see what happens. You willing to part with it?"

"Hell, it's just sitting in storage right now. I have a courier heading to Washington tonight. You should have it tomorrow morning. But I want you to promise you'll let me know if you discover anything concrete."

"Whatever I can, Captain. Whatever I can."

CHAPTER 68

TOMADUS AND PEREGRINE walked down a wooded path running beside the Sequana River as they approached its northern apex within Parisius, a mid-sized town in the western-most section of the Mahdian Muslim Empire. Tomadus looked to the north and saw the Sultan Akbar Mosque atop the only real hill in town. From this vantage, the mosque dominated the town both physically and culturally. But that was not their destination. They were heading for the Forumaparisium on Quay, where Tomadus expected to find Isa speaking this morning.

"He will remember you," said Tomadus.

"Why?" asked Peregrine. "He only met me once, and that was over three years ago."

"Trust me, he will remember. Do you believe in his god?"

"We are both Romanus technologists," Peregrine replied. "Must you even ask?"

"I'd wondered if the visions had changed you," said Tomadus.

"You know they have, but they have not yet wiped my mind clean of my training," Peregrine said.

"Did you believe in God in the other world?"

"Did I believe? Look, I see visions, but I do not yet accept as you do that I actually lived in this other world. The visions are not so clear."

"Yet you have memories of experiences there?"

Peregrine shook his head. "I see it through a frosty window, though I admit I seem to see through the eyes of only one person."

"Yourself?"

"I see only bits and pieces, but I think this person was a student. I can recall a few pieces of his college life, but no occupation, at least not yet. The memories come to you in waves?"

Tomadus nodded. "They still come from time to time. It is as if I am currently living his life, and the visions just appear in my mind as new memories as they occur."

"You said he is some kind of spy for the American government? That seems strangely familiar, though I cannot pinpoint it."

"Not a spy, not really. But yes, he seems to be investigating some type of terrible terrorist plot, winding his way through unusual puzzles and clues left for him."

Peregrine tilted his head. "How odd."

CHAPTER 69

"I'll have the NSA nerds on it in minutes," Kira said with her most gracious smile. "Is there anything else I can do for you, boss?"

"No, nothing more for now."

Kira rose to leave.

Huxley snapped his fingers and pointed at Kira. "There is one thing—thanks."

"Thanks?"

"Yep. Thanks for putting up with my bullshit. I know I can be a bit demanding at times. You put up with it and keep coming through—and all without even calling me an asshole."

"Yeah, well, maybe not to your face." After she laughed, she smiled softly. "Thanks for saying that, though. You okay?"

"Sure, I'm fine. Just a bit down on this case, I guess. I talked to the boss man and it appears nobody can find anything about this Pardus prick. He's going to blow up a couple cities and we might just have to watch it happen. I feel like the answers are lying right in front of me, but I'm too stupid to see them."

"You'll get there," she said softly. "You always do."

"I don't know."

The office phone beeped and he saw reception was calling. He smiled and nodded to Kira, who left the room. "Hello."

"Mr. Huxley, you have a call from Ambassador Kadir al-Razin al-Asr. Shall I pass him through?"

"The Ambassador himself?"

"It appears so. He is quite the gentleman."

"That would be him. Sure, put him through." Huxley paused and waited for the light clicking sound. "How is the one and only true Ambassador of Peace?"

"Always a smartass," came the response on the phone. "You need to show a little more respect for your betters." They shared a short laugh.

"To what do I owe the pleasure of a call?"

Kadir said, "Just doing my part to keep the world safe for Americans."

"You must just love us. What have you got this time?"

"Some intelligence on a former Catholic cardinal. You want it or should I talk to someone else?"

"I'll pass it on if appropriate."

"Okay," said Kadir, "I heard this guy, Armondo Fine, recently became mixed up with some bad-ass Islamic terrorists. Kind of hard to understand the connection, but that is the information that has been forwarded to me. I do not know the names of the terrorists, though someone mentioned a leopard. Anyway, they have got something big cooking. My source said he heard the plan would make 9/11 look like a pathetic Molotov cocktail. He swore he knew no more details. Oh yes, they believe the cardinal is hiding in Rome. Something is apparently planned there as well. I do not know if it is just a meet or the location of the target. This connected to any of that shit you have been rolling in?"

"Do I smell that bad?" Huxley asked.

"In fact, I did not know until just now that odors could travel through telephone wires."

Huxley shook his head. "Funny man. Any idea where he might be in Rome?"

Kadir took a few seconds to respond. "No, sorry. Anything else I can help you with?"

"Nah. Thanks for your help."

"No problem. So how is that new Italian beauty you have been seeing?"

"I'm not sure."

"What? She bored with you already?" Kadir used that taunting tone of his. "You need your handsome friend to show her a good time?"

"You're just full of yourself today, aren't you? No, I think I've fallen for her, but…"

"But what?"

Huxley said nothing for a few seconds.

Kadir said, "Come on Sko-B, don't you trust me?"

"Of course I trust you, Kadir. I'm worried she is somehow involved with this terrorist I've been trying to find."

"That would not be good. Your boss know that?"

"You kidding?" Huxley said. "I'm not going to hand her over to the CIA to water-board her."

"Well, good luck with that one, Sko-B. Hey, did I mention my new Sunseeker yacht arrived? It's a gift from my second cousin, the sheik. Quite a craft. We should cruise the Potomac one of these nights and enjoy some scotch and Cubans. It has been awhile since you let loose. You sound stressed out."

Huxley leaned back. "No shit. I'll take you up on that one of these days. Too much crap to wade through now, though." *Like finding that viper cardinal.*

"OK. Just let me know, Hux. If I am in the District and not busy kissing ass with one of your governmental officials, I can head out almost any evening. Just give me a couple of hours so the crew can prepare. But now I have other important matters to which I must attend. Take care of yourself, Sko-B."

Huxley smiled when he lowered the phone receiver. A cruise on Kadir's yacht would be nice, but it was a diversion he could not afford. Kadir had confirmed his views of Cardinal Fine, so he still had one hard lead to follow up along with the puzzles Baqir Najwa had left him. *No, Hux, don't be a chump. Not Najwa.* Someone else was yanking him around by a nose ring with those clues. *Pardus.* But the clues had been helping him solve the case. Without the clues, he probably would not have found the missing warheads in Pakistan. Without the puzzles, he might have never noticed the disappearance of the Israeli chemist. They had not led him astray. *Not yet.* Therein lied the problem. If this were Pardus's handiwork, a trap would eventually await him, unless Pardus made a mistake. Even the Ghost Leopard could make a mistake. *I must seize on the mistake and recognize his ruse at the proper time.* He needed to find Anwari. Hell, he needed to find the cardinal.

CHAPTER 70

TOMADUS AND PEREGRINE approached the upper streets of the Forumaparisium on Quay and saw the crowd dispersing below.

"They say he is the Mahdi. Do you doubt it now?" said one man to his friend as they walked past Tomadus and sat on a bench within earshot. Tomadus stopped.

"I hope so," said the friend quietly. "We could use a little more justice and a bit less tyranny."

"Hush, you could be overheard. Besides, if he is the Mahdi, then the world will soon end. Is that what you wish?"

"The end of the world? Phhht. Only morons think that way. But I hope he will bring the end of the world for our despotic rulers."

"Quiet yourself or I will be forced to report you." The man looked around and saw Tomadus and Peregrine looking in their direction.

Tomadus pretended to be looking beyond them as if he were waiting for someone else. He pivoted and continued down the street with Peregrine. "This is dangerous," he whispered to Peregrine.

"What?"

"A man does not criticize the Emperor in the Mahdian Muslim Empire openly—not even a Mahdian."

"So? It is one man. The empire will deal with him if they like."

Tomadus looked at Peregrine. "Only a fool steps on a termite in his home without worrying about the hidden decay of the entire structure. The Three Emperors have long understood this and will not hesitate to fumigate before it is too late. I fear the repercussions for Isa's movement. Ah, but here they are."

Isa and the Ten were sitting on the quay eating apples, figs and nuts, their legs dangling above the slow current of the Sequana. Isa saw the two men approaching and stood up to greet them. "Tomadus, welcome. We missed you in Tetepe."

"Greetings, Isa." Tomadus kissed him on the cheeks. "Let me introduce you to my new friend—"

"Peregrine, it is good to see you again," Isa said.

Peregrine nodded his head slowly and asked, "You remember me?"

"Of course," replied Isa. "How could I forget such a distinguished astro-technologist?"

Tomadus smiled knowingly. "I told you." He and Peregrine laughed.

While still chuckling, Tomadus noticed Jochi standing a few feet behind one of the Ten. He almost had not recognized her, now stripped of her Romanus trappings and fitting comfortably with other women of the Way, wearing a simple chador. But he could not miss her bright face and coy smile, which she now displayed again to Tomadus. The Light struck him quick but deep. He began sweating as several emotions swept through him rapidly: love, guilt, heartache, loneliness, joy and finally, distrust. The emotions tracked his vision of a confession to a woman close to Huxley— the woman from the investigation, the woman Huxley loved yet could not love, could not trust. This last realization gripped him just as Huxley departed the scene, and then the vision and emotions faded away.

Isa seemed to notice the change in Tomadus's visage and glanced over his shoulder. At this, Jochi hunched her shoulders and looked down and away. "Have you just experienced the Light, Tomadus?" Isa asked.

Tomadus swallowed and breathed deep, coming back to reality. He nodded in Isa's direction, then gestured to Peregrine. "Isa, this man has also experienced the Light."

Isa smiled but said nothing.

Tomadus crossed his arms. "He can see many of the same things in the other world that I see."

"Other world?" Simeon bellowed, wrinkling his nose and raising his lip like he smelled a dead rat. "Does our favorite rich man believe in another world?"

Tomadus had not seen the man coming up behind him.

"I don't...I don't believe...in anything," Tomadus said.

"Well, that is no shock," responded Simeon, "for surely you still do not believe in God and probably would not even do so if he kissed you on the cheek. If you do not believe in anything, then how is it you can see another world? Are you cracked?" Now surrounding them, several of the other Ten roared with laughter.

Isa stepped between Simeon and Tomadus. "Do not ridicule what you do not understand, Simeon. All of you must keep your eyes and your ears open to everything, for the Father speaks to us all in different ways. Like Tomadus, admit your ignorance and search for the truth wherever you can find it." The laughter stopped. "Though his path has differed from yours, you know not whether it will lead him to even greater illumination." Isa turned toward Tomadus and Peregrine. "You have each independently searched for an explanation of your visions. Now that you have found each other, share with us what you know."

Tomadus's cheeks reddened and he forced a fake smile. He had never shared the visions with the Ten. "Well, it is complicated," he said. "We are hoping that you will help us find the answers."

Isa smiled softly and looked at Peregrine. "What do you think?"

Peregrine blurted out, "I think we have somehow seen or crossed through to another universe."

Tomadus's eyes widened. "Another universe? What can you mean?"

Peregrine shook his head. "I don't know, but I have heard of a theory held by some astro-technologists. They believe our universe is just one of an infinite number of universes. Many of these are very similar to ours. Others are very different."

"But how can that be?" asked Tomadus.

"There has been research into mathematical and physical laws to support it. They talk about decoherence between certain states of matter for small points of time, but it remains controversial."

"I may be able to think of another explanation," Isa said. "But let us assume there is such a thing. Do you think you two have somehow physically traveled between these distinct universes?"

Peregrine's eyes narrowed. "No, I really do not know. Maybe our minds just act as windows to the other universe."

"No," said Tomadus. "If there is another universe, then I feel like some part of me has traveled between the two. It is just too real. It is not like a visi-scan display. It is not a story. It is in my memory. Somehow, I was this person. I see through his eyes; I sense his thoughts; I feel his emotions. I was this man. I am this man. I am sure of it." He looked at Simeon to see if he were snickering; instead, the man's face looked thoughtful. The Ten were all in deep thought.

Isa interrupted the silence. "How would you make this physical transfer from one universe to the next? Do you recall choosing this course? Is your body the same in both worlds?"

"No. I look different. I don't know how it happens, but I know we both began having the visions right after you touched us."

Isa smiled. "I have touched many people, but they do not speak of visions. Why do you now assume the science of astrophysics holds your answers, and why do you assume something physical? Have I touched you in any other way? Could there be another explanation?"

"I have not been able to think of any," replied Tomadus.

"Ah, how miserable is the body that depends on a body, and how miserable is the soul that depends on these two," said Isa mystically.

"What does that mean?" asked Tomadus.

Isa looked into Tomadus's eyes. "I sometimes forget that you do not yet believe in souls."

"Yet?"

"There is always hope," Isa said. "Perhaps you two are like the Buddhists or Hindus—your souls travel a path toward the enlightenment of God through multiple worlds."

A murmur arose among the Ten.

"Is this the Father's plan, Master?" Simeon asked.

Isa looked around the group. "I see many of you are disturbed by this. It does not bother Tomadus and Peregrine because they do not, yet, believe in souls. But for you others who dispute this possibility, do you also dispute that there is a Heaven and a hell?"

Anders, the Muslim, weighed in, "The Great Book says of Heaven, 'These will come face to face with their evil, but those who repent, who believe, who do righteous deeds, will enter Paradise. They will not be wronged in the least: they will enter the Garden of Lasting Bliss, promised by the Lord of Mercy.' It also says, 'For those who defy their Lord We have prepared the torment of Hell: an evil destination. They will hear it drawing in its breath when they are thrown in.'"

Simeon guffawed. "So, Tomadus, tell us—are you now in Heaven or hell?"

The other nine of the Ten joined his laughter until Isa frowned and shook his head. "You think this is a joke? Why do you assume the duality of Heaven and hell? If your soul is not ready for Heaven, Simeon, will you forever be condemned to hell? Could there be yet another possibility?"

Simeon lowered his head and muttered, "I am a sinful man. Perhaps there is no hope for me."

"Simeon," said Isa, "when you sin you risk separating yourself from the Father, but have I not taught you that the Father forgives? You need only ask and he will save you from Gehenna, for I will bring you back to him."

Adin blurted out, "So then there is only the different worlds and Heaven and hell!"

Isa grinned and put his hands on Adin's big shoulders. "Adin, you always see the truth so clearly. Let me ask you something."

"Okay, master."

"When you joined us, your parents were both dead, is that right?"

Adin nodded several times.

Isa smiled gently. "Do you remember your earthly father?"

"Oh yes, he was very nice. I loved him."

"Did you ever do anything wrong in his eyes?"

"I tried to be good, but I made mistakes."

"Of course," Isa said, "you are human. When you erred and your father discovered it, did you ever ask for his forgiveness?"

"Oh yes."

"And did your father forgive you?"

Adin nodded excitedly. "He told me he forgave me right away. He was kind."

"Yes, Adin, he was a very good man," said Isa. "Now, I want you to think hard about this. After he forgave you, did he punish or try to correct you in any way?"

"Uh huh, but I didn't mind so much 'cause he wasn't angry at me. He said I had to do that so I would learn to be better in the future."

"Thank you, Adin. Your father did a wonderful job raising you."

Adin beamed. "Thank you, master."

Isa turned toward the others. "You all should take a lesson from this gentle man's father, who taught him so well. Would not my Father in Heaven also find such a way to teach his children, to help their souls find the way?" Isa smiled and began walking away.

Tomadus and Peregrine walked after him, pleading for more explanation. Isa turned and nodded. "Like most children, you still have much to learn. Be neither afraid nor stubborn, and you may still find your way in this world or the next. Remember, I am the Light. I am the Sun. Turn your ship toward me." Isa turned away and this time ignored their pleas for more.

Simeon shouted out to him, "Teacher, please, do not walk the streets alone. Do not forget the rumors."

Isa responded, "Thank you for your concern, Simeon, but my time has not yet come." He shuffled down the street alone. Simeon asked two of the Ten to follow Isa, and they obeyed.

Peregrine and Tomadus returned to Simeon. "What is that about?" asked Tomadus. "What rumors have you heard?"

"Some friends of the Way have told us there may be a plot against Isa by someone in authority. We do not know if the rumors are true, but it would be just like the bastards to grab him when he walks the streets alone."

"Who told you this?" demanded Tomadus.

"It was someone highly placed. It is not the first time we have heard such things, but I begin to worry."

CHAPTER 71

CRUISING IN A DC-10 that had just taken off from Reagan International on its way to Rome, Huxley stared at the glimmering Atlantic below, his thoughts flowing gently with the waves. Why was this cardinal still in hiding? Government agents were looking for him along with half the Carabinieri, yet they had found no traces. Maybe his Vatican friends could help, if they weren't hiding something themselves.

The long plane ride gave Huxley time to try his new favorite game. He had Najwa's phone in his hand and kept plugging phantom passwords into The Apostle app, without luck. The NSA's super computers were still crunching the Jefferson Memorial and Jeff Thomas, III, clues. Something had to be missing. He figured the app had some sort of answer. Maybe he should have turned the phone over to the NSA, but he had to have a shot at it first.

He had inputted various portions of the Jeff Thomas entry, including the phone numbers, the address, the real address for the Jefferson Memorial, and the fake name of Jeff Thomas, III. The screen remained blank. He thought about the clue that had made him examine the Jeff Thomas entry closely: "Apostle of Democracy." Nothing. He exited again and tried, "Jeff Thomas, III, Apostle of Democracy." Still blank. He tried, "Thomas Jefferson, Apostle of Democracy." The visible screen did not stir, but the phone vibrated. Nobody was calling and there were no texts coming in. He turned on the volume, exited and restarted the app, and again entered, "Thomas Jefferson, Apostle of Democracy."

The screen remained blank, but a metallic voice said, "Speak so that you may hear."

Huxley stared at the phone a few seconds, then he noticed a small microphone icon had appeared at the bottom left corner of the screen. He pressed it and said, "Thomas Jefferson, Apostle of Democracy."

The metallic voice responded, "Voice match. Ask and you shall receive." Huxley smiled. Yes, he would very much like to receive.

He hit the microphone icon and said, "What is the message?" Nothing happened. He exited and started over again, this time saying, "What is the key?" Again nothing. He tried a number of other variations on this theme until he considered the Jeff Thomas entry. He said, "Jeff Thomas." Nothing. Then he exited and repeated the name along with "III." Again nothing.

Huxley tilted his head and stared at the phone. He repeated the entire process, but this time he said aloud the first digit of the home telephone number from the Jeff Thomas contacts entry: "Two."

The phone's screen lit up for the first time with a smiling emoticon followed immediately by a series of seemingly random numerals separated by dashes:

☺ –1-1-1-2-1-3-1-3-1-1-2-1-3-8-4-2-1-6-3-2-1

Huxley grabbed his pad and pencil and wrote out the symbol and numbers. Then he spoke the second number from the home phone entry, "0," and a small, hand-printed "t" appeared followed by a much shorter set of numerals:

† – 1-1-3-1-1-8

After writing these down, Huxley continued through the digits of the home phone number, proceeded through the digits of the other two phone numbers and continued until he had reached the "o" in "Washington" in the home address. At that point, no entries produced any further output in The Apostle game.

Huxley sat back and looked at the sheets of symbols and numbers he had written:

☺ – 1-1-1-2-1-3-1-3-1-1-2-1-3-8-4-2-1-6-3-2-1

† – 1-1-3-1-1-8

⚭ – 8-5-5-2-1-5-1-5-2-2-3-3-2-3-1-2-5-2-13-1-1-2-1-1-1-5-4-1-4-2

Δ – 1-5-2-1-3-2

☺ – 2-7-1-1-2-2-2-5-1-1-7-4-3-6-4-1-4-2-1-4-1

† – 2-1-1-1-4-3-14-4-1

⚭ – 1-5-3-1-1-2-2-5-5-1-1-1-1-6-4-2-1-6

Δ – 1-3-3-2-1-2-1-5-8-1-2-2

☺ – 2-5-3-4-1-6-1-4-4

† – 1-2-2-1-4-2

⚭ – 1-1-7-1-2-3-1-4-1

Δ – 2-1-7-2-1-2-1-2-1-2-3-1-3-2-1

☺ – 5-3-2-4-3-6-1-3-4-1-4-6

† – 2-4-5-5-5-4

⚭ – 13-1-4-2-5-1-3-3-6-1-6-2-2-2-1

Δ – 3-1-1-1-7-3-14-7-3-1-5-4-1-3-1-4-1-4

☺ – 7-5-7-3-4-4

† – 2-2-1-3-3-5-2-2-2-1-1-7-3-3-6-1-4-6-2-4-8-3-4-5

⚭ – 2-6-1-3-1-1

Δ – 3-5-1-15-3-7

☺ – 1-2-3-1-1-2-5-5-3-1-5-1

† – 8-5-8-3-5-1-2-6-5

⚭ – 1-7-2-2-5-4-2-5-8

Δ – 2-3-3-4-1-1-1-4-1-1-5-7

☺ – 1-7-1-1-4-5-2-4-1-1-7-3-2-4-1

† – 3-2-1-1-5-3-2-2-1-1-1-1-1-1-2-2-3-1

☺ – 2-5-6-2-4-2-3-2-2

Δ – 5-4-1-1-5-1-1-4-2-14-7-3

† – 3-4-2-2-1-3-2-3-2-1-1-4-14-6-1-2-2-3

☺ – 2-3-2-1-4-3-5-2-1

⚭ – 1-3-2

Δ – 4-6-1-1-6-3-1-1-1-1-7-6-2-3-4-1-7-8

☺ – 4-2-1-3-3-2-6-4-1

† – 2-6-2-2-2-4-17-1-9-2-4-4-3-5-2

⛓ – 2-5-1-2-5-7-1-3-3-3-3-2-1-1-3

Δ – 5-8-1-2-1-6-1-7-1-1-6-2-1-7-2-4-5-3

⛓ – 7-7-1-1-7-1-2-5-9-3-1-3

☺ – 8-4-1-1-5-3-8-5-1

† – 17-1-2-16-4-3

Δ – 17-2-6-17-2-8-17-1-8-16-6-1-16-6-2

☺ – 16-2-1-16-2-12-17-1-5-17-1-1

† – 17-1-12-17-1-10-17-1-7

⛓ – 16-7-1-15-7-1-16-3-1-16-5-5-15-7-2-17-2-5-17-2-4-14-4-2

Δ – 16-3-1-16-3-2-15-3-7

☺ – 16-5-1-17-1-2-16-5-4-17-2-1-16-5-7-17-2-6-16-5-8-'

† – 17-1-5-16-3-5-15-3-3-17-2-1

⛓ – 16-5-6-16-4-2

Δ – 16-4-5-14-7-3-15-4-1-14-5-2-17-2-9

☺ – 17-2-4-17-2-5-17-1-4

† –16-2-2-16-2-6-16-3-1-16-2-7-16-3-3-16-4-1

⛓ – 10-4-1-16-1-1

Δ – 17-1-3-17-2-4-17-2-1-17-2-3-14-4-1

☺ – 15-4-5-17-2-3-17-1-6

† – 15-5-7-13-4-2-16-2-3-16-1-3

⛓ – 7-5-3-17-2-2-17-3-1-16-5-4-17-3-4-6-1-6-17-4-1

Δ – 14-5-1-16-6-3

⛓ – 15-7-8-16-5-1-16-3-5-12-1-4

☺ - 17-2-2-16-7-2-16-7-3

† – 17-1-1-16-5-1-15-2-2-14-1-7-15-6-2-17-1-11-15-5-4-15-1-3-17-1-8-15-5-2-14-6-2

Δ – 14-2-1-16-6-4-15-3-6-14-2-2

☺ – 13-6-5

† – 12-3-4-15-5-3-16-4-2-16-1-2-14-3-8-12-4-3-14-4-1

⛓ – 13-5-2-16-2-3-14-6-4-15-7-6-14-6-3-13-7-5-15-6-3-11-3-3

Δ – 17-2-2-17-2-7-13-5-1

☺ – 15-4-3-12-8-2-16-2-4

† – 16-1-1-14-1-2-16-3-4-13-6-2-15-3-4

⌯⌯ – 17-3-3-16-7-2-6-1-3

Δ – 14-3-4-12-1-4-16-4-6-16-4-7

☺ – 13-4-1-16-2-5-17-1-3-15-5-6-16-5-6-15-5-4-17-3-1

† – 14-1-4-15-4-1

⌯⌯ – 12-1-4-16-6-2-15-1-3-14-2-3

Δ – 9-6-2-16-4-4-15-3-1

☺ – 13-5-1-13-1-7-14-3-7-15-5-3

† – 16-4-6-15-3-2-15-1-2

⌯⌯ – 11-2-1-14-4-3-15-7-7-16-4-1

Δ – 14-3-3-16-5-1

☺ – 11-1-4-15-3-2-15-4-7-15-4-6

† – 7-1-9-15-2-3-13-5-8-16-3-2-14-3-2-13-5-7-4-5-1-17-2-1

The list contained only 4 repeating symbols, but at first the number arrays did not appear to follow any cryptographic methodology he had seen before. Then he noticed a few interesting patterns. First, the symbols were generally in sequential order throughout the clue: ☺, †, ⌯⌯, Δ. Second, there was one instance of a symbol—it looked like an apostrophe—that was different than the other four symbols and appeared not at the beginning of a line but at its end. Then he noticed that the total number of digits on each line was a multiple of 3: the first was 21, the second 6, the third 30, and so on.

This multiple of 3 could not be a coincidence. He split the numbers in each line into units of three numbers each. Now the first line read: "☺ – 1-1-1/2-1-3/1-3-1/1-2-1/3-8-4/2-1-6/3-2-1." After he did this, he saw that the first number of each grouping in the first half or so of the clue was almost always a smaller number between 1–4 while the first number of each grouping in the second half was generally between 14–17. That must signify some other demarcation point.

This was no simple substitution cipher. If it were, then each group of three numbers would refer to a single letter. He could then decode it through frequency analysis. This technique made simple ciphers ridiculously easy to break by assuming that the most frequent number combination in the message likely represented the letter "e," the most frequent letter used in English. The next most frequent number combination was the second most frequent letter, "t," and so forth. But as he viewed the cipher, he realized the units almost never repeated themselves, except across symbols. The symbols probably conditioned each three-number unit, so in actuality each unit consisted of four elements—the symbol plus three numbers. If he were right about that assumption, then the entire cipher contained only nine repeats, and a collection of 282 unique letters. That seemed highly unlikely in any alphabetic language.

What if the message was a book cipher? In those, the message contains location references within a piece of writing, such as a book. These location references specify either words or letters within the book. The trick to deciphering was to find the right book. Without more, it would be difficult for anyone to decipher, though the computers with vast libraries of books stored in them might be able to do it with time. But he had more.

The writer of this cipher had wanted Huxley to figure out the messages himself—that much had been obvious for some time. He had only to find the "book" the writer must have "told" Huxley to use as his key. The Apostle of Democracy. That was it. There were four inscriptions from the Jefferson Memorial on his phone picture gallery: four inscriptions = four book keys.

He reread the inscriptions, looked at the symbols and smiled. The second symbol was not the letter "t" in hand printing but a simple cross, which matched the inscription containing quotes from Jefferson about the role of religion. Then there were the three links in a chain, which must represent Jefferson's admonition against slavery. He stared at the triangle symbol. Three parts, three angles, one whole. He looked at the two remaining inscriptions. Nothing clicked. Let's see, what does a triangle represent? Of course, delta—the Greek symbol for change. It had been used by mathematicians and scientists for eons. So that matched the Jeffersonian quote about the need to continually renew the nation's institutions "to keep pace with the times." The happy face must default to the excerpt from the preamble of the Declaration of Independence. Perfect—Jefferson had included among our inalienable rights "the pursuit of happiness."

With these keys in hand, the message proved easy to decipher. The symbol for each line of the cipher pointed to the key, or Jeffersonian inscription, to be used for that line. Each three-number unit acted as a three-dimensional letter locator—not three dimensions in space, but three dimensions in a writing: line of the key, word in that line, and finally the letter to be used in the message. So he converted the first line of the cipher from the inscription pulled from the Declaration of Independence as follows:

The first unit, 1-1-1, designated the first line and its first word ("We"), and, thus, the first letter in that word: "W." So the first letter in the deciphered message would be "W." The next unit, 2-1-3, designated the second line, first word ("Evident"), and the third letter in that word: " i." So the deciphered message now read, "Wi."

Huxley continued through the first line and soon realized that the cipher used punctuation in the inscription key as if it were a word in the key. So 3-2-1 converted to a comma because the second "word" in the third line of the inscription was a comma. Since the next line of the cipher started with a cross, he switched to the Jeffersonian inscription on religion to decipher that line. It produced "my" with no punctuation, so by now he had determined that the message began: "Within, my." It sounded promising. A few minutes later, Huxley had deciphered two full sentences:

Within, my principles do comfort me.
Forget them not or you shall miss my plea.

He read the two together. They employed the same now familiar rhythm: iambic pentameter. *Another poem. Good grief.* When he completed the cipher and added the demarcation point half way through, the poem read:

Within, my principles do comfort me.
Forget them not or you shall miss my plea.
Beyond my fortress on my left you see
What shall befall the many unlike he,
A priest who never lived before just me.

On truth lies yet obscured thy fathers' end.
To myths our hearts do reach and then depend.
We seek our consolation with a friend.
Remember now the Maine and then ascend.
To know his fate you must to hell descend.

With this accomplishment, Huxley's heart did not leap with excitement; to the contrary, his throat closed up, and he wanted to chuck his pad of paper down the aisle, for once again his path to understanding seemed blocked by another thicket of delusions.

Much of his frustration had arisen from the second stanza. Pardus had found yet another way to personalize the pain. And yet again, it hurt just a little too much. Damn him all to hell. Damn Pardus? Certainly. Damn his own father? Why not? The bastard deserved it as well, didn't he? Anyway, the poem obviously expected, no exhorted, Huxley to follow his father's lead to the depths of hell. But he planned to send Pardus there first…

∇   ∇   ∇

…As another vision subsided, Tomadus tried to shake off this latest revelation, the four symbols still dancing in his head along with the words "you must to hell descend." Even he, still clinging to his disbelief, shivered at the thought of descending *ad infernum*. He closed his eyes hard, pushing the images to the back of his mind so he could cope with the present. What could he do about strange clues from another world anyway? It was like watching a vid-drama and trying to figure out the ending—fun but not much use in his current reality.

Putting those thoughts aside, his heart soared again and nearly lifted his feet above the stone path. Tomadus had spent the afternoon with Peregrine and many of the Ten, discussing a litany of permutations on various theories trying to explain the bizarre feelings and visions he and Peregrine shared. The open discussion with his brethren had made him feel truly welcome among the community for the first time. However, Simeon's warnings about potential plots against Isa gnawed through his immediate bliss, and so he set off toward one of the several communication pods in the city, which was less than a *mille passus* down the path beside the Parisius Gardens on the Sequana River.

As he approached a portion of the path separated from the gardens by ornamental bushes, he heard Jochi's gentle voice. He slowed his pace until he noticed a small opening in the bushes where he could see Jochi sitting next to Adin on a garden bench. Adin was shaking his head rapidly from side to side as he held it in his hands, his giant body trembling.

Jochi lightly stroked Adin's massive arms and shoulders and said soothingly, "It's ok Adin. Everything will be all right. You must not worry yourself so."

"Someone is going to kidnap Isa!" blurted Adin between his tears. "They might kill him! I will be alone again. Why? Why would they kill someone who is so good? Simeon said it!"

Jochi caressed Adin's hands in her lap. "You do not know this will happen. It is all rumors and speculation and fear. Simeon fears what might happen because they know Isa is good and speaks the truth to everyone. Some people cannot accept this. They see only a man who wants to change their world."

"But he does want to change it!" shouted Adin. "He wants us all to be better. He wants us all to love God and love everyone else—even our enemies. What is wrong with that?"

"Nothing, Adin, nothing. But it is a new way of thinking for many. People fear what they do not understand."

"Do they?"

Jochi tilted her head and pursed her lips for a moment. "Well look, do you remember when we were in New Jutland and you saw the dragon's head on the ship there? You were frightened, were you not?"

"It was a monster! I ran away."

"Then I showed you it was only made of wood and iron and was very old and you understood."

"Yes, it was just part of the ship—it wasn't real."

She smiled and nodded. "Well, it is like that for some people, but in reverse. They do not understand Isa as you do. They do not want to believe what is real. Because he says things that do not match their own views of the world, they fear him, and they fear the power of his words."

"Why would they fear his words?"

"Not the words themselves but what those words could mean. You see how many people are excited when they hear Isa speak?"

"Of course. He says nice things that make us feel good."

"To some, yes. To others in power, those words sound like a threat. If all of Isa's followers begin acting as Isa asks, they might seem like a new army to them."

Adin shook his head several times. "But Isa hates violence. He don't want no army."

"No, not that kind of army, Adin. Sometimes governments fall not from swords but from ideas, though it seems even then that swords and bloodshed soon follow."

"Then Isa should stop saying these things that make those people afraid."

"Should he? What is worse: to challenge injustice and tyranny and die in the attempt or to shrink from the shadows cast by these two demons and leave the world in darkness? No, Adin, Isa must continue to speak, for to stand mute would allow mere shadows to hide the light of truth."

Adin's brow furrowed. "Shadows? Demons? I don't understand."

"Sorry, Adin. Isa must keep fighting for what is right, for truth, even if the bad guys threaten him." When Adin nodded, Jochi turned her head toward the path.

Tomadus froze. She must have seen him. Yet when he looked into her eyes, he saw something he never quite understood. It was empathy for Adin, no doubt, but it felt like something more.

She sat there looking at Tomadus for a few seconds and then looked back down at Adin. "My advice to you, Adin, is to let loose your worries and trust again in Isa, for he so loves you that he will never abandon you. Look into your beautiful heart, for it knows this better than your brain will ever admit."

A sharp tingle shot down Tomadus's spine as he heard these words, and his eyes darted between Jochi and Adin. He had heard something like them before, and the look on her face had been identical to the one in his dreams. He walked toward the clearing and around to the garden where she and Adin sat.

Adin looked up, and a smile filled his face. "Tomadus! I was just talking to Jochi about the bad men who want to hurt Isa. Don't worry—Isa will take care of everything!"

Tomadus drew his lips together. *If only it were that simple, as simple as Adin's faith and love.* "Adin, you are right to put much faith in Isa. I shall not worry, nor should you. And know you have friends around you who will never abandon you—never." He gave Adin a big hug, his hands barely reaching around the giant's shoulders.

As they parted, Adin continued smiling innocently, cocked his head and said, "Thank you, Tomadus. I love you, too. I think I will go try to find Isa now." He patted Tomadus on the shoulder as he walked past him on the path back toward the quay.

"You have a way with him, Tomadus," Jochi said.

"I was about to say the same thing of you."

"You overheard our conversation?"

"Much of it," Tomadus said. "Sorry for eavesdropping, but I couldn't help myself. Adin was quite upset but seems better now. Simeon and I spoke recklessly in front of Adin. I had not considered the effect upon him."

Her smile turning down, Jochi began to nod. "Sometimes we all forget the effects our actions have on others." She looked down at the ground for a few seconds and then up at Tomadus again. Sadness seemed to have settled upon her. "I am sorry I did not contact you when I was in Tetepe, Tomadus. Things were just, I don't know, so magical, so spontaneous. It was as if I were in a trance—I never thought of anything but Isa and our mission."

Tomadus cocked his head. "Did you see the Light?"

"The light?"

"Tell me, has Isa touched you in any way?" Tomadus asked.

Jochi scowled at him. "What are you suggesting?"

"I'm sorry, but our visions—Peregrine's and mine—began after Isa touched us. Have you begun to see visions?"

"No...I...I don't think so. I have had some strange dreams, but I...I don't know. Why do you ask?"

He shook his head. "I guess it might explain a few things."

"Like what?" she asked.

"Like why I see you in my own visions."

"Me?"

"No, not you, not really, but…I don't know."

"If it is not me, then how can you say you see me?"

"You both just have a way about you and you…I don't know…I guess you both make me and Huxley feel the same. We both love…"

"Oh." She looked down and away, awkwardly. "Look, I…I don't know what to say."

Tomadus stiffened. "Forget it. They are just dreams."

Jochi closed her eyes. "Yes, just dreams."

CHAPTER 72

HUXLEY'S MIND HAD been pre-occupied by the latest poem for too long. Without greater insight, it would get him nowhere. But he still had a tangible clue to explore, so he had sought an answer to that riddle at its source.

"I'm sure you understand that these matters are highly confidential and quite sensitive," Colonel Zaugg said. "I cannot help you further."

"I understand the delicacy here," said Huxley, "but do you understand the risk? Let me be plain: We think you may be the target of a very dangerous group of terrorists who might be able to destroy much of this city—and I am referring to not only Vatican City but all of Rome. I cannot say more about the specific nature of the risk, but you might hazard a guess. We believe that former Cardinal Armondo Fine may be mixed up with these terrorists in some way. He may even be helping them. Unfortunately, he may represent our only real chance of finding the terrorists at this point. If necessary, the President will contact His Holiness, and we both know you will be briefing me after that call. The question is, do you really want to require that we go above both of our heads, or should we just cut to the chase now and avoid wasting critical time?"

Colonel Zaugg sat back in his chair and clasped his hands together beneath his chin. For a good twenty seconds, he just stared Huxley in the eye.

Huxley stared back. He had made an impression, but now he had to soften the blow. "I have brought with me a document from my government assuring the Vatican of the confidentiality of the information you share with me here today." He pulled the agreement out of his pocket and handed it to Zaugg. "I assure you personally that what you say will not hit the presses. Even if we arrest the man, we will never bring up information about this particular past in public. Access to the information will be limited even within Homeland and the CIA. Please, do the right thing here."

Zaugg studied the document carefully and consulted with a Vatican legal expert in an adjoining room. Returning to Huxley, he said, "All right, I will dispense with any additional formalities, but let me make myself clear: if you do not satisfy your commitments, there will be serious repercussions. While we may not have many soldiers, Mr. Huxley, the Vatican does have a somewhat unique ability to persuade its followers of the folly of their secular leaders and institutions. Though the pope only rarely chooses to exercise this power, do not forget that it exists."

"Understood. Now tell me, why was Fine drummed out of the Vatican?"

"The better question might be why was he ever made a cardinal, or a bishop, or even a priest, for that matter."

"I take it you are not terribly fond of him."

"Have you found anybody who is?"

Huxley smiled wryly. "I know members of his former diocese still call him a snake."

"How deserving a moniker."

"So why did the snake rise so quickly through the church bureaucracy?"

"I wish I knew," Zaugg said. "He became a cardinal before the new pope was elected. Nobody ever asked the former pope why, so I guess we'll never know. Some believe they just found themselves on the conservative wing of the church and shared a common cause. *Senza senso!* There are many conservative bishops in the clergy and this man could just as easily have been overlooked. No, knowing the Snake, as you call him, I personally believe he found some way to apply some sort of leverage that the former pope found irresistible. But I have no real hard evidence of that. His Holiness never raised any issue of improper influence with me."

"So what happened once he was at the Vatican?"

"He caused no trouble until the new pope was elected. Fine had worked to oppose his election and had even put feelers out for his own nomination. However, the other cardinals had no serious stomach for him as a leader. His actions before the election were not unusual. We try to keep the politics out of the press, but these are powerful men with strong beliefs."

"What happened after the election?"

"He went off the deep end politically. Never accepted the election of the new pope."

"Never accepted the election?" asked Huxley.

"Well, it turned out that he continued working behind the scenes to find a way to force the new pope to resign."

"How?"

"There are a substantial number of cardinals in the Curia at the Vatican who remain staunchly conservative. Many were appointed by the former pope, so what would you expect? They were stunned by the election of the new pope. Not only was he much more liberal than the former pope, but also he was the first pope to be elected from the Western Hemisphere. Well, apparently Cardinal Fine used this collective shock to form a secret cabal among several of the sitting cardinals. The cabal had little real power because the pope calls the shots here, but they used their connections within the administrative arms of the church to undermine the wishes of the pope for a time. They had become quite adept at that."

"So the pope struck back?"

Colonel Zaugg shook his head. "Such actions alone would not have caused His Holiness to take such drastic measures against Fine. The pope is a very patient man, and no doubt he would have found ways to slowly change the makeup of the Curia and diminish the strength of the conservative cabal. This is not the first time in history that has happened."

"So then why the dismissal?"

Zaugg smiled. "Fine acted like the snake he is."

"How's that?"

"We discovered that Fine had hired private investigators to dig up dirt on the pope from his earlier days as a priest. He hoped to use that dirt to blackmail the pope into resigning."

Huxley nodded. "I'm guessing he failed."

"Correct. His Holiness has led a holy life. He will admit he is not perfect, but nothing in his past could rise to the level of blackmail."

"So the pope was upset with this underhandedness and decided to cut off the Snake's tail?"

"No. He confronted Fine privately with the evidence we had supplied. Fine confessed and begged for the pope's forgiveness, which the pope immediately granted him on behalf of himself and God. Fine then promised he would cease any further attempts to undermine the papacy. His Holiness thought the matter at end until we discovered that Fine had begun meeting with some pretty scary people outside of the country. Since he couldn't find any real dirt, Fine had been working to manufacture an embarrassing story."

"What was that?"

Colonel Zaugg sat back and shook his head. "I do not think it worthy of repeating, even here."

"It may be important, especially if the same terrorists were involved."

"Let us just say they had tried to bribe a few of the pope's former servers."

"Altar boys?" Huxley asked.

Zaugg nodded slowly. "They are grown men now. This group had tried to convince these men to invent allegations about inappropriate conduct. You can probably figure out the rest since the papers are full of such stories about priests around the world."

"How do you know they were invented?"

Colonel Zaugg gave a pained expression and shook his head slightly. "Thank God, one of the former altar servers refused the bribe and contacted us. Before this all blew up, we put an end to the matter with the others. Then His Holiness had no choice but to unceremoniously laicize the Snake. We set his options out clearly for him: if he called off his dogs, we would not press criminal charges. However, if even one allegation were made against the pope, he would serve many years in prison. He selected the route of least resistance."

"Now I get why you don't want this to hit the press. Why didn't you just demote him and stick him in a monastery somewhere where he could do little damage and the matter would not become public?"

"His actions were just too extreme," Zaugg said. "Besides, the pope had taken that step after Fine's first blackmail attempt, and it obviously didn't have the effect he had anticipated. No, I think this was appropriate. If we had just left him on an outpost and he ultimately made some other allegations, how would His Holiness defend himself in the press when he had not punished the man severely for this travesty?"

"I see," said Huxley.

"Do you?" Zaugg leaned forward. "Could you imagine what such lies would do to undermine the pope's ability to address this scourge that has harmed so many innocents and has marred the church's reputation for the past several decades? It would set us back another thirty years. Many expect the pope to wave his hand and immediately end the misery that has infected the church for so long now, but there are few simple truths or solutions, and his power to bring change through the huge bureaucracy and rigid power structures of the church is much more limited than the outside world understands. The conservative cardinals and bishops have seen that as an opportunity to drive a wedge between the pope and the flock."

"I get that it is complicated. But if they moved against the pope for a false allegation, couldn't the Vatican demonstrate the witnesses were bribed into committing perjury."

Zaugg shook his head. "Unfortunately, such recourse often proves difficult. When an allegation is made, the public assumes the worst. Do you really think that would matter if we proved his innocence after the fact? The immediate glaring headlines would swallow the truth whole. The facts would emerge out the crap hole only after it was too late. Look, you are an experienced investigator, so you know that people like to believe what their preconceived notions tell them. The actual evidence often seems irrelevant."

Huxley nodded. "Your Vatican secrets are safe with me. But they may prove quite helpful because they give me an insight into the Snake's mind. Thank you so much for your assistance."

"You are welcome, Mr. Huxley."

"Can you give me any leads on his scary friends?"

"Not much, except they had close ties to some of the terrorists you have held in Cuba for a few years."

Huxley nodded. "Guantanamo?"

"Yes. There was reference to Abu Dakar."

"He died."

"Yes. Also, someone named Baqir Najwa."

Huxley's head jerked up. "He has also died, though I find that interesting. Any details you can add?"

"Not really. We never located him after the U.S. released him. His was just a name that came up in the investigation. Our security budget is a bit smaller than yours."

"I understand. Any connections to anyone who is still alive?"

Zaugg shook his head. "Sorry."

"Any idea where we can find Fine?"

"If I had known that, the Carabinieri would already have arrested him. We had an understanding with Italian Immigration that we would be notified if Fine ever tried to re-enter Italy, but someone over there screwed up or was paid off. We only learned he was back when the Carabinieri informed us a few weeks later. We've turned over every bit of personal contact info we had on Fine, but we understand they are still looking for him."

Huxley nodded.

"I'm sorry," Zaugg said. "If you find him, will you let me know so we can keep tabs on him? Based on the dire picture you have painted, I must also worry about some kind of attempt on the pope or other members of the Curia."

"Sure. I'm wondering, though, how does someone just disappear in Italy?"

"You joking? It happens all the time."

CHAPTER 73

AFTER LEAVING JOCHI, Tomadus found the communication pod and called a special number in Roma. "I hope I am not disturbing you. I am at a public pod in Parisius, though nobody is within sight at the moment."

"Parisius?" said First Consul Khansensius. "Then you are with Isa again?"

"Yes, he has returned to the continent from Tetepe—safely I might add."

"I understand. That is quite…fortunate. Does he plan to return?"

"I don't know, but I would think so, eventually." Tomadus paused. "They need him there."

"I thought you said we need him here, in the Three Empires."

"I think he may be able to bring the world together."

"So you have restored your faith in him?"

"I wouldn't quite call it that."

"But he has faith in you?"

"Perhaps. There is a rumor that some authority will soon arrest Isa and may bring harm to him. It might help my credibility with the Way if I could ferret that out. Have you heard anything?"

"No, I have heard nothing of the sort. However, if he returns to New Jutland too soon, who knows? As I have shared with you openly, we need to find a way to change the religious leaders into supporters of his. If the

Grand Imams turn too strongly against him, well if even the Jewish Abh Beyth Diyn makes a fuss, the situation could become, shall we say, delicate? He needs to prove his bona fides. Have you given that any more thought?"

"A bit, but I haven't yet had a chance to talk to him about it."

"What do you plan?"

"I'm thinking about a worldwide broadcast on the visi-scan."

"By Isa?"

"Yes, if the leaders can see him speak themselves, if all the people can see him speak…"

"I don't know. I doubt you could convince the broadcasters to cover his speech. It is expensive and closely-controlled, you know."

"I might be able to pay for it. Perhaps you could help with some of the approvals?"

"I don't know. I've already stuck my neck out for you with Yohanan."

"Yes, you tried. Thank you again for that. But this could mean even more. You've seen the impact he has. He might succeed. The peace could be lasting."

After pausing a few seconds, the First Consul said, "I shall take it under advisement, Tomadus. Just realize that if the religious leaders oppose Isa, my hands may be tied. Surely you have studied the Wars of the Three Empires, have you not? The emperors have, I assure you. Differences in their beliefs caused death and destruction for nearly two hundred years and weakened all of the empires. That is why Roma has some small power today—to keep these empires from squabbling over their little differences so that we can preserve our proper place in the world and maintain the balance. The balance is everything, Tomadus. So do not count on me openly taking sides in any religious fight—even if your friend Isa is one of its participants."

∇　　∇　　∇

While he slowly approached the quay, Tomadus thought about that other world and the fate of Jesus—the man of God whose martyrdom served as a foundation for a religion known as Christianity. Was that where Isa was headed? Emperor Acamapichtli, Yohanan and now Simeon had seemed to worry about that possibility. Tomadus would not let it happen again. He had promised to protect Isa, and he kept his promises. The broadcast might just do that. Even if the religious leaders were still against him, the broadcast would make it that much harder to take action. The resulting popularity for Isa would certainly hinder Skjöldr from moving against Isa in Tetepe.

A few last rays of the day's sun shimmered on the Sequana River in Parisius as Tomadus stepped off the garden path and onto a street heading toward the town center. In front of Tomadus ran a small black and white dog, its articulated ribs testifying to the depths of its hunger. Tomadus tilted his head in contemplation as a strange tingle went down his spine. The dog was so familiar, but his family had never owned one. When he closed his eyes and thought of Huxley, a few flashes of a similar dog drew across his memory. Huxley had only been a child then. Tomadus opened his eyes and smiled, feeling in his pocket for the heel of bread he had left over from his noon repast. "Come here boy," said Tomadus, but the dog just looked back at him and continued sniffing the ground and moving forward.

Tomadus followed the dog around a building to his right, through a narrow alleyway, behind a garbage container and through a small pedestrian passage, where the dog stopped and stared at him with a strange look of hunger, almost a look of longing. Tomadus broke off a scrap of bread and kneeled down to convince the dog he meant no harm. The dog approached and took the first chunk of bread in one gulp. His tail began wagging, and he lifted his paws to Tomadus's knee. "You little beggar," Tomadus said tenderly. He handed him another piece of the bread and the dog quickly swallowed it down and came back for more, this time licking Tomadus's face, which Tomadus shook as he smiled and held out another piece. "Here you go, fella."

As he handed the dog another piece of bread, Tomadus noticed the light from the door across the way begin to wash through the courtyard. A few seconds later, Adin appeared through the doorway, followed quickly by Isa. They were speaking in hushed tones as they walked, with Adin telling Isa he did not understand.

"This is for the resurrection, Adin," Isa seemed to repeat as he held out an open hand toward Adin. Tomadus could see a small item in Isa's hand, but could not discern its nature in the twilight. "You must take it," said Isa. "Trust me. It will be fine."

Adin replied, "But I don't want to if it means—"

"You must put that out of your mind," Isa said. "You must do this for me. This will be a sign to all."

The dog jumped up against Tomadus's chest and licked his face, forcing him to fall backward, causing him to lose a few seconds of the conversation. He picked the dog off of him and petted it as he scrambled to his knees to catch a few more words. All he could hear was a snippet at the end of a sentence from Isa: "…come back to the living."

Adin stopped, nodded slowly with a pained look, and looked down as he took the small item. Isa smiled and touched Adin's shoulder, and the two turned and walked away.

Tomadus remained kneeling in the alley a long time, petting the dog and trying to parse through what he had just seen without success. When the dog barked and jumped on him, Tomadus smiled and fed the little rascal his last scrap of bread. "I'm sorry boy, but that's all I have." The dog licked his face and trotted away. "Left again to myself," Tomadus said aloud. "I, too, must return to the living."

CHAPTER 74

HER DARK ROSE lips parted and reunited with a gentle grace while words flowed through them with perfect elegance. The lips and words fashioned their own couplet full of beauty and style, sending tremors of longing though Huxley's heart. But could he accept her words as oracles of truth? Like the oracles of the ancient world, perhaps they were nothing more than carefully crafted illusions leading him to a pre-ordained, horrific end. That he could not be certain terrified him. Her recent inability to identify Cardinal Fine as Tocelli's Florentine snake had only raised his suspicions. But her contributions to his case had bothered him even more—a trail of careful breadcrumbs left cleverly along his path, always helping him find the way just when he thought he was lost.

"Chris?" Sonatina asked.

"I'm sorry, I must have zoned out for a second. You were saying?"

"I asked you if you had found Armondo Fine."

"No," Huxley said. "We haven't. Why?"

"Why? You came all the way to Italy to find the man, didn't you?"

"Is that what you think? No, I just needed an excuse to have dinner in Rome with a most enchanting woman." He flashed a huge, over-the-top smile, playing the love-struck schoolboy.

Sonatina lowered her jaw, tilted her head to the side and raised her eyebrows above nearly pouting eyes. The entire look screamed incredulity. "I'm supposed to believe this puffery from a man whose every move suggests he does not trust me?"

He would never live that down. "Sonatina, you know I trust you. There are limits to the sharing of state secrets, you know. They could throw me in a dark cell with really bad dudes."

She mouthed silently, "I know." She grinned. "I do love to tease you, you ugly American spy." They shared a laugh.

But the truth still hung in the air, a heavy cloud of cynicism, though they both pretended not to notice. He needed her to trust him, to believe he trusted her. It was the only way this would work. *Bring her back. But how? The dream.* "It would be nice if this ugly American spy could get some sleep."

"Oh, are you tired of me already?"

"No, its just…I keep dreaming crazy dreams and waking up in the middle of the night."

"Crazy?"

"Crazy in that it keeps repeating, yet it has nothing to do with me, not really."

"How so?"

"Well, I see Scooter, my old black and white border collie in the dream, at least at the end. I haven't dreamed about him since he died."

"Was that recent?"

"No, ancient history. His heart gave out a few months after I started college. That might be why I keep having the dream—I loved that old dog." He smiled.

"What is strange about the dog?"

"The dog? No, he's not that strange. He doesn't come in until later. I'm in some part of the world where we all wear robes. There is one man in white robes, and we are talking about parallel worlds and strange things like that."

"Parallel worlds?"

"Yep. I don't quite remember the conversation, but I remember the man in white quizzing this huge, gentle man, asking him about how his father treated him when he did something wrong. The large man agreed that the father corrected him even though he forgave him. Then he looked at all of us and asked us if his Father in Heaven would also find such a way to teach his children, to help their souls find a way. It was all kind of mixed up. You know how dreams are. But this one…" He stopped when he saw her puzzled reaction. She had tilted her head, narrowed her eyes and begun to twirl the hair by her ear. "Something wrong?" he asked.

She shook her head. "No, I…I don't think so. Have you told me about this dream before?"

"No."

"Funny, I could swear I remember it vividly. Deja vu, I guess." She shrugged. "Who knows, maybe God is talking to you, and you are too bull-headed to listen. Where is he helping your soul to go—Heaven? Are you looking for Heaven, Chris?"

"Right." He snorted and shook his head. "I haven't searched for that in a while. Maybe that's where all these clues lead—a stairway to Heaven?"

"Do not tease about Heaven, Chris. You still hang onto that crucifix?"

He tried to hold back his smirk. "You know that is just to remind me of my mother. But you might be right. Maybe the guilt is pulling me down again. The guilt is telling my soul it needs help."

"Maybe it does."

Huxley bit his lip, holding back the rising heat. *Trying to convert him back again.* She had always seemed so rational, but then religion… Damn, he hated that. *Just change the subject, Hux.* "Anyway, I'm still trying to find Fine. Any ideas where to find the cardinal?" Huxley said quickly.

"Why would I know? I barely knew him when he was a cardinal. He probably wouldn't even remember me—except maybe from his time in Florence, although I was pretty young back then."

"I'm just gasping for a breath of air here and hoping that maybe you would find it in your heart to rescue me."

"Well, maybe later, after dinner." She smiled coyly.

He had to use every bit of self-restraint not to whisk her out of the restaurant. Giving into temptation could not work. Not yet, not for him. He still could not figure her out, and that scared him, but he had to play this thing out anyway. "We must find Fine soon. He might be a key player in this. We have to figure out a way to flush him out."

"I doubt you will have much luck. He knows you're looking, so he'll stay close to his hiding spot, no? You might need to force a break. Have you thought about using the press?"

"We have, but how do we explain the importance of finding him without unduly alarming the populace?"

"Unduly? From your tone, they should be very alarmed."

"At this point, we can only speculate. We don't even know where the event will occur, just that there is a possibility. Mass hysteria generally leads to mass chaos and often death. Do you know how many times a year we stop terrorist plans before they occur and the population never hears about them? Now that would really scare you."

She put her fingertips to her lips. "Why don't you create a little story to explain the situation? Maybe inform the press that he has Alzheimer's disease, has disappeared and the authorities fear he may be in trouble?"

"Not a bad idea, but that might not sit well with the Vatican. I doubt they want him to be portrayed as a sympathetic character. And if we do catch him, then what? We have arrested and are now questioning an Alzheimer's patient? The press would have fun with that one. Nah, we might just have to say he is suspected of links to terrorists and leave it at that. If we are wrong, he sues us, but I think the reward is worth that minor risk."

"I wonder if he will try to leave the country before you catch him."

"If he does and has Pardus's help," Huxley said, "we'll never see him again."

"Why?"

"Because Pardus never leaves anyone alive for long once they can identify him and have any risk of capture. Maybe the cardinal doesn't know Pardus directly. If so, that might save him. But otherwise, Pardus knows we have a few methods, employed only at times of desperation, that might squeeze out something we can use." As he said this, Huxley watched her eyes to see if a little truth might appear, but she was a stone to him. *It might still work. If she's playing for the other side, this little warning might just flush him out.*

She sighed heavily. "You sound perfectly awful. That is not you."

"Well, I wouldn't engage in those practices myself anymore, but I don't have to tell you what others might do, especially with what is at stake."

"The man is a snake, but I doubt he deserves that. Unless you are right about his plans, of course."

"Of course, but isn't that the conundrum?"

She frowned. "Any other developments you can trust me with?"

"Did I send you the latest verse?"

"The latest?"

"Yep, it appears we have an aspiring Shakespeare in our midst." Huxley brought out his phone with the latest deciphered poem and read it to her:

> Within, my principles do comfort me.
> Forget them not or you shall miss my plea.
> Beyond my fortress on my left you see
> What shall befall the many unlike he,
> A priest who never lived before just me.

> On truth lies yet obscured thy fathers' end.
> To myths our hearts do reach and then depend.
> We seek our consolation with a friend.
> Remember now the Maine and then ascend.
> To know his fate you must to hell descend.

Sonatina's face gave nothing away. "It seems like nonsense. Do you have more context?"

"Well, assume you are reading this at the Thomas Jefferson Memorial in Washington, DC."

"I've never been there, so I probably can't help you. Looks like you need to look to Jefferson's left."

"You never miss." Huxley smiled. "Yep, just over the bridge lies Arlington National Cemetery."

"A cemetery? So death, then," she said slowly, "death will befall the many unlike he."

"Sure seems like it," Huxley said.

"But who is the 'priest who never lived before' Jefferson? That could be just about any clergyman who lived after Jefferson was born."

"I agree, and what good would it do anyway to find a priest? I don't know, but I wonder if we are both missing something."

"Let me think about it," Sonatina said. "But I must admit I am not well versed in American history or the life of Thomas Jefferson."

"What do you think of the second stanza?"

She read it again. "Did your father die mysteriously?"

Huxley nodded slowly. "When I was young."

"I think whoever wrote these things loves to toy with your emotions. Have you considered that this poet knows you pretty well?"

"I have no doubt as to that."

"But why would he telegraph that so—just to get you off your game?" Sonatina asked.

"When I can answer that question," said Huxley, "maybe the fog will finally lift."

"Then let us hope the fog clears before you hear a bang from beyond the mist."

❧ ❧ ❧

Huxley was sitting in an enormous Gothic cathedral supported by high pointed arches and adorned with beautiful stained glass windows casting a rainbow of color on intricately carved wooden pews. Twenty feet in front of the pews on a raised dais, a plump, baldheaded Asian man sat quietly in the lotus position, smiling contentedly at the spectacle before him. There an Arab man in white robes and a white turban waved his arms in perfect 4/4 time. He held a short baton in his right hand and appeared to be directing a choir of eleven angels hovering about twenty feet in the air, their wings flapping to the beat as they sang out gloriously: "Meet me at Mary's Place, we're gonna have a party." To their side stood a man wearing dark robes and a tiny cap just covering the back of his scalp, bouncing and singing, "Turn it up, turn it up, turn it up, turn it up!" On the altar stood a golden candelabrum with seven flickering candles. Nearby, a silver-haired man in a tall, pointed hat and a red robe displaying a large, golden monogram of overlaid Greek letters, chi and rho, danced with his arms in the air waving above him. The angels began singing, "Tell me how do we get this thing started?"

just as Huxley's eyes opened. The hotel room was pitch black, except for his phone on the nightstand lighting up as it played his familiar ring tone.

"Hi boss," said Kira Sampson cheerfully, "I hope I'm not calling too late for you."

"It's 2 a.m."

"Yeah, well, its early evening here. Doesn't this time difference suck, especially when you're on the wrong side of it? I think it is time for you to wake up anyway, Mr. Huxley."

"I will get you back for this, Ms. Sampson."

"You mean you will thank me for it. I have some news and thought you might want to start making some preparations."

"Okay, I'm game. Whaddya have?"

"I found your little friend Anwari."

He sighed. "Dead?"

"No. Why would you think that? He's alive and well in American custody in Afghanistan."

"You had him detained? I told you—"

"No, I didn't have him detained. Ken Mayer took care of that for you a couple of days ago. Anwari is sitting in a CIA cell at Camp Chapman near Khost. Mayer didn't bother to tell you that?"

"No. No, he didn't, and I just spoke to him yesterday."

"Well, I only found out because a friend who has been helping us in Kabul gave me the scoop. He said everything was hush-hush, but he knew I was looking for the guy."

"Any idea why?" Huxley asked.

"He is suspected of terrorism. That was all I could get. Oh, and you would think Mayer might be heading there himself, but my guy said Mayer had no interest in seeing Anwari face to face. In fact, he didn't want anyone interrogating him for quite a while. Mentioned something about softening him up first."

"Thanks, Kira, you've done it again. Have you told anyone about this?"

"No, and I agreed with my friend not to mention this to Mayer or anyone who might let it blow back on him, so I doubt Mayer knows you know. You guys really ought to have a talk, don't you think?"

He nodded. "When the time is right. For now, keep this to yourself. Anwari is a minor character in this investigation, remember?"

"Who's Anwari?"

He laughed. "Exactly. Oh, and by the way, I will still figure out a way to get you back for your kind little wake up call."

"Yeah, well, good luck. My cell's going on moonlight mode tonight."

He hung up the phone and sat staring in the darkness a few minutes. Mayer didn't know about Anwari from him. Why would he have the man arrested when Anwari's a frickin Afghan hero? And if Mayer suspects Anwari's involvement in this thing, why would Mayer wait to interrogate him with the world hanging in the balance? If Mayer had been keeping an eye on Anwari, why not ask Huxley about Anwari before blowing this up? Or was that his intention? Does Mayer want Anwari out of the game? *Could Mayer be the link to Pardus? Or worse?*

CHAPTER 75

HUXLEY GLANCED AGAIN at his watch, wondering when they would finally begin boarding. It was a colossal waste of time, but travelling to Camp Chapman by military transport from Aviano would have tipped off Mayer way too early. No, he had to fly commercial from Rome through Dubai to Kabul and then drive to Chapman, but that itinerary meant he had to wait most of the day for a flight out of Leonardo da Vinci Airport. At least it gave him more time to study the latest poem from his tormentor:

> Within, my principles do comfort me.
> Forget them not or you shall miss my plea.
> Beyond my fortress on my left you see
> What shall befall the many unlike he,
> A priest who never lived before just me.
>
> On truth lies yet obscured thy fathers' end.
> To myths our hearts do reach and then depend.
> We seek our consolation with a friend.
> Remember now the Maine and then ascend.
> To know his fate you must to hell descend.

The first two lines opened the verse with an admonition: do not forget the principles or risk missing his plea. The principles must be the Jeffersonian inscriptions, but whose plea—that of Jefferson, the poet or some other unknown person?

The next three lines clearly referred to the death of many, but who the hell was the priest? Did he live after Jefferson or just after the poet or other person? If Huxley found the poet, would he have found Pardus? Or was the poet just trying to help him? No, the writer must be Pardus. But he needed Anwari to confirm that.

The second stanza was all about his father's suicide. The "myth" must refer to the crazy story of his father's "accidental death." After all, his mother's heart and his own had wanted to reach out to that conclusion, and both had depended on it: a finding of suicide would have cancelled the life insurance death benefit that helped his mother keep them just above the poverty level for years. Still, he could not recall any friend of his mother with whom they sought their consolation at the time of his father's death. Certainly no friends of his had demonstrated any particular willingness to console him.

Why now remember the Maine? This appeared to be the famous call to arms from the beginning of the Spanish-American War in 1898. The Spanish had allegedly blown up the armored cruiser USS Maine in a Cuban port, killing over 260 U.S. sailors. Huxley had seen many of their graves in Key West. What would that tragedy have to do with his own father's death? Maybe it was just a reference back to the many myths we often grasp during our worst tragedies. Before the explosion was even investigated, the yellow journalists of the day managed to blame Spain and push America further towards war, thereby creating a convenient cover for one of America's first weak forays into imperialism. Imperialism—was the poet using the Maine to chastise America as an imperialist? That was the slur Latin American revolutionaries commonly employed against the U.S. in the twentieth century. But in this context, that label seemed quite a reach.

The last line of the poem spoke with the greatest clarity. To truly understand his father's death, Huxley must himself die and descend to hell. A personal threat? A call to suicide? *Does he think I am as unstable as my father before me?*

Huxley's phone began singing. He looked at the screen and answered it quickly. "Hello Sonatina, do you miss me already?"

Her hushed and hurried tone told him she was not looking for another date just yet. "Of course, but listen, this is important."

"Yes?"

"I found him."

"Who?"

"Armondo Fine," she whispered.

"How?"

"No time for that now. Look, I'm following him. Can you come pick him up?"

"I'm at the airport. I'll call the Carabinieri. Where are you?"

"Near Vittorio Emanuelle II."

"Who?" he asked.

"The King who unified Italy," Sonatina said. "There is no time for a history lesson. It is near the Forum. Near Capitoline Hill. Chris, he's on foot and he's still on the move. I'll try to keep following him."

"Sonatina, get out of there. You could be killed. I'll call the Carabinieri. They'll find him."

"No, he'll be gone by then. I'll let you know when he goes into a building or stops walking."

"No—"

"Have to go. *Ciao*." She hung up. He called her back, but she didn't answer. He began racing toward the airport entrance while trying to call Lieutenant Patismio. The Carabinieri said they could have someone to the site within a few minutes.

As he hailed a cab, he received a text from Sonatina: "No worry. Cant talk, but K. 4got to say - poem - lots of fathers - not all yours - priest is a father - same 4 cardinal - that help?"

She's texting this while following the guy? He moved his fingers over the phone as fast as he could and sent: "Get away. Cops coming. Don't want u hurt."

Not a half minute later, he was in the cab and received another text: "Aw ur sweet—guess u do luv me."

He texted back: "Of course. U?" *What the hell are we doing?* She was in mortal danger and they were expressing love for each other for the first time in blubbering text messages? But somehow he couldn't help it.

The response came ten seconds later: "*Certo!*" Another message arrived a minute later: "AF w/Arab man near statue at Piazza del Campidoglio. Gave him package."

Huxley shouted an obscenity, then typed: "Get out of there!" He called Lieutenant Patismio with an update on the location. Huxley shouted in Italian to the cab driver, "How close are we to Piazza del Campidoglio?"

"This traffic—probably forty minutes" the driver responded.

Huxley typed: "Where u now?"

No response.

He typed in: "U OK?"

No response.

He tried: "Sonatina?"

Nothing again. He sent: "U there?"

After about a minute, a new text arrived: "She be OK after wake at hospital - head might hurt."

Huxley's heart dropped. He called her cell. Nobody answered. He texted back: "Who r u?"

A minute later a text came back: "Never mess with the leopard, my friend. He pounce on you before you even see his spots."

❃ ❃ ❃

When Huxley rushed into the hospital room, Lieutenant Patismio was standing with his pad and pen out at Sonatina's bedside. When she saw him, she flashed that big Italian smile and said, "A little late for the American cavalry, no?"

Huxley assumed his best stern look. "Did I tell you it was dangerous? Pretty ballsy for a Vatican administrator."

"Now I am just an administrator with testicles?" she said, deliberately overplaying a pout.

"You're damn lucky you're not a dead administrator," he said.

Huxley held her hand gently, and her soft eyes told him everything. Although Patismio took a step back, Huxley could still feel the lieutenant watching them stare at each other for a few seconds. An hour ago, they had shared a high stress, contextual, textual moment. Was it real, or just the stress? What should he do now? Hug her? Kiss her? She had certainly proven herself more than worthy of his love by getting knocked on the head for him. So why was he holding back? He looked at Patismio and said, "I'm sorry, Lieutenant. I didn't mean to interrupt your interview, but would you mind if I asked her a few questions myself?"

Patismio flashed a sly smile and twirled the corner of his mustache. "Not at all. We were just wrapping up." Patismio turned to Sonatina and bowed slightly. "*Grazie, Signorina D'Amare.*" After she smiled broadly, the lieutenant turned toward Huxley. "Thanks to Ms. D'Amare, we have apprehended Armondo Fine. My government has already instructed me to allow you to interrogate him yourself."

Huxley's eyebrows rose. "*Grazie*, Lieutenant. Did you arrest the Arab?"

"Arab?"

"Shit." In the excitement Huxley had forgotten to tell Patismio about the Arab. That was just plain incompetent. Stop letting your emotions control you, Hux. "Wasn't Fine with anyone?"

"No. Do you suspect another?"

"I don't know. I'm sure he is gone now. *Mea culpa.* I'll be there shortly and we can go over it."

After Patismio left the room, Sonatina looked at Huxley coyly. "You want to question me? What about—Armondo Fine or your undying love for me?"

"You remember that text, huh?"

"Even a crack on the head won't wipe that one out."

"Is that what happened—you were hit on the head?"

"What else?" Sonatina asked. "Someone grabbed me from behind, I struggled and everything went black. I awoke with a headache. Patismio said it was probably one of Fine's men, though my phone was stolen, so there is always the petty thief."

"I doubt that."

"Why?"

"Know any thieves called 'The Leopard?'" Huxley asked.

"Eh?"

"He texted me after you were unconscious. I'm not sure why he didn't kill you."

She shook her head slowly. "Never saw him."

"Still, you are a loose end. How'd you find Fine?"

Sonatina perked up. "Just luck. I went on my usual run by the Colosseum and down *Via dei Fori Imperiali* next to the ancient Forum. I saw an older man with a hoodie covering his head walking suspiciously down the sidewalk toward *Piazza Venezia*. He kept checking behind him like he thought he was being tailed. Seemed strange. I thought of Fine hiding and I took a chance and followed him. He pretended to take in a view of the Vittorio Emanuelle II statue and I stopped to watch him. When he turned around a few minutes later, I recognized him and called you."

Huxley nodded a few times with his lips tight. What was the probability that his girlfriend, who seemed to be caught up in this terrorist plot in some way, would be the one person to spot the cardinal—and all by chance? "You have any reason to suspect he would be there?"

"No, why do you ask?"

"Oh, just trying to figure out how lucky I am." *Or whether I should keep my guard up—way up. She's still alive, but why?* "Hey, I'm worried about you. Pardus doesn't leave loose ends, and you have seen too much." Huxley stopped and sent a message to Patismio requesting a security detail for Sonatina's hospital room. He looked back up. "You mentioned a package Fine gave to the Arab he met. What was it?"

"*Non lo so*," she said. "It was small, not bigger than a pack of cigarettes. I could not see it very well."

What about the Arab man—you ID him?"

"No, I tried to give the nice lieutenant a description—told him the Arab had a bloated face—but he said it would be best if I could look at some pictures tomorrow after I am discharged. I feel ok except for the headache, but they want to keep me under observation."

"Makes sense," Huxley said. "Been there. You feel a bit fuzzy?"

"Not a bit. He must not have hit me that hard."

"He? Did you see your assailant?"

"No, no. I just assumed…"

"Uh huh," he replied blandly. There was that strange tingle that would not leave the back of his neck. Something doesn't add up. *What are you holding back, Sonatina? You go unconscious from a blow to the head and you feel fine?*

It was only later, after an awkward silence or two and an equally awkward farewell kiss, that the attending physician told him she had suffered no symptoms of a concussion whatsoever, though she had presented with a small bump on her head. It seemed almost a minor miracle, but then Sonatina had always seemed quite capable of producing those.

CHAPTER 76

JOCHI SAT ON the bench in the flower garden, staring at ripples of water flowing down the Sequana. It had been her habit in Parisius to come here alone after Isa finished speaking to the crowds. Tomadus watched Jochi's gaze and saw her twirl the waves of hair by her ear over and over again. She must be deep in thought. *How do I know that?* A tingle swept down his spine. *Sonatina. Could she and Jochi be the one and the same?* Ever since he had met Jochi at Yohanan's shack, he had felt the strange sense of déjà vu. But Jochi said she had seen no visions. Perhaps there were those who somehow appeared in both worlds but never knew of their other selves. Hell, very few had even had visions of the other world. Sometimes it all felt like nonsense, like the other world existed only in his own mind. *Do I dream of Sonatina because my psyche wants Jochi to love me? But then why does my alter ego harbor his suspicions? Do I distrust my love of Jochi as well?* Tomadus shook his head. Peregrine's story had proven this world existed outside of his own mind. Of course, Peregrine still did not see the visions clearly, but with time? *Maybe Jochi will see it someday. Maybe then she will understand.*

Tomadus took a few steps forward and whistled a song so that she would not be startled by his approach. She seemed not to notice until he came around her left flank and appeared before the bench. When he nodded and smiled, she looked up and smiled back. When he motioned toward the bench, she nodded. "Hey, sorry about the other day," he said. "I can be such a clod sometimes. I didn't mean to make you think... These visions get to me sometimes."

She nodded with a slight smile.

"Great," he added. "I noticed you were in deep thought. Care to share?"

"It was nothing...and everything."

Tomadus's eyes narrowed. "Well that answer reveals a great deal."

"I am sorry, Tomadus." She looked down. "You have been so good to me. I wish I could return the favor right now."

Tomadus waved his hand in dismissal. "Hey, it was stupid. I don't know what I feel anymore. You have seemed to be avoiding me these past few days."

She looked at him, now studying his face, then dropped her chin to her chest and closed her eyes gently. "I have."

Tomadus nodded. "That's ok. I'd probably avoid me, too."

"No." She smiled sadly. "It isn't what you said the other day." She took a deep breath and sighed. "Whenever I see you, I remember that day in Jerusalem. You were so good to me, but the memory of Yoh—of Yohanan—on that...that thing, I...I can't...it still..." Tears fell down her cheeks.

"I am sorry, Jochi. I wish I could help."

"You are kind. Your friendship means a great deal. I wish I could return your...affection, but I can't right now." She closed her eyes and leaned her head on his shoulder. Tomadus saw another tear roll down her cheek.

"It's all right," he said softly, petting her hair. "I'm here as a friend."

She wiped her eyes and then laughed. "Thanks. It should be so easy. I've always had this unusual connection with you, and I must admit you are pretty gentle on the eyes."

He stiffened. That little spinal tingle again. He had heard that before. "Have I told you about Sonatina?"

"Sonatina? Is she the one from the other world, the one this Huxley..."

"Yes. How stupid of me. I shouldn't say anything, but you just used the exact words she had said to Huxley. I'm sure of it."

"I am not her, Tomadus. I'm just Jochi."

"I know. I know."

"Will you be going with us to the Aegyptian Province?" she asked.

"I think so."

"Good. Isa needs you. He really is amazing, isn't he?"

Tomadus nodded slowly. His heart began pounding. "Do you love him?"

"Of course, don't we all? But there is something more, something… special. It has me all confused and excited at the same time."

Tomadus bit his cheeks, his chin falling to his chest. "I see."

"There are times—don't take this wrong—there are times when I am with Isa and it is like there are rockets bursting and stars gleaming—all while my eyes are open."

Tomadus perked up. "Have you seen the Light?"

"You said that the other day. I…I don't know. I have not had any visions, just this burst of sunshine."

Tomadus's voice betrayed his excitement. "That could be it. I saw only glimpses of visions at first."

"Tomadus, stop hoping that I'll be Sonatina. I don't know her. This whole thing is just too strange, too personal. I don't think I saw any visions, not really. Let's not talk about it."

"Well, if it isn't the Light, then what would it be?"

Jochi looked up at Tomadus with a hopeful smile.

"Oh," he said. He kissed her gently on the forehead and stood up. "I'm heading back to camp. Care to join me?"

"Thanks, but I think I'll sit here a bit longer."

"As you wish," he said. "If you don't mind, let's talk again. Maybe we can help each other."

"I'd like that," Jochi said. "Thanks for listening, Tomadus." He smiled, nodded and walked away.

CHAPTER 77

"You speak with an air of authority that I have seen only among kings and emperors," said the distinguished looking man bowing gently toward Isa as the crowds dispersed on the Alexandrian shore. He was dressed luxuriously in gold and platinum-laced silken robes accented with various pieces of fine jewelry filled with precious gems.

Isa shaded his eyes from rays bouncing off of the *Mare Internum*, nodded briefly to the man, and said, "There is only one true authority."

"So you have said, although I have many masters," replied the man. "I am Aujani. Perhaps you have heard of me? Some say I am one of the wealthiest men in this empire."

Isa replied with a surprisingly sarcastic tone: "Interesting, but I am not familiar with either your name or your worldly wealth."

Though the visitor initially seemed upset by the insolence of this lowly preacher, he managed to swallow hard and force a thin smile in return. "I see," he said. "Well, sir, I have been following your movement for some time. Your words and your works amaze me. You have done wonders. Allah has blessed me with much wealth, and I wish to repay him. I would very much like to help you."

"All the help I need comes from the Father." He looked deeply into the man's eyes. "But I do have a suggestion for you if you truly wish to repay God."

"And what is that, teacher?"

"Sell everything you own and give it to the many poor who look only for a mouthful of bread each day. Then follow me, and your soul will find the freedom it needs to truly live."

The man looked down and shook his head. "What you ask is impossible! I cannot throw my riches away on those…people. I cannot follow this path you suggest. Isa, I offer you my financial help to promote your message. We could market you and your speeches. You could become rich. I would ask for only a small percentage. Allah would certainly be well pleased with that."

Isa replied quickly and sternly, "You understand nothing of His will. We seek only one treasure, Aujani, and you have now told me you are unwilling to pursue it. Return when you are prepared to open your heart."

After the man had walked away, Isa turned to his followers and noticed a few disappointed faces. "What would you have had me do," he asked them, "accept his assistance?"

Several of the Ten chimed in, saying such things as, "We could have taken his money and given it to the poor. Now he will just hoard it all the more," and "It would have been nice to eat well for a change," and "He could have helped us so much—why would you turn his help away?"

Now frowning, Isa shook his head. "My friends, where is your faith? Our father in Heaven will provide for us just as he provides for the birds of the sky. We do not need his money. This man wished to turn us into a commercial enterprise. He does not believe. He thinks he can buy his way to faith."

Many of the Ten shook their heads or looked down.

"I tell you now: worry not about the coin of the empire but about the coin of my Father's realm. What would happen if I left you all with a legacy of Earthly wealth? How long would you truly follow me? Would my words be written in your hearts or would they be abused for the sake of personal gain? Do not fool yourselves: you cannot truly follow my Father and me in your heart while yearning for gold. No, the coin your soul seeks cannot be minted by any government but only by your kindness, your charity, and your devotion to God."

The followers looked away silently. After a few seconds, Tomadus broke the silence. "Look, all of you, this man Aujani cannot be trusted. I know of him. He is an oil magnate, a facilitator in the Sunni Muslim Emperor who sells oil to parts of the world deemed unworthy of contact to believers of the Muslim Faith. I suspect he wanted Isa to accept his proposal so they could discredit you all for corruption. Beware my friends, for there may be other attempts at such subterfuge. Isa is becoming a target of those in power."

Simeon began a slow, mock applause, his hands slapping each other hard once every few seconds. "Good. Very good," he said slowly, nodding to Tomadus. "You speak a truth, but it hides your own lies. Like this Aujani character, you too are wealthy and connected, Tomadus. Should we suspect you of a subterfuge as well?"

Others joined in the fray, hurling insults at Tomadus about his wealth and powerful connections. Until that moment, he had never quite understood how much he remained an outsider to the Ten. Only Peregrine and Adin spoke in his defense.

Isa raised his hand to silence them all. "Listen to yourselves! You feed at the trough of hate and threaten to swallow one of your own brothers. Your hate blackens your souls, your jealousy closes your hearts, your anger dampens your reason. This man has done nothing but act as our friend. He must play his own role as all of you must, can you not see that?"

"But he is an infidel, without faith," shouted Atuf. "He can be no brother to us!"

Isa lowered his voice. "Atuf, you do not understand him, and if you hate him, you never will, and hatred leads to nothing but evil. What does it hurt you if someone does not believe as you do? Who are you to judge their beliefs? They will be judged on the last day. Do you think our Father in Heaven needs your help to make that judgment? No! Look to yourselves and damn the evil within you wherever you find it, but do not try to be God's judge on Earth."

"But you said money was evil, and he has money! Should we not try to destroy evil?" said one of the Ten.

"You have ears, but you cannot hear," responded Isa. "You have eyes, but you cannot see. You see only black and white, good and evil, friend and foe. Such simplistic views cheapen the beautiful intricacy and complexities of the world the Father has created. I tell you no tangible thing is either good or evil in itself. Anything susceptible to evil can also be good, and anything that can be good is also susceptible to evil. This applies to nearly every person as well. For even the kindest, gentlest creature can harbor a deep darkness in their hearts, and no person, no matter how evil, totally lacks even a kernel of goodness."

Simeon looked confused. "I do not understand this, master."

"Listen, all of you. During your lives, you have come to think of many things as purely evil. But objects are only evil when we make them so. Everything that can be used for evil purposes can also be a tool for the promotion of good. Do you doubt me? Take fire. Could we seriously live in our society without it? Yet the flames of war and shaitaanism have wreaked death and destruction on millions."

"But surely there are things that are always evil or always good."

"Are there? Name one, then."

"Money," Simeon responded glancing in Tomadus's direction. "It is the root of all evil."

"An oversimplification, perhaps, but yes, money has been at the crux of many an evil act in this world. However, it is greed that taints money, not money itself. When money is used to help feed the poor, is this not good? When money is used to bring our message to the people, is this not good?"

"All right, then. How about death? When is death ever good?"

Isa shook his head. "Death is not a tangible thing but an event. Nevertheless, you speak with some insight, Simeon, for true death is the most horrible fate awaiting anyone. However, if you have ears, you know what the Father promises—what I have promised you—and soon true death will no longer hold power over you."

"Then how about something good?" asked Anders. "How could the sun ever be used for evil?"

"You might as well ask how the Light of the World can be used for evil, but I assure you that He can and will by those who abuse His love. The sun's rays may easily be redirected and focused to kill. Recall when you were a boy and you or your brother used a small magnifying glass to kill an innocent ant for no purpose. Were you accomplishing good through this action? What worse could men armed with such weapons do to destroy their foes? And what of the secrets to its power to shine and heat our world? Could those, too, be used to for evil?"

Tomadus shuddered. The secrets of the sun. He knew that Huxley sought those who would unleash that power to kill millions. And what an evil that could be.

Isa continued, "And let us consider the opposite—darkness. We have always used darkness as a metaphor for evil because it is so much easier for evil to thrive in the absence of the light. But cannot the darkness sometimes hide a good person from harm? Has not darkness even sometimes brought an end to military battles?"

Diego asked, "But if there is no distinction between good and evil, then why do we bother?"

"Let me be clear," said Isa. "Good and evil both exist and are mutually exclusive in themselves. But many things are neither. And just because good and evil are opposed to one another, it does not follow that things or people or even philosophies and religions cannot be filled with or capable of both."

"Like your words?" Tomadus asked.

"My words?" asked Isa.

"You speak in parables and with vague pronouncements, and generally we think we understand you, but what if we do not? Or what if we are confused and you are not around to explain? Could not someone misinterpret even these words for evil purposes?"

A smile slowly appeared on Isa's face. "Of course, my words and those of the prophets before me."

"Then why do you not speak more clearly to us?" Tomadus asked. "Why do you use parables?"

Isa looked around at each of his closest followers. "I have explained many of my parables to you, my disciples. And so knowledge of the mysteries of the kingdom of God has been granted to you; but to the rest, they are made known only through parables so that I may fulfill the prophecy that 'they may look but not see, and hear but not understand.' But why, you ask, when this confusion could allow evil to flourish? Let me ask you this: even if I teach all with utter clarity, do you think my words will never be abused?"

"I do not know," answered Tomadus.

"I do," said Isa. "Evil will always find a way to accomplish its ends as long as there are men and women willing to accept it into their lives. I am sorry, Tomadus, but evil shall survive until the last day. I cannot change that. What I can do is tell you this: If each of you can remember only one thing I have taught you, then remember to love everyone including God, and do this with all of your heart, all of your mind, and all of your strength. And if you truly understand this, if you can lose your hatred for others—even for your enemies—and if you can comprehend that there is some good worth saving in nearly everyone, then perhaps a little good can prevail on this Earth awhile, even if only within your own soul." Isa nodded slowly, smiled gently, and walked away.

∇   ∇   ∇

In the early evening, Tomadus found Isa sitting on a bench near the *Mare Internum* seawall. As Tomadus approached, he studied the face of the man now staring blankly out to sea. Isa appeared tired and older than he remembered. The strain must be wearing on him. Tomadus sat beside him.

"I listened carefully to what you said today."

"Only today?"

Tomadus laughed nervously. "Your take on good and evil is…different. I noticed you said money could be 'good' if it helped bring your message to the people."

Isa nodded.

"I think I may have a way to use my money to do that," Tomadus said.

Isa raised both eyebrows.

"I think I could pay for the broadcast of one of your speeches on the worldwide visi-scan. Think how many more people you could reach."

"I thought the visi-scan was reserved for what they call news but most of us know as propaganda."

"That's true, but I think we could harness its power for our purposes. For a sizeable contribution and a little urging from the First Consul, I think we could arrange a broadcast."

"So you would bribe them?"

Tomadus shook his head. "I would simply offer an open contribution with nothing expressly guaranteed in return. The First Consul would urge them to support my wishes."

"And you do not call that a bribe?"

Tomadus shrugged. "What is in a name? There are no promises. What do you think?"

Isa stroked his beard. "You think the First Consul will help?"

"We have discussed it. We are both worried about what the religious leaders think of you. We need to change that."

"Tomadus, you know they have not shepherded their flocks."

"I know. I understand your criticism. But if you could turn them in your favor…"

"They have ears but do not hear. Have you listened?"

"I understand," said Tomadus, "but you are showing everyone a new way. Sometimes it takes time. Still, if you are to have a chance, the leaders must trust that you yourself believe in what you say."

"I speak every day in the Empires. They need only listen and observe."

"They cannot be seen at your events. But with a broadcast it will be easy for them to see you speak. Even if you do not move them, you will be much safer if we can get the entire world behind you. You don't think you're safe walking in Tetepe, do you? Skjöldr now fears you. He will act when you are there next. But he will be powerless to do so if you expand your support among the people in the Three Empires and around the world."

"Tomadus, you think of power as men do. Remember the lessons I taught Yohanan. Do not seek to change governments. Seek only to change the hearts of the people."

"And your broadcast could change the hearts of many, including these religious leaders."

Isa sighed and looked into Tomadus's eyes. "You put much faith in the First Consul."

"He has proven to be a friend."

"The government will distort my message. We would not control the broadcast. They might edit it."

"True, but we may be able to change that. I need to return to Roma for a few days. Where can I next rejoin you?"

"We are heading to Jerusalem." Isa looked at Tomadus with a slack expression. "If you wish to act, you must act quickly."

CHAPTER 78

ARMONDO FINE SAT alone, staring at the brick wall and fidgeting with his fingertips but otherwise remaining composed. Except for Fine, the interrogation room contained only a table, three chairs and a video camera visibly hanging in the corner.

"He seems pretty calm. Do you think it will work?" asked Lieutenant Patismio to Huxley while they viewed the cardinal through the two-way mirror.

Huxley replied, "You think his manner means anything?"

"You tell me. You are the expert."

"Unless we are dead wrong, it tells me he fully expected to get arrested. He's already prepared for this interrogation. Looks to me like he's going over the script in his head."

"You can tell all that from looking at him?"

"Nah, just guessing," Huxley said. "Let's see what he says."

The two men walked out of the observation room. Patismio waived his card by a reader.

Fine looked up and smiled at them as they entered. "Finally," he said. "You have obviously made a mistake here. I have done nothing wrong."

Patismio said, "That is what all the criminals say, Fine. I would have thought your education would at least allow you to dispense with the clichés." Fine scowled and shook his head at this latest form of disrespect.

Huxley used a kind tone, "I'm sorry, Cardinal. Please forgive my colleague's presumptions. Lieutenant, please do not prejudge this man. He is well known as a great supporter of true Catholics around the world. I know of him and his famed reputation for honesty and supporting the traditions of our great church. So please, I am sure he can help us clear up this matter so we can find the real culprits."

Fine smiled and nodded at Huxley, "*Grazie, signore.* May I know your name?"

"I'm sorry. It's Huxley. Christian Huxley." Good time to pull out his full first name and give it a little emphasis. "I work with American Homeland Security."

"You are a Roman Catholic?"

"I was proudly born to an Italian-American mother. Still, it is hard to find the Latin masses in America anymore. It was nice to see that St. Peter's Basilica still honors that tradition, but I wonder how long that will last with the new pope changing everything." Although he had not lied, he certainly ensured the prisoner drew a few misleading conclusions about his status and opinions. "I was shocked by the Vatican letting you go, Cardinal."

"I am no longer a cardinal. I am not even a priest. They stripped me completely for simply guarding our heritage."

Huxley shook his head, frowning. "How unjust that must feel! That must be why the Carabinieri decided to arrest you. Lieutenant, was this arrest ordered by the Vatican authorities, or do you have any real evidence here?"

"*Atroce!*" yelled Patismio. "You take the side of this defrocked terrorist? This is the last time we shall cooperate with you Americans. Finish your little love fest and then leave." He stormed out the door.

Huxley did his best to look surprised as the door slammed but then turned toward Fine and shrugged. Huxley paused, looked at Fine as if in contemplation, and then looked over his shoulder at the camera with the red light. Slowly, he walked over near the door and pushed a red button. "*Sergente*, please turn off the video camera. I don't think we need any recording of this discussion." Huxley and Fine looked back at the camera and watched the red light go off. Huxley returned to the table and sat down casually.

Huxley flashed a smirk. "I'm sorry to say I think the fix is in here, Cardinal. As you know, the Vatican's arms are pretty long here in Italy. Unfortunately, I am only an American and have no jurisdiction, but if you can tell me your story, I might be able to pull some strings and get you transported to the U.S., where we might be a bit more, shall I say, flexible?" Huxley could see Fine considering this vague offer, but the man was no fool.

After a few seconds, Fine said, "There is nothing I can tell you or I would. I think I am but a dupe in this whole thing. I do not even know with what I have been charged."

"Oh, I can help you on that one. They think you are in league with some Islamic terrorists and bent on revenge against the Vatican. They believe you have already killed a Vatican spy, Dante Tocelli."

"Tocelli? I do not believe I even know the man. He is dead, you say?"

Huxley answered, "Well, they can't actually prove that. He just disappeared after he returned from Tel Megiddo. He said he saw you there. I'm guessing these guys are just jumping to conclusions because you happened to be on a sightseeing vacation, and he just happened to see you there. Am I right?"

Fine beamed. "That must be it! I did go there to see the dig and the beautiful history surrounding it. I have had considerable free time following my dismissal from the Vatican."

"See, now that is what I told them, but they just don't seem to care about the truth here. Does the new pope have it in for you or something?"

"It would appear so. I can go nowhere without constant interference from his agents."

Huxley shook his head. "Such a tragedy. Hell, you should have been the pope—a true Italian pope—instead of that, that—" Huxley stopped speaking, pursed his lips and scrunched his eyebrows close together and shook his head, then finished with "—that South American."

"*Precisamente.*"

"So how long were you at Tel Megiddo?" Huxley asked.

"Oh, no more than a week. I saw the site and was intrigued, so I stayed on and learned more of its history from some of the people working there."

"I see. And did you see Tocelli there? I think he was participating in the dig. I'm sure you must have seen him."

Fine opened his palms to Huxley. "Oh probably, though I doubt I would have noticed him much. Was he a student?"

"Exactly. I'm sure he knew you but you didn't know him."

"Certainly."

"He also mentioned seeing a wild jungle animal at Tel Megiddo. Lord it is a wonder these people believe anything the man said."

"A jungle animal?" asked Fine.

Huxley studied the cardinal's eyes. A hint of worry leaked from their depths. Fine was trying hard to keep it all inside. "Yes," Huxley said, "a leopard or something ridiculous like that." Now a deep pain trembled the lashes. The man was fighting himself.

Fine laughed, but it was too tight, too forced. "How silly."

"I agree. He even said you met with this animal, but he called him by the Latin name, I forget it now." Huxley looked up as if he were trying hard to think of the word. "Oh, what is it, again?" Huxley snapped his fingers a few times.

"Pardus?" the cardinal said.

"That's it!" exclaimed Huxley, but he was secretly relishing the obvious recognition of the name reflected in Fine's voice, chin and eyes. "Do you know him?"

"Him?" asked Fine. "I thought we were speaking of an animal."

"No, I think he meant a person named Pardus. What do you think? Did you meet with a man named Pardus at Tel Megiddo? I'm sure he is just some bit player in this. Maybe a digger or something?"

"Yes, I think you are right. I do seem to have met someone with that nickname. He was just a digger, but we had *caffè* together one time. I think he may have been Arab, no…, yes, I believe he was. He spoke with an Arab accent anyway."

Huxley nodded. "Oh, that makes sense. I know they use Arabs at those sites sometimes. Do you remember his name, just so I can cross that one off my list?"

"Hard to remember. I doubt I ever knew it."

Huxley leaned in. "Think hard. That may help me wrap enough of this up to bring you back to the States. You ever been there? I could show you a few sights when this is over."

"No, I have never managed to visit."

Huxley sat back. "Great, then let's do it. Now what did you say Pardus's name was again?"

Fine looked down, pressing his lips together for a few seconds, and then shook his head. "I just cannot recall. *Mi dispiace.*"

"No problem," Huxley responded quickly. "Let's just move on and see if we can finish this up. Now, let's see." Huxley flipped through his pad. "It looks like you returned to Italy at almost the same time as Tocelli. We haven't seen him since. Nobody had seen you since, either, so naturally they thought that you either had suffered the same fate as Tocelli or were responsible for his. So help me out here. What have you been doing for the past few weeks behind closed doors?"

"Nothing of interest to you, Mr. Huxley. Remember, despite the Vatican's orders, I remain a holy man in my heart. I often spend weeks in seclusion simply praying that God will deliver me from this torment."

"I understand, Your Eminence. So you never saw Tocelli during that time, right?"

"I would doubt it."

"Okay, great. I think we are almost there." Huxley smiled gently at Fine, and Fine returned the smile. "You meet with anybody during this period? Anyone at all?"

"No. I was in seclusion. My landlady brought me groceries and the like. Otherwise, I was devoted to God."

"So no visits from anyone? Not even your new friends from Tel Megiddo?"

Fine shook his head.

"I see." Huxley shifted forward in his chair. "Say, with all of this time on your hands, have you thought about starting a grassroots movement?"

"Eh?"

"Well, like-thinking Catholics might follow you quite a ways, you know." Huxley whispered, "You ever think about getting something like that going?"

"I have my moments."

"I'm sure. You ever discuss it with any Arabs?"

"Arabs?" the cardinal asked slowly.

"Well, look, I know you are just forgetting, because I know you want to be open with me, but we know you met with an Arab man last night at Piazza del Campidoglio—not ten minutes before you were arrested. Can you enlighten me on that?" Huxley saw Fine's neck muscles tighten and his eyes widen. They betrayed Fine's surprise. How was it possible Fine had not realized he knew about the meeting? Could it be that it was not Fine's henchman who "knocked out" Sonatina after all? But the man revealed his nervousness now. It seemed Fine had thought this was a secret he would be able to keep, but now he was wondering just how much Huxley knew. Huxley saw Fine look up at nothing in particular to his left. He was trying to invent a response that would satisfy.

After staring at the wall a few seconds, Fine said, "Oh, I, uh, I am sorry I forgot to mention that. I thought you were asking about visitors to my sanctuary. How stupid of me. Yes, I just ran into a man I had met at Tel Megiddo. It was no big deal. Just spoke with him for a minute or two and then moved on. I had forgotten all about it."

"Of course, no problem. Did you give him anything at the meeting?"

"I don't think so, did I?"

Huxley smiled. Now the guy was asking him. Fine wanted to know if he had to make up another lie. "Well, so I have been told. What was it?"

"I cannot recall. Maybe it was a cigarette or something." Fine was now sweating profusely.

"Uh huh, yeah, makes sense. Oh yeah, I know I forgot something. So tough to remember stuff sometimes. Where is this sanctuary where you lived?" When Fine gave him the address quickly and willingly, Huxley smiled, hiding his disappointment. The Carabinieri would not find any more evidence there.

"*Grazie*, you have been very cooperative, Cardinal. If I can just get the name of the man you met last night, I'm sure I can clear everything up."

Fine stared back at him, shaking his head slowly, signaling he just could not recall.

Huxley grimaced and shook his head. "I'm sorry. I'd love to help you more, Cardinal Fine, but I just don't have enough to convince my guys it is worth the political fallout." Huxley stood up to leave.

"No, wait," said Fine, and Huxley sat down. "I think…I think it was just that insignificant digger from Tel Megiddo." *Now he's slipping into a half-truth, hoping that will save him. Let's see how far he will go.*

"Oh yes, what did you say his name was again?"

"Bakeer Nawa, or something like that."

Huxley bit both cheeks and his bottom lip without showing any expression, thus performing another small miracle of self-restraint borne of his long years of interrogations. "Okay, let me see." He looked at a pad with some scribbling on it that had nothing to do with Tel Megiddo. "I have a guy on my list from the Tel Megiddo dig called Baqir Najwa. I think he might be an Arab. Could that be it?"

"Yes, yes, that is it!" exclaimed Fine.

Huxley nodded gently, though inside every nerve cell in his body was firing at once. What the hell? Najwa's cold, dead body should have been resting in an Israeli morgue for several months now. Is this just another ruse, or have we been fooled all along? Confused, Huxley nearly stood up to go and let Patismio have his turn as the bad cop, but then he decided to explore one more aspect of this case that was still bothering him. "Hey, I forgot to mention, I met a woman from the Vatican Museums who said to say 'Ciao.'"

"Sonatina D'Amare. A lovely lady, indeed." Fine's eyes glistened as he looked up and away from the table and slowly spread a smile across his cheeks.

Huxley bit the inside of his lip. *Shit.* He smiled warmly. "Oh, she didn't mention how she knows you."

"We go back to my Florentine days, of course. I was a bishop there, you know. But I also worked with her awhile when I served on the Vatican Museum Oversight Board. She gives a great tour—lots of spark, if you know what I mean." He winked at Huxley. "You should ask her for one."

Huxley could feel the heat rising up the back of his neck. *The cardinal cherishes more than just the tours.* He forced a smile, happy the blood boiling inside him would not release steam out of his ears. "Perhaps I will."

CHAPTER 79

"**T**omadus, it is good to finally see you again. You have done well." First Consul Khansensius nodded slightly toward him as they stood in the First Consul's office in Roma.

Tomadus bowed deeply and suppressed a grin. This powerful man was looking out for him. "*Gratias*, but I am not sure what I have done except follow my heart."

"You have ingratiated yourself with Isa and his…followers. That allows me to help you help him. Is that not where your heart has taken you?"

"Yes, but I fear this plot against him. I must find a way to stop this before it goes too far. I cannot bear to see the tragedy play out again."

The First Consul raised both eyebrows. "Again?"

Tomadus rubbed his face, trying to cover up his gaffe. "I just mean, you know, what happened to Yohanan."

"Yes, I see. After a few inquiries, I have discovered what we have feared, Tomadus. A few of the Grand Imams and Jerusalem's Abh Beyth Diyn have been mounting a secret attack against him with the Three Emperors. They argue he is just another religious hack who will make a mockery of their beliefs and eventually rile up the crowd for his own benefit. We must turn them to his side before this becomes serious."

Tomadus scratched his beard. "How about the visi-scan speech? When they and the Emperors hear him, they will see his sincerity come through."

"You think that is the answer? I don't know. It is risky and could blow back on both of us."

"Risky? He will say nothing that he doesn't already preach openly. Anyway, you have said his sincerity is the issue, haven't you?"

"Yes. We both know his message is one of peace. We can all get behind that if it is genuine. But if they think he is seeking something else…"

"He is not. How better to prove that sincerity than by speaking sincerely in front of the Emperors and millions around the globe?"

"I understand, Tomadus, but not everyone sees Isa like you do. Do not the very best swindlers often seem the most believable?"

Tomadus remembered a few charlatans from his days running the streets of Roma. The First Consul was right. And it appeared Isa was copying this Jesus from the other world, wasn't he? Tomadus believed Isa was sincere, but a broadcast might not be enough to convince others. "What else can we do?"

"I'm not sure. I suppose we must somehow show that Isa would not alter his message even if he might personally gain by doing so."

"He would never do that," Tomadus said. "He does not care about personal gain."

"You and I know that. How do we convince the religious leaders and the Emperors? If these men could be made to believe he is genuine, they might even choose to follow him rather than persecute him. It is a possibility, Tomadus. Have you thought of a way to make that happen?"

Tomadus rubbed his forehead and said softly, "You could test him."

"Test him?"

"Sure. They could try to force him to renounce his views under a little pressure. He will not succumb to the pressure and will thereby demonstrate his earnestness."

The First Consul put his palms together in front of his jaw, bouncing his forefingers against his lips. "How would we accomplish that?"

"I don't know," Tomadus said. "We'll have to figure it out. But he must not be harmed. I need your assurances of that. He just needs a chance to prove them wrong when put to the test."

The First Consul's teeth glimmered back to Tomadus. "No, of course he should not be harmed. There must be a way we could accomplish this. If you think it would help, I shall consider it."

"*Gratias*. But we still need the broadcast first. Isa must lay out his ideas for the whole world. That by itself will help him."

The First Consul sat back and bounced his fingertips on his lips again for a few seconds. Then he leaned forward and smiled. "Yes, I see it now. It could help."

"I can make a sizeable payment. Can you convince the visi-scan broadcasters to cover the speech?"

"Do you see this as just a simple speech?" the First Consul asked.

Tomadus shook his head. "He excels in the give and take of a crowd. We will begin with a sermon followed by a question and answer session. That will show his best attributes."

"Of course—an excellent idea. It will demonstrate the passion of his beliefs. I can use that with our Emperors."

"Can we do it live? Isa is rightly concerned about potential editing. You know what they can do with pre-recorded programs."

The First Consul nodded. "I would not have it any other way. Where are you headed?"

"Jerusalem."

"I could not imagine a better location."

CHAPTER 80

"Damn it, you telling me you guys never checked the CIA's dental and DNA records on Najwa?" Huxley asked.

"Why would we?" Yadin said. "He was dead. We had his phone and identification card. We returned his body to the UAE authorities, but we never heard we had ID'd the wrong guy. Sure his face was disfigured, but why would it matter to the terrorists whether we knew who he was?"

"I'm guessing Najwa was hoping to disappear. I have certain information suggesting Najwa may himself be Pardus."

"The Ghost Leopard? What is your source?" Yadin asked.

Huxley looked up. "That's, uh, something I'm not able to officially share with you at this point, but it is fairly reliable. Our source met him at Tel Megiddo."

"I understand," Yadin said.

"He may also be tied up in this plot. But our source is in custody, so we think part of this escapade may be over, or at least sidetracked, for now. We need to find Najwa and the goods, but first I'd like to confirm he's not already dead. Tell me you guys took some blood samples so we can run a DNA match with our records from Gitmo."

"We are not incompetents, Huxley. We'll forward a sample today. You think Najwa is in Israel?"

"No, I think he's in Italy. But please keep a special eye out for him. We just don't know."

Huxley hit the red icon on his phone and looked up at the info board for Gate 45. Too damn much was happening too damn fast. Although he had delayed his trip to Afghanistan by a day, the interrogation of Fine had been well worth it. Had he finally discovered the identity of Pardus? It all seemed to make sense, and the cardinal sure seemed to believe his own story. Still, throughout the interrogation, Fine never appeared to appreciate the significance of identifying Najwa as Pardus. That apparent ignorance made his statement all the more believable. He probably overheard some other player at Tel Megiddo refer to the nickname but never knew it mattered. If Pardus realized that Fine had made the connection, Fine would have disappeared with Tocelli weeks ago.

Unfortunately, Huxley and Patismio had not been able to coax any other really critical information out of the cardinal. He had tried to discover if the man knew of the nuclear warheads, but Fine's blank look suggested he knew nothing. Was Fine just another Pardusian pawn in this grand plot? After spending the day with Huxley and Patismio, Fine still had not given up anything more about the package he handed Najwa, if there ever was one.

Then there was Fine's take on Sonatina. The more Huxley knew her, the less he understood. She had feigned only a passing knowledge of the snake, yet the cardinal recalled her with great kindness and a sparkling twinkle and wink in his eye. Why then had she lashed out about the man and denied knowing him well? After his fall from grace, had she become too practiced at such denials to save face, or was she hiding something else? If the two had some sort of relationship, then why would she have turned him in last night? That made no sense—even if she had faked a knock on her head to lend an aura of credibility to her story. Still, if that whole scene were a sham, then she also must either be connected closely to Pardus or strangely playing the part. The texts from her phone that night could mean nothing less. But maybe he was making too much of this. She could merely be an honest victim and sublime ad hoc analyst. That would be nice, but the little connections darting through his brain kept screaming their little warnings at him, overwhelming even the desire still coursing through his veins.

CHAPTER 81

HUXLEY WATCHED THE live video feed of the holding tank from the control center at Camp Chapman. Anwari was kneeling as he faced what he must have believed was the direction of Mecca. He lowered his face to the floor and remained there for some time. Huxley looked away from the screen and back at the special agent. "You hear from Mayer, yet? I need access yesterday."

"Sorry sir, but he is in a meeting in Washington and cannot be disturbed. We were told he would be out soon. I cannot give you access to the detainee without his approval."

Huxley turned around and began pacing. *Meeting my ass. He's delaying so he can pull his next move before I interrogate Anwari. At least Anwari will not suffer any mysterious "accidents" while I'm here.* Contacting Mayer had probably put Anwari at further risk, but it was the only way Huxley could get through CIA security. He had been fortunate enough to talk his way into this facility with Kira clearing the interference. He needed to press Mayer to make this happen quickly. *And I need to talk to Anwari alone.*

Huxley's phone began singing "Highway to Hell," a special tone reserved for Mayer. Huxley said, "Mayer, thanks for calling back. I need to see Anwari right away."

"So I have been told. What does he have to do with you?" Mayer asked.

Huxley's eyes narrowed. Was Mayer playing with him? "You mean you don't know?"

"Why would I? We grabbed him because some satellite footage caught him sneaking into Afghanistan from Pakistan through the mountains on one of the terrorist trails. We have been wondering what an Afghan hero is doing on that trail. I thought we might let him sit for a week or two and then see how he might explain that."

Huxley nodded. *You need this. Take the chance.* "I think he might be connected to the Pardus case. It is a long shot, but I'm here, so let me speak with him."

"Holy hell, Huxley, you know you could screw it up. You haven't managed a deep terrorist interrogation with special tools in quite awhile."

"And I don't plan to."

"What? You going to dance with him or something?" Mayer asked.

"Something like that," Huxley responded. "I might even need to release him. Look, you know what's at stake. I'm not sure what he did in Pakistan, but if he was involved, then we have to use him. I've met him in some passing encounters, so I have an outside chance of turning him. But I have to play the game right."

The silence that followed gnawed at Huxley's gut. Had he blown it?

Mayer said, "Okay, I will cut the orders, but you're responsible for him. Anything happens and it is your ass, not mine."

"I accept that. Thanks." Huxley looked suspiciously at his phone after disconnecting. That had been just too easy. These CIA guys were assholes when you wanted to interrogate their detainees, and Mayer was the biggest asshole of all. *Maybe he is finally seeing the big picture. Or maybe he is trying to scramble mine.*

Fifteen minutes later, he faced Anwari in the sparse cell. "I am sorry to see you under these circumstances, my friend. What is this all about?"

"You tell me, Chris. They yanked me out of my home and stuck me here. They have not even had the decency to tell me what they think I have done wrong."

"You must have some idea."

Anwari looked around the cell as if trying to find something hidden, looked at Huxley and then shrugged.

Huxley nodded slowly. *Okay, I'll take the hint.* "Abdul, you look like you need to stretch your legs. Might that help to clear your mind? Let's take a walk on the base."

"That would be nice. Thank you."

A few minutes later, Huxley and a handcuffed Anwari walked outside the building but well within the perimeter of the base. "I have no wires on me, Abdul. Do you want to check?"

"No. I trust you. You are not the Leopard."

Huxley stopped and faced Anwari. "The Leopard? Do you know him?"

"Do you?"

"Let's say I know of him from the bodies of his former colleagues that we keep finding hanging in the trees he has visited. We think he killed a platoon of soldiers in Pakistan after they did his bidding. He will eventually do the same to you, Abdul, even if you remain loyal to him. He despises loose ends."

"When he finishes with me, I will die, unless you protect me—and I do not refer to hiding me in a jail cell."

"What you asking?" asked Huxley.

"Asylum, pardon, protection in your country."

"Why would we do that?"

"When I tell you, you will understand."

Huxley studied Anwari's face. "If your information proves critical, that may be possible. Do you need something in writing?"

Anwari shook his head slowly. "I trust you. You know, I was going to fly to Washington to warn you after you called me. Allah spoke to me through you on the phone that day. You are blessed, Christian. Allah shines his light on you though I fear you do not see it. I decided then to help you with Pardus, but the CIA arrested me a few hours later. The CIA has at least one mole loyal to Pardus, so when they arrested me, I figured it would not be long before Pardus found me. No, Chris, if I do not trust you, who can I trust?"

"I see." Anwari's statement had sprayed the unavoidable mist of truth into Huxley's face—yet another emphasis on trust. Just like Sonatina. He frowned. Luckily, Anwari had not been watching his face, or Huxley's expression might have blown the growing connection between them.

Get her out of your mind, Hux, or you will regret it. Focus. "Give me an idea of what you might have to exchange, and I'll let you know what I think. But know I can't make it happen myself. It will take time and a little arm twisting."

"I could wear a wire and call him—but not from here. He might have the technology to track the call's origin, so I have to be in Kabul."

"If you can call Pardus, why don't you just tell me his real identity?"

"I do not know it. I do not know if anyone does. Maybe Dracoratio."

"Dracoratio? You know him?"

Anwari nodded.

"He the alias for Esnanimen Kharun Udani?"

Anwari nodded again. "Anyone other than Udani finds out, they are dead. I am pretty certain Pardus is an Arab, though I have never met him face to face."

Huxley straightened quickly. "What? You must have met him when he recruited you."

"No. He sent only Dracoratio in person. We talk only on the phone—in English to reduce the surveillance tracking. He has an Arab accent."

Huxley nodded. Mayer could speak with a perfect Arab accent. "Does he call you from the States?"

"I do not know." Anwari raised his eyebrows. "Sometimes he uses American slang."

"You ever hear the name Baqir Najwa?" Huxley asked.

"No, who is he?"

"Just wondering. Anything else you can tell me?"

"Pardus is a Muslim, or at least pretends to be. I used to believe that was his motive—to serve Allah. But he slipped during a tense moment with me, and now I know he is no different than most of the other terrorist leaders—selfish men consumed by power and willing to sacrifice even the words of Allah in the fires of their lust for glory and power."

Huxley nodded, but then his eyes narrowed. "Why did you decide to help him? You were an Afghan hero."

"Hero?" said Anwari. "I killed my brother."

"What?"

"To you Americans, I was a hero. To my own family, I was a murderer.

On my last raid with your army, I killed my brother and his family when I called for a thousand pound bomb to slam into a building in Jalalabad. My brother survived a few weeks, all along demanding revenge against the Americans. Then he died in my arms. I was bewildered and disillusioned and vulnerable to Pardus's influence. His call for revenge kept speaking to me. We screwed up, but it was because we relied on a damn CIA spook for bad intel. The bastard didn't care, and then when we reported him, a good man paid the price instead. The mass murderer went free."

Huxley frowned and shook his head.

Anwari nodded. "Pardus convinced me that that the problem was the American incursion. He made me believe Allah wanted to rid my country, no this whole world, of the men who seemed bent on the destruction of His people. I am sure I was an alluring target for Pardus just because every-one still thought I was a hero and friend to the Americans. I have tried to play the role Pardus set out for me, but in the end, I failed because Allah would not permit it. I have searched my soul. I have searched the Qur'an. I simply cannot reconcile Pardus's plans with my devotion to Allah. So I have now decided to stop Pardus."

"I see." Huxley closed his eyes for a couple of seconds. Could he believe Anwari? The man had apparently switched sides because Allah spoke to him through Huxley? *Is it even possible to know what God wants? With enough certainty to sacrifice yourself to do his bidding?* Eyebrows raised, he glanced over at Anwari. "You act as an instrument of your god?"

"We are all instruments of God's will. Sometimes we just cannot see it."

Huxley shook his head and grimaced.

Anwari smiled. "Someday you too will see it, Chris. Look hard and open your heart."

Huxley shook his head again. "Instruments. You think we lack free will?"

"No, we are not puppets. We serve Him by serving the truth."

Huxley grinned. "But what is truth?" He meant it as a subtle joke, but that thing in his abdomen pinched his muscle hard. He frowned and said again lowly, "What is truth?"

Anwari nodded. "Ah, well, that is always the problem isn't it? For the Deceiver hides the truth. But we must keep searching. The Qur'an says,

'His signs are that He shows you the lightning that terrifies and inspires hope; that He sends water down from the sky to restore the earth to life after death. There truly are signs in this for those who use their reason.' We search for the Light from the sky, for it is God's Truth, and He sends His rain to assure us of everlasting life. You see we are not that different, I think."

Huxley sighed. "Perhaps. Tell me, had you been following me for Pardus?"

"Will you satisfy my requirements?"

"Do you have knowledge of his current mission?"

Anwari chuckled. "You mean stealing the nuclear warheads?"

"Okay, I get it. Yes, I'll make it happen if you help and don't hold back. Our meeting before was no coincidence, was it? Had you been following me for Pardus?"

"Yes. I am not the only one he has misled. My role was to ensure you were as well."

"What do you mean?" Huxley asked.

"He created the clues in the cell phone you discovered at Ramat David. He wanted to divert your attention away from his real objectives. He wanted you to believe that the clues came from some traitor in his organization. My role was to ensure you figured them out. He had heard you like scavenger hunts, so he gave you one, but this hunt leads you not toward the truth but away from it."

"And where is he leading me?"

Anwari stared at Huxley for a few seconds. "Washington, DC."

Huxley grinned and nodded. "Can you help me with this poem?" He pulled out his phone and pulled up the latest verse.

"I have no details on that clue. Sorry. But I am sure it must point to Washington."

"So if Washington is the ruse, what is the real objective?"

"I can't be sure, but I heard him accidentally call it the Apple."

Huxley's eyes grew big. "As in Big Apple? New York City?"

"I assume so. That is all I heard. Pardus is not much of a free talker."

"We need to know for sure."

"I might be able to help you with that. Put a wire on my phone. I'll call him. But it must be in Kabul."

"Do you know where the nukes are being kept?"

Anwari shook his head. "You think Pardus would trust me with that when I do not even know his real name?"

"Were you involved in stealing them?"

"Does it matter?"

"Only if you might have a clue about where they went."

Anwari looked across the dessert for a full five count. "Nothing I can say would help you there. I was not involved in removing them from Pakistan."

"Then I guess we need to call your friend."

CHAPTER 82

I T HAD BEEN a longer trip than planned, but Tomadus had stayed in Roma just long enough to complete the broadcast deal after Isa consented by communication pod. Isa would speak in Muhammad Square in Jerusalem—the same square where Yohanan had been put to death. Isa would speak to the crowd assembled and the visi-scan would cover the speech live to the world. Tomadus's excitement kept him going through the long nights of negotiations until the broadcasters finally agreed, though he knew their change of heart more likely came from the back-room workings of the First Consul.

When an exhausted Tomadus arrived in Jerusalem, a somber Peregrine greeted him in the *aeroportus,* speaking above the loud engines of the *aeronaves* taking off and landing. "Welcome, Tomadus, it is a great comfort to see you again in these troubled times."

"It is good to see you as well," responded Tomadus. "Where is Isa? We have much to discuss."

"He, Simeon, Atuf and Diego traveled to Medina a few days ago. They return today, though they are too late."

"Too late? Too late for what?" He saw Peregrine's lips tremble and eyes glaze over. He grabbed his friend by the shoulders. "Peregrine, what has happened?"

Peregrine paused and took a deep breath, swallowing hard to hold in the tears. "Adin died yesterday."

"No!" Tomadus yelled and turned his head away, biting his lip. A few seconds later, he exhaled hard, looked up at Peregrine and asked quietly, "How?"

"He wandered into a field near our encampment to pick some flowers for Maryam and Jochi. Apparently, he found a stretch of mushrooms and decided to pick them for dinner. He ate a few in the field and collapsed. They were poisonous. They found him clutching the flowers and mushrooms he had picked. Even in death, he was smiling."

Tomadus swallowed hard, closed his eyes and saw Adin stumbling through the pots and pans while taking care not to squash the precious insect with a "torch in his butt." This simple, gentle man had been so sweet, so insightful, and so loyal to both Isa and Maryam. Then another image from the back alley in Parisius briefly fluttered through Tomadus's mind, and he shook his head to dispel it.

An hour later, Tomadus arrived at the camp of the Way members just outside a hilltop town a couple *milia passuum* west of Jerusalem proper. He found Jochi and Maryam dressed in black robes, their faces covered with black veils. Wailing loudly, Jochi ran up to Tomadus and threw herself into his arms.

Tomadus held her tightly to his chest. "He was a wonderful man. We will miss him greatly."

"If only Isa had been here. He would have saved him."

"But I thought he was found dead in the field."

"Oh, these physic-techs in Palestine are so primitive. They did nothing to try to revive him. If only we had been in Roma!"

Behind him, he heard Maryam shout, "Isa! You have come, finally!"

When Jochi turned and saw Isa standing with Simeon, Atuf and Diego, she pushed away from Tomadus and ran to Isa. Maryam followed her, and Isa's arms swallowed them both. Isa comforted them gently for a few minutes until Jochi's face appeared away from his robes. "Isa, why did you go to Medina? You could have saved him if you had stayed! But even now, I know that whatever you ask of God, God will give you."

Isa said quietly, "Adin will arise."

"Yes, on the last day as you have told us," Jochi said through her tears.

"I am the resurrection and the life; whoever believes in me, even if he dies, will live, and everyone who lives and believes in me will never die. Do you believe this, Jochi?"

"Yes, oh yes, for I know you are blessed by the Father."

Isa touched her shoulders. "Where have they laid him?"

"In the mortuary in the little town on the hill. The funeral will be tomorrow."

The group walked up to the mortuary. Tomadus joined them, and a woman greeted them at the door. She noticed the crowds gathering behind Isa and asked what he wanted. He said, "We wish to see our friend Adin."

"But you must wait for the funeral. The mortician has already begun preparations." She gestured toward a door near the back.

"Please, show me the body now," said Isa, perturbed.

"You cannot. Nobody can disturb the dead during preparation!" she proclaimed. Nevertheless, Isa simply walked past her and a few from the crowd followed.

He opened the door without knocking and walked in. The mortician was standing by a table with a scalpel in his hand, leaning over Adin's massive, limp, pale body, preparing to cut.

"What is the meaning of this intrusion? It is unholy."

"The Father determines what is holy, not man," Isa said firmly. "Please let me do His work." The mortician seemed humbled by Isa's words and stepped aside.

Tomadus moved closer and felt Adin's wrist and neck. Although the coldness of Adin's flesh disturbed him, he held on long enough to search for a pulse that did not register. He stepped back and shook his head at Isa and then looked down.

"Tomadus," Isa said, "you must have the faith of your friend's sister, for then you will see the glory of God. Please leave me to do His will." Reluctantly, Tomadus and the mortician stepped outside and shut the door behind them.

When the door opened a few minutes later, Isa walked out of the room and toward the crowd with a soft smile on his face. He paused a moment, turned back toward the door and commanded loudly, "Adin, come out!"

Adin moved into the doorway. Adin's skin remained sallow, his eyes nearly shut, but there he stood, a bit shaky but alive. Cries and gasps filled the air. The mortician let his scalpel fall out of his hands as he collapsed to the floor.

Tomadus shook his head back and forth, his heart racing. *How could this be?* Tomadus's mind flew over recent events and eventually remembered that little black and white dog, so much like Huxley's dog, eating his bread in a Parisian alley. It had led him to the strange scene he had witnessed while the dog licked his face. "Back to life," Isa had promised to Adin as he handed him the package—and Isa had delivered. Happy to have his gentle friend back, Tomadus grinned at Adin and held back a hearty laugh. He turned to Isa and said with a smile, "Brilliant. Absolutely brilliant." But the First Consul's words echoed in his brain, "They must not think him a fraud." *Is he a fraud? Should I continue to help him?* Tomadus winced and rubbed his belly as the creature began gouging the insides of his gut.

CHAPTER 83

"You must believe in him now, Tomadus," Jochi said in a low tone. "The whole world must believe."

The two were sitting together alone by a small fire near the women's tents, which lay about a hundred feet from the roaring campfire where most of the Ten now celebrated Adin's miraculous return surrounded by a growing crowd of believers. He could hear an oud playing and men and women singing joyfully.

Tomadus breathed deeply, feeling the smoky air swirl through his nostrils. He turned and smiled weakly at Jochi. "Well, it makes for a good show and an even better party, though I would prefer to have some *vinum* to cherish the moment."

"You call it a show? It is a miracle."

"You really believe in all of these miracles?"

"You do not?" Jochi's eyes looked like they would punch Tomadus if they could. "There is no other explanation. You told me you checked Adin's pulse and felt his cold skin. He was dead. He had been dead for over a day. Not even the best physic-tech in the world could have brought him back. Isa asked, and God answered. There is no other explanation."

"Perhaps," replied Tomadus. "Or maybe…"

"Maybe what?"

Tomadus looked her right in the eye. "Maybe there is another explanation."

"Like what?"

"I saw Isa speaking quite secretively with Adin in Parisius. He told Adin something about bringing him back to life so others would know who Isa was. Then he gave Adin a package."

Jochi said, "So, Isa has the power of foresight. So what?"

"I think the package contained a very powerful drug that might have simulated death in Adin. I think the very loyal Adin reluctantly took the drug at Isa's request. It is lucky we got to him before the mortician began emptying his bodily fluids."

"You are insane! What kind of drug does that?"

"I don't know, but Isa seems to have a way of finding these things. He is quite widely traveled, you know. He could have come across it anywhere. But the big thing is that I know Isa is doing his best to mimic another holy man from the other world. I do not blame him. He is brilliant, and his attempt to follow this path will accomplish much in our own world, so I help him. He is very good at what he does. He almost had me with that Adin thing, but I know too much of the other world now to fall for these tricks."

"Tricks?" She shook her head a few times. "You are mistaken. Do not utter this opinion to anyone unless you have absolute proof."

"Of course not. Do you think me mad? Oh yes, you already called me insane."

Jochi slumped in her chair, a dejected expression taking over her face. "I do not believe that, Tomadus. In fact, I am beginning to wonder about my own sanity."

"Your own? What has happened?"

"A light, followed by some visions," Jochi said.

"The Light of Our Yesterdays—like Peregrine and me!"

"I don't know about that. They are strange visions I do not yet understand." Jochi looked down. "Tell me more about this other world you see. You mentioned Huxley and Sonatina."

Tomadus leaned forward. "It's hard for me to describe. While it's completely different, it is somehow similar. I feel like in this other world I am chasing some kind of evil, yet I am not sure of the truth or even what is good and what is evil."

"You? You are chasing? Is this more than a dream or a vision?"

"It feels like it. I always see this other world through the eyes of Huxley, who seems bent on trying to find a man they call Pardus, the Leopard. Hey, are you OK?"

Jochi's face had changed to the same ashen expression he had seen when Adin first appeared at the mortician's door. "Yes, I…I'll be fine. Go on," she said haltingly.

"Look, in this other world, I am just an investigator trying to find this Leopard, Pardus, a shaitaanist bent on killing millions of innocents. But it isn't like I am a hero or anything. It feels like a bad dream—like the whole thing is nothing more than a jumbled game my brain has invented to turn me in circles. I'm sorry if I cannot explain it further. Does any of this make sense?"

"A little bit. This Sonatina you mentioned—what does she do?"

"She runs an art museum that is part of a huge church."

Jochi gasped. "I…I'm sorry…I…"

"What? What have you seen of this other world? Are you Sonatina?"

"I…I…I'm sorry. I can't talk about it. Not until… Sorry." She buried her head in her hands and began to shake.

Tomadus kneeled in front of her folding chair, placing his arms around her shoulders and stroking her hair. "No, I am the one who is sorry," he said softly. "Look, this thing almost tore me apart when it first happened. Don't let it confuse you. You must separate it from your life here—see it as a story instead of just a part of you. It is the only way to cope. You will be all right. I'll help you through it."

Her shaking stopped. She wiped her eyes and raised her head as she caressed his arms. "So it isn't real?" She swallowed hard. "These are just visions? What happens there won't ever happen to us here? Will it affect us here?"

"I wish I had the answers," he replied. "What have you seen?"

"I…I can't say." He hugged her more tightly to his chest.

After awhile, he heard steps behind him and looked over his shoulder to see Adin lumbering over. Maybe it was just the light of the fire, but

Adin's complexion was off. Nevertheless, he still wore that typical, goofy, loveable Adin smile.

"Hi Tomadus!" Adin said. "Are you coming over to join the party? Jochi, are you OK? You look sad."

"I will be fine, Adin," she responded, wiping her tears as she and Tomadus separated. "I am just so happy you are alive again."

"Me too!" beamed Adin.

Tomadus seized the moment. "Adin, it is so good to see you well again." When Adin just continued smiling, Tomadus added, "Tell me, do you remember anything about what happened before you died?"

"Not much."

"Well, tell me what you do remember."

"Okay," said Adin. "Let's see. I remember feeling sick. I was going to puke. Then everything was spinning and then went dark, except this one bright light."

"What happened with the light?" Jochi asked.

Adin's eyes lit up. "It was strange. I kept walking toward it, but it was rocky and slippery under my feet and I couldn't seem to get anywhere. I fell down and started crawling on my hands and knees, but the rocks under me were crumbling, and I got nowhere. I almost gave up, but then I heard a voice say to me, 'Your faith is strong, Adin, but you must return to the living. I still have plans for you.' I woke up and Isa was standing over me and smiling. I love Isa."

"Did Isa tell you how he brought you back?" Tomadus asked.

"You know that, Tomadus. He asked the Father, and the Father answered him like he always does."

"Yes, Adin, I understand. But I am wondering, was there anything Isa did in front of you that looked like he helped it out? Did he have a vial or syringe in his hand or anything?"

Adin shook his head slowly several times. "He just had his hands stretched out above me."

"I see," replied Tomadus. "Now, this is very important, Adin. Can you search your memory to the time just before you started feeling sick?"

"Sure."

"Did you eat or drink anything strange?"

"Yes, the mushrooms. They tasted funny. Maryam said I can't eat those anymore."

"Did you eat or drink anything Isa gave you just before you got sick?"

"No. I don't think he gave me anything to eat or drink. Why?"

"You don't remember him giving you something—back in Parisius?

Adin closed his lips tightly and looked down, shaking his head rapidly. "I'm…I'm not supposed to say anything about that now."

"It's okay, Adin, Isa trusts me," said Tomadus, feeling the creature somersault wildly over such an exaggeration.

"Well…I guess he does trust you. Okay, Tomadus." Adin pulled a silver chain from out of his tunic and over his neck and head. Sliding on the chain was a simple silver pendant in the form of an inverted triangle. "He gave me this and said I could show this to the others before the resurrection to give them faith. It would forever be a sign of God's love for the world."

"Before your resurrection? Did you show it to anyone before he brought you back to life?"

Adin giggled. "No, Tomadus, before Isa's resurrection."

Tomadus dropped his jaw as he looked at Jochi. She smiled and nodded. "Let's get back to the party," she said. "I'm hungry."

"I'll catch up with you later," Tomadus said. For a long time, he sat and stared at the stars in the sky, his mind turning over again and again everything that had happened since he had met the preacher from Palestine. Occasionally, an image of Adin's silver triangular pendant would flash in his brain, and each time he would see the image in Huxley's hands of his mother's silver crucifix as Adin's words echoed in his ears: "Isa's resurrection." Tomadus was no longer sure what he believed, but it didn't seem to matter. Either way, Isa must make the speech. He must convince them.

CHAPTER 84

HUXLEY WIPED THE comingled dust and sweat off his brow as he and Anwari drove up the long dirt road back to Kabul. *Washington, DC—how does the first stanza of Pardus's little poem point there?* If he could figure that out, he could confirm Anwari's story to his boss. Deputy Under Secretary Blount was a career guy—an old SES officer who would get the intelligence nuances and explain it to his political boss, the Under Secretary. Still, that would not be enough. The Secretary would need to be in on such a major shift of critical equipment. Hell, the President would need to approve the switch. He focused on the last three lines of the first stanza:

> Beyond my fortress on my left you see
> What shall befall the many unlike he,
> A priest who never lived before just me.

Sonatina had pointed out that priests and cardinals are "Fathers." She had been right so many times that he could not avoid trying the suggestion. So if he said, "A father who never lived before just me," what would that mean? A father to whom? Not to Jefferson, because his father could not have first lived after the son. What did it really mean that the father "never lived before just me?" It was an odd construction obviously employed to shroud its real meaning.

So what else did these words mean? How about the word "lived?" When you live, you exist as a being, but that is just the typical meaning. When you live, you choose to act in a certain way regarding your life. You can live off of some type of food or subsistence, so it is like surviving. Nah. What else?

There was the Christian view of life after death. According to John, what did Jesus say? Something like, "whoever believes in me, even if he dies, will live, and everyone who lives and believes in me will never die." Could that be it? It would make sense if the words in the poem were reordered, because then someone could live both before and after another person forever. Is that what the writer meant? But where does that point? Such a construction could refer to almost any Christian.

What else could the word "lived" mean? Where do you live? In a home. That is a location. Hmm, that has possibilities. A father who never lived in a home before just me. What home is before just Jefferson? That's it: "before" indicates not time but place—"in front of." So what home lies just before Jefferson's statue? Crap, it's the White House. OK, it is a mile away, so what? Jefferson looks right at it, almost longingly.

Well, then who never lived in the White House? Many people, but only one U.S. President—George Washington. He resided in an executive residence in Philadelphia before the first White House was finished. And many consider him the father of our country. It all fits: Death shall befall the many in Washington, because this father of our country never lived in the city named after him, unlike its many current inhabitants. That confirms it: Pardus wanted him to think the danger lied in Washington, just as Anwari had predicted.

He needed more, though. The President would not order the UNGARD moved without additional proof, and that would leave New York City open for Pardus's real attack. He glanced over at Anwari, who seemed to be contemplating the upcoming call. There was one thing Huxley still didn't get. "Hey, Abdul."

"Yes?"

"Why did you try to kill me?" Huxley asked.

"Kill you? I never—oh, you mean the bomb in Florence."

"Yeah that little bomb in Florence. I was in the hospital for a couple weeks, remember?"

Anwari shook his head and laughed. "I screwed up."

"You wanted me dead?" Huxley asked.

"No, you were not supposed to get hurt—not badly anyway. I actually reduced the C4 from the recommended quantity. I think the wall was older and weaker than I had estimated."

"Why would you bomb me if you didn't want to kill me?"

Anwari tilted his head. "Why did you think?"

Huxley looked at Anwari. "I figured I was getting too close and Pardus wanted me dead."

"Then the C4 served its purpose."

"Pardus enjoys the art of deception."

Anwari nodded. "Yes, he is the Deceiver. 'The Deceiver tricked you about God.'"

"The Deceiver?" Huxley asked.

"Words from the Qur'an. Let me see if I can recall—"

"You've memorized the Qur'an?"

"Only parts. There are many who have memorized every word. I am worthless." Anwari closed his eyes, breathed heavily and translated from his memory:

> On the same Day, the hypocrites, both men and women, will say to the believers, 'Wait for us! Let us have some of your light!' They will be told, 'Go back and look for a light.' A wall with a door will be erected between them: inside it lies mercy, outside lies torment. The hypocrites will call out to the believers, 'Were we not with you?' They will reply, 'Yes. But you allowed yourselves to be tempted, you were hesitant, doubtful, deceived by false hopes until God's command came—the Deceiver tricked you about God. Today no ransom will be accepted from you or from the disbelievers: your home is the Fire—that is where you belong…'

Huxley swallowed hard. *The Fire.* "Yes, I have been deceived."

Anwari turned his head toward Huxley, bit his bottom lip and shook his head. "No, it is I who have been deceived. Now I must find my way back to the light before it is too late."

Huxley recalled the counsel from his own mother. "Jesus said, 'See that no one deceives you.'" When Anwari's eyes narrowed, Huxley smiled and added, "It is not the end, my friend. You and I can stop this Deceiver, this beast, and undo his deceptions before it is too late."

"I thank you for that," said Anwari. "I pray to Allah that you are right and that we may both return to the light."

Huxley tilted his head toward Anwari for a few seconds but said nothing, then returned his view to the dusty road ahead.

❀ ❀ ❀

They were in Anwari's apartment, surrounded by a mess of extra electronic equipment. Anwari held his phone with the scrambler chip. A wire ran from the phone to a black box that would digitally record the conversation and simultaneously search for the location of the call. Another wire led from the black box to a set of headphones over Huxley's ears.

Anwari shook his head. "The locator is useless. Pardus has technical resources and likes to use them."

"We have to try," responded Huxley. "You ready?"

Anwari nodded slowly, and Huxley returned the gesture. Anwari hit the button to place a call to Pardus. A strange metallic sounding voice answered, "Yes?"

"Who is this?" asked Anwari.

"Be not alarmed, Abdul. It is I, your imam, the Leopard."

"Your voice is different."

"Yes. I am continuing to improve my security and am trying out this new voice scrambler. I am using it on all of my calls now."

"Were you trying to reach me earlier?" asked Anwari.

"Yes. Why did you fail to answer?" Pardus demanded.

Huxley gave Anwari a smirk. Because the guy had been rotting in a CIA detention cell, of course. But they had anticipated this query.

Slowly and lowly, Anwari said, "I am sorry, Imam, it is unforgivable, I know, but I dropped my phone into the toilet and destroyed its electronics.

Fortunately, I did not have the security chip in it at the time. I was unable to procure a new phone until today since the shops remained closed for the holidays. But now we are 'back in business' as the Americans like to say."

"I see," replied Pardus. After a slight pause, he added, "Do not be ashamed, for I have suffered that misfortune myself. But remember, we are nearing the end of this play, and we must not make any mistakes—not even little ones. Do you understand?"

"Yes, Imam."

"Good. I think it is time for you to come to DC. Huxley is not here, but I think he may need a few more breadcrumbs to find his way home. I think he will return soon. Be here in the next few days and I'll contact you with more."

"But how can I help him? You haven't told me the answer to the latest clue."

"Ah, but I have."

"You have?" Anwari asked.

"I told you he must focus on the District."

"So the clue tells him that?"

"And more. I'll give you more details after you arrive."

Anwari looked at Huxley and back at the equipment. "What is the real target?"

"You need not concern yourself with that, my friend."

"I would not care, but I would rather not be too close if the thing goes off."

"Well then, just be sure to avoid taking a tourist trip a few hours north, and you should be fine. Hopefully, we'll have you out of the country before anything happens anyway."

"Thank you, Imam."

"Thank you, Abdul. *Allahu Akbar.*"

"*Allahu Akbar.*"

After the phone disconnected, Huxley smiled at Anwari. "You have done well."

"Should I have pressed him on the location?"

"If you pushed any harder, he might have suspected something and then changed his plans. No, that confirmed things nicely. Thank you."

"Did you get any location info on his phone?"

"Nothing that this little machine can determine—too many reroutes and sidetracks. He must use multiple telephonic control devices interlinked to avoid location analysis. But it captured all of the data. I'll ship it to the shop and see if our analysts can make anything of it."

Huxley stared at the equipment, the hair bristling on the back of his neck. A synthesized voice. Why pick this call to begin using a new security device with Anwari? Just a coincidence? Or did Pardus suspect Huxley had turned Anwari? If Pardus were really either Mayer or Najwa, Huxley would have been able to recognize the voice, but not now. Then again, maybe there was another way. "Tell me, what is Pardus's voice normally like?"

"Deep. Rich. Very authoritative. Arabic accent."

"Similar to anyone you know?" asked Huxley.

Anwari shook his head. "Not really. Only voice I recall that deep was Half-Moon Mole, but he had no Arabic accent. More of an American drawl."

Huxley's eyes narrowed. "Half-Moon Mole?"

"Yeah, the OGA operator who killed my brother in Jalalabad. Never knew his name."

Huxley's mouth opened but he said nothing. *Mayer. He has a deep voice. And that mole on his face—hell if it wasn't shaped like a half moon.* "Why you call him 'Half-Moon Mole?'"

"Asshole wouldn't tell me his name. I guess that's standard OGA crap. Anyway, he had this mole on his cheek in the shape of a half moon."

Huxley stared intently at Anwari. "Half Moon. Ever hear any of his real name?"

"No."

"What's he look like, other than the mole?" Huxley asked.

"Big dude. Rippling arm muscles. Likes to roll up his sleeves and show them off just for intimidation."

"That's him," Huxley said, without thinking.

"Who?"

"Sorry, can't say."

Anwari shook his head. "Doesn't matter, though. I think I would know if he were Pardus. Not the same cadence or inflection. Definitely the same pitch, though. I don't know. I suppose if he were careful and tried to change his inflection with his accent, but…no, I just don't know. Anyway, it's been awhile since I've heard Half-Moon Mole speak and then it was only a few times. I could be remembering it wrong. He capable of that?"

Huxley sat back in his chair, hands below his chin. *Mayer. A long shot, but it could explain a few things.* Huxley grabbed Anwari's phone and disconnected the wire. He plugged in his own phone and handed Anwari the headphones. "I'm going to make another call. You listen and tell me if the voice sounds familiar." He hit the entry for Mayer. Nobody answered until the voice mail picked up. That would have his voice. Nope. Mayer used an automatic machine greeting that repeated the telephone number. Standard CIA protocol. Huxley looked at his phone to see if he had any old messages from Mayer. "Damn. Never mind. We'll have to try it later."

Huxley studied Abdul for a few seconds. There was one other possibility. "Hey, Abdul," he said, "how can I be sure you aren't still working with Pardus and setting me up here?"

Anwari looked him in the eye for a few moments, shrugged and replied, "I have trusted you. Now you must trust me."

Huxley pulled his lips in. *Yeah, I've heard that one before.*

CHAPTER 85

WHEN TOMADUS HAD planned a short procession into Jerusalem to excite the crowd before Isa's sermon, he had never imagined the march would grow like this. Thousands from Jerusalem and small cities around Palestine greeted Isa and the Ten before they arrived in the city. The buzz about Adin's miraculous revival had changed everything. That excitement played out in front of the visi-scan cameras all along the parade route as the visi-scan news brought the spectacle live to the world. The impact of the broadcast would be greater than Tomadus had ever dreamed.

As the procession reached the old city gates, the crowd began chanting, "Isa, Isa, Isa," "Savior, Savior, Savior," and "Mahdi, Mahdi, Mahdi!" Isa stopped for a moment, looked around at the crowd with his arms wide open and his palms toward the sky as if to welcome them all. The crowd responded with even louder cheers.

The procession made its way to Muhammad Square, where thousands already had taken the best viewing positions. Isa approached the makeshift stage followed by the Ten, Maryam, Jochi, Tomadus and Peregrine. The Dome of the Rock towered above and behind. Isa stood silently near the microphone for a few minutes, waiting for latecomers from the parade to make their way into the crowded square.

Tomadus stared in awe at the size and intensity of the crowd, which now began chanting Isa's name again. Would a similar reaction follow around the globe? Tomadus beamed with pride, and the creature stirred within, but he misinterpreted it. What must he be forgetting? Would Isa be careful? He took a few steps over to Isa and whispered, "Remember to stay away from criticizing the emperors or the religious establishment. You need to show them your beliefs are real but not threatening to them." Just smiling back, Isa acknowledged nothing.

After the crowd settled down, Isa delivered a short sermon. His message differed little from the many lessons he had taught over the past year, but then again, most of the world had never heard him speak. He spoke of forgiveness and welcomed all into the Father's forgiving arms: "If you forgive others their transgressions, your Heavenly Father will forgive you," he said. "But if you do not forgive others, neither will your Father forgive you. Blessed are the merciful, for they will be shown mercy. Only those who are merciful will be shown mercy by the most Merciful." He spoke of love and hate, chastising those who choose to hate "others," decrying it a pathetic and sad substitute for greater understanding and compassion. "You must love even your enemies," he reiterated. "Blessed are the meek, for they will inherit the land. Good and evil cannot be equal. Repel evil with what is better and your enemy will become as close as an old and valued friend." When he had finished these remarks, he raised his hands and said, "Now, please, what is in your hearts?"

The visi-scan broadcasters had hired microphone runners throughout the crowd for this very purpose. Not more than twenty feet from the stage, a bearded man with a white turban approached the microphone. "Teacher, you instruct us about what God wants for us, but how are we to accomplish it? You have said nothing about our wonderful emperors and the generous First Consul. What should they do to ensure that we all do what you tell us God commands?"

Tomadus held his breath. *Watch out. He's baiting you to proclaim the government must abide by your words. Such a claim would be very dangerous indeed.*

Isa took a different tack. All he said was, "Nothing."

"Nothing?" the man replied. "How can you say this? If God commands it, should not our leaders enforce his commands upon our people?"

"Before I answer your question, let me ask you this: do you believe God is all powerful?"

"Of course he is," said the man. "The Great Book says that it 'is to Allah that you will all return, and He has power over everything.'"

"Good. But if God is all powerful, as we both agree, then why would He need emperors to exert His will upon His people?"

The man's voice faltered a bit as he said, "I don't know."

"Then neither do I," said Isa. "Our Father has given us all a great gift—free will. Do you think He gave us that free will just to take it away? Do you think He would like to or need to use the power and instruments of the state to enforce His will upon ours? Why would He do that?"

"Because He wants people to act justly."

Isa nodded. "He does, but you miss His intentions completely. He loves us and wants each of us to choose for himself or herself to find the path of righteousness. But if the state compels you through force of arms to believe in God or perform one of God's commandments, have you chosen to do so?"

"No, but at least I will have done so."

"True, but the Father cares about what is written in your heart as well. If you are forced to do something, does it come from your heart?"

"No."

"Then neither should the power of the state be used to enforce His will upon our own."

"But shouldn't we punish the wrongdoers?" the man said.

"I am quite certain the Father can take care of that Himself on the judgment day."

"But we cannot allow killers or robbers to go free, can we?"

Isa shook his head. "Of course not, for society must keep the peace, but you would have emperors govern by imposing their interpretation of God's will upon their people and even possibly upon the people of other nations who do not even share your beliefs. Emperors are not the agents or enforcers of God on Earth."

Tomadus winced. *The Emperors themselves claim to be appointed by Allah.*

Isa gestured to the crowd with his palms forward at his sides. "So why should the Emperors act as God's enforcers with the force of the state machinery behind them?"

Tomadus began sweating profusely. *Is Isa crazy? Does he want the Three Emperors to silence him?* These were officially Muslim empires—everyone knew that. The empires permitted a few other religions like Judaism to continue to practice their beliefs, but only in limited regions and in a very limited way. *Isa must see that! Why does he challenge them so?* Tomadus began walking over to Isa to bring him back from the political abyss, but Isa glanced in his direction, and Tomadus knew at once he would fail.

Another grabbed a microphone and yelled, "You claim the Three Emperors are not God's agents, but what about you? You make proclamations and act as if you know God's will. You have no authority and yet you would do the same thing! Is your authority greater than the Emperors?"

Isa smiled and paused a count. Then he replied slowly, "Do you not still see the difference between my actions and those of an emperor? I do not pretend to have the earthly power of an emperor, nor do I ever wish such a thing."

Tomadus let out a long breath. *Good.*

Isa continued, "So when I or my followers tell you to act a certain way, I am merely instructing you about the path you should follow because you will ultimately be judged by God. If I am wrong and you choose another path, what harm would come to you? No guard would come to your house to drag you away in the middle of the night for breaking the law. God would judge you well. But if I were instead the Emperor and made the same mistake, whether intentionally or not, and you chose to defy me, what would happen to you then?"

When a hush went over the crowd, the man backed slowly away from the microphone, his arms open and raised nearly to his head.

Isa nodded to the crowd. "Now let us assume, instead, that you comply with my edict, not because of what is in your heart, but because of your fear of what may happen to you on Earth from me as the Emperor? If I have truly followed God's word, what good is your compliance in God's eyes when it is not from your heart? Yet if I as the emperor am in error about God's will and you comply because you fear the Emperor, what consequences do you think might await you upon the judgment day?

"Find your way to God's grace by changing your own heart, not by demanding that the Emperor change the hearts of others. Do not hope the Emperor imposes his views of God's will on those with whom you disagree, for who knows when a new emperor may come to a different view and exercise a new policy against you? Perhaps you now see the danger of covering the Emperor with the mantle of God. Do you also perceive how destructive it is to cover God with the robes of the Emperor?"

A young man near the stage yelled, "Can't you see this man is crazy! Who can put the Emperor's robes on God!"

Isa replied graciously, "I am sorry, young man. I speak, of course, with a simple metaphor. But consider history, and the truth will emerge. Now let me tell you a story:

"There once was a mighty king who ruled his subjects well, but a few discontented princes challenged his right to rule their provinces. Troubled by this, he approached a religious leader whom nearly everyone believed was just and righteous and who helped lead the spiritual lives of many souls. The king proposed that the two men work closely together: the religious leader would openly bless the king, crown him officially as the "King of Kings," and proclaim that he ruled by the will of God. In turn, the king would praise the religious leader, name him the kingdom's official leader of souls, grant him various lands and money for places of worship, and even give him the right to rule lands around his home.

"'What a great thing for God,' said the religious leader to himself. 'This king is a good king, so why should I not do this when it will benefit my church so?'

"Now the two carried out the king's plan, and at first it worked beautifully for them both. No longer did any princes openly challenge the king, and the religious leader was able to expand his influence by opening more and more houses of worship. The religious leader also discovered the great generosity of the communities served by his new assistants—the new church leaders—as they began sending him portions of their collections from their various congregations around the kingdom. With this money, the religious leader grew incredibly wealthy and acquired more lands within and without the kingdom.

"But by now, the growing riches and power had made him greedy for more. So he asked his new church leaders how they could raise more money from their congregations. The church leaders told him the people were giving everything they could, so he would have to be satisfied. But the religious leader did not like this response, and eventually he struck upon an answer. For a long time he had been granting various privileges to his congregations, including certain spiritual benefits in the name of God, and appointing important additional church leaders, and he had been doing all this without any charge whatsoever. 'How stupid of me,' he thought. 'Why not charge for the privileges and appointments, for I have no doubt that the leaders and many in the congregations will pay handsomely for them, and I will eventually put that to good use for God.' And so he did. And his wealth and authority increased even more.

"Meanwhile, the King of Kings was growing weary. It was wonderful that none of the princes openly challenged him as before, and he discovered that since he now officially served God's will, he had much greater power to do as he wished without facing any serious challenges from others. But he had a problem: the religious leader was accumulating so much property and wealth that the king was having trouble raising sufficient taxes, and he feared that the religious leader's control over so many of the church leaders could ultimately undermine his own rule. So he issued a decree requiring any leaders of churches within his realm to be appointed by him. This would give him both additional resources (because the candidates would pay him for the appointments) and the allegiance of powerful local leaders.

"As you might imagine, the religious leader strongly opposed the king's actions. If his church leaders were not beholden to him and had not paid him for their offices, his power and resources would be severely undercut. So the religious leader sent a message to the king complaining that this new edict broke their longstanding agreement and warning the king of serious consequences that could follow this breach.

"'What can he do to me?' thought the king. 'I am the King of Kings.' So he ignored the religious leader.

"Now the religious leader became enraged and announced publicly that the king neither ruled as the King of Kings nor by the will of God but only by his own despotism. The king soon found that his power had suffered greatly. Many princes began to revolt against him and many of his people followed them. So the king, crown in hand, traveled to the religious leader's palace, but the religious leader would not even consent to see him. The king then humbled himself by kneeling in the snow before the palace for several days. Finally, the religious leader allowed the king to enter his palace, where he pleaded for his forgiveness and agreed he would revoke his decree. Satisfied, the religious leader again anointed him as the 'King of Kings' and proclaimed he ruled by divine will.

"The religious leader was quite pleased with his demonstration of power and thought to himself, 'how crafty of me to bring the king to his knees.'" However, the religious leader had greatly underestimated the force of his words and actions on his congregations, the princes and even some of his church leaders. Many of them began to question his motives and wonder whether he truly spoke for God, not only concerning his king and the need to pay for privileges and appointments but also now concerning his church and the need to support the religion and him.

"Meanwhile, the princes began to conspire to determine how they could dethrone the King of Kings. 'The people will not join us if they believe God is on his side,' said one prince. The others agreed and decided to support some of the upstart church leaders who had begun to oppose the religious leader. This gained the princes considerable favor among certain rich men in their provinces who did not want to pay the religious leader any longer. With this new religious power on their side, they fought a series of long wars with the King of Kings and his supporters, including the original religious leader."

"Eventually, the King of Kings found his power and territory had dwindled mightily with many territories being swallowed up by the princes, who now proclaimed themselves kings. The religious leader discovered that many of his former churches were now led by his former church leaders who now opposed him and preached many things he did not like, but he knew there was little he could do."

Isa paused for five seconds and looked straight down at the man who had asked the question. "Now let me ask you, young man, in the end, do you think either the king or the religious leader was happy with their cozy arrangement?"

The young man shook his head quietly.

A middle-aged man with light hair approached one of the microphones and said, "Teacher, I believe we understand what you say in general, yet surely you must believe that our current religious leaders and emperors have done God's will."

Isa replied, "Your question illustrates my point, for if I say they have done God's will, I have now clothed them with the mantle of my Father, have I not? But if I say they have not followed my Father's commandments, then they could use the power of the state to either try to change my views or end them. Do you not find that to be a problem?"

The man shook his head and left the microphone.

"But this brings to mind another story. A man planted a vineyard, put a hedge around it, dug a wine press, and built a tower. Then he leased it to tenant farmers and left on a journey. At the proper time he sent a servant to the tenants to obtain from them some of the produce of the vineyard. But they seized him, beat him, and sent him away empty-handed. Again he sent them another servant. And that one they beat over the head and treated shamefully. He sent yet another whom they killed. So, too, many others; some they beat, others they killed. He had one other to send, a beloved son. He sent him to them last of all, thinking, 'They will respect my son.' But those tenants said to one another, 'This is the heir. Come, let us kill him, and the inheritance will be ours.' So they seized him and killed him, and threw his body out of the vineyard. What then will the owner of the vineyard do? He will come, put the tenants to death, and give the vineyard to others."

A murmur rose from the crowd. Like Tomadus, they were unsure of the meaning of this parable. Who was Isa chastising here? Who were the tenants? Who was the son? Fortunately, another question came quickly: "I see that you have included women on the stage with you? What gives you the right to raise them up this way?"

"Raise them up?" Isa lowered his chin to the man and gestured to Jochi and Maryam. "It is God who has the power to raise people up. I asked these two followers to join me and to open their hearts and minds to my words. They have accomplished that better than most, so what is wrong with that?" Yet another murmur rose from the crowd.

A man at a different microphone quickly fired another question at Isa,

"I have heard that you recently traveled to Tetepe and demonstrated against the government there. What do you think should happen to the region?"

"First, let me correct your misunderstanding. I did not demonstrate, for that would suggest I have taken sides in a political conflict, and I am no politician."

Tomadus nodded and smiled. *Good answer, now just let it go.* He frowned when Isa did not.

Isa said, "But I will say this: Tetepe has become a tragedy for us all. God loves all people, and all people should be allowed to live together in peace and security regardless of their backgrounds, their ethnicity or their beliefs."

Another man in the crowd shouted without any microphone, "You were a friend of that shaitaanist, Yohanan, weren't you!"

Isa responded, "In the end, Yohanan sought the way of God. He wished for peace on fair terms. He transformed himself into an agent of peace and the mouthpiece of God."

The man, now with a microphone, shouted, "But he tried to bomb Hugleikr on the steps of the Dome! Everybody knows that! Do you support shaitaanists?"

"I support the truth, not lies. Do you?" said Isa. "I support love, not hate. Do you? I support forgiveness, not vengeance. Do you?"

"Shaitaanists should be put to death!" the man shouted.

"And so he was," Isa replied evenly, "though I doubt it was because of any shaitaanist act on his part." The din of the crowd now rose to new heights and several fights broke out as some thugs in the crowd attacked obvious Way supporters. The broadcast looked like it would end in a riot, until Isa shouted, "Be still! All of you! Have you so little regard for my words that you seek violence in the streets at the first opportunity?" And then, almost inexplicably, no almost miraculously, the fighting stopped.

"Yes." Isa nodded several times, turning his head to various sectors of the crowd. "Yes, Yohanan was sentenced to death in this very square, and many of you may still suffer pangs of despair from this event while others seem still to applaud it. But while Yohanan was the first, he shall not be the last! Those of you who thirst for blood and hunger for destruction will feast upon those horrible toxins long before you comprehend the poisons they contain! Yet I tell you now, if you destroy this temple," Isa said with his arms raised to the sky, "I will raise it up in three days!"

It seemed to the crowd that Isa was referring to the Dome of the Rock that lie behind Isa and up the hill, and they murmured to each other, "How can he say this? It took many years to build."

An older man grabbed a microphone and asked, "By your crazy words, you seem to believe you can work amazing miracles, Isa. Is that what you call that trick you played on the crowd with your loyal idiot, Adin?"

Isa looked at the man with amazing compassion while Tomadus looked at him only with disdain. They both recognized him as one of the local residents who had seen Adin come back to life at the mortuary.

"I am sorry to see your faith runs so shallow that you cannot believe even the evidence of your own eyes," Isa said. "Yes, I saw you there when Adin awoke. Did you see me perform any tricks, as you put it?"

The man said nothing.

"No, I do not play 'tricks,'" Isa said. "I merely asked our benevolent Father to save Adin from the mortician's table, and he sent Adin back to us." He gestured to Adin and Adin joined him near the microphone. "I will not discuss this further," Isa continued, "but listen carefully to my words." Isa looked around at he entire crowd for a few seconds. "Unless you open your hearts, you are doomed."

Isa put his arm around Adin and reached his other arm out to the crowd. "This uncomplicated man understands far more about God than most of you ever will. Despite your obvious contempt, I ask my Father to forgive you, as I ask him to forgive you all."

Isa turned his head to Adin, who was smiling as usual. "Blessed are you when they insult you and persecute you and utter every kind of evil against you because of me. Rejoice and be glad, for your reward will be great in Heaven." With that, Isa nodded to the crowd and walked away from the microphone, with Adin arm in arm.

CHAPTER 86

ABDUL SABOOR ANWARI exited the jet in Dubai on the first leg of his trip to Washington. Huxley had flown ahead of him on American military transports to make a pitch to his boss. Anwari flew commercial to avoid tipping his hand to Pardus. As far as the Leopard knew, he was just travelling to DC at Pardus's orders to give Huxley a few helpful hints. Pardus had planned the trip long ago and Anwari had passed the security checks, so Anwari had already procured a temporary visa. Huxley's assistant had ensured the latest detention hadn't blown that. However, the last minute flight preparations eliminated any possibility of a direct DC flight; instead, he could only fly to Dubai in the afternoon, pick up a morning flight the next morning heading to Boston, and then fly to DC that evening. America could be his sanctuary from the Leopard. Maybe he had found his way out of the jungle.

Anwari left security and began walking toward the airport hotel, gazing around now and then to be sure he was not being followed. He saw nothing suspicious over his shoulder when he stopped at a fruit stand and bought a pomegranate. But as he turned away from the stand, he ran into an old colleague now playing the role of the raven: Dracoratio. Anwari's heart raced. After a few moments, he dug deep, smiled and tried his best to keep his tone even. He had revealed no wavering, no worry, had he? "I did not expect to see you here," said Anwari. "Where are you heading?"

"Nowhere important." Dracoratio let out a slow, guttural breath. "Stuck here with a flight delay. I travel with an old friend, Baqir. We dine at Hatam in a few minutes. Care to join us?"

"Sure. Baqir?"

"Yes, Baqir Najwa, though I rarely call him that anymore. Have you met him?"

"No," replied Anwari, wondering if he had actually spoken with Baqir many times on his cell but by another name. He swallowed hard. Had the terror in his eyes or the lump in his throat given him away?

❈ ❈ ❈

During his layover at Aviano AFB a few hours earlier, Huxley had desperately tried to reach Mayer without success. The nice people at the CIA had said the spymaster was "indisposed" and would "return the call at the first opportunity." In other words, standard CIA bullshit meaning they would never tell Huxley where Mayer was nor when he would surface. Mayer was ignoring his cell. Huxley really just wanted to record the bastard's voice so he could share it with Anwari and see if he had found the crowning clue to finally capture Pardus. And if there were no match, he could begin targeting the formerly dead, and now merely missing, Baqir Najwa. Either way, he had to know about Mayer.

He had shared just enough with his boss to get a meeting without tipping off any mole lurking at the agency. Huxley had berated Blount about keeping the matter close. The boss had asked him if Mayer knew. "No," Huxley had replied. "And it is critical—absolutely critical—that he not know. Trust me on this, and I'll tell you more when I get there."

The boss had responded, "What the hell, Huxley? Mayer isn't even here. He's checking out a lead in Dubai."

"Dubai?"

"Yes. Udani—who Mayer suspects is Dracoratio—has been spotted there, so Mayer thought he might just help us find this Pardus character."

Huxley had hung up and called Anwari. No answer. Probably still in the air. He had left a text message telling Anwari to beware of both Dracoratio and Mayer. Then he had been forced to make a choice—Washington or Dubai? Now sitting in the transport on its way to Langley AFB, Huxley covered his face with his hands. He had promised to protect Anwari but may have put him in harms way. Still, if he had tried to intervene in Dubai, he might have tipped off Pardus. No. This had been the only good option: play the thing out. *Come on Anwari, just check your damn messages.*

❆ ❆ ❆

Sitting across from his two Arab colleagues, Anwari fought off the nearly irresistible instinct screaming in his ear to get up and run the hell away from the obvious danger radiating from these two men. Dracoratio had always scared him. Pardus's right hand man kept his secrets close and publicly acted the part of an elite Emirati—Esnanimen Kharun Udani—but beneath the veneer he normally hid an efficient ruthlessness only visible to his terrorist colleagues. He had never shown any hesitation or regret during the capture of the chemist's family. In fact, he seemed to rather enjoy the work.

Yes, Dracoratio could be deadly here. He could be deadly anywhere. Huxley had warned him as much in the same text in which he had warned him about Half-Moon Mole showing his ugly face here in Dubai. But he had not seen Half-Moon Mole at all, and the danger from Dracoratio was nothing compared with the potential danger coming from the man he had just met, Baqir Najwa, the fat-faced Arab sitting across from him. Was this man Pardus? Despite a few attempts, Anwari could not push the conversation into English, since they all spoke fluent Arabic. But Anwari had only heard Pardus speak English, albeit with an Arabic accent, and then only on the phone. Sure, Najwa shared the same deep, intelligent, soothing tone, but was it the same voice? And what if he were Pardus? Anwari was simply carrying out the man's orders, so he had nothing to fear, right? But then why would Pardus be meeting him at the airport? No, if Najwa and Pardus are the same man, I shall not survive this day.

Maybe I should leave. Make an excuse and go to my hotel room. He knew that would be useless in the end. Pardus would find a way to get to him in Dubai, and Anwari would never even see it coming. *This may be a trap, but it's also an opportunity.* If he could figure out if Najwa was truly Pardus, it might prevent a nuclear nightmare.

"Tell me, Baqir, how do you know Esnanimen?" Anwari said in Arabic.

"We have known each other since we started in the Emir's security detail together so many years ago."

"Are you two still in that detail?"

Dracoratio put his hand on top of Anwari's forearm. "Not a matter we discuss. Tell me, Abdul, are you heading to America at Pardus's request?"

Anwari bit his lip. "Pardus?" he asked, with a look of ignorance indicating that Dracoratio should not be using that name. He tried to see how Najwa reacted, but his eyes revealed no sense of surprise.

"Najwa is one of us," Dracoratio said. "You need not be so circumspect."

Anwari looked at Najwa. *An opening.* "You are? How do you know Pardus, Baqir?"

"The same as you—from afar. Are you off to America?"

"Yes."

"For what purpose?" asked Najwa.

"That is between Pardus and me. Sorry."

"Of course. You have come from Afghanistan?"

Anwari nodded. "Kabul."

"Oh, I had been under the impression you may have been further south awhile." Najwa smiled.

Anwari leaned forward. "Why would you think that, Baqir?"

"It is nothing. Pardus just mentioned you had gone south for a few days. Perhaps he was speaking metaphorically?"

Anwari stared straight back into Najwa's eyes. Why would Pardus think that? Why would he tell Najwa? Anwari's breathing cadence had increased dramatically as his heart began pumping faster and harder. He tried a laugh but wasn't sure he pulled it off as authentic. "I dropped my phone in the toilet. He was probably just venting."

"Ah, perhaps you are right," said Najwa. "Are you warm, Abdul?"

"Warm?" Anwari asked.

"Yes, you appear to be sweating heavily on your brow. On second thought, I am sure it must be this food. Very delicious but very spicy, no?" Najwa picked up his napkin and dabbed the corners of his mouth and then continued, "Thank you for a delightful dinner, my friends, but the sun is about to set and *Maghrib* calls. Will you join me in the Airport prayer room, Abdul?"

Forcing a smile, Anwari rubbed his beard. Could he discover anything more? Was it the jaws of the trap snapping shut? If no other Muslims were in that room, walking in would be like walking alone down a dark alley in a downtrodden section of the city after showing a tavern full of vermin the wad of cash you were carrying. No cameras, no security personnel—just an empty, soundproof room where shouts and screams could reverberate but not easily escape. "I think I will just go to my hotel room and pray *Maghrib* there, but thank you for the offer."

"Oh, but prayers are always so much more fulfilling in congregation, do you not agree? Dracoratio?"

Dracoratio said, "Yes, we shall both join you, Baqir. Abdul, you will be in transit for the next day. You should take advantage of your last opportunity to pray communally. You are Sunni?"

Anwari nodded. They seemed sincere. The prayer room would likely be filled at this time of day. He could not afford to let them become suspicious. He forced a big smile. "You two are very persuasive. Yes, I will pray with you."

Najwa led them to the second prayer room for men. That was a problem. With two prayer rooms, either one was more likely to be poorly attended. On the way, Dracoratio stopped quickly for a drink from a water fountain and then paused shortly afterwards, studying the framed glass-covered painting above the fountain. Dracoratio turned back to join them with a slightly pinched expression on his face, his eyes narrowing quickly and his lips tightening. A moment later he smiled. As they approached the room, Dracoratio pulled out his cell and looked at it. He waved at Najwa and Anwari. "Go on in. I will join you in a few minutes. Pardus wants to speak with me." He touched the screen and said, "Yes? Of course." Then he strolled away, and Najwa opened the door for Anwari.

When the lights turned on automatically, Anwari winced. They would be the room's only inhabitants. *Too late to turn back.* Anwari kept Najwa to his front during the entire cleansing ritual and again as they assumed their prayer positions on the floor, but the door to the airport and Dracoratio loomed behind him, for even the depth of his fear could not change the location of Mecca. In the middle of their prayer, he heard the door open. Peering secretly under his arm, Anwari saw only a pair of legs clothed—not with Arab robes but with a pair of tan slacks. Anwari put his lips together, exhaled quickly, and relaxed his muscles back to his praying posture. When he heard a deep melodic voice calling his name and Najwa's, they turned in unison and grimaced. The man smiled at them both and said, "Well, hello again, gentlemen."

It was not Dracoratio. Anwari remembered the man's deep voice and immediately recognized his face with the half-moon mole. He wanted to jump at the spook who still haunted his memories, but froze at the gun pointing at his chest. He heard Najwa laugh nervously. Every muscle in Anwari tensed, every artery pulsed with his hot blood as the twin bullies of anger and fear overcame him. "You," was all he could say.

"Indeed. It is time to bring this to an end." Mayer looked at Najwa and smiled.

The conversation and charade that followed proved highly unusual and terribly short—far too short; nonetheless, it would bring Anwari great enlightenment. Unfortunately, this enlightenment would also prove short lived, as would Anwari himself. Anwari gave the best performance of his life, and so managed to tell a lie about Huxley as his last act on Earth. He doubted it would send him to hell. Nevertheless, just before he died from a bullet to the temple, he spoke only one word: "*Astaghfirullah*," which means, "Allah forgive me."

CHAPTER 87

I SA SAT WITH the Ten, Maryam, Jochi, Peregrine and Tomadus in a hillside garden outside of Jerusalem. The morning sun danced off the dew dripping from the leaves of the palms as the crested larks chirped their morning songs. The fresh scent of flowering mandrakes and irises filled the air. Isa seemed to prefer this spot for early morning prayers, which he typically followed up with a time for group reflection with his closest followers. This morning everyone seemed focused on the previous day's speech in Muhammad Square.

Simeon said, "You were magnificent." Many of the Ten echoed this view. "Obviously," he continued, "our enemies placed some hecklers in the crowd, but you handled them beautifully."

"Our enemies?" responded Isa. "Is that still how you think?"

"Whatever you want to call them," Simeon shrugged. "The people who don't believe."

"The Father loves all people, regardless of their beliefs. They can still find their way. Have you learned nothing?"

Simeon nodded humbly. "Yes, of course. I am sorry."

"Teacher," Anders said, breaking the awkward silence. "I was confused by the story of the religious leader and the king. I understand how people might suffer if we do not truly follow God, but what if we could garner the support of the Three Emperors—what if they sanctioned what you said? Think of your ability to get others to believe!"

Isa sighed. "I see you have entirely missed the point, Anders. The righteous often assume they and their leaders will always remain so. This is impossible because men are flawed. Power tends to corrupt the powerful, and even if there is no corruption, the people will suspect it in every room where earthly power holds sway. So what happens when the Way becomes tied too closely with the political power of the state? Will people trust the Way more? Or will some worry that the Way is becoming corrupted by this power? Those who have much faith and hope may begin to doubt the intentions of their own religious leaders and the purity of their beliefs. And thus, by seeking to use this political power to prop up our church, we succeed only in sinking it down into the muck."

"But surely you would not let that happen!" replied Anders.

Isa looked around at each of his followers. "I must leave you soon, and you all must carry on. Heed what I say and avoid these traps, for I assure you our Father in Heaven does not wish to so tempt the souls of those who may lead after me."

The Ten all looked queerly at Isa.

Isa turned to Tomadus and said, "What say you, Tomadus? I sense your views of my speech may differ from the others."

Tomadus frowned. He had hoped to speak with Isa privately. "I fear for you, Isa. The speech was not broadcast in its entirety in the Three Empires and Roma. Despite the First Consul's efforts, the visi-scan network ran it with a small delay, cutting the parts they did not like. I worry you may have angered the Three Emperors, for why else would they censor the broadcast?"

"What was cut?" asked Simeon.

"I was told several parts, some large, some small. Most of the discussion about the links between God and the state. Do you think the emperors would allow that colloquy when they claim to rule by the hand of Allah?"

"Was any of the message distorted by the cuts?" Simeon asked.

"I don't know. I have not seen a replay. I have only heard from a tech friend."

Isa blinked slowly. "I thought your First Consul had arranged for the entire speech to be broadcast live. What do you think went wrong?"

"He tried and was given assurances. I guess even he has limited power in such matters. I assured him you would avoid criticisms of the emperors, as you and I had discussed. That might have caused the problem."

"I did not criticize them at all. I merely pointed to the disease in the underlying structure."

Tomadus shook his head. "That is a little bit like telling a man you didn't push over his chair when you merely cut off one of its legs."

Isa laughed. "Very good, Tomadus. The image is quite…amusing. But allow me to ask you a question, if I could."

"Of course."

"If that part of the speech reached no one of consequence in the Three Empires, then why would the Three Emperors be angered?"

"It reached all of the people in the square in a different manner than on the visi-scan. Word may spread among your followers that the Emperors are not to be trusted."

"Won't the broadcasters simply blame any differences on technical problems? Nobody will discuss it openly anyway."

"Perhaps. But I fear the Emperors' motives. I wonder if we did anything to convince them or the religious leaders of your bona fides. It is imperative."

Isa nodded. "So you have told me. In any case, if they worry about the possible impact of this speech, do you think it might have such an impact? Do you believe we accomplished some good?"

"Yes, I suppose, but at great risk to you and the others here."

"Then tell me, what is it you wish to accomplish—to preserve our lives in relative comfort and safety or to follow my lead and God's will?"

Tomadus frowned as he took in Isa's words. *Does he truly believe his lead and God's will are one in the same?* He forced a weak smile. "I wish only to help you, Isa."

Isa stared at Tomadus for a few seconds and then opened his arms to all of them. "There was once a group of people living on a large island in the middle of a vast ocean before there were *aeronaves* or any long sea voyages. Nobody ever visited or left the island, and nearly everyone who lived there thought they were alone in the world.

"The people on this island divided themselves into groups that engaged in interminable fights over the island's limited resources, which constrained their resources even further. And so the people generally struggled for survival, living just well enough to keep them alive, and often not even that.

"Finally, a leader emerged who told his people about a great vision he had seen of a wonderful land across the sea, where all people lived in peace and plenty. Anyone from any group that helped him build a grand boat according to his own design could accompany him on his trip to this great land.

"Many ridiculed him, saying, 'Show us the vision so that we may understand the way to this wonderful land. Otherwise, you are threatening the death of us all on the treacherous sea with your pure fantasy.' And a few from the other side of the island thought him dangerous, believing that the boat would end up being a warship that would attack them on their shores. But a few from each group believed him and began the arduous process of building a larger boat than had ever been attempted before.

"Now, one of the most brilliant men from the islands began to study what this new leader was doing. He did not believe there was any other land across the sea, let alone a beautiful land full of peace and plenty, since he had neither seen nor heard any hard evidence of such a land. Though he had heard stories of other lands many years earlier, he thought those stories were simply myths told to comfort the weak and feeble minded.

"Nevertheless, something drew this brilliant man to the new leader. He saw that the new leader's project was bringing people together from many of the groups on the island, and it seemed to him that this project might be the way to help everyone on the island live better, happier and more peaceful lives. So he joined the new leader and began to help him construct the boat.

"The brilliant man was a very talented organizer and manager and seemed to understand the principles of building boats like none of the new leader's other followers. He relished how many of the people of the island were beginning to cooperate and learn to live together through the building of this boat. When the boat neared completion, he worried incessantly, thinking that the community accomplishments would evaporate when the new leader departed on the boat. Worse yet, he feared that the leader and all of his followers would ultimately perish on the seas. He truly loved the leader and could not bear to see this happen.

"So the brilliant man approached the new leader with a plan, hoping to stall for time. 'You must convince everyone that we need to build more boats, and then the entire island will come together in peaceful cooperation.' But the new leader simply smiled and told the man that there was plenty of room on his boat for all who wished to go. Building more boats would simply delay their departure to the paradise that awaited them across the sea.

"Now this man became disconsolate. He felt sure that after the leader left, the island would descend into chaos. After brooding about this and the coming loss of his good friend, a new plot entered into the brilliant man's mind: 'If I destroy the boat by convincing one of the other leaders to attack it,' he thought, 'we will need to build at least one more boat.' After some garnering support among his old friends from the other side of the island, his plot was hatched and ready to come to fruition. The boat would be attacked and destroyed in the morning, well before his new friends were scheduled to board the boat for the rich land.

"But in the middle of the night, the leader awakened the brilliant man, saying: 'We are leaving on the boat tonight with the tide. Gather your things and join us.'

"'But you are not supposed to leave until tomorrow night,' responded the brilliant man.

"'Why, so your old friends can destroy our boat?'

"'How did you know?'

"'That matters not,' responded the leader, 'but your heart was in the right place, and I forgive you your misguided actions. You are a good man and have helped begin to realize my vision for all of us. You are my friend, but where I am going you may not follow unless you, too, can believe in my vision. So tell me, will you come with me?'"

After pausing for a few seconds, Isa looked directly at Tomadus. "And what do you think this brilliant man did?"

Tomadus looked down and mumbled, "I do not know."

Isa tilted his head, smiled and said, "Then neither do I." He looked up at the others. "Rest assured all of you: that ship will soon sail, not three days after I tell everyone it is finished."

CHAPTER 88

JOCHI REMAINED IN the garden alone, thinking about Isa's latest words. She struggled to reconcile them with what she now knew of the other world of this Jesus that Tomadus and she had seen. Would they soon sail to paradise? When would the ship be finished? She shook her head and kneeled down in prayer. "Dear Father, I thank you again for sending Isa to us. Please let me travel with him on his ship to paradise. Dear Lord, help me understand these visions you have sent me of this other world. Isa calls this ability a gift, yet it confuses me so. Please help me to understand why you have given me this gift."

Jochi looked up at the sky. She saw the glow of the sun, its comforting rays warming her cheeks. She smiled. The sun's rays seemed to grow in intensity until she could see nothing but light. Then the visions of the other world began. She saw a beautiful city from a distance, like she was on a mountain above. Suddenly, the brightness of the sun seemed to envelop the city for a second, evaporating into a cloud that covered the city from view. When the cloud finally cleared, much of the city had simply disappeared among the ashes. Except it had not just disappeared, it had been ruined, for the rubble began to appear through the smoke along with the burned bodies of now unrecognizable humans. As she began screaming in terror, a gentle man appeared—was it Isa? He smiled softly at her and touched her on the shoulder. When she covered her hand with his, he waved his other hand, and the city began rebuilding itself before her eyes.

When the light subsided, Jochi found herself on her hands and knees, sobbing. On the ground before her, she noticed the former contents of her stomach. She returned to her knees and yelled out, "Why have you shown me this? I do not understand."

The light flashed again and the former vision of the sun exploding over the city repeated many times, though each episode differed. Yes, she was on a mountain above a beautiful city. And yes, the beautiful city was destroyed. But each time the destruction came to a different beautiful city. And this time, a man in black hair and a black beard sat next to her on the mountain watching the destruction. The man had a tattoo on his upper left arm consisting of tiny identical black dots repeating in equidistant spaces in increasingly larger rows to form the shape of a perfect equilateral triangle with "T_{36}" written below it. The other arm displayed the tattoo of a leopard. Each time a new city was destroyed, he looked at her and bellowed as if gloating over yet another victory. The light began to subside, but the images had overwhelmed her, and she collapsed.

When she awoke, only a few long rays of the sun still found their way through the line of trees to the garden. She felt the dampness of her chador against her body, the abundance of sweat still cooling her body late in the day. She returned to her knees and tried again to pray, but the visions would not return. When she began to shake and cry, she bit her lip and thought of Isa. *He could help me understand.* She took a few deep breaths and the shaking stopped.

Jochi soon found her way back to the small house in Bethany where Isa and many of the Ten were staying. When she entered the common room, Diego stopped playing his oud, stood and walked over to her. "Are you all right, Jochi?"

"I…I don't know. I think I'll be OK. Have you seen Isa?"

"He's in the bedroom upstairs."

"Asleep?" she asked.

"No, praying I think."

"Oh."

"You look like you need him." Diego gestured up the stairs.

She looked up the stairs and hesitated. "I don't…I don't know."

"He won't mind. He and I are the only ones here. You can go—it is Isa."

Just before she arrived at the door, Isa opened it. "Jochi, welcome. You feel great pain. Come, sit down and tell me what troubles you."

After Isa closed the door quietly behind them, Jochi sat on the bed with Isa beside her. "I have told you before that I am having visions of the other world Tomadus mentions."

"Yes. A gift from the Father."

"I know you have said that, but I am having trouble believing it is anything but a curse."

"A curse?"

"The visions I am seeing grow increasingly horrible. Tomadus has mentioned none of these. He talks only of threats from a Pardus his Huxley is trying to stop. Why do I see these other terrors when he does not?"

"Like Tomadus, you must find your own answers, Jochi."

"I know, but please help me down that path. These visions are tearing me apart. I passed out for several hours after the last vision. I don't know how much longer I can continue."

Isa smiled gently and patted her shoulder. "Be careful not to become fixated with time."

"Fixated with time? You mean my visions may be of a time different than Tomadus's? But how? I feel like I see this world through Sonatina. I have seen his Huxley with my own eyes."

"And yet…"

"And yet I see things he doesn't see. Horrible things. They must be the other world in his Huxley's future."

"Must be?"

"Yes. No. Wait. I had two very different visions. The first made me wretch in horror, but then you…"

"Me?"

"Well, someone like you. He seemed to make things better. But then I woke and began praying again. The next vision made me whimper helplessly. It was worse, far worse. The wicked man just kept laughing as everything was destroyed."

When she began crying, Isa put his arm around her and pulled her head to his chest. "These two visions seem to conflict."

"Yes, it is as if they are two different futures, two different versions of this other world. What can this mean? I beg of you Isa, please tell me. You must know. You know everything."

"Do you have faith in me, Jochi?'

"Of course. You were sent by the Father. I believe."

"Then you understand what must happen here, in this world."

Jochi pulled back and looked into his eyes, which gazed back into her, as they always did. She nodded and burst into tears. "There must be another way."

"Tomadus must play his role. I believe in you, Jochi, as you believe in me. If only Tomadus could…"

"Could what?"

"Jochi, you and Tomadus play an important role in this other world. Can you see that?"

She nodded.

"And Huxley and Sonatina play an important role in this world. Can you see that?"

"I hadn't thought about it that way."

"This gift you and Tomadus share is exceedingly rare. Such gifts are not granted without purpose. Your awareness of your intertwined souls can benefit both worlds."

She tilted her head and narrowed her eyes.

"Our Father works in mysterious ways," Isa said. "If each of you have faith, you shall do what is right. Have faith. You shall save yourself and so many others."

Jochi begged Isa to explain, but he would say no more. They stood and embraced, the tears still running down her cheeks.

❊ ❊ ❊

Despite so little sleep, Huxley had struggled to nod off in the transport back to the States. And every time he managed it, he awoke thinking of the same strange dream. When his transport reached Andrews AFB, Huxley saw that Anwari had sent him a brief text: "Is Najwa Pardus? In Dubai w Dracoratio." *I should have flown to Dubai.* His chest pounding, Huxley tried calling Anwari, but there was no answer. *Damn!* He could not call Emirate Security forces. That would completely blow Anwari's cover. All he could do for Anwari now was hope.

Sonatina had called but left no message. The only voice mail was from Lt. Patismio, who told Huxley that he was heading to bed, so Huxley should call him tomorrow.

Huxley's phone started singing to him, and he saw Sonatina's name pop up. When he closed his eyes, he envisioned not the gentle smile of her pleasing visage but the winking eye of a cardinal's conceit. He looked at the phone again, began returning it to his pocket, then stopped and hit the green button. "How is my favorite Vatican art administrator? I hear you give a great tour."

"*Che cosa?* Chris, you all right?"

"Just tired."

"Tired—you still having that same dream?"

"No, onto a new one."

"Tell me." After a few seconds of silence, she added sweetly, "Please, Chris, I can help you."

Huxley tilted his head, his eyes darting. *Why not? She needs to believe you still trust her.* "Ok. On the transport I kept dreaming that I was sitting in a garden on a hill in a strange land. I was with a dozen or so men and a woman—I think it was you. No, not quite. Anyway, we were all sitting in a circle, listening to that same man in white robes. He was telling us a story about a boat builder on an island and how the boat builder planned to take his followers across the sea to a land of paradise revealed to him only in his visions. He wanted one of his followers to believe his vision, but he couldn't. He said he could only go with him to paradise if he believed the vision. He stopped the story and looked right at me. I was wearing a strange robe as well. He asked me what the brilliant man did and I told him I didn't know, though I knew he was talking about me."

"What…uh…what did the man in the white robes say when you said that?" Sonatina asked.

"He just told me that he didn't know either."

Sonatina gasped. "Chris, these dreams are from God. Don't you see?"

Huxley laughed. "It is just a strange dream. I always get those when I have gone too long without sleep."

"But what about me?"

"You?"

"I had the same dream, but from the woman's perspective. I've had many crazy dreams lately, but this is at least the second time I've dreamed the same thing as you."

"You're joking. You must have heard me talk about it."

"No. You were on the transport. We've never talked about boat builders or paradise. It is not coincidence. You must listen to your dreams."

"Listen? To what? A man in robes talk about building boats?"

"You know who He is."

"I know who you want him to be."

"He said He didn't know."

"So?"

"So, He's telling you that you still have a chance. You must believe in Him."

A tingle slinked slowly down Huxley's back. Huxley closed his eyes and shook his head. *She trying to screw with me—another Pardusian tactic?* "Why do you keep doing this to me?"

"Doing what?"

"Trying to shove God back in my face."

"Chris, I don't dream for you. I don't carry the crucifix for you. I don't have conversations with priests about the existence of God. Just admit it to yourself. You still need Him."

"Look. Just drop it, will you. I'm tired. Yes, I dreamed again. But let it go. I am so tired from this long journey."

"Your flight to Washington," she said.

"Yeah, that too. No, I mean this much longer journey."

"Oh, the terrorist's game."

"Game? Yes, his game. Know anything more?" he asked.

"I identified the Arab who received the package. Patismio said it was some guy named Najwar, or something like that."

"Najwa? Baqir Najwa?" Huxley asked with excitement.

"*Si.* Is that helpful?"

Huxley shook his head. "You never disappoint."

"I hope not, yet you sound disappointed."

"No, just worried."

"About what?" she asked.

"Sorry, can't share that."

"No. I guess not." Now she sounded disappointed.

Huxley stared at two F-22s taking off. Should he say more? If she were with him, it wouldn't matter. If she were not, then it would help confirm for Pardus that he believed in Pardus's fake target. "I do have some good news. I figured out the latest poem, well, most of it. You were right on the father angle. Washington is the father of my country. Washington never slept in the White House, which lies in front of Jefferson's statue. And it appears Washington was not murdered like all those Washington residents may be soon if I can't manage to wrap my head around this thing."

"Brilliant," she replied enthusiastically. "Then you have reached the end of the line. It makes sense because Washington is the American capital. Yes, that is where a terrorist would strike if they could. It even fits my…"

"Fits your what?"

"Nothing…uh…my thoughts. It fits my thoughts. You have found your answer."

Huxley cocked his head. *She really excited or just priming the pump for Pardus? Keep playing.* "Not quite. I still don't know who Pardus is, unless…" He paused to see if she would fill in the blank.

She accommodated. "Pardus is Baqir Najwa?"

"Why would you say that?" he asked.

"Why not? He's obviously tied in with Fine. Maybe you could find out for certain if you arrest and interrogate him?"

Huxley frowned. *Are you tied in with Fine too?* "Kind of hard to interrogate a dead man."

"Dead? I saw him. You have to believe me, Chris."

He tried to make his voice upbeat. "Of course I do. Yet there is still something quite disquieting about a supposedly dead Arab receiving a package from a corrupt former cardinal in the middle of the night."

"You being funny?" she asked tensely.

He shook his head. "How else can I be? You?"

"Funny?"

"Yeah."

"I don't think so." Worry tightened her voice. "You all right?"

"Just tired, I guess." That and he couldn't get the cardinal's wink out of his mind. "You said you didn't know Fine well, right?"

"Yeah, but…"

"But what?"

Sonatina spoke quietly. "I forgot to tell you one thing about Fine."

"What's that?" Huxley asked.

She paused a few seconds. "He was on the Vatican Art Board for a year or so. He was a creep and kept looking at me with wanting eyes."

"He think you were the Mona Lisa?"

"More like Venus de Milo. And that man has taken a vow of celibacy. Now you know why I think he is a snake."

Huxley frowned. Was this honesty or had he tipped off that the cardinal had mentioned something to him and now she was covering? "You just thought of telling me this now?"

"*Si. Mi dispiace*, but it did not seem important to your investigation, and I…I tend to block it out. Have you ever done that, Chris?"

He sighed. "Sure. I'm a bit worried about you though. Washington may be one target, but I have a feeling Rome is the other."

"Should I come to see you there? I have plenty of vacation time saved."

"No. It's probably more dangerous in the States right now. I'll let you know if I think you should get out."

"I trust you with my life, Chris. Do you trust me?" she asked.

He held back a sigh. "How could I not?"

"Do you trust me when I tell you that I love you?"

"That takes a warhead full of trust for me, but I think I'm almost there."

"Almost?" she asked, this time pouting genuinely.

"Hey, Venus, it doesn't matter, you know, because I would love you even if you favored my worst enemy. How could I not?" His tone had made it sound like a joke, but he wasn't sure…

∇   ∇   ∇

…As Tomadus climbed the stairs to Isa's room, he paused halfway up to let his latest vision wash over him. Huxley had struggled to trust Sonatina again, but this was not just another episode in Huxley's life. Huxley had told her of a strange dream with a scene so familiar to Tomadus that he had not even realized Huxley had dreamed it because it overlapped with his own memories in this world. Huxley had dreamed it, but Tomadus had lived it. He still felt pangs of doubt when he thought of Isa's last question to him: "And what do you think this brilliant man did?" After he closed his eyes to dispel the vision, its import finally struck him—if Huxley dreamed of him and he heard Huxley's dreams, then maybe the two could find a way to communicate across the divide of these parallel universes. But why was Huxley dreaming of Tomadus now? And how could he cause Huxley to dream of him again? He shook his head. He must discuss it with Jochi. He continued up the stairs.

Not wanting to disturb Isa from prayer, Tomadus quietly opened the bedroom door. What he saw in the dimly lit room sent his heart to his stomach: Jochi emerged from Isa's arms as she wiped a tear and turned to leave. When Isa held her hand firmly and looked at her with such a soft look of pure love, Tomadus nearly turned away in embarrassment. She nodded at Isa gently with a loving yet slightly restrained smile and turned to the door, seeing Tomadus for the first time. She smiled at him too, and he wanted to return the expression, but a somehow familiar verse clouded his thoughts: "Poor king of love, in my own law forlorn. To love a cheek that smiles at me in scorn!" Where had he read that? Scorn? She had only been kind to him as had Isa. He forced a nod and smile to Jochi as she left the room.

Isa stood silently, his arms crossed. "You must forgive her," Isa said softly. "She is being pulled in many directions, but she, too, will eventually understand."

"Do you love her?"

"Of course," Isa replied as if Tomadus had asked him whether he breathed air. "You wanted to see me?"

"Yes, I would like to share my plan with you."

Isa raised his eyebrows. "Your plan?"

"Yes. The broadcast was only a beginning. In some ways, it may have made things worse. We need to change your path before it is too late."

"My path?" responded Isa woodenly.

"Yes, you know as well as I do what happened to Jesus. You seem to be going down the same path, but we can find a new way. This time we have a friend on the inside who can help us."

Isa laughed.

"What?"

"Tomadus, you have a conflicted soul. You often suspect the worst of those who love you the most, yet you are blinded by those who love you the least."

"The First Consul trusts me and I trust him. Do you know how many times he has helped me? How many times he has helped us both?"

Isa closed his eyes slowly and then reopened them.

Tomadus pulled his lips together and exhaled hard through his nose. "You are in danger, Isa. We must change the story. We tried through the broadcast, but we need more. We must convince them you are sincere. The First Consul and I believe you can right the ship if we do it at once."

"Right the ship? Are you sure you do not seek to destroy the boat?"

Tomadus shook his head. "You do not understand. The Abh Beyth Diyn and the Grand Imams apparently still believe you to be a fraud. The First Consul has confided this in me. He believes, I believe, you must convince them you actually believe in what you say. If we can turn them, the First Consul can keep the Emperors on your side."

"What do you believe, Tomadus, about me?"

Tomadus checked for the creature, but it did not stir. He did not know what he believed, and everything had become so confusing since the Adin miracle. "What does it matter? We believe—"

"We?" Isa interrupted.

"The First Consul and I believe that if you were put to the test and passed, you would win them over. It would make all the difference. Your mission could continue. You could even return to Tetepe."

"It is written, 'You shall not put the Lord, your God, to the test.'"

Tomadus bit his lip hard. *Now he is God?* "They are not looking for miracles, Isa, only your sincerity. Think of it like when God tested Abraham by asking him to sacrifice his son Isaac on the altar. God did not go through with it, nor shall they. If you do not back down in the face of their adversity, you shall win. We all shall win."

"And what would I 'win'?"

"Stop parsing my every word!"

"Then what adversity do you anticipate?"

Tomadus lowered his voice, "I don't know exactly. They will probably threaten to harm you, but the First Consul will control the proceeding. He has promised you will not come to harm. I know you think your fate remains inevitable—that you must follow the same path as Jesus. You need not. I'm telling you we have the means to change what happened in that other world. Your mission will continue. Isa, think of the things you could accomplish."

Isa closed his eyes, clasping his palms together for a few seconds. He opened them and stared for a few seconds into Tomadus's eyes. "Do what you must. It seems your efforts are necessary."

"I'm glad you finally see it," replied Tomadus triumphantly.

Isa's eyes misted over as he regarded Tomadus for several seconds. He bit his lip, turned and slowly walked away.

CHAPTER 89

"Damn it! The target is New York City. We have to move the UNGARD there now!" Huxley had blurted out his conclusion without any explanation. What had happened to his carefully crafted speech artfully leading up to that point? Well, it went right into the shitter as soon as Huxley had walked into Deputy Under Secretary Blount's office. His boss had acted strangely, asking him a few surprising questions and seeming to probe for hidden answers. The oddity had forced his hand. It was almost as if Blount were revving up for one of his famous, torturous tongue-lashings. What the hell had Huxley done wrong now?

His lips lined and eyebrows raised, Blount crossed his arms and asked in a skeptical tone, "And how did you come by this conclusion?"

"It has been a long path, but the clincher came just before I hopped on the plane from Kabul. You know we have been trying to decipher the clues in Najwa's phone contacts list. Well I did that, and it points conclusively to Washington as the target."

"DC? Then why the hell are you telling me the target is New York City?"

"Because Pardus told me the whole contacts list thing was a sham. He was trying to misdirect the investigation to waste my time and convince me to ultimately focus our efforts on Washington."

"You spoke with Pardus?"

"Not exactly. He spoke with one of his agents, whom I have now turned, and I was able to listen in on the whole conversation without Pardus's knowledge. He did not specifically ID New York, but he told my informant to avoid the area a few hours north of DC if he wanted to be safe. Plus, the informant said he had previously referred to the target as 'The Apple.' Where else could it be?"

"I see," said Blount. "Then you have identified Pardus?"

"No, not completely. My informant says he has a deep, resonant voice and speaks in English with an Arabic accent."

"That does not narrow it down much. Who is your informant?"

"A former Afghan army hero, Abdul Saboor Anwari. He is on his way here. We need to protect him from Pardus. But keep Mayer out of it. I'm worried he may be helping Pardus…or worse."

Blount put both hands on his desk and leaned forward. "Are you suggesting Mayer may be Pardus? Are you nuts?"

"No. Look, I don't know for sure, but I don't want to compromise the mission here. If we screw this up because of misplaced loyalties, there will be no way to reverse a nuclear explosion in Manhattan. I have plenty of reasons for my suspicions. Whoever put together the contacts list on that phone had way too much personal information on me—information I know Mayer knows, but not many others, not even in the CIA or Homeland. Pardus has to have an inside contact, plus Mayer's been squirrely about this entire mission. I hate to say it, but it feels like he has given me too much rope—way too much for him given his personal style—and I can only think he is doing that to lead me astray. He can speak with a perfect Arab accent. He was the CIA intel agent in Afghanistan when shit went bad and Anwari's brother was killed by a JDAM ordered by Anwari. Mayer also had Anwari stuffed in cold storage without even having someone interrogate him. That's tough to understand when nukes are hanging in the balance. I was able to get to Anwari only after a specific plea."

"Wait, you told Mayer you had turned Anwari?"

"No. But I had to tell him I was interrogating Anwari and trying to turn him just to get Mayer to agree that I could meet with him and release him."

Blount sat back in his chair. "What if Mayer knew you turned him?"

"That was a risk I had to take. I was out of options. But look, if he is

Pardus or his informer, they still don't know if I turned Anwari. They just know I tried."

"But the call with Pardus would be the clincher. Did Pardus ask about where he had been?"

"Yes, we expected that, but we had a good excuse. You cannot buy a phone in Afghanistan during the Islamic holiday—all the stores are closed. So he had dropped it in the toilet."

"But if Mayer is involved, they would know he was lying. That would give him up."

Huxley shook his head. "You might think so, but everyone knows about Pardus's reputation for eliminating loose ends. It would be a death sentence for anyone from Pardus's gang to admit to having been caught by the CIA. They would watch him after that, but they could not be sure without more. I told Mayer I might have to spring him and watch him awhile to find out anything. So he can't be sure. The last thing is the voice. Anwari has heard Pardus's voice. I just need to get a recording of Mayer's voice in Arabic to Anwari and see if he IDs him."

"Why would Mayer do this? He passed all of the psych and background tests years ago. Never heard he was disgruntled, so why?"

"That is the toughest question," said Huxley, "but who the hell knows? He has made connections all over the globe and they don't pay CIA operators that much. Why does anyone shit on his own country? Money? Maybe. Or maybe he likes the power. Some people just like to pull their little levers and laugh when they see nobody even realizes what little puppets they have become. I know Pardus cherishes his own cleverness. He undoubtedly is arrogant as hell—just like Mayer. Still, I really don't know. Nevertheless, we can't risk taking a chance right now, not with nukes at stake. So we keep him out of the loop, okay?"

Blount grimaced, looked out the window and then back at Huxley. "What if Mayer's voice doesn't match Pardus's?"

"Then I have one other principal suspect, and I'll focus on him."

"Who would that be?"

"Baqir Najwa."

Blount raised both of his eyebrows and stared for a full five count. "I thought you said a few months ago that he died at Ramat David."

Huxley shook his head slowly. "Turns out that was a dodge we missed because Aman was a bit careless. I just got a call from my contact there—they finally ran a blood sample against the DNA we had on Najwa from Gitmo and confirmed the body at Ramat was not his. No, Najwa is more heavily involved in this thing than I had originally thought—he either is Pardus or is working closely with the Leopard. I've heard his voice and it matches the voice Anwari described. If Mayer's not our guy, then I'd bet on Najwa. The other possibility is Dracoratio—Esnanimen Kharun Udani. Anwari confirmed that alias. We've always seen him as the lieutenant, but I suppose he could also be Pardus himself. I doubt it, but it's possible. If Pardus is none of the above, then your guess is as good as mine. Hell, he's evaded our detection for ten years, would it surprise you if he had managed that again?"

Deputy Under Secretary Blount sat back in his chair and rested his chin on his clasped hands, his eyes focusing and refocusing on different parts of the room.

Huxley cocked his head. *The old man's trying to decide whether to tell me something. He wondering if I'm going off the deep end again?*

Blount leaned forward and nearly whispered to Huxley, "You won't have to worry about Baqir Najwa anymore, nor do we need to provide any protection to your informant."

"Why?" Huxley asked weakly.

"Because they were both found this morning in a prayer room in Dubai International Airport with 9mm bullets in them."

Huxley swallowed hard, trying to keep his emotions inside. He'd let Anwari down. The man's blood was on his hands. "How?"

"We don't know with certainty yet, but it looks like they were both shot by the same gun."

"Murder-suicide? Anwari had no weapon. He'd been on a plane."

"Najwa did and so did the shooter."

"The shooter wasn't Najwa?"

"No," said Blount. "It was Ken Mayer."

Huxley's jaw dropped.

"That's right," Blount said. "He was found dead alongside the others. Looks like Mayer shot Anwari first in the head execution style and then shot

Najwa in the gut just as Najwa was pulling out his own pistol. Apparently Najwa had the last say and killed Mayer with a shot to the head. Najwa tried to get up a few times, crawled across the floor but bled out in the prayer room. That's just the preliminary report. No witnesses. Nobody heard any shots. Bodies were discovered early this morning."

"Why didn't you tell me this right away?" asked Huxley.

"Given Mayer's involvement, I had to see what you knew first. We're still trying to figure this out."

"If you are right on the sequence, it seems that I was right about Mayer. Anwari was unarmed. Mayer must have executed him as a loose end, and Najwa saw a hair too late that he was next. That suggests Mayer was either Pardus or his agent."

"Sounds about right," nodded Blount.

"What about Dracoratio?"

"What about him? He wasn't there," said Blount with a note of authority.

"Oh, but he was." Huxley showed Blount the last text he had received from Anwari.

"Crap!" Blount chewed on his bottom lip and shook his head for a few seconds. "So he may still be engaged."

"No doubt. And as the second in command, he will still be moving to deploy the nukes."

"And you're sure he'll try to take one of the warheads into New York City?"

Huxley leaned forward, placing both palms on Blount's desk. "If we don't stop him. I saw Anwari's face and heard his inflections. He was smart, but he was no great actor. He believed New York was the target. He was a loose end, so Pardus killed him. It all fits. No, the clues were the ruse, not Anwari. Washington's the red herring. New York's the target. The only risk is if they figured out I discovered the truth, then they might try to change the location. But I suspect that would take time to plan. For now, there is only one choice: we move the UNGARD from the Chesapeake Search Zone to the New York Bay Search Zone. We've had the Continuity of Government plan in place for a few weeks now to help DC. We raise it up a level or two. Anyway, in the meantime, just in case we are wrong, the Coast Guard searches every boat, every pleasure craft—hell, every raft and log—that gets within 15 miles of the Chesapeake's entrance, and we hope they can find the warhead. But Pardus's plan points to New York. We don't tip our hand there."

"They have two nukes. Why not both New York and Washington?"

"I think the other is targeted for Rome. Just a hunch, but it's the only thing that explains the cardinal."

"Cardinal?" asked Blount.

"Yep, a former Catholic cardinal, Armondo Fine, is mixed up in this. He would seem extraneous if Rome is not a target."

Blount raised his eyebrows. "You tell the Italian authorities?"

"Well, I hinted as much to a Carabinieri lieutenant, but I figured the official warning should be made by you or the State Department, given our confidentiality commitment to Pakistan."

"What if you are wrong and they are also targeting Washington?"

Huxley shook his head. "Doesn't make sense. Why would they lead me to the District if they plan to target it? Could be another city, but DC seems pretty damn unlikely."

"OK if we are going to get the UNGARD moved, I'll need you to help me convince the Under Secretary, then the Secretary and the President."

"Of course." Huxley got up to leave his boss's office, but then turned. "Was there anything else in the prayer room in Dubai—any other clues that might help?"

"Not that I've heard. Oh, there was one quirk."

"What's that?" Huxley asked.

"Anwari had a picture of a young family in his hand. We haven't ID'd it yet."

"His brother's family. Saw it at Chapman. He probably grabbed it to comfort his distress."

"I doubt that, since Anwari had ripped the picture down its middle, right through the man's face."

CHAPTER 90

HUXLEY LOOKED AROUND at the three officers with the mic'd aviation helmets. The sound permeating his own helmet—the constant vibration and the thwack, thwack, thwack of the Jayhawk—nearly took him back to his days in Afghanistan years ago. But this was no Black Hawk. There were no rugged mountains below. The Coast Guard whirlybird sped over the cool waters of the Atlantic, taking him farther from the Staten Island Coast Guard Station where he had spent a few weeks waiting for this one ride out to sea.

Those weeks had passed without Dracoratio blowing up any cities—at least not yet. The UNGARD ships had moved into the Atlantic about twenty miles out of the New York Harbor. The Coast Guard had also begun individually harassing every boat captain and crew on their way to the Chesapeake—from large container ships to smaller pleasure craft. The higher levels of the COG (continuity of government) plan had sprung into effect. Huxley had moved into a dingy little temporary office on Staten Island, waiting for the call that the UNGARD had found its prey. Nothing for two weeks.

Well, nothing except an outpouring of complaints about the Chesapeake searches that had already hit the national news. The official word was that the Coast Guard was testing a new search protocol. The unofficial response from many of the private vessel captains was that the government could take their new search protocol and shove it. And the politicos were no different. They had work to do and were tired of staying out of Washington to meet the additional security precautions triggered by the COG. In New York, only the UNGARD had changed. They could not allow the terrorists to realize they had learned the truth. It was the only chance to get those nukes back before they were used somewhere in the world. It was a risk, but everyone at DOD had verified the UNGARD would work. They had better damn well be right.

Huxley knew that for the purposes of this mission he was what the Tier 1 door bangers (the SEALs) would call an REMF—in less vulgar terms, rear echelon non-essential personnel. He waited for the mission anyway because doubt kept creeping into the conclusions he and Blount had reached. Everything fit, but a little too snuggly. He had spent the time reviewing reports, waiting for others, and obsessing about the remaining holes in his case. The Dubai Airport shootout seemed to convince his boss and the CIA boys that Mayer had gone rogue. All the forensics evidence—from powder residues to bullet trajectories to blood splatters—seemed to confirm the original story. But Pardus had led Huxley through the maze far too deftly for this thing to end so simply and stupidly. Each time he closed his eyes, he saw Deputy Under Secretary Blount asking him again: Why? Why would Mayer do this?

Then the CIA had found a comforting answer. They had searched Mayer's home and uncovered a hidden number and key, which led them to a safe deposit box in a Swiss bank holding 2 million Euros in cash. So it was the money after all, or at least that supplied the official motive for the reports. But Huxley could still smell the stench of a decaying investigation. If Mayer had been Pardus, he would have had infinitely greater resources. If he had been working for Pardus, would he really have kept the account number and key in his apartment? And in either case, who is willing to destroy a couple of cities for a few million Euros? You would have to be an awfully greedy and callous son of a bitch to do that. Sure, Mayer was an asshole, but even he didn't seem so greedy he wouldn't mind killing millions of people at less than a dollar a pop. Maybe there was more money somewhere else. But could a sane person put any price on a few million heads? A good solid motive for Mayer would end Huxley's self-interrogation, but nothing emerged to remove the subtle hint of deception.

Frickin' Dracoratio had not resurfaced despite every resource the U.S. had expended looking for him. Was he now dead somewhere or still working the nukes? Was he the real Pardus? It probably didn't matter, because they could not have spent more resources searching for him if he were the reincarnation of Adolph Hitler with a couple of mini nukes in his back pocket. *Hell, maybe he is.*

What about Sonatina? He never had anything tangible on her. She just seemed too damn right too damn often to be fully trusted. But she had never really said anything requiring some secret knowledge, had she? He had ignored her these last few weeks, telling his assistant to report that he was "indisposed" and would "return the call at the first opportunity," but "it might be awhile." Hopefully, she just figured he was in deep cover or something. If he slipped and she found out he believed a nuke was heading for New York and she did have some connection to Pardus, then what? Then they switch the plan and we never catch the bastards. *But I won't let the CIA torture her.* Would he still love her if she were his worst enemy? There should have been an obvious answer, and yet…

One day last week, he had begun obsessing about her. She was still in Rome. Damn, he had thought, that was one of the possible targets. If it were live, would they set it off when the Coast Guard found the nuke bound for New York? Patismio had confided that the Carabinieri had made no further progress with Armondo Fine and were now at wits end on where to look next. He had stopped and picked up his phone and stared at her name in his contact's list, but he simply could not bring himself to hit the phone icon. Maybe a text? Why not? He could craft it without risking giving up anything with his tone. He had typed the message:

> Hey - sorry I know its been awhile. Really miss you. Cant talk
> now. But want to warn you - leave Rome at once. Hell - leave
> Italy and go on vacation. Stay away until I tell you otherwise.

The text was long, but he had only one chance. This could not turn into a long discussion string. He hit send.

A few minutes later he saw Sonatina's reply: "OK, will come see you. Where r u? Love u."

He had not known how to answer that. If he had said he was in New York, then she would have wondered why he had not called. Worse, if Pardus had learned he was in New York, then he might think they were not taking the DC threat seriously. He typed a response and sent it: "Cant say. But stay away from US—may be just as deadly."

"Had a bad dream about ur friend. Beware. Hey - U still love me?"

Ur friend? Maybe she had not known Anwari and Mayer were dead. Then there had been the love thing. Huxley had begun typing into his cell and stopped. He had reached for the delete button and stopped again. Finally, he had shaken his head and hit send: "Like a Leopard loves his spots."

It took a few minutes, but the response had come: "Im no leopard. U?"

He had typed: "Maybe we should go on a safari together."

She had responded with only a happy, excited emoji.

He also had spent more time studying the last stanza of the poem Pardus had written for him. Pardus had promised Anwari that the entire poem revealed the location of the bomb "and more." What other secrets did the last stanza hold? He pulled it up again:

> On truth lies yet obscured thy fathers' end.
> To myths our hearts do reach and then depend.
> We seek our consolation with a friend.
> Remember now the Maine and then ascend.
> To know his fate you must to hell descend.

What could this mean other than the obvious personal references to his father descending into hell? Why would Pardus know or care about what had happened to his father?

When the Jayhawk jumped with the turbulence, it tickled Huxley's belly and brought him back to the current mission. He said into the intercom, "ETA to the *Finis Lineae*, Lieutenant?"

"Five minutes."

"How far out from New York is she?"

"Nearly 20 nautical miles. Our cutter, the *Egeria*, forced the *Finis Lineae* to halt just a few minutes after they got the alert."

"They aboard yet?"

"Waiting for reinforcements. Could have a well-armed crew given the expected cargo. Navy SEALs will arrive about the time we do. The *Reliant* should arrive about the time we get there. Her bird will be armed in the air. We'll land on her pad and drop you, then join the air patrol. You can check out the cargo after the SEALs do their thing."

Huxley nodded. "You think we'll need 'em—the SEALs?"

"Not likely. Word from *Egeria* is that the master of the *Finis Lineae* has agreed by radio to comply. Says he doesn't understand what this is about. Sounds sincere. SEALs will handle the boarding to make sure."

Huxley nodded. "Sounds like a plan. We got air cover?"

"Roger. We have coordination as planned." He tapped on a screen showing several concentric circles over a map with little diamonds moving here and there. Each little diamond was accompanied by a plus or minus sign, a two or three digit number, and a line in front of the direction of the movement of the diamond. The Lieutenant pointed to the diamonds with +150 and +180 ahead of their position. "Heavy movers are already above the target." He pointed to the diamonds to the southeast that were plus or minus 001 or 002. "Whirlies on the way."

Coordination—such a nice, positive, friendly word: Navy and Air Force jets ready to chip in a few bombs and destroy this vessel at sea if need be along with Army Apache helicopters available to stick a quick missile up the butt of any perceived threat. Of course, any of those coordinated resources might kill Huxley, the SEALs and the Coast Guard crews as well, but who is going to cry about a few friendlies when a nuclear bomb is at stake? He wouldn't. He just hoped nobody had a quick trigger finger. If Pardus had some rocket attached to that thing and set it off out here, the jets might even have a chance to shoot it down before it got anywhere. Always good to have resources. Coordinated resources.

A few minutes later, the Lieutenant nodded to the front. "There she is."

Huxley saw the huge *Finis Lineae* ahead carrying hundreds of inter-modal containers stacked five to six deep along her deck, the hull swaying slightly with the waves of the ocean, the USCGC *Egeria* before her bow, the *Reliant* approaching to her port side. The ships' two CG Jayhawks were already in the air, ready to deploy their M240J machine guns at anyone thinking of firing a shot from the deck of the container ship.

As they landed the Jayhawk on the *Reliant,* the Apaches arrived and pointed their guns and missiles at the bridge castle while hovering a few hundred yards to the side. About 20 men stood on the top of the bridge castle, their hands locked behind their heads. Several SEALs rappelled down lines from two Sea Hawk helicopters to containers at two corners of the ship. They immediately crouched and took aim at the bridge castle. Another Sea Hawk moved above the bridge castle, the wind from its rotor rippling the uniforms of the *Finis Lineae's* seamen. Four SEALs rappelled to the bridge castle in seconds, their rifles pointing at the twenty or so crewmen as the leader motioned to them to lie down on steel grate top deck of the bridge castle. Another Sea Hawk moved to the bow of the giant ship and ten SEALs dropped to the surface of the ship. They began moving down the long outside aisles of the ship toward the stern, carefully checking each aisle between containers for any targets.

With the *Finis Lineae* substantially secure ten minutes later, Huxley came aboard and signaled to the Coast Guard captain. The two Coast Guard ships now began to slowly pass down either side of the ship, the UNGARD device sending signals between them, trying to pinpoint the location of the target container. When he reached the bridge, Huxley found the master of the *Finis Lineae,* his hands already pinned behind his back with high-strength straps. Beads of sweat ran down the captain's cheeks, flowing around and through hyper-wide-open eyes that kept darting between Huxley and the M-16 rifles pointing at his head. "You speak English?" Huxley asked calmly.

"*Si.* A little."

Huxley switched to Italian. "Do you know why we have boarded you?"

The master shook his head slowly and deliberately. "I have been boarded before for inspections. This is different? What have we done?"

"We are looking for a particular cargo aboard your ship that might have been placed by some terrorists. Are you carrying anything unusual?"

The master shook his head slowly but deliberately several times. "Standard voyage. Garabundi, chief mate, handles cargo details."

Without much trouble, Huxley found Garabundi. He was calmer, more talkative, but no more helpful. They searched the manifest. Nothing looked out of place, but they wouldn't list "nuclear weapons" on the manifest, would they? They reviewed the inspection certificates from the U.S. CBP for each port under the CSI initiative. All of the inspections seemed in order. Either Rosenthal's device was fooling the gamma ray detectors or an American inspector in one of the ports had been compromised somewhere. Could be both.

Huxley stared back at the master. "Any of your crew new to the ship?"

"Sì, due. But they have been vetted."

"Show me."

The master walked out of the bridge toward the men lying face forward on the steel grating, their hands clipped behind their backs. He nudged one with his foot and the man looked up. Huxley nodded to a nearby SEAL, who picked the man up and led him back to the bridge for questioning. As Huxley turned back to the line of men, he saw one on the far side scrambling to the edge of the bridge castle deck. "Stop!" yelled a nearby SEAL, pointing his weapon at the man's head from ten feet away. The man ignored him and slid under the railing head first off the bridge castle, his arms still tied behind his back. A clang sounded from the metal deck six stories down. Huxley peered over the railing at the mess below, the man's head looking much like a squashed watermelon, a pool of dark red splattered about. They would get nothing more from this terrorist, but his desperate suicide confirmed a nuke was probably aboard. After interrogating the other rookie seaman for a few minutes, Huxley was quickly convinced the man new nothing.

A voice in Huxley's ear piece said, "Mr. Huxley, we think we have found it—at least the aisle—two to the fore of the bridge tower. Narrowing the vector now to see if we can get a distance between the cutters."

Huxley shot back, "Roger that. We'll be there in a few minutes." He approached the chief mate. "You got the keys to these containers?"

"No keys. I have passwords for the few that are locked. In the safe."

A minute later, Huxley had the password manifest in his hand—a spreadsheet with container numbers in one column and eight digit codes in the other. "Any other security?"

The chief mate responded, "If the contents are valuable enough, they use tomographic motion detectors that trigger alarms we see on the bridge electronically."

"Tomographic?"

"*Si.* Node to node radio signals. Something moves in them, we know."

"Which containers have security in the second aisle to the fore from here?"

The chief mate nodded to a security panel in the center of the bridge. "Hit that second button and the schematic lights up the security net. Those with green have tomographic. When they go red, there is motion and a siren sounds. The container has its own siren as well. Container numbers are identified on the schematic."

Huxley looked at the schematic and focused on aisle two, then shifted to the password manifest. Five containers in aisle two, each with locks.

The Coast Guard Captain spoke to Huxley through his intercom, "Mr. Huxley, looks like we have a fix. Somewhere within a twenty-foot radius of the center of aisle two, likely the top container or two."

Huxley looked at the security schematic. At the center on top, container AG93728B was locked and incorporated the tomographic motion detection system. He pointed to it. "Where's this headed?"

The first mate looked at a small code on the schematic next to the container. "Red Hook. First stop. That is why it is on top."

"Red Hook?"

"Container port in Brooklyn, no more than a mile across the East River to Manhattan."

"That's gotta be it." Huxley nodded and the four-man SEAL team escort followed him out of the bridge. With the help of a few of the Navy helicopters, they made their way to top of the container mountain near aisle two. Four other SEALs joined them as they peered down the six-story canyon between containers. With container AG93728B standing across the canyon just below them, Huxley looked at the SEAL commander and spoke softly, "How you want to do this? Could be hostiles inside waiting for us to open the door."

The SEAL commander nodded. "We could drill and fill, but that might alert them if they don't know anything yet.

"Drill and fill?"

"Drill a hole and fill the thing with gas to incapacitate them. They might hear the drill, though."

Huxley shook his head. "If they do, they might detonate the device. Can't take that chance."

"But they must know the boat has been stopped."

"Could be a routine inspection as far as they know."

"Alright, assuming the thing unlocks, we open and swing in ready to pop them. Otherwise, we'll use detcord."

Huxley nodded. He handed the code to the commander. The SEALs hooked up some ropes around the tops of the nearby containers, carefully avoiding container AG93728B. After they all signaled they were ready, one SEAL pressed the code into the lock, and quickly opened the door. A piercing alarm came out of the container. Almost simultaneously, two SEALs swung into the opening, their weapons ready to fire. Two others followed immediately. Huxley tensed up, waiting to hear shots fired, but nothing came.

Huxley's earpiece rang out. "Clear. We have the packages but no tangos. All clear."

Huxley sighed. "Any launcher, actuator, anything counting down?"

"Negative. Ticker might be hidden. Weird wiry liquid contraption around them, though, and a small control panel. Nothing counting down."

"Alright, I'm coming down." A nearby SEAL threw him a rope, and he swung into the poorly lit container. He smiled when he saw the two warheads looking exactly like the ones that had disappeared from Pakistan. At least what he could see of them. They were surrounded with a strange wire and plastic-like mesh filled with an odd clear viscous liquid. The whole contraption was connected to a control panel glowing with various green and amber diodes.

"Good work, men," Huxley said as he walked toward the SEAL team, but something was wrong. Their eyes narrowed, and they began crouching down and raising their rifles in his direction. They moved quickly to each side and fired several rounds as he spun around.

"Down, Huxley!" yelled the commander. More small arms fire screamed from behind Huxley as he fell on his back to the steel floor of the container.

He heard a loud explosion well to his rear and then silence. "Any tangos left?" the commander asked.

"Moving in now to confirm."

Huxley raised his head just in time to see two SEALs entering the container opposite, its door now open, smoke still billowing out. A few seconds later he heard, "All clear. Two tangos neutralized. No packages here."

Huxley looked back at the warheads. They were still intact. He moved closer and found their serial numbers beneath Rosenthal's handiwork, snapping a few pictures to send to Blount. He brought up the notes in his phone. The serial numbers matched the warheads stolen from Pakistan. Both of them. Rome would be safe as well. Sonatina… He fell to his knees, looked up and laughed, shaking his fists in the air. It was finally over.

CHAPTER 91

A FEW HOURS LATER, Huxley was gathering his things in his makeshift Coast Guard office on Staten Island when a familiar old face peeked around the door. "Well, well, it looks like you were right, Hux." Deputy Under Secretary Blount walked over, slapped him on the back and shook his hand. "NNSA gave us a preliminary confirmation. The warheads are the same ones that were stolen from Pakistan—well, except for all those wires and plastic and liquid shit that surrounded them. That was the Israeli chemist's work. His fingerprints were still on the control device."

Huxley smiled gently and nodded.

"Stop being so humble you son of a bitch. It's your doing. Outstanding work, Huxley! When we get back to DC, we'll have a party and toast a few to the savior of the world—or at least New York. Oh, and I'm guessing there might be a presidential or congressional medal in this for you. You are a goddamned hero, Hux, a goddamned hero. Maybe we should hold a ticker-tape parade for you or something."

Huxley grinned. "Thanks. You know you can shovel bullshit with the best of 'em. Parade—hell, you know damn well none of this will ever go public. You and I will just have to celebrate with a beer as always. Tonight?"

"No can do, unless you're staying here. I need to calm down the New York folks before some crazy fake news story about nukes on board makes them all paranoid."

Huxley chuckled. "A Guard chopper will take me back in a few minutes. Three long weeks here."

"Yeah, well, when I get back in a few days, the President is going to want to thank you and me in person. Probably not over a beer, though." The burly man laughed loud and hard.

Huxley nodded with pride, but caught himself glowing too warm in the praise. His smile turned sideways. "The real heroes are Anwari and Jinnah. They died for this."

Blount nodded slowly. "Anyone on the *Finis Lineae* talk?"

"Nothing useful. I suspect everyone who knew anything on the ship is now dead. They were on a suicide mission and must have known it. Just didn't end the way they'd hoped. SEALs are searching every container, but I doubt they'll find anything. The ship was supposed to slide in under the radar, not end up in a fire fight."

Blount nodded. "Figures. Chances are the container itself was hijacked before being loaded and was re-purposed without anyone knowing it. It looks like the plan was to remotely detonate the warheads when they hit port."

"Warheads. Plural. Why?"

"Why what?"

"Why both?" Huxley asked. "Each was big enough to devastate much of Manhattan, if not a good chunk of the whole city. Why waste two here?"

"Apparently they really hate the Yankees," Blount said sarcastically. "Hey, I don't know, but you said there were no rockets, right? If they had no system to get them up in the air, that reduces the blast radius. Maybe they thought they needed both to do the job. Or maybe they were worried that one wouldn't work and they wanted the other as a backup. Who the hell knows? But I do know we have both of them. Pakistan has also confirmed based on the pictures we sent them."

"You have someone dismantling them just to be sure?"

"They are the right warheads, Huxley. We've confirmed that. But, yes, NNSA will have a full report in the next few days."

"Good. Can we keep the UNGARD protecting New York Harbor until then?"

"Of course. Why wouldn't we?"

As Blount left, Huxley grinned. With both warheads recovered and pretty much confirmed, Sonatina would be safe as well. Maybe it was time to reconnect. A text to break the ice? He typed out: "Looks like crisis averted. When should we meet in the Maldives?" Could he do that without thinking of Hannah? Without thinking about his mother? He hit send.

A text came back: "Why, Mr. Huxley, did you forget that I am a good Catholic girl?" Then a few seconds later, another text arrived. "So when do I pack?"

He smiled. That should smooth it over a bit. He hit call. When she answered, he said, "*Ciao, la mia piccola musa.* Good to hear you safe and sound."

"Your little muse? What have I done now?"

"I told you, crisis averted. Thanks for all of your help on this. I think you can return to Rome now."

"I never left."

"But Sonatina, I texted. You weren't safe."

"I should be different than the rest of Rome?"

"I'm not in love with the rest of Rome."

After a pregnant pause, she said, "What did you mean, crisis averted?"

Huxley drew his lips in. Could he tell her now? They had the nukes, so it wouldn't help Pardus if she were somehow connected. Pardus was probably dead, but he still had to track down Dracoratio. She was still sore over his lack of trust. *Here's a chance to change that.* "We recovered the missing packages—not in Washington but near New York."

Sonatina did not hesitate, "That makes no sense. The poem led to Washington."

"It is complicated, but that poem was just a ruse."

"I don't think so."

"Why? We have the packages. They were headed to New York."

"Your government is in Washington. That must be the target."

"Half of our wealth is connected to Manhattan and the stock market. Can you imagine the dislocation? Remember that terrorists struck New York in 9/11."

"They also struck Washington."

Huxley felt the heat rising in him. He was tiring of this. Could she not let go? "Well, this time it was New York alone. There were only two packages."

"Are you sure? Have you descended to hell yet? That was in the poem."

Hell. Now she was dragging God and Satan back into the picture. "Yes, I am sure. I don't plan to go to hell. I think Pardus is already there."

"Chris, I'm telling you something is not right. I...I had one of those dreams."

"Those dreams?"

"Yes, did you have it, too? It was different, though. Like the world of the people in robes and our own world all mashed up. I was sitting on a hill in my simple outfit looking at a city below. A man in black hair and a beard laughed when the city blew up."

"It blew up?"

"*Si.* Mushroom cloud and all. The man kept laughing, but then the man in the robes—"

"The merchant?"

"No, not you, the man in the white robes. Jesus. He came and touched me on the shoulder. As He did this, the city began to rebuild."

"Have you been to the city?"

"No, but I know it."

"How?"

"I've seen many images of it—of its beautiful capitol, its long mall split by a phallic symbol, its White House."

"Washington?"

"Yes, that's why I think you must be mistaken. It is Washington they are after. I am certain."

"Certain? It was a dream, Sonatina."

"Yes. You said you've had them. It is strange, but I know it is more than a normal dream. Just like your other dreams. Our other dreams. They are some kind of premonition. They are a warning from God. You must do something."

Huxley banged his hand on his forehead. "Pffft. Come on. Dreams? From God? Just because we share a few dreams? You got the idea from me. You are scared. Now you attribute them to God? You might as well say your Fairy Godmother told you. Not exactly actionable intelligence."

"Don't be sacrilegious, Chris. I thought you believed. I thought you believed in Him again."

Huxley felt the twitch from that thing in his gut. He said lowly, "Look, I want to, but…"

"You will get there, Chris. I know it. But trust me, now. You must focus on the District."

Huxley exhaled hard and shook his head. *Why is she trying so hard? This is over.* Then her words echoed in his mind. *"Focus on the District."* Where had he heard that before? Pardus. Those were Pardus's exact words to Anwari. *Did I repeat that to her?* No, he had never even told her about Anwari's call with Pardus. Then why had she used the exact same words? A tingle slithered down his spine, and he began to sweat. *Could there be another bomb? They want us to pull the UNGARD away from New York. Thank goodness I told Blount to keep it here.*

"Chris, you still there?"

"Sure, just thinking. I probably should get going."

"OK. When are we going to the Maldives?"

"I, uh…I don't know. We'll have to see. Gotta go."

"You OK? I didn't mean—"

"I'm fine. Thanks again for your help, *Signorina. Addio.*" He hung up.

He stood there for a few minutes, trying to lose the foul taste of distrust from his mouth. It was a common phrase, wasn't it—"focus." So was "District." Everyone called it that. Everyone from DC. He had never heard a foreigner call it that other than Pardus. You put the two together and it sounded like words she must have heard someone say before. Had she slipped? Then there was this whole God thing. Why was she pushing that so hard? *Is she trying to weaken me? Trying to drive me back into my emotional abyss?*

He took a deep breath and looked at his phone. His old friend had called. Why not? He deserved that. He was a Goddamned hero—Blount had said it. He should celebrate, not wrap himself in Sonatina's cold, wet, righteous blanket.

When Kadir answered his call, Huxley said jovially, "Hello, Mr. Ambassador of Peace."

"Yeah, well, screw you, too." They laughed. Kadir continued, "You in town? You ever coming over for drinks and a cruise on my yacht? I cannot promise you any wild women this time, but we can still have a few laughs over some scotch."

"Hell, why not? I could use a drink and a friend. How about tonight? I've got nothing going."

"Excellent. Come at 7pm, Slip C-10, Southwest Wharf."

"Great. See you then." Huxley hung up and his stomach tightened. He closed his eyes and saw the image of his father hanging from the cables at that wharf so many years ago. *You can do this.* He smiled. For the first time in a long time, he actually believed it.

CHAPTER 92

TOMADUS WAS EATING alone at a small café in Jerusalem when Jochi strode by and stopped at his outdoor table, her arms stiff and her expression tortured. The anger in her voice matched her gestures. "There you are. Why are you not eating with the Ten tonight? Isa has something important to tell us."

"He will forgive me."

"But will he forgive your betrayal?"

"What?" he asked.

"He told me about your ideas to put him to the test. He asked me not to confront you, but… Are you insane? Has your obsession with the other world scrambled your brains? Why are you doing this?"

"He asked for it."

Jochi started slowly, but her momentum, tone and volume grew quickly. "He asked for it? Why? Has it something to do with me? He has done nothing but help me grasp the truth. Or are you still hung up about his refusal to rescue my brother from the authorities? Dear God in Heaven, Tomadus, it was not Isa's fault. Would you have preferred to see him die next to Yohanan on the *triangulum penetrans*? He has done nothing to harm you and everything to help you. How can you do this to him?"

Tomadus stared back and took a few breaths. When he spoke, he chose a low, measured voice, almost in monotone. "Do you think I'm evil? I love Isa. I want to help him—that is all. He wants this. Maybe he didn't initiate it, but he agreed it was best. You don't understand what is going on with the authorities. It is the only way to save him from the same fate, to save him for the world. We cannot afford to lose him. But you wouldn't understand."

Jochi wiped the tears from her eyes and took a deep breath, her lips pursing to prevent another round. Swallowing hard, she asked, "And why not?"

The emotion welled up into Tomadus's face, and he tried to squish every opening together to prevent it from coming out, but he failed. "Because you don't know what happened in the other world," he said.

"You mean when they crucified Jesus?" she asked.

Tomadus gasped. "You…you see the other world that well now?"

"I am beginning to…to see too many things. The visions are coming so rapidly. But the other world is not just one. It splits in two. We must have faith, Tomadus. Isa has told me… But you are going the wrong way—do you not see where this will lead? You will become the new Judas. Can you not see that? You are betraying him!"

"No, I am helping him. It doesn't have to be the same. We will change the outcome. He doesn't have to die!"

"You have heard him, Tomadus. Have you not understood his words? They will put him to death. You have not the power to control events as you believe. He will die horribly, and you will be to blame. Do not do this, I beg of you. You may think you can destroy God, but that is impossible! He will be with you always."

Another tingle squirmed down his spine…Sonatina…but he could not let this allegation go. "Kill God? Are you insane, Jochi? Do you now believe Isa is God? What is wrong with you people? I want to save him, not kill him." Tomadus threw a few coins on the table, stood up and began walking away, ignoring Jochi's last few pleas to him.

Heading toward his meeting with the First Consul, Tomadus looked down and sighed. Was he fooling himself about his own motives? Was this whole plan the result of his emotional backlash for Yohanan's horrible death, or, worse, had some growing jealousy rotted his heart and mind? Was that why he was so willing to take such a horrendous risk with Isa's life? He closed his eyes and shook his head. He loved Isa. He would die himself to save him. Tomadus felt a chill go down his spine as he recalled Jochi's last words to him: "You think you can somehow save Isa, but it is He who must save you."

CHAPTER 93

ENTERING THE LARGE visi-scan studio, Tomadus spotted First Consul Khansensius speaking with an assistant on the stage. The floodlights illuminated the set, indicating a broadcast was imminent. The stage in this visi-scan studio had obviously been designed to accommodate grand indoor spectacles where the sound could be controlled better than in the great outdoor amphitheaters and squares. A dozen or so rows of seats permitted a small audience to add to the ambience of any particular political production. Behind and above the seats, a large glass wall separated the sound stage from the sound booth, where several technologists worked, apparently double-checking various technical aspects of the upcoming production.

As he approached, Tomadus saw the First Consul dismiss his assistant and waive Tomadus up to the stage. He obeyed this as well as the First Consul's arm gesture indicating he should sit in the chair at the table opposite him. The First Consul flashed that calming smile at him. "Sorry for the odd meeting place, but it cannot be helped. I have to prepare for another broadcast presentation soon. Can I have my assistant get you anything?"

"No, I'm fine. *Gratias.*"

"Wonderful. Are you feeling well?"

"Yes, why not?"

"Good. Now, I have ensured that all of my assistants are tasked with other matters, so we can speak frankly."

Tomadus nodded slowly. "I think that is wise. *Gratias.*"

"I try. Now, I would say your plan seems to be progressing nicely. Do you agree?"

"Perhaps. Isa has agreed to it, but I have some doubts."

"As to?"

"I am concerned about the impact of Isa's broadcast speech. Did he say anything that might have offended the emperors? Do they fear he will try to usurp their power?"

"No, no, not in the least. The emperors found it refreshing. But I must say that the Grand Imam and Abh Beyth Diyn still secretly challenge him. He must step up and demonstrate that he is no fraud. He must show he believes in himself."

Tomadus smirked. "Oh he believes in himself all right. He will not yield, I guarantee you of that." Then he added sarcastically, "No more than God Himself would yield to the Abh Beyth Diyn and Grand Imams."

"Does he say he is God?"

"No, of course not." Tomadus's eyes narrowed. "No, I don't think he has said he is God." *At least not that I would ever admit to you.* "Please, First Consul, do not put words in my mouth."

"Oh, I am sorry. I just thought those words might be coming from him."

"No, not those words. I admit, though, that I still do not quite understand him."

"Were you with him at the so-called "Adin Miracle?"

"Yes," Tomadus said slowly. *Where is he going with that?*

"I've been wondering how he did it."

"I do not know. He has traveled widely, you know. Some say it was a simple pharmaceutical trick, but I know otherwise. Adin swears he did nothing but eat the poison mushrooms, die and then be brought back by Isa. Adin would have told me otherwise. He is a simple man totally lacking guile. I myself felt Adin's body as he lay on the table. He was dead, yet when the door to the mortuary opened not two minutes later, he was alive! How do you explain that? Perhaps it was a miracle."

"You don't believe in God now, do you? I thought you were a good Romanus technologist."

Tomadus looked away. His honest response might scare the First Consul. Could he speak truth, even now? "I don't know. I wish I did."

"You wish it?"

"Well, I wish I could understand these, these…" Tomadus lowered his head.

"These what?"

Tomadus shook his head slightly, still looking down. He recalled Emperor Acamapichtli's warning.

The First Consul smiled. "You mean your visions?" When Tomadus looked up in shock, the First Consul continued, "Yes, I am aware of them. I think I can help you there. We shall find the answers together, Tomadus. You need not fear of that. Let us continue our work together, and you shall understand everything."

"You sound like him."

The First Consul grunted a laugh. "Patience, Tomadus."

"So what more can I do to complete the plan?"

Just beneath his chin, the First Consul bounced the tips of his fingers off their opposites for a few seconds. Then he said easily, "Well, you could help us collect him tonight."

"Collect him?" asked Tomadus. "Why? Can't he just come himself?"

"No, you know this cannot look like he is cooperating or else the Abh Beyth Diyn and the Grand Imam will never be convinced. Remember, Tomadus, this is a performance. We need to put on a show for them to believe."

"But why not collect him during the day?"

"You know these crowds are unpredictable. Some of his opponents could see him arrested and think they had license to harm him. You do not want to see that happen, do you?"

"No, of course not. Not a hair of him should be harmed. Is there anything else you need from me?"

"In fact, we think you should be there throughout, to tell us your thoughts and help keep an eye on things. We may want to interview you on the visi-scan for the record."

Tomadus smiled and leaned forward. "Certainly, I can attest to his strong beliefs. Now remember, he must not be harmed. When he refuses to yield to their threats and questioning, you must have the leaders ready to proclaim him genuine and then release him."

"Of course, that has always been your plan, our plan, but you must be patient, Tomadus. You must let the process run its course until they are convinced. If we move too early, we will do more harm than good. You once asked me to trust you with the Letter of Transit, and I did. You must now return that trust. I will help you find your answers. It may get ugly at times, but that ugliness is what will save him in the end."

"Is that even possible?" Tomadus mumbled.

"What?"

"Nothing. Sorry. Yes, I will be patient."

"Then we are agreed?"

Tomadus nodded.

CHAPTER 94

THE SUN WOULD not yet rise for several hours as the full moon lighted the group's way. Tomadus led three of the Grand Imam's guards to the garden where Isa had told him they would be praying. The guards came through the garden gate with their rap rifles held at the ready like they expected some kind of resistance from this tiny group of pacifists. Simeon, Atuf and Adin slept by a tree off to the right. About fifty feet away, Isa was kneeling with Jochi by his side. Isa appeared to be praying with his eyes shut. It looked like Jochi was also trying to pray, but her body trembled. She looked at Tomadus with tear-filled eyes and gasped. "No! Tomadus, no…"

Tomadus noticed the last 'no' had fallen off dramatically, like she had caught herself. Had she lost her remaining energy or had she finally resigned herself to this? A small black and white dog came from around one of the hedgerows and began barking at the intruders. Tomadus tipped his head at the dog. Wasn't it the same dog in Parisius—the one like Huxley's dog?

Tomadus walked quickly over to Isa and Jochi as they both rose from their knees. By now, the barking dog had awakened the Ten, and they walked over to join the group. The guards held their rifles up and yelled, "Close enough. Everyone keep their hands where we can see them."

Before Tomadus could gesture to Isa, he opened his arms to welcome

Tomadus. "Will you greet me properly, my friend?" Isa asked. When Tomadus came to him, they kissed cheeks. One of the guards seized Isa.

Adin tried to move in and get between the guard and Isa, but another guard hit Adin in the head with the butt of his rap rifle, knocking him to a knee. Another kicked him in the gut. Adin bent over but rose quickly and came toward the guard. Another guard struck him on the head with his rifle butt. Adin fell to the ground as a third guard pulled back the pin on his rap rifle and pointed it at him.

"Stop," Tomadus yelled to the guards, "or you will face the wrath of the First Consul!"

"Shut up, Romanus," replied the sergeant. "You have done your part. Now let us do ours."

Isa dropped to a knee, touching Adin gently on the head and stomach as they all watched. Adin seemed to recover quickly and sat up in a slight daze. He looked into Tomadus's eyes and a tear fell from his own. Adin shook his head slowly and frowned.

Simeon moved forward yelling, "You traitor, Tomadus!" Several of the other Ten joined in. Peregrine looked at him in disbelief and said only, "Why?"

Simeon yelled over to Isa, "We'll gather your followers. We can contact Emperor Acamapichtli. He has the resources. We can save you."

"No, Simeon," Isa yelled back. "Did you not hear me at supper? Shall I not drink the cup that the Father gave me?" Simeon, Jochi and the Ten bowed their heads.

Torn by the entire scene, Tomadus frowned and said softly in Jochi's direction, "I am sorry to you. I am sorry to you all. But this is the best thing for him, for everyone." He turned and followed the arresting party as they led Isa away, keeping an eye on the guards so they would treat Isa well. As the group reached the gate, a gentle hand pulled on Tomadus's shoulder, nearly spinning him around.

Jochi's wet eyes nearly drowned Tomadus in her emotion. His face fell with his heart, and again he said, "I'm sorry. I'm sorry. It will be alright."

She forced out a few barely audible words among her tears. "No...it won't... You are killing him... You are condemning the other world to a horrible end... You must stop... You must have faith... The only way."

"What?" asked Tomadus.

"We—you and I—must save them. We must have faith to do what is right…" Her sobbing consumed her words as she dropped her chin.

He felt her pain in every extension of his body. How could he stay and comfort her? She probably still thought he was the source of her misery, the evil that had come in the night to kidnap her hero. And now she was talking crazy about the other world like Sonatina had overtaken her. She had lost her grip on reality. He nodded with a weak smile, trying to tell her it would be all right, but her eyes were wild and filled with tears. "I," he said, "I am doing what is right. You will see."

▽   ▽   ▽

Not long after Isa was taken, Jochi found herself alone in the garden, still crying and trying to make sense of what Isa had said to her. *Our Father works in mysterious ways. If each of you have faith, you shall do what is right. Have faith. You shall save yourself and so many others.* Well, she had faith, but Isa had been taken anyway, just as he had said during their supper just hours ago. Isa had meant something more. Something about this world and the other. What was it? The images from the two horrible visions replayed in her brain and she shuddered. She could not grasp Isa's meaning.

She shook her head. "Have faith," she repeated, this time aloud. She nodded and began to pray. "Dear Father, I need your help so badly. Please. Isa has told me to have faith, and I do, but Tomadus? If we must both have faith, how can we ever save ourselves? How can we save this other world from its worst torment? Help me understand. Help us help them. Please let Tomadus find a way to protect Isa. If you must take Isa away as he says, then please help Isa save Tomadus. He does not understand. He needs you, Lord. I need you."

Jochi began sobbing and could say no more. She lay down in the garden by the stately cypress, where Isa had last prayed with her. The black and white stray dog that had been hanging around the garden came over to her and nuzzled against her cheek. When she petted him, the dog lay down beside her. She put her arm around him and soon drifted off to sleep.

The same two visions began alternating in her dream, but this time she saw Huxley and Sonatina and Tomadus on the hill with her. Then the image of Huxley merged with Tomadus and the image of Sonatina merged with Jochi. She heard Isa's voice repeating, "Have faith and do what is right."

The man in the black hair and beard was laughing at Tomadus/Huxley, telling him to do something. Tomadus/Huxley looked utterly bewildered and confused. He turned toward Jochi/Sonatina. "What should I do?"

Jochi/Sonatina shook her head sadly. "I...I don't know."

Isa stood on the hill beside them and Jochi/Sonatina stared at him for a few seconds. Then she looked at Tomadus/Huxley and reached her hand, palm up, toward Isa. Tomadus/Huxley closed his eyes for a long time, but finally opened them and stared at Isa. "What shall I do?" he asked him.

Isa smiled and nodded to Jochi/Sonatina. Suddenly, she knew what to say. "You must do it, Chris. Sacrifice yourself and you will save billions."

When Jochi awoke, she was shivering. The first rays of the sun were becoming visible over the horizon. The dream had been so real that it stayed with her. She knew what she must do. She looked up to the sky and smiled. "Thank you." With all of the guards around, she may not be able to see him, but she could get him a note. She leapt to her feet and headed for Jerusalem.

CHAPTER 95

I T WAS A lovely evening in the District, a perfect night to cruise the Potomac with his old roommate. Huxley had not yet seen this famed yacht, but he figured it would be a beauty since Kadir never did anything small. A glass of aged scotch, a fine cigar and a watery sunset…

He heard the GPS in his car warn him about the upcoming turns, "In one quarter mile, turn left onto Maine Avenue, then in two hundred feet turn right onto Seventh Street, and immediately turn left onto Water Street." He ignored the slight tingle travelling down his spine.

Huxley pulled into the Southwest Wharf parking lot, saw the sign for slip C-10 to his left and walked over to it, deliberately looking away from the north end of the wharf. Was he still so weak? He looked back at the place where his father had strung himself up by the neck over a quarter century before. It seemed different though he had only seen a picture in the newspaper. Huxley smiled. *Ghosts. We always act like we have buried them, but then we resurrect them again and again.* He saw a sign for slip C-10. The object just beyond the sign opened his eyes wide: a huge, three or four story luxury yacht big enough to sail across the Atlantic. "*Infernum*" was written boldly at the bow of the beast. A slight shiver crawled down Huxley's arms, but he shook it off and walked up the stairs to the gangplank, where he called out, "Permission to come aboard this ridiculously ostentatious vessel, Mr. Ambassador of Peace, sir?"

He expected Kadir to respond; instead, an Arab crewman emerged from the bridge. When they reached the open deck on the bow, Kadir was seated and smiling at him with his glowing set of beautiful white teeth. Kadir rose, bowed slightly, shook Huxley's hand and gave him a hug. "Welcome, my friend, to the Ship of Fate."

Huxley laughed and tilted his head at Kadir. "You always seem to have a flair for overstatement, Ambassador. Good to see you again."

The two old friends sat back while a steward in a white tuxedo brought them glasses of 30-year-old Royal Lochnagar. A few minutes later, the yacht pulled away from the wharf and reached the Potomac as the waiter brought out a box of Cuban cigars. Huxley smiled. Kadir lived the life and knew how to ensure his friends never forgot it. But it was nice to occasionally partake in the pleasures of real wealth when given the opportunity. "So this is how the rich people live," joked Huxley.

"Those who deserve life's riches the most find time to enjoy them," responded Kadir with that deep melodic tone of his.

Huxley pulled his lips together. That was a bit arrogant, even for the Kad-man. "I'm sorry, I forgot to kneel before you when we met, Mr. Ambassador of Peace, sir." That should do the trick.

Kadir did not laugh. "You know," replied Kadir, "you have been joking about that title quite awhile, Hux, but I think I will really adopt it some day."

"Why, because Prince of Peace is already taken?"

"I see you remain tethered to your Catholic upbringing."

Huxley grimaced. "You okay? You seem a bit, uh, strident, tonight. You seem out of character."

"I do? Perhaps, I am a bit anxious over a few coming events, or maybe I just don't feel like acting the part."

"Acting?"

Kadir sat back and rested his chin on his folded hands for a few seconds. He put his hands to his knees, leaned forward and said with a strange smile, "Please, ignore my oddities this evening. Tell me, how is your love life old friend? Have you progressed with that Italian beauty?"

That was more like it. "Enough that I won't tell you her name."

"Why not?"

"I'd be heartbroken if you stole her from me."

"Ah, but I think you performed the only woman stealing in this friendship, no?"

"What? You mean Hannah? You had long passed her off like a piece of Jewish meat."

"Yes, but she was a pretty fine cut, my friend." They laughed, and then Kadir added, "Nevertheless, it is quite improper to topple your close friend's former lover, even if she is a mere courtesan, would you not agree?"

"Courtesan? Not when it has been fifteen years." *What the hell is wrong with him?* "I'm sorry, Kadir, did my relationship with her really bother you? You never said anything."

"No, I was long over her. But friendship sometimes demands greater deference. You never asked for my permission, and that demonstrated a terrible lack of respect."

Eyes narrowing, Huxley sat up straight, confusion wrinkling his brow. "Then I am truly sorry. I meant no disrespect. I just never thought about it."

"Precisely. Anyway, forget it now. It is of no importance, and I should not have raised it. Here, Sa'id, bring us each another glass." The waiter filled the order and Kadir raised his glass to Huxley. "Let us drink to friendship. You have done much for me, my friend, more than you can now imagine. I thank you."

Huxley nodded in acknowledgment. What had he done to deserve that? He accepted the toast as one of the practiced diplomat's common tools. Good time to change the subject. "Your cousin gave you this yacht, you said? It must have cost him a pretty penny."

"I imagine so."

"Why did he name it '*Infernum*'? That is Latin, isn't it?"

"I named it. Yes. It is Latin for hell."

That tingle ran down Huxley's neck, spine, arms and legs. What was he missing? Had the scotch gone to his head?

Kadir raised his eyebrows. "Does that surprise you?"

"It's a strange name for the ship of the Ambassador of Peace."

"Is it now? It serves its purpose as a useful reminder of past failures."

Huxley nodded slowly. Something was creeping to the periphery of the now hyper-extended tendrils of Huxley's gray cells. Something about hell and something he had heard earlier this evening were linked.

"You seem spooked. What is the matter? I thought you had recovered from your childhood indoctrination of angels and demons. Do they haunt you still today? Did the wharf remind you of anything?"

Huxley's muscles tensed as he held his breath. *Was Kadir doing this intentionally?* "You know my father died there. Why are you bringing this up?"

"You told me he killed himself there. By Catholic doctrine, that would send him to hell, would it not?"

"I don't know. Why do you—" Huxley grabbed his head as a pain shot deep through its corridors. He realized he was having trouble thinking clearly. He looked at his drink, which appeared blurry. As he closed his eyes, he could almost hear his GPS tell him to turn left on Maine Avenue and nearly see the name "Infernum" on the stern of his friend's ship. "No, that couldn't be. My head hurts. Is there something funny in my drink?"

"Do you think so little of me, my friend? What a cliché!"

Huxley rubbed his temples. *Need to get away. Need to think. Excuse. Excuse.* "Sorry, I...I gotta...go to the head."

"Certainly. Down the stairs and aft—you cannot miss it. Would you like Sa'id to assist you?"

"No, no, I'll be alright. Just too much scotch, I think," Huxley mumbled as he began to stumble to the stairs.

Kadir shook his head. "You never could hold your liquor."

❆ ❆ ❆

Huxley splashed water on his face. He must be delusional. The scotch, the cigar, the pressure of the case. Kadir had been his friend for nearly twenty years. They had traded a few words about a difficult part of the past and now Huxley was beginning to draw strange suspicions, just like he had with Sonatina. His emotions always messed things up. *Just get it together, Hux.* He shook his head and wiped his face, but the fog drifted further down and confused every thought now racing through his mind to God knows where. *Calm down, Hux.* There was Sonatina's face saying over and over again, "Do you trust me?" The image transmogrified into an image of Anwari repeating over and over, "Now you must trust me," and finally morphed into Kadir's face. Now it was Huxley's own voice that kept repeating, "I trust you, Kadir," while Kadir laughed loudly in his face. Could he have been so wrong? He shook his head to dispel these images with limited success. *Need to question him. Need her forgiveness.* He pulled out his phone to text Sonatina. Fumbling over the keys, he managed to text:

> Sorry abandon u. Sorry doubt u. Love you still. On Ship of Fate sailing away. Pardus lives. Where will Fate take me? Where will it take us all? My loud friend will give answers.

He hit send, took a few deep breaths and walked out of the bathroom. As he stumbled toward the bow of the yacht, he saw a door on the center side of the hall now slightly ajar. He heard a few strange beeps and saw a few flashes of colored light and could not resist ducking in for a look. Inside were cameras and enough monitors and electronics to run a war room. *What the hell?* He heard a noise behind him and turned quickly in the darkness. A light flickered on. In the periphery of his still muddled vision, he saw an Arab man dressed all in black. *Dracoratio? How'd he get here? Why's he raising his arm?* Huxley's instincts kicked in and he tried to move, but his motor skills were equally impaired. Darkness came quickly. Less than a second later, Huxley's limp body slammed to the cabin floor.

CHAPTER 96

THE LATE-MORNING SUN filled Muhammad Square with bright rays sparkling on the temporary stage. Perhaps the glow presaged good things to come. How glorious it would all be after Isa convinced the authorities of his own convictions! But the scene in front of him dried his mouth and turned his stomach into knots.

Everything looked disturbingly similar to that day when Yohanan had been executed, except this time a *triangulum penetrans* device stood not outside the gates but on the stage itself. Another prop employed by the First Consul in his grand show. Tomadus stared at the horrible monster while the creature within him stirred.

A crowd had gathered and looked an unruly sort. Tomadus saw no Way members. Where were Simeon and Atuf, Diego and Anders? Adin surely would have come if he could. And certainly, Jochi… He shook his head. She probably hated him now. When this was all over, she might finally understand him, finally love him.

Tomadus searched the huge square for the First Consul without success, but also without any real disappointment. Khansensius was probably ensuring the success of the proceeding. One of the cameras for the visi-scan was already live. It would not be long before the First Consul would appear on stage to direct the spectacle.

Without warning, the ground began to shake, and many in the crowd screamed in fright. Tomadus had never encountered an earthquake in Jerusalem before, but they were not unheard of, and this was only a minor tremor. He regained his balance and waited for it to end. The rumbling ceased but was soon replaced by the sounds of the traditional procession entering the square on the right. Three ancient wagons rolled slowly by, their wooden wheels chattering on the cracks between the pavers in the square while the hoofs of the magnificent draft horses clattered out a dreadful beat he had never forgotten. They were the same wagons he had seen at Yohanan's execution, except this time the final wagon held only one prisoner—Isa.

Tomadus looked around in astonishment as the crowd let out a collective cheer, which was followed by individual screams of derision at Isa, each person calling him yet another despicable name. These could not be the same people who had repeatedly proclaimed him "Savior" just a few days ago. Had Isa's speech turned the people against him or was something else amiss?

Isa's head was covered with blood, his face and forehead bruised and cut. While the First Consul desired a sense of reality, did he really need to denigrate Isa by forcing him to wear but a single strip of clothing around his private parts? Did he need to wear those terrible metallic bracelets and collar around his wrists, ankles and neck? The First Consul had gone too far.

Tomadus began to shake. It was like watching Yohanan executed all over again. *No, control yourself. This will be different. You heard the First Consul. Be patient and we shall prevail.* He took a couple of deep breaths and the trembling ceased.

The carriages nearly followed the familiar routine: The Governor appeared out of the first with his red robe with purple fringes and was followed by the Grand Imam and the Abh Beyth Diyn. This time no First Consul emerged from the carriages. Could something have gone wrong? Tomadus madly scanned the square. There, the First Consul walked inconspicuously into the square from the left and stopped well short of the stage. Tomadus made his way through the crowd and over to the Romanus leader.

When Tomadus reached him, Khansensius put his hand up and waved it slowly toward the ground a few times.

Tomadus ignored the gesture, walking right up to the First Consul. "What has gone wrong? Why are you not on the stage?"

The First Consul motioned for him to lower his voice. "Quiet, you fool!" he said in a low voice. "We should not be talking in public. Remember, patience."

"I need to know—are we on track?" Tomadus asked.

"Everything is fine. I can accomplish more here."

"Why has Isa been beaten?"

"The guards did that against my express orders. I am sorry. They will be severely punished."

"But why is the crowd so against him?"

"Tomadus, it is your plan. You asked for adversity. Isa must appear as a man against the world. If the Grand Imam and the Abh Beyth Diyn do not believe his sincerity after this, how could they ever? I made sure the guards only allowed the right kind of spectators into the square today."

"You excluded followers of the Way? How could you?"

"All according to plan," said the First Consul. "Now calm down."

Tomadus turned back to the spectacle. The guards forced Isa out of his mobile jail cell to the front of the stage. As Isa turned away from the crowd, blood oozed out of fresh whip marks on his back. "My lord," Tomadus exclaimed, "they have whipped him." The First Consul sighed heavily and then shook his head along with Tomadus.

The Governor stepped to the microphone. "Isa of Palestine, you have been accused of crimes against Allah and the Sunni Muslim Emperor. In light of the severity of these crimes, I have decided to take this case myself and adjudicate your fate, with the assistance of the Abh Beyth Diyn and the Grand Imam of Palestine. Your immediate release or punishment shall follow. Do you understand?"

Now standing and facing the Governor, Isa neither spoke nor moved.

"Do you understand?" the Governor repeated, this time with greater vehemence.

Isa said nothing.

One of the guards struck him with the shaft of his spear. "Respond, prisoner!"

Isa stood mute.

The Governor waived off another potential beating from the guard and spoke, "We shall take your silence as assent."

The light of the sun had darkened visibly. Tomadus looked up and saw foreboding clouds rolling in, threatening the proceeding. A thunderclap tumbled across the square.

"Prisoner, we would like to hear your defense first," continued the Governor. "What say you?"

Isa stood mute and still.

"Do you not understand that I hold the power to release you or punish you on this *triangulum penetrans*?"

Isa now responded for the first time, "You only have the power my Father gives you."

"You hear that!" yelled one thug in the crowd. "He has said he is the Son of God! Kill him!" Several others began yelling the same. Another group began chanting, "Triangulum, triangulum, triangulum."

"Silence!" yelled the Governor, but the unrest in the crowd grew. They now hurled not only insults but also rocks and bottles. The guards tried to quell the crowd by shooting their rap rifles into the air, but it had little effect. The governor yelled, "This man deserves an impartial trial in accordance with the laws of Allah."

"Kill him! Kill the blasphemer!" the crowd kept shouting.

"Since you begin to riot and disgrace yourselves, we shall move this proceeding to a more austere location. Guards, escort the prisoner inside."

"Inside? Inside where?" asked Tomadus.

The First Consul smiled. "All according to plan, Tomadus. We retire to the stage where we can remove ourselves from the crowd and better control the outcome of this play."

As the guards dragged Isa into the official building, the crowd surged forward, hitting him with bottles and spitting at him. "False prophet!" they cried.

As Tomadus followed the First Consul, he was separated for a few seconds and feared he would not be let in. As he neared the door, a hand reached from the angry mob and pulled him back. He was ready to punch his way out when he saw Peregrine's face.

"Dear Lord, Tomadus, what have you done?" Peregrine said.

In the face of the near riot around them, Tomadus said, "It is under control. Isa will be vindicated."

Peregrine shook his head sadly. "I managed to get by security. They would not let anyone else from the Way in. Jochi tried but could not push past them. She wrote this letter to you. She said you must read it now."

After Tomadus grabbed a folded letter, several guards pushed Peregrine and the rest of the mob. One of the guards pulled Tomadus by his arm toward the door. "The First Consul wants you inside. What is that?" he said, pointing at the letter.

"Nothing," Tomadus said, and put the folded letter in his pocket. *Probably just another dagger through my heart.* Nevertheless, he knew he would read it when he could.

CHAPTER 97

WHEN HUXLEY AWOKE, a hammer struck repeatedly inside his head, his vision bouncing with each blow. This time he quickly found the cause of his pains: a thin layer of dried blood caked on the back of his head. He looked at his sore left arm and saw the needle mark on one of his cuffed arms. He was leaning back on a counter with two-foot long chains connecting his wrists to two metal bars hanging from the ceiling of that same interior cabin of the *Infernum* where he had blacked out. He could move only a few feet across the center of the cabin before the chains tightened, grabbing his wrists, yanking him back.

He was alone. He winced and tried to grab his head, but the chains stopped him. Lights were still flashing on various electronic displays, and several cameras pointed at him. The monitors were on but merely showed a still picture of the graceful *Infernum* at sea. A huge console, busy with buttons, dials, needles and lights, stood in the center of the room—too far away for him to reach with his feet. Why was he chained? Why was he not dead?

The pain shooting through his brain muddled any cogent attempt at recall. He tried to isolate the pain and then ignore it. He focused on the monitor in front of him and blinked slowly. He kept seeing a few tidbits of the strange conversation with Kadir, his old friend, or so he had thought. *What a strange side of Kadir.* A few fragments of the poem slithered through his neurons, and he saw the boat and heard the GPS voice from his car again. His heart sank anew. "Shit," he uttered lowly—low enough that nobody would hear him on the deck of the ship. Nonetheless, his word triggered a response.

"Welcome back, Scholar Boy." Kadir's face now replaced the picture of the ship on one of the monitors, his face grinning with the same cocky look the Kad-man would always give him after administering another beating on the squash court…

∇   ∇   ∇

…As the guard gestured to Tomadus to take a seat near the First Consul, the glowing light in his eyes softened, and the remaining image of his old friend from that other world still burned hot in his head. Tomadus whispered, "You are The Leopard."

The First Consul stiffened and turned quickly toward Tomadus. "What did you say?"

"Nothing. I… Nothing," Tomadus shook his head to dispel the residual glow of another reality.

When his eyes cleared, Tomadus fixed his gaze on the large contraption towering over him on the sound stage. While the thing resembled the *triangulum penetrans* on its exterior, there was something quite different about it: the many little holes that normally covered the inverted triangular slab had been replaced by tiny glass lenses.

The First Consul crossed his arms. "I see you have noticed the upgrades to this version."

"What do they do?"

"All in due time. Quiet now, the proceeding resumes."

The Governor and the Abh Beyth Diyn and Grand Imam stood on the stage. Next to them were the same table and chairs in the same spot where Tomadus had spoken with the First Consul last evening. Isa stood below the stage, not ten feet from Tomadus. From this distance, Tomadus saw Isa's bare back and could almost feel the pain of the cuts and bruises that drew a strange purple and red pattern on his skin. The entire theater itself was empty, except for the guard standing with his spear just behind Isa and another guard with a rap rifle off to the side. However, technicians worked behind the glass wall of the sound booth to the rear of the theater. The public would view this proceeding only through the live visi-scan broadcast.

"Isa of Palestine, how do you respond to the charges?"

"I have spoken publicly to the world. I spoke on your visi-scan and in your square not three days ago. I have always taught in the open. Why ask me? Ask those who heard me what I said to them. They know what I said."

"Perhaps we shall," the Governor said slowly. "Can you name a witness?"

Isa said nothing.

The First Consul interrupted, "Governor, I wonder if we could hear from one of this man's closest friends. Here is Tomadus of Roma. He has followed Isa closely this past year. I can vouch for his integrity. He has done much to help the Three Empires."

The Governor nodded and gestured Tomadus up to the stage and to the same chair he had sat in the evening before. Tomadus felt a rivulet of electricity surge up his chest and through his arms, so he stretched out his fingers to expel the nervous energy. The creature paced over every *uncia* of his gut. He looked down as he was led to the very chair he had occupied last evening in his discussion with the First Consul. The stage lights baked his skin and the sweat trickled down his forehead. *Focus. He needs you.*

The Governor spoke, "Tomadus of Roma, you are brought before this hearing to speak only *veritas* about Isa of Palestine. Do you agree?"

"Yes, of course." Tomadus responded quietly.

"Please, speak up. Tomadus of Roma, what say you? Who is this man and what does he believe?"

"I have followed Isa and the Way for nearly a year now, and I have been with him in many of his discussions with his followers. I do not understand the nature of the allegations against him, because I have heard none. I have heard you would like to determine whether he really believes he is who he says."

The First Consul nodded to him.

Tomadus looked at the Governor and straightened up. "I can say this without any reservation whatsoever. Isa believes in everything he preaches. He loves his God more than anything in this world, and he loves others nearly as much—yes, even his enemies—he loves them more than you or I could possibly love even our own families. He is a man of peace. He is—"

"Thank you, Tomadus," the Governor interrupted. "That is enough." Tomadus began to rise from the chair, but the Governor continued, "Just a few questions, though. Why have you followed him?"

"Because I believe he is the best hope for our world."

"Hope? Tomadus, despite being a Romanus technologist, do you believe in God?"

"Well, I…I—"

"A simple yes or no will do."

"I don't know." *Why could he not just say no?*

Isa smiled gently at him.

The Governor asked, "Were you with him at the so-called "Adin Miracle?"

"Yes."

"Please explain what you saw." Tomadus told the story plainly, never mentioning anything about Adin receiving any packages from Isa or ever doubting the nature of the miracle or anything at all about any potential pharmaceutical tricks.

"Just a few more quick questions, then. Tomadus, have you ever heard Isa say he is the Mahdi, returned from occultation to now lead us to peace and justice?"

"No, I heard only a few Mahdians say that among themselves," Tomadus said. "He has never acknowledged that he believes that."

"Very well, then have you heard him say he is the Messiah promised to the Jews?"

Tomadus bit his lip. *Damn, how do I answer without condemning him?* "I… I—"

"Yes or no?" the Governor demanded.

"I don't understand who this Messiah is. I am a Romanus technologist, not a Jewish scribe. May I be dismissed, now?"

The Governor looked at him for a few moments in silence. "Has Isa ever said he is God or the Son of God?"

"No!" Tomadus responded strongly. *Not to me, not exactly. But does Isa believe otherwise?*

"Has he said how he will try to work with the Three Emperors?"

"No. He is not political, so I do not think it matters."

"I see." The Governor nodded a few times. "Very revealing. Thank you, Tomadus, for your honest testimony. You are dismissed."

Tomadus left his seat and walked off the stage.

As he neared Isa, Isa looked up and said, "Forgive him Father, he knows not what he has done."

Tomadus tilted his head, staring back at Isa. *How would Isa's words apply to him?* When he sat down by the First Consul, he leaned over and whispered, "What is this travesty? They are not testing him as we anticipated. They seem to be trying him for blasphemy! We have had enough of this, now. Please, intervene and release him."

"Calm down," the First Consul whispered back. "You must be patient. You have said nothing damning, have you? The Governor is with us. We just need to put him on the new device to convince the Grand Imam and the Abh Beyth Diyn."

"No!" yelled Tomadus audibly to the sound stage. The Governor looked down at them, but with a quick gesture, the First Consul had the other guard escort Tomadus quickly toward the back of the theater and into the soundproof control booth.

CHAPTER 98

HUXLEY SHOOK HIS head at the image of his old friend on the monitor. Was this some kind of elaborate prank? The guy had pulled a few good ones in college and since. But Huxley's mind kept sifting through the poem and his last conversation with Kadir. He recalled his desperate thoughts just before he sent Sonatina a text last night. *No, it could not be.* "Kadir, good to see you. I seem to have hit my head on something and somehow gotten myself tangled up in these chains. Would you mind terribly coming down and releasing me?"

"Why would I want to do that?" Kadir bared his teeth like a wolf.

"Ah, let me see…because you are the Ambassador of Peace?"

"That is precisely why I cannot release you."

"Okay, how about because you are my friend, although right now I am having some serious doubts about that."

"It might be wise to reexamine your assumptions in that regard." Kadir raised one eyebrow, and then added with a sarcastic tone, "Hux."

"I take it this is not some stupid practical joke, then?"

"That is the first thing you have said that makes sense."

"Did you write the Jefferson poem?" Huxley asked.

"I had hoped your little brain had made the connection."

"So now I suppose you are going to tell me about the fate of my father, for when I stepped on your boat, I obviously must have descended to hell."

"Good. Good. You understand that as well. You always did need a little help, even if you thought you were smarter than the rest of us." Kadir grinned and added with an acrid tone, "Sko-B."

"And how would you possibly know my father's fate? You were under 10 years old at the time just like me."

"Once again, you underestimate me. I have many connections with many governments—a few closer than you might imagine. It was a small matter to find out he was murdered. I have known that for years."

"Bullshit, he committed suicide."

Kadir shook his head slowly. "I am afraid that even that little double myth you have contrived must be sacrificed on the altar of truth. Oh, you wanted to believe it was an accident—so did your mother—but in your hearts, you always believed he killed himself. You told me that in college over a few drinks one night. Do you not recall?"

"Of course," said Huxley. "I told you about catching him in his little love affair. You even agreed he probably killed himself to avoid the embarrassment to his family."

"Affair? You idiot. Did you forget he was a CIA spy?"

"No."

"Well then, do you think he was really sleeping with an Ambassador's wife because the sex was so good? No, he was trying to obtain information on a particular Emirati in the secret service whom he suspected of complicity with the KGB. Like you, he underestimated an Arab and suffered death for it. The security officer learned of the plot from the Ambassador, who was more than willing to sanction your father's death. Even your own CIA knew he was killed because of the mission. Too bad they chose not to share it with you or your mother."

Huxley asked. "If you knew this, why didn't you tell me earlier?"

"What, and wreck the fun? It was ever so much more enjoyable to scramble your emotions during your pathetic little investigative adventures."

His blood beginning to boil, Huxley took a deep breath. *Control.* Kadir was trying to pull his strings again. He needed to play the emotion back to Kadir, but keep cool inside and find a way to use the deception. He hissed, "I suppose you had fun playing around with my mother's death as well!"

"That I did, old friend. Actually, since the wound was fresh, the salt stung all the more, I am sure. I had a good laugh when Anwari told me you nearly cried at the Church of the Annunciation. I always knew you were just a little baby inside. You act like a big, tough, clever investigator who knows all of the answers, but in reality you are incapable even of dealing with your own mother over a little Jewish harlot. Hanna saw it in you as well. You are weak, Huxley. You gave her up rather than challenge your mother. Worse yet, when Hanna was ready to leave you, you played the coward and dumped your mother as well."

"Is that why you are doing this? Are you still pissed about Hanna and me?"

Kadir laughed heartily. "You still do not comprehend, do you? You think this is all about you."

"No, Pardus, I know it is not."

"Well, well, at least you understand who I am…"

∇   ∇   ∇

…"Pardus," Tomadus said to himself, slowly opening and closing his eyes. He repeated, "Pardus." A tingle went down his spine and his little creature began clawing at his gut. He sat in the control booth, shaking his head while struggling to connect the wild thoughts washing over his latest glowing revelation. He felt the betrayal, and it had come from his friend. No, not from his friend, but Pardus. They were just images of the other world, of Huxley in D.C., yet they seemed so real, so present. He'd made a mistake then. He could not repeat it here. The room seemed to close in on him as the sweat poured out of his face. While several technicians worked intensely at their terminals in the control booth, he could still see the proceedings on the stage through the glass and hear it through the speakers in the booth.

The Governor said, "Let us recall what you said on visi-scan a few days ago. You claimed to be able to perform miracles. You said you could rebuild the Temple of the Rock in three days if we tore it down? Now, tell us, how can this be?"

Isa stood mute.

The Governor stepped away from the microphone and conferred quietly with the Grand Imam and Abh Beyth Diyn. When he returned, he said, "Since you refuse to speak, we find we must assist your memory with our newest version of the *triangulum penetrans*, equipped with the new technology of light amplification."

Tomadus gasped. The Three Empires had adapted part of his invention to further demonize their methods of punishment and torture. But how effective would it be? Thank goodness he would not find out today. They would stop before the pain had begun, wouldn't they? As the guards scrambled on the stage to hoist Isa up to the inverted triangle, Tomadus saw a technician in the booth smile with satisfaction, eject a storage disk and place the disk at an unoccupied desk next to the First Consul's three-jeweled letter opener.

More sweat dripped down Tomadus's brow. When he reached in his pocket for a handkerchief, the folded letter grazed his fingers. *Jochi.* Now trembling, he closed his eyes and bit his lip. Could he manage to read the letter in this state? She had seemed prescient. Could he live with himself if he didn't? He unfolded the paper and began to read:

My Dear Tomadus,

You honestly are so dear to me. I know you may not believe that now, but you must. I only realized a few hours ago how much I have truly loved you and for how long. I know I would love you now even if you favored my worst enemy. How could I not?

I fear for you as I fear for Isa. Isa wants to die as a martyr. No, that is not quite right. He believes God wants him to die as a martyr. We both know what happened to Jesus. It now happens again. Only this time, maybe you can save him. I don't know.

You have put so much faith in your friend, the First Consul, but you will find your faith misplaced and your error will again undo you. Did you not learn this from the other world? Your friend was and is a destroyer, but you have never seen it. Stop him before it is too late!

If you cannot save Isa, Tomadus, at least let him save you. Let him save Huxley and Sonatina and their world. You have never quite believed me; you have never quite trusted me—even in that other world, even when I was Sonatina. I loved you then, and I love you still. You must trust me now.

You might think me insane, but I believe I have seen two very different worlds through Sonatina's eyes —two different futures for that world. The first made me wretch in horror. The second made me whimper helplessly. The second is worse, far worse. I think we can help, Tomadus. Both of us, together. Isa told me that the Father has granted both of us beautiful gifts, and we must use them. He said that if we have faith, we will do what is right and save ourselves and others.

I did not understand him then, but he would say no more. I know he has always wanted you to believe in the Father, but it seemed like he was saying something more this time. Then, after the soldiers took him away last night, I prayed and fell into a dream that repeated these horrible visions of the other world. The evil man—I think it was Pardus—taunted you to do something and you looked at me and asked me what to do, but I had no answers. Then Isa appeared and you finally asked him. He nodded to me and suddenly I knew. "Do it, Chris," I said. "Sacrifice yourself and you'll save billions."

I'm not sure what this dream means, but I know it is the key. Somehow, you must get this message to Huxley. You said you thought he sometimes dreamed about you. Find a way to tell him, Tomadus. Tell him, and he may hear! You must have faith. Chris Huxley must have faith. He must sacrifice himself, whatever that means.

I love you and shall wait for you,
Jochi

Tears streamed down Tomadus's face. Across two universes, he had known, but somehow refused to believe; across two worlds, he had loved, but somehow refused to trust.

He looked around and saw the technicians were preoccupied with their tasks. He slowly reached over, picked up the disk and inserted it in the monitor near him. A vid of his testimony began playing. He quickly put the monitor's headphones to his ears and was sickened to hear his own voice say things he could never possibly utter aloud. But it was unmistakably his voice—how had they altered it?

Turning his head slowly toward the sound stage, Tomadus stared at the chair he had sat in during his testimony. It was the same chair in exactly the same place as during his conversation with the First Consul the evening before. The cameras must have been rolling when he was being candid with the First Consul. But he had said nothing damning, had he?

It turned out that had not been necessary. The splices in the vid were obvious, but only to someone who knew what they had done. The vid carefully interspersed the questions and snippets of answers, showing an image of the Governor instead of Tomadus whenever a clip was too short to seem real. He knew it was fake, but nobody else would:

"Tomadus of Roma, what say you?" said the Governor.

"I have followed Isa and the Way for nearly a year now, and have been with him in many of his discussions with his followers."

"Thank you, Tomadus. Why have you followed him?"

"I don't know."

"Were you with him at the so-called 'Adin Miracle?'"

"Yes. He has traveled widely, you know. Some say it was a miracle, but I know otherwise. Adin…told me. It was a pharmaceutical trick. I myself felt Adin's body as he lay on the table. He was alive!"

"Tomadus, have you ever heard Isa say he is the Mahdi, returned from occultation to now lead us to peace and justice."

"Yes."

"Very well, then have you heard him say he is the Messiah promised to the Jews?"

"I can say this without any reservation whatsoever. He has said he is God."

"Has he said how he will try to work with the Three Emperors?"

"He will try to usurp their power."

"I see. That is revealing. Thank you, Tomadus, for your honest testimony. You are dismissed."

Tomadus slunk back in his chair and the light once again consumed him…

❈ ❈ ❈

…Huxley stared back at Kadir's image, Pardus's image. "If you wrote the poem, who else could you be? But if the end is not about me, then why is the last stanza all about my father and me?"

"They must have used a rather large hose to suck out all of your intelligence when you became a spy boy. You were pretty damn smart in college."

Huxley stared at the monitor, moving his mind rapidly over the last stanza, searching for more:

> On truth lies yet obscured thy fathers' end.
> To myths our hearts do reach and then depend.
> We seek our consolation with a friend.
> Remember now the Maine and then ascend.
> To know his fate you must to hell descend.

Pardus laughed. "You think the last stanza is only about you and your father?"

Huxley's lips curled in as he closed his eyes. There was something about the first line that had always bothered him. "The apostrophe."

"There you go."

"It came at the end of 'fathers,' not before the 's'."

"Exactly, so it refers not to just one father but two or more. Hell, Huxley, do I know English grammar better than you?"

"I filed it away as a typo."

Pardus clicked his tongue and tilted his head. "Bad idea."

"So it must also be another reference to Washington."

"Of course."

At first Huxley nodded, but then shook his head. Did he dare let on what he knew? There was nothing Pardus could do now—the NNSA had recovered the stolen nukes. "It doesn't matter, you know. I didn't fall for your little deceit. You never realized I turned Anwari to our side. He helped me figure out you planned the whole scavenger hunt as your little ruse to make us look at DC and ignore New York. Well, we stopped your plan cold yesterday when we recovered the two nukes on their way into the harbor."

Pardus grimaced.

Huxley smirked and nodded. "That's right—you might kill me you son of a bitch, but the world will be safe. And, just think, you could have just killed me in my sleep so many years ago if you had wanted, but now you have spent what—a few hundred million bucks of your family's money? And what do you get out of it but a dead friend? Kind of crappy return on investment, don't you think?"

"Interesting," responded Pardus with a curious smile.

Not the response Huxley had expected. "What?"

"Right to the end, you remain clueless. Let me translate the last stanza of the poem for you. If you had been capable of translating it yourself, you might have figured out the whole thing. I am of a sporting nature, Huxley—you know that. I gave you a chance, but you blew it."

Sneering, Huxley shook his head in defiance at Pardus. *He's just full of shit.* The poem hadn't given him any clues except about some fathers. But wait, what was that about the myth? *We reach our hearts out to myths and then depend on them.* The myth had made Huxley believe Washington was the target, or had it? *No!*

Pardus interrupted his thoughts, "I see from your expression that you may have finally found enlightenment. How wonderful for you."

"So what is the myth?" asked Huxley quickly.

Pardus's teeth gleamed with his pride. "Why all of it, of course..."

∇   ∇   ∇

..."All a myth," Tomadus said, the yellow light beginning to fade. A vid-tech squinted and cocked his head at Tomadus. Tomadus blinked hard and brought himself back from Huxley and Pardus and the other world, back to the control booth. Undoubtedly, the vid of his fake testimony was just one weapon in the First Consul's arsenal of deception. Tomadus winced.

He was helping this devil kill Isa. Worse yet, he had provided the tool to kill Isa's message for good.

The display of the terminal reflected in his eyes as he looked at the technicians in the room. They didn't know he'd uncovered the deception. They were too busy working on their next counterfeit. *I know the technology better than they. I still have a chance.*

Tomadus leaned forward and tapped on the terminal's keyboard. The screen showed exactly what he had feared. He could switch it over now, but that would not be enough; he must mask reality from the technicians themselves or all would be lost. He began typing on the terminal and soon found the kernel. A little segment of code in just the right spot would do the trick. He hit the button, the little routine ran, and the screen returned to its steady state. He sat back satisfied, though his smile lasted but a fleeting moment.

"Tomadus, what have you been up to?" the First Consul said from over his shoulder. The First Consul reached over to the keyboard, hit a few buttons and the vid of Tomadus's testimony began to play. "I see my technicians have done an excellent job with this…testimony." The First Consul stood up straight and looked at the two technicians on the other side of the control booth, his almost sinister smile now so much different than the gentle, calming smile to which Tomadus had become so accustomed. "Well done, men!"

When Tomadus scrambled to leave the booth, a quite distinctive clicking sound stopped him cold. A guard holding a rap rifle aimed it at Tomadus, its bolt now cocked back. "Very wise, Tomadus," taunted the First Consul. "You did not wish to miss the remainder of the show, did you? After all, we have you to thank for our new torture device."

Tomadus swiveled his head toward the glass wall and looked out at the stage. Isa was now hanging on the modified *triangulum penetrans*, his arms outstretched. The many small glass lenses now glowed red. Isa gritted his teeth in pain.

The First Consul laughed. "This is a prototype, of course. It is just one application of your wonderful invention. The remaining military applications will be so much more useful in the long run. Thank you so much for your assistance, by the way. You really did deserve that medal."

"It's killing him."

"Oh, not yet, not for a good while," the First Consul replied. "You see, one of the advantages of your enhanced light rays is that we can use them to fine tune the instrument itself. We can determine when we have hit a key organ and deactivate a particular beam. It allows us to keep the marshmallow browning nicely without setting it on fire. But I am afraid, eventually, he will die."

Isa screamed. The First Consul looked up and rubbed his hands together. "Wonderful! It looks like they have increased the intensity. I do so enjoy a good cookout."

Tomadus nearly retched and began shaking at the scene before him. Smoke rose from the *triangulum penetrans* behind Isa's body. He could smell the horrible odor of burning flesh. Jochi had been right—he was responsible, in more ways than one.

The light flashed across Tomadus's eyes and another vision entered his brain…

❃ ❃ ❃

…Kadir, Pardus, let out a long, derisive laugh. "Please, let me explain. While it is quite enjoyable to watch you struggle to peel the layers of the onion away, I have no time for this childish entertainment. Now, recall that the first line of the last stanza was: 'On truth lies yet obscured thy fathers' end.' And what is 'truth' but what one thinks is 'right'? So from Jefferson's view, the truth about the end of Washington stood to his right but obscured. Of course, the Southwest Wharf is to the right of Jefferson. Your father met his end there, but it is also the home of my lovely boat, the *Infernum*, which obscures the means of Washington's end."

Huxley wrinkled his brow. What did the *Infernum* have to do with Washington's end?

Pardus said, "And further nested is the word 'lies.' Because the 'lies' remained obscured there as well—the 'lies' that I allowed you and your government to adopt as their truth. You all so wanted to believe you had found the warheads in New York, and so you did, even before they were dismantled. Thus, your heart reached out to this myth, as in the poem, and then you all depended on it. More on this myth in a minute, but I wish to finish the poem first. It is great fun, is it not?"

Huxley just shook his head.

Pardus shrugged. "So after depending on this myth, you sought consolation with me on my boat. How nice of you, Hux. Similarly, your nation's spy agencies have sought consolation with me as their good Arab friend. How many times have I provided insights to help them find those terrible terrorists! And, of course, let us not forget that the organization I founded, The Brotherhood of Arab Nations for Peace, has been at the forefront of bringing Arabs together to assist America's obsession with mollifying the less compliant segment of the Arab populace. You are welcome for that, by the way."

Huxley kept shaking his head slightly, almost imperceptibly.

Pardus leaned forward. "The remainder of the poem clearly refers to you coming aboard my lovely Ship of Fate, the *Infernum*. While you did not need to be here, it is terribly satisfying to me that you should be aboard the ship that launches a nuclear bomb over Washington, D.C."

His head sunk low, Huxley mumbled, "So the warheads in New York were also fakes."

"A little slow, but then you have been on an emotional roller coaster. For some reason you all seemed to think it was impossible to take the warheads apart and just use the weapons-grade plutonium. Making a new warhead is pretty easy when you have the material and a few hundred million dollars to work with. I left enough nuclear material in the original warheads and lowered the resistance of Rosenthal's device just enough to ensure it set off your little UNGARD device."

"Why me?" asked Huxley in a low voice. "Why did you involve me?"

Pardus, who seemed no longer to resemble his old friend Kadir, stared back at Huxley through the monitor. "Why not? You were the perfect dupe, Huxley. God has long been dead to you, and you constantly try to prove it. You wanted to believe in Anwari not just to save the world, but also to validate yourself. Deep inside, you wanted to show that when the chips were down, you would take a Muslim's word the same as a Christian's. But this isn't about the glory of God. It never was. With a little help from me, Anwari figured out that the love for Allah could not possibly be my true motive. No, my motives differ quite significantly from that, I am afraid. You might say they are quite the opposite. Hell, when are politics and the wars of men truly motivated by the love of God? You know better."

Huxley said, "Anwari truly was a man of God. You obviously are the opposite. You want to start something that could ultimately kill us all. You are truly evil."

Pardus merely smiled. "Anwari a man of God? Are you a Muslim now, Christian? Pathetic."

Huxley glared back at the camera but said nothing.

Pardus laughed. "Of course, I also knew you were an emotional wreck. Oh, you managed to fool your boss at Homeland, but I knew you too well. It allowed me to distract you just enough to confuse you. At your best, you might have figured this thing out. I could not have that, so I added a little fuel to the fire of your emotions and you tumbled into the abyss."

Huxley closed his eyes. *Damn. Sonatina asked if I had too much emotional baggage to see through the fog. But I did see through it!* "I saw Anwari. He told me the truth. I could read his expressions. The hunt was a ruse to get me to look away from Washington!"

"You and your blessed ability to read people! You must know that anything good can be twisted to other purposes with enough finesse. I needed only to figure out where to twist it. I knew if Anwari and Jinnah truly believed what they told you, you would believe them because your deepest faith has always been in your ability to read people. So I simply needed to make them believe a few things themselves. That was ever so much easier than trying to slide a big lie by you directly."

Huxley raised his chin high and sighed.

Pardus snickered. "Do you think I was stupid enough to let Anwari know my true motivations? I fed him a little vitriol when I thought the time was ripe. The man was so damn loyal that I had a hard time getting him to turn back to you. But I knew he would. Why do you think I employed him in the first place? He was never a real terrorist, and I knew it. He loved Allah and he loved his brother dearly, so he thought God had called him to retribution. My spies heard his brother in the hospital the day he died. From that point, it was simply a matter of seizing the opportunity by turning a few emotional screws that would divert him into my hand awhile.

"But I could never ask him to really harm someone innocent. He would have bolted, which is precisely why I used him. Real terrorists usually don't give a damn about their targets. Hell, some of them actually enjoy killing. It stokes their hatred. Anwari was full of remorse before I even engaged him, so I knew he would turn against me when the pressure came to bear. All I needed to do was make him believe the real target was outside of Washington and he would eventually feed that information to you. Your old friend Jinnah served a similar role, but there I just needed to release enough information to him at the right time and ensure he knew you had entered Pakistan."

Gnawing on his cheeks, Huxley nodded. "That's why the scavenger hunt brought me to Pakistan. You wanted me to know the nukes had been stolen."

"Of course, although I was a bit worried you might figure out those clues too soon and arrive a little too early, which would have been a real disaster. The bomb in Florence both made you think you were on the right path and forced you to take a little time off while a few other moving parts came together. I saw you used that time well."

"You talking about Sonatina?" Huxley asked. "She in on this, too?"

Pardus laughed. "I find it terribly ironic that in the end an American Catholic altar boy believed an Arab Muslim who was not even his friend and instead suspected his Italian Catholic girlfriend. Why do you think that is, Christian? Will your little rebellion against the Church never end? Perhaps I should recruit you, huh? Mmm, no, we both know that wouldn't work. No, Scholar Boy, Sonatina never knew a thing. However, once you shared your concerns about her with me, how could I resist playing her off as yet another of my decoys?"

"Decoy?" asked Huxley. "You hit her on the head and texted me that you had done it."

"Well, I merely directed that action from afar. Najwa took care of it. He performed a brilliant piece of acting, I might add. We knew you had set your mind on Cardinal Fine. We knew you would do that when we set him up at Tel Megiddo by carefully releasing information to Dante Tocelli.

Tocelli was such an amateur spy. We were able to monitor his communications and ensure he told just enough that Fine would ultimately be implicated. And if you were too dense to figure that part out, we would have found another way to help you just like we did in Tel Megiddo and every other time you got stuck. But I had faith you would implicate Fine. His history just made for too juicy a Vatican conspiracy theory for you to reject out of hand."

During Pardus's lecture, Huxley had looked at the ceiling and noticed something he had not seen before: an aluminum nozzle. He quickly looked back down to the camera. Maybe, just maybe, if he had time. *Keep him talking*. "But Fine was in hiding for weeks in Rome."

"Of course," replied Pardus. "I never said he was not working for us. He just never understood the stakes. Remember, he became involved with some of my lower echelon terrorist friends awhile back. They convinced him that if he stayed incognito in that little apartment for a few weeks, they would find a way to rid the Church of the pope, and he could emerge afterwards as a savior for the Vatican. We had no difficulty stroking his ego. Surely you have noticed he carries an enormous one with him wherever he goes."

Huxley nodded weakly.

Pardus continued, "Then we just set up a meeting with Najwa near the same place Ms. D'Amare always runs in the evening. So we created a little opportunity for D'Amare to spot Fine, knowing it would be just too damn unlikely a coincidence for you. The little sleeper hold followed by a slight bump on the head gave her one of the worst lame excuses you could imagine. Remember, she did not know if she had been hit from behind. You started thinking that when you saw Najwa's text telling you she would have a little headache. She simply had no idea what role she was playing.

"I had worried about her awhile. She could pull you out of your emotional handicap, and she had helped you find a few answers way too quickly. Alas, I hated to interrupt your little love affair since I don't recall you ever having managed to hang onto a lover for long. However, the deception did help confuse things further for you and kept her out of the action when it could have hurt us most."

"The last few weeks."

"Yes. Do you comprehend yet what happened in Dubai?"

By now, Huxley was seeing it all too clearly. "Dracoratio performed a nice triple murder and made it look like Mayer was Pardus. It had to be him."

"Very good, but what luck that Mayer walked into our midst! Dracoratio happened to see Mayer following him in a reflection. He faked a call from me and then improvised. Najwa and Anwari were already scheduled to kill each other, but Mayer's propitious entrance into the prayer room changed the plan. The new plan took another counterweight out of the equation and placed greater credence on your story. It is amazing what people will do when there is a gun to their heads. Dracoratio demonstrated his own brilliance that day."

"So you waited for me to convince the President to move the UNGARD to New York and then what?" Huxley asked.

"That was the whole point of the plan. I always wanted to destroy Washington. It is terribly nice of all the politicians to return to the area now that your Continuation of Government plan has been lifted. Perfect timing, do you not agree? With most of the politicians dead and the government in disarray, the bomb will create exactly the kind of chaos I desire—even better than destroying the financial center of this nation. I knew through other sources you had the UNGARD searching ships heading to the Chesapeake."

"How'd you hear of the UNGARD?" Huxley asked. "It's compartmented, so maybe 20 or 30 people know of it."

Pardus raised his eyebrows and lowered his chin. "You aren't my only friend."

"Who?" Huxley demanded.

Kadir just smiled and nodded. "It was the only thing that stood in my way once that Jew chemist figured out how to block your other detectors. How do you eliminate the one device standing in your way when it is impossible for you to get to it? You find a way to have so-called Homeland Security move it on its own. That was your role, Huxley. Without you, I never could have accomplished it. So thank you for your substantial assistance."

"But we searched every boat entering the Chesapeake!"

"That is where the poem comes into play. You see, not only your heart but also the hearts of your boss and the President reached out to that myth of warheads heading to New York Harbor. When they thought they had found them, they chose to depend on that myth and stopped the intrusive searches of watercraft heading to the Chesapeake. Predictably, the searching had become incredibly unpopular, and politicians hate that so. My captain was waiting for the magic window to open, and sailed right through it as soon as it did. Besides, you came aboard the Ship of Fate —did you see any nuclear weapons?"

Mayhem wrecked the walls of Huxley's gut, like a creature trying desperately to leave his body, clawing at his stomach lining, pulling his heart down to his bowels, and devouring any good left in him. When Blount had called him a goddamned hero, he had been right about one thing—he would be damned for all time. He had been a blind man believing he was leading the world to the light, when he was actually condemning it to hell.

Huxley shook his head. "You have led me like the lamb, unknowingly, to slaughter."

Pardus chortled. "I prefer, 'And all our yesterdays have lighted fools the way to dusty death. Out, out, brief candle!'"

"Macbeth?" Huxley said. "How fitting. Your delusions will undo you in the end."

"It is you who have been deluded."

"The warheads are on this boat?" Huxley asked lowly. If so, he would be alone with all of this equipment —the equipment that must be controlling the warhead.

"No, not warheads, just warhead. Why would we need two? I saved the other for your girlfriend in Rome—well, actually for her and her friends in the Vatican. It is a shame that the rest of Rome must suffer such an ignoble end. I rather like the Italians and all those ancient buildings. But, alas, it is just too damn poetic. And, of course, it fits my plans."

Was it possible that Huxley's heart had sunk deeper? With so many people dying, with his own death imminent, it still hurt worse to learn of Sonatina's coming end. A tear came down his cheek. "Your plans?" he said in a voice he would have sworn he had never heard before. "How can there be more?"

Pardus grinned. "There is always more. You did not think I was doing this out of some psychotic attempt to avenge a small slight by you, did you? Oh, I must admit that when you told me you were marrying Hanna, I was quite miffed. However, the revelation just made it more enjoyable for me to abuse your trust. I saw the way Hanna looked at you back in college. You ruined her for me and then confirmed your pathetic affair when you jumped her in the Maldives."

"I never had an affair with her in college."

Kadir shook his head slowly. "It is of no matter."

Huxley began to shake his head and then he saw it—an extra mooring rope coiled on the floor. Was there a metal clasp attached? He dared not risk allowing Pardus to see him move toward it. *Where the hell is the pull?* He looked nonchalantly around the cabin and kept the conversation going. "So was that when you began to hate me?"

"You misunderstand me. I have never hated you. Oh, you were always the typical American sympathizer who congratulates himself on his tolerance and respect for other cultures: 'See what a great person I am for showing my love for all of you poor, inferior Arabs and all of these other poor souls around the world who are unfortunate enough not to have been born an American?' Bah! You Americans are just as corrupt and greedy as the rest of the world, but you fail to see it because your world power fuels your ignorance. You think you do everything for the good of mankind, but you are just protecting your own damn wealth and dominance. Well, I have found a way to use your dominance to my own advantage, and so change the world."

"What are you going to do?" Huxley asked.

"That is for another time, Hux. Unfortunately, your time and that of your fellow Washingtonians has run out."

"But why? I still don't understand. How can a little arrogance by the U.S. be your motive for killing so many? You do not seem mad, so there must be a reason. Why?"

Pardus paused for a few seconds. "What is my name?"

"Pardus. The Leopard."

"That is my nickname, and it should give you all you need. What is my birth name?"

"Kadir al-Razin al-Asr."

"Yes, and there is your answer. You forget your Shakespeare, Huxley."

"What?"

"Well, not quite. Remember, Juliet said 'A rose by any other name would smell as sweet,' but she knew the world did not agree. Sometimes our names define us. Sometimes they guide us. Sometimes they are our destiny. Look, I am perfectly positioned. The Ambassador of Peace will emerge from your country's predictable overreaction to the nuclear attack. 'An eye for an eye' will be the cry from your citizens, and the new American government emerging from the ashes of Washington will give it to them or face violent revolution."

"But they will know a terrorist was responsible," Huxley said. "No other nation is at fault."

"They will not. Nuclear explosions have a way of destroying the evidence at hand. But there is other evidence that will not go unnoticed. Just as I left you a few breadcrumbs, I have ensured that the blame will fall squarely on another Islamic nation. Who will doubt this in America? Nobody. And once your country has nuked an Islamic nation's capital, the world will seek a new savior to prevent Armageddon. The Ambassador of Peace will serve that role nicely."

Hopelessness filled Huxley's heart; the creature inside of him seemed to die. "I'm sorry. I was wrong," replied Huxley.

"In so many ways."

"Yes, but mostly in this: I judged you a sane man but now finally comprehend the depths of your insanity."

Pardus laughed. "Think what you like, my old friend. I have not changed. You simply never knew me. I have full knowledge and appreciation of my actions and always have—even in college when I suggested you use your brilliant mind as an analyst for the CIA. You could have made megabucks on Wall Street, but you were a sucker and took the bait. And in the past ten years, I have fed you tips to catch a wayward terrorist here or there. Was I insane when I turned you into my clueless agent and helped you rise through the ranks of your intelligence services? No, you were nearly the insane one, Huxley. You almost ruined all of my work with you when you took a career dive at your mother's misfortune. Unlike you,

I have always been perfectly rational. I have taken these steps because they are my destiny. So it is written. So it shall be. People always underestimate the power of one man to change the course of history. I shall prove them wrong."

Huxley spit out the sour saliva poisoning his mouth. "I have always wondered what evil looked like, but now that I see it up close I still cannot comprehend it. Why does such horrid evil exist? Why do you live?"

"Good and evil?" Pardus asked. "Do you still believe in such archaic concepts? Well then, perhaps you should consider this: Without evil, how would we know what is good? Without good, how would we know what is evil? I am the yang to your yin, my old friend. Hey, I'm such a sporting guy that I'll even give you a chance to save your girlfriend."

Huxley's voice cracked, "Sonatina? How?"

"You do love her, don't you? An amusing thing, love. It makes otherwise rational people do the most reckless things. You see the button hanging above you? With just enough energy you should be able to reach it."

Huxley saw the metallic device hanging in front of him. He had thought it was just a broken electrical conduit, but now he noticed the button at its end. A long wire led from the device down to his cell phone on a counter five feet away. Another wire led from the cell phone to the central console. Hoisting himself up on his chains, he could barely reach the hanging device with his right hand as his left held him high. He yanked on the device, but it remained bolted into the ceiling. The cell phone did not move on the counter. He fell back and nodded to Pardus.

Pardus smiled. "Good, I see you are not completely useless. Push that button, say a few words, and it will give Sonatina a little head start on leaving Rome."

Huxley's eyes narrowed. "How?"

"By sending her a text message, of course."

"What's the trick?"

Pardus grinned broadly. "Trick? Must there always be a trick? No, there is no trick, but perhaps I have not explained the whole situation. You will be sending her a text message that I have drafted myself. Here, let me put it up on the screen for you."

Pardus's face was replaced on one of the screens by an iPhone screen with an unsent message cued in:

> Sonatina, leave Rome immediately! You have 30 minutes. I will set off nukes in Rome and Washington at that time. You must leave to escape the devastation. I have lied to you. I am the Ghost Leopard. I am Pardus. This is my final act of retribution against the corruption of these two cities; my final redemption for the wrongs I have committed on their behalf. With the help of my sponsors, I have now brought the world a new beginning. But I cannot let you perish, for you still are so dear to me. Leave Rome immediately!

Huxley snorted. "How ridiculous! Even you cannot think Sonatina would believe this. She would know someone stole my cell phone and sent this fake message."

"I will not allow the message to transmit until you add a voice clip to convince her. You must push the button and say, 'I am sorry, Sonatina, but it is best for the whole world. These cities must die. Forgive me.' That should do the trick, don't you think?"

"You pathetic beast. Why do want to blame me? What about your little plot to blame a Muslim country? You willing to forgo that to stick it to your old friend?"

"Oh, do not think yourself so important, Hux. This is merely for fun. Those breadcrumbs I mentioned can run to you, to Ken Mayer or to another. It matters little to my plans, but I do so enjoy seeing what you will do. It is a nice experiment for humanity, don't you think? Eternal condemnation to save your girlfriend. Oh, and I forgot to mention that the message will also be sent to James Cargill, the columnist at the New York Times. He's on vacation in Hawaii. What a nice little scoop that will give him when he finally checks his messages."

Huxley suppressed the rage bubbling within. "They'll check my record. They'll know I'd never do this."

"You think so? How about that little CIA meltdown a few years ago? You think the press won't be able to find a motive after you were drummed out of the agency? Especially when you clearly set up Ken Mayer in Dubai?

You've had contacts with terrorists around the world—your name even showed up in one of their cell phones. And you released the main terrorist, Anwari, from a CIA prison just weeks after he stole the nukes from Pakistan. Don't worry, we have plenty of evidence to link you to him and him to the nukes. Oh, and I forgot to mention—we did put $50 million into a Swiss account for you. Too bad you won't be able to spend it. Of course, you already spent much of your illicit funds from that rogue Islamic nation when you bought this Ship of Fate using an alias that will be traced back to you. That is right, Huxley, it has been registered in that name from the time of its maiden voyage. But look, I want to be sporting with you, my old friend. If you so choose, I can put all of this baggage on Mayer instead. You'll just be the dupe, not the bad man. But then, Sonatina will surely die. Your choice." Kadir smiled broadly while glaring at Huxley through the monitor.

Huxley closed his eyes, drew his lips into his mouth and exhaled hard out of his nose. *Keep your head. Why does he need to frame me?* He remembered his text to Sonatina before he blacked out and looked back at the camera. "You are worried about Sonatina. She's read my texts. They point to you, my loud friend."

"They do no such thing. You wrote:

> Sorry abandon u. Sorry doubt u. Love you still. On Ship of
> Fate sailing away. Pardus lives. Where will Fate take me? Where
> will it take us all? My loud friend will give answers.

"Nothing but the nonsense of a crazed, love-struck killer. The Ship of Fate is your own and you are sailing to hell. You are Pardus and you live. Your loud friend is your nuclear bomb. Of course, your final text today will end any speculation that might provide. It doesn't matter, though. If you don't push the button, she will be dead, and the texts will be long forgotten in the ashes of DC and Rome. Just do it. Push the button, Hux, and your little girlfriend Sonatina will get her chance to live. Of course, you will be vilified forever as the destroyer of cities, but that is not too much to ask, is it? So what will it be? I'm running out of patience."

Huxley's head fell to his chest and he closed his eyes…

▽   ▽   ▽

…Tomadus sunk back in his chair, shivering as the glow subsided, still too devastated to move. He had seen his other self, Huxley, in chains, pleading with a man on the screen who just taunted him, "Just do it. Push the button…" The button had been linked to a small device with a message—a message of warning, a message of despair, a message that would condemn Huxley for all time. How had he gone so wrong in both places? He remembered Jochi's words in her letter. That was it. Somehow, she had known before him. Were her visions ahead of his? Had she experienced something else? He had to trust her now. Somehow, he must tell Huxley to do it. *Do it, Chris. Sacrifice yourself and you will save billions.*

Tomadus heard the Governor resume his interrogation. "Now that you feel the wrath of God, renounce your teachings and you will be spared."

"I am here to testify only to the truth," Isa said, the words barely audible.

Tomadus shot a look at the First Consul. "You are a fool to believe he will renounce. His death will make him an even greater martyr in the eyes of the Way. Millions will rally to his cause. The Empires will not be able to stop the movement. And Heaven knows what wrath God will bring you."

"Quit acting like a religious zealot," said the First Consul. "You know God has nothing to do with this because God has long been dead to you. This isn't about a deity. It is about power. And your little Christ isn't going to gain any power for himself or his little band of brothers over this execution."

"I thought you were politically astute, Pardus," Tomadus said indignantly.

The First Consul raised his eyebrows.

Tomadus sneered. "Yes, I know who you are. You think you can act the destroyer across both time and universe, but you will suffer the same end in both."

"And you are ignorant, my old friend. You still do not understand, do you? I have planned this with the help of the Governor, the Grand Imam and the Abh Beyth Diyn all along. We do not play at politics like you do—we control the masses. You really thought I tried to save Yohanan from the *triangulum*. You fool. We will torture your Isa awhile, just to see if we can 'coax' him to renounce on his own. But do you think I am stupid enough to let this man martyr himself like Jesus before him, and this time on worldwide visi-scan? No, my friend, we are employing a little broadcast delay to give merely the impression of a live show. Right now, we are broadcasting only the preparation for this trial and punishment. In a little while, if he refuses to relent and dies on us, we will use the magic of editing and a few camera tricks to show him admitting, apparently live to the world, that he is nothing but a fraud."

Tomadus sneered at the First Consul. "He is no fraud!" Then the light struck again…

❆　❆　❆

Kadir/Pardus shouted, "Decide! No more stalling. Do it, Huxley. Sacrifice your reputation and you save her."

Huxley raised his head slowly and pleaded, "Thirty minutes is not enough. She won't make it. Give her 2 hours."

"Nice try Scholar Boy. No chance. Too much time for your government to figure out your text is real and determine there is a credible threat."

"An hour then."

"Twenty minutes."

"No. No. Please."

"Last chance. Thirty minutes."

"How can I trust you?"

"Hey, I'm your old friend, remember? What is your choice? She dies for certain if you don't. She has an outside chance to survive if you do. Just push the button."

"Will you promise you won't kill her after?"

Pardus laughed raucously, as if he and Huxley were sitting in a bar in DC having the time of their lives. "No promises. But she will despise you, anyway. You used her to destroy the Vatican and all of Rome, even if you managed to save her petty little life. You will have, as I wrote in the poem, descended to hell like your father before you. She will hate you so badly I might even want to give her a little taste of the Ambassador of Peace to comfort her. That might be the best way to rid her of the foul taste of Huxley. What do you think, Hux, you banged my old girlfriend—how about I bang yours?"

Huxley lost control of himself. He rattled the chains holding his arms, struggling against hope to somehow free himself. He threw every expletive he knew back at the camera. Pardus just laughed. Eventually, Huxley became still, absolutely still, his head hanging down with his eyes closed…

∇ ∇ ∇

…When the glow dissipated, he saw the First Consul standing over him, laughing. Tomadus's voice thickened as he slowly asked, "Why have you done this?"

"You must ask that?" the First Consul asked. "Just who or what do you think I am? Obviously, you do not yet comprehend. Perhaps your skepticism does blind you at times. You were a tool, Tomadus, a simple but useful tool. I saw this Isa heading down the same path as Jesus in that other universe, but I was prepared this time, and He was playing on my home field. He predictably followed his time-honored martyrdom strategy, but you helped me remain a step ahead. Finally, I will extinguish his message forever—at least in this instance of the universe." First Consul Khansensius cackled and then stared at Tomadus for a few seconds. "Here," he added with a smile of pride, "let me show you what we have done."

When the First Consul started toward the console, Tomadus's head jerked toward it. Would he discover Tomadus's ruse?

Isa screamed again, and Tomadus winced. How many times had it been? With his courage now refueled by desperation, Tomadus lunged out of his chair, knocking the rap rifle to the side, grabbing the First Consul from behind, and twisting him around toward the guard. In nearly the same motion, he whisked up the First Consul's letter opener from the desk and held its point to the First Consul's throat as he stood behind him. "Tell the guard to give me the rap rifle," Tomadus said calmly.

Khansensius nodded to the guard, but the guard did not move. "I cannot give you my weapon," he said.

Tomadus glared back, motionless. "Then the First Consul will die."

Tomadus heard Isa yell out, "My God, my God, why have you forsaken me?"

Although the guard ignored Isa, he could not entirely ignore Tomadus. The guard let the rap rifle fall into his left hand, holding it away from the trigger. He slowly showed both hands to Tomadus and moved toward the wall where he opened a refuse chute and tossed the weapon in, the sound of metal echoing through the room as the weapon clanged its way down.

Tomadus nodded to the guard but kept the letter opener tight to the First Consul's taut neck. "Fair enough," he said. "Now back away from the door." When the guard complied, Tomadus ushered the First Consul out of the control booth and into the theater, down its steps toward the stage. With each step, he struggled as the visions kept flowing through his brain…

❧ ❧ ❧

…Kadir/Pardus sneered. "What's the matter, Hux, have you lost all hope?"

Huxley barely heard the words, but they echoed in his brain. The echo came first in the voice of the Old Priest: *Hope… My hope is my belief… Because of my faith in Christ, my hope is my belief: I believe that the world and my own soul will not end in death or nothingness…* Huxley shook his head slowly, but the echo continued. This time Anwari's voice rang through his brain: *Hope. He shows you the lightning that terrifies and inspires hope… The Light from the Sky is God's Truth.* Huxley's eyes opened as he raised his head.

The Deceiver looked back at him with a pathetic look of sympathy. "You done pouting, now, Hux? You going to cry? Hey, have a little faith. Your little love will survive somehow. Just do it. Push the button."

Huxley glared back, but Kadir's voice once again echoed through his brain until it transformed into Sonatina's voice: *Faith…love… Faith and love… Have a little faith, and love will come back to you.* A tear ran down his cheek. He watched it fall to the floor and splatter there. *Had love come back to him?* Still looking down, his eyes began to refocus when they noticed the bulge in his pocket. The crucifix. Now his mother's voice echoed with Sonatina's: *Love… God's Love… Every gift can be used for good or evil. You must trust your heart and fill it with God's love, and He will guide your way.*

Huxley's chin sunk further into his chest. *Hope, faith and love…* He held back more tears and swallowed hard, but his heart and soul rose anyway through his throat and into his brain. *Can I believe again? God. My God. They have all tried to bring me back to you. Forgive me. My mother is dead. Anwari is dead. Sonatina—please, save Sonatina. Please save humanity. Forgive me. Must my penance now forever condemn me as the Destroyer?*

Please, show me the way. Show me the way! Huxley took a deep breath. *What am I doing? Is this a last act of desperation? Who but the wind will listen to my prayer?* Huxley shook his head. *He must hear me. Accept my sacrifice as you sacrificed for all. Please, hear me…*

▽   ▽   ▽

…As he moved down the stairs, knife to First Consul Khansensius's throat, Tomadus fought with himself. *What am I doing. Is this a last act of desperation?* He looked up at the stage and saw Isa still hanging from that damned wooden contraption, sweating and smoking and spewing his precious blood. His eyes were closed, and his head hung to the side.

A tear fell down Tomadus's cheek.

Isa raised his head slowly, opened his eyes and looked at Tomadus.

The unbelievable compassion from Isa's eyes reached into Tomadus and hugged the creature shaking in his belly. *Could this man, even now in this horrible condition, reach so deep within my soul?*

Tomadus breathed, "Forgive me." When Isa gazed back at him, Tomadus knew Isa had already granted him absolution. As he looked into Isa's eyes, words of atonement from Jochi entered his head again. *Do it, Chris. Sacrifice yourself, and you will save billions.* Tomadus shook his head. *Who but the wind shall hear me? No. Trust Jochi. Trust Isa. Trust the Father. I must have faith.* He focused on Jochi's words and repeated them in his brain over and over again. Finally, he burst out, "Do it, Chris. Sacrifice yourself, and you will save billions!"

The First Consul jerked in his left arm, but Tomadus pulled him closer and pushed the blade of the letter opener tighter into the man's throat. A small trickle of blood appeared, followed by the Light…

❈   ❈   ❈

…Huxley hung from his chains, his body nearly limp. He felt himself blacking out and soon found himself dreaming. Or was he awake? He was not certain. His eyes were shut as a strange scene played out before him. He was wearing a silken robe. No, it was that merchant from his dreams. He was standing very close to another man in a robe, hugging him. No, not hugging. He had one arm around him holding the man in place. The other held a tri-jeweled letter opener with its point to the man's throat. In front of them on the stage hung the man he had seen from his earlier dreams—the man in the white robes. Now nearly naked, this Jesus was being crucified. No, that wasn't quite it. This Jesus's arms and legs stretched out in the same way as he stared back at Huxley, but this Jesus hung not from a cross but an inverted triangle. Smoke was rising out of Jesus's back, the putrid smell of burning flesh poisoning the air. In his dream, the merchant mouthed, "Forgive me," to this Jesus. Then the merchant's thoughts and words turned to a single chant: *Do it, Chris. Sacrifice yourself, and you will save billions.* The thoughts dissolved into voices. He heard his mother: *Do it, Chris. God will know the truth.* Then it was Sonatina's voice. *Do it, Chris. Sacrifice yourself, and you will save billions.* No, it wasn't her voice, not quite, was it? As the chant played over and over, this Huxley stared at Jesus, and Jesus nodded gently. Then Jesus mouthed to him, "Tell her."

When he awoke, Huxley's eyes opened to Pardus glaring at him on the screen in the cabin of the *Infernum*. Huxley did not glare back. With a strange sense of calm, he smiled at Pardus. He hoisted himself up and grabbed the device, pushed the button, and said slowly, "I am sorry, Sonatina, but it is best for the whole world. These cities must die. Forgive me." As he did this, the phone lit up, showing it was recording the audio clip. He released the button but could not release himself. She would hate him forever. The world would hate him forever.

Kadir/Pardus smiled broadly and nodded to Huxley. "I always knew you were pathetic. How sad a fate for the Destroyer of Cities? You are the Destroyer of Cities, Hux, and I am the Ambassador of Peace." Kadir/Pardus snickered.

"Ambassador of Peace. How can you even call yourself a man?"

"Sometimes, Huxley, your insights amaze me. But now I must go. Please, enjoy the view. I owe you that, at least. Until we meet again." Kadir/Pardus nodded as his image faded to black.

❈ ❈ ❈

Sonatina twirled her hair, lost in deep thought. She had awoken early that morning and seen the bizarre message from Chris about abandoning her and loving her and sailing on a Ship of Fate. She had never felt abandoned by him, not really. She felt in her heart that they would soon fully reconcile. But what was the Ship of Fate? Where was Pardus? Who was this loud friend? She pursed her lips and shook her head. If Chris had responded to just one of her many replies, she might now know the answer. But after this strange confession from him, he had ignored her. First her texts, next her calls, then her voice mails. So he had gone dark once again. Becoming desperate, she had thrown logic to the wind and leapt head first with the faith she could save him. She knew he needed her. She knew she needed him.

She tipped the few remaining drops of merlot over her lips and set the glass down on the half-folded table above her lap. The woman in the neat blue suit and red scarf with the stylized wings noticed it immediately. "Would you like some more wine, Ms. D'Amare?"

"No, thank you. You can take the glass." She looked out the window, down at the clouds that puffed like giant pillows, tempting even the largest of the gods to lay down their heads and rest. She was tempted to do the same but heard the familiar ping of a text from her cell phone. When she pulled it out of her purse, her heart leapt. *Finally, a message from Chris.*

Instead of singing, her heart sunk. *It is some sort of sick joke. No, Chris wouldn't find that funny. A lie then. Someone had stolen his cell and was making fun of him. Or maybe his friend thinks he is funny. That must be it.* Then she saw the audio file at the bottom of the message. She gasped and her brain stopped searching for another rational explanation. She closed her eyes, inhaled deeply, and pressed the play button. When the words came from Chris's voice, they exploded her heart, taking with it nearly every fiber of her being.

∇   ∇   ∇

Tomadus tried to separate himself from Huxley so he could manage the scene in front of him. His chant to Huxley had finally gained the Governor's attention. He paused the interrogation and saw Tomadus with the sharp point to the First Consul's throat. "What is this? Have you gone mad?"

"Let him down or your First Consul dies."

The Governor stared back at Tomadus without the least flinch. "Release the First Consul at once if you want to live."

"No Governor, you first. Release Isa. First Consul, care to weigh in on this discussion?"

The First Consul responded, "Why should I weigh in on your pathetic little martyr?"

Isa responded weakly, "People always seem to underestimate the power of one man to change the course of history."

"So it seems you too can see the other world," said the First Consul. "But then you are not just a man."

Isa responded, "You have said that."

Tomadus sighed and the Light again blitzed through his brain…

❊ ❊ ❊

…Kadir's image on the monitor in front of Huxley was soon replaced by a shot of the Vatican, focused on St. Peter's Basilica. Superimposed in the corner of the picture, a digital clock was counting down—now less than 29 minutes remaining. A second monitor to the right began showing a close up view of a warhead mounted to a large device that appeared to be some type of small single-stage rocket. The same numbers counted down in its lower-left corner. To the left, another monitor clicked on and showed a view of the Washington monument. While it also contained a superimposed digital countdown clock, this one lagged thirty seconds behind.

To its left, a third monitor showed the top of the *Infernum* with the other nuclear warhead and another rocket assembly, again with a countdown clock synchronized to the monument clock. The warhead and small rocket assembly were disguised as a part of the radar, satellite dish and arch assemblies at the top of the yacht, so they would not be visible as anything nefarious from the shore or a passing boat. Hell, he had been on the boat itself and had not seen them.

He had one last chance, and he was going to take it. Huxley still had not found the pull. Could it be directly behind him? He lifted his feet up, tucked his legs and twisted backward until he was hanging upside down with his hips above. Now looking at the wall behind him, he saw the red fire alarm pull staring back at him. He tried to kick at it with his feet, but they would not reach. His shoulders ached, but he managed to right himself, kick off his shoes and slide his right foot over by the rope on the floor. In a few moments, the coil was beneath his body. When he pulled the rope with both feet, the metal clasp at one end appeared. He grabbed the rope a few feet above the clasp with his two feet, lifted them up and twisted backward again. Hanging upside down from the chains and facing the back wall, he gradually swung the rope with his feet, trying to catch the pull with the metal clasp. The clasp struck the pull on the second try, but the pull remained in place.

Something began sliding out of his left pocket. When the crucifix fell toward his eyes, he opened his mouth and just caught the chain in his teeth as the crucifix smashed the underside of his nose. He sighed. Though he was conscious, an image and voice returned. He saw the man in white robes mouth, *"Tell her."* But he had told her. Now she would despise him forever. He could see Pardus kissing her. He shook his head. *No. God help me!*

❈ ❈ ❈

Sonatina spoke into the air phone as calmly as she could, but her words were getting nowhere. "Damn it, I tell you Washington will be ashes in a few minutes. You must believe me. Evacuate the President, Congress, the whole city!"

"Tell me again the source of your information."

"Huxley, Chris Huxley. He works for you. He said in a text that Washington and Rome would be nuked in—God, it will be less than 15 minutes now."

"We cannot divulge our employees' names Ms...."

"D'Amare, Sonatina D'Amare."

"Ms. D'Amare. But if he were our agent, don't you think he would have told us instead of you? What is your relationship to Christian Huxley?"

"My God, you are wasting time. He is my boyfriend. Look. I don't know why. Maybe that was the only message he could get out. I don't know."

"Is there something you are not telling us?"

She bit her lower lip hard and suppressed her tears. "I...I...can't."

"You can't what?"

Sonatina burst out crying. "It can't be true. It can't."

"Ms. D'Amare, if you are right, there is little time. What can't be true?"

She inhaled deeply and closed her eyes. "He didn't call you because he is the one setting off the nukes. He wanted to warn me to leave Rome, but I had already left. But it can't be true!"

▽   ▽   ▽

Tomadus saw the guard's movement at the far edge of his peripheral vision. He tensed, turned his head and poked the point tighter into the First Consul's neck. "Tell him to move to the Front, where I can see him."

"You heard him," said the First Consul. "Nothing stupid."

When the guard moved back toward the stage, Tomadus saw he had no weapons. Still, he needed to maintain a perimeter. "Governor, I am waiting, but I will soon run out of patience."

"Your arms tiring, Tomadus? How long can you hang on? Just release me."

"You'll soon be dead if they don't take Isa down. I can wait that long." But he fought the strain and exhaustion of the last two days. He knew he was forgetting something. What was it? The rapidity of the visions had shaken him. He struggled to stay in his own world. *Focus!* The adrenaline kept him going, but his shoulders tired. He pulled the First Consul even closer just before the Light flashed again…

✠   ✠   ✠

…Huxley grunted under the strain of his tired shoulder muscles. The chains were slowly pulling his arms from their sockets. He stared at the alarm pull again and refocused on the rope. *Calm. Be calm.* His heartbeat slowed. After a few more tries, he realized he needed to hit the wall above the pull and let it slide down to have any chance of linking the clasp with the top of the pull. Several attempts later, the clasp finally hung on the pull. When he yanked the rope, the clasp slid to the side, the pull still in place, laughing at him in defiance. After repeating the process a few times, the clasp hung on the pull again. This time, when he gradually applied downward pressure on the rope, the alarm pull shifted down.

The siren sounded in the cabin, but that was not his purpose. It would be far too long before a passing boat might hear it and stop to make any difference. An instant later, water began shooting out of the sprinkler system into the cabin and onto the console. If he could just get the thing to short out, it might stop the warhead from shooting off. Maybe it would stop both warheads.

He righted himself and watched the water cascade down while the crucifix hung from his lips. As the water splashed on the console, the panel began to spark. He looked at the countdown clock—only 4:55 left. He looked back at the console. It was still lit up. A few more sparks came and went, but when he looked again at the monitors and saw the clocks still counting down, he gasped. The crucifix fell from his mouth to the floor and sunk beneath the rising water. He hung his head, closed his eyes, and saw his mother on her death bed, handing him the crucifix. She said nothing, for her mind was gone. But her expression. He saw it now and understood it for the first time. He felt it deep: *I go with God and so shall you.* He looked up and cried out, "I am damned for all time."

He thought again of Sonatina and the dream and words Jesus mouthed to him. *Tell her.* He had told her. He had pushed the button and told her. There had to be more. Would the thing still work? Had Pardus forgot? He reached up and spoke into the device, but he could see the phone remained black. His words would never reach Sonatina.

What could he tell her anyway? *The truth. Tell her the truth.* Huxley closed his eyes and sighed. "I heard the voices. Could she hear me?" He began chanting in his thoughts, *"Sonatina, I am not Pardus. Pardus and Kadir are one. Pardus and Kadir are one. Sonatina, Kadir and Pardus are one."* He fell back on his chains, totally spent.

"God," he said, "if you are there, hear me now. Tell her. Tell her I am not Pardus. Tell her Pardus and Kadir are one. Sonatina, Pardus and Kadir are one…"

▽   ▽   ▽

…Tomadus tried to shake off the Light, but it still seared through his eyes. He repeated the words from his vision: "Sonatina! Sonatina, I am not Pardus. Pardus and Kadir are one. Pardus and Kadir are one." The Light released Tomadus's brain. He exhaled hard and stared at Khansensius. "Pardus, Kadir and the First Consul are one."

Isa smiled slightly as the First Consul Khansensius tried to jerk away, but Tomadus held him tight, pressing the letter opener hard against his throat. The First Consul sneered and said lowly, "You speak nonsense, you fool. They will never understand your point. Nonsense. It will never work."

Tomadus's muscles tightened. "First Consul, consider the point at your throat for a moment. Are you sure you do not care to give some direction to the Governor and his men here?"

❆ ❆ ❆

Sonatina stared ahead, her puffy red eyes now masking the dark circles under them. When her phone pinged, she saw the message from Colonel Zaugg: "Evacuating the Vatican. Pope is away. Homeland now agrees. God, I hope you are wrong." She exhaled and put her head against the window. *God, please let me be wrong.*

No way she could sleep, yet she felt her head spinning slowly toward the irrational, toward the world of dreams. Let them come… She was that woman in her simple outfit, surrounded by men in robes as they stared at what appeared to be a television screen depicting a passion play. No, that wasn't quite it. She could see a nearly naked man hanging in pain on a device. It was the man in the white robes—this Jesus who talked to her and Chris in their dreams. He was not on a cross but on a wooden inverted triangle. An officious man dressed in a red robe with purple fringes stood before a microphone near him. Off-screen, another male voice yelled her name, "Sonatina!" She knew that voice. It was Chris! No, not quite, but she knew that voice from her other dreams. "Sonatina, I am not Pardus. Pardus and Kadir are one. Pardus and Kadir are one. Pardus, Kadir and the First Consul are one!"

Sonatina awoke with a start. Her eyes narrowed. "Kadir," she said. "Chris's friend, the Ambassador. But who is the First Consul?" She bit her lip again, her eyes squeezed tight to hold back the river. "God save you, Chris. Dear Lord, please save him. My God, save us all."

CHAPTER 99

"You think you've won?" the First Consul asked. He was glaring, but not at Tomadus. He spit in the direction of Isa.

Isa was too close to death to respond. He hung nearly limp on the *triangulum*, his eyes focused only on Tomadus. Tomadus stared back, amazed. But he knew he had forgotten something. What was it again?

The First Consul wiggled, but Tomadus hung tighter, the point of his opener nearly opening the First Consul's jugular. He gurgled. "You want me to give directions to them, Tomadus? I can barely speak. Loosen your grip." Tomadus pulled back the opener, but only a touch. "Thank you."

Tomadus had hoped that would end it, and in that, he was not disappointed. But the standoff ended differently than he imagined. The First Consul turned his head quickly to the side, causing blood to trickle down his throat. Just before the First Consul spoke again, Tomadus remembered. The other guard at the door. The guard with the ancient, ceremonial spear.

"Kill him," said the First Consul.

Tomadus began to turn, but it was too late. Tomadus's eyes bulged as fluid rushed through his mouth. Had his lung just exploded through his chest? He looked down and saw the point of the guard's spear protruding out of the front of his left rib cage. He toppled face forward onto the floor, the shaft of the spear sticking out of his back like a fence post anchored in the ground.

His head was turned sideways, so he could still see Isa suffering on the *triangulum*. Looking straight down at Tomadus, Isa struggled to say, "Today…you will…be with me…in paradise." He saw the Governor signal to the technicians to turn a knob and Isa's body trembled with pain, but he screamed no more.

Tomadus lay motionless, gurgling blood out of his mouth. Who was this man who would say such things while suffering intolerable pain? Who was this being who would forgive the very man responsible for his own torture and death? Who was this man who despite all of this would still take him with him to paradise? *He has given everything for me. He has believed in me. Can I now believe in him?*

Laying on the floor away from the stage, he heard a door slam and a technician yell from the back of the theater, "First Consul!"

"Not now!" the First Consul responded.

"But First Consul, you must know!" yelled the technician.

"What is it?"

"The broadcast—it was not delayed. He must have done something to the broadcast computer. This whole thing has been broadcast live worldwide!"

"Shut it down, now!" the First Consul yelled.

"I've tried. I can't. He revised the security protocol. It will take another ten minutes at least."

"Then pull the damn plug on the machine!"

But it was too late. Isa looked up to the ceiling and exhaled, "It is finished," and bowing his head, he handed over his spirit.

❊ ❊ ❊

Huxley flashed back to his discussion with the old priest when he had asked, "What if God gives up on us?" The priest had responded with a jest: "Then God help us all!" *That is all that I ask, dear God. Do not give up on us. Do not give up on me. God, help us all!*

He looked at the monitor showing the Vatican: the clock had ticked down to 0:55. He closed his eyes and saw Sonatina flicking her hair that way she always did when lost in thought. *You were brilliant, Sonatina. I should have listened to you. I should have trusted you, but I confused good and evil. God help us!*

A moment later he heard a loud crackling from the control console, and it went dark. No lights, no instrument readings, no sounds, no displays. Nothing. Had he done it?

He looked up at the monitors and saw the countdown continuing. *Damn it all to hell!* As the clock counted down from :05, he saw the rocket ignite in Rome. The warhead was headed just a thousand or so feet above the ground—just high enough to spread the blast throughout the city. Huxley screamed, "Damn you, Pardus!" and kicked his legs forward out of control. The tip of his foot connected with one of the monitors and tore out some of the connections to the other monitors. All of the screens went blank. He kicked again and more equipment fell. Could that have stopped this?

Huxley heard a loud bang above him; a portion of the cabin ceiling flipped down, revealing the blue sky of the Heavens above. The deck of the ship rumbled for a few seconds as flames shot to the sides. He saw the small rocket launch above the *Infernum,* the hellish Ship of Fate, on its way to a thousand feet or so above the District of Columbia.

"Oh God, Oh God, please forgive me!" he screamed.

He wanted to close his tear-filled eyes, but they remained open, taunting him. A moment later, his eyes saw a flash of light so brilliant that they were instantly blinded—just a moment before his body and everything around him turned to ash…

∇   ∇   ∇

…A light began to glow and Tomadus saw the rocket shooting upward into the night sky. A hot-white light flashed across the eyes of the investigator as the power of the sun was unleashed on the other world. The light did not blind him but permeated everything—glowing, piercing, searing a hole in his consciousness and eventually washing the entire scene in a yellow-white hue. But this light was neither new nor unusual to him: it was the Light of Our Yesterdays.

He blinked a few times, and the glow dissipated slightly but still filled most of his vision. It no longer touched the periphery but encircled Isa. No longer the beam of destruction, it had become the light of rebirth. Could the others see this aura cover Isa's limp body? No, he could hear most of them still scrambling to end the broadcast. But he could see the three officials on the stage—the Governor, the Grand Imam and the Abh Beyth Diyn—and though they all looked right at Isa, they saw nothing but death.

As he lay there, his blood slowly draining onto the theater floor, Tomadus and the creature within became one. For the first time he could recall, he smiled with a feeling of true contentment. When his eyes shut for the last time, he searched for and felt the warmth of Isa deep in his heart, deep in his soul. He knew. He finally knew.

❈ ❈ ❈

The next day, a predictable headline ran nearly the full length of the front page of the New York Times: "Democracy and God Dead: Washington and Rome Destroyed." The subtitle was nearly as large, but few understood the nature of its untruth: "Martial Law Declared After Rogue Homeland Security Agent Nukes Capital Cities."

▽   ▽   ▽

Published much later, *Liber Vitae* was filled with many truths, truths that Jochi would never doubt unto her Earthly death. But she knew one sentence was false. It had to be. She had heard, and she had understood. But when Simeon would not relent, the Ten followed his lead. And so the official publication included the lie nonetheless:

> *"Then Tomadus, lamenting his betrayal as he watched Isa suffer on the triangulum, stabbed himself through the chest and died."*
>
> *— Liber Vitae—Di. 27:3*

▽   ▽   ▽

Not long after his death, Isa stood smiling above him, waiting for his answer.

"I am ready," he said. He reached out his arm to Isa.

Isa laughed and grabbed Tomadus's arm and pulled him onto the boat. "Then come with me, for where I am going you may now follow. We shall set sail to that beautiful land across the sea."

APPENDIX A

Detailed Excerpts from: "Plinius's Condensed Study Guide for the Advanced Technologist Exam: History Since the Founding of the First Romanus Empire"[1]

Year(s)	Region(s)	Development
649 BH (726 AUC)[2]	Roma	Augustus Caesar (Octavian) proclaimed First Emperor of Roma.
579 BH (823 AUC)	Palestinian Province	Removal of Jews from Jerusalem following defeat of Jewish Zealots at Masada.
502 BH (888 AUC)	Palestinian Province	Death of the "Messiah" Simon bar Kokeba, the leader of a Jewish insurrection, at the hands of Iulius Severus, general of the Romanus army. Kokeba is the only man ever proclaimed as the Messiah by a prominent rabbi.
307 BH (1077 AUC)	Romanus Empire	After a series of civil wars, Flavius Valerius Aurelius Constantinus Augustus (*Magni Constantini*) consolidates power in the Romanus Empire.
303 BH (1081 AUC)	Romanus Empire	Magni Constantini issues *Edictum Oroculorum*, requiring investigations of all pagan temples with oracles claiming messages from the gods affecting the Romanus Empire. Investigators are permitted to use torture where they deem it appropriate. Paganism wanes in the Romanus Empire, and no other religious movement fills the void.

---

1 The unabridged "Plinius's Complete Study Guide for the Advanced Technologist Exam: History Since the Founding of the First Romanus Empire" is available online at www.lightofouryesterdays.com.

2 Years are given in AH or BH and, alternatively, in AUC. BH = Before the Hijra. AH = In the Year of the Hijra (denoting years since the time of the Hijra). AUC = Anno Urbis Conditae, or years since the founding of the City of Roma. Note that the Hijra occurred in 1376 AUC

Year(s)	Region(s)	Development
301 BH (1083 AUC)	Eastern Romanus Empire	Magni Constantini founds the city of Constantinopli at the small town of Byzantium near the Bosporus leading to the *Pontus Euxinus*. He makes it the capital of the Eastern half of the Romanus Empire and forbids the construction of any pagan or other religious temples in the new city.
291–90 BH (1093–94 AUC)	Eastern Romanus Empire	Imperial Reforms of Constantinus II. After ending a civil war with his pagan brother, Emperor Constantinus II (son of Magni Constantini) stabilizes the Romanus Empire with a set of "Imperial Reforms" that substantially eliminate the civil wars that had plagued the empire for centuries, preserving Romanus armies for wars with barbarian tribes on the periphery. The reforms include rotation of generals, involvement of Senate in selection of the succeeding emperor, and inclusion of provincial governors and generals in key Senate matters. He also begins to withhold imperial funds from pagan temples throughout the realm.
253–77 BH (1130–1300 AUC)	Romanus Empire in Europe	Barbarian Tribes Repelled. Remaining strong in the absence of internal strife, the Romanus Empire defeats various barbarian tribes migrating west from the Asian steppes. Forced to fight further among themselves, the barbarian tribes deplete their men and resources.
77–72 BH (1300–05 AUC)	Romanus Empire	Loss of Gallia to Germanic Union by Romanus Empire. Through mismanagement, Emperor Vergilius loses the region of Gallia in northwestern Europe to a conglomerate of German–speaking barbarian tribes.
70–38 BH (1307-38 AUC)	Romanus Empire	Balkan Split. Slavs move south through the Romanus Empire into the Balkans, cutting off Constantinopli and Eastern Romanus Empire from Roma.

Year(s)	Region(s)	Development
57–47 BH (1320-29 AUC)	Romanus Empire	Forced to fight his own battles, Governor Balbinus of Constantinopli defeats Sassanid Persians at Tarsus and declares the Eastern Romanus Empire to be independent of Roma.
54 BH (1323 AUC)	Arabia	Muhammad is born in Mecca.
38–5 BH (1338-70 AUC)	Eurasia and North Africa	Union of Eastern Empire and Slavic tribes. Following a resurgence of the Romanus Empire in the Balkans, Balbinus, now Emperor of the newly named Eastern Empire, enters a joint protection agreement with Zdravko, leader of a Slavic army from north of the *Pontus Euxinus*. The pact permits some settlement of Slavic peoples in various abandoned cities in the eastern Balkans, especially along the eastern shores of the *Pontus Euxinus*.
12 BH (1363 AUC)	Arabia	Muhammad is called to be a messenger of Allah by an angel.
0 AH (1375 AUC)	Arabia	Hijra: migration of Muhammad and his followers from Mecca to Yathrib (later named Medina by Muhammad).
8–23 AH (1384–97 AUC)	Arabia	Muslims conquer the Arabian Peninsula.
10–124 AH (1385–1495)	Europe	Civil wars in Germanic Union, with Franks and Goths defeating the Huns and fighting with each other for control.
10 AH (1385 AUC)	Arabia	Muhammad dies.
17–18 AH (1391–92 AUC)	Palestinian Province	Muslims Blocked in Palestine and Aegypt. Muslims attack the Eastern Empire in the Palestinian Province and in Aegystian Province. Strengthened by its peace accord with the Slavs, the Eastern Empire succeeds in holding them off to the south and east of the Fertile Crescent and the Sinai Peninsula.

Year(s)	Region(s)	Development
21–28 AH (1395–1402)	Mesopotamia	Muslims turn attention to the east and defeat Sassanid Persians in Mesopotamia and drive the Sassanids back to central Persia.
35–41 AH (1409–15 AUC)	Arabia	First Muslim Split. Civil war breaks out in Muslim lands between the followers of Ali ibn Abi Talib, husband to one of Muhammad's daughters, and Mu'awiya ibn Abi Sufyan, kin to the recently murdered Caliph 'Uthman. This split eventually evolves into a permanent split between Sunni factions (following Mu'awiya) and the Shiite factions, following Ali.
82–155 AH (1454–90 AUC)	Eurasia	Shiite Expansion/Slavic Integration. Shiite armies attack remnants of the Sassanid Persian Empire, capturing Baku and bringing them into contact with Slavic peoples to the north. Baku becomes the eastern capital of the Muslim Empire. Shiites begin integrating Slavic tribes into their society.
155 AH (1525 AUC)	Southwestern Asia	Treaty of Baghdad. Ending civil war between Sunni and Muslim factions, the treaty divides the Muslim Empire into the Shiite Muslim Empire and the Sunni Muslim Empire.
156–165 AH (1526–35 AUC)	Palestinian and Aegyptian Provinces	Conquest of Jerusalem and Alexandria by Sunnis with the military assistance of the Shiites.
156–439 AH (1526–1800 AUC)	Western Asia	The Shiite form of Islam gradually spreads from the *Caspium Mare* north as many of the pagan Slavic tribes of Western Asia, including the Rus, convert. To the south of Baku, the Shiite Muslim Empire spreads across Persia after defeating the remnants of the Sassnid Empire, all the way south to the Persian Gulf and eastward to the mountains. Tehran becomes a key Shiite city to the south of the *Caspium Mare*.

Year(s)	Region(s)	Development
165–252 AH (1535–1619 AUC)	Southern Mare Internum	Expansion of Sunnis across the Maghrib (North Africa). Sunni Muslim Empire moves slowly through the Maghrib, defeating the Romanus Empire in various battles along the way. By 227 AH, most of the Maghrib has been converted to Islam and considers itself part of the Sunni Muslim Empire. By 252 AH, Sunnis have crossed to Iberian Peninsula (Andalus) and defeated Romanus Empire at Barcelona.
206 AH (1575 AUC)	Northern Europe	Viking raids begin: the Northmen (later called "Vikings") in the Jutland Peninsula develop more advanced seafaring navigation and ships. They begin raiding towns in Britannia and northern continental Europe.
253 AH (1620 AUC)	Romanus Empire	Retreat to Italian Peninsula. When the New Germanic Union attacks the Romanus Empire in the north, the armies of the Romanus Empire in the west retreat south of the Alps. This is the beginning of the end of the Romanus Empire.
261–69 AH (1621–36 AUC)	Southwestern Europe	Germanic Reshuffling. When New Germanic Union is torn apart by royal marital strife, Frankish House of Martel (occupying most of western Europe), led by Charles, fights a series of wars with the Gothic House of Theodoreich (controlling most of central Europe), pulling Jutland Vikings into the fray. After Peace of Verdun, House of Martel attacks Sunnis in Iberian peninsula, driving them back to the Maghrib.
273–74 AH (1640–41 AUC)	Balkans	Ognjen leads a revolt of his Slavic peoples from the Eastern Empire. Eastern Empire is now limited primarily to Constantinopli and the Anatolia Peninsula.
275–79 AH (1642–45 AUC)	Romanus Empire	Ognjen, leading a Slavic army, attacks the Eastern Army of the Romanus Empire and drives them back to Italia. The Romanus Empire now exists only on the peninsula of Italia.

Year(s)	Region(s)	Development
275–82 AH (1642–48 AUC)	Romanus Empire	End of the Romanus Empire. Goths and Franks sack, burn and loot Roma and other cities in the Italian Peninsula, generally returning with their loot to their current homelands to the north.
282–1200s AH (1648–late 2500s AUC)	Europe and Western Asia	Period of the Dark Ages. With the loss of the Romanus Empire and eventually the Eastern Empire, much of classic western civilization is lost to antiquity. Within two decades, with no independent institutions preserving ancient ways and texts and the governmental repositories of information destroyed, very little remains of the Romanus (and its preceding classic Greek) culture in the west. When Constantinopli falls to a Slavic army a few decades later, the same fate befalls the East. The New Germanic Union, still just a conglomeration of illiterate tribes, lacks any interest in preserving the culture. Muslim conquerors generally adopt the view of one of their great conquering generals, Yazeed ibn Ziyad, who, when he conquered Alexandria and found the great Alexandria library, said, "If what is written in these scrolls agrees with the Great Book of Allah, they are not required; if they disagree, they are not desired. Destroy them therefore."
431–550 AH (1793–1908 AUC)	Caspium Mare Region	Seljuk Turks attack the Shiite Muslim Empire in Persia. After initial losses, the Shiites bring in an army filled with Slavic tribesmen from its northern regions, defeating the Seljuks at Tehran. The Seljuks retreat to Turkish territories directly east of the Caspium Mare and eventually convert to Shiite Islam, becoming vassals of the Shiite Muslim Empire.

Year(s)	Region(s)	Development
480–750 AH (1840–2100 AUC)	Central Europe	Shiite Islam moves slowly into Europe from the east, partly by conversion, partly by conquest. This Eastern migration is initially led by a group of Twelver Shiites who emphasize the return of the Mahdi. This emphasis is continued as the religion spreads into the Germanic areas of Europe, particularly after the Shiite Muslim Empire is split in two by the arriving Mongolian Empire.
534–44 AH (1893–1902 AUC)	Northern Europe	Jutland Viking ships in the north Atlantic discover a volcanically active island with lava fields and geysers near mountainous glaciers. Settlors from Jutland establish first settlement on the island, which they call Islandia.
595–640 AH (1952–95 AUC)	North Atlantic	Islandia sailors discover an enormous island in the North Atlantic that is nearly covered with glaciers. Settlors call this "Grœnland" or "Greenland," hoping to attract other settlors.
604–81AH (1960-2035 AUC)	Eurasia	Genghis Khan unites the Mongolian tribes and begins westward conquests by the Mongolian Hordes. The Mongols reach the Caspium Mare by 629, sack Baku by 656, splitting the Shiite Muslim Empire in two, and, by 681, capture much of the Shiite Muslim territory to the north of the Caucasus Mountains.
681 AH (2053 AUC)	Northern North Aztalan	Calder, a Viking from Jutland, seizes on the mythology of the Inuits of Greenland concerning a vast land to the southwest. He sails across the sea in that direction from Greenland and discovers extreme northern areas of North Aztalan.
704–71 AH (2057–2122 AUC)	Europe	Mongol armies sweep west, capturing the Anatolia peninsula and the Balkans, all regions around the Pontus Euxinus, the Eastern Alps, all land south of the *Danuvius*, and ultimately the entire Italian Peninsula, including the remnants of Roma.

Year(s)	Region(s)	Development
Circa 710 AH (Circa 2063 AUC)	Northern Europe	Islam reaches the Jutland Peninsula, but does not initially gain many adherents due to the strength of the Vikings' beliefs in Norse gods such as Odin and Thor.
722–825 AH (2075–2175 AUC)	North Aztalan	Viking warriors/settlors from Jutland, Islandia and Greenland begin raiding and settling extreme northern sections of North Aztalan, eventually arriving in Tonquizalixco Tetepe, where they raid Iroquois and Algonquin settlements and ultimately settle on an island with a large natural port. There they found the city "New Åarhus," named after the great port of Åarhus in Jutland. They begin calling themselves "Jutes," reflecting their roots in Europe.
810–35AH (2160–84 AUC)	Europe	Kaidu Khan, leader of the Mongol Empire, breaks from the policies of past Khans, taking residence in Roma and beginning to rebuild it. In addition to his many other titles (including King of Kings and Mongol Emperor), he declares himself, Kaidu Khan Augustus, Emperor of the reconstituted Mongol–Romanus Empire, and successor to the Romanus Emperors before the fall.
907–935 AH (2254 AUC)	Eurasia	A rebellion in China diverts Mongol-Romanus Emperor Ogeiadah's attention from Europe and Southwestern Asia. Returning to China with nearly half of his army, he is ultimately defeated near Cumuda.

Year(s)	Region(s)	Development
915 AH (2262 AUC)	Tonquizalixco Tetepe	Gustav, a Mahdian cleric, is banished from the Jutland peninsula for proselytizing his religion and sails for Tonquizalixco Tetepe. During the long voyage, he dies from scarlet fever but not before first converting a few Viking settlors to Islam. When Kustaa, one of the converted Vikings, reaches New Åarhus, he begins preaching his version of Islam to others without great success. However, a small mosque is established in the new city with a handful of adherents.
918–952 AH (2269–98 AUC)	Eurasia	The Sunni Muslim Empire and the southern portion of the Shiite Muslim Empire defeat the remnants of the Mongol-Romanus Empire in the Fertile Crescent, Anatolia, Mesopotamia, the Caucuses, and Persia. The army in Anatolia retreats to Constantinopli and the Balkans. The remainder of the Mongol armies retreat to the east, eventually beyond the borders of the Shiite Muslim Empire.
930–957 AH (2276–2303 AUC)	Europe	During the Mongol occupation and separation from the remainder of the Shiite Empire, the western portion of the Shiite Empire had become increasingly focused on the return of the Mahdi. After the Mongols retreat, the western leadership refuses to reunite with the Shiite Empire and declares itself the Mahdian Islamic Empire. After various battles between the two empires, the Treaty of 957 establishes an initial border between them running north from the Caucasus Mountains to the White Sea.
934 AH (2280 AUC)	Southern Europe	Upon hearing of the defeat of Mongol army in China, Governor Togul declares himself Emperor Togulus Augustus in the substantially shrunken Mongol-Romanus Empire. Pledging to remain a European emperor, Togulus drops all references to Mongols and renames the empire *"Imperium Romanum Secundum"* (or Second Romanus Empire).

Year(s)	Region(s)	Development
1012 AH (2356 AUC)	Tonquizalixco Tetepe	After an Islamic cleric and physician miraculously cures his infant daughter from scarlet fever, Helge the Great converts to Islam. Within a few short years, most of the Jutes convert with him. They now call themselves "Juteslams."
1015–90 AH (2359–2431 AUC)	Tonquizalixco Tetepe	Isolation of Juteslams. Successive severe winters cause the abandonment of settlements in Islandia and Greenland, isolating the Juteslams from Europe since their small ships cannot reasonably return directly without immense peril.
1019–22 AH (2363–66 AUC)	Northern Europe	Using newly developed guns and cannon, the Mahdian Muslim Empire conquers the Jutland peninsula, where they burn Viking ships along with other symbols of the Norse pagan gods. Previous plans for resettlement of Islandia and Greenland are abandoned.
1034–1123 AH (2377–2463 AUC)	South Aztalan	"Wise Men from the Sea" from China arrive on the shores of the fledgling Aztec Empire. Emperor Mochtezacatl welcomes them and begins integrating their technology into Aztec society.
1065–95 AH (2407–36 AUC)	Northern Europe	Mahdian Muslim Empire conquers *Britannia* and *Hibernia* and ultimately the Kingdom of Frankereich (near Parisius), consolidating northwestern Europe into the Mahdian Muslim Empire.
1161 AH (2500 AUC)	Aztalan	Juteslams begin raiding and slaughtering settlements of the Aztec Empire just north of the Achahuitl Peninsula (at the extreme southeastern end of North Aztalan)

Year(s)	Region(s)	Development
1162–95 AH (2501–33 AUC	Tonquizalixco Tetepe	Aztec Empire sends a large Army east to the region "Over the Eastern Mountains," in their language "Tonquizalixco Tetepe," to attack the Juteslams. The Juteslams, having no significant firearms or cannon, are overwhelmed, but fight valiantly using a hit and run style of defense and attack permitting them to steal and use firearms. Nevertheless, by 1195, the Aztecs conquer all of New Jutland and move into New Åarhus, where King Cnut of the Juteslams pledges tribute to the Aztec Empire.
1221–98 AH (2558–2633 AUC)	Europe and Southwestern Asia	First War of the Three Empires. Caused primarily by ethnic and religious differences, the three Muslim Empires fight a series of wars with each other (with multiple changes in alliances) while the Second Romanus Empire remains neutral.
1222 AH (2559 AUC)	North Aztalan	The Great Displacement. Fed up with the constant rebellions and of the Juteslams, the Aztec Empire sends a larger army to Tetepe and destroys New Åarhus and other major Juteslam cities. To prevent further unrest in the area, the Aztec Empire removes several thousand remaining Juteslams on a forced march to the stable Latisilolal Province on the Pacific coast, which lies closer to Tenochtitlan and remains loyal. A third of the Juteslams die along the way. Tonquizalixco Tetepe is now almost entirely depopulated, except for the remnants of various Iroquois and Algonquin tribes and a few limited outposts of the Aztec Empire.

Year(s)	Region(s)	Development
1224–circa 1350 AH (2561–2683 AUC)	Aztalan	Freed from their only legitimate enemy (the Juteslams), the Aztec Empire gradually expands its frontiers to the north to cover the entire habitable Aztalan continent. As usual, it primarily relies on a tribute system, allowing local governments to maintain some control of their own peoples. The wealth of the Aztec Empire grows and they begin to devote more resources to technology, the arts, and literature. They also begin to build larger ships with cannon. Due to their conflicts with the Juteslams, they are generally aware of a vast continent to the east from which the Juteslams ancestors, the Jutland Vikings, originated. Because of the Wise Men from the Sea, they are also aware of a vast continent to the west. With few enemies in Aztalan, they become increasingly concerned about their readiness to defend Aztalan from any invasion from across the great oceans. Therefore, they devote many of their military resources and technology to naval warfare.
1257 AH (2593 AUC)	Aztalan	Juteslam Declaration, requiring all Juteslams in Latisilolal to live in one of ten different settlement regions outside of the cities and limiting other rights of travel and ownership of Juteslams.
1298 AH (2633 AUC)	Europe and Southwestern Asia	Treaty of Florentia. Mediated by Emperor Flavius's First Consul, Khanattinius, the Three Empires agree to cease hostilities and establish regular borders between them. The Sunni Muslim Empire agrees to turn over governance of Andalus (southwestern Iberian Peninsula) to the Second Romanus Empire in exchange for the assurances by Emperor Flavius to remain neutral with respect to the practice of Islam within the region.

Year(s)	Region(s)	Development
1300–1410 AH (2635–2742 AUC)	Europe and Southwestern Asia	Golden Age of the Three Empires. The entire region flourishes in relative peace. Romanus technologists begin developing the technological method. The Three Empires independently resist the technologists, finding them anathema to Allah.
1365 AH (2698 AUC)	Europe	A scouting expedition of 5 tall ships from the Aztec Empire arrives on the shores of Gallia in the Mahdi Muslim Empire. The Mahdians engage in some limited trade with locals, but both parties remain very wary of each other.
1370–1395 AH (2703–27 AUC)	Second Romanus Empire	Emperor Marcellus begins building ships for long voyages designed by his technologists in part based on drawings of ships from the Aztec Empire from local Mahdians. Concerns grow among the Three Empires about the strength of the new Romanus navy. Marcellus assures them he is merely trying to preserve all four empires from an attack by future naval expeditions of the Aztec Empire.
1402–09 AH (2734–41 AUC)	South Aztalan	A naval expedition from Roma crosses the Atlantic to scout the Aztec Empire. It encounters ships of the Aztec navy in warm islands to the east of South Aztalan, where two Romanus ships are easily destroyed. The Aztec Empire eventually permits the remaining Romanus ships to return with both a stern warning against further attempted incursions and a proposal for future trade. Trade delegations travel the Atlantic for the next several years.

Year(s)	Region(s)	Development
1416–17 AH (2747–48 AUC)	South Aztalan	An army from south of Huitzlampatetepe (the southern mountains) moves north and raids an Aztec village. With its large navy, the Aztec Empire is able to transport a sizeable army to the northern shores of Apukallpa (the continent south of Aztalan), where it begins attacking the villages that it believes were the source of the raiding parties in South Aztalan. However, the raiders actually originated from small tribes at the extreme south end of Aztalan. Instead, the Aztec Empire has attacked the periphery of the primitive but enormous Incan Empire in Apukallpa. The Aztecs have inadvertently awoken a sleeping giant.
1416–28 AH (2747–59 AUC)	Europe	The War of Romanus Aggression. Emperor Valerianus of the Second Romanus Empire rashly attacks two of the Three Empires, initially making huge gains against each of them. When they and the third Muslim Empire finally unite against the Second Romanus Empire, their unity buys them time to rebuild their armies and navies and eventually turns the tide in the war. As losses mount, First Consul Fabianus leads a palace revolt, killing Emperor Valerianus. Fabianus sues for peace, but the Three Empires insist on unconditional surrender. He refuses to surrender. When the Second Romanus Senate votes to proclaim Fabianus emperor, he refuses the crown and argues that the Age of Empires in Roma has come to an end, renaming the country the Second Romanus Republic. However, he continues to exert powers similar to an emperor. Eventually, during peace talks at Barcelona (after the Second Romanus Empire has retreated to the Alps and Italian Peninsula), the Three Empires split over their own post-war borders, triggering the Second War of the Three Empires.

Year(s)	Region(s)	Development
1418–1510 AH (2749–2838 AUC)	Aztalan and Apukallpa	The Aztec Empire and Incan Empire fight a series of battles in the northern reaches of Apukallpa and eventually in the southern reaches of the Aztec Empire. In 1425, the Aztec Empire returns much of its army to Aztalan proper, but keeps several limited outposts in North Apukallpa. The intermittent wars with the Incan Empire continue to drain the resources of the Aztec Empire and weaken it, particularly with regard to provinces in North Aztalan.
1428–1452 AH (2759–82 AUC)	Eurasia and North Africa	The Second War of the Three Empires. With the Second Romanus Republic no longer a threat, the Three Empires begin fighting among themselves. The Second Romanus Republic remains neutral and actually withdraws 50–100 *milia passuum* from its previous positions to avoid conflict with the Three Empires. The war rages back and forth on four borders.
1437–40 AH (2768–71 AUC)	Eurasia	Religious Revolts in the Three Empires. During the middle of the war, various Islamic sect minorities are mistreated by the majorities in their native empires. It begins with the mistreatment of Mahdians by Shiite vets in the Shiite Muslim Empire. When nothing is done to protect the Mahdians, they revolt, but their revolt is met with extreme force by the Shiite Emperor. Over ten thousand Mahdians, including women and children, are killed. Similar mistreatment and revolts occur in the other two Muslim Empires concerning their own minority sects.

Year(s)	Region(s)	Development
1452 AH (2782 AUC)	Eurasia and North Africa	1452 Peace of Roma between the Three Empires and the Second Romanus Republic. As part of the peace, the Second Romanus Republic agrees to become the Romanus Protectorate, an independent nation that will remain neutral with respect to any wars between any of the Three Empires. Each of the Three Empires pledges to protect the Romanus Protectorate by coming to its aid in the event it is attacked by either of the other two Muslim Empires or by any outside party.
1455–1575 AH (2785–2901 AUC)	North Aztalan	Dismantling of Northern Aztec Empire. Various provinces in North Aztalan rebel from the Aztec Empire at various times during this period. The Aztec Empire generally regains some level of control over many of them, but by 1575, the Algonquatl and Absáalobke Provinces in the far north have established permanent independence from the empire, and the empire's hold on the Nepantla Province remains tenuous.
1457–90 AH (2787–2819 AUC)	Europe	Limited trade resumes between the Aztecs and commercial enterprises of the Romanus Protectorate. This trade slowly expands to the Three Empires despite their frequent conflicts and rebellions.
1465 AH	Aztalan-Asia	The Aztec Empire sends ships across the Pacific to the western continent of Asia. When they ultimately land in the Chíeng Empire in southeastern Asia, they open up trading between the regions.

Year(s)	Region(s)	Development
1481–1537 AH (2810–65 AUC)	Europe	Age of Islamic Purges. The Mahdian Islamic Empire forces the removal of Shiites from the cities of Nuremburg and Leipzig. They are forcibly marched to the borders with the Shiite Muslim Empire, which reluctantly allows them to enter. In reprisal, the Shiite Muslim Empire begins its own purges of Mahdians from its territory. The Sunnis follow suit and eventually each Empire begins to force either conversion to its brand of Islam or expulsion from their respective empires. Jews throughout Europe and Southwestern Asia are also caught up in these purges. Though the Sunni Muslim Empire permits Jews to live in Andalus and Jerusalem, the other two Muslim Empires expel Jewish populations along with unwanted Islamic sects. At the behest of each of the Three Empires at different times, the Romanus Protectorate agrees to permit immigration of the expelled refugees from the various purges to areas within its borders.
1491–1585 AH (2820–2911 AUC)	Tonquizalixco Tetepe	Tetepe Immigration. From among the purged populations of Eurasia and the Maghrib, a desperate number seek a new life in the depopulated region of Tetepe. Most of these are Jews, but a few are purged Sunnis, Mahdis and Shiites who have tired of the religious and racial battles in their former lands.

Year(s)	Region(s)	Development
1515–16 AH (2843–44 AUC)	Romanus Protectorate	Florentia Protocol. Civil war nearly breaks out in the Romanus Protectorate in various skirmishes between Sunnis, Mahdis, Shiites and Jews of various ethnic sects. The First Consul arrests the leaders and threatens to expel them and all former refugees and their children if they do not agree to the terms of a "settlement" reached among a few leaders in Florentia. This agreement becomes codified as the Florentia Protocol and is ultimately approved by all of the Three Empires as well. Under its terms, any persons coming into the Romanus Protectorate pledge to withhold from any proselytization of their religion within the Romanus borders, subject to criminal penalties from each of the signatories. After this Protocol, many of the refugees in Roma begin to join the exodus of refugees to Tonquizalixco Tetepe rather than live with the restrictions.
1535–1615 AH (2863–2940 AUC)	Tonquizalixco Tetepe	Many skirmishes occur between the new Tetepian settlors from across the Atlantic and the previous Iroquois and Aztec inhabitants, especially over the Tetepian's expansion down the Atlantic Coast. After a raid by the Tuscarora tribe in 1584, settlors attack the tribe, capture their chieftain, and execute him.
1585 AH (2911 AUC)	Tonquizalixco Tetepe	Non-Alien Proclamation of 1585. Troubled by instability in the region, Emperor Itzcoatl VII of the Aztec Empire forbids additional immigration into Tetepe.

Year(s)	Region(s)	Development
1603–15 AH (2929–40 AUC)	Eurasia and North Africa	When the Romanus Protectorate and Mahdian Muslim Empire try to intervene to stop a war between the Sunni Muslim Empire and the Shiite Muslim Empire, the two empires turn on them. In the Treaty of Baghdad in 1615, the Romanus Protectorate agrees to dismantle the remainder of its navy and army and never raise forces in the future. The Three Empires enter into another mutual defense pact with the Romanus Protectorate in which the Three Empires individually agree to defend the Romanus Protectorate against foreign invaders and against each other.
1615–25 AH (2940–50 AUC)	Tonquizalixco Tetepe	When the Aztec Empire attempts to re-establish control over Tetepe, a war erupts and the Tetepians seek help from the Three Empires and Roma. Sent by the Three Empires as their emissary, the First Consul of Roma brokers a peace between the Tetepians and Aztec Empire. The Tetepian Province will remain nominally a province of the Aztec Empire but with a quasi-independent government. A governor for the entire region is appointed by the Aztec Emperor from among 4 candidates chosen by majority vote of the inhabitants of the region. The Governor must rotate every four years between the five major ethnic/religious groups in the province (Iroquois, Algonquin, Aztecs, Jews and all sects of Muslims). Various joint cultural events are established to try to harmonize the populations.

Year(s)	Region(s)	Development
1635–42 AH (2960–66 AUC)	North Aztalan	Nepantla and Chgantlo provinces obtain quasi-independent status from the Aztec Empire when they threaten to secede. Instead of tributes paid by the provinces, the people agree to pay taxes on their international trade in products grown and manufactured in the area to compensate the empire for its protection of commerce through navigable waterways.
1655 AH (2979 AUC)	Eurasia and North Africa	Technologies Treaty of 1655. The Three Empires enter into a joint treaty with the Romanus Protectorate relating to the development of technologies and operations of the growing numbers of technologists. Under the pact, the Romanus Protectorate agrees to remain neutral with regard to the dissemination of technologies to the Three Empires. In exchange, each empire agrees that the Protectorate will be its primary supplier of any new technologies and that it will respect the rights of technologists to the exclusive rights to their inventions.
1737 AH (3058 AUC)	Tonquizalixco Tetepe	Tetepian Constitution of 1737. By now, the Tetepian settlors have become fairly well integrated with each other and with the Tetepian natives; however, all residents resent the control of a weakened Aztec Empire. When the Aztecs seek to enforce new taxes against Tetepe through their local governor, he refuses and resigns his post. He and other Tetepian leaders come together and write a new "Constitution" in which a new government will be elected through a form of representative democracy and the nation will be called the Tetepian Republic. Because the nation consists of many different ethnic and religious groups, they fear the powers of pure majority rule. Therefore, they include an article entitled "Rights of the People" in the new Constitution.

Year(s)	Region(s)	Development
1743–1833 AH (3064–3152 AUC)	Tonquizalixco Tetepe	Imperial Boycott of Tetepe. Emperor Acamapichtli VIII of the Aztec Empire confers with the Sunni Muslim Emperor about the new, radical form of representative government and minority rights established by Tetepians. The two emperors jointly agree to boycott trade with Tetepe to undercut this threat. The other Muslim Empires and the Romanus Protectorate join the longstanding boycott, condemning the region to relative poverty and general isolation for over a century.
1743–52 AH (3064–73 AUC)	North Aztalan	Wars of Western Independence. Nanooko and Latisilolal rebel, this time successfully. The Aztec Empire officially agrees to treat Nanooko and Latisilolal as independent sovereign nations. Nanooko and Latisilolal monarchs agree to pay nominal amounts for naval protection by the Aztec Empire and to allow the Aztec Empire to maintain naval ports in their nations. Most of the merchant vessels are owned and operated by Juteslams, who have kept their seafaring expertise after The Great Displacement. Most Latisilolals distrust the Juteslam captains and crew and welcome the assistance of the Aztec Empire in keeping them in line.
1750–1800 AH (3073–3120 AUC)	Latisilolal	Latisilolal aggression. As Latisilolal grows increasingly wealthy with trade in the Pacific, it becomes more aggressive with the Aztec Empire and ramps up its mistreatment of Juteslams, resulting in the Juteslam Anarchist Edict of 1800, under which all Juteslam ships and property are confiscated.

Year(s)	Region(s)	Development
1805–10 AH (3124–29 AUC)	World	War between the Sunni Muslim Empire and the Shiite Muslim Empire expands into Aztalan, with the Aztec Empire joining the Sunnis and Latisilolal siding with their Shiite trading partners. Nepantla and Chigantlo side with the Aztec Empire and send armies west. The two Asian empires refrain from joining the war. Latisilolal loses, its king is deposed, and an oligarchy of five prominent families gains control. In Eurasia, the Romanus Protectorate arranges a truce between the Three Empires and they pronounce the First Consul of the Three Empires as their official arbiter and representative in future conflicts among themselves and around the globe.
1811–17 AH (3130–36 AUC)	Latisilolal	Ahuacatl, leader of one of the five Latisilolal families, consolidates power when he promises to restore order in the nation and then executes the heads of the other four ruling families based on trumped-up charges of treason.
1820 AH (3139 AUC)	Latisilolal	Ethnic Prioritization Edict of General Ahuacatl, granting natives in Aztalan priority over any Juteslams and requiring all Juteslams to wear a three-horn insignia outside of any settlement areas to identify them as Juteslams.
1822 AH (3141 AUC)	Latisilolal and North Asian Empire	Latisilolal King Ahuacatl enters into a "Special Trade Partner" compact with North Asian Emperor Dae-Sung, whereby Latisilolal is provided with various economic assistance in rebuilding its industries, and Latisilolal gives the North Asian Empire "Special Trade Status" with respect to any goods or services travelling between the two, including those shipped through the nation to other parts of North Aztalan. King Ahuacatl begins to re-arm Latisilolal.

Year(s)	Region(s)	Development
1823 AH (3142 AUC)	North Aztalan	King Ahuacatl proclaims that all Juteslams who do not live in the former settlement areas shall be required to serve the government as laborers in various critical state projects to rebuild Latisilolal.
1827 AH (3146 AUC)	Eurasia and North Africa	Technologists Act of 1827, granting greater rights to Romanus technologists for their inventions.
1827–39 AH (3146–57 AUC)	World	The Great World War begins in Asia over claims between the North Asian Empire and the Chíeng Empire to the Islands of Nippon. The Three Empires and Romanus Protectorate enter into the war on behalf of the Chíeng Empire, forming what becomes known as the "Alliance." Latisilolal and the Incan Empire enter the war on behalf of the North Asian Empire. The Aztec Empire and most of its former provinces join the Alliance. Latisilolal is the most prepared for war and it conquers most of North Aztalan up to the Tonalixcotetepe. In 1835, the Tetepian Republic enters into a peace agreement with Latisilolal in which it agrees to remain "neutral" in the war, but also licenses "merchant ports" on the Atlantic Coast in the southern city of Brest to Latisilolal ships. A year later, the Latisilolals commandeer the port and ships at Brest and convert it to a military naval base. Following a major naval victory in the Pacific, the Alliance begins to reverse the gains of the North Asian Empire and the Latisilolals and ultimately defeats them and the Incan Empire.

Year(s)	Region(s)	Development
1839 AH (3157 AUC)	Worldwide	The Treaty of Roma, also known as the Great World Peace of '39, ends the Great World War. Bemoaning the travesties inflicted on the Juteslams by the Latisilolals prior to and during the Great World War and upset with the "neutrality" of the Tetepian Republic, the parties to the treaty also agree to return the Juteslam people to their former "homeland" in the northern regions of Tonquizalixco Tetepe, where they are expected to form a joint government with the existing Tetepian population in the Tetepian Republic.
1840 AH (3158 AUC)	Tonquizalixco Tetepe	Various skirmishes between Juteslam and Tetepian peoples occur throughout the Tetepian Republic when the Tetepian Republic refuses to seat elected representatives from newly settled Juteslam areas. The Three Empires send military equipment to a band of Juteslam rebels to "enforce the terms of the Treaty of Roma."
1841 AH (3159 AUC)	Tonquizalixco Tetepe	After forming a Juteslam army, Hadingus sets himself up as a king to govern Tetepe independent of the Tetepian Republic. When the police and army of the Tetepian Republic seek to arrest Hadingus for treason, the Juteslam Army defends him and other Juteslam leaders, triggering the War of Juteslam Independence. The Juteslam army, supplied by the Three Empires and the Aztec Empire, quickly outguns the army of the Tetepian Republic and deposes the Tetepian leaders. A general civil war erupts. Uzziel, a former president of the Tetepian Republic, forms a separatist military group from among the remaining Tetepian forces. He calls them the Demoseps. Their declared goal is to rid Tetepe of the Juteslams and return true democracy to Tetepe.

Year(s)	Region(s)	Development
1842 AH (3160 AUC)	Tonquizalixco Tetepe	The Juteslam army defeats the Demosep army in what later becomes known by Juteslams as the Battle of New Åarhus.
1843 AH (3161 AUC)	Tonquizalixco Tetepe	King Hadingus declares northeastern Tetepe the new Kingdom of New Jutland, with New Åarhus as its capital.
1844 AH (3162 AUC)	Tonquizalixco Tetepe	The Juteslam Army defeats the Demoseps at the Battle of New Hedeby. The remaining Demosep forces scatter throughout the countryside of Tetepe, principally to the mountains and forests.
1844 AH (3162 AUC)	Tonquizalixco Tetepe	Treaty of Parisius. Representatives of the Three Empires (Sunni Muslim Empire, Shiite Muslim Empire and Mahdian Muslim Empire) and the Aztec Empire conclude the Peace Conference of Parisius with this treaty negotiated by the First Consul of Roma (Romanus Protectorate) declaring that the Kingdom of New Jutland shall hereafter be recognized as the rightful government of the Tetepe region. The accord is also signed by the King of New Jutland and other nations in North Aztalan. Mordecai, an unelected, but self-proclaimed Tetepian representative, signs the accord, but the conference and accord are boycotted by all Demosep leaders. Shortly after, Mordecai is found dead near Shenandoah.

Year(s)	Region(s)	Development
1844 AH (3162 AUC) –present	Tonquizalixco Tetepe	Demoseps regroup as a loosely organized paramilitary force and begin attacking various Juteslam strategic targets on a hit-an-run basis. They are normally able to hide in various mountain retreats when the Juteslam army is sent in. After a few years, they begin to attack civilian targets as well. Eventually, Muslim leaders begin calling the Demosep attackers "shaitaanists," for shiataan, the devil, because their actions are considered "works of shiataan." The Juteslam government develops a "No Tolerance" policy toward shaitaanist attacks, not only punishing responsible individuals, but also indiscriminately shelling Tetepian cities in reprisal for any such attacks.
1855 AH (3173 AUC)	Asia	The Chíeng Empire officially annexes its Nipponese and Cantonese Protectorates, forming the East Asian Empire.
1875 AH (3192 AUC)	Aztalan	Chicahtoc leads a bloodless revolt by prominent Aztec families and military leaders against the hapless Aztec Emperor Otlananquili. Rather than executing him, Chicahtoc banishes Otlananquili, an action that gains him considerable favor from among the Aztec elite. Chicahtoc declares himself Emperor Acamapichtli X, and begins rebuilding the Aztec Empire.
1890 AH (3207 AUC)	Roma	Lumenology Conference of 1890 AH.

APPENDIX B

English-Language Contacts in Baqir Najwa's Cell Phone

Jonathan Ascott
Associate Professor, Archaeology
Oxford

Notes
who has checked out this guy's
background?

Vanessa bartley

work
302-712-0076

home
302-762-7821

mobile
302-872-4524

---

michelle been

work
212-288-8892

mobile
516-326-8867

home
beeneverywhere@gmail.com

Orlando Bickel
Antiquities restored, inc.

Notes
best 18th century furniture
restorations

Janine Bligh

mobile
757-287-8776

home
captainbligh@yahoo.com

Notes
Who's The Boss?

Hiram Blunderbuss

mobile
44-20-2870-2860

home
blundersrm@crotchett.uk

Josiah Bratsworth
Janitor, main building
savant security systems

work
301-289-6109

mobile
202-287-2687

work
bratswor@savantsec.com

Notes
when lies become lives, fact
becomes fat

Brickhouse Grill

work
269-887-9982

Marilyn cable

mobile
432-287-8791

Notes
Not here nor there but
everywhere

Franklin P. Calley
pastor
Franklin lutheran church

work
317-871-1086

work address
32 all saints drive
Indianapolis, IN 46220

---

mary cantor

mobile
312-879-9828

home
cantorific@msn.com

Jeremy Carston
Lickety split cleaners

work
202-729-7908

work address
2743 14th st., n.w.
washington, dc

---

madrea celeste

home
212-379-2869

home address
Cheshire, apart ment 914
666 7th avenue
new york, ny

birthday
17-May-1942

spouse
Papea

child
Figlio

Grace Condamine
lady in waiting
the palace club

work
212-887-2878

work address
131 w. 47th st.
new york, ny

Thomas Cooley

home address
Apartment two, 433 graven drive
sacraement, ca

Devante culbertson

mobile
404-879-2897

Cadance Culling

mobile
320-201-2978

Notes
We While Away the Hours and
Lose Ourselves in Time

---

roman darius

home
207-287-8797

---

kenneth j. détente
tech support supervisor
The source electronics, inc.

work
209-818-3206

work
détente@thesource.com

work address
751 Martin Luther king jr. Way
Merced, CA 95341

Harold Dixon
Fredericks of Hollywood

work
323-297-8978

Alfred Doddridge

mobile
44-12-2387-2798

home
adoddridge@cam.ac.uk

home address
twenty thee alister lane
Cambridge, eng

Notes
an old prof with nothing to lose

Francis Dorsey

home
201-198-8972

mobile
201-532-8892

John doth
lincoln park zoo

work
312-287-2897

work
john.doth@lincparkzoo.org

Thomas Flaherty
Seneca hold and ship co.

Work
201-289-1872

Notes
container ships around the world

Percy gillingham

mobile
44-75-7087-9879

home address
310 a
436 chestershire cir.
windsor, eng.

Birthday
6-Nov-65

spouse
penelope

Desmond Hansel
vp of sales
The simpler solutions, inc.

work
928-785-8782

mobile
697-329-9862
home
928-918-7767

work
DHanse@simplersol.com

Harbor view resort

work
207-287-7530

Christian Huxley
CIA

work
703-486-0623

mobile
723-135-1171

other phone
413-333-4011

work address
Central Intelligence Agency
Washington, DC 20505

other address
2K927 Kings Ridge Dr.
Arden, DE 22329

Notes
A Th. Meet.
Mother: Maryam
Mobile-Other: Main

Maryam Huxley

home
993-485-0010

mobile
993-534-0120

home address
Apt. 3
3 Wiggin St.
Boston, MA 02113

other address
3971 North St. Joan Way
Kingston, Mass. 01723

Notes
—Forsaken & Deceased
—No? A dozen times at least.

Donald Jacobs

home
802-794-6682

mobile
802-361-3977

home
djacobs32@gmail.com

home address
2457 Just Lane
Burlington, VT 05401

birthday
18-March-62

spouse
Donna

Chaiang Feng Jiang
owner
Chaing's take out

work
202-121-9812

mobile
301-507-2233

work
cfjiang@chaiangstake.com

home
chaiangaling@gmail.com

work address
1672 a Street, NW
Washington, DC 20002

Notes
Best cashew chicken in the city

___

Connar Killarney

home
617-712-4949

home
connarsbrew@charter.net

___

Samantha look
associate
Robbin, Allause, Blind, Attys at
Law

work
212-941-6663

work
silook@robball.com

Notes
Met at Hakim's party

___

anastasia luden

mobile
202-888-1415

home
annaluden@yahoo.com

home address
Apt. 1449
1333 14th St., N.W.
Washington, DC

Notes
Got her email from Jamil

___

Camille Lysector

mobile
44-20-3124-6099

___

Eve MacCollough

mobile
325-404-7912

spouse
Frank — the Man

child
Jesse

Notes
Lot's of fun

___

Frank MacCollough
asst. manager
Mac's do it Center

work
325-917-1616

mobile
325-404-7861

work
macattach@macdoit.com

spouse
Eve—a blast

child
It's not Jesse

Notes
Does he know?

Jamil Maroun

mobile
202-753-2609

home
tinkertailor41@gmail.com

Notes
I believe he drives a yellow Jag

Felecia Menendez

mobile
325-272-6910

home
feliznavidez@icloud.com

---

robert murdoch
Under The Sea Productions

work
954-222-0011

mobile
954-796-3171

work
theshark@underseaprod.com

work address
1001 seabreeze blvd
ft Lauderdale, fl

Notes
By Word of mouth, he's the best
scuba instructor in Fla

Ishmail Nabali

home
971-4-3986692

home
whalehunter@emirates.ae

birthday
22-Sep-81

spouse
begot

---

anita nicoli

home
862-301-3798

mobile
862-573-5521

home
annanicoli13@icloud.com

Nights from heaven strip club

work address
1532 G Street
Washington

James Norwick
Warwick, Smith and Donne,
Clothiers

work address
13 saville row
london, uk

Notes
They altar suits perfectly.

Malika Numchencka

mobile
7-812-360-0293

home
malika@svetada.ru

Kelly O'Brien
Production writers exec.
Emerald Isle Productions

work
353-1-235-9022

work
kobrien@emeraldislepros.ie

work address
121 clarendon street
dublin, ie

Notes
Checkered past—IRA?

Jermichael Ochren

work
205-271-9163

mobile
256-777-1329

home
terminator205@yahoo.com

home address
3965 we shall overcome drive
Birmingham, AL 35211

spouse
Shanaqua

Notes
Jerel's buddy

Sumit Om
Stylist
Heir do of Kings

work
202-599-7575

mobile
202-218-2622

work
peakout32@icloud.com

work address
918 New Hampshire Ave, N.W.
Washington, DC 20037

Notes
Better believe the best beard work
in DC

Kate Orwell
man. dir.
W.A. Fowler Enterprises

work
44-20-7634-3972

work address
2607 but terfield road
london, uk

Paul Parkinson

mobile
206-398-2772

home
parkinsn@havaball.com

Dave Pouslon
We just win sports

work
608-227-3981

work address
313 Main Street
Waunakee, WI 53597

Notes
Nice cardio/bike trainer

Armondo Pyzcheski
Armondo the Magnificent
Magicians r us

work
208-226-7939

Hammond query
lead counselor
the simple Life

work
707-239-8619

Home
707-239-8885

mobile
707-286-4320

work
hquerry@simplelifeworks.com

Sojourner Truth Rayburn

mobile
404-971-1828

home
truthserum10@icloud.com

home address
apt. 16-d
1037 juniper st. nw
atlanta, ga

Elizabeth Raynke
Here We Go Childcare

work
240-549-9781

home
301-226-3976

mobile
301-222-3961

work address
632 keokee st.
Langley park, md

Notes
I pray they don't close this place

Everett Reynolds, Jr.

mobile
505-279-9981

Notes
Ev's better at shooting pool than
shooting guns

Taniquioa Runion
women within

work
212-327-8809

Hakim Safar

mobile
971-4-8907292

home
kimsafar@cmail.ae

Notes
He's The Best Poker Player

Joquin Santiago
Mail cour.
Lloyds

work
44-20-1877-0997

work address
1512 bawd st.
london

Emily Sarchuk

mobile
312-260-0828

Hefaz Saxo

mobile
202-278-2882

Notes
works where Jamil hangs

Georgia Seals

home
212-286-8781

mobile
212-756-7782

home
gseals@temperfoam.com

___

Seekers only

Work
626-289-3992

Mobile
980-263-8891

Home
626-332-9812

work address
201 s dacotah st.
los angeles

Notes
Is He Ready?

___

Peter Stanibruck
low lying scum
Larry's bail bonds

work
956-291-8989

Notes
Where Did He Go?

___

Eloise Starcraft

work
303-926-3355

mobile
303-260-0103

home
skistar35@gmail.com

work address
767 soar st.
denver, co

birthday
15-June-90

spouse
Kirk

Notes
fav ski bunny

___

amann subil

home address
15 so. 22nd st.
chicago

spouse
Kalili

child
Nadir

Notes
ghost recon

___

Hafiz Tannous
chief, high command

mobile
971-4-0122876

Morgan Taylor

mobile
202-913-7675

home
morgantaylor25@yahoo.com

Notes
goes above and beyond the call of
duty

Jeff Thomas, III

work
202-987-1295

home
202-693-4721

mobile
202-579-7979

home address
Apartment three
1252 Maryland Avenue, S.W.
Washington, DC 20024

Notes
If I could play The Apostle, would I
know the truth?

Thurman's chocolates

Han Torbold
buyer
The centuries past

work
212-639-2777

work
torbold@centuriespast.com

Notes
great antiques

Tamera Touchstone
Parts Now

work
618-870-2288

merissa unterhyme

mobile
504-490-2877

home
munterh@cherishem.com

Notes
I cherish every moment I spend
with her

Anthony Watry

home
970-396-8802

work
970-212-2868

home
tonywattsman5@yahoo.com

home address
267 deep gorge drive
fort collins, co 80525

birthday
21-Dec-82

spouse
Lara

child
Jess

Notes
tight turns on snowy roads

---

charles within
yankee imports

work
617-826-8713

work
cwithin@yankeeimps.com

home address
259 sea port blvd.
boston, ma

Woltham our Christ redeemer church

work
434-798-1862

mobile
434-896-2286

work address
Route 2, Highway 57
Lynchburg, VA

Notes
nice location for a little celebration

Carrie words
harmony publishing company

mobile
206-879-9871

home
words@harmonpubco.com

Sauron Yandor
Councils of Troy & Rome
The Aeneid Company

work
39-06-265-8718

mobile
39-06-222-8760

work
syandor@aeneidco.it

Notes
The Lord of the Rings?

Dakota Yeller

work
541-386-8876

mobile
541-587-2862

home
yellerbell3@cerendo.com

home address
16B The Palisades
1919 Ocean Way
Winchester Bay, Oregon, 97467

birthday
17-Feb-75

____

Your time assisted living

work
304-897-7128

____

Felicity yorke
london times

work
44-20-2369-7866

____

dominique yves

mobile
33-1-23-66-24-69

home
dyves@malibuleit.fr

Notes
enjoyed her company in Paris

____

Thomas Zaccaro
Tragic Flaws International

work
202-542-3131

work
zaccar@tragicflaws.com

Notes
A forlorn hope?

____

william zobrist

mobile
775-893-3292

work
wzobrist@harrahs.com

home
zobdealer@icloud.com

____

zor shrine circus

work
608-982-2996

ACKNOWLEDGEMENTS

WHEN I BEGAN this complex novel as a first-time author, I had only a small notion of just how much help I would need to pull it off. Fortunately, the early guidance I received from so many good friends quickly reminded me that our greatest journeys are rarely travelled alone. I owe much to them and the many others who helped me through this adventure.

First, I would like to thank everyone who gave me such valuable feedback concerning an early draft of this book, including Jacob Craft, Lori Tomaselli, Greg Lynch, Dan Aiman, Bill Toman, Tyler Hansen, and Emili (Tischer) Hansen. Your thoughts helped point me in the right direction and gave me encouragement to find answers to the many challenges I faced.

Linda Kampe, you deserve special thanks. I still cannot believe how much time you must have spent on this work to give me so many perceptive comments and edits. In particular, you deserve much credit for pushing me to work harder on the development of Sonatina and Jochi and their relationships with the central characters of the book.

To Father Dick Aiken, thank you for guiding me through some of the religious aspects of the book—particularly regarding matters relating to the Catholic Church. I have always found you to be an insightful spiritual leader and a wonderful friend. Of course, any mistakes or exaggerations in the novel concerning Catholicism are solely my fault for not listening to your expert wisdom.

One of my very best friends, Col. Joseph Buche (ret.), made it possible for me to attempt to find some realism when it came to scenes involving the U.S. military. I was pretty naïve about quite a few military/spy things until Joe straightened me out more than once with a "Ken, I love you like a brother, but…" Thanks for being honest with me, Joe. And thank you for your service to our country and the many tours of duty that put you in harm's way. You probably never thought those experiences would come in handy when helping a friend write a novel. I do want to be clear to readers, though. I didn't always listen to Joe because, as Joe is fond of joking, "Nothing ruins a good war story like the truth." Readers will have to divine for themselves what is close to reality and what is simply a fabrication of my little daydreams.

My wife, Jenny Hansen, deserves the "Hopelessly Dedicated Award" for reading three different versions of this book and giving me outstanding feedback every time. I am not sure how she managed that since the basic stories remained the same throughout. I guess she must love me (as I do her). There is no way this book gets written in the absence of her love. She and my children (Tyler, Ben and Jenna) deserve credit for putting up with me during the years I wrote and edited this. I bounced so many ideas off of them that they probably felt like bumper cars at a carnival. I hope they enjoyed the experience as much as I did.

A huge thank you goes out to Tim Cavanaugh. Readers may have noticed a few Latin terms in this book. The only Latin I ever learned was while trying to decipher a few legal phrases during law school and beyond. Fortunately, those seem to be dropping out of common use in the law *(res ipsa loquitor)*. However, this supposedly "dead" language seems to keep trying to make a comeback in other circles, so I suppose there may be some readers out there who might actually notice a mistake in Latin grammar. Tim graciously looked at a list of my Latin phrases in this book and saved me great embarrassment by correcting my many errors. If any terms remain questionable, they no doubt are *mea culpa* resulting from my own clumsy failure to apply his adept guidance to my specific uses.

From the beginning, a major challenge I faced was allowing two seemingly different stories to unfold separately and slowly come together without leaving the reader in complete confusion or total dismay. No doubt, that would have been the result if it were not for the keen insights and persistence of a top-notch editor, Paul Dinas. He helped me in many ways but perhaps most importantly by pushing me to rethink the entire organization of the book, which underwent a number of rewrites. While we did not always agree about how to slice through the complexity of this work, in the end the novel owes much of its better parts to his thoughtful recommendations.

Thanks also to Allison Merten for her excellent work as a copyeditor. With my legal background, I figured I had developed a pretty solid foundation for editing my own words. Thank goodness she saved me from that particular foible.

The maps at the beginning of the book and on my website owe their artistry to Christine Vande Voort. I can barely draw a stickman, so I think readers should have a sense of her level of effort on these maps. Thanks for your expertise, Chris, and also for your kindness when making all of those "final changes" that became not so final after all.

I'd like to applaud the folks at Damonza for their excellent work on cover and book designs. Momir Corocki came up with a great cover design from the beginning and was patient during my attempts to get it just right. Chrissy Hobbs was always very responsive and a delight to work with throughout the interior book design process.

Finally, I would like to add my most important thank you last. I want to thank God for…well, everything…but especially for Love. Sometimes Hate consumes our lives and becomes a driving force in our world, threatening even to tear this wonderful globe apart. If we can all remember to try to Love each other despite our differences, even our differing religions and political beliefs, and yes, try our very best to Love our "enemies" even when they Hate us, then the glow from that Love will truly light our lives, our nation, and our world.

Peace.

AUTHOR BIO

Ken Hansen is now a writer, pilot, biker, woodworker and occasional scuba diver but never again attorney. Though he majored in political science at the University of Wisconsin and graduated magna cum laude from Harvard Law, his early political naiveté took him to a lobbying law firm in Washington, DC, where he discovered a few too many ugly truths. Turning his ambitions toward more productive endeavors, he ultimately served as VP & General Counsel of Epic Systems Corporation, a health care software company that grew much larger than he ever thought possible. He retired in 2013 to once again explore that seemingly simple question posed so many years ago in a philosophy class: "Why?" Luckily, his incredibly patient wife of thirty years, who helped him raise three great kids, keeps asking him, "Why not?"